THE SEAS
OF DISTANT
STARS

THE SEAS OF DISTANT STARS

FRANCESCA G. VARELA

OWL HOUSE BOOKS

RETURNING TO OUR STORYTELLING ROOTS

Published in 2018 by Owl House Books
Front Cover Image © By Tithi Luadthong | Shutterstock.com
Cover and Interior Designed by Leslie M. Browning
ISBN 978-1-947003-92-7
First Edition Trade Paperback

OWL HOUSE BOOKS
An Imprint of Homebound Publications
WWW.HOMEBOUNDPUBLICATIONS.COM
WWW.OWLHOUSEBOOKS.COM

10 9 8 7 6 5 4 3 2 1

PROLOGUE

Her name back then was not *Agapanthus.* It was Aria. Aria like the song the wind made through cottonwood trees. They reminded Aria's mother of feathers, and she often watched the cotton tufts as they floated through the dusk air. She loved when they melted into the flowing, pebble-braided creek, high with water after a storm, or even as they joined the summer trickle when the creek lay stagnant. On summer nights the water shone thick with flies, with dark red clay and the sticky tips of fallen leaves that caked together at the bottom. The freeway hissed in the distance, cars and blackness glimmering just beyond the blackberry bushes.

Aria's mother pretended the freeway didn't exist. She often sat alone, or with Aria scrunched between her thighs, while the trees creaked, and the air stunk of pollen. When the cold air spread bumps over their skin she raised her daughter to her feet and draped Aria's long blonde hair over her shoulder so she could wipe the dust from her pants.

They held hands as they emerged from the ravine. There was the sky again, pale and waning. There sliced the blurred traffic, blazing as always in front of their one-story house. There glowed the fields, the sheep far beyond, the hills broken by dirt patches that always shone reddest at sunset. But sunset was past, so Aria's mother nestled her daughter inside.

Her husband's stomach propelled, jiggling, upward and downward with his sleeping breaths. His hands clenched the armrests of the yellow recliner, the remote wedged between his side and the seat. Aria's mother patted Aria toward the kitchen and kissed her husband's forehead. He smelled like cinnamon and orange peels, soft remnants of the tea he had finished after dinner.

Aria's father woke up slowly. He scooped his wife into his lap. She murmured something about Aria's bath, and then she burrowed her head into the warmth of his shoulder. They breathed together. The screen door slid open, but neither of them heard it. They didn't hear Aria's lithe footsteps against the wooden stairs. They didn't hear her slide down, crawling on her knees into the grass, unsure of how to balance on the changing surface. She couldn't speak yet, so she didn't know what the trees were called, but she knew she wanted to stay with them for a little longer.

The grass massaged her bare feet and made them itch. Aria looked up at the clouds. The moon was there, too; strangely thin, strangely weak. It wasn't dark enough for the moon. A bright star shined over the hill already. It grew brighter. Brighter. Then there was darkness. Claws on her shoulders. Flashes of light so hot she cried out as they teared at her, pulled her up, gripping her shoulders until she felt they would pop from their sockets. And then smooth black stone. And then—nothing.

1

AGE: TEN EARTH-YEARS

Agapanthus *hated the check-ups.* She hated the cold click of the measuring band around her arms. She hated standing against the wall with a straight back while the scientist leaned forward, sniffing and sniffing, like he was about to sigh, only to never breathe the air out again. He scanned her with a cool blink of light to measure her height, her weight, her bone density. Then he nodded, and he looked into her eyes, pulling gently on the lower lids where her eyelashes hung down. Agapanthus stared at the scientist's eyes as he did this; she thought it was fair to analyze him since he was analyzing her.

He had orange eyes. They were a dim, pooling, saturated orange, the same hue as the gauzy shadows encircling Aamsh and Jord, the homes of the Gods. Agapanthus breathed in. Her cheeks puffed with air.

"What's that? What are you doing?" the scientist asked, pointing to her inflated cheeks. His voice was soothing; kind. "Now, turn to the side."

She did, and, with an exhale, she stopped holding her breath. The scientist scanned her again. That was another thing she hated; the way the light pricked her, like spiked rocks scratching her arms, her thighs, her forehead. She half expected to see white streaks left behind, tattooed onto her. But when the scientist turned off the scanner, the itching dissipated, and her skin returned to its usual pale-pink.

"Alright, we're all done here," the scientist said. He pressed the button on the side of the stick.

Agapanthus licked her lips because the measuring light had dried them out. She waited for the scientist to rest his hand on her head, the manner in which all adults said hello and good-bye to each other. Sometimes adults did this with children, but rarely outside of the family. Yet, last time Agapanthus had visited, the scientist had done it—simply, casually, like he'd forgotten that she was a child and not an adult.

She hovered near the open doorway. "Bye, Feol Vatker," she said to the scientist's back.

He bent closer to the polished black countertop, huddling over the measuring stick and its data screen like a red-breasted-sper over its prey. Agapanthus lingered a moment longer. Would he do it? Was she an adult, today?

"See you next year, Agapanthus Caracynth," he finally said. He tilted his eyes toward the soft skin of her shoes. "Take care."

Her foster mother, Leera, stood outside, leaning against the wall, watching the open end of the breezeway where the red sunlight glowed.

"How did it go?" Her warm hand fell to Agapanthus's scalp. Leera bent down so Agapanthus could reach her head as well. "I hope they're not sending you back quite yet?" Leera led the way outside the building, onto the coarse ground.

"I really have to go back?" Agapanthus looked up at Leera's thin cheeks; at her matte, red skin. "Can't I just stay?"

"Oh, Aga," Leera laughed. "I wish you could stay here with us. But when the Gods say you have to go back, you have to go back. And no one knows when that'll be."

They were silent.

"Maybe if you're good they'll let you stay until you're an old woman." Leera patted Agapanthus's back. "It's happened before. So say the Gods, I can only hope it happens again." She held her outstretched hand in front of the twin stars, Aamsh and Jord, whose slow chase through the sky marked the passing of days. The home sun, Imn, shimmered steadily next to them, high above the rock-carved canyons. Imn burned half the sky with rich, purple-red light.

Agapanthus glared at the stars with an intensity she hoped Leera would find pious. It wasn't hard to stare at them; Agapanthus often found herself watching their dim movements anyway—their wispy breath, like fire and water wrapped together, mesmerized her. What would it be like to stand on them? How did the Gods do it? How did they stand on those mounds of rolling fire? Did they have feet like stone? Were they shell-bearing, hiding within their coverings and floating over the flames? That seemed undignified, to Agapanthus, but also kind of fun. She wished she were a God, just to see what it was like. Or maybe just meeting one would be good enough.

But she would never say any of that out loud.

Instead she mimicked Leera's prayer symbol, and held her own hand to the two stars.

An older woman walked toward them, across the scuffed place in the ground where everyone walked. Her breasts shook with each step, even wrapped tightly in her tunic dress. Leera quickly grasped Agapanthus's wrist. She unfolded it from the prayer symbol and dropped it to her waist.

"You're getting too old to be copying me, especially in prayer. Don't forget where you're from," Leera whispered. "Don't forget that these are not your Gods."

"Then why do I have to do what they say?"

Leera's wiry lips came together. As the old woman passed— her wide eyes unnaturally pink from vision-enhancement- lens surgery—the two women made eye contact and nodded. Agapanthus blinked at the rocky, red-brown soil.

When the old woman was behind them, Leera said, "I don't expect you to understand. You're not Deeyan."

Nothing more was said during the walk home. Agapanthus ignored the stark, folded cliffs, beaming red against the darkness of the Waters. Usually she loved to take them in, and the heavi- ness of the sky, and the warm, dry wind as it caught her blonde hair by the roots; sneaking, sluggish, full; catapulting her long hair outward in all directions. But, for now, in the windy silence, she took big steps to keep up with Leera.

Agapanthus's nose constricted with effort. She opened her mouth so she could breathe more easily. Even on short walks, her thighs burned along the insides, so much so that she imagined hy- drothermal vents were magically popping out of the ground just to burn her. She had only seen a vent once, during the last Festival of the Underworld. It was on one of the other islands, just a pool of black water. The distant steam rising from it.

"This is what keeps us alive,"The guard standing next to the vent had said.

He bent down close to her. She remembered how he smelled like sweat, and, the vent, like dust.

The lights were on in the men's side of the house. The women's windows were dark, as black as the stone that framed the win- dows, and so were those of the children's hall and the meeting hall connecting the two wings.

"Looks like we're the first ones back," Leera said. The door slid open as it recognized her body signature.

The white orbs high on the ceiling lit up. Leera and Agapanthus stepped inside. It felt, as always, surprisingly cold inside the thick walls. Geometric carvings patterned the crack between ceiling and floor. Leera swept into the next room, but Agapanthus stood in the front hall a moment. She tilted her neck to look at the recessed mural of the Waters, right above her head, ornately carved into the wall directly facing the door; each stroke was a tiny etch, the work of the ancestors who had first inhabited the house. The picture of small waves was flat and gray, but realistic in its illusion of movement. Agapanthus didn't like the mural. She didn't know why, but it wasn't beautiful to her. It always looked dusty, even though it wasn't, and that made her want to touch it and scrape her fingers against it to wipe away the powdery sheen. She wasn't allowed to, though. Oh, no, of course not. It was too old—too precious—to soil with the hand-oils of an alien, or even a Deeyan— none of the women had ever touched it. Not even Grandmother Surla, and she was the oldest of all of them.

Agapanthus didn't feel like following Leera around until the other women came home, when they would meet with the men to walk to the cafeteria. She was the only child living in the house, so she escaped to the children's hall to be alone.

The floor was lined with animal skin. Agapanthus kneeled, and its softness embraced her bare knees. She dug out her storyteller from her chest in the corner. A deep, woman's voice rose from the hand-held machine. Agapanthus stretched back on her bed of leathery-soft skins. It was the story of how the Gods brought the Deeyans to Deeyae. She listened to it often enough that she had memorized certain parts.

"The Water Planet was the first home of the Deeyans," the recording and Agapanthus said in tandem. "There, they ate plants, and they climbed trees. They lived off the sun, not the hydrothermal vents."

That was all Agapanthus knew about her home planet. There were more audiobooks with information about it; after all, most scientists exclusively studied the Water Planet and its inhabitants, at the request of the Gods. But neither Leera nor Pittick would buy them for her. They told her she was too young for that sort of thing, and the Gods may not like it. Besides, she would go back someday, and then all of her questions would be answered.

Her eyes began to close. The weight of the data-reading with the scientist came over her. She felt it in her limbs; every step, every turn, every motion she had made throughout the day pulled her down further into her bed.

When she sat up again, the storyteller had shut off automatically. She'd missed the end, where the Gods drop the first Deeyans on their new planet and the First Age begins. Agapanthus swallowed hard. Using all the strength in her thin arms, she pushed herself up. She needed to stay awake, or else she would miss the meal. She plodded toward the men's wing through the other door in the hall.

There stood Pittick. As he smiled, his forehead wrinkled all the way up to his scalp, a red swath behind a veil of black hair.

"We're leaving soon, Aga," he said, tapping her on the head. "But first, come look at this."

She followed her foster-father to the study room. Comfortable piles of blankets dotted the marbled floors. Aunt Imari's husband, Uncle Sonlo, sat on one of them with his naked legs crossed. Both men carried the faint scent of the water creatures which they harvested. They managed the fisheries together.

"Hey, how did the visit go?" Uncle Sonlo asked her. He smiled, and his white teeth seemed to glow against his dark lips.

"Fine," Agapanthus said.

"I can't believe they still make all of you exchangers go there every year," Uncle Sonlo said. "They must be busy, with all those test subjects. You'd think they would cut back a little. Don't they have enough data yet?"

"They'll never have enough data, Sonlo," Pittick mumbled. He picked up a thick, crunchy-looking sphere. "Ah, here it is." He squinted at her, smiling.

"What is it?"

"Take it."

She pinched it lightly from his hand. It was bumpy, unmoving; like a strange, orange stone.

"It used to be a karap shell," Pittick said. "I found it just underneath the boat, floating in a shallow area of the Waters. It's not even molting season."

"Good thing it's not, or you'd be in trouble," Uncle Sonlo said loudly.

"If it was molting season I wouldn't have taken it."

Pittick knelt in front of Agapanthus. Of everyone's eyes, his were the yellowest, she thought. They were nothing like the orange scientist's.

"This is very valuable. It's breakable, and it's rare, and it's beautiful, too. If you were to buy one of these, it would cost a lot of money, more money than anyone has, except maybe the Contact." He took the shell back from her and shook it in front of her nose. Agapanthus shuffled backward slightly.

Pittick continued, nodding as he spoke. "You have to get lucky and find one. And I did. And I want you to have it."

Agapanthus nodded, too, mimicking the short pulses of his neck.

"But you have to promise me you're not going to lose it. It's worth a lot."

"I promise."

Pittick placed the shell back in her cupped hands.

"Why do you have to put so much pressure on her? Don't give the shell to her if it's that valuable," Uncle Sonlo said as he stood up, stretching his thick arms in front of his chest. "She's just a kid. You know she's going to drop it or something."

"No I won't!"

"She's responsible," Pittick said lightly. His wide jaw settled into a smile. "I trust her."

Agapanthus took big steps to her trunk in the children's hall. She wanted to run there, but her legs were too tired. Sometimes, after a good long rest, she could run for short bursts, but then her muscles began to ache, and so did her spine, and her lungs. Even the bones in her neck seemed to tighten. Most of the time she preferred big strides instead of running.

She delicately nestled the shell next to her pile of folded clothes, along with the collection of pretty rocks she'd found out by the Waters. Now she had fifteen, counting the shell. It fit in perfectly with her collection. She only picked up rocks that were different; one was shaped like a triangle; one had a crack down the middle, exposing light-yellow sparkles on the inside; another was a purple so dark that it looked black unless she held it up to Imn.

"We're leaving now, Aga!" Leera voice echoed through the hollow walls.

"Coming!" Agapanthus called back. She rushed out into the women's hall. Aunt Imari, Grandmother Surla, and Great-Aunt Tayzaya waited there.

Aunt Imari rushed happily toward Agapanthus, her delicate hand ready to meet her head. "There's my little one!" Imari's sons had married off to different houses just before Agapanthus was adopted. It was a hard thing for a mother to have only boys, because they always left. Sometimes they even went to different islands, and then you could only see them at festivals. Leera had once told Agapanthus that this was why Imari was so kind toward her; she missed her own little ones.

"Hello there, Agapanthus," Surla said. Grandmother Surla and her sister Tayzaya rarely offered their hands to Agapanthus. Today they simply smiled at her. Neither looked as old as they sounded. Their voices seemed to be the most aged part of them. Everything they said came out sounding feeble—at least compared to Leera and Imari's warm, hefty voices.

Imari withdrew her palm from Agapanthus's head. She walked outside without giving Agapanthus a chance to reciprocate.

Sonlo and Pittick were waiting, their backs turned to the bi-sloped house. Sonlo looked like a giant, compared to Pittick. They were the same height, but Uncle Sonlo's body was just bigger—more bulky and laborious. Agapanthus liked Pittick's smoothness better. She thought curvy muscles looked better than sharp-look-ing ones. Hopefully Pittick wouldn't end up like Sonlo when he grew older. But, then again, older men usually looked more like Sonlo. He was a strange match for Imari. Her shoulders receded into her neck with smallness, meagerness, fragility. Sometimes Agapanthus wondered if something was wrong with her, but she was afraid to ask.

In a long line, the family headed toward the cafeteria. They walked along without speaking. Each footstep crunched against the gravelly dust.

Then a scream surged over the cliffs. Then another and an-other, building upon the echoes of the first, until they all blended together into a tunneling, quavering, mass. Grandmother Surla led the family in a slow succession toward the chanting. They walked expertly sideways over the unsteady, sloping ground. As they made it over the top of a red cliff, the Waters came into view. Agapanthus had come to think of the Waters as a person; a very old woman, her arms spread wide to encircle the center of Deeyae, and the warm sky above it, too, and all the Deeyans and the wa-ter beings and the Others and even the exchangers, like her. She wished she could speak to the Waters. Well, sometimes she did, while she practiced swimming along the shoreline; she muttered into the musky-tasting water while her lips were submerged. What she really wanted was for the Waters to say something back to her in a velvety, kind voice. *Agapanthus, good things are in store for you*, the Waters would say, oh so wisely, with each word un-rolling like a slow, curling wave. Of course the Waters would be all-knowing; a future-seer. A goddess. To Agapanthus, the Waters were more godly than the Gods themselves.

A growing crowd hovered at the edge of the Waters, all dressed in sleeveless shifts made of thinly stretched leathers—some of better quality than others. Tayzaya and Imari drifted into the mass of people, but the others stayed back to survey them.

"Another coming-of-age attempt?" Leera said to Pittick, her gaze still latched onto the crowd and the dark expanse in front of them. "I don't even see anyone out there. They must be pretty far."

"I see them. Way, way out there."

A man wearing a black-stone chain around his neck pushed his way from the crowd and lowered his head toward Surla. "Surla Caracynth," he said in a deep, creased voice.

Grandmother Surla patted his nearly hairless scalp. "Akinan Pelloi."

The man was tall enough that he could touch the top of Surla's head without her even bending at the knees. Agapanthus recognized him; he was a member of the Council. He had only been added on two years ago. Everyone had been surprised; he'd come out of nowhere, some boat-builder from the other side of the island. But apparently the Gods had been happy with him, because the Contact called Akinan up during the yearly island-wide meeting, and he'd made the announcement right then and there.

"Do you think he's going to make it?" Surla asked.

"Who is it, who's swimming?" Leera stepped closer to Akinan.

Akinan coughed. "He's the son of Lapars Rq," he said. "And I think he is going to make it. He's already halfway to Shre."

"Do they have the boats ready over there?" Leera asked, her voice high, her fingers to her lips. "Did someone tell them?"

"I'm sure," Akinan said. "He picked a bad time, though. Yes, the wind is calmer now, but it's about meal time. He's keeping everyone from the meal."

"Maybe he was hoping everyone would be eating so they wouldn't stand here and watch him," Pittick said.

"If that's what he wanted, then he was stupid about it." Sonlo laughed with his shoulders. "He should've started after everyone was already inside eating."

"As long as he makes it," Leera said. "I always get so nervous."

"I still remember your swim across, Leera," Grandmother Surla said.

"I do too," Pittick said. "That's when I first saw you, it was right after the Festival of Imn, right as I was going to head home. You swam fastest of all the women that year. And remember the celebration after? I don't think I've ever eaten more."

"See—if Lapars's kid does it today, we won't have to worry about missing the meal. Maybe this is all a genius plan to get more food," Uncle Sonlo said.

"We don't have much in the stores," Akinan said. He crossed his arms, and his necklace rattled. "And today was a slow hunting day. The celebration will have to wait until tomorrow, I think. If they can catch enough."

"The kid probably won't even care," said Pittick. "He'll be a man after this. That's why he's doing this. So his life can start."

Agapanthus sat down in the dirt, stretching her legs in front of her. Her knees were too tired to continue standing. She imagined herself swimming like this boy; swimming like all children did to become adults—the flowing, transient Waters wrapped around her from all sides, floating, in space; blackness as she closed her eyes, as her arms flew in rhythm with her breath, like the water drums at festivals. Very few exchangers could make the long swim from their own island, Yeela, to the neighboring one, Shre. Some even drowned trying, because it was forbidden to help anyone attempting the rite of passage swim. All anyone could do was stand and watch.

The shore of Shre was clearly visible on the far side of the Waters. It appeared shaded; a dark, dark, red, like the dry skin on the bottom of someone's foot. Well, not Agapanthus's foot.

A Deeyan foot. Unless, of course, Agapanthus walked barefoot through the dirt to "paint" her feet red. Even then, it wasn't quite the right shade; the pink of her foot always broke through the dust—glaringly, shockingly, lifelessly.

Against the distant hump of the neighboring island, the swimmer dissolved. First he was there, a bare speck against the churning Waters, and then he was gone. The screams dissipated into muttering. Waves sloppily crested over the rocky shores. They sounded brittle, shattering ceaselessly.

"He's out of the sight line now," Leera said. "May the Gods watch him carefully."

No one said anything back, they just swallowed, or adjusted themselves slightly, or shifted their weight, so Leera continued. "This is the worst part. That place between the islands. No one can see him from that side, and no one can see him from this side, so no one would know if he sunk. He would be completely alone, just slipping down into the belly of the Waters. Completely alone—"

"Oh Leera," Grandmother Surla said. "No Deeyan has drowned in here for more than three-hundred years."

"I know, but you just never know when it might happen again."

"Really, Leera? Swimmers twice a year or so, and you're still not over this nervous habit?" Uncle Sonlo raised his thin, black eyebrows.

"It's because she saw her friend almost drown," Grandmother Surla said. "At the Water Festival, many, many years ago. Roslg Boea. She was practicing for the rite of passage, and she lost her strength halfway through. Thank the all-watching Gods it was only a practice swim. There was a boat not too far from her. They saved her."

"Why was she practicing at the Water Festival anyway?" Uncle Sonlo laughed.

"So no one would be paying attention," Leera said.

"With all those boats in the Waters?" Uncle Sonlo shook his head. "Wait, so, what happened, though? Why didn't she make it?"

"She was just a weak girl. Weak-bodied," Grandmother Surla said. "Almost as weak as the aliens."

"Surla." Leera's wide eyes fastened to her mother's strict face. "Most people say 'exchangers' these days. You know that." She glanced down at Agapanthus.

"Why are they 'exchangers' if we don't send anyone over there? What's the exchange?" Sonlo asked.

"We get their children, and they get honored on the Water Planet when they go back," Pittick said. "We get them, they get respect."

After listening to the adults for so long, Agapanthus had the sudden urge to jump into the crooked shoreline of the Waters. Not to test herself; just to swim; just to enjoy the cool brush of the breeze against her wet cheeks. Despite her tiredness, she seriously considered throwing off her clothes into a homely, dusty pile, and bowing gracefully—as gracefully as she could—into the blackness.

"I say we go ahead and eat," Akinan said loudly. "It's going to be a while." He walked off into the crowd.

"I won't argue with that," Uncle Sonlo said.

"I'm going to stay and watch." Leera clasped her hands in front of her stomach. "Aga, go tell Tayzaya and Imari it's time for the meal."

Agapanthus stared at her foster-mother, who watched her with unblinking fierceness. Leera really was beautiful; wide-statured, with wide cheeks and a high forehead and thin features. She seemed more skin than anything. Leera was like the edge of a cliff—red, solid, but ready to crumble.

Another wave of exhaustion came over Agapanthus. It felt like she had been asked to rise from the dead. To journey down the hill, into the quavering, warm-moist conglomeration of bodies, to fetch Great-Aunt Tayzaya and Aunt Imari, then to leap wide strides back to the cafeteria? Just getting to the cafeteria sounded impossible.

"But—" Agapanthus began.

"It's okay, I'll go," Pittick said quickly. He lifted Agapanthus by the underarms, bringing her to her feet. His hands felt dry, scratchy from work. Agapanthus laughed.

"Go on with Surla." Pittick stepped away. "Go on, get a head start. We'll catch up."

"Oh yes, you'll catch up no problem," Grandmother Surla said. She exhaled, and her eyelids clamped down roughly. They began walking. "You know, Agapanthus, I used to be fast, and strong. I was a good swimmer. I could hold my breath until I reached the bottom of the Waters. Not the deep water, but the shallows. Now look at me. I'm no faster than an alien." She shook with muted laughter. "Sorry—'exchanger.'"

The cafeteria was one of the few buildings on the island without the two-winged design. Instead, it was a large rectangle borne of the usual black stone. One room to butcher and prepare the food, and an open hall with skin-draped floors. Half the island sat there at the prescribed daily meal time. The room smelled like food already; metallic, blood-like.

Grandmother Surla and Agapanthus lined up at one of the two doorways where the preparers handed out stone bowls. The lines already stretched the length of the room, even though much of the crowd remained near the Waters.

In front of them stood a girl whose eyes were very far apart. Agapanthus often saw her running in the higher cliffs with some of the other children. They had spoken once, at one of the festivals—the Marriage Festival? Or was it the Water Festival? It was so long ago, Agapanthus could barely remember. The girl had come up to her, asked her something about why Agapanthus looked different. Agapanthus couldn't remember what she'd said back. Had she pointed out the other exchangers in the crowd? Had she shuffled away without answering? Every festival and meeting and mealtime since then, Agapanthus had avoided this girl. What was her name, again? She reminded Agapanthus of one of the herded inner-island creatures, whose black-mirror eyes sat very far back on their heads.

"Looks like there's not much, today, huh?" the girl turned and whispered hoarsely. Her smile revealed two missing teeth on both sides of her mouth.

"I can't really tell from back here," Agapanthus said. She glanced back at the entrance to look for Pittick and the others.

"The bowls are basically empty!" the girl said. She patted her thick mound of a stomach.

Agapanthus nodded, smiling gently. She didn't know what to say.

"You hate me, don't you?" the girl asked in a dull, flat tone.

"What?"

"We don't run into each other that much, and it's not like the island's that big. You hide from me."

"No. I just don't look for you. I don't even know you." Agapanthus swallowed. "What was your name, again?"

"Geleria Serenop. You're Agapanthus Caracynth."

"How did you know that?"

"I have a better memory than you." She held her flabby chin higher. Her red skin shone ashily under the lights. "But it's not your fault. All Deeyans have better memories than your kind."

Agapanthus held her breath. She nodded, her eyes to the floor. The smell of food, of heaps of raw animal flesh in the doorway beyond, disintegrating into the floor—blobby, flopping, dead—it made her suddenly uneasy. She licked her lips again and tilted her head to the side. She knew she had to say something back.

"Well at least I'm not fat." Agpanthus paused as Geleria's mouth tightened into a pinched circle. Yes. That was the right thing to say. "How did you get so chubby if we're all eating the same amount? You must have something wrong with you to be so different from everyone else. Look around, who else is fat?"

Geleria glanced hurriedly across the room; at the seated figures, those waiting in line, the servers. Most people were squat, wide, and hefty, but toned. And the other children were usually thinnest of all.

"It's still better than being a scrawny alien," Geleria said. "A scrawny experiment-subject. I'd rather be dead than be one of you."

"You could never be one of us, anyway. That's impossible," Agapanthus said, each word growing quieter. "That doesn't even make sense."

"Who cares?" Geleria locked eyes with her. "No wonder you don't have any friends." She turned around and stepped in front of her parents.

Agapanthus stared at their backs for a moment. She wanted to collapse to the floor and rest her head on her knees.

Grandmother Surla coughed. Agapanthus had forgotten she was there. "I wonder what's taking them so long?" Grandmother Surla surveyed the crowd as she spoke. She paused. Her breath expounded wispily from her chest, and she swept her shoulder-length black hair away from her face. "Agapanthus. Don't you play with the other children? You spend so much time out by the Waters. I thought you played with them there?"

Agapanthus thought of the mushy sand wrapping over her feet as she waded into the Waters. She thought of the coarse, rich smells, the dim heat of the red sun. She thought of the arching cliffs, heavy with dust, and the row of children running down them. Down the hill, down to the shadowed sea, down to the expanses above which Aamsh and Jord billowed. She thought of the clipping noise of ripples against rock. The slimy, black water plants stretching their stalks above the waterline. The other children, screaming down the opposite edge of the shore, yelling because there might be water creatures under their feet, racing each other as they swam to the distant fishing boats. She watched them and they never glanced her way. They knew she was there, they must, but they never looked at her.

"I go there to play in the Waters."

"By yourself?" Surla finally met Agapanthus's eyes. "Don't they ever ask you to play?"

"Not usually."

"Even the others like you?"

Agapanthus shook her head. She liked to think that she was left out because she wanted to be. They had invited her once, long ago; a mixed group of exchangers and Deeyans who liked to play chase. She'd declined because she wanted to hunt for pebbles. She told them she would join them the next day, but they never asked her again. That was her one chance, and she'd lost it.

"Well you need to fix that," Surla said. "No use being anti-social at such a young age."

They made it to Kopri Karia, one of the servers handing out the meal. All the servers and food preparers were required to shave their heads. On most it looked strange, but it made Kopri look regal. Her highly arched eyebrows looked both sharp and kind. She didn't smile, but she nodded at them. Agapanthus clutched the cold bowl to her chest. Inside were small, filmy chunks of red-breasted-sper meat. Its rawness made it gelatinous—clear but bloody, freshly killed that day. Surla and Agapanthus sat on the floor.

"I don't see anyone here," Surla said. Her lips already shined from the blood of her first bite. "No Balia, or Fetru, or Lopor. Where is everyone?" She dug her fingers into the mass of food and brought some to her mouth. As she chewed, she said, "And where are Pittick and the others? Watching that swimmer, still?"

Agapanthus clenched her teeth together as she worked through her first bite. The food tasted better than it smelled. But, still, she wanted to run out of the lukewarm air of the cafeteria. Away from the saliva noises and the fragrant blood and the scattered words of mostly-strangers. The island wasn't very big—in fact, it was one of the smallest—but there were still a lot of people she didn't know.

Surla and Agapanthus both ate sloppily, and loudly. Agapanthus couldn't remember spending this much time alone with Grandmother Surla. It made her nervous. She tried to focus on her food, but her gaze was drawn to the rustling clusters of people, the stragglers still procuring their food. She watched the door, too, hoping Leera or Pittick would save her from being alone with Surla.

Finally Pittick rushed in. He bounced to his knees, his white teeth barred as he breathed through his mouth.

"The food is losing its freshness," Grandmother Surla said. "May the Gods tell me, what took so long?"

"They didn't make it. Lapars's son—" Pittick said, his words rushed and clattering together. "And Lapars, he went out and—"

Static pierced the speakers near the ceiling. Then the Contact's steady voice poured through. "All residents of rightwards Yeela. At the shore."

Grunts overtook the room as people stood. They adjusted their dresses away from their necks or down lower toward their knees, and left their bowls—stained, half-empty—on the floor. They scurried out into the redness. Once under the blushing sun, panic hit. Agapanthus could see it in their faces. Tight, pulled; yellow eyes flickering.

"His arm!" a woman said from deeper in the crowd.

"No, that happened in the water," a man's voice answered her.

Pittick sighed and continued pushing his way through. He nudged shoulders and ribcages gently, with just the tips of his fingernails; a light, tapping invitation to shift over.

"There she is," Pittick muttered, and they were once again next to Leera, Tayzaya, and Imari.

Agapanthus stepped forward, head bent, assuming Leera and Aunt Imari would greet her. Neither of them did, because there, with his thick necklace of black stones, stood the Contact. Agapanthus could barely see him over the rows of people. She could see him only from the chin up. The rest of him was muffled by skin-clad backs and thin black hair.

He was young, for a Contact. The last Contact had been one-thousand years old when he died. Agapanthus still remembered his death festival well, even though she had been very young— she remembered his pale lips slightly parted, his stomach sunken down like an empty crevasse underneath his clothes. They carried his body up to the highest cliff. All members of the Council slid their hands under his frail body and carried it above their heads. Some of them, almost as old as the Contact had been, struggled to keep their arms from shaking. But it had to be done. He had to be left there so that, within moments, he could disappear. There was a feeling of static in the air, and then a low *whomp*. And then he was gone. By then the new Contact had mounted the cliff. He looked down upon his subjects and said something about hearing the glimmering voices of the Gods. That was how one got to be a Contact; the voices. From then on it was his duty to listen to them—the voices of the all-watching—to tell the island of Yeela how to live. It had been that way since the Awakening, and so, they said, it would be forever.

"Look here," the Contact bellowed. "We know this isn't right. We know it's forbidden to aid those who are swimming the rite of passage. If they aren't going to make it, then it's their time to return to the Gods. It's not our place to help them in that journey." The Contact swallowed roughly. His soft-looking, hefty chest rose and fell. "In this case he was bitten by a water creature; we assume it to be a Ltran, by what the fishermen are saying."

Pittick leaned in closer to Leera. "Can't he hurry this up? Poor Lapars's son is just sitting there bleeding."

Leera grunted. "And look how pale Lapars looks, himself."

Agapanthus fell to her knees. Through a forest of legs, she saw a boy on his side, his whole arm and stomach and neck slathered with burgundy, clotted blood; an older man, lips moving, eyes shut, desperately covering the wound with his palms.

The Contact slowly faced the twin stars. All remained silent, except the Waters and the wind.

"So say the Gods: It is their destiny to drown." The Contact's face became thinner as he spoke. Grimmer, and harder. But in the deep yellow of his eyes, Agapanthus thought she saw suppressed tears. Certainly there was sadness there.

"But why? That doesn't do any good," Agapanthus whispered to Leera. "Why would they—"

"It's what the Gods want. And if that's what they want, we don't question it."

A small, leather-wrapped boat was pulled to shore. The Contact helped heave Lapars and his unconscious son into its bowl-shaped center. Two members of the Council carried in large rocks. Then they paddled out with great speed, the Contact solemnly looking down, the Waters wisping by underneath him. When they stopped, still close enough to shore that Agapanthus could make out their startled faces, the Contact held up a rope of finely braided animal skin. Hunched over, he slipped it through a hole in the rock and tied it around Lapars's ankles. The Council members stepped closer, their mouths weighted and creased. Everyone breathed heavily. The boat trembled as they helped push Lapars over the edge, into the immeasurable Waters. There was no struggle; almost no splash. He simply disappeared. Like he had never existed.

The son would be next. No one in Agapanthus's family could even remember his name, yet he was going to die. Agapanthus tried to blink her tears away. No one else was crying. Her throat ached and her nostrils flared, and she tried so hard, as the second rope was tied, to withhold her chest-rattling sobs. She tried to think of good things, like swimming, like listening to stories, like walking with Leera and Pittick. But it didn't work. And as they threw him down he flopped over sideways. A great splash of purple, of blood and water mixed, sprayed out from under the body. He was a body already. No longer a boy, no longer a living being. Just a lump of fleshly matter coursing through the depths. Lapars surely waited at the silty bottom. Through his barely open eyes, he would see his son drifting down, just the outline of him, the silhouette against the eternal presence of Imn high above, his hair fanning out around, his one arm dangling above his head, the other still streaming blood. And Lapars would feel that knot, that horrible knot, at his core—that he needed to do something, he needed to help his son. He would be crying without realizing it; the tears, of course, would blend right into the water. Then, finally, as his son hit down on the sand, too far away to hold, to touch, to say goodbye to, the water would enter his lungs.

Leera pulled Agapanthus into her arms. "It's alright, Aga," her hot breath said against Agapanthus's hair. Leera kissed the top of her head. "It's alright."

Pittick joined in too. All three of them hugged each other, submerged in the hushed crowd. No one left to the meal, or to their homes. They stood and spoke softly to one another. The boat returned to shore much slower than it had left. The Contact drifted back up the cliffs without saying anything at all.

"This is—" Pittick said, "—this is tragedy."

"Don't say that, Pittick," Leera answered. But she grasped them both in tighter, and, when they pulled away, she was the last to let go.

They walked home; through the buzzing silence, through the steady, sweet-warm glow of the inescapable sky, lit aloft by the home sun and the quiet meanderings of the God stars, which Agapanthus now hated—hated, hated, hated, with all her gut and her clenched jaw and all the strength she could pour into the limbs of her weak, young body.

Could the Gods sense this? Could they see or hear inside her mind—inside anyone's mind—just as they could with the Contact? Was the Contact only special because he could sense their presence there, while all the others remained blind? She hated them. Suddenly she understood how the Others must feel. They were the ones living on the fringes of the frozen lands to the south and the great deserts to the north. Right on the very edge, next to the Waters. During the Awakening, the Gods had only spoken to Contacts living around the equator. The islanders. The Others were not the chosen people. They were primitive; they didn't have access to the technology of the Gods. No; they still worshipped the old god, the single, fierce god of the underbelly of Deeyae, who they believed controlled the hydrothermal vents, and, thus, all life. But those who worshipped the Gods knew this was not true. They knew that They controlled everything from their high perch on Aamsh and Jord. Without them, the Deeyans would not exist, and all of Deeyae would crumble.

Agapanthus didn't know whether the Others believed in the Gods. But how could they not? Their touch was everywhere—in the science labs, in the healing centers, in the portation center, in the exchange program headquarters, in the electricity, in every advanced device, every planet-transport machine, every light. But maybe the Others didn't know about this evidence. Either way, she knew they must hate the idea of the Gods. The idea that the islanders were better than them. Superior, chosen, brilliant. Agapanthus had only seen the Others once, on the way to the Star Festival in the ice lands. They had passed their camp—animal-skin tents, round and low to the ground, and a small gathering area of stones where they probably sat and spoke of their underworld god. But the only Other in view was a young woman. All Agapanthus saw was the back of her head, right outside one of the tents. And then, she remembered, Great-Aunt Tayzaya said something, like, "Poor things." And they had all gone on, farther and farther from the eternal sun of the equator, into the dark half of the planet. It was always night there; always. They wore special fur suits that covered every speck of skin and body except their eyes. Onward they had walked, over the strange, ticking, cracking ice that smelled of water and soil at once. It was so tiring that Pittick had to carry her in his arms. She fell asleep pressed against his chest. His warmth. When she opened her eyes they had arrived. And that was when she looked up; above them, the sky had melted from red to—to everything. A black sculpture painted with stars, with lights that bulged, and soared, and cascaded; that reflected on the unending ice fields until ground and sky became one, rolling the world into a sphere of light.

"Aga," Leera had said, crouching to Agapanthus's level. Her words were muffled through the furs. "There is your home world." She pointed to a certain light, faintly yellow, unblinking.

It was disappointing. It looked like nothing. Like anything. Like any other star.

"Isn't it beautiful?" Leera said. "That is your home sun."

"It looks just like the other ones."

"Exactly. And they are all beautiful."

2

AGE: THIRTEEN EARTH-YEARS

"*'m sorry. I'm so sorry.*" Agapanthus didn't know why she kept
repeating that—she knew it wasn't her fault in any way—
but it just slipped out again and again, like tears or vomit.
"I'm sorry. Sorry. Sorry." She said it with her hands cupped over
her mouth, shaking her head, shivering. "I'm sorry."

Grandmother Surla's body was stretched out on a pile of skins
in the meeting hall. Aunt Imari and Leera had hauled her there
on a blanket-stretcher, tenuously lifting her all the way across the
house. That way the men could see her before she was reclaimed
by the Gods. Now she lay with her head dangling sideways, her
skin almost orange in its paleness, with dark, ugly blotches under
her eyes.

Leera knelt at the side of her mother. She reached out tenta-
tively for Grandmother Surla's curled, stiff hand. When their skin
touched, Leera quickly pulled away. She opened her mouth; closed
it; parted her lips slightly again, so just her front teeth shone.

"Mother," Leera whispered.

She's not going to wake up, Agapanthus felt like yelling. But she didn't. Of course she couldn't say that.

Aunt Imari cried freely. Between each breath, she heaved and choked. She sounded like a dying animal. Agapanthus knew she was really crying for her own mother, Tayzaya, who was quivering in her room with the sickness. Most likely, she'd be dead soon as well.

Static pierced the air. The small hairs on Agapanthus's arms stood up. There was a zipping noise, the smell of intense heat, and then Grandmother Surla's body vanished in a flash of light.

"She's with the Gods now," Uncle Sonlo said in a deep, lifeless voice.

Leera swept her palm over the soft coverings, which were still impressed with the curves of Surla's body. She pulled the blankets taut. Her nose dripped, but she didn't brush it away.

After a moment Leera stood curtly and left the meeting hall. The windowless room felt dark and tight, all of a sudden. Aunt Imari continued to sob.

"Do you think it's really the exchangers?" Agapanthus asked Pittick. "Can the sickness really come from us?"

"That's just a rumor. They're very careful about the disinfection regulations. You're just built differently; it protects you from it, for some reason."

"But, Pittick, we're all from the same planet, originally. Wouldn't you be protected, too?"

"That was a long time ago. A very long time ago, Aga. That's why we look so different now."

"Not that different," Agapanthus said quietly. "But couldn't it be because it's a disease from the Water Planet? So we're tolerant of it, but it's dangerous to you?"

"You heard them talking behind us at the meal the other day. I thought so." Pittick glanced up quickly, then rested his hands on Agapanthus's shoulders. His mouth curled up on one side. "The

Contact has said it's a Deeyan disease. Don't worry. It's not your fault."

Agapanthus stared at him. She wished her eyes were his color; that bright yellow.

"It's not your fault," Pittick repeated. "No one can control these things, except the Gods."

"Anyway," Uncle Sonlo said. He left Imari's side and stepped over to them from across the room. "Maybe all any of this means is that you scrawny exchangers are stronger than you look."

Agapanthus tried to smile. Her cheeks felt too stiff, like they were composed of small rocks, or gravel, and would fall apart at any moment.

"You're not going out today, are you?" she asked Pittick.

"We have to. People need to eat. Especially now, to keep up their strength."

"What about the—"

"And the stores are still low."

"But they said everyone should stay in their homes, besides meals."

"Except the food gatherers. Fishers and game-managers still need to go."

"Then I should come too."

"No—"

"Why not? I won't get sick."

"But you don't have to, Aga," Sonlo said. He moved back toward Imari, wrapping his arm around her shoulders. "None of the other children are going to be apprenticing today."

Pittick nodded, his eyes absently shifting over the walls. "Go sit with Leera," he said. "She needs someone with her."

She imagined coming up behind Leera, hunched over in the corner of her room, her back curved as she cried into her hands. She imagined tapping her on the shoulder; Leera whipping around with her face damp and faded, no expression but what could be described as withering. "It was you," she imagined Leera growling. "It was you."

Agapanthus ambled into the women's wing. She could still hear Aunt Imari's sputtering cries, even through the extra-thick walls of the meeting hall, built with two layers of black stone to withhold the impassioned noises of men and women joining together. Maybe she was also crying for her married sons. Imari would never know whether they lived or died.

As she passed the mural in the entryway, Agapanthus felt more tempted than ever to touch it. Just one finger. Just barely, fleetingly. But instead she continued on, into the chilled center of the house. The skin-carpeted common room. The bathing room. Surla and Tayzaya's room, in which Tayzaya lay dying. And, finally, Leera and Aunt Imari's shared room. The black-stone door was closed. It would only open for Imari or Leera. Agapanthus leaned her nose against its cold surface. It smelled fresh, sterile.

"Leera," Agapanthus called. That was all she said. She knew she should say more, something comforting, but what was there to say? If Leera wanted her company—her words—she would open the door. Agapanthus sank to her bottom and leaned against the wall. She had no idea how late in the day it was. It had been so long since she'd gone outside. How far along were Aamsh and Jord on their daily journey?

She waited, listening to her own breath. Maybe Leera had fallen asleep. Agapanthus thought of the Waters. She gave a little grunt of effort—something she only did when she was alone—and pushed herself up.

Then the door swept up and open. Leera's face was broken; it was changed. Even her lips, usually so thin, were burled with puffiness. She clasped Agapanthus's wrists. Her hands felt clammy with dried, old sweat. She pulled Agapanthus in for a hug. Her wild hair fell directly over Agapanthus's face, but she didn't dare pull away, or brush Leera's stale-smelling hair away from her eyes. If she moved, she knew it would be ruined. So Agapanthus held Leera tightly. She wondered if she should say, "It'll be alright," or, "She's with the Gods now." Or, maybe, again, "I'm sorry. I'm sorry." Inexpressible sorrow. But she said nothing, and they stayed wrapped up against each other. Agapanthus had never known anyone that had died. Sure, the old Contact. Lapars and his son. Some people on the island whose names she'd forgotten. But no one she really knew. No one like Grandmother Surla. She would miss her—even her roughness; her meanness. Where was she now? On one of the God stars? Her body burnt and evaporated?

A heavy sigh echoed against the stone hallway. Leera pulled away. There stood Aunt Imari, her unusually slender legs shivering.

"Has anyone checked on her?" Imari tilted her head toward Tayzaya's door. Her voice was that of someone already dead; hollow breath unsupported by timbre or sound.

"Not yet," Agapanthus said.

"She's dying, you know," Imari whispered so loudly that it hurt to listen to. Agapanthus wanted to clamp her hands over her ears.

Leera must have felt the same, because she curled her fingers over her lips—the symbol for quiet.

"I'm sorry," Imari said, and she repeated the same gesture over her own mouth. Her orange-yellow eyes looked like the reflection of the sun in the Waters.

"We're all sorry," Agapanthus said. She felt useless, like she shouldn't be standing there. Like she wanted to hide. She didn't know where to place her gaze, and everything about her felt too loud; her breathing, her throat as she swallowed, the faint rustle of her knee-length dress. The moment pulled and stretched and wandered on—the three of them staring at nothing, standing next to doors and doorways but unwilling to move through them. Agapanthus licked the dryness from her lips, and that, too, felt out of place. Her shoulders dropped. She looked solemnly at Leera. "I'm going to the Waters," Agapanthus said.

Leera nodded. A nod; a short, quick nod, and that's it. Agapanthus rushed past Aunt Imari, past the tempting mural, out the front door. The warm air fell upon her. It sunk into her paleness, absorbed into her weak bones. But she was growing stronger. Now she could run all the way from the house to the edge of the cliffs.

And so she did; all alone on the dirt paths, in the windy silence, under the enormous face of Imn, she ran. The hill spat dust as she coursed down it. Agapanthus bent over to allow her heart to slow, and to will her sweat to cease its pouring. The shore smelled especially like mud. Against the redness of the world, Agapanthus felt pasty and uncertain. She dropped her head back, still heaving and trying to calm her clenched leg muscles. Underneath the sky and the red clouds, underneath the unmoving light of the sun, she knew the stars were hiding. If Imn could be stripped away the stars would be there, just as she had seen them in the frozen lands. She wished she could see them now; all the other stars with planets around them, all the other Waters, and herd animals, and sicknesses, and girls staring alone at the sky. And her home sun, too. That was there, too.

Agapanthus pulled her soft, leather dress over her head. She dropped it over a boulder and dove into the Waters with her hands in a triangle over her head. Underneath, all sound was muffled but bright. She heard great whooshes and yawns unfold from the ripples and waves. Today the Waters were calm. She danced, each movement unburdened and weightless. Arms overhead, legs fluttering. For as long as she could hold her breath, she reveled in this freedom. Finally, Agapanthus surfaced. The wind cooled her face. Her neck immediately tensed against the weight of the sky.

There was something about the pink-orange-red of the sun. When she glanced at it quickly, without thinking, it made a certain emptiness come into her chest. Like she had nothing to grab on to. In those moments she became a cloud, or a plume of dust dissipating against the rocks and the dirt-scratched pebbles. She was made of little pieces, little dots, coming together to form a shape that was weak and breakable; a shape that, ultimately, was nothing, and would soon drift apart, or crash against the red-cliff canyons, and, finally, disappear.

She swam sloppily on her back over to the line of water plants. Far off in the deep Waters sat three fishing boats. If she listened with her ear cocked toward them, she could hear their voices, even over all that distance. Not words; just grumbles and coarse, brisk yells. Sonlo and Pittick were out there, too, nestled within the enormous fishery station. Good thing they were too far away to see her.

Agapanthus looked down at the still water; at her muddled reflection. She tried to splash it away but ended up staring at the ugly, blonde hair on her arms. Instead she dove back under. Though the Waters always shined darkly, its underbelly was clear. If she let herself sink down and down, Agapanthus could still see the sky. That's what it must have been like for Lapars Rq. Sinking. Sinking. Her back hit the bottom. She could even make out the God stars from the shallow floor. Flopping wildly, she searched the mud for rocks. Like a fish, like a water creature. She rushed to the surface for air.

Another exchanger stood on the far end of the shore. It was Glaux Lari, one of the much older exchangers. He was technically still a child, since he had never made the swim to the other island, but his hair was white and his skin looked thin and fragile. That was how the Water People aged; through the skin and hair, instead of the through the voice and the eyes. With Deeyans you could just sense someone's place in life. With exchangers it was hard to tell, because some of them looked very old but most were still children. She wondered when Glaux would be sent back. She wondered if she'd be allowed to stay that long, too

Glaux stepped closer. He walked along the waterline, each foot steadily imprinting on the tiny rocks. Why was he there? Why did he have to ruin everything? Agapanthus crept out of the sea, slipped on her sun-warmed dress, and, still dripping, ran barefoot up the hill. It was about time she went home, anyway.

She walked slowly past the scattered bi-lobed, black-stone homes that looked just like her own. People were dying inside them. Old people especially; unable to breathe, unable to think. Dead, dying, ceasing to be anything more than muscle and skin. Agapanthus kept her arms close to her sides and pushed each footstep deep into the dusty soil.

As soon as the door opened, shadow replaced the resonant outdoor heat, and, instead of the movements of the Waters, she heard Imari's wailing.

"Gone!" Imari screeched. "Gone!" It was almost a song; almost the accompaniment to a water drum.

Something thumped against the floor. Agapanthus rushed into the common room to find Aunt Imari on her knees. A thin lock of hair was stuck to the wetness of her sallow cheek. Agapanthus asked her what happened, if she was alright.

"Go—" she couldn't even finish the word without dissolving into trembling tears. Agapanthus stepped back slightly. She crouched down to Imari's level. For a brief moment all she could think of was that people sobbing looked insurmountably dirty. Leera had looked that way, too. They suddenly devolved into such an unkempt, harrowed state. Agapanthus had never cried like that. They were adults; was it okay to act like this, even in such times?

But how could she be thinking about that when Imari was there in front of her, grasping her stomach, rearing her neck up and down? She had devolved into something ancient. *Our ancient predecessors*, the audiobook called them. *The animal-people whose most striking difference from modern peoples was their inability to make art; and, perhaps, their inability to dream.*

Agapanthus covered her eyes. Why couldn't she just focus? Why couldn't she just help Imari stop crying?

"Is it—" she was going to say Tayzaya, but she didn't need to. Imari's eyes—the sharpness of her stare—told her that, yes; Great-Aunt Tayzaya, too, had died. "Does she need moved, like we did with Surla?"

Suddenly Imari calmed her shuddering. She breathed in through her mouth, still hunched over. "She's already gone. Oh, Aga," she said. "Oh, my little Aga, you're all I have."

"But you have Sonlo. And Leera."

Imari said nothing. She wiped the snot from her nose with the side of her hand. "My aunt is dead. My mother is dead."

Agapanthus clasped her lips together, and she glanced at the ceiling. Suddenly she felt hot. So hot she wouldn't have been surprised if a hydrothermal vent opened under her feet. She could imagine herself blistering and rubbed bare with burning liquid.

"Where's Leera," Agapanthus stated. She did not ask it, could not ask it. Could not give Imari the chance to hold her there any longer. She slipped around Imari's folded knees; her oddly skinny thighs.

"We're the elders now," Imari said when Agapanthus's back was turned. "Unless Leera has her own daughter, this is it. By the Gods, she's been trying long enough. And I'm not having any more children; I'm too tired. So this is it. Our house will be given away. We're the last ones."

Each word died a little as Agapanthus stepped further down the hallway. Agapanthus was not a real daughter. She'd never imagined herself to be. Pittick was foster-father. Leera was foster-mother. They were substitutes. So was she.

Leera's door was closed. "I heard," Agapanthus said through it. She wasn't an adult. She didn't know how to comfort. Maybe she should stop trying. But she was the non-relative, the one who shared no blood. She was, on some level, the guest. And so she could not cry. And so she could do nothing but yell through Leera's sealed door: "Have they delivered the meal yet?"

Of course they hadn't, or she would've seen it in the front hall.

If it wasn't for all of this, it might have been kind of fun to have the meal delivered; to eat together in a circle on the floor, all alone, all private, their chewing abnormally loud.

The door opened. Leera was sitting on her cushions in the darkness. It was like the world was falling apart, Agapanthus thought.

"Come sit with me." Leera patted her side. Agpanthus rested on her knees, upright, stiff-backed. She squinted through the darkness, trying to find somewhere to focus her eyes. She ended up staring at the polished box in the corner of the room, where Leera stored her clothes.

Leera's voice startled her. "I hope you're happy here."

That was the worst thing she could've said. Agapanthus stretched her legs out in front of her, then bent them and rested her chin on her knees. Her dress had grown damp from her dripping hair.

"All of this change has made me realize how fast everything moves. Everything and everyone is slipping away. I just hope we've done well with you. I hope you're happy."

"How can I be happy when Surla and Tayzaya just died?"

"I don't mean today. I mean over time. I mean over all. I hope you consider yourself a happy girl."

Agapanthus nodded. Her eyes remained on the box. The darkness covering the room felt unsteady. It was gray, not black. Drips of light leaked in from the open doorway. It felt like everything was buzzing. Like the air was alive.

Leera rubbed Agapanthus's back. "Did you have a good swim?"

"Yeah," Agapanthus said, even though she really just wanted to nod and creep away. "I'm getting a lot better at it. A lot stronger."

"That's good. Good. Pretty soon you'll be across the channel, right?" Leera laughed through her nose; a loud huff.

"Maybe," Agapanthus said. "Other exchangers have done it. Why not me?"

"But not—"

"Someday, not now. I'm not ready yet."

Leera grabbed Agapanthus's hand. "You have no idea what it's like, Agapanthus. It's not just another—another swim, another strengthening exercise. Think about it. Think about how far that is, how choppy the Waters are out that deep. You've seen it in the fishing boats. It's rough. Can you even visualize yourself doing it? Can you visualize every moment, every boring stroke when you're halfway out? Not just the finish. Not just the send-off. You have to think of that time in the middle where you're too tired to keep going, and you can't catch your breath, and the wind is blowing water in your eyes. You can't just go into it—"

"I'm not. That's why I said I'm not ready yet."

"You need to realize you might never be ready, Aga."

Agapanthus weakened her grip. Leera's hand was no longer clammy, but Agapanthus's was.

"Most exchangers never do it," Leera said.

"Who cares, anyway," said Agapanthus. "Why does it matter? I'll be leaving someday. Why does any of this matter?"

"You're here now," Leera said. "And Pittick, and Sonlo, and Imari, and all of us; we love you. And we don't want you to drown." She paused. "Besides, it's unseemly for an exchanger to swim the rite of passage. There's just no need for it."

They sat in silence together for some time. Agapanthus finally wandered into the children's hall. Imari, too, had gone to bed. Agapanthus wondered if the men were back yet, or if the meal was waiting outside the door. But she didn't care enough to find out. Instead she wound herself up in her blankets and tried to sleep; to sleep for so long that, when she woke up, the sickness would be past.

Eventually the sickness did pass, but it took nearly half a year. By the time the Contact announced that it was safe to return to work, and to eat meals in the cafeteria again, about half of Yeela's elders had died, plus a handful of adults and children. No medicine was manufactured to treat it. The sickness simply fled, as though it had grown tired of those it tormented.

The Contact called the people to the shore and announced that three of the seven Council members had died. "I'll heed the guidance of the Gods as I look for worthy successors," the Contact said. His hair had grown longer. It hung by his chin, framing his face. Red and black; the contrast was beautiful. And his cheeks looked so high and structured, Agapanthus thought as she watched him speak. He must have grown handsome with worry. She imagined him sitting in his shell-decorated black-stone palace, combing his hair, his brow furrowed.

Agapanthus wanted to laugh; to startle the silence of the crowd. She didn't, of course. Could she not focus? Why did she think of weird things like this? Maybe she was just giddy at the return of normalcy. The return of life. Without the Deeyans and other exchangers roaming the shores, the only life nearby were the water plants. Everything else was relegated to the center of the island—where vents sputtered and shell-bearing orscops were hunted—and the fisheries of the deep Waters—where the water creatures swam free, and the fish circled restlessly in their net prisons. The wind sometimes felt alive, and the rocks, too, but she knew they weren't.

Maybe the Waters were. She wasn't quite sure about that.

This came to her mind again the next day as she rushed over the Waters on the little round boat that led out to the fishing vessels. She felt the immensity of the Waters; its calmness, its kindness, its power. She could see it breathing. The ripples out this far were dark purple, and the choppy surface heaved and rolled. She decided that, yes, the Waters were alive.

"Are you nervous to get back to work?" Pittick asked. He sat closely next to her, looking over the side of the boat as the boatman paddled.

"No. I'm only going to be observing, still."

"Yeah, but you've got to keep up with me."

Agapanthus smiled. "I can handle it."

The boat slowed. Pittick stepped out on to the floating dock, made of smoothly sanded bone. That step was so easy for him. He held both of Agapanthus's hands and helped her out of the boat.

"Well, thank you, Aravi Murialis," Pittick said to the boatman.

"It's my job, Pittick Caracynth," Aravi—slender but strong-looking—said. His face was so round; Agapanthus thought he was the perfect person to captain a circular boat. "Good luck with the Council. I hope you get it."

Pittick laughed, and he led Agapanthus up the dock, into the square, metallic vessel.

"The Council?" Agapanthus said.

"Just a rumor. Probably not true."

Inside the vessel, rows of hanging, triangular lights reflected off the silver walls. Nothing creaked or shook with the water beneath. Everything was immobile. Unmovable. The vessel had been a gift from the Gods long before Agapanthus—or even Pittick—was around. It was ancient, dating back to the Awakening. After all this time, it had never browned, nor dirtied, nor lost its shine. It still smelled crisp. The windows had not fogged. Even dust had resisted landing on the silver walls, or the shining floors. The vessel was perfection. It was immutable.

"Agapanthus Caracynth," a small voice said from behind Agapanthus's shoulder. It was Lekrish Pfierq's daughter/apprentice.

"Erabet Pfierq! I'm so glad you're not dead." Agapanthus rested her hand on Erabet's head, and Erabet did the same to her. It was good to see her friend again; her first friend, her only friend.

Pittick and Erabet's father continued walking, their heads bent together as they spoke.

"I knew you wouldn't be dead, you exchanger, you. Good thing. I would've missed you." Erabet sighed, carefully gripping a blonde lock of Agapanthus's hair. "And your hair."

"My hair?" Agapanthus laughed.

"It always gets me. It's yellow. Yellow!"

Pittick and Erabet's father glanced back at them from down the hall. Agapanthus and Erabet began walking to catch up with them. Erabet's quick, fluttering steps forced Agapanthus to fast-walk. It felt more like a jog.

"My hair's light brown. Just like yours, but way lighter," Agapanthus said breathily.

"And a lot thicker."

"Not that much." Agapanthus gathered her hair, twisted it, and rested it over her shoulder. She looked at the floor, trying to disappear from Erabet's yellow-orange, large-pupiled eyes. But Agapanthus's reflection lurked on the mirrored floor, and the shining walls. She tried hard not to close her eyes, though she desperately wanted to.

Instead she looked over at her friend. Erabet had tiny, black hairs above her lip. They were barely noticeable unless you looked for them, but Agapanthus always did. She rejoiced in Erabet's flaw. She liked her more for it. As they continued down the tall, narrow hallway, through the glass doors and out to the nets, Agapanthus glanced sporadically at Erabet's shadowed upper lip. Some of the exchanger men grew hair on their faces, but the women didn't; and certainly Deeyans didn't. Before Erabet—before those tiny little hairs, like those in an eyebrow—Agapanthus hadn't even thought they could grow hair on their faces. She wondered if other people noticed it.

"It smells today," Erabet said as the wind blew wildly over them.

"Yeah. Some of the fish probably snagged on the net."

Their fathers stood together at the edge of the dock. The Waters churned grayly in front of them, and the metal rings holding up the nets bobbed like water plants. Imn painted the mirrored building red, orange, and an unmistakable black. The neighboring island, Shre, looked broken. It looked bulky and overturned, with its hills and the haze of its shoreline jutting rudely above the deserted expanses. Even this far out, it seemed a long swim away.

Agapanthus and Erabet leaned against the building. The workers filed around all seven nets, checking ropes, stirring the water with metal poles, pouring in massacred chunks of vent-feeding fish they bought from fishermen. Voices and clanking metal muffled the warbled song of the Waters.

"You're going to do it, right?" Agapanthus nodded toward Shre. "Swim over?"

"Of course."

Yes, obviously; all Deeyans do. All real Deeyans.

Agapanthus nodded. She felt her throat constrict. It suddenly hurt to swallow. Why did it bother her? She'd known the answer even before she asked it. Now she wanted to ask when Erabet was going to do it, but she didn't. She couldn't. She didn't want to be left behind.

"Are you?" Erabet asked. Smiling, laughing, her face wide, thick, so strong the strings of muscles showed through her cheeks.

Agapanthus's eyes remained wide. She raised her shoulders up to her neck. She wanted to shrink away. To disappear. What could she do? Run? Hide in the fish-slaughtering room? Jump into the nets and swim? She wanted to push away Erabet's laughing, squinting, yellow-toothed face. Or punch her. Or shove her to the ground.

"Are you girls watching?" Pittick's voice echoed toward them. He waved. "This is how you pull the dead fish out of the water."

"We've seen this a million times." Erabet tilted her head toward the fathers. "Let's get closer."

As they watched the bulky fish-sifter burrow through the water, Agapanthus finally relaxed her shoulders. Even as the mechanical scooper resurfaced with steady, neat droplets of red slipping off its sides, she felt better. Pittick steered the feathery chunks into an open stone container, which would later be poured into the deeper Waters. The farmed Marbar fish didn't eat each other, but water creatures would devour the pieces in mere moments.

"Erabet, do you think everyone is blaming the Sickness on the exchangers?"

"Why would they?"

"Exchangers were the only ones not to get sick."

"That doesn't mean you caused it, though. No one's saying that. If anything, I think everyone looks up to you guys a little more."

"That's what my Uncle Sonlo said."

"Where is your Uncle Sonlo today?" Erabet asked. The machine's loud whirring finally receded.

"He had a meeting with the Council. To see if they can add another net onto the fishery."

"The Council? He should've just waited until Pittick was added on." Erabet pushed her lips together. Her face-hair caught the dim light. "I heard my father saying yesterday that the Contact's going to announce it today, right after the meal."

"And how would he know?"

"He's good friends with Akinan. And they always ask the Council who they want on, and of course everyone said Pittick. How could they not after what he did during the Sickness?"

"I hope he's not added," Agapanthus whispered. Pittick's back was turned toward the container.

"Why?"

"Because then I'd have to stop my apprenticeship. I don't want to shadow Leera at the electricity-control center. That would be so boring."

"Just petition to work with Sonlo. Or someone else. You could do anything!"

"I guess," Agapanthus said. Pittick still had the control device in his hand. She thought back to the first time she'd followed him to work. How he introduced her as "my daughter, Agapanthus." And, during the break, as they sat alone on the edge of the front dock, with their bare feet dangling over the edge, Agapanthus had asked him, "Why did you tell them that?"

"Tell them what?"

"That I'm your daughter. I'm only your foster-daughter."

"In my mind, there's not much of a difference," he said.

"Well in my mind, there is." As soon as she said it, she wished she hadn't. The words sat unpleasantly in the air, right between their noses. Echoing, revolving, muttering.

Pittick had nodded once, biting his lip. Then, with a quick turn of his head, he'd smiled at Agapanthus. "Well too bad I'm the one doing the introducing." He jumped up and jogged toward the front door, like he wanted her to chase him. And she jumped up as quickly as she could, which was a deliberate and aching speed, like pushing a sore muscle past the point it was able to stretch to. And she followed him back into the building, where she was now "my foster-daughter, Agapanthus." But Pittick had patted her proudly on the shoulder as he said her name; as it fell from his mouth like smooth clay stretched taut. He had kept her close all day, and made sure that she understood what she was watching. She loved working with Pittick.

So when, that night after the meal, the Contact's voice came over the speakers, she clenched her teeth tightly together. As she walked to the shore with Imari, Sonlo, Leera, and Pittick, she said nothing. She focused her eyes on the hem of her dress, which she finally grabbed and rubbed between her thumb and finger to try to calm her nerves. They waited for the crowd—now slightly thinner after the Sickness—to surround them; for the Contact to stand at the confluence of water and rock-sand, with his slip-on shoes and tri-colored dress.

"The Gods have spoken to me, and they have told me who to appoint to the Council," the Contact boomed. "Their choices are based on the generosity, selflessness, and ethical nature of the following individuals. Here are their names."

Agapanthus grasped her hands together in front of her stomach. She dug her fingernails into her knuckles. Leera rubbed Pittick's arm, wearing a quickly-flashed smile.

"Elish Gryu, Pittick Caracynth, and Remera Quorquor."

Pittick didn't smile, nor did he raise his eyebrows in surprise. He simply walked to the front, took his place next to the Contact, and looked back at the audience with his lips slightly, barely turned up. Elish and Remera—older, especially bulky women who worked together at the health center—stood on either side of him. The four existing Council members drifted to the front as well, looking sleepy and hunched. Akinan reached for Pittick's scalp, but Pittick was too distracted by the roar of voices to notice. Agapanthus thought she saw his mouth form Pittick's name, but still, Pittick remained turned, half-smiling. Akinan finally dropped his hand and eyed the audience. He smiled forcefully at the cheering, word-jumbled mass; at Agapanthus and her family.

The Contact greeted each of the Council members. None of them were allowed to touch the Contact's head; that was forbidden, because that was the receiving station—that was where the Gods whispered and shouted and spoke in their strange, unknown language. Agapanthus imagined it sounded much like someone breathing loudly through their nose.

She glanced at Leera—bellowing wildly, her thin lips perched open—and at Aunt Imari and Uncle Sonlo—his hands funneled around his mouth; her tiny nose scrunched in delight. Agapanthus suddenly felt self-conscious for her own yells. They were too low-pitched. Too undulating, too back-of-the-throat. She stopped cheering, but pretended to by opening her mouth wider.

The Contact finished his greetings. He nodded to the people of rightwards Yeela, his long hair brushed loosely behind his ears. The outline of his strong, muscle-hewn body was silhouetted against the home sun. His skin was that exact red. The exact shade of Imn's eternal glow. The Contact was a piece of the sky. He saluted the God stars, watching them for a moment. Then, without saying anything else, he walked up the hill. Every time he did that, Agapanthus wondered if it was an act to make him more relatable; to make him seem like a regular person. Or maybe he was a regular person. Maybe he'd never wanted to hear the voices. Maybe he was the one person who didn't care about the highness of the position, or the shell necklaces, or the big house. Maybe he wanted to be in the crowd, not in front of it. But there was nothing he could've done. You couldn't ignore the Gods. You just couldn't.

At home, all five of them sat on the red dirt, which, though dry, morphed around their bodies like a spongy fabric. They sat in a circle, legs crossed, arms flying as they spoke. Aamsh and Jord had fallen very low; only their top halves could be seen above the cliff that hid the sea. Most people were in bed already. It lurked at the edges of the conversation, but they kept it at a safe distance.

"I wish they would've said why exactly you were picked," Imari said. "What exactly caught the eyes of the Gods."

"You know that's not a question we should be asking," Leera said.

"I know. But I do wonder. If it was just going into the fisheries during the Sickness—" she stopped herself, glancing at Sonlo. He readjusted himself so he was sitting on his knees.

"Pittick's done a lot more than that," Uncle Sonlo said. "He's the one everyone goes to. The one everyone looks up to. Or, he was." He laughed slightly. "Now I guess you're just one of those distant Council people, always serious. You ever notice how they don't smile? Or if they do, it's obviously forced. Like Akinan today. What was that about?"

"He was embarrassed," Agapanthus said as she pulled on the end of her hair. "Pittick didn't see him reaching out."

"Yeah, I saw that too," Leera said.

Pittick bit his lip. "I hope he doesn't think I did it on purpose. I was distracted. They usually don't greet each other when they first get up there—I didn't know we were on those terms."

"He was only doing it because of Surla, anyway," Sonlo said. "You know, because they were so close."

Imari exhaled so heavily a small cloud of dust blew up onto her bare knees.

"Well I'm just happy you made it on," Leera said.

"Yeah. One step below the Contact!" Sonlo said.

"Yes, congratulations, Pittick," Imari said quickly.

Agapanthus traced a circle in the dirt. She suddenly felt like she was watching something she wasn't supposed to. She focused instead on the amber glow of the world. The air smelled distantly like the Waters, and, even more distantly, like rain. It hadn't rained in such a long time; it was so long ago that all Agapanthus remembered about it was the open smell, and the *tick-tick-tick* right before the water sloshed down in heaping gusts. They'd stayed inside all day, except for the meal, when Pittick had carried her through the rain as they all sprinted—even Surla and Tayzaya. And, with their hair frayed, and their faces moist, they all huddled together in the cafeteria, listening to the roof shudder. No one even went to work that day. The rain seemed to last forever, but it was only one day. And, afterward, the cliffs were maroon, and the Waters were grayer than ever, and it all made her inexplicably sad. It was the same loneliness that Imn sometimes made her feel.

As they stood up to go inside, Agapanthus said to Sonlo, "I was thinking, Sonlo. I was thinking I could petition to apprentice with you. Then I can stay at the fisheries."

He shook his head as he brushed the dirt from his knees. It was almost hard to tell where his skin ended and where the dirt began. "I'm sorry, Aga, but I don't think so. I'm going to have enough work to do, running everything, without someone following me around."

Agapanthus froze. "Pittick never had a problem with it. And he was running everything, too."

"Yeah, but Pittick had my help." His eyes met with Pittick's. Everyone was waiting to go inside, shuffling, turning their faces away from Sonlo. "We were co—we were co-leaders. Co-supervisors. Now I have to figure out how to do this alone."

"You could always hire someone to take my place," Pittick said.

"I probably will."

Leera slapped her hands against her sides. "You both get some prestige out of this. Pittick's on the Council, and Sonlo's the executive leader of the fisheries." Her voice was balmy, as she said it. Her eyes flickered between the two men.

"I was already the leader. Or one of them, at least," Sonlo said. "But that's great for you, Pittick. Great for you. Like I said. Moving up in the world."

"Thanks," Pittick said expressionlessly.

Agapanthus swallowed hard. "But who am I going to apprentice with?"

"You can always come with me," Leera said.

Agapanthus nodded because that was what she was supposed to do. She couldn't force herself to reciprocate Leera's smile, but she twisted her lips into a slightly-more-uplifted-than-normal-straight-line. "I guess," Agapanthus said.

"Or, hey, you could come work with me," Imari said, "at the water portation center. You've never been inside, have you? I think you'd like it. You love the Waters so much." She stepped closer to Agapanthus, bending her knees as though she were going to bend down to Agapanthus's level. But Agapanthus had grown, and she was now the same height as Imari, and slightly taller than Leera. Aunt Imari must've forgotten. Her eyes gaped. They reminded Agapanthus of holes. She couldn't help thinking back to the Sickness; back to Imari's howls and deathlike hollowness. It seemed to her that that was the real Imari. This smile that pushed her cheekbones up to her eyes; this light-brown dress that clung to her nearly-flat chest; the soft roll of wispy, clean-smelling hair that framed her high forehead; all of it seemed fake. Imari on the floor; that had been real—like watching someone as they slept, or from the corner of a room when they didn't know you were spying on them.

"Wouldn't you like to learn how water gets into our homes? Oh, you would love it, Aga." She looked at Leera. "She would just love it." She looked back to Agapanthus again. "What do you say?"

"Sure," Agapanthus said. She nodded at first, but then stopped because she worried Imari would realize she was faking her enthusiasm.

"I'll file for the petition tomorrow," Imari said. "And, aren't we in luck now? Pittick, you'll make sure it gets through, right?"

"I'll try my best."

As the men and the women drifted into their separate wings, Leera wrapped her arm around Agapanthus's shoulder. "This will be good for you," she whispered, her mouth so close to Agapanthus's ear that her hot breath burned. "And it will be good for Imari, too." She gave Agapanthus a squeeze, then pushed her forward through the door.

"Great! Now you can get a few days off while the petition goes through," Imari said. Her voice filled the empty front room. "And don't worry if you end up not liking it, Aga. I won't mind. But I think you will. I really do."

"Great." It came out sounding stiffer than she'd intended. Imari didn't seem to notice. She continued down the hall, her footsteps lighter than they had been since Great-Aunt Tayzaya died.

Three days passed while the petition was waiting to be approved. Agapanthus felt the same dread she felt before a check-up. Water portation? That sounded almost as boring as Leera's job.

She went alone each day to the Waters, just as she'd done when she was younger. She practiced rolling her arms over her head; clenching her stomach and legs—muscles that she only felt power in when she was underwater. She practiced the rhythm of kick, reach, kick, reach. Stretch, lengthen, kick, reach. After all these years she could hold her breath for a long time. She rarely had to turn her cheek to the side and suck in quick spurts of air. Which was good, because that slowed her down. Agapanthus treaded water as she re-tied her hair with a delicate ribbon. The waves slapped up against her chin. She pursed her lips and sipped some of the water. Clean, sun-warmed. As she was just about to fall under, to re-moisten her wind-dried face, she heard footsteps behind her on the sand. And there was Pittick.

"Shouldn't you be at work?" Agapanthus yelled, smiling. She stroked closer to shore.

"I just got off. Good news, Aga! You're approved!"

"Good!" Agapanthus called automatically, but her eyes fell to the great dark Waters surrounding her, and she concentrated on her head-above-water swimming.

When she pushed herself up onto the rocky sand, Pittick handed Agapanthus her dress. Imn was warm enough that Agapanthus didn't even want to cover her body. The air felt only slightly cooler than the Waters. If she was younger, she might have walked home naked. But, at this age, it was only acceptable to be clotheless when swimming.

"Is this what you've been up to all day?" Pittick asked.

"Yep. Training," Agapanthus said. She wrung out the tip of her hair so it wouldn't drip down her back.

"Training—for what?"

"You know," Agapanthus said. "The rite of passage. The channel."

"That again?" His back hunched over as he crossed his arms. "You're not really thinking about it, are you?"

"Pittick, I can't stop thinking about it."

"Well think about something else. Your apprenticeship."

Agapanthus was silent. She exhaled. "Does that mean you don't think I should train?"

"No. I can't allow it, Aga."

"You can't *allow* it?"

"I'm your foster-father, Agapanthus. Leera and I are your guardians here. We're in charge of your safety. And there is nothing less safe than crossing that channel." He pointed toward the Waters. Heavy, crisp; both moving and still at once.

"I don't care how safe it is. So many people do it, think of how many people—"

"How many Deeyans. How many *Deeyans* do it. You're not Deeyan. You're an exchanger. You're different. Your body is different. You're not built to do things like that. Some exchangers get lucky, but they're bigger than you. Stronger than you."

"But I can do it. I know I can."

"Please, Agapanthus. Please don't put yourself at risk. It's not worth it."

"But it *is* worth it. Because it's always been there—because I've always *wanted to do it*. It's like something is calling me to do it. Like the sacred Waters are calling me."

"The Gods wouldn't like to hear you talk like that. The Waters aren't cognizant. They can't be sacred."

"You're starting to sound like Leera."

"But it's true. The Gods—"

"That's all any of you care about. The Gods, the Gods. The stupid Gods! I'm not even allowed to worship them. What have they done for me? Why should I give a fuck what any of them say?"

Pittick grabbed Agapanthus's wrist mid-gesture. In contrast to his deep, red skin, her hand looked even paler than usual. His grip was tight. She felt it against her bone. "You're going to have to ask Their forgiveness now," he said quietly, through his teeth. He pulled her toward the hill. "I'm taking you to the Contact."

By the time they arrived at the Contact's meeting hall, it was about time for the meal. A short man stood next to the tall glass doors, a bowl of red-breasted sper meat in his hands. Agapanthus realized how hungry she was. She wished she was in the cafeteria. She wished she was anywhere else.

"Can we go in first? Please?" Pittick asked him. "We won't be very long."

The delivery man nodded. Pittick shoved open the door. He tightened his grip on Agapanthus's arm. She had never been inside the Contact's building. From a distance she'd seen it, and his enormous home not far down the road, both bulky and strange. They were the two biggest buildings on this side of the island. But she'd never been inside either one.

It smelled a lot like the inside of the fishery vessel. It must be the smell of the Gods, then; everything they'd built had that same smell—that new, wrapped-up, airless smell that was so different from the sweet warmth of stone buildings.

"Hello?" Pittick's voice echoed. His yellow eyes traced the metallic walls. The room was empty. Agapanthus realized that Pittick didn't know what to do, either. She sighed and looked up, and there was the sky.

"The ceiling is made of glass," she muttered, because she thought that maybe if she tried to be normal, Pittick would like her again. But he ignored her.

"We request a meeting with the Contact," Pittick said to the concrete floors.

A door opened. Out stepped the Contact. Agapanthus's cheeks grew hot. He was handsome. So, so handsome. That was all she could think. So handsome! Look at his strong chin, his matte skin, his small, flat nose.

"Pittick Caracynth," the Contact said. His leather shoes clicked as he drifted toward Pittick. He greeted him, hand on head. "Didn't I just see you earlier today at the Council meeting? What's this about?"

"My foster-daughter, Agapanthus. She said some things she shouldn't have. Concerning the Gods."

"Oh." The Contact shifted his gaze toward Agapanthus, then back at Pittick, who still hadn't quite stood up straight. "Well, most of their kind does that at one point or another. Questioning their identity. Questioning their place on our planet. Nothing unusual. For the first offense, I usually just deliver the apology to the Gods." He raised his eyebrows at Agapanthus. "But only if you're really, really sorry."

Agapanthus nodded. If she tried to speak, she knew her voice would be gone. Or, at best, it would be squeaky, rough, stuck in her throat.

"If this happens again, you'll have to be punished. And we don't want that, do we?" After a short pause, he clapped his hands together. "Alright, time for the meal. You two better be off." He turned. "Oh, and Pittick; as a member of the Council, I expect you and your family to display model behavior. I expect others to emulate you. Understand?"

Pittick nodded hurriedly. "Of course," he said, a little too loudly.

The Contact retreated into the wall-door. As it closed, the walls reverberated—smack—and the sound wobbled overhead like the whole building was shaking. The meal-deliverer bent his neck inside the front door. "All set?" he asked without any hint of laughter; without any glint of a smile. He looked tiny against the towering entryway.

Pittick nudged Agapanthus forward. Her eyes suddenly felt tired. She realized that she'd been afraid to blink; afraid to look away from the Contact's high cheeks, and the deep gully between his nose and upper-lip, so unusually pronounced, up that close, and so strangely beautiful, like he had carefully dug it into his own face, and wore it purposefully like an adornment. And the polished, bright red stones around his neck; they looked like something out of the collection in her box at home. Maybe she would string hers together? All the different colors and shapes, all in a row, with the carap shell Pittick had given her right in the middle, on display against her pink skin and the thinness of her neck?

"I hope you took that to heart," Pittick said when they were back on the pathway. "The Contact knows you as a troublemaker now. Think of how that reflects on me. And Leera."

Is that what this was about, Agapanthus wanted to shout at him. Is that why I suddenly matter? Because you're on the Council now? Is that why you don't want me to swim the channel? But she didn't say anything at all. Her nose whistled with heavy breathing; with trying to keep up with Pittick's brunt stride.

"Just be more careful with your words, Aga. Be more careful with your thoughts, even. They can hear you. They may not be your Gods, but They're the Gods of Deeyae, and you're on our world, Their world, so you have to respect them. Okay?" He waited. "Okay, Agapanthus?"

"Okay," she grumbled. But she was lying. She hated them now. She hated the Gods. She hated Aamsh and Jord. She hated the handsome Contact who made her feel sweaty and small. And most of all she hated Pittick, walking alongside her. She hated the way his hands dangled bulbously at his hips. She hated his downturned lips, and the way they made his chin sag, just slightly. She hated how his bright yellow, round-oval eyes avoided her own face. Tears burned at the back of her eyes. She'd let him down. And soon she would let Leera down, too, when Pittick met her in the meeting hall and told Leera what had happened.

Agapanthus's stomach gurgled with hunger. Angrily, she tried to ignore it, tried to gaze stoically at the amber sky. She should run away. She should steal a round boat, paddle out to the al-most-invisible southern shoreline, the cusp of the frozenlands, and join the Others. What did they think of exchangers? They would probably call her Alien. They would make her their slave. Come, Alien, wash the bowls for us! Did they use bowls? Did they

build with stone, like the Deeyans did? Or did they use snow?
Ice? Did they even speak Deeyan, or had it been so long since the
Awakening that they had formed their own language?

Her stomach growled again. She felt hollow. Almost queasy.

"Sorry you missed the meal," Pittick said. "I bet you worked up
an appetite with all that swimming."

"Being hungry is my punishment, I guess." She should've said
something nicer, but they were almost home, and she was so over-
come with dread.

"Listen, Aga. Let's just keep this quiet, alright?"

"You mean—"

"I mean everything that's happened today. No one needs to
know."

"But you're going to tell Leera?"

He stopped; stared at the dirt. "I don't think we even need to
tell Leera. Why worry her?"

Agapanthus's hollowness fled from her abdomen. She felt as
though Imn had crawled inside her stomach, or her chest, and she
was warm. Her dripping hair no longer annoyed her. Her pains
of hunger dulled. Pittick was on her side. "Thank you, Pittick,"
she said, and she flung her arms around his middle. They hugged,
out there on the dirt expanses, all alone, everyone else just home
from the meal. She listened to his heart through his soft-skinned
dress. It was just like her own. Always counting, always humming,
like stones falling, like the Waters running up against the cliffs.
Her eyes felt wet, just from the pressure of closing them so tightly.
Pittick held Agapanthus by the shoulders, and he stroked the rich
blonde hair—mixed with brown, mixed with gold—right above
her forehead. Just once, just one pet, but it was so kind, and so
gentle, like he thought of her as glass, as a tiny, gangling carap
shell. And she knew then that she was his daughter, and that he
was her father, and that the word "foster" didn't matter. It had
never mattered.

She entered the house through the women's side, and she leaned close to the mural—the Waters, angularly carved. Each time she looked at it, it looked less real. It was just too thin. It didn't have that—that fullness that the Waters had. She poked her finger out, and she whispered, she actually whispered out loud, "Just once." She ran her fingertip over the concave edge of the carving. It felt like regular black stone. And nothing was left dented or sullied. It looked like she'd never touched it. It looked like she'd never even been there at all.

3

AGE: SIXTEEN EARTH-YEARS

"*Agapanthus.*" Aunt Imari stepped close, her mouth moving. "*Something-something* today?"

"What?" Agapanthus called back, because, even with Imari standing right at her shoulder, she couldn't hear over the clucking and sizzling of Portation Machine #6. The metal block was filled with water, which poured into it from the ceiling. Behind all the rattling, Agapanthus could still pick out the waterfall's sweetness. She could still focus on its tin drip, and the way the bright-white ceiling-lights made it, somehow, lusterless, like a solid sculpture of stone rather than water.

"I said—there's a new apprentice today," Imari yelled into her ear. She pointed at the glass wall on the side of the machine. "Push the button now; push the button. It's full."

"I was going to." Agapanthus clenched her teeth together. She slapped the button with the back of her hand, so her fingernails clacked against the shining God-metal. The water sashayed side to side—one, two, three, four times—and then sunk into the air as smoke. It would be split up, reappearing in several different homes, where portation receivers would deliver the water into bathing bowls—large bowls made of the tightly woven skin of water creatures—and into household drinking carafes.

What a relief, once the machine quieted. Then just the water trickled. It was like everything was finally still. Agapanthus felt as though she'd run up one of the tallest cliffs, and had finally made it to the top.

Imari stared at the portation machine as she spoke. "That's your one job, just to push that button. You need to be extra careful, because, if it overflows, the machine might break. We already lost a machine last year, and the Council said that the mechanics haven't figured out this technology yet. And certainly the Gods won't fix it for us."

"I know, Imari. I was here the day it broke, remember?"

"So just—watch. Be extra careful, okay? We don't want to have to move you back down to the observing stage." She finally looked at Agapanthus. The lights made Imari's cheeks look thinner than usual. "Now, why don't you take a break? Let's go see the new kid. I think she's your age. Just transferred from an apprenticeship with the audiobook makers. She's going to be working with Gmel Serenop." Imari paused. "Don't forget to turn it off."

"I know," Agapanthus said. She bit her lip and flipped off the switch.

"All the way off?"

"Imari, I do this every day when you're not here watching me. I know what to do."

"Okay; but if it overflows—"

"It's not going to overflow," Agapanthus said quietly. But Imari had already started walking.

There was the new girl, at the end of the dark hallway. Her silhouette was rounded on the sides of her stomach, jutting out right at the ribs, and her arms shook with a light layer of fat. Agapanthus recognized her immediately—Geleria Serenop, the girl she had been avoiding for years. *I'd rather be dead than be one of you.* Agapanthus considered running back into the portation room, pretending she'd forgotten something. *Experiment-subject.* But then she'd have to face Geleria eventually. They would be working in the same building, after all. Great.

And what had Agapanthus said to her? She'd called Geleria fat. Agapanthus rubbed her palms nervously together. That was so long ago. So, so long ago. She suddenly wished she'd worn a better dress today. The one with the dark brown stripe across the bust, and the covered shoulders. She felt disheveled. Her hair kept slipping across her forehead, itching, sticking in her eyelashes. And she kept hearing Geleria's young, high voice saying, *your kind,* with that squinted look. *Your kind. Alien.*

"Ah, there you are," Imari said when they were closer. "We were just coming to introduce you. This is my apprentice, Agapanthus Caracynth."

Geleria smiled. Her eyebrows curved sideways, and her thick, red cheeks puffed out. Agapanthus bent her knees so Geleria could reach her scalp. She was taller than most people now, except the other exchangers.

"Agapanthus Caracynth," Geleria said. Her voice wasn't as deep as Agapanthus expected it to have become. It sounded just like it had when she was a child. "I'm Geleria Serenop." Geleria pulled back her cold hand and it caught one piece of Agapanthus's hair—pulled it out with a sharp snap—but Agapanthus didn't say anything.

She knew it was her turn, but Agapanthus waited. She waited for some recognition, some glaring look, or snort, or half-smile. Was it because Imari was standing there silently? Just nodding like that?

"Nice to meet you," Geleria finally added with a throaty, nervous laugh.

Agapanthus shook her head, pretending like she'd forgotten her manners. "Oh, sorry," she said breathily. She touched the top of Geleria's head—cautiously, deliberately, careful not to appear too rushed or repulsed. "Nice to meet you, too."

Did she really not remember?

"I'm going to go see how they're doing upstairs. Aga, can you show Geleria around?" Imari nodded once more, then shuffled into the shadowed edge of the hall.

"Your hair is so pretty," Geleria said. Her voice was throaty. "Is it naturally like that?"

She couldn't take it anymore. "Geleria, we've met before. Do you really not remember me?"

"What?" Geleria furrowed her eyebrows together. "Where? When?" That's when Agapanthus knew she must be faking it. Geleria probably remembered every word. She had probably been avoiding Agapanthus all this time, too. And now she was just pretending. She was just trying to be nice.

"At the cafeteria. We were waiting in line." Agapanthus wasn't going to let her be nice.

"Okay. Sorry, I don't—"

"It was the day Lapars Rq and his son were drowned. You have to remember that."

"Well, yeah, but I don't remember who I was in line with before it happened. That was a long time ago."

Agapanthus began walking, her arms crossed over her chest because she didn't want them floundering at her waist; she felt Geleria's eyes on her, analyzing her alienness, searching for things to make fun of.

"Sorry," Geleria said, and she touched Agapanthus's shoulder. It wasn't an apology for not remembering, thought Agapanthus. It was Geleria's apology for all the things she'd said. For the first time, she realized that Geleria had been young. She'd probably just been echoing her parents. Now she was old enough to think for herself.

"Don't worry," Agapanthus said. "It's not important."

Although, it was—it would always be important to Agapanthus. She would often think back to that day in the cafeteria, how Grandmother Surla overheard the whole thing. She would think back to how she had returned to the shore in the following days and saw the Deeyan children running high in the sun-mottled cliffs, chasing each other, expending their boundless energy, running, just running forever without even breathing heavily, and on the days that they swam, they stayed on the opposite side of the beach from her, and, even though Geleria herself had moved on to play with a different group, Agapanthus never asked that group if she could join, and they never asked her either, nor did the mixed group of exchangers and Deeyans, and she pretended like it didn't matter, because she had stones to sort through, and the Waters to explore, and swimming to practice, but, really, she watched the other children constantly, and she relished their cheers and yells as they cut through the watery silence, because then she could at least imagine she was one of them. She'd always avoided the small group made up of only exchanger children. They were different from her. They weren't like her. Agapanthus didn't have friends until she met Erabet at the apprenticeship. Until she'd been *forced* onto Erabet. And Erabet had been kind, but for the longest time there was pity in her eyes. Now Agapanthus trusted her. She sometimes met with Erabet at the meal, where they sat facing each other as they ate bloodied hunks of raw meat. They talked about how things had changed. How Erabet was going to swim the channel any day now. How Agapanthus planned to stand at the edge of the Waters and cheer the loudest for her. Screams, yells, warbles, all the way until Erabet swam past the sight line, and maybe even then. All the way until those on Shre sent their signal, and carried her back on a small, fast boat. It was strange to think that the people on Shre didn't swim back the other way across the Waters. No one ever swam all the way to Yeela. They had their own rite of passage on

He was annoying. The way his head had moved when he talked, just slightly back and forth at the neck. And his too-long teeth sticking out of his brittle, wispy, bottom lip, flashing as he spoke, like fish teeth.

Geleria followed Agapanthus into the portation room. Just as the door was halfway open, Agapanthus imagined the machine bleeding with water, the silver floors glistening, the waterfall no longer trickling, but gurgling profusely. But this was not so, and, in the metallic, silver-washed room, everything was fine; the receptacle was only halfway filled; the filter-lights lining the inside of the cube colored the water a fierce yellow; the waterfall was whispering, lengthening, writhing.

"It's weird how the water just comes out of the ceiling like that," Geleria said.

"Not really. It's just another portation machine, up there. Like the ones in everyone's houses."

"I know. But it looks so different. It looks like it's coming from a miniature version of the Waters, shoved up there in the ceiling." Geleria looked up.

Agapanthus had often thought the same thing. She wouldn't admit it, though. She pressed her lips together and ran her fingers over the control panel of the machine, pretending to adjust things.

"So have you been here awhile?" Geleria asked. "I couldn't stand my last apprenticeship. I felt bad for leaving my father, but I couldn't take it anymore. It was at the audiobook producers. My job was to greet the readers as they came in. That's it, that's all I ever did. It's like I was never good enough to try the editing or the recording or anything else! Can you imagine? Being stuck at the same mindlessness for years and years? I couldn't take it anymore. So I said, I have to change. And I left."

Agapanthus nodded. She knew she should answer Geleria's question—have you been here awhile—but it was too lost within the rest of her words. Geleria didn't ask it again, either. She just stared up at the ceiling with the plump underside of her chin exposed.

"Yeah, I think I'm going to like working here." Geleria heaved in the air through her nostrils, and let it out through her mouth. "So. Are there any good guys here? Anyone handsome?" But she paused, and then said, "Oh, but I guess you wouldn't be looking, huh."

"Why not?" Agapanthus faced her. Her shoulders hunched over. She didn't like being so tall.

"Not that you don't like men, or that you wouldn't notice how they look. Just that, being an exchanger, it wouldn't matter to you as much, since you won't be mated. At least, not here."

Marriage was reserved for adults. Very few exchangers married, and, if they did, it was to other exchangers. Even then, it was looked down upon. No Deeyan had ever mated with an exchanger. At least, not officially.

"You never know," Agapanthus said.

"Yes, that's true. You never know. Some of you are very strong."

Agapanthus didn't even nod.

"I love your look, too. I wish that I was taller like that. You remind me of water plants, only pale."

You. That's what bothered her. *You*, the generic *you*. You people. You others. Aliens. Your kind. Aliens.

"Are you actually trying to be nice?" Agapanthus held her breath. She ran her finger and thumb over the hem of her dress. "Or are you purposefully trying to insult me?"

"What did I say?" Geleria's lips parted and her eyes widened. Within her large, black pupils, there was some sort of remorse. Some sort of sadness, or desperation. Maybe she was trying to be nice, but she just didn't know how.

"Never mind. Let's just keep going. I'll show you the other rooms."

They popped their heads into the other portation rooms. Every time, Agapanthus held out her hand and gestured to the

machine, scowled at it, and, if the operator was in there, she introduced them quickly. Then she hurried off to the next room without even giving Geleria a chance to touch heads with the other
person. Agapanthus felt like her limbs were filled with sand, and,
yet, she felt jittery at the same time.

At Portation Machine #2 they found Loao Tretn; Agapanthus
thought he was handsome, and he had recently moved up in his
apprenticeship, just like her, from observationship to actual work.
His skin was the reddest she'd seen—so red, red, red, deep, bright,
saturated red, that it was orange and pink and yellow, too; all colors at once, somehow blended into this beautiful, complex shade.

"Loao Tretn." Agapanthus couldn't help stepping all the way
into the room. He wasn't quite a friend yet, but she often came
in like this and spoke with him on breaks. Yesterday they'd been
talking about the Star Festival. They were both excited for the
next one, only two years away.

"Agapanthus Caracynth!" he said, and they lowered the crowns
of their heads for one another. Agapanthus had to bend her knees
and back so he could reach her. He was shorter than most Deeyan
men.

Geleria lurked behind Agapanthus. "Loao Tretn," Geleria said
quietly. "I'm Geleria Serenops."

"Nice to meet you, Geleria Serenops." He greeted her much
more easily than he had Agapanthus. Geleria was already the
same height as Loao. She barely even had to tilt her neck forward.

"It's Geleria's first day as an apprentice here," Agapanthus said.

"Oh really?" he said. His whole body was turned toward
Geleria. He rubbed his wrists as he spoke. "Who are you apprenticing with?"

Agapanthus hadn't even thought to ask how Geleria was related to Gmel Serenop. She hadn't cared enough.

"My uncle, Gmel Serenop. He's sponsoring me. Just got approved by the Council two days ago." She nodded and looked between the two of them.

"Okay, okay. And how do you like it here so far?" Loao asked. He was so kind, thought Agapanthus. It seemed like he cared about everyone he talked to. Like he loved everyone.

"It's nice," Geleria said. She opened her mouth like she would say more, but then she closed it again.

Loao's laugh overtook the silence. It was nasally; chuckling. Agapanthus realized it sounded a lot like the portation machines as they first turned on. She realized that, sometimes, she visualized his face on top of the machine. Sometimes she pretended he was the machine. Agapanthus laughed, too.

"Hopefully this place grows on you," Loao said to Geleria. "Don't worry, the first day is always hard. Everything's new."

"Yeah," Agapanthus weakly agreed.

She was about to say something more, when Geleria said, "It's just all so much at once."

"Overwhelming," Agapanthus added. "I remember my first day so well."

"Me too," Loao said. "My mother shoved me in here and didn't introduce me to anyone. Anyone! She didn't even have me shadow her. I was afraid to leave the room, afraid to walk around, or ask anyone, because I thought people would be all—I thought it would be—I don't know. It sounded intimidating. But then the second day she was less busy, so she showed me around some more, and I started doing the observing, and then working at the machine."

"And then you met me," Agapanthus said.

"And then I met you."

"So you two like working here, then?" Geleria asked, with her arms crossed just like Agapanthus's, under her breasts but over her stomach.

"It's alright," Agapanthus said. She half-smiled at Loao.

"I like it," he said. "It's pretty easy."

"Does that mean it's boring?" Geleria asked.

"Exactly," Loao said, nodding enthusiastically, his hair dangling darkly next to his yellow eyes. "That's exactly what it means."

"Yeah," Agapanthus said again. "It's boring, but it's something. At least we get lots of breaks."

"Yep. But we should probably get back to work soon," Loao said.

Agapanthus agreed, even though she didn't want to leave Loao. He told Geleria it was nice meeting her; that they should talk again tomorrow, if she had time. He didn't say anything to Agapanthus, but she assumed this was because she came in every day, anyway. She didn't need an invitation.

When they were back in the hallway, Geleria asked, "Do you guys talk a lot?"

"Yeah. All the time."

"Does he ever come into your room like that?"

"No." Agapanthus paused. "No, he doesn't. Maybe because he just expects me to come into his."

"Hmm."

"Do you like him?"

"It's kind of soon to tell. But he's cute. Yeah." Geleria inhaled deeply. "I hope you don't mind. If he and I got together, I mean. If I end up liking him."

"Why would I mind? It's not like he and I could ever be together, anyway."

"Exactly," Geleria said, gesturing toward Agapanthus. "Exactly."

"Do you—think he likes you?"

"Too soon to tell. But why wouldn't he like me?" Geleria looked at the silver floor, at her wide, flat feet shrouded in plain leather shoes. "Unless he thinks I'm ugly?" Then her eyes hit Agapanthus's, straight on, eyebrows raised, lips tightened together. "Unless he thinks I'm fat?"

So she did remember. Agapanthus wanted to say something. She wanted to shout at her, or shake her by the shoulders. Or yell, you *are* fat. Something. But she didn't. All she said was, "Don't worry, it seems like he likes you already."

And Geleria smiled. It felt, to Agapanthus, that they had made some sort of non-verbal agreement; they'd agreed to acknowledge the past without re-living it, and they'd agreed to be friendly in the future. At least, that's what Agapanthus got from it. Who knew what Geleria was thinking. She had eyes that always seemed shaded, or distant. Agapanthus couldn't read true emotion anywhere within the broad planes of Geleria's face. And whenever Geleria laughed her shuddering giggle, or smiled broadly, both rows of teeth showing, Agapanthus didn't believe her. Her emotions seemed forced. They seemed hollow. Over the days, they met in Loao's room during breaks, and the three of them talked easily. And, when they were all together, Geleria seemed much more real. Agapanthus actually liked her, then. But when it was just the two of them, she didn't trust Geleria's eyes. The dark red around their rim. The gold-flecked yellow surrounding that dull, black dot. Her eyes, though yellow, reminded Agapanthus of the sunless sky of the frozenlands to the south. Or maybe they were more like the yellow heat of the deserts to the north—at least, how she imagined them to be—so hot that smoke rose from the sand, so hot that Imn cracked the ground, and pierced it into pale, orange triangles. *The north is a land without water, the man's voice of her audiobook had described them. The interior of the deserts are entirely uninhabited, but the coasts are peopled. It is a harsh climate, and they are, understandably, a harsh people, whose customs pre-date the Awakening.* The Others must be the only people thought of as lower than exchangers, thought Agapanthus.

She wondered if Loao liked Geleria better than her because she was an exchanger. She wondered if they secretly met up together in his portation room. If they talked about her. If they agreed, laughing, that she looked like a pale water plant. She wondered if Loao held Geleria's hands—both hands at once, just held out there between their chests, as the machine rumbled, and she wondered if they made plans to swim the channel, if they made plans to become adults and marry at the next Marriage Festival and live in Geleria's house.

And Agapanthus missed being outside. She missed the open walls of the fisheries, and the warm smell of the Waters as the wind carried drops of mist onto the floors of the vessel, onto her forehead. Here was a piece of the Waters, dripping down in front of her, but it wasn't the same. It was like comparing a piece of red-breasted sper meat to a living red-breasted sper. The portated waterfall wasn't alive anymore. She almost felt like she was stealing it. Stealing from the Waters. Maybe they all were, each time they took a drink, or bathed; maybe they were all thieves.

"So, Agapanthus, I've always been curious; what do they do when you guys go in for your check-ups?" Geleria asked one day, leaning against the wall in Loao's room.

"They take measurements. And—I don't know. They put me out for most of it, now that I'm older."

"As in, you're unconscious?" Loao asked, his eyebrows scrunched.

"Yeah. They make me breathe this smoke and then I fall asleep. They give me vitamins and stuff when I'm out—when I'm asleep—whatever we don't get here on Deeyae that we—"

Aunt Imari walked in. Her thin body sliced out of the shadowed hallway. If anyone reminded Agapanthus of a water plant, it was Imari. Suddenly, Agapanthus wanted to run over and hug her poor, weak foster-aunt. "Imari!" she said so loudly her words echoed against the portation machine.

Imari's words were rushed together, one long line, in her strong, full voice: "There's going to be a solar flare, so, by the will of the Gods, we have to stay inside; it's too dangerous, and everyone is being called into the nearest building, so stay right here, don't leave this room until I say so. Alright, Aga?" She clapped her hands together. "Don't go out there."

"Yeah, fine. Alright."

"And you two keep her in line, alright?" Imari said to Loao and Geleria.

"Alright," Loao said, just as Geleria was saying, "Of course."

Leera whipped back into the hallway, the sound of her footsteps still creeping into the room until she had turned the corner into the main entryway.

"That was weird. Why would anyone go out during a solar flare? Purposefully?" Loao said.

"I've tried to go out every time," Agapanthus said. "And every single time I get pulled back inside by someone."

"Why would you want to be out there?" Geleria said. "It's so dangerous."

"No it's not. If the Gods put up that net thing to protect us, why would it even be dangerous? Why do we have to hide?"

"Why would you *want* to be out there, though?" Loao asked.

"To see if it's real. To see if *They're* real. I want to see the black ring surround the sky. I want to see if They really protect us."

"Of course They protect us. Otherwise we'd be dead. Everyone on Deeyae would be dead," Loao said.

"And the Gods want us to stay inside. Maybe there's some residual radiation leaking through their—whatever they use to protect us," Geleria said. "Imagine if we had to sit through full-strength solar storms? Loao's right. Without the Gods, we would be dead."

Agapanthus nodded without purpose. "Could you imagine if the Gods weren't real, and I went out, and the solar flare was full strength?"

"If the Gods weren't real? There's not really much debate, is there?" Loao said.

"I don't know. I wonder, sometimes."

"But They've given us so much. Technology and all."

"Well. Yeah. You're probably right." And she said it again, so the words encircled her tongue, and she imagined the letters scraping off the little pink bumps on top. "You're probably right."

But Agapanthus still wanted to go outside. She still wanted to see what was not to be seen. So she decided to run, and look, and come back. Imari would never have to know about it. Geleria and Loao wouldn't follow her. She could see the sky in the tangled fires of Imn; she could see the black tendrils of the Gods' planet-shield, planet-shroud, planet-protector, whatever it was called; and then she could drift back inside, dazed but, for once, knowledgeable. She looked at Loao's handsome, tired face, with the gentle curve of his jaw, a shade slightly darker, slightly deeper, in his rich, red skin. She looked at Geleria. The more time she spent with her, the less fat she seemed. She could no longer imagine Geleria thinner—improved—as she once had, with a graceful contour to her chin and neck, rather than a pocket of softness. Geleria's softness, her fullness, was a part of her, just as Erabet's face-hair was a part of her.

Agapanthus told them she was going to the pit room—the bright-white room with the long, metal-lined trench where they relieved themselves, and where their waste was subsequently dissolved into nothingness. They couldn't question that, could they? And they didn't. Agapanthus walked carefully out to the hall, until she'd turned the corner, and then she ran. The soft soles of her shoes skidded over the floors. In that first moment she felt weightless—as her feet thump-thump-thumped, as her stride widened, as she felt the hardness of the ground rise up through her bones and into her teeth, tasting like metal, and her arms and legs clenched. As she ran, she felt that her body actually held something. Some shock of energy that spun over her muscles in blinks of hurried light.

By the time she made it to the front doors—amazingly, unseen—she felt the familiar heaviness begin. It was like each stringy fiber in each muscle was pulled upon, twisted and muffled. She felt this often, even when she hadn't been running, especially at the end of a long day of standing. It made her stomach sore to think about it, as though she'd swallowed rocks—how often it happened. She hated that this hadn't gone away. That she hadn't grown out of it. That she hadn't grown strong enough to avoid it. The heaviness of the sky always pushed down on her, except in the Waters. That was the only place where she didn't feel the tiredness anymore. She was as good a swimmer as any Deeyan.

Outside, it smelled like heat. Like raw, yellow, heat, just like she'd felt standing next to the hydrothermal vents at the Festival of the Underworld. Only it was drier. And the smell was stronger. It reminded her of something, but she couldn't think of what it was. It made her sad, whatever it was. It made her lonely.

Imn looked strange; shadowed, or watery. The God stars had disappeared entirely. Agapanthus wanted to walk toward the Waters, shimmering blackly in the great distance, but she was afraid to. Everything felt like it was buzzing. It reminded her of the measuring light at the check-ups, the way it bristled against her skin. That was always the last thing she remembered, now. Something in the light put her to sleep. She woke up every time, dry-mouthed and dizzy, with her back sore like she'd been lying there for days. Sometimes there were bruises on the thin, pale skin that covered her spine. She thought they were probably from the vitamin injections. But she didn't ask.

The sky looked naked with Aamsh and Jord missing; over-shadowed by the growing light of Imn. Maybe this was why the Gods didn't want anyone outside. They didn't want anyone to see the fragility of their homes. To see how life would look without them, without the yellow-red light of their stars. Maybe that was why everyone always went to sleep when the God stars sank below the horizon. And maybe that was why the Gods didn't come to the Others during the Awakening. Down at the edges of Deeyae, where Imn, at times, disappeared, the Others could see all the universe, all the other stars—even Agapanthus's home sun. Aamsh and Jord were only pieces. Only dots. Agapanthus wasn't sure if she would like living there all the time. She liked the specialness of it—saving the night sky as a gift, as a present at the Star Festival.

Suddenly she felt cold. She dug her hands into her armpits to keep them warm.

"Agapanthus! I knew you would be out here."

She wanted to turn and see Loao, with his thin hair flopping at his ears, but it was Geleria.

"Come on out," Agapanthus said. She raised her arms up to the sky. "Nothing's happened to me yet."

"Yet!" Geleria yelled from the doorway. She pressed her lips together. "I was wondering what took you so long in the pit. I thought you fell in."

Agapanthus smiled out toward the barren, red fields; the dense, square homes in the distance. She stepped farther from the Portation Center's entryway. Just one step.

"Aga," Geleria said. It was the first time she'd called her Aga. "What are you doing? Please."

Agapanthus said nothing. She realized, thinking back, how unbearably silent it had been before Geleria came outside.

"There's not even anything to see out here. Come on."

"Didn't you notice? Aamsh and Jord?"

"We're not supposed to be seeing this. Doesn't it feel wrong to you? Don't you feel guilty? Like you're about to be ripped apart? Like you're about to drown?"

"I feel—prickly—"

"Then let's go in. You've already seen more than anyone else ever has." Geleria exhaled deeply, and her breasts shook. "Let's go inside."

"It's kind of unfair that the Others get the protection of the Gods without having to do everything They say. The whole planet benefits, but only the islanders have to obey the Gods?"

"What? What are you talking about?"

"Never mind." Agapanthus took one last look at the muf-fled sky, and then she followed Geleria into the front hall. They walked in silence down the dark corner to the portation rooms. Agapanthus's skin cooled further. She rubbed her hands over her forearms.

"Please don't tell my aunt, okay?" Agapanthus said suddenly.

"Tell her what?"

"That I was out there. I know it would look really good for you to—"

Geleria waved her hand in front of Agapanthus's face, sharp-ly, stiffly, like she had changed her mind about waving halfway through the gesture.

Loao called out to her from across the room. "She's back!"

"I'm back!"

"You're troublemaker of the day then, aren't you?" He smiled with his eyebrows turned up. It was a sad smile. It was a pity smile.

"I guess I am."

"What did you think you were going to see out there?"

"Something. Just—something worth seeing."

"And did you?"

Agapanthus glanced at Geleria. She wasn't sure if it had been worth it. "Yes," she said in a forcedly loud voice. "Completely. I got to see how the sky changed."

"And you got to feel prickly," Geleria said, and she laughed through her shoulders.

"I'm not even going to ask," Loao said.

Agapanthus laughed, too, but with her eyes unfocused, unin-terested, staring at the floor. She realized that she hadn't liked see-ing the red sky blurred, or the twin stars hidden. She hadn't liked how different it looked. Her throat hurt like it did before crying. Like all those times, before she slept, when she rested her forehead on the crook of her arm and cried into her skin-blankets, because she knew everyone would leave her. Those times, surrounded by stone walls, in the windowless children's hall, with her collection of rocks and shells sprawled proudly across the floor; when Pittick and Leera were asleep. That was when she mumbled to the Gods. That was when she prayed to them.

4

AGE: TWENTY-ONE EARTH-YEARS

gapanthus didn't want to be here. She hated Marriage Festivals now. They were loud, as the water drums shrieked, as the Contact yelled over the rows of waiting couples: "The Gods approve your joining! The Gods give their permission!" And every person on the island was clustered together at the edge of the cliffs, along with the families of men from other islands who were marrying in to Yeelan households. There was barely room to move. It made Agapanthus sweat, all that warm body-heat. She saw others' wet foreheads and shiny noses, and the delicate droplets of sweat lining their arms, and she half-expected to smell the saltiness or the musk of this great mass of sweating people—of all this bare, red skin—but it was too windy for any odors to stagnate. For once she was glad to be tall—she stood in the back of the crowd, and she could still see over everyone's heads. Agapanthus kept her arms tight at her sides. She left them there, stiff and dangling, for the whole ceremony, as she stared at the marriers—like Erabet and her new husband, Roif, who met each other at the last Molting Festival. "He's the guy version of me," Erabet had once told Agapanthus at the meal. After that, Agapanthus expected Roif to have hair on his face, a small patch just under his nostrils. But he didn't. He looked—normal. Plain. Like the kind of man who would have a high, whining voice. Erabet would probably introduce her later, and then she could find out for sure. Agapanthus watched as they grasped each other's arms, waiting in the first row of couples to feel the Contact's hands upon their heads.

Two rows behind stood Geleria and Loao. They'd swum the channel one after the other, and celebrated at a joint feast, where they'd pulled Agapanthus aside. Geleria put her hand on Agapanthus's arm, and, through smiling lips, said, "Aga, guess who's decided to mate?" And Loao, too, was smiling, stupidly, handsomely. Agapanthus had pretended to be happy, but her cheeks hurt from the forcedness of her own smile.

The Contact began greeting the couples. He looked older. It wasn't his skin, or his eyes. It was his shoulders. They seemed slumped, now. Tired. Every time he appeared in public he looked worse. Agapanthus wondered if, at times, he didn't want to be the Contact anymore. Or if he even let himself think such thoughts, when the Gods could so easily hear the words in his brain. She thought back to the day Pittick took her to the Contact to ask forgiveness. The red stones around his neck. He wore them today, too. From far away they looked like pieces of his skin showing through the light-brown of his dress. Shiny cut-outs in the fabric.

Suddenly she couldn't look anymore. She couldn't stand to see all the couples. Erabet and Roif. Geleria and Loao, pressed together, he, whispering into her ear, his arm around her chubby waist, the graceful slope of his forehead lined up against Imn's light, saturating him, saturating *them*, in red-against-red-against-red. She closed her eyes for a moment, then pushed her way past another exchanger, a brown-haired woman who had been breathing heavily behind her. There were deep shadows under the woman's eyes. Agapanthus stared at the ground. She'd worn her good shoes. New; still stiff along the back of the ankle, where the seam had been stitched. She wished she'd worn something older. Something more comfortable. No one was even going to be looking at her feet.

As she backed away from the crowded cliffs, the wind picked up. It swept through her hair, which she gathered over her shoulder to keep from blowing in her face. Dust caught in her eye. She rubbed it, and it watered.

It didn't bother her that she was choosing to walk away at the moment her friends were truly, officially married. It didn't matter. In her mind, they had already been married since they swam across the Waters. It was as though they'd been left over there, in Shre. It was as though they had died.

Pittick appeared beside her. Agapanthus perked up her eyes with false interest. False happiness.

"I thought you said you were going to come find us?" Pittick asked.

"I didn't see you guys."

"We're near the front." He nodded his head toward the mass of people. Agapanthus fuzzed her vision so she was looking just beyond his ear. She couldn't look him in the eye. She couldn't talk, or laugh, or do anything, because she knew she would cry. She wasn't a crier. Not in public. She was sharp, she was strong. She was not a crier. She would not cry.

"You're not going to watch?" he asked.

Agapanthus swallowed; blinking, blinking, blinking, pulling in everything. "I just got tired of the crowd." She swallowed again. "I just wanted to be alone for a second." Immediately, she regretted saying that. "I mean, alone, away from the crowdedness."

"It's even worse than the Molting Festival. Remember how bad that was?"

A cheer erupted behind them—intense; rolling.

"Looks like we missed them," Pittick said, widening his eyes. "They're going to be done soon. I better get back up there."

"Oh, that's right. The Council."

Pittick turned, his hand between Agapanthus's shoulder-blades as he led her back up the cliff. "Did you have time to finish?" he asked as they walked, stretching his voice over the whoops and yells.

"Yep. They're right here." She patted the front pockets of her dress.

"Can I see?"

Agapanthus stopped. She dug out one of the bracelets. It was made of rounded, orange stones she'd gathered along the shoreline. She remembered digging out each one from the sand, right on the cusp where the shore became the hill, as Imn heated the soil with warm breath. Then she'd stabbed holes into them with a laser-tool Pittick brought her from work, and she strung them onto fine, leather bands she'd braided herself.

"That came out great," Pittick said. Agapanthus couldn't hear him anymore, because the cheers had risen, but she followed his lips. He rubbed one of the stones between his fingers. "Really great," he shouted. "They'll love them."

"Thank you," she said, but he put his hands over his ears to signal that he couldn't hear her. She didn't repeat herself. It had sounded stiff, anyway; the way she'd said it. Thank you. Not even thanks. Thank you. Like he was a stranger. This was Pittick! Agapanthus followed him back to the rest of the family. She nestled the bracelet back in her heavy pockets and stroked the hem of her dress to keep her hands busy.

"You found us," Leera said cheerfully. "Just in time for the celebration."

This, more than anything, made Agapanthus want to run down the cliffs and kneel helplessly at the edge of the Waters. And

Aunt Imari and Uncle Sonlo, smiling up at her. And Pittick's gaze on her nervous, moving hand.

"When are you going to give them to them?" Leera asked.

"The bracelets?" Imari asked. "They're finished?" Agapanthus couldn't tell if she was asking her or Pittick, so she said nothing and let Pittick's nod serve as the answer. "Oh," he said, stepping backwards. "I almost forgot. I have to get up there."

"The Council," Sonlo said. "Good luck."

Pittick nodded again and slipped back into the crowd, toward the front of the cliff.

"Well, show them to us, Aga, before your friends take them away forever," Imari said.

So Agapanthus once again drew a stone bracelet from her pocket. They passed it around. Sonlo looked as though he might crush it, with his thick, wide hands. He brought it to his nose. "Smells like—stone." He laughed, blowing air through his nostrils. "What a surprise."

"And what did you think they would smell like?" Imari asked.

"Water," Sonlo said.

"And what does water smell like?"

"I know what it smells like," Agapanthus said.

"Course you do, Fish," Sonlo said.

Her gaze met the large, yellow circles of Sonlo's eyes. Creases formed alongside them as he squinted warmly at her.

Agapanthus wondered if her eyes made people uncomfortable. If people thought her eyes were ugly— brown, with all that white around them, and such a small black pupil in the center. No one on Deeyae had eyes like that, except the other exchangers. Even the shelled water creatures, and the herds of red-breasted spers, and the paraas and velis of the inner island; they all had yellow or orange or dark, dark black eyes. None of them had white-brown oddly flat-looking eyes.

"I think they're done," Leera said. "You should go find them before they get too distracted by the food." She handed the bracelet back to Agapanthus. "Go on."

Agapanthus breathed in deeply. This was stressful, for some reason. It felt like she was walking up to the Gods, not Loao and Geleria, who were standing aside, face to face, close enough to the edge to see the Waters below.

"Agapanthus Caracynth!" Geleria shouted, drowning out the water drum with her voice. "We're mated, can you believe it?"

"Congratulations," Agapanthus said. She forced a smile. Were they not even going to greet each other properly?

"Did you like the ceremony? I thought the Contact did a great job," Loao said.

"Yeah. It was—yeah. He did a great job." She swallowed. "You know, you've always reminded me a little of the Contact. The way he looks."

"You're so right," Geleria added. "That same jaw. And the hair."

"You both are too kind," Loao said. He clasped his hands behind his back.

"Who knows," Agapanthus said. "Maybe you'll be the next Contact."

"Yeah, when I'm one-thousand years old. This Contact's not going anywhere."

"True," she said. Then, quickly: "Also, I wanted to give you something, as a marriage present." She dangled the bracelets in front of them, holding them gingerly, one in each hand.

"Aga! I love it." Geleria wrapped it immediately around her wrist. The beads stretched out, revealing the string tying them. "It's a little tight."

"No, it looks fine," Agapanthus said. "But if you want, I can take it out a little."

"Did you make these, then?" Loao asked with his eyes scooping up, tracing Agapanthus.

"I did." She laughed for no reason. It felt tight and unreal, un-furling itself from her stomach like that.

"They're just so beautiful," Geleria said. "I'm impressed. I didn't think you were this talented." Her eyes narrowed and she half-smiled at Agapanthus.

"Well." Agapanthus looked away. Everything was going to change. Everyone was melting away, drifting away from her, leav-ing her curled in a ball as they walked away together toward great-er things. "Oh, there's Erabet. I have something for her, too."

"Oh, yeah," Geleria said.

"We'll see you later, Agapanthus," Loao said. He held up his braceleted wrist. "Thank you."

Agapanthus didn't say anything. She pressed her lips together like she might smile again, but she didn't. She couldn't. So she stepped away and took large strides toward Erabet. Agapanthus looked behind her, over her shoulder, to see if Loao and Geleria were still looking. Mostly to see if Loao was still looking. But they were talking to each other. Closely; wrists at their sides, the brace-lets already forgotten. When she looked forward again, her cheek ran into someone's chest.

"Oh, sorry, sorry," Agapanthus said. Then she saw who it was. The Contact. She held her breath and jumped back. "I'm so sorry, I wasn't looking."

"Agapanthus Caracynth," he said. His hand rested upon her hairline. He couldn't reach the crown of her head.

She couldn't believe he remembered her name. And she didn't know what to do. How should she greet him, if she wasn't allowed to touch his head? Her eyes fell to the indent beneath the tip of his nose and above the curve of his upper lip. There was some-thing flaky just on the edge of his lips; dead skin, or something. She hadn't thought it possible for someone as glorious and power-ful as the Contact to have something on his face. "You remember me," she finally said.

"Of course I do. You're the foster-daughter of Pittick Caracynth. I keep an eye on all my Council members. And their families." He breathed in deeply. "It's been some time since we've spoken. You've grown. You've grown to be lovely."

But I'm an exchanger, she wanted to say. *Exchangers can't be lovely.* It made her angry with him. As though it was his fault that she was an alien.

"Let me know if you ever need anything," the Contact said. "I know that it's sometimes hard for your kind to adjust to Deeyae over longer-term exchanges."

"Longer-term? Do you know how long mine will be?"

"Ahhp." He held out his finger. "No, no. That's not a question we should be asking. That's the domain of the Gods, Agapanthus."

When he said her name, all she saw was the color gold. Swept, brushed, fraying gold that drained from the sky. *Ag-a-pan-thus*, he had said, each letter stretched from rounded lips. *Ag-a-pan-thus.*

"It'll come when it comes," he added. "There was a little exchanger boy—Lomatium Gereiq, I think his name was—I have that kind of memory—and his study was only twenty years long. He just arrived here and then he had to leave. Deeyan years, of course. Years on your planet are much longer."

"They are?"

"They have very long years there. Very long. You haven't done much research on your home planet, then, have you? You should listen to some books on it. You know. Just to avoid the shock factor when you get back there."

"My foster-parents thought the Gods might not like me to focus too much on my birth planet," Agapanthus said.

"No, not at all. They wouldn't mind. You should, really. It's a fascinating place."

A small part of her wondered if the Contact was tricking her. Maybe he knew the Gods would hate her reading about the Water Planet. Maybe he wanted her to be sent home. "Have you seen it?" she asked. "Have you actually been to my birth planet?"

"That's another question you shouldn't be asking. But I'll tell you this much; I'm not much older than you, so I remember being your age. I remember being pre- rite of passage. And I was just like you. Full of questions. And, you know what I learned? The moment you stop asking questions is the moment you'll find your answers. Simple as that."

Then I won't stop asking, she thought. Because then I'll be sent back to the fucking Water Planet. She nodded slowly at the Contact, as though he'd said something profound, as though she were still digesting his words, pulling them out of the air to re-hear them.

"Take care," the Contact said, and, without any other warning, he left.

Agapanthus crept slowly toward Erabet and her husband. Once again, she passed by the Contact—who was now talking with the Council—on her way over. Should she meet his eyes? Should she even look? He embarrassed her, now. What if he was looking at her? She felt the heat of someone's eyes on her face. What if it was Pittick? But, no. When she looked up, it was the Contact. She smiled at him with her mouth closed. Her lips felt chapped. They burned. She wondered if she had any dry skin around the edges, like the Contact had. She wondered if any of the Council members noticed it, there, like fish skin, like the crackly sap that spilled from the buds of water plants. Even from a distance, she could see it. Maybe Pittick was looking at it. Maybe he would tell her about it later.

Finally she made it to Erabet, dressed in a dark-red dress with extra fabric hanging thinly behind the shoulders. Her face-hair was gone. There was no red fuzz framing her lip. No stubby, black hairs protruding weakly around her smile lines. Instead it looked waxy, there, on her bare skin. Maybe a slightly different shade of red. Agapanthus couldn't help but stare. She didn't want to say anything, though. They'd never talked about it, because

Agapanthus didn't want to embarrass Erabet, even though, for some reason, she'd assumed it never bothered her. Otherwise, wouldn't she have removed it sooner?

Erabet loved the bracelets. And so did her husband, who had an average voice after all. He was all-around-average, with his wide stance, his shortness, his thickness, his well-cropped black hair, his smooth, red, features, all small and straight except for his enormous orange eyes. He was the epitome of average. And, now, so was Erabet. Now they would move into the separate wings of Erabet's home. They would join together in the meeting hall, wearing the stone bracelets Agapanthus had given them, and they would stay up talking, long after Aamsh and Jord had fallen and risen again. They would sit with their legs crossed, barefooted, their dresses riding up along their thighs, just talking, talking and noticing everything about each other, every small thing; the shifts in tone on certain words, the calculated drifts of eye contact, the soft, wet noise their lips made when they clashed together. Agapanthus had never known anyone that well. Not even half as well. Really, she'd never known *anyone* fully. She wanted to, but it scared her. It seemed like, if someone knew too much about her, she would have nothing left. She didn't want to be hollowed out from the inside like that. There was already a certain emptiness that followed her around. She assumed it was the future. She imagined the return to her birth planet to be something like dying. Everything rolling, swirling. Sourness—sour smells; sour, metal tastes in the back of her mouth. Then, pain in the abdomen. Numbness.

Sometimes she pictured a blonde-haired exchanger woman. She had thick, wide thighs, and eyes like half-circles, filled in murkily, and breasts that swung freely in her loose Deeyan tunic. Agapanthus didn't know whether this was a memory or an imagining. Either way, it was her mother. Her birth-mother. And her birth-father had brown hair, and all she thought of on his face was a nose. He was just a giant nose.

The Marriage Festival stretched on. Agapanthus left early. She ate some of the delicacies—the w'rr meat, and the asasd fish, both served in the giant, metal festival bowl, where everyone dug their hands in and ate as they stood, dripping blood or water on the ground—and then she took her time on the way back to the house. The water drums became slight thuds. The cheers became echoey giggles.

Twelve couples married. Most were her age, but some were older.

She thought of the Contact again. Even with his fallen posture, he was still handsome. She wondered if he would ever mate. Secretly, she hoped he wouldn't. No matter what, it couldn't be her, of course—even if she swam the channel, an exchanger would never be allowed to marry the Contact. It embarrassed her just thinking about it. But, at the same time, she didn't want to see him with anyone else. Suddenly she flashed back to Lapars and his son. The Contact's steadiness as he declared their death sentence. *So say the Gods: it is their destiny to drown.* Was it his fault? No. It was the Gods. It was all the Gods. *So say the Gods. So say the Gods.*

Agapanthus wondered what the Gods would do if the Contact disobeyed them. Would they yell inside his head, scream at him? Would they burl into his brain? Would they somehow kill him; shoot down from their stars and force him to bend over and spit up blood and die? Just thinking of it scared her, because, it could, very likely, come true. She tried to focus instead on walking. On Imn's saturated orange light. But, for the rest of the day, and the days that followed, Agapanthus couldn't focus on anything. Her mind curled inward to some blank, dry funnel infused with memories. Sitting with Pittick and Leera in front of the house when she was a child; their knees touching, their legs angled to make a distorted triangle, as they played the game where you guess the creature the other is thinking of. "Red-breasted sper!" Agapanthus had shrieked. Agapanthus had looked out, then, at the sky. Aamsh and Jord were so close to the cliffs. As though they were melting into them. "You guess that every time, silly," Leera said, adjusting her stance, nestling her bottom into the dirt. "Which is a good strategy, because, eventually, it's bound to be true," Pittick said. He smelled like crushed stone. Like mineral. "You win, Aga; you win!" And they lifted her up and they both hugged her at once. Back when she was smaller than them. The moment had seemed to last a long time. They sat her down but continued to hug her; her head up to their belly buttons. Red, soft arms. Hearts beating. Agapanthus wondered, thinking back, if that was when Pittick and Leera finally began to feel like they could forgive themselves for not having a real daughter. She had always loved them, but maybe it had taken gentle moments like that, a compendium of those moments, for them to love her.

Each day after coming home from the Portation Center, Agapanthus tried to read. She could buy her own audiobooks now, and she had filled her Storyteller with books about the Awakening, and about how portation machines functioned, and about the wild herds that dined on hydrothermal vents in the interior of the island. She meant to buy a book called *The Workings of the Water Planet* but she was waiting until she finished the ones she'd already bought. The money—tiny, black, rare stones—for audiobook purchases was taken out of her apprenticeship pay before she received it, so it was hard to keep track of how much she'd spent. Agapanthus liked it a lot better when she went to the clothing store, or something, and paid using real money, hand to hand. She didn't make much as an apprentice, so she wanted to be careful.

Sometimes, after the meal, she just couldn't read, or sleep, so she snuck out the front door of the men's wing—Pittick and Sonlo were heavy sleepers—and she walked quietly to the Waters. When she was younger she used to imagine that the Waters morphed and changed while everyone slept. She imagined the ripples glowing red, or shading in, darker, darker, until they became a shiny, thick, mirrored surface like ice, only warm. But the Waters looked the same. The only difference was the absence of Aamsh and Jord. Agapanthus rested her knees in the sand. She leaned into her thighs, stretching the tight muscle running down the back of her leg. No one was there to watch her. She pinched at the sand, lifting it up into her palm and letting it spill back through her fingertips. Each grain maroon. Each grain coarse but somehow spongy. She dropped some on her legs. Drip-drop, drip-drop; she could almost hear the sound they made as they landed on her skin. Light scraping sounds. Whispering. As though she were asleep, or her head were underwater. Agapanthus pictured her arms in front of her, brushing through the filmy charcoal depths of the Waters with her eyes open. Her skin always looked paler underwater.

It had been so long since she'd *really* swam—train-swam, counting her strokes and holding her breath until either her forehead ached or the upper, back end of her throat began to complain. Now she just floated, usually. Maybe a steady, parallel lap from one end of the shore to the other. She wasn't even sure what she thought, anymore. Part of her had given up on the rite of passage, but the other part of her wanted to prove it to them. What if she did it? What if she really did it, and she emerged from the small round boat to a feast and cheering crowds and Leera would cup her chin in her warm hands and say, smiling, "I can't believe it," and Pittick would at first rest his hand on her head, but then hug her, and she couldn't even imagine what he would say. Something about how he was wrong. About how much stronger she was than any of them had guessed. Something about being proud.

Agapanthus looked down at her legs. They were coated completely in sand, no skin showing at all. She stood and brushed off the clinging particles. They felt like little teeth boring into her. Drops of mist speckled the edge of her cheek as the wind climbed over the Waters. She was going to brush the droplets away, but, instead, she left her fingers splayed over the side of her face as she stared out toward Shre. If anyone saw her, they would think she was odd—just staring with her hand up like that, her other hand wrapped over her ribs, her shoulders fallen, like the Contact's had been. But no one was there to see. That was the good thing about being alone. One of the few good things.

The next morning, walking to work, Agapanthus heard a dull groan, like trilling, multiplying voices bellowing out against the Waters. Imari had left early for work, so Agapanthus was alone. It wouldn't hurt to be just a little late to her apprenticeship, would it? To stop and see what the cheering was about?

Among the crowd, the back of Pittick's head stood out. She tapped him on the shoulder.

"What's going on?" Agapanthus asked after they'd greeted each other.

"Someone's swimming."

"Who? Who is it?"

Pittick licked his lips. He stared at the edge where the Waters and Imn met. "We don't know for sure yet."

"Well who do you think? Who are people saying?"

Pittick nodded and scrunched his lips together. "Aster Hibierl."

"I don't remember him." She shifted her gaze from Pittick to the Waters. The clouds painted murky red stripes across Imn, and the cliffsides farther down the shoreline looked especially steep, especially ribboned with facets and edges, and crumbling towers soaked with the sweet stink of long-dry stone. Shadowed. Everything was shadowed. And the Waters—blacker than ever. As though they didn't like being looked at, and were trying to disappear.

Pittick said nothing. He adjusted the arm of his tunic.

"Oh," she said. "He's an exchanger, isn't he." She could tell. She could just tell.

"If that's who's out there. Yes." He exhaled. "He didn't warn anyone. We sent someone over to Shre to see if he's even alerted them."

"Oh." Agapanthus tried to pick out the frenzied, white blur of his strokes, but she couldn't. "He's past the sight-line already?"

"Looks like it."

"He might actually make it, then." She opened her mouth and squinted, desperate not to see him. She wanted to believe that he was looking at the tall hills rising from the center of Shre, heavy with fog. Each swing of the arm brought him closer. He was so close, she hoped; so close, so close, in the lukewarm water.

"Aga, I know what you must be thinking. That it's not fair that another exchanger gets to swim the channel, when you can't—when I've—but it's not a normal thing. You have to recognize that—it's not a normal thing."

"I know that."

"And you're a girl. A girl exchanger has only done it maybe twice. Ever, since the Awakening."

"I know."

"Okay." He put his hand on her head again. "Just so you don't get any ideas, now." He paused. "I can't pretend I know what it's like being an exchanger, but I—when I first married Leera, and I moved to this side of the island to move in with her, I remember feeling like everything was too big. I didn't know anyone, and I—I had Leera, but everything was just so different. You've been over to the leftwards side. There are no cliffs, and just that long coast of gravel. Remember how much you liked picking out pebbles from there, when they held the Festival of the Underworld? It's so different. It was a shock, when I came to this mountainous, busy place. But then I started in at the rightwards fisheries and it all became routine. And everything felt right."

Agapanthus took a deep breath and held it there, right where she imagined the top of her stomach would be.

"If you don't love working at the Portation Center, you can always try something new, as long as you find a mentor. Then you could work your way back up. What's important is, wherever you work, that it fulfills you."

"I know. I don't mind working there. I don't."

"Imari sure loves having you."

"Don't you miss the fisheries, though?" Agapanthus asked, still looking for the swimmer. "Is the Council really better than working there was?"

"It's different. I don't know. I guess it's like comparing Imn to the God stars, or—" he pointed at her with a flat, upturned palm, "—comparing an exchanger to a Deeyan. They're too different. You can't compare them."

"Do you think Sonlo will ever let me apprentice with him?"

"Probably. I think he's gotten over his weird, jealous rage by now."

"But how could I leave Imari? Especially for Sonlo? If I left for another industry, with someone unrelated to us, it'd be one thing, but to ditch her for Sonlo? Doesn't that sound mean?"

"Imari would understand. I mean, you're right, she'd secretly be crushed, but she'd understand."

"The Portation Center is okay. Really, I don't mind it."

"Well it's up to you, Aga. Always up to you."

They were silent for a moment. "Should I go to work today?" Agapanthus asked.

"If he makes it, it'll be cancelled anyway, for the feast. You can stay, if you want. As a Council member, I give you my executive permission."

Agapanthus laughed. She didn't really feel like laughing, but she knew that was what he wanted from her.

Aamsh and Jord drifted steadily away from Imn, toward their resting place at the right edge of the sky. Jord was always just barely ahead, and just barely higher, than Aamsh. Agapanthus wondered if the Gods living on Aamsh were jealous of those on Jord. Maybe the true Gods lived on Jord and their servants lived on Aamsh. Or maybe it wasn't even better to be first, or highest, or above all else. Maybe, to them, being low and comfortable was good. But they were Gods. Of course they must like looking down on others; they looked down on Deeyae all the time.

She thought about saying all of this to Pittick, but she didn't want him to reprimand her for speaking that way about the Gods. It was bad enough when Leera grew angry with her, but when Pittick did, it was unbearable.

"Is that a boat?" asked Pittick. He pointed to a round, bowl-like object scouring through the Waters. "Really then. He's made it."

"Yes!" Agapanthus said. "Yes, yes, yes!"

And the bone-and-leather boat blundered up against the sand, right onto the shore. A pink face stood out from two red ones. He slumped over the side of the boat, his head held high like he was pretending not to be tired; but he was betrayed by the slowness with which he swung his legs around to hop out onto the shore. His hair was cut very short, right up against his head. How strange. Agapanthus didn't like that. It made his cheekbones seem angular, but his ears and his nose looked hefty. The hair itself, at least, looked fuzzy. Each tendril was still alight with water-jewels. She wondered what it would feel like to run her palm over the top of his head. Probably like running her hand over the surface of the Waters on a calm day.

The crowd yelled coarsely, shoutingly, just as they would for any Deeyan. He was as close now to being Deeyan as he could ever be. His arms were great, rippling cliffs. No wonder he'd done it. He was more muscular than Sonlo, twice as muscular as Pittick. His arms even rivaled those of the Shreyan rowers, still sitting silently in the boat behind him, waiting for the food to come out.

The water-drummers carried their metal rods down to either side of the shoreline. Their skin blended into the cliffs, so,

from afar, it looked like only the drums existed—the poles rising, slicing downward, piercing the skin of the Waters and erupt-
ing in a low *graaaaaarn*. One side and then the other, until the
rhythm surfaced. The communal bowls were placed at the base
of the cliff. Lines formed behind them for the initial taking. More
people scurried down the gentle slope of the hill; more and more,
as they heard about the exchanger who swam the channel. Soon
the beach was thick. Still, above it all, Agapanthus could smell the
Waters. That particular warmth. That particular heaviness.

She looked around for Aster Hibierl. He'd been swallowed up
so quickly when the crowds came.

"Only good thing about the exchangers swimming the channel
is the food," a man behind her said. Agapanthus wanted so badly
to turn around and glare, but she also wanted to hear what else he
would say. She clasped her hands in front of her stomach, burrow-
ing her fingernails into her skin.

"I don't even know if it's worth it. There's just something wrong
about them becoming adults. They can't be adults. They're not
Deeyan," a woman said. Her voice was deep, for a woman. "It's like
a water creature becoming an adult. It just doesn't make sense."

"Can I eat your share, then?" He laughed.

"I wasn't saying that, Pgar."

"If he did it, he did it," another voice said. "He's proved himself.
That his body's grown."

"But an alien body grown is not the same as a Deeyan body
grown. If he's trying to be Deeyan, he'll never get *anywhere*," the
woman said.

"Maybe they should have their own rite of passage," Pgar said.
"Maybe we should just make them walk one end of the beach to
the other. Besides this kid, most of them wouldn't even be able to
do that."

Laughter. Agapanthus looked back over her shoulder, pretending to gaze over the crowd, just so they would notice that there

was an exchanger standing in line right in front of them. Whether they noticed or not, their laughter lingered as short gasps through the nose and deep, hearty throat-chuckles.

"They're a little old-fashioned, don't you think?" Agapanthus asked Pittick. She didn't even bother making her voice quieter.

"Who?" Pittick's eyes swept toward her. They seemed less yellow than usual. Like he had a small cloud inside each eye, casting them with the tiniest hint of transparent-red. Maybe he was still thinking about his childhood on leftwards Yeela. She'd never thought to ask him about it before.

"Do you ever miss your family, Pittick? The one you grew up with?"

"I did at first. They're all with the Gods now, except my sister."

"Oh, I forgot. How did they—?"

"It was an illness. A lot like the one that took Surla and Tayzaya."

"I remember your sister. From the Festival of the Underworld." She was beautiful—as short as Imari, but filled out, strong-looking, with a heavy chest and curving, muscled legs. She had smelled like sweet, fresh leather, and her house was very clean. The mural on their front entry was a red-breasted sper, all six legs splayed forward as it bowed, ready to jump forward and join the herd. It looked strange. How could it be a red-breasted sper if it was carved in black stone? Why didn't they touch up the skin on its breast with red dust so it could be more realistic? But she knew that that would defile the ancient mural, so she hadn't mentioned it.

"Here we go," Pittick said. He grasped an especially large handful. Agapanthus did too. The meat jiggled between her fingers. It felt cold and taut. It smelled like metal.

"This is from the storage, isn't it; not the hunt?" asked Agapanthus with her mouth full. "What could they have caught, this early?"

"It's a mix of both, I'd say. They'll bring in more later, as they catch it."

"That's not fair; the hunters have to keep working while everyone else gets the day off."

"That's always how it is. That's the trade-off for having the best jobs; hunters and fishers. It's hard to get time off." His lips shined with meat juice.

"Maybe it's good that we're not at the fisheries anymore, then," she said. But that wasn't true. She missed the fisheries so badly. The only reason she didn't want to go back was because Uncle Sonlo had said what a nuisance she would be. Following him around. Maybe that's what she had always been, at the fisheries; a nuisance. Maybe Pittick had been glad to move on to the Council so, for the most part, he would be rid of her.

Sometimes she thought about her Water Planet family. She knew it was a great honor for them to send their child to Deeyae. They probably bragged about it. "Our daughter is an exchanger," they probably said, in their Water Planet language, which was probably thick, and stiff, and ugly. She was sure that, in the vestiges of her mind, she would recognize the language if she heard it. She wouldn't understand it, but she would recognize the rhythm of it. "We are so proud of her. When she returns we will throw her a magnificent feast." She imagined them, for some reason, to live in holes they'd dug for themselves over the generations. She had no idea why. Just these giant, crumbling dirt pits that they stood helplessly in while they stared angrily at their sky. Ugly dirt pits. Ugly pink faces.

Leera and Imari showed up. Loao and Geleria, and Erabet and her husband. They ate and talked and listened to the heavy thuds of the water drums. The feast ended. Aamsh and Jord lowered themselves from sight. As she began to follow her family back home, Agapanthus glanced around one more time. The empty metal bowls, stained red. The water drummers heaving their instruments up the hill. Two older men sitting on the ground with their legs folded beneath them, staring at the hazed outline of

Shre. Emptiness and quietness blossomed over the shore. It was like everything became light, again. Like a solar flare had ended and the Gods' cover had been lifted, and everyone was allowed to go outside again.

Aster Hibierl stood with his feet in the shallows. The Waters drifted sleepily over his calves. He reached out to the black stem of a water plant, and it curled down and hid beneath the waves. Those enormous, burly arms, and he'd touched it so gently. Then he stood and looked out. At his feet. Out again. Crossing his arms across his stomach. Then Agapanthus stepped beyond the crest of the pathway up the hill, and she couldn't see him anymore.

She couldn't sleep again, so she rejoined Imn's deep glow and ran toward the Waters. Yes, she ran, even though it burned at the end of such a long day. She wanted to dive down, arms strong around her ears, stretched long, body taut, slicing beneath the black surface, down to where everything was soft, where she could swim and trace long, spiraling ribbons through the water, and look up and see Imn's shadow fall upon the surface in a wash of bright orange light.

When she came to the cliffs she had to slow down; her chest hurt. She stepped sideways down to the shore. It was empty, the rocky sand disheveled; dotted with the sunken remnants of footsteps. She plucked off one shoe, then the other, and she laid them on top of each other alongside the cliff. Why hadn't she left them at home? She should've left all her clothes. Why hadn't she run here, naked in the starless night? She pulled off her short-sleeved tunic, next, and the silver-stone necklace she'd made herself. Then she dove in, just as she'd imagined. Arms over her head. Quick, lithe, long. Water replacing air. Everything muted and compact but somehow enormous at the same time. She kicked and stroked until she couldn't hold her breath anymore. Then she floated on her back. She was nearly past the drop-off, already; past the slight bay the cliffs cut the Waters into. Just those few strokes, and look how far she'd swam already.

She should join the water creatures, she thought, smiling at the sky. She should live with them beneath the Waters. Borrow one of their shells after molting season—with their permission, of course—and fit it over her shoulders. Maybe her own ancestors were like the water creatures. They lived on the Water Planet, after all.

With her ears submerged, Agapanthus could hear nothing but the forever-moving, blurry whisper of the Waters. She could almost fall asleep. Maybe she would wake up somewhere near Shre, and she would return to Yeela an adult without ever even trying. Unless the currents took her somewhere else. Somewhere landless and deep.

Agapanthus saw a brown shape flit beside her. A water creature? She sat up and treaded water. She looked around for it but saw nothing besides the marbled surface and its enormous reflection of Imn. Then, almost soundlessly, with nothing but a crisp whipping noise, an exchanger boy pushed his head above the surface. He looked at her, his eyes threaded with red lines throughout the white part. Inside the middle, they were a very light, very warm brown that matched his eyebrows but not his hair, which was darker, and cut so close to his head that she could see his scalp underneath it.

"Wow, sorry," he said, shaking his head, rubbing his eyes. "I didn't see you. I didn't think anyone else would be out here." His voice reminded her instantly of heavy rain. Each word piling up, joining the others, multiplying.

"You're—you're Aster, right? You swam the channel today?"

"I did." He looked away from her, back toward shore.

"Congratulations. Really. That's impressive." She smoothed her hair behind her ears.

"Yeah, thanks. I trained so hard for it, for years."

"I'm surprised you're out here now. Aren't you tired?"

"Surprisingly, no. I couldn't sleep, so I thought I'd swim."

"Same with me. It's perfect, with no one out here." She laughed throatily. "I mean, except you. Which is good, actually, because I kind of wanted to ask you. How you did it."

"How I swam across, you mean?" He cleared his throat.

"How you trained. You didn't just get up one day and decide to go for it?"

"No, I trained. Just like this. Swimming. Building muscle. Every day—or night. Whenever I could."

"But I never saw you here before. And I come all the time."

"I timed it so I was here when no one else was; so I could concentrate. That's part of it. Concentrating on each movement so—so hard that eventually whatever you're concentrating on dissolves, slips from your mind, and you don't even know what you were thinking about in the first place."

"That's how you did it? When you swam across?"

"That's what I tried to do. What I was supposed to do."

Agapanthus was silent for a moment. She let her lips dip underwater and then resurface. "Did you really do it?" She creased her eyebrows together. "Did you really make it all the way to Shre? I just can't believe it. It was—I don't know; so sudden."

"It wasn't sudden. I told you, I worked and worked and worked for it."

"I know. I meant—it felt sudden to me. That doesn't even make sense. Sorry, I guess I'm the tired one." She laid her hand across the bridge of her eyebrows. "Or, it's like I'm in shock. I just can't believe it. *An exchanger.*"

"They shouldn't even call it a rite of passage unless it's an exchanger doing it. It takes no effort from them. It takes no skill. Their bodies are built for it. But us—we really have to push ourselves, prove ourselves." He paused. "You know the Deeyans came up with it just so we would have less power."

We? Agapanthus thought. *So we would have less power?* She didn't want to be part of this we.

"Although, really, what kind of power would we have even if we were all considered adults? It hardly makes a difference. They would still treat us like their prisoners."

This was why she didn't hang around exchangers. Who would say things like that? She began kicking her legs more quickly, warming them up so she could swim back. "Why did you do it, then?" she asked him, her voice heavy. "Why swim all that way if you don't care what anyone thinks?"

"To prove to myself that I could."

"Well you did," Agapanthus said. "Now what?"

"That's the big question—exactly the question I've been asking myself."

"Maybe that's why you couldn't sleep, then."

"Maybe. Maybe that's why you couldn't sleep either. Now what?—the big question." He breathed in deeply so his shoulders rose like white hills from the water. "You want to know the biggest secret? To getting across? This." He kicked his legs out so his body was flat. He floated on his back, his neck curving bulbously, his fingers spreading wide, skimming the water. Agapanthus's eyes strayed to his waist—his pale pink underparts. Nakedness was nothing new, at the Waters, but she still felt strange about it. Especially with an exchanger. She concentrated on kicking and waving her arms. Treading. Treading. Thankfully he lurched forward and treaded water again, too. "There's no time limit, you know? You could take days, if you needed to, and just keep resting. And, you know what else? Ask the fish. *Follow the fish.* There are currents that'll make it easier. I doubt there's a Deeyan out there who even knows about them, let alone one who really cares." He flipped onto his stomach, and then he stared intently at the cliffs. He began to paddle with his arms, so quietly that all Agapanthus could hear was a slight clipping, a slight shiver in the rippled fabric of the Waters. "Oh, and another thing," he shouted, straining his neck to look back at her, eyes squinted, teeth exposed above his lip. His voice boomed. "You might want to bulk up." He swam a little farther. "Your arms are tiny. You don't have the body for it."

She felt the warmth of her breath reflect off the surface, clouding it like glass. She realized that she'd believed everything he said. It was the way he said it. Kind of like Pittick—that same tone, like the narrator of an audiobook, like everything from their mouth was fact.

"Why even bother telling me any of that?" she said as loudly as she could without yelling. "You think I'm going to swim across?"

Aster stopped mid-stroke and treaded again. "I'd like to see another exchanger make it. I'd like to see as many of us do it as can do it. And you can. You've just got to work."

Agapanthus didn't know what to say. She was suddenly glad that the water was dark enough to hide his body; her body. She hated the long, white line of her silhouette. The flat, soft flesh over her stomach. The coarse blonde hairs coating her legs and groin. Her arms were the least of her problems. She suddenly worried, for some reason, that he could hear her thoughts like the Gods could.

"I think I'm done for tonight," Aster said. He dove under and resurfaced next to the beach. How did he move so quickly? Standing naked on the shore, so far away she couldn't make out his features, he shouted at her: "You've got to work on your agility, too!" His voice echoed against the cliffs. If it were a color, she realized, his voice would be red. Red-orange, orange-red, subtly striped along the slopes—that was how she imagined it. This great, booming cloud that rushed from his chest and his mouth and flung itself wildly across the basin the Waters had long ago cut and now sat at the bottom of. His voice was a sculptor. A boat builder. It brought things into being. She knew this intrinsically and she knew this because she wanted it to be true. She wanted to swim through the choppy Waters with the wind scrubbing her face and her hair messy and loose and dripping down her neck, water mixing with sweat, disgusting exchanger sweat, different from Deeyan sweat, certainly. She'd never stopped wanting to swim the passage.

So, the next night, she returned to the Waters. She looked around carefully and then she undressed. Once she was in the warm water, her shoulders shrank down. Here she was. Now she could relax. She focused on her breath; the fine movements of her muscles; the perpendicularity of her head in relation to the surface. *Guide me*, she mouthed with her head underwater. The thick, open taste drew itself into her nose, her eyes, her throat. She drank as she swam, determined not to return to the air until her lungs curdled. *Guide me*, she said again, this time in her head.

When Agapanthus finally whipped herself above the surface, she floated on her back. Warm, dry air sank onto her warm, wet belly, and goosebumps coated her skin. She watched Imn. Breathing, breathing. Aster had been right. She'd swam almost all the way to the fisheries in half the time just by concentrating a little harder. And she wasn't even tired. If she periodically floated on her back, she could make it all the way to the distant bulk of Shre. Right here, right now, at the end of a long day, she might just make it. And if she kept training, getting stronger, planned it out—of course she could do it.

Back on the shore, Aster was sitting with his knees bent up to his chest. He picked at the pebbles with his fingernails. Agapanthus darted to her dress and slipped it on so hurriedly that the arm hole tore slightly. She slapped her arms down and adjusted the neckline so it was straight. Was he staring at her? No. He was still looking at the sand. She sat down next to him. His thigh was even stubblier than her own, and the hair was dark. It didn't surprise her to see him out here again. She'd known he would come. She'd hoped for it.

"Did you used to play in the cliffs here? With the other ex-changer children?" she asked while sitting, while sighing, while breathing in all the glorious air.

"All the time."

"Was it the group with only exchangers, or the one that was a mix of Deeyans and exchangers?"

"Both. I played with whoever I felt like. But mostly the exchanger kids. Most of them are still my friends now. But some of them, I don't know. We forgot about each other." He shook a pile of sand in his palm. The rocks rattled; they sparkled against Imn's enormous red face. "We probably played together, didn't we?" He angled his chest toward her. "Did I forget who you were?"

"No. I was just curious."

"Who did you play with?"

"I was too busy to play."

"Too busy?"

"Swimming. Rock-collecting."

"Rock-collecting? How's this?" He held out a translucent golden pebble.

"I have one just like it already. They're pretty, but they're everywhere."

"So you're looking for rarities?"

"I look for the ones that no one else would notice. The strange ones."

"Oh. Well, how about this one?" He held out a flat, red rock.

"Those are really everywhere. That's not unique at all."

"But maybe there's something unique in its mundanity. You have to admit, no one would notice it. It fits your criteria."

As she reached to grab it from his hand he held it higher, out of reach. She drew her hand back like he'd hit it. Did he lift it on purpose, to tease her, or had she just reached at the wrong time? He was squinting at the rock, turning it around against the light. She couldn't tell what he was thinking. Why was she so embarrassed around him? He wasn't the Contact, he wasn't a Council member, he wasn't anyone exulted or chosen or above her. Just look at him, with his lips slightly parted, gaping at this plain, red stone.

"Let me see it," Agapanthus said, and he placed it in her cupped hand. The rock did have some nice little light gray speckles on one side. And it was exceptionally smooth. "Maybe I *will* keep this one."

"Woah, now. I'm the one who found it."

"Yeah, but do you even collect rocks?"

He said nothing, for a moment. "But what do you do with them?"

"I keep them all in a box."

"Are you ever going to trade them? Are you saving up?" He grabbed the rock from her again. His fingers swept against her skin. Warm, sticky.

"No. I just—like having them there. I like looking at them." She only noticed how strange she was when she was with new people. "But sometimes I make jewelry out of them. Bracelets and things."

"Well, here, then. You keep it." He held it out. "Molded from the planet, from the soil and the stars, for quadrillions of years, and now its destiny is to sit in your house, or, at best, on your wrist."

"It's not cognizant. It's just a rock."

"Yes—a rock that's more Deeyan than we'll ever be. A rock that's more Deeyan than the Deeyans."

Agapanthus didn't know what to say to this. "Maybe that's why I collect them, then," she said, and she immediately wished she hadn't. It was too true, a truth she had never acknowledged before. She hoped he would think she was kidding. She smiled at him, close-lipped, eyebrows raised, trying to convince him of her light-heartedness. Suddenly she felt very tired. It took a lot for her to smile like that.

"Fine. I have the perfect compromise. It's still mine, but you can look after it for me. I would probably lose it, anyway." He tucked the stone beneath her fingers, wrapping his own hand over her own.

"You're really strange, you know that?"

"Don't even think about it," he said. "You're not collecting me."

5

AGE: TWENTY-TWO EARTH-YEARS

They met every day they could, whenever she was sure Pittick wouldn't see her. At night; on their days off—which, at first didn't match up—Aster was off on the days she had to work. It went on like that for a while—three days with Agapanthus at work and Aster off, three days with Aster on and Agapanthus off, over and over in a cycle, until, finally, Aster asked to be switched to the other shift. And he was.

Aster worked at the Hydrothermal Power Plant. Agapanthus had no idea what exactly he did there. It was too complicated; she didn't understand how you could even begin to capture the raw heat-energy of the vents—fierce, wild, and revered—let alone how you could send it all over the island to power the automatic doors and lights and even the audiobooks of thousands of people. Aster, after proving himself an adult, had worked his way past apprentice. Now he was the assistant manager of one of the divisions within the Plant. An overseer, mostly, he said, but he still remembered how to do the technical stuff. His foster-father worked there, too. One of the department heads. Aster had been worried that his foster-father wouldn't allow him to switch shifts. He said that he was a man with hard eyes. Thick, round, barely moving eyes of a dull, putrid yellow. He had raised him in the house of his dead wife's unmarried sister, who they rarely spoke to. It was just her in the woman's wing, and just the two of them in the men's wing, now. Aster said it was too empty. He would rather be outside.

Sometimes, after the meal, Aster's exchanger friends came to the Waters. Agapanthus loved swimming with them; they were slow, and floppy, as though their muscles were brittle and spasmic. One of the girls, Collinsia, the one with very dark brown skin, contorted her mouth into an awful, teeth-baring frown whenever she swam. Like the water hurt. Like it scared her. The two boys, Oenanthe and Daucus, splashed wildly when they kicked their feet. And the rest of them—the other two girls, Urtica and Dicentra—were decent, but slow. They could only hold their breath for two strokes. Agapanthus and Aster reigned over them as the fastest and sleekest swimmers. But they still trained together, all of them. Aster had long ago convinced his friends that they needed to swim the channel.

"He has this whole exchanger-movement idea going around in his head," Oenanthe said to Agapanthus one day, when they were the first two wading into the Waters. "Some sort of liberation scheme. If we all become adults, we can make things better for ourselves."

"I don't know. I don't think things are so bad."

"You must have a good foster-family, then." Oenanthe splashed carefully through the Waters. His cheeks were especially prim and shrunken. Against the fractured light of Imn—colliding against the ripples—his skin looked beige, yellowish. Agapanthus glanced down at her arms. Pink-white as ever. She wanted so badly just to dive in, but she didn't want to leave Oenanthe behind. It was a strange thing, to have to think about other people. She was used to just taking off and being alone. But she waited, and Collinsia, Daucus, Urtica, Dicentra, and Aster caught up with them. Soon they all stood in a crooked line, water up to their waists at the edge of the shallows. She could see it on their faces—we're all here now, let's get in. She could see the ritual pull at them. They had grown up swimming together. They'd been doing this all their lives. These were the children she'd watched from afar. The children who once invited her to play, just that once; the ones who she'd said no to, who had never asked again.

Without anyone counting or shouting or anything, they all dove in at the same time. Agapanthus waited a moment to watch them slop around her. Everyone besides Aster and Urtica pushed sheets of water up in their wake. Agapanthus let the Waters churn around her knees. Finally, she, too, dove in. She pushed her toes into the sand and shoved as hard as she could. The warmth blew over her. She locked her limbs. Keep tight, keep strong, keep straight. When she came up for air, she'd glided twice as far as even Aster. Her hair clustered around her ears. Thick, wet. She hoped it looked thinner when it was wet. Dicentra had yellow hair, too, but it was much lighter than hers—almost white. All the rest of them had some shade of brown, with Collinsia's being the darkest. Collinsia was making that face again. Her chin dropped below the waterline as she rubbed water from her eyes.

"Ah, it feels so good," Agapanthus said to her. Her voice sounded especially crisp and authoritative as it soared over the Waters.

Collinsia's mouth became a long rectangle. She nodded.

"You'll stay afloat better if you kick your feet more," Agapanthus said.

"Oh?" Collinsia's head rose slightly.

"That's better," Agapanthus said.

Collinsia never said much. She just wasn't talkative. Agapanthus wondered how the group had become friends with someone so shy. Why was it okay for Collinsia to be that way? She felt like if she was that quiet, no one would bother spending time with her. It was like Collinsia wasn't even there. But, then again, Agapanthus hadn't made many friends being how she was, anyway—in-between; not talkative, not silent.

"Do you guys ever wonder what the water's like on the Water Planet?" Oenanthe asked. He floated on his back with his neck craned up over his chest. He flipped to his stomach, then to his back again. "I mean, I assume it's just covered in the stuff. What color it is?"

"Water's always black. Maybe silver," Dicentra said.

"I think it looks reddish, here, sometimes," Agapanthus added.

"But that's because of the reflection," Dicentra said. She gestured, with stern eyebrows, toward Imn. "The real color is that dark-black-translucent."

"Sometimes Imn reflects against my skin, so when I look down at my reflection in the Waters, it looks like my skin's turned red," Urtica said, her voice choppy from the exertion of treading water.

"So—sometimes—you look Deeyan?" Daucus asked, laughing.

"Oh no—all this time, you've secretly been a Deeyan in disguise?" Aster yelled. He somersaulted backwards and flipped underwater. When he came up, his skin was coated in a sheen that was also, somehow matte. It reminded Agapanthus of a pile of sand glued together with water.

"No, no, no, I've noticed that, too," Agapanthus said. "When the Waters are still enough. When they become quiet and glassy."

"Well I'm glad I've never noticed it," Aster said. "That would be terrifying. Who would want to look like a Deeyan, even for a second? Tiny nose, giant eyes, that weird, impenetrable-looking skin?"

"Aster! Don't be so mean," Agapanthus said.

"I'm not being mean. Just observant."

"I wasn't talking about the features, anyway. Just the skin tone," Urtica added.

Aster continued. His eyes were locked on Agapanthus. "Like—they're short. They're short compared to us. We look down at them. They are short, little, stocky people." Aster swam closer to her. "Is that mean?"

"I think it's a little mean," Aapanthus said.

Daucus rubbed his large nose with the side of his hand. "It really is true, though. My foster-mother is only up to my waist. The other day we measured it. We stood back to back, and she was only to here." He brought his arm to the lower edge of his ribs. "It's so weird. When I was a little kid, I remember her being so tall!"

"My foster-parents aren't that much shorter than me. My foster-father's about up to my shoulders," Agapanthus said. "Still. I liked it better when I was shorter than them."

"The Deeyans liked it better then, too. They don't like it now, how we watch them from above, like the Gods."

"Aster!" Agapanthus looked around at the others. None of them looked shocked—they plied their hands eagerly through the Waters, or stared off absently at the cliffs—treading water, floating haphazardly on their backs and stomachs, everyone doing their own thing, Collinsia even humming to herself as she practiced winding her arms backwards. But everyone listening, everyone waiting. "How can you—what—"

"Everyone tells us all the time: they're not our Gods. Our whole lives, we've heard that. Why should I care what they think of me? What are they going to do—send me back? Send me home? Release me from this prison?" His words were strained; saturated in overly forced control. Agapanthus could tell that he was trying to keep his tone light. It wasn't working. His water-sleek lips attempted a smile before deflating.

"Sometimes I think—would I really want to go back? They did give us up, after all," Oenanthe said.

"But only because it was an honor to come to Deeyae. To be part of the exchange program. Everyone there probably wants to send their child here. When we go back, we'll be—well, we'll be heroes, I guess," Agapanthus said. "Explorers. We'll come back and tell them all about Deeyae."

"So what must the Water Planet be like, then, if they didn't want us living there?" Dicentra asked.

"I don't think it's that they didn't want us living there," said Agapanthus. "It's that they wanted us living here."

"Why? So we could be ordered around? And treated like we're beneath everyone?" Aster shifted onto his back. "Truth is," he said without looking at anyone, "no one knows anything for sure. That's it. That's all. Done."

There was a long silence, suppressed only by the light slosh of the Waters. Back and forth, slosh-slosh-slap. The warm wind curled itself around their faces. Warm air, warm water, warm wind. Such a perfect temperature. Agapanthus thought this must be the temperature before you were born—inside the womb. But that was also kind of gross to think about.

Daucus started talking about water creatures—why they so rarely attacked people. No one since Lapars's son had been attacked. Collinsia spoke up for once and said it was because of the balance at the fisheries. If the Deeyans didn't overfish, and left enough for the water creatures, then the water creatures left them alone, for the most part. Of course this had been arranged by the Gods. The Gods didn't rule over the water creatures, but apparently they kept in contact with them.

Then Urtica started talking about whether they had language, whether the water creatures spoke aloud to one another just like Deeyans did, whether they could learn their language.

Aamsh and Jord had fallen entirely. Without any group consensus they all started toward the shore as they spoke. The rest of rightwards Yeela would be in the cool centers of their homes, asleep or, at least, trying to. Agapanthus wasn't ready to leave yet. She wasn't ready to go back to the Portation Center tomorrow. And she hated the idea of curling up alone in the children's hall, on the new blankets she'd just bought; the stillness echoing, and everything grey, unless she slept with the light on again. That always made her think of Aster at his job the next day, making that power, pointing at people and at strange, bulky metal boxes.

Agapanthus slowed her strokes. So did Oenanthe.

"He was in a bad mood today, wasn't he," Agapanthus whispered.

"He gets rough like that sometimes. Maybe not rough—I don't know. You saw it." Oenanthe splashed closer, his arms limp and obviously tired. "He has good reason. You ever notice the scars on his back?"

Agapanthus nodded. "I thought they were from the check-ups."

"He would never admit this, but we all know anyway—we've always known—his foster-father used to—he used to hurt him." Oenanthe's thin face seemed to close up, close in, like a tight shroud. "He used to hit him. How could we not know, when he came out the next day, bleeding, or bruised up all over? And it was more often than the check-ups. No. It wasn't the check-ups."

"I never would've—I didn't—think that happened. To anyone. I had no idea."

"You can't say anything. He wouldn't want you to know. But now you can understand." He swallowed. "He likes you, you know."

Agapanthus nodded again and glanced down at the water. She hadn't even noticed that she and Oenanthe had stopped swimming; that the others were already on shore, scrambling nakedly into their clothes. "Come on, we better get back," Agapanthus said. She kicked off and billowed forward on her stomach. But then she sat up again, and she turned around, and said, "Oh, and thank you, Oenanthe." His name still felt stiff when her lips formed it. Everyone's name did. She was always secretly worried that she would get them wrong; what if she called Daucus Dicentra? Or Urtica, Oenanthe? The only person she felt completely safe with was Aster.

Aster, who stood in his light-beige-skin dress, short-sleeved, hanging perfectly over his heavy shoulders. Aster, with water dripping down his ears and his high forehead, over his close-cropped hair and along his neck. Aster, who kicked at the pebbled sand, coating his bare feet in red powder, not looking at Agapanthus as she slipped the soft leather of her dress over her scalp and nose and neck. Aster, who Agapanthus stood next to. Said nothing, just stood next to, as Daucus, Urtica, Collinsia, Dicentra, and Oenanthe filtered away and up the hill. Aster, who rested his hand on the top of her head, and then leaned forward and kissed her cheek. Aster, who she hugged beneath the light of Imn, with the Waters sputtering madly with the heaviness of the wind. Aster, who looked at her with so much white around the colored part of his eyes, and said nothing, though he looked like he wanted to. She wanted to say, *I know, I know where you've come from, I know why you hate your foster-father, I know why you're so driven, why you're so hard on the Deeyans, I know everything and you don't have to worry anymore because, somehow, I can share your pain with you.*

Then, over Aster's shoulder, high in the cliffs, she saw something red move quickly past. A face? A person? Who would be out so late, except their own group of exchangers? Agapanthus returned her gaze to Aster, and she said, "We should get back," even though she didn't want to. She couldn't bear it, really. She wanted to stay out here all day, all night; watch Aamsh and Jord rise and fall over the fragrant hull of the Waters, and lie on the beach with Aster at her side. They could search for stones. Swim. Become water creatures.

But they didn't. Aster and Agapanthus walked together in a slow, sauntering pace up to the plateau, where they could see the Waters churn with fullness. One more hug. His hands pressed flat against her shoulder blades; her nose pressed up against his shoulder. She breathed in. He smelled like the Waters, or maybe like a stone that had been buried so deeply for so long that it felt damp when pried from the soil.

"I'll see you tomorrow, then," Aster said. His voice rumbled through his entire body and into hers.

"After work?"

He nodded. "We better train you extra hard tomorrow. We hardly swam at all today."

"How much more do I need to train? You know I'm faster than you by now."

"Faster! Who needs faster? You need endurance."

"Does that mean you're afraid to race me?"

"Tomorrow?"

"Tomorrow."

And then they smiled at each other and at the red ground, and they walked away toward their ancient, stone homes. Agapanthus couldn't help but think of Aster stepping quietly into his dark house, trying desperately not to wake his foster-father with the empty echoes of his footsteps. Did Aster have his own room now, she wondered? Now that he wasn't in the children's hall? She wondered what the mural in his front hall looked like. She wondered if Aster, when he was younger, with wider cheeks, with bruises along his back, had ever brought his hand up, slowly, to the mural, and let his skin sully its pristineness.

Agapanthus entered through the men's wing, as usual. It was heavy with cool, quiet, darkness. She sidled through the automatic door into the children's hall. But then the door on the other side beeped—the door to the woman's wing.

"Yeah?" Agapanthus said in what she thought would be a normal voice, but which ended up being a whisper, stuck in the back of her throat. She stood in front of the door so it would open. There stood Leera. Straight-backed, mouth creased.

"What are you doing up?" Agapanthus asked.

Leera cleared her throat. She rested her hand on the upper edge of her chest, right at the cusp of her neck. "Imari and I were looking for you after the meal. She forgot to tell you that tomorrow is recalibration day. You'd said you went home, so we looked all over. No sign of you. And you didn't answer when we knocked, here, so I went out, walked around. Back by the cafeteria. Along the cliffs."

Agapanthus dug the tip of her finger, right between the skin and the nail, into the thread of her dress's hemline. "We were swimming."

"And that exchanger boy?"

"What?"

"The one you were pressed up against."

Agapanthus was afraid to speak. She felt like her voice wouldn't work. Her throat felt dry, as though her tongue was stuck to the roof of her mouth. She wanted so badly to close the door and curl up within her pile of blankets. Disappear into them.

"Who is he?" Leera asked.

"He works at the Power Plant. I thought I told you about him. We've been friends for a while."

"Why were you out so late?"

"It was a whole group of us. We were swimming. They're my friends now, too. The whole group. We swim together a lot. For years now." *And you haven't noticed*, Agapanthus wanted to add.

"I don't think the Gods would like you being out so late. Aamsh and Jord had already fallen from sight. That's not the time for swimming. And you know that, Agapanthus."

"We were just about to head back up."

"But first you needed to hug each other."

"What's wrong with that?"

"It could give people the wrong idea. That's not the kind of crowd you should be fraternizing with."

"What? What's wrong with them? Tell me one thing that's wrong with them."

"He's an exchanger, Aga."

"Hmm. Oh, look. Look at my arm. Look at what I am." Agapanthus held her forearm shakily up against Leera's. Red next to pink. Smooth next to speckled. "Why am I not allowed to fraternize with my own people?"

Leera pinched the bridge of her nose. "Maybe I shouldn't have—I didn't mean you shouldn't see them. I just meant you shouldn't stay out so late. And you shouldn't give people the wrong idea about anything. You don't want anyone to make the wrong assumptions."

"What if their wrong assumptions are right? What's so bad about that? It's not like I'm out hugging Deeyan men."

"Agapanthus, you are *not adults.*"

"*He* is. He swam the channel."

"So *that's* who it is. Is that why you like him?"

"I—"

"It doesn't even matter. You're not an adult, and he's not good enough for you."

"You can't get mad at me for being a child when you won't let me do the rite of passage. You just want to keep me from having any say. Any power. You just want to keep me under your control."

"I just want what's best for you. And the only man good enough for you would be a Deeyan man. And since you can't be with a Deeyan man, you're better off being independent."

"Leera, I'm not some separate species somewhere between a Deeyan and an exchanger. If an exchanger isn't good enough for me, then you're saying I'm not good enough."

"No, I'm saying that that boy at the Waters isn't good enough for you. And you need to be careful with him. Don't hug him again. Don't kiss him. Don't—don't. Just think, before you go anywhere with him. Everything we do has consequences, Aga. It helps to think of them before we make our decisions, instead of after. Some consequences never go away. And just like that, your whole life is ruined."

"Well if I ruin this life here I'll get another one on the Water Planet."

"That's not how it works. If you got pregnant, you would have to leave your baby and be sent back. They would kill your baby."

"Pregnant? I'm not going to get pregnant."

"Just be careful. That's all I'm saying."

"Okay, fine. I get it. Fine."

"We all care about you, Aga. We all love you."

"But you don't want me to grow up, do you."

"I don't want you to swim the channel, no. We've talked about this." Leera stepped back from the doorway, her chin just bare-ly turning away from Agapanthus, ready to whip the other way, escape, retreat. She did this every time Agapanthus tried to talk about anything important. She edged away, gradually, footstep by footstep. Like she didn't care at all what Agapanthus thought.

Not this time. Agapanthus stepped forward. She clasped her hands on either side of the door frame.

"I'm going to do it," she said, and then she clenched her teeth. She swallowed. Suddenly she remembered how thirsty she was. "I've been training and I'm almost ready. Any day now, and I'm going to do it." She felt like her words were stuck in the air. They hung there in front of her. They embarrassed her, made her cheeks hot. She pulled her hands down from the doorway because her underarms were sweating.

Leera stared at her. Her eyes gleamed hollowly. They remind-ed Agapanthus of how they'd looked during the Sickness—like a cloud on the opposite side of the sky from Imn—the empty edge of the sky, away from the God stars, and the Waters, and the cliffs; the side of the sky that was all red-pink expanses, and looked down upon the interior of the island with a blankness that led everyone to forget about it, that made it almost cease to be sky; to become the absence of it. That's how Leera's orange eyes looked. Her eyes were the absence of sky.

"I'm sorry to have failed, then," Leera said. "Obviously everything we've given you hasn't been enough."

"I just want to be a person now, I want to be a real person, not property—"

"Property? How could you even think that? You're everything, in this family. Aside from the Gods, you're our greatest joy. Property—how could you even say that? You're my *foster-daughter*, Aga. You're my foster-daughter."

"Yes, I'm your foster-daughter. Not your real daughter."

"I couldn't have a—"

"A real daughter?"

"I couldn't have—"

"I'm sorry I wasn't enough to make up for it. I'm sorry I can't inherit the house. I'm sorry I could never make it better, I'm sorry you couldn't have your own children, I'm sorry you couldn't somehow trade me in to fix whatever's wrong with you that you can't get pregnant. I'm sorry, okay? I'm sorry that I exist. I'm sorry that you're messed up."

"Don't be ungrateful. We took you in. We've given you a good life."

"Why did you take me in?"

"It was a—"

"Because all the Council members have foster-children, right?"

"Stop it. Stop it right now. Stop interrupting me." Her voice rose. It grew thick. "You ungrateful child. We took you in because it was an action endorsed by the Gods."

"Is that the only reason?"

"And because I wanted a child. Pittick and I wanted a child," Leera said quietly. She said nothing for a moment. "And I was infertile. I should tell you. I should probably tell you. I've always thought—I brought it upon myself, I think; my infertility. There was this exchanger boy. When I was young. He had dark, dark brown skin. I thought he looked so handsome. Like he was glowing from the inside. We walked together to the interior of the island one day. Just to walk. And that way we knew no one would see us. I knew it wasn't a good idea to be spending time alone with an exchanger boy. Especially since he always liked to rub my shoulders, or, sometimes cup my chin in his fingertips. But he was so kind. So soft-spoken. I had to lean in to hear what he said." Leera paused. "He was the first man I joined with, like that. It just happened, so fast. I didn't even think about it. It just happened. And the Gods did not like it. Not at all. Obviously. They sent him back not long after. And I—they took away my ability—I just know they did—it's my punishment—" Leera placed her hands over her eyes, and then over her ears.

"Does Pittick know? Or did Grandmother Surla?"

Leera shook her head. "No," she said breathily, like she was sighing. "And you can't let Pittick know. He would blame me. He would know it was my fault."

"You don't know that for sure. Maybe you would've been—maybe you wouldn't have been able to have children anyway. Maybe it made no difference at all. Didn't you ever go to the healing center and try to find out?"

"No. What if they knew, somehow? What if they could see some evidence that the exchanger boy had been there? Or, what if I was simply born wrong? What if I was broken? What then?" She exhaled. "No. I couldn't do that."

"Did you love him?"

Leera said nothing.

"That dark-skinned exchanger boy?" Agapanthus grumbled.

"No, of course not. Over the years I grew to hate him—the memory of him—for what happened." Leera's tongue moistened her thin, bottom lip. "You don't love the exchanger boy from the Waters—?"

"I don't know yet."

"Please be careful, Aga. I know you're both exchangers, but if you get sent back, you'll probably be separated. Just keep in mind that nothing you begin on Deeyae is going to last forever. The life of a Deeyan is like Imn. Steady. Static. The life of an exchanger is like Aamsh and Jord. Always moving. Always rising, and falling, and traveling throughout the sky."

"I'm surprised you wouldn't call that blasphemy," Agapanthus said. "Comparing exchangers to the God stars."

"No, my dear. Advice. That's just advice. Do not waste your life here. You never know when it will end."

Agapanthus couldn't sleep after that. She bundled herself in her blankets, inhaling the sweet, new-leather smell. She turned the lights off, and then turned them on again. She tried to focus on the deep aches buried in her shoulders and her upper back; the tightness along the back of her legs. Couldn't she pull that physical tiredness inside, and let it make her sleepy? All she wanted was for everything to stop. For it to stop—for it to stop—for it to stop. Leera's voice: *you never know when it will end.* Agapanthus kept hearing that over and over. She wanted to cry but, even alone in the children's hall, she felt, for some reason, like she was being watched tonight. Maybe Leera's presence had somehow saturated the hall, even though she'd gone to bed. Or maybe it was the Gods that Agapanthus felt. Maybe they were judging her right this very moment. Well, let them judge her. She unfolded her body slowly, tiredly. Then she turned off the light and migrated quietly through the men's wing, out into the warmth. It was so late that surely Aamsh and Jord would rise again soon. Agapanthus sauntered to the Waters. She kept thinking, *the world is a heavy place;* kept rendering it with her lips without saying the words aloud. Then she saw the Waters illuminated in red-black, and she nodded to them. But before she even made it to the shoreline, she slipped while sidling down the hill. Her thigh was bruised. She lay there, in the pebbled sand, right in the middle of the foot-worn path, with her blonde hair caked over her face so she could see noth-ing—so she could hear the Waters mumbling in the strange night. Her cheek and ear itched with sand but, still, she didn't move. She tried to listen. In one ear, she listened to the Waters. In the other, she tried to listen to Deeyae. She thought maybe the planet would roar or shift or something. She thought maybe, if she listened long enough, it might say an actual word. But she waited, and waited, and waited, and, still, nothing.

After the meal the next day, Agapanthus drifted away from the family—from Leera's obvious quietness—and she met Aster at the base of the cliffs. He was waiting with his back against the rock and his arms crossed over his chest. As she walked toward him Agapanthus felt his eyes roll over her. She watched him and tried to smile, but then she realized how desperately unhappy she was. His arms uncrossed, and he walked out to her and gently grabbed her shoulders. Then they greeted each other, hand to head. Aster bowed so Agapanthus would be able to reach. Although he had to do this, although he always did this, Agapanthus felt, for some reason, like this was the kindest thing anyone had ever done for her. She pulled him in and hugged him. "Are you ready to race?" she asked with her lips rubbing against his tunic.

"I think, Aga, this is the perfect final test. If you beat me, you're ready."

Agapanthus stepped back. "Ready to swim the channel?"

"Yeah, I think so."

"Come on, then. Should we start in the Waters or dive in?" She stepped toward the waterline.

"Let's start once we're already in. I don't want to have an unfair advantage."

"Hey, I'm just as good at diving as you are. Maybe better."

"Okay. Let's start in the Waters so *you* don't have an unfair advantage."

Agapanthus swept off her dress and dove in anyway—gracefully, with her back arched. She felt the Waters fall over her, wrap around her and lift her up. Aster was already beside her when she drew breath at the surface. Agapanthus brushed her hair back from her face and wiped water from her eyelashes. Aster looked up. His chest rose as he inhaled deeply. "Ready, Aga?" he asked. His voice sounded smaller today. Like, instead of magnifying it, the Waters had swallowed his voice. Maybe he knew she would beat him.

"To the other end of the bay?" Agapanthus asked.

"On the count of three."

Agapanthus's stomach clenched. She held her breath.

"One," Aster began.

"Two." Agapanthus breathed in as much air as she could; through her stomach, her nose, her mouth. She filled her body with air.

"Three!" Aster shouted. They leapt downward into the filtered, choppy light. Agapanthus focused on long strokes. Short leg kicks, long, lunging arm movements. She'd swum across here so many times. Red haze above, silver shadows below. Usually she kept her eyes open underwater, but now she closed them. She didn't want to see Aster beside her. She needed to pretend that she was alone. Just her and the Waters. She thought that it must be like this in space if you were a God. They probably swam through space all the time. They floated and spun and swept their way between the stars in that black nothingness that was probably actually water. The stars were like beautiful pebbles. Surely They went hunting for them.

Guide me, Waters, Agapanthus thought. Over the usual hum of the ripples came a distant clipping noise. She thought it was probably a fishing boat. Just in case, she opened her eyes. She was so close to the cliff. Where was Aster? She didn't let herself look behind her until her hand touched the stone—bleached orange beneath the water where it had worn away over time. Aster was only halfway. Did he know? Had he seen her? Agapanthus dove back under and swam toward him. Then she turned around and swam toward the cliff a little more slowly. She wanted to win, but not by that much. When had Aster become so slow? Was he letting her win? Hopefully he hadn't seen her. Hopefully he would think it was a pretty close race. Or maybe he was letting her win.

"Aster, why did you swim so slowly?" Agapanthus asked when they'd both made it to the edge of the bay.

"I'm not slow. You've just gotten fast."

"Am I really that fast?"

"You're really that fast." He stood up, and the water only barely covered his waist. She saw his hip-bones, and the thin, veiny skin that clad them. "But the real question is, are you tired? Do you feel like you could swim that distance twenty times over?"

"I'm not tired at all."

"And do you know how to feel the pull of the currents? And if you see a fish, to follow it?"

"I'm ready, Aster. I'm completely, absolutely ready. I have strong arms and stamina and I can hold my breath forever. If I get tired, I'll float on my back. I'm more comfortable in the Waters than out. I think I should just do it."

"Me too. I mean, I think so too."

"Tomorrow?"

"Tomorrow." Aster nodded absently, staring out in the cloud-heavy direction of Shre. "Are you going to tell them?"

"No. They'll just try and stop me. They can find out when the Shreyans paddle me back over for the feast."

And so they swam a little more, and then they went home and slept. Agapanthus got started early the next morning—just as Aamsh and Jord joined with Imn's light. She crept outside in her usual tired, quiet way. Aster was waiting for her at the shore.

"I'll wait until you're near the line of sight, and then I'll tell someone, and they can get the word to Shre. There'll be a crowd by then. I'll be sure to tell them it's you. It's Agapanthus, everyone; an exchanger! They'll go crazy over it."

Agapanthus said nothing. She just hummed, *mmm,* and wrapped her arms around his ribs. "I wish you could swim it with me," she said, after a moment.

"You're doing something great. Something bigger than you. Think about how this will change the perception of exchangers."

"Aster," she said suddenly. "What if I see a water creature?"

"Just stay calm. And don't touch it. That's when they attack, if you accidently touch them."

Aster, Agapanthus wanted to say. *I'm scared. I don't want to do it anymore. This is all I've wanted to do my entire life and now it's here and I'm terrified.* She wanted to run home and tell Pittick and Leera everything; let tears spill from her eyes. She wanted to be a good foster-daughter and go to work at the Portation Center and not be friends with Deeyans or exchangers or anyone at all. Leera didn't make sense. Agapanthus wasn't supposed to spend time with exchangers, because they weren't good enough for her, but, then, none of the Deeyans wanted to spend time with her, because she was a forever-child? What was she supposed to do, when all her life they'd told her to make friends with the other children, Deeyan or otherwise? And now she had? And now it was wrong because she was older? But even though she was older she was still, technically, a child? Agapanthus bit her lip and stared heavily at her bare feet. She hadn't even bothered wearing shoes. She hadn't bothered washing up, either, since she'd be in the cleansing Waters soon enough. Suddenly she felt dirty. What if she smelled like sweat? Or dust? What if Aster was repulsed by her? She breathed in deeply; nodded for no particular reason.

"Okay," she said. "I'm ready."

She wanted to swim because that was what Geleria and Loao had done. She wanted to swim because that was what Aster had done. Because that was what Leera, and Pittick, and Imari, and Lapars's son, and Leera's nearly-drowned childhood friend, and all the Deeyans before them had done.

Aster brushed a stray hair from Agapanthus's eyes. His fingers were hot against her forehead. "You're my inspiration, Agapanthus." He laid his palm on her hair's part, right on top of her head. She looked straight into his eyes, those light-brown orbs, intersected, as usual, with red veins of tiredness. She wished she could look at his eyes without him looking back at hers. She hadn't spent much time looking at her own—she knew they were brown, just brown. What was there to look at? And they were so oddly shaped, so long and drawn.

She couldn't take it anymore. She glanced away from Aster, at the roaming waterline. It seemed like it was breathing. Like it was waiting for her; gently tossing the pebble-choked sand. Agapanthus suddenly thought of her rock collection.

"Aster, if anything happens to me, I want you to break into the child's hall at my house, and take my rock collection. I want you to have all of them. All the rocks."

Aster's eyebrows clenched together.

"And, I want you to pick out one, whichever one you like the best, and I want you to keep it. And I want you to throw all the rest into a hydrothermal vent. But not at work; wait until the next Festival of the Underworld." Her lips felt numb as she spoke. Her voice had grown shaky.

"Agapanthus, it won't come to that. You're going to make it across. Just remember: float on your back. Follow the currents. Listen to the Waters." He kissed her on the cheek, then. Very softly, and surprisingly quietly. There was no smacking-suction-lip-noise. Not even their breathing. He smelled warm—like warmth, like Imn. Agapanthus listened to the whole of the Waters; every wave, every clash against the cliffs, every sparkling moment lit to red, orange, pink.

"I'll see you on the way back, then." Agapanthus smiled with her lips closed. Then she turned sharply, drew off her red-breasted sper skin sheath-dress, and left it on the sand. She slid her feet under the lukewarm shallows. She waited—one, two, three—counting the pulse of the Waters, and then she dove in.

She didn't resurface until she was far past the drop-off. Even then, she only came up for a quick gulp of air before resuming her lunging swim forward. As she swam, she tried not to think about swimming. She thought about Collinsia. Whether she had always been that quiet, whether she was born that way, or whether, when she was younger, she had been a talkative, free sort of girl, and had only grown inward because she had been broken, somehow.

Agapanthus thought, also, about Loao. What was it like, living in the dark, open halls of the men's wing? It must be hard to move into a new house, and then to be alone there. He'd probably sat outside a lot with Geleria, at least at first. Maybe they were so used to everything now that they stayed in their opposite wings, like Leera and Pittick, and Sonlo and Imari. Agapanthus rarely saw Loao and Geleria anymore. They had both been given positions in the upstairs at work, where the Waters were cleansed before cascading down to the portation rooms. She wondered what would've happened if she had somehow—*somehow*—mated with Loao. Of course it was impossible. But what if somehow her skin turned red? If she became Deeyan? Would Loao have chosen her over Geleria? Would Aster still have kissed her cheek? What about the Contact? Would he have called her lovely? Agapanthus had watched that memory revolve in her mind, over and over. She realized that he'd meant lovely *for an exchanger*. So if she was a Deeyan the Contact wouldn't have said anything at all.

If she was a Deeyan. But she was not Deeyan, even though she had wished for it. She'd once tried to paint her skin red with a mixture of sand and water. There was no way to change her eyes to orange or yellow. The white circles around the brown were indistinguishable. And her hair would always be pale. She pressed into the water. Not only would she swim all the way to Shre, she would do it as quickly as Aster had. She felt the current hinge itself to her abdomen. Underwater there was nothing to see but a twisting of color and light. No fish, no water creatures. She brought her head up and looked behind her; there was Yeela's hill-sloped outline. There was the great fishery vessel, hazy, fogged, almost invisible. Pittick would be angry with her after this, but he would be proud.

The farther she swam the less tired she felt. She must be halfway already; the Waters had grown choppier, and the wind drummed heavily against her ears. She'd never been out this far before, except in a boat. The bottom was so distant. Maybe there was no sand, no pebbles, at the bottom. Perhaps it was only water forever, all the way down into the core of Deeyae, where the Others believed the god of the underworld lived.

Agapanthus screamed with her mouth underwater. The sound was caught in the fabric of the Waters. Torn up, kept secret, carried down to the unforeseeable seafloor, where it would sit for millions of years, until someone swam past it, in that exact spot, down low at the bottom, and it echoed again. Agapanthus had never screamed like that before. She didn't know why she did it. Maybe because she was completely, irrefutably alone. Or, maybe, because the Waters were listening.

The waves grew rough. Agapanthus couldn't move very far without a spray of water flushing up her nose, or knocking her sideways. Some of the wind-spurred waves were so large they loomed over her head. They catapulted her down, below the surface, until everything spun. She couldn't even tell which way was sky. Agapanthus found her way to the top, breathed again, and another wave hit. Her arms groped in panic. When she came up again, she noticed the sky had darkened. Deep, red clouds encircled Imn. Another wave hit. This time, Agapanthus breathed as deeply as she could and dove. Finally it was quiet again. She would stay under here as long as she could—under this blanket of water. There would be no floating on her back. There would be no resting. Her success depended on the sinewy paddling of her arms; the strength of her stomach; the fluttering of her legs. She just had to remember that her body was strong and well-trained. She heard Aster's voice: *You're going to make it across.* And then Leera's: *You need to realize you might never be ready, Aga.* Both of them spoke to her at once, rotating between yes and no. And all the while Agapanthus couldn't breathe, but she was afraid to break the surface. She didn't want to get knocked down again. The helplessness of being pounded and flung frightened her. What had happened to her dear, benevolent Water goddess? Evidently she was fiercely powerful. Evidently she cared nothing for Agapanthus.

Which way was Shre? Which way was—another wave pummeled over her head. Water rushed into her open eyes, down her throat. She felt burned, singed, betrayed. Once again she shoveled down into the lower water. She had never worried about going the right way. Shre was so obvious on the horizon, but, underwater, she couldn't see it. What if she ended up overpassing it? What if she swam all the way to the frozen southlands? Would the Others save her? Would she die of cold before she made it to their shore?

Then, just above, she saw a fish. Flat-bodied, black, with multiple fins on its sides. Like a glistening circle. Like a fallen piece of night-sky. At first Agapanthus was glad not to be alone. Then she remembered the current. Follow the fish. She swam up, closer to the surface but still beneath the breaking of the waves, until she felt the tug. This current would take her all the way to shore.

Every time she went up for air, the waves knocked her down again. She began to feel like her head was stuffed with a bundle of leather. It would be so nice to just fall asleep. Right here, suspended weightlessly in the Waters. For a long while that's all Agapanthus thought about as she swam—the soft comfort of sleep. Little bumps coated her skin. She felt like she was in the middle room of the woman's wing. It was always coldest in there, insulated from the warmth of Imn by layers of heavy stone.

She wanted to be done. She wanted to be done so badly. It almost made her want to cry, she was so desperate. Her throat itched with a subtle knot and the sour taste of panic. Since when was she a crier?

When she peeked over the waterline again the wind was slightly calmer. Agapanthus breathed until her chest felt cool and softened. Shre loomed in the distance. Its peaks were taller than those on Yeela, and, from this distance, the whole island rose from the Waters like one giant mountain, tinged gray by distance. Red clouds were just beginning to clear off its summit.

The wind chilled the damp skin of her face; the back of her neck. Agapanthus stretched out and floated. Her body rose and fell with the Waters—sloshy, rhythmic, up-and-down movements that made her want to fall asleep even more. "Thank you," she said to the Waters. Her voice was surprisingly clear and calm, though she'd expected it to be raspy.

There was the sky. The unending sky. Aamsh and Jord had fallen. That meant Agapanthus had been gone an entire day. There was no way she'd be faster than Aster had been. How long had he taken? No more than a day, certainly. It had already been a day for her, and Agapanthus still had so far to go.

But he hadn't told her about the waves! He hadn't warned her. Agapanthus moved her arms at her sides, feeling the water flow through her and around her, propping her up, displaying her pale body to the sky. Her hair cascaded around her ears. Each tendril stayed constantly in motion, like long, slippery fingers, or like the stems of water plants cowering, always timid. How she wished to be in the shallows, at that moment. How she wished to be on the shore, legs sprawled in front of her, splotched with sand, while Aster dug up pebbles at her side. She wished that, somehow, they could see the stars, there, in Yeela's warmth, and lie there side by side, so close that they could share their breath; their heads against the ground, her hair splayed out, accidently spilling over onto Aster's shoulder; she wished they could point upwards at their Water Planet, and all the other multitudes of stars that shimmered, that seemed almost to chime as their steady, ancient lights bounded together and stroked the sky. *I wonder what our home is like, Aster would say. I wonder if we'll ever be there together.* And Agapanthus would tilt her head toward him, and, with her voice heavy, she would say, *We already are.*

But that would be taken away, someday, and she would be hurled alone into the vastness. It seemed impossible that another family waited for her on the Water Planet. She wondered if they talked about her. Did they love her? Maybe they gazed at their own sky and looked for her. Maybe they whispered that they would like for her to come home.

What if they had already died? What if they were all dead, and she would really be alone?

And what if she died, right here, swimming the rite of passage, and she let the Waters permeate her lungs? Her shoulders hurt. Her thighs felt like they were compressed with tightly wound ropes. It would be so easy to stop; to sink. But she chased the current anyway. Arms, legs. Kick, glide. Lips above water. Breathe. Glance up. The God stars revolved above her. Whenever Agapanthus floated on her back she held her arm up in deference. *Please help me,* Gods, she asked the stars. *Please help me, Imn,* she asked the sun. *And, Waters—please, please help me.*

She felt like the rest of Deeyae had slowly dissolved and melted down into the wind, and she was inhaling small pieces of it; scattered remains of the red-dust cliffs and bits of skin from the creature-herds of the inner island and the thin black hair of the decaying Deeyan people. Every face, and every nose, and every breadth of sentience, all absorbed into her own body; all the wide desertlands seen from the tops of hills; every dull pigment of redness, every rainstorm lingering for days imprinted upon the soil; every subtle movement of Aster's forehead and his eyebrows, every punch and gouge his foster-father had imprinted upon him as he refused to cry; all those moments when Agapanthus had felt like she was not there, like she wanted so badly to belong with Leera and Pittick but was afraid to feel comfortable; like that one day, when she was very young, as they walked, three in a row, back from the meal, and, when the house first came into sight, Leera said: "We love you, Aga"—that was the moment Agapanthus realized that she had never believed them, and she never would believe them. Maybe she would never believe anyone.

And then she saw the rocks, deep below. And she saw the Shreyan cliff-faces jut sharply from the Waters. They looked so much like those on Yeela, but meaner and stronger, and gouged with thick, burgundy scars. The waves echoed around her on both sides as the cliffs boomed. On her hands and knees, she crawled up out of the shallows and touched the sand. It was fine; powdery; very light orange. And there were so few pebbles. Part of her mind realized that she had done it—that she was there, kneeling on Shre, out of breath, worn, and aching; that she had done what Pittick and Leera had always doubted, what Erabet and Geleria had always laughed at, what Aster had always known she could do—but the other part of her mind was stuck beneath something heavy and was unable to think of anything other than sand.

She rolled over onto her back. She still felt like she was floating.

Two Deeyan men appeared above her. They wore the longer, frayed tunics typical of Shre. One of them had a cut on his chin, half-healed, only slightly darker red than his skin.

"You're the one who swam the rite of passage?" the one without the scratch asked.

Agapanthus nodded. The back of her head dug into the sand.

"Obviously," the man with the cut said, staring at the other man. Then he looked down at Agapanthus. "Are you alright?"

"I'm fine," Agapanthus said, and, this time, her voice really was raspy. "You got the signal? You knew I was coming?"

"We knew someone was coming. We didn't know it would be an exchanger," the one without the scratch said.

The man with the cut raised his eyebrows at the other man. His low forehead wrinkled profusely.

"Are you the boaters, then?" Agapanthus asked.

"We're the *rowers*," the one without the scratch said. His voice reminded Agapanthus of Surla's, for some reason. Something about the rhythm of his words, and the breathiness behind them.

"Are you ready to head back across?" the man with the scratch asked.

"We're ready for that feast," the other man said quietly as he bounced up onto his toes.

Agapanthus curled up so she was sitting. Her whole body hurt, but she could do it. "Where's the boat?"

"Just over there." The man with the scratch pointed to the other side of the bay, where a round boat and bone-hewn paddles rested on the sand. "And we have clothes for you."

Very slowly, Agapanthus stood. She pulled on the dress. It was too big, and hung down at the underarms.

"Here, give her—give her the light thing," the man with the scratch said. "Then she won't be so tired anymore."

"It probably won't even work on her. She's an exchanger."

"What are you *talking* about? It worked on that exchanger guy a few years ago! Remember Vulehoof talking about it? How surprised he was that it worked on their kind?"

"Okay, let's do it, then."

And then there was a flash of dirty yellow light, and then she was perched, cross-legged, in the back of the boat, while the muscular shoulders of the men turned the paddles. The Waters sifted beneath the thin fabric. Agapanthus's eyes were still worn with tiredness, but her body was no longer a writhing slump of turmoil.

"Did you get that machine from the scientists?" Agapanthus yelled over the wind. "It's just like what they use at check-ups."

The one without the scratch said something, but his words spilled forward and were lost in the air.

"What?" she asked him. "What?" But he didn't seem to hear her, either. Agapanthus watched the Waters skim by. They were halfway between Shre and Yeela already. The waves looked docile compared to when she had been swimming through them.

"What was it like?" The man with the cut turned his head over his shoulder. "I haven't tried it yet, but I've heard it's like being asleep. You were walking, though. But just—blank. I don't see how you can be asleep and awake at the same time."

"The light? It felt like nothing. There was nothing, and then I was awake, and now I feel better," she said hoarsely.

"I shouldn't have questioned whether the light would work on exchangers—I guess that's what they're here for," the one without the cut said to the other man. "Experimenting on. Testing new technology on before we use it. That's why the scientists love them."

The man with the cut glanced at Agapanthus, who pretended she couldn't hear them, and continued to stare placidly at the horizon.

"Don't say that," the man with the scratch said, slightly more quietly. "It's not the scientists. The Gods asked for them to be here. We shouldn't question it."

"I'm not questioning it. *I'm just understanding—*"

"Well not even that. Focus on paddling, alright? We're starting to turn. You need to keep up."

And then their heads shifted forward again and Agapanthus could no longer hear whether they were talking or not.

Yeela spouted into view, swollen and asymmetrical. There was the tallest cliff at the interior, the empty fields at its base, the sea cliffs, and the walls of the bay. The sand would be cluttered with cheering people, and the water drums would announce her arrival as the food bowls were brought out. She would leap from the boat and slosh ankle-deep through the Waters, her bare feet quickly coated in sand, and she would run to her family, and Aster, and all his exchanger friends. The Council would congratulate her. And the Contact! He would rest his hand on her head. She would feel the warmth of his fingers through her hair. And from then on she would be an adult.

But as they rowed closer to the shore, it still looked barren—boulders, the usual pebble-sand, one Deeyan man sitting along the cliffs. They passed the fishery vessel. Small fishing boats. Did they not know she was coming? Had they given up on her?

"What, no feast?" the one without the cut said.

The Deeyan man stood as they came closer, and then Agapanthus recognized him—the Contact. He waited on the cusp between wet and dry sand as Agapanthus waded onto shore.

The Contact's eyes remained on the God stars until Agapanthus was directly in front of him. Her breath suddenly felt very loud. She wasn't sure whether she should say something, or whether that would interrupt his communion with the Gods, so she waited silently. Finally his gaze shifted to her. He didn't smile. His face reminded her, then, of a house; of cold, dark stone built with ancient hands. "Agapanthus Caracynth," he said as he reached up for her head. "You've done it. Congratulations."

She pretended to smile. What she really wanted to do was rush back into the Waters so she could hide. Or, if she could find the strength, maybe she could dash up the hill and run home. As handsome as the Contact was, she didn't want to talk to him right now. That was the last thing she wanted to do. Her fingers went nervously to the hem of her dress, but it was fringed. She'd forgotten it was a Shreyan dress.

"I know you must be upset that there's no feast. No celebration. But I made sure there wasn't one. I thought you would rather skip it when I gave you the news—so you have enough time to make preparations, and say your goodbyes." He swallowed with grotesque loudness. "Agapanthus Caracynth, the Gods have told me that it's your time to go home. To the Water Planet."

Without thinking, she crouched down and clasped her hands over her face. "Is it because I swam the channel?" She looked up, then back down. The Contact was barefoot, too. Her eyes didn't know where to rest. She closed them again.

"It was decided before that point."

"And you let me swim anyway?" She couldn't believe she was talking to the Contact like this; so irreverently. But she felt that he owed the answers to her. His status as Contact meant nothing now that she would be leaving. She had nothing to lose, anymore. "You let me swim across?"

"I didn't know you were going to. I didn't get to you in time."

"All that for nothing."

"It's an accomplishment that will be remembered here on Yeela for some time."

"Without a feast? I'm sure."

The Contact held out his hand to help her up. She slowly placed her palm in his. Her body felt like mud. Like wet sand crushed beneath a rock.

"I wish I was dead," she said. "I'd rather die than go back."

"No, no, that can't be true. The Water Planet is a lovely place."

Lovely. Lovely. Tears pressed at the backs of her eyes. She held them in. "What about Aster?"

"What about him?"

"Will he be sent back, too?"

"No. It's not his time quite yet."

"And can we find each other, when we're back there?"

"You'll both be sent back to your home locations. You could end up close together or across the world from one another. I, personally, don't keep track of those locations."

"So probably not."

"No, probably not."

"But I—love him."

"I'm sorry. I really am. These things happen, and there's nothing I can do. Nothing at all." The Contact sighed. He rubbed a bead of his black-stone necklace between his thumb and forefinger, and then dropped his arm to his side. "You should go to your foster-family. We've told them already. They'll be waiting to say goodbye."

Agapanthus rushed up the hill just as she'd imagined doing. When she made it to the top she was exhausted already, and she walked the entire path home with drudging slowness. She knew she should look around and take in Deeyae's beauty, but she couldn't focus on anything except her terror and dread and unbearable numbness. Her worst fear had come true. She felt herself harden. Her eyes became glass. Her lips locked together. This must be what it felt like to be dying.

"Aga, Aga!" Leera was waiting outside the front door. She flung her unsteady arms around Agapanthus's neck. "Come inside. Come on."

Everyone was waiting in the meeting hall. In turn they hugged her. First Imari, then Sonlo, and then Pittick, who stroked her back, and reached up to kiss her cheek.

"You did it, huh?" Pittick said with his hands still on her shoulders. "You swam the channel?"

"That's not why I'm being sent back. The Contact said it was already decided."

"I spoke with him already. I asked if there was any way you could stay just a little longer. Another year. Another day. Anything."

"And what did that worthless man say? He said it wasn't his decision. So what is he here for, if he can't even speak to the Gods for us? Isn't that his job? He's worthless," Uncle Sonlo spat. "Worthless."

Leera's thin mouth scrunched up. "The Gods don't *need* anyone—"

"You honestly aren't going to stand by the Gods at a moment like this?" Sonlo said.

"You honestly aren't going to *turn against them*? Sonlo, that won't help anything."

"This is beyond the Gods. Below them. This is the cruelty of Deeyans. This can't be the Gods' decision. If it is, I want nothing to do with them."

Aunt Imari stepped forward. This motion brought them all into watery silence. "Pittick, tell them what Akinan told you. What you told us just before they walked in."

"What? What happened?" Leera said.

"Some of the Council found out Aga will be leaving. They came up to me and they said, you know her memory will be wiped? You know she'll forget she ever knew you? That's what they do, when they send them back."

Leera leaned against the wall, rested her chin on her hand, and shook her head. "Impossible. We can't let that happen. At the very least, you need to remember us, Aga."

"What, is she going to have a blank hole in her life? How can they just take away her memories?" Sonlo asked.

"They implant false ones," Imari said. "Weren't you listening earlier?"

"False Water Planet memories," Pittick added.

"No," Agapanthus said. "I thought I would go back as a hero? And tell everyone about Deeyae? I don't get it. The Contact told me, learn more about the Water Planet since I'd have to go back someday. Why would that matter if—?"

"They are all disgusting liars. All of them," Sonlo said. "This is injustice. You swam the rite of passage, little fish. You should be an adult now."

"This isn't fair!" Leera said, loudly, shakily. She began to cry. "I knew you shouldn't have swam across. How could you do that without telling us?"

"It doesn't matter now. She didn't know this would happen," Pittick said, wrapping his arm around Leera.

"It's not because of the swim. I asked the Contact!"

"The one who already lied to you about the memory wiping?" Sonlo said.

"You have to remember us somehow. You have to remember us!" Imari swept into the woman's wing. Leera followed her.

Agapanthus sat on the floor with her legs crossed. Her hair was still slightly damp at the tips. She looked up. Pittick's yellow eyes wouldn't leave her.

"I need to see Aster before I leave," Agapanthus said.

"The exchanger boy? Who swam the channel?"

"I met with him every day at the Waters. For years. Years and years."

"Oh," Pittick said. "I never knew."

"I didn't want you to know."

"He taught you to swim across?"

Agapanthus nodded. "I always watched for you. I always made sure you wouldn't see us."

And then Imari and Leera came back in, clutching handfuls of Agapanthus's rock collection.

"You went into the children's hall?" Agapanthus stood. "How?"

"The door's open to everyone now," Imari said. "You're not a child anymore."

"Take some with you," Leera said. She held out a palmful of tiny, golden pebbles. "Maybe they'll help you remember."

"They'll never let her take those," Pittick said.

"It's worth a try." Imari held up a smooth, black stone that Agapanthus remembered finding deep in the Waters when she was little, one of the first times she'd swam all the way to the bottom, past the drop-off. She'd kept the rock so she could remember that she'd made it to the floor.

"Take the Carap shell," Sonlo said. "The one Pittick gave you when you were young."

"You remember that?" Agapanthus looked at Sonlo. He nodded slowly with his stocky neck.

"Yes, take the Carap shell," Leera said. "It's lighter. Maybe they won't notice it." She turned to Pittick. "Didn't they say there was any way around it? Didn't they tell you what to do?"

"No, they just warned me, that's all."

"Worthless," Sonlo said breathily.

"The Carap shell is bulky. I'll never be able to hide it." Agapanthus rubbed her hands together. "I—I need to find Aster. How long do I have?"

"Until the end of the day," Pittick said.

"Go find him." Leera nodded. Her eyes were half-shut and still profusely wet. The tears dripped down her nose.

"He should be here. He should've been waiting," Agapanthus said absently. She felt like the world was muffled. Every sound was turned into a high-pitched, metallic echo, and every color had blushed to a matte burgundy. Out in the woman's wing, alone, she said, aloud, "He should've been waiting. He should've been at the shore." Her voice sounded like it had been stretched through a long tube.

Everything was moving so fast, and yet, she couldn't make herself run. Still shoeless, she reverted to the stride of her childhood. One foot, and then the other, almost leaping. Aamsh and Jord were past Imn's face already. The day was almost half over.

She passed two people without even looking up to see who they were. Her gaze remained on her gait, and the dirt path. Every so often she shook her head. It was impossible. All her life she'd known this was coming, but she'd never quite believed it would actually happen. It was something that was supposed to happen to another version of herself; an older version that had moved past all troubles and doubts, a version that was complete, and kind, and selfless.

That was what growing up was supposed to be. She was supposed to be someone else when she grew up. Someone better. All the irritating parts of her adolescent-self were supposed to have been smothered away, leaving only the deep, strong, self; the part that belonged. But, as a true adult, Agapanthus felt the same as she had the day Pittick gave her that Carap shell. And that's how all adults probably felt. No one swam the rite of passage and was suddenly new. Maybe no one was really an adult at all. Everyone just felt the same inside for the whole stretch of their lives. And, maybe, all their lives, everyone was just trying not to be scared, and trying to convince themselves—prove to themselves—that they weren't children anymore.

Agapanthus yelled at Aster's door. She yelled his name, over and over. It hurt her throat, and her voice cracked, but she tilted her head back and bellowed at the stone house. She felt, for a moment, like his house was a person, like all the houses were people, and she would miss them. She would miss everything about Deeyae.

"Aster!" She tried one more time. Nothing. She lunged back to the path. Maybe he was at the shore by now. Someone's shoes passed by her, but she kept her head down. They stopped. She felt eyes on her back.

"You made it, then. You made it! Agapanthus, I was just at your house." It was Oenanthe. His skin looked especially pale. "I was looking for you, to see if you were back."

"Where's Aster?" Agapanthus threw her hands on his shoulders. Suddenly she felt like she might cry.

"He's out there," Oenanthe pointed to the Waters. "He stole a fishing boat. He was going to find you."

"During the rite of passage? We both would've been—they would've killed us."

"He heard that you're leaving. And you were taking so long, he thought you might be in trouble. He wanted to run away with you. He said he wanted to escape."

She clasped her fingers over one eye. "Why would he do that? That would never have worked. And now he's not here. How is he supposed to get back in time?"

"Maybe—he might. Or you could steal another boat. You could follow him and you two could run away."

"I don't want to die, Oenanthe. If we run away, we're going to get caught, and we're going to die." She said this even though she felt like she was already dying. The words felt false coming from her mouth, but tiredness was seeping back into her limbs, and she knew she didn't have the energy to paddle, or to search for Aster's boat. "Don't you remember Lapars and his son? I was there, for that. I saw it happen. I don't want that to be me. Or Aster." Without thinking, she hugged Oenanthe. His body was much softer than Aster's. "If he comes back, tell him I said goodbye."

"Is that it?" Oenanthe said into her shoulder. "Goodbye?"

"And I want him to have my rock collection." How could she tell the Contact that she loved Aster, but she couldn't tell Oenanthe? It was just—for some reason she couldn't let herself. Oenanthe, with his sunken cheeks, and his deep-set eyes, was just too open, and too kind, and she didn't want to talk to him anymore, because she didn't want to leave him, she couldn't leave, she couldn't leave Aster. Her throat felt like it was filled with leather.

"We'll all miss you, Agapanthus. Maybe we might see you again on the Water Planet."

Agapanthus tried to smile, but her lips were tight with sorrow and it ended up being more of a grimace. She didn't say anything. She made her way home. For the rest of the day she sat with her family on the floor of the meeting hall. In near silence they huddled close together—Leera, Pittick, and Agapanthus, knee to knee along one wall, and Sonlo and Imari across from them along the other. Leera ran her fingers through Agapanthus's hair. Every so often, she said, "I can't believe it. I can't. It went by so fast." Imari wept openly, the tears slinking down past her chin, onto the floor, and, occasionally, dripping down her neck; her skin was radiant with sleek water stains. Sonlo stared at an empty corner of the room. Pittick held Agapanthus's hand in both of his. There was something tentative in his grip, like he wasn't sure this was what he was supposed to be doing, but he still didn't want to let go.

And then the Contact's voice came over the speaker. "Agapanthus Caracynth. Please report."

Sonlo, Imari, Pittick, and Leera walked her to the building. She hugged them each one at a time, and, as she did, she realized she hadn't bathed in several days, and she was still wearing the ugly Shreyan dress. Was this how she would present herself to her birth planet? There was a small, very small, part of herself that curled with dark excitement—she was finally finding out where she'd come from. It horrified her that she felt this way, but she knew it wouldn't last. By the time she arrived on the Water Planet, she would have forgotten she ever lived on Deeyae. That, too, was horrifying.

She left her family and huffed down the breezeway, into the science labs. Where she had gone for check-ups her whole life. This was, presumably, where she arrived as a child, and, of course, it was where she would leave. Feol Vatker was standing behind the door.

"Agapanthus Caracynth," he said. His orange eyes hung heavily on his face. He slung his hand up to Agapanthus's forehead.

"Congratulations. You've provided enough help to us and the Gods. We have all the data we need, so it's finally time to go home." He said this so stiffly that Agapanthus knew it must be memorized. "We'll miss you, around here, Agapanthus," he added. "Can't say I'm glad to see you go." And then he motioned for her to follow him into the next room.

The Contact was there. He looked stiff and unreal against the familiar, sparse, brightly-lit room. He didn't greet her. "Don't worry, we'll make sure you have a safe journey today," he said.

Agapanthus had a sudden vision of herself pummeling alone through space. Broken in half. Eyes open but unseeing. "How am I getting back?" As she spoke, Agapanthus realized she hadn't said goodbye to Geleria, or Loao, or Erabet, or the other exchangers. She hadn't sat in the children's hall one last time. She hadn't kneeled at the Waters and given her thanks.

"It's extra-solar-system. So, portation, of course," the Contact said. He leaned close to her and spoke with his chin turned up, close to her nose. She worried his breath would smell, but it was odorless. "You'll live under a new sun. I think you'll like it there—I think you'll be happier there than you ever could have been here on Deeyae. And I hope you will look up at their stars, and find Imn among them, and I hope you will gaze upon us in wonder."

Agapanthus left her face as neutral as she could. Her body felt numb and shaky. She bit her lip. Tears filled her eyes. She stared through them at the Contact. This was the last she would see of his handsomeness; his hunched shoulders. She reached down and gently, so gently, let her fingers run across the red, taut skin of his cheek.

And Aster? Could Aster sense that, at this moment, she was leaving? Did Aster love her? He must, if he was willing to run away with her. If he was willing to die for her. All she wanted was to see him. She should have taken a boat.

"I shouldn't be leaving," she said, desperately. "I'm not like the other exchangers. I swam the channel."

The Contact stared at her motionlessly until she drew back her hand. She was sure that no one had ever touched his face like that; it was forbidden, after all. "Agapanthus," was all he said, mumbilingly, the word unfolding from his lips. Then he glanced at the scientist, who was breathing heavily. Then there was a flash of light. Then a coldness in her abdomen. Agapanthus's head felt like it had been shot through with freezing water. Blackness veiled her sight.

*   *   *   *

Grass. Dry, yellow grass. Her elbows itched with it, where it had left red imprints on her skin. She turned over onto her back. Everything felt sticky and cold, even her lips, even her chin. She wanted to take a warm shower. But where was she? There was some old one-story house with a rusty yellow bicycle by the back steps. Farther in front of it, she could hear the freeway. Behind her, wind through a cluster of trees. The sun beat through an overcast sky, but it provided no warmth.

She was annoyed, irritated, but she didn't know why. In an obscure, unreachable part of her mind she knew why she was there, but she couldn't bring forth that information. Instead, she focused on the goosebumps on her bare arms. She was wearing a draping, extra-large blue t-shirt—now saturated in random spots, thanks to the wet grass—and faded jeans that cut into her hips along the sides. Her shoes were a pair of off-white Keds sneakers that, surprisingly, fit pretty well.

A heavier cloud blotted out the weak sun. She knew she should stand up, knock on the door, and ask for help, but she couldn't bring herself to move. Not yet. The wetness of the earth seeped up through the bottom of her jeans. Her fingers plied through the grass, and down to the mud beneath it. All of this annoyed her. It made her angry. There was something—something right there, in her mind, *right there*, but she couldn't remember what it was. And it was so important. So, so important.

The back door squeaked. "Hello?" A teenage boy stuck his head outside. His eyes were very dark brown, but his hair was pale, blonde. She wondered if he had dyed it. He waited a moment, eyes wide, lips drawn in. "Are you—lost?"

"Can you help me?" she asked automatically. "It's so cold. I really need help."

A man pushed his way forward, opening the door further. "Max, who you talking to? Who's that woman out there?" He had a large stomach, glasses, and a mustache.

"Can you help me, please?" she asked the man.

"With what?"

"Can I come inside? Please, it's so cold."

"It's sixty-two degrees outside. You homeless?"

A woman's face emerged from the doorframe. The other two stepped outside to let her pass by. The woman scooped her blonde hair over her shoulder, and a lock of it caught in the button of her shirt. She fumbled with it for a moment, then left it there. "What's going on?" she asked. The woman's voice was spring. It was light green, early afternoon rain, the smell of a stream at dusk.

Then—she remembered. "I think—you're my mother," she said. She forced herself to stand. It made her forehead pound. "I think I've found you."

The woman walked down one step. Even though she was thin, the wooden step creaked. She stuck out her foot to take the next one, but stopped herself. The woman stared. Her eyes were lined with wrinkles. She brought her hand to her mouth.

Wearing only socks, the woman strode through the grass. She cupped Aria's chin in her cold fingertips, and she cried.

She thought back to the first night she'd spent on this cot. Her mother and Derek had set it up in the living room, originally. It was louder out there—everything buzzing, the house full of electricity, the refrigerator murmuring—but Aria had fallen asleep easily with the relief of being warm. In the middle of the night she woke up. Her heart was echoing in her ears, burning in her chest. She remembered. Suddenly, just like that, she remembered everything about Deeyae. Everything about the Contact, and Aster, and her family. Sweat clustered onto her skin. She walked around the room along the strange beige carpet. But how did she know it was carpet? She just knew. And she knew that she was thinking in English, not Deeyan. And then she realized there was another memory there, a very fuzzy image from her three-year-old mind. She had been picked up by a woman with dyed-red hair, who led her to a car that was pulled over on the side of the freeway. Her next memories were from when she was older, four or five. She remembered driving to hotels around the city. In the car, the man smiled at her in the rear-view mirror, his teeth yellow along the edges. Once he had turned around—while driving—and given her a small teddy-bear toy, the size of Aria's palm. She played with it while they did "grown-up things" at the hotel, which she later learned were drugs. No, this wasn't right. These memories were flat. They must have been implanted back on Deeyae. She couldn't feel them. She couldn't—no, she hadn't been carted around by druggies who wanted to make themselves look like a nice, innocent family. No. But the memory was there. And it was startling how clear certain things were. The smell of that car. Like Velcro. Like vacuumed carpet. And the ticking noise it made when the turn signal was on. She used to click her tongue along with it, and Meredith would shush her because she was usually on her cell phone. And Aria remembered sitting on the floor of so many bathrooms, yellow and green linoleum tiles against her bare thighs.

They'd told her that she was an orphan and they took her in. She should be grateful to them. And when they checked into new hotels, the front-desk-person sometimes gave her a free cookie. Or, at the very least, they usually smiled at her, or asked how old she was. That lasted until she had her growth-spurt, and ended up taller than Meredith. Then she wasn't cute anymore. Then she stopped being so valuable. Her name was Paula. That's what they called her. What an ugly name. Paula. It reminded her of the water damaged paper of Max's book.

She ran away when she was seventeen. Right after Richard tried to kiss her. He was like her father, until then. And his breath had smelled like beer and something else, some drug smell that always clung to him like rot, like mold. She imagined his insides coated in a horrible slime whose fumes seeped out through his ears, his nose, his mouth. She'd been trying to take a nap. Meredith was in the shower. The rush of the water drowned out the TV, the volume turned low. There were empty food wrappers on the floor from Burger King. All Paula/Aria/Agapanthus wanted to do was sleep. Then he was there on his hands and knees, on the bed— and she was lucky to have a bed that time; sometimes she had to sleep on the floor covered in towels. Richard stuck out his lips, like two worms beneath his mustache, and said, "Come here," and he tugged her closer to him, gripping the back of her head. She wriggled away from him, across the room, and she wrapped her arms around her middle, and she stared at him with hard, hurt eyes. Then the shower water turned off. That night, Aria left them. For years she walked along highways. She washed her face in public bathrooms, splashing lukewarm water on her underarms to try to clean herself up a bit. She sat on picnic tables in parks and blew the wisps off dandelions as they aged. If she went to the police or anything, she would be put in a foster-home for a year. How pointless. She would rather be homeless. So she'd wandered. She had found fresh, perfect food in dumpsters behind grocery stores.

She had been alone. Then, sitting beneath an oak tree, a very distant memory had come to her—of her mother. Her mother and trees. A house by the freeway. Maybe Meredith and Richard had lied to her. Maybe she wasn't an orphan. And she began searching.

No. None of this was true. These must be false memories implanted by the scientist. All of these conflicting memories had come to her, that first night, and she had been so confused. She'd turned on the big overhead light and kneeled on the dusty wood floor in the kitchen. Through the half-slanted blinds she could see outside. It was dark. There were a few stars. This was, all at once, a normal thing that she had seen nearly every night of her life, and a rare dream that reminded her of the frozen southlands. Her mother and Derek led her back to her cot. "Here you go, now," her mother said in a high-pitched voice. "Here you go. Just watch some TV until you fall asleep. You're here now. It's alright." She rubbed Aria's back and they left her perched on the edge of the cot, gripping the remote, illuminated by the flickering light of an infomercial.

"Are you even sure she's your daughter?" Derek asked her mother in their bedroom down the hall, so loudly that Aria could hear it over the TV. "How do you know she's not some homeless freeloader who read your story in the newspaper? She could have something wrong with her, Joyce." And she couldn't hear her mother's answer, but she guessed it had something to do with a motherly sense of knowing, or how Aria looked like she had when she was a teenager, even though Aria, of course, was no longer a teen.

The next day, Aria's mother had brought out the age progression photos from missing posters that were printed in the newspaper, and on missing children websites, and in free coupon magazines that came in the mail. They were supposed to estimate what Aria would look like when she was fifteen. She looked only slightly older now, in real life—higher in the cheekbones, and maybe a little thinner. But the resemblance was obvious.

Aria's mother called her father, who had moved to Florida three years ago. He said he would fly over as soon as he could get off work at the restaurant where he bartended. Two days later, he arrived. Derek and Max picked him up at the airport while Aria and her mother stayed home. They sat at the kitchen table together, eating grilled cheese sandwiches. Aria didn't like the way the cheese stuck to her teeth. It made her feel like they were coated in something. It was grotesque, to think that this came from the fluids of an Earth animal. And, yet, she also remembered sitting at a ripped diner-booth with Meredith and Richard, and ordering a miniature grilled cheese off the kid's menu. And then she'd asked if she could play on the indoor play-structure, and Richard had said no. She was beginning to wonder which set of memories were real.

"I'd been writing a lot, lately, before you got here," Aria's mother said with her mouth full. "About your disappearance. I had five chapters done. I was hoping someone would see it, you know? I was hoping it would help me find you. But I don't need it, anymore." She rested the sandwich back down on her plate and half-smiled, half-chewed, with her eyes so squinted they looked closed. "And I'm so glad. Do you like to read, hon?" She finally swallowed her bite. "You didn't go to school. They taught you, didn't they? You do know how to read?"

"Of course I know how to read."

"Sorry. It's just that I want to know all about you. Everything. Like, your name. What should I call you? Would you prefer Paula? Or is Aria okay?"

"Agapanthus."

"Agapanthus?"

"Or Aga. Call me Aga."

Her mother smiled. She had nice teeth; especially wide, and strong-looking. They reminded Aria of wood. "Is there a story behind that?"

"Never mind. Aria's fine. Anything but Paula." She tore at the crust of her sandwich. "What should I call you? Mother? Mom?"

"Call me whatever you like."

"I'll call you Mother, then."

Mother nodded twice, folded her hands under her chin, and glanced at her empty plate. "I want you to know I'm here for you. Whatever it takes, I want to make everything okay. I took the whole week off work so I can be here."

"Where do you work?"

"Oh—there's an animal shelter in town. I work there part-time."

Animals as pets. That could never happen on Deeyae. A red-breasted-sper in the house? How would you feed it, without a hydrothermal vent around? Exchangers were the closest Deeyans came to owning pets.

Aria was about to say something, but in walked her father. His hair was dark, ear-length, slightly frizzy at the tips. He had a tidy mustache and goatee, and a huge, very straight, very narrow nose. The smell of rain wafted in behind him. Max and Derek slipped off their coats and tossed them over the back of the lounge chair. Her father wound across the table and kneeled in front of Aria's chair. He grabbed her hands. His skin was browner than hers. She worried her fingers were sticky with cheese.

"My daughter's here," he said softly. "My sweet daughter's back. My girl."

Aria slumped forward and hugged him while he still knelt. His neck was warm. He smelled like licorice; something spicy-sweet.

"You've lost weight, Greg," Mother said. Her voice sounded hollow.

"So have you. You look good, Joycey," Aria's father said. His voice was somehow bouncy. A bit scraggly. He smiled at Aria. The creases on his forehead sprung up as his eyebrows rose. "And you. You look like a grown woman. My god."

"I'm twenty-two."

"I know, Aria. I've been counting. I bought you a card every year on your birthday. Here, I brought them, you know." He dug through his black backpack—the only luggage he'd brought—and pulled out a Ziploc bag. "Started since you were four."

Aria opened each one. Cards shaped like teddy bears holding balloons. Plain, white cards with glittery butterflies journeying across the front. *Happy 12th Birthday, my little Aria. Happy 17th, Happy 5th, Happy 9th.* She had never gotten a birthday card before. Not in either set of memories.

"Thank you so much, Father," she said.

"Father?" He scrunched up his enormous nose and looked at Mother. Her eyes widened at him. "It's so good to hear that," he said. He swallowed loudly. "I always thought I'd be Dad, but Father—I'll take it."

Derek poured a beer into a freezer-chilled glass with a rose printed on it. "You want any, Greg? Joyce?"

"That's alright, Derek. Thanks," Father said tiredly.

"Sure, hon, I'll take one," Mother said.

"And, Aria? How about you?" Derek asked.

"I don't drink. I never have."

"Dad, I'd like some," Max said from the couch.

"I know you would. But you've still got three years."

"Erick's allowed to drink at home," Max said. "He's been allowed to since he was sixteen. It's a European thing. His mom's German."

"Well we're not in Erick's house, are we?" Derek said. "Or Europe?"

"It's legal here too, if you're at home."

Derek shook his head.

Father finally shifted from the floor to the open chair between Aria and Mother. He rubbed his palms together above the table. "So, Max, how's school been?" he asked over the pop of the second beer being opened.

"I'm done."

"You graduated? Already?" He turned around in the chair so he was sitting backwards.

"No. The ceremony's in two weeks. But we're done with classes."

"Oh, good, good. Well congratulations, Max. You have any college plans lined up?"

"Just community college." Max walked into the kitchen. He stooped down to look through some lower cabinets.

"Well that's a good start. Any idea what you want to study down the line?"

"Maybe botany."

"Oh. Well that's something you don't hear every day. Interesting."

Max nodded. The wooden cabinet thudded shut and he drifted down the hallway to his bedroom, shoulders down, lips frozen in a straight line.

"Did I upset him?" Father whispered to Mother.

"No, no. He's been like that lately. Tired, I think. Quiet. It's that transition time. High school to college. It's hard on everyone."

"I thought college to real life was harder," Father said. He patted Aria's knee. She was still wearing the tight jeans that flared slightly at the ankle. "How about you, kid? How are you holding up?"

She wanted so badly to fling herself into her mother and father's arms and sit quietly with them and finally feel safe and—and at home. Her parents were both kind, both a peculiar mixture of soft-spoken and forceful. She wanted to love them but at the same time she wanted to hide. She wanted them to stop staring at her.

This world was a bright place full of strange colors. She had gone outside for a walk with Mother and Father, later that afternoon. The sky was overcast, again, but a small tear sheared the clouds just across the freeway, and the sun spilled down onto the hills. That blue was so magnificent, so alien and startling, that Aria was suddenly sure that Deeyae was the real reality. It had to be. She had never seen that color before—pale and deep and matte all at once, bending, immutable. Unimaginable.

Yes—before that moment, a blue sky had been unimaginable. The Contact had forgotten to give her a false-memory of it. Under Imn's red light, it would be easy to forget that such a shade of blue existed. The sky's blue wasn't like her jeans, or like the indigo of her oversized shirt. It was incomprehensible. It could not be captured. It could not be faked.

Her parents swayed a few steps behind her, talking quietly. Aria watched two sheep standing across the old metal fence at the edge of their property. They looked scrawny without their wool. Tight, and sinewy. One of them was smaller than the other. Maybe a mother and child? Both sheep kept their soft pink noses to the grass.

"You told the investigators already?" Father asked in a hushed voice.

"No," Mother answered. "I wanted to wait to get more information."

"We have to find them. We're going to find them. I'll do everything I can to make sure that happens."

"I know, I know. I agree. They need to be held accountable."

"Held accountable? They need to pay. They need to pay for what they've done. They need to pay for stealing her childhood. They need to pay me for having my daughter taken away from me. One hundred million dollars wouldn't even come close to enough. Nothing can come close."

"Shh, Greg. She's here. She's back."

Aria turned. Mother was stroking Father's arm. His white collared shirt was rolled up at the sleeves, and Mother's fingers brushed over his arm hair. Aria pretended she hadn't seen them. It seemed like such a private moment. She leaned against the mossy wood framing the fence.

"I just wish we could get those years back," Father whispered.

"We can't. But look how many are still to come." Mother coughed. Her hiking boots squeaked against the wet grass. She rested her hand on Aria's shoulder, and they went inside to start dinner.

Aria sat on the step outside while Mother boiled water for spaghetti. Father took a shower, and Derek and Max watched TV. Aria knew she should be inside with them. She knew she was being forlorn and strange. Half the time she chose a direction and stared until her vision blurred into abstraction. She spoke as little as possible. It was all too painful. Too confusing. The air here was lighter; she actually felt like she could run up those hills—her feet digging into the mud, torn grass sticking to her shoes. She felt like she could run the whole way to the top and look down upon the musty, stinking cars, and the fields clothed white with sheep, and even the blue-green hills curling up against the opposite horizon. She could look down on all of them like one of the Gods.

The sun was so bright. Even from behind its haven of clouds, it felt oppressive. She didn't like it. She missed Imn, and the God stars. Nothing could fix that. Nothing could make that pain go away. And why did she even remember Deeyae? She wasn't supposed to remember.

What she had to do was fall numb. She had to instruct herself to move, to do anything: *Stare at the dead, crunchy leaves molding into the grass. Go inside when Max calls. Sit on the fold-up deck chair Mother has pulled up to the table, even though she insists that you take one of the real dining chairs. Eat dinner, which is not true spaghetti after all, but pasta shaped like conch shells soaked in a soupy white sauce that smells of raw garlic and wine. Tear off the inner fluff of the French bread and arrange it on the side of the plate until the pasta is gone, and then take a bite, and decide it's too much like sourdough, and leave it on the napkin. And then, even after everyone has finished, after Father is handing Mother the oily dishes, and Derek is emptying the clean dishwasher, even after Mother turns and asks you if you've had enough to eat—stare.*

Aria knew that she must stare. Stare at nothing. Stare at numbness. Dissolve.

After a week, her father went back to Florida. On his last day, before Derek and Max drove him to the airport, he stood stiffly in front of Aria and said, "I'm coming back here to live. I'll find a place in Eugene, as soon as I get a job. Close as I can be. Nothing can keep me away, now that my girl's home." And he lifted his hand, as though he might tickle her chin with his fingers, but instead he hugged her. "God, I love you. Always have. Always will." His underarms smelled like peppermint deodorant.

Now five months had passed and he still hadn't come back. He called once a week, before he left for work on Monday evenings at around five Oregon time. "I'm working on it," he said every time. "I've got to get things wrapped up on this end. I'll be out there as soon as I can."

Aria wanted to care, but her mind was too busy. She could finally allow herself to look back at her last day on Deeyae and analyze it fully. The rite of passage, and her family, and not seeing Aster. The realization that she loved him. Admitting it to the Contact, of all people. So much had happened that day. But, as she tried to sleep on the squeaky cot in Max's room, Aria's memories focused on the boat ride from Shre to Yeela. The scientists had been testing new technology on exchangers. That was what the Gods wanted them there for. Why did this bother her? She had always known that exchangers were there to be studied—how they grew, how their bodies adapted to Deeyae, how they differed from Deeyans. Why was experimenting on them any worse? Either way they were there to be used. They were nothing but pets.

Other thoughts came to her, too. Geleria and Loao and Lapars's son and Erabet and Oenanthe—they spun around her in long sheets of memory. Everything was red. Everything spun, and spun, and she worried the memories would become thin if she thought about them too much, like over-chewed gum stretched long and transparent. She wasn't supposed to have these memories. Something must have gone wrong.

"Aria, it's almost two-thirty," came Max's hoarse voice. "In the morning."

"I didn't mean to wake you up."

"Why are you awake?"

"This has happened every night since I got here."

"What, being awake at two-thirty in the morning?"

"Except the first night, I've never fallen asleep before four."

"Why?" Max's twin bed rattled as he sat up and leaned against the headboard. There was just enough freeway-light seeping in between the cracks in the closed blinds that Aria could see Max's nose and lips, how pale and close together they were. His eyes were lost to the darkness.

"I can't sleep. I can't stop thinking about everything."

"You mean—how it was for you? Before?"

No. She thought about why her memories weren't stolen—was it luck or did this only happen to her, or had other exchangers gone through this, or had it only been a rumor that they would wipe her memories, and, if so, why had they implanted new Earth memories?—and she thought about, what if they actually found Meredith and Richard? That would mean they were real, that those memories were real, that she was crazy. And that was why she hadn't told anyone about Deeyae. No one here knew about Deeyae, or the exchange program. It wasn't an exchange program at all; that would imply that there was consent involved. No. She had been stolen. And no one here would believe her. Maybe she didn't even fully believe herself. Sometimes doubt came to her as a tightness in her chest. It was just barely there; just above her stomach. In those moments she felt like her body was burning on the inside, curling inward, fingernails scraping at her intestines.

"Yeah," Aria finally said. She exhaled heavily and wrapped a tangled strand of hair around her finger. "It's hard to forget that stuff."

"You need to try thinking of something else. Everyone keeps focusing on that same old shit—the investigation, the questions, the check-ups at the doctor, the psychologist dude with those stupid glasses pulled up on top of his head, your dad calling all the time. It's like they're doing everything they can to make it so you can't move on."

"That's the thing—what else is there?"

"I don't know. Hobbies. School. People. Life, I guess."

Aria suddenly wanted to cry. She thought back to that time she snuck out of the Portation Center during the sun storm. Back then, she had been fearless. Now she was either an empty, cold, vessel, or she was crying.

"This is a good time to start fresh. You just had your birthday last week. It's going to be winter soon—maybe it'll even snow this year." Max's voice sounded tired.

She wanted to tell him. Sitting there in the dark, with her knees pulled up to her chest, Aria felt safe. She felt like, if she was ever going to tell him, it should be now, and then at least she would have someone to talk to about it.

"Everything can be new for you," Max added.

"Yeah. Everything is new for me. Everything on this planet, everything on Earth," she said. Her voice felt forced and flat. "It's weird, calling it that." She paused. "We used to call it the Water Planet."

And Deeyae surged forth from her words. The Waters, dark fields of liquid beneath the sprawling blush of Imn. The shore, hewn into the burnt-red cliffs of square, crumbling stone. She told him about her life there. About everyone she'd known. About the festivals, and the rite of passage, and her apprenticeship at the Portation Center. She talked until her throat grew dry. Max listened without even grunting or nodding—he gave no indication that he was listening. After a while, Aria assumed he had fallen back asleep, but she kept talking anyway. When she had finished, she listened for his breathing.

But he was awake. "There you go, Aria. Be a writer," Max grumbled. "Write that shit down."

"Like a biography?" Aria's chest burned as she said this.

Max sat up further. He rested his elbows on his knees so his silhouette looked like a little ball. "You don't really believe you're from another planet, do you? Like, really, honestly, do you?"

Aria didn't respond. The moment stretched out into buzzing silence.

"It's four in the morning now," Max said. "Let's just go to sleep."

The next morning Max's white sheets were crumpled in an empty, tangled mess. Aria zipped on a hoodie and crept down the wood-paneled hallway. Rain crackled against the roof. Derek had his arm around Mother on the couch, where they sat with coffee mugs on their laps, watching a DVR recording of The Amazing Race. The toilet flushed down the hall behind Aria—Max must have been in the bathroom.

"Morning, hon," Mother said.

Derek paused the show. He nodded at Aria and said, "Morning."

"Good morning." Aria stepped quickly to the fridge, then the cupboard, looking for breakfast. The TV was playing again but Mother kept glancing at Aria over the back of the couch. Aria finally opened a packet of strawberry pop-tarts. One had broken in half inside the bag, and crumbs spilled out onto the counter. Aria stuck the whole pop-tart into the toaster. Great, now she would have to wait there while it cooked, and pretend she didn't know she was being watched. Pretend that she didn't know that Max must have told Mother about Deeyae.

"There's some new orange juice in the fridge," Mother said. "Aria."

Aria looked at the floor.

"It's the kind with pulp," Mother added.

Yes, Mother definitely knew. The pop-tart shot up. Aria jumped.

"Aria, hon. Don't forget that tomorrow's your appointment with Dr. Wendell."

"I have them every Monday, Mother." She pinched the hot pop-tart from the toaster and dropped it on a plastic plate that had foxes drawn on its edges.

"I know." Aria's mother paused the TV. "I know. I want to make sure you're telling him everything, alright? Max mentioned something you said about—space—"

"He told you about Deeyae?" Aria said softly.

Mother placed her hand around her mouth and turned her head toward the TV again.

"Our insurance doesn't cover psychology, and these sessions aren't cheap," Derek said. "We want you to get the most out of them that you can."

"You need to tell him everything so he can help you," Mother said in that high-pitched tone her voice sometimes slipped into.

Aria couldn't respond. She looked down at her pop-tart. It smelled like sweetness and bread. She took a bite and carried the plate to Max's bedroom. Then she ate it, staring out the window from her place at the edge of the cot. She watched the rain slow. She watched the colors burn forth from morning to early afternoon.

"Come on," Max said from behind her. His hair smelled like shower—soap and peppery boy shampoo. "Come with me. Fresh air, you know? Exercise. And you'll really like the bright colors right now. The vine maples are awesome." He waited a moment. "It's not like I'm going very far. It's like, what, a minute walk? Don't tell me you're that lazy."

"You told Mother."

"Yeah, I told her. Was I not supposed to?"

"I'm not stupid. I know how it sounds. And I don't want everyone to think I'm crazy." She pushed her hands into the pockets of her sweatshirt. "I told you because you actually listen to me. And I thought you might actually understand."

"I never said I didn't believe you. Just because I told Mom what you said—that doesn't mean anything. Hey, I'm completely open to letting you convince me that your story's true." He licked his upper lip, which was usually chapped because he refused to wear lip balm. He almost licked his nose, it was so closely situated above his mouth. "Come on, let's go before it rains again."

Aria put on the new jeans Mother bought her, a soft long-sleeve shirt, and her thick down jacket. She stuffed a collapsible umbrella in her pocket.

"Really, an umbrella?" Max said when they were outside. His forehead looked heavy under the overcast light.

"It's freezing. I don't want to get wet."

"It's not that cold."

"But you have to remember that my home planet was warm. The only cold place was deep inside people's houses, because the stone cooled the inside." She felt wild, saying these things. She felt like she was telling forbidden secrets.

"So you had a dark red sun. And two smaller suns?"

"Stars. The God stars. Their names were Aamsh and Jord. That was where the Gods lived. And everyone—well, the Deeyans—would hold their hands up in reverence." Her jacket crinkled as she lifted her arm to the sky just as Leera had done so many times. It felt wrong to be doing it to this heavy, white sky.

"That looks like the hail Hitler thing," Max said, laughing. "What the fuck."

"What thing?"

"The thing where all the Nazis lift up their arms and salute Hitler. Like in those old videos. Didn't you ever—?" He paused. "You never went to school."

"We didn't have school," Aria said. "We didn't even have reading, or books. Just audiobooks."

"Audiobooks?" Max looked at his bulky, worn tennis shoes, and so did Aria.

They waded through the overgrown grass. Crows bellowed from across the field. Their sound reminded Aria of metal; of coins being scraped together.

"I really like the sound they make," Aria said.

"Crows? I think you're the first person to say that. Ever." Max scrunched up his nose and eyes, his whole face squinting. "Did you know they're as smart as some humans? Smarter, even, if you think about all the really dumb people out there?"

"What do they eat?"

"Crows? I guess if they're not picking McDonald's off the street, they eat worms and stuff."

"Worms. It's hard to remember what eats what. I think it's strange that so many animals eat plants here."

"Well I think it's strange that your world is so similar to Earth. Think of all the animals on Earth, how different everything looks, all that diversity. And that's just on Earth. One planet. How is it possible that there's a planet in another galaxy—"

"Solar system."

"—a planet in another solar system that has aliens on it that look basically just like humans? And you have audiobooks and houses and clothes and hail Hitler arm movements basically just like ours?"

"Because we came from here. I told you, Deeyans came from Earth before the Gods brought them to Deeyae. Of course there would be similarities."

"And now the Deeyans go around abducting all these random people, like, little toddlers and babies, and, so—so, okay, okay, here's the part I don't get. You spend your whole life on Deeyae thinking that everyone on Earth knows what's going on. Then you get sent back and you find out no one knew a thing about it, and they think you've lost your mind. So no one believes you. Why, then, do the Deeyans even bother erasing people's memories? Erasing people's memories. See, that sounds like a sci fi movie. I don't get how that's real."

Aria rubbed her eyes. "I mean, that could have been a rumor. I'm not sure about the memory erasing. Maybe they just give us new memories to help us adjust better, and we still keep the old ones, too. Or maybe something went wrong with me, and, really, we're supposed to adjust by forgetting everything about Deeyae."

"So do you think they jack up people's memories because they're being nice, or because they don't want humans catching on? Like, if everyone who was abducted started telling this exact same, super detailed story, people might actually believe it, right?"

"I thought it was—I don't know. It's probably whatever the Gods told them to do."

"And the Gods are basically just another species of aliens spying on everyone? Can they see us right now?"

"I don't know. I think they can see everything. Everywhere in the universe."

"And that Contact guy? You think he can see us?"

"Maybe. I think he visits Earth sometimes."

"Are we being watched?"

"I don't know."

"And why do you even want to go back? After they used you like that?"

"I never said I wanted to go back," Aria said fiercely. "I know I can't."

"So why do you keep worrying about it?"

"Because that's the problem! I can't go back!"

"This is about that swimmer dude, isn't it. What was his name? Asteroid?"

"Aster."

"Aster? *Aster subspicatus*, Douglas's aster. He's named after a fucking Earth plant."

Aria opened her mouth to speak, but Max continued.

"And, wait, what did you say your name was, there?"

"Agapanthus."

"Aga—?"

"Agapanthus."

"Lily of the Nile? Lily of the Nile. Praecox? Agapanthus praecox."

He looked up like he was trying to find the answer within the naked limbs of the cottonwood trees. "Yeah, Lily of the Nile. Tall stem. Purple flowers. Wait, were you all named after plants, then? Earth plants?"

"I don't know. Just stop. Stop, please. I don't want to talk about this right now."

"You have to realize how ridiculous all of this sounds," Max said breathily. "You can't expect me to believe it?"

"Please shut up."

"Okay, fine. I don't care. I was just trying to help make sense of things."

"You make everything sound small. It wasn't small. It wasn't ridiculous."

With each step their heels sunk deeper into the mud. The sky was cut through with branches. A cold wind wrapped around the tree trunks and found its way onto Aria's neck. She zipped her jacket up further.

"Now it's cold," she said.

Tree noises. Empty wind noises. Max didn't respond. Another gust came. The cottonwoods tossed in circles, shedding the last of their wilted, yellowed leaves, which curled slowly to the earth. The stream swept forth, chokingly full of silver and brown pebble-water. Aria stared at it as she followed Max. It was such a small strip of water. Sometimes it had trash in it; granola bar wrappers, plastic water bottles, random pieces of busted tires, all washed in from the stream's journey through the silver pipe underneath the freeway. Now that the rain fell almost daily, and the stream was heavy, the water was brushed clean from the inside. Yes, there was mud, and there was murkiness. But it was clean. And she was glad.

The vine maples popped out from the naked bushes around them. Their leaves were an intense, saturated red. Max didn't say anything. He plucked off a leaf and ran his hands along the stem so it twirled.

"Are you mad at me now?" Aria asked.

"No. You just didn't want me to talk to you."

"That's not what I meant, Max. You know that's not what I meant." Then, smiling, she said, "You were right. The trees are beautiful." She thought her voice sounded forced as she said it, even though she was telling the truth. They were beautiful trees. She was glad to have seen them, especially on this dark day when their colors seemed even brighter.

"Yeah," Max said. "Beautiful."

They made their way through the mud, back onto the grass. The wind poured over Aria's face. Her hair swirled forward onto her forehead. A strand stuck to her nostril, and she brushed it away. The air smelled like ice. It smelled like something sad, something lonely.

"You know I only brought you out here to cheer you up," Max said.

"I know," she said. "And it worked. Thank you, Max." Once again her words sounded stiff, even though they were true.

"Say something in your alien language, quick," Max said.

"The Gods came to the Water Planet and forever changed the course of history," Aria said in Deeyan, mimicking one of her audiobooks. "The Water Planet was the first home of the Deeyans. There, they ate plants, and they climbed trees. They lived off the sun, not the hydrothermal vents."

"Holy shit, that sounds fucking demonic. You didn't make that up?"

"How could I make that up?"

"I don't know. People make up languages. Like in *Avatar*. They made up the language for that. And *The Lord of the Rings*." He wrapped his arms around his midsection. "Ugh. What the fuck, Aria. I didn't like that. Chills, all down my arms."

"Are you sure that's not just because it's *freezing?*"

"You didn't make it up, then? You really didn't make it up? Say something else."

She said something about the Water Portation Center.

"It's not just gibberish?"

"I swear it's not."

"It sounds like a real language."

"That's because it is!"

"Okay. I'm not saying I believe you," Max said as he slid open the back door. "But I'm not saying I don't believe you either."

"Thank you, Max," she said, and for once her voice sounded sincere. "That actually means a lot."

Aria's mother watched her closely for the rest of the day. She asked Aria to watch TV with her, and they sat together on the couch for hours. Then she made Aria an omelet with green onions for dinner. Aria ate alone at the kitchen table. Max was doing homework, and Derek had gone to the store. It was only five o'clock. "You need to go to bed early tonight," Mother said. "We have to wake up early and drive down to Eugene tomorrow morning."

It was a forty-five minute drive. The fields turned into buildings and bridges, all cloaked in a veil of gray concrete. Mother kept the air conditioning on even though Aria had her down jacket zipped up to her chin. The car's vent brought in outside air. Aria hated that smell, the smell of the city—distantly like manure, or like bark mulch. It reminded her of her of walking along the pathways in the park at sunset, when the wind was blowing in off the river; back when she slept under leaf-stuffed garbage bags on the banks of the water. That was one of her first nights after leaving Meredith and Richard. But—no. It wasn't. That was a false memory.

The turn-signal clicked. Tick-tick-tick. Aria wished that Mother would turn the radio on. The oldies station, maybe. But Mother never put music on when they drove into the city early in the morning. Maybe she wanted to give Aria the option of sleeping in the car. Maybe it was because of the sunrise outlining the hills over Mother's left shoulder. Maybe sunrises deserved silence.

Dr. Wendell's waiting room had a globe on display next to the plastic chairs. It was painted a metallic gold. "It's the golden globe," Mother had said the first time they saw it. Today, Mother leaned against the counter to talk to the thick-armed receptionist. Aria struck the globe with the very tips of her fingers so it would spin. The continents were outlined with thin black lines, but they weren't filled in. It was a gold ocean with gold land and probably gold people, too. Gold like the sunrise. The stand, even, was gold, but a different shade of it that seemed more like the cheap yellow of a cereal box.

"There she is!" Dr. Wendell said from the doorway. "Welcome in. It's good to see you, Aria."

She glanced at Mother before following Dr. Wendell into his office. The room smelled heavy and warm—like oatmeal. Dr. Wendell pushed his round-framed reading glasses on top of his head, just above his hairline. His blue eyes looked murky without lenses over them.

"Feel free to take your coat off," Dr. Wendell said slowly, choppily—as always—in that soft tone of voice that was kind of like wind blowing through a roadside of litter. Plastic bags waving.

"I'm cold," Aria said.

Dr. Wendell laughed. Aria thought of crumpled soda cans. "Alright, then. However you're comfortable." He stared at her for a moment. She stared back, focusing in on the wiry hair just above his ears. "Well, Aria. How are we today?"

"I'm sure Mother told you."

"Told me what?"

"About Deeyae."

"Your mother told me about your belief in another planet. She says you believe you were born there."

"Not born there. Raised there. I was born here. That's why Mother's my mother."

"Oh," Dr. Wendell said. "So you believe you were raised on an alien planet?"

She told him everything, just as she had told Max. Dr. Wendell leaned forward in his high-backed leather chair. He rested his scrawny palms on the desk, where they pressed into a pile of papers, a manila folder, and a Sharpie. When he moved his hands back to his lap, an imprint remained on the paper, vague and crumpled but not sweaty. Aria stared at it as she spoke.

"So, essentially, you are faced with two realities, and you're struggling to decide which one is real."

"I know which one is real."

"And by that you mean—"

"Deeyae."

"And why do you believe that's the ultimate reality?"

"The memories are stronger. I can feel everything, smell everything, see it so clearly. It's like I'm still there. And the other memories, they just feel like I'm watching a screen or something. They surprise me. I can't anticipate what's going to happen next—"

"Aria, you must admit that it's much more likely that you grew up here on Earth." He took a breath. He waited for her response. When she gave none, he continued. "Sometimes when we want to escape the harshness of a true reality, our brain tricks us into thinking that things happened differently. This is what we call a defense mechanism. Your brain is trying to protect itself from the pain. And it may feel real to you, but my best guess is that those alien memories are just your brain's way of helping you make sense of a traumatic experience."

"So you think I'm imagining it?"

"I never said that. And I never said I didn't believe you. I'm just telling you what is most likely. Only you can decide what you think happened." He grabbed a smooth, purple stone from a pile of colored rocks on his desk, and he rolled it around in his hand.

"What is that?" Aria asked.

"Amethyst." He handed it to her.

It felt almost like plastic. "Is it real?"

"It sure is real. And I have a few others, too." He picked up a light blue one with a white streak through it. "Mostly birth stones. I have some crystals, too. Petrified wood. And a thunderegg, of course."

"Do you collect rocks?" Aria asked.

"Mmhmm." He nodded in a way that reminded Aria of a chicken.

"Oh," she said. "Me too."

The session lasted forty-five minutes. In the waiting room, Mother had *Better Homes and Gardens* spread on her lap. "All done?" she said in that high voice. "Thanks Dr. Wendell." She waved.

He held up his hand. "Have a good one."

Mother switched the radio on in the car and then turned the volume low. "So how did it go?" she asked, whipping her hair over her shoulder as she backed out of the parking spot.

Aria didn't know what to say. She didn't know how it had gone. "Did you—talk about things?"

"That's the whole point of it, Mother," she said, forcing a smile so Mother would know she was joking. "That's what we do. We talk about things."

Mother nodded and said nothing. She glanced out the window, then back at the road. Aria looked out her own window. The glass was dusty and streaked with old raindrops. Aria looked past it; she focused on the skinny, leafless trees planted along the sidewalks; at a girl with close-cropped hair and a loose white blouse buttoned all the way to the neck like some frilly old-fashioned thing, walking in the bike lane with her brightly patterned bag swinging against her hip.

When they were past the buildings and out into the expanses of grass and hills, Aria's mother turned the radio low again. "I just wanted to let you know—" she paused. The turn-signal ticked as she changed lanes. "I wanted to make sure you—that I told you—I needed to—tell you that I'm sorry. So inexpressibly sorry. I'm sorry I wasn't there to protect you. My little girl." Mother inhaled sharply and licked her lips, which reminded Aria of leaves, for some reason. Her tone deepened and her words became choppy, straight-forward, like she was listing things off. "I should have been there. I should have kept my eye on you every second. I should have been watching you. I should have had the door locked. I should have heard you open the door." Her eyes were wet. "We live next to a freeway. I should have been more careful."

"It's not your fault," Aria said. Once again it was that tone of voice that sounded fake even when she was being sincere. Aria didn't understand why she sometimes said things that way—maybe it was because she was uncomfortable saying whatever it was she was saying. She wondered if others picked up on the fakeness of it; maybe she was the only one who noticed the minute curves of her lips after the words fled, and how every twitch of her muscles seemed to reveal an insincerity that she was incapable of acknowledging; an insincerity she didn't understand.

"It's not your fault," she said again, trying to add a pleasant roundness to her tone. Like the way Leera spoke, and Imari. "It's their fault."

"Whose fault?" Mother asked, gruffly, through tears.

"The Gods."

7

AGE: TWENTY-FIVE EARTH-YEARS

ria pressed upload. This one was about the day she swam to Shre. It was the first blog post she'd added in two weeks. It had taken so long to write; a few words in the mornings before class, or after dinner when she didn't have a lot of reading to do.

The royal-blue, star-littered background of her website loaded first, then the banner—**The Girl From Another Planet,** written in stiff, timeless font—and the **New Blog Post!** notice underneath the menu. Aria scrolled down past her old entries; all stories of her childhood, written in first person like a diary. She had a Facebook page, too, and a Twitter account where she announced new posts.

Max had told her that nothing was ever truly erased from the internet. That was part of why she was doing this—to preserve her memories. But she also wanted as many people as possible to read her story. Or, really, she wanted someone else from Deeyae to see it. Someone who remembered.

For now she only had one-hundred Twitter followers and twenty Facebook fans. Her ultimate plan was to polish her blog posts into articles and send them to *Nexus Magazine, Paranormal Magazine, UFO Magazine,* even *The National Enquirer*—anyone who would publish them.

Maybe it would become a book someday, she thought. It would be published as "fiction", but, if an ex-exchanger read it, they would know it was really true; it would match their own story, and they would recognize Deeyae in it.

Of all the people who had ever been sent back from Deeyae, she couldn't be the only one who remembered. Whether it was a mistake or a superpower or just luck—she couldn't be the only one. And that was why she wrote.

"How's it coming?"

Aria turned around and there was Max, long-haired, stiff-shouldered, with his arms crossed over his chest. "Max! I didn't know you were coming home this weekend."

"Yeah, well. Neither did I. My roommates were being douche-bags so I decided to drive down."

"Didn't feel like getting hammered this weekend?"

"I just needed a break from them. From people," he said. He sat on the edge of the bed, sinking into the flower-print duvet cover Aria had bought with Mother at Target. "Hey, did you look into those podcast interviews yet? Or the YouTube shows? I messaged you the links."

"Not yet. But I will."

"You could get a lot of views that way. And you get to let someone else do the work. You'd just have to do a decent job answering their interview questions."

Aria exhaled and wiggled her hands in front of the laptop screen. "First I need to finish this. The writing side of things."

"It's not going to work. Fuck, no one even reads paranormal magazines."

"Well how many people listen to UFO podcasts?"

"It's more likely someone'll see it online. They might just randomly stumble across it. No one randomly stumbles across magazines."

"Unless they're looking, too."

"Looking for what?"

"Looking for me. Other exchangers. Maybe they've immersed themselves in UFO, alien-conspiracy-theory culture so they can reach out. Like I'm doing."

Max was quiet for a moment. He buttoned and un-buttoned the cuff of his shirt—a dark blue and green flannel. "And what are you going to do if you don't find anyone? How long until you give up?"

"I'm not even going to think about that."

"What if they found your kidnappers? Would you give up then?"

"Well they haven't found them yet." The muscles of her arms and stomach constricted. "Right?"

"Right. But would you?"

"Obviously. If they found them, it would mean I've just been crazy this whole time."

"Too late for that. Either way, you're crazy."

"Ha ha. And I was just about to feel bad for stealing your room. Not anymore."

"Honestly, I would rather sleep in the living room. It looks too empty in here. Too bright and sparse. It's like a prison. Like, how have you not accumulated things yet? What, you have a dresser, a desk, a bed, and some clothes?"

"And books. And my phone. And this computer."

"But that's it."

"It's better for the environment. Less materialistic."

"It makes me feel like you're ready to leave at any moment. Like you're ready to take off."

"College?"

"Did you look into scholarships?"

"No, but—"

"I told you, don't say anything to Mom and Dad unless you know you can get a scholarship. You know they can't afford it. You'll just make Mom feel like shit."

"I thought I'd apply to U of O and OSU and see what I can get out of it."

"No, no, no. You're not coming to OSU."

"Come on, you don't want me there?" She smiled.

"What do you even want to study?"

"I don't know. Geology, maybe. Or history. Natural history? Do they have that?"

"Why? You hate Earth. I thought you were going to say astronomy."

"Or that. That's a good idea."

"Why do you want to go to college, again? You can get a job with an associate's degree."

"Isn't four-year-school the next step? And it would only take two years after community college. I mean, why did you go?"

"To study botany. You don't even have anything you want to study. You just want to go to go."

"And that's not normal?"

"It's normal for normal people, but not for you." He paused. "It's normal for people with money. And on top of all that, do you think Mom's really going to feel comfortable with you living on your own? After everything that's happened?"

"I'm twenty-five. Twenty-five! I'm a grown woman for fuck's sake."

"Ooo, Aria swore."

"Shut up."

"Look how mature you are, swearing and shit."

"You're the one who swears all the time."

"You're the one who thinks she's an alien." He said this more harshly than he'd meant to; Aria could tell by the way his eyes seemed to darken, how they shrunk back inside the hollows of his face with regret. Max's phone buzzed in his pocket. He typed something with the screen nearly to his chin. As he shuffled into the hallway, he mumbled something Aria couldn't make out.

She counted to five to make sure he wouldn't come back in. Then she covered her face with her hands. She sat back in the desk chair—an old dining chair, really—and fanned her fingers out against her cheeks. There were little blonde hairs all along her skin. So small, so invisible, that they could only be felt. For some reason she thought of Leera; the way she sometimes paused between bites in the cafeteria, and tousled Agapanthus's bowl if she hadn't finished it. Leera never said anything. Just pinched the edge of the bowl and shook it as if to remind Agapanthus that it was still there. And then, when Agapanthus dug in with her fingernails and sloshed the rest of the raw meat into her mouth, Leera looked away; *it was your idea,* she seemed to say. *It was all you,* with the slightest kindling of a smile on the thin corners of her lips.

These memories came randomly. Usually it was during the car-ride to Eugene for class at Lane Community College or a Dr. Wendell visit. Just the other day, Aria had been staring at a kestrel perched on a fencepost along the freeway—at its plump, mottled belly and its quivering eyes—when she suddenly remembered one of her earliest days at the fisheries, before the apprenticeship; just a visiting day. She had accidently followed Uncle Sonlo down a hallway, dimly lit and oddly bleak smelling, oddly devoid of odor. Although Sonlo's thick shoulders were much bigger than Pittick's, they were equally familiar, and she hadn't noticed who she'd been following. Agapanthus realized it and turned around. She lunged—in her aching, slow way—back to the net-room without Sonlo seeing her. Pittick had said they would be heading home soon. All day she had been worried she would be left behind.

Big steps. Hurry. One foot, other foot; tightness at the thighs. She stopped midway down the hall—what if Pittick was waiting for her at the entrance instead of the net-room? Where was it, again? Which shadows should she follow? The high ceilings scared her. Everything was big and lofty. What if he'd left without her? Would she have to stay there and wait for Sonlo to finish so he could guide her home instead? She didn't want Sonlo. She wanted Pittick. And then the door slid open and there he was, sitting alone on his knees in front of the water. "There you are," Pittick said. Lithely, he uncurled his knees one at a time. "I wasn't sure whether I should look for you." Then, standing so close she could smell his fish-smell as it mixed with the fish-smell of the air, he'd added, timidly: "So I waited."

Sometimes Aria wanted to tell these memories to Mother. She came so close sometimes that she clenched her teeth together in anticipation, or bunched her lips and swallowed the words before they slid forth from the back of her throat. Then, instead, she would say something about the way Mr. Douglas still wrote on a chalkboard in class, and always used too-short chalk that sometimes made his fingernail screech against it. Or, once, she asked Mother why they didn't have sheep—"We used to, before you were born. They just weren't bringing in money. But I still have some wool yarn left over. There are bundles of it in my closet."—or why they had built their house so close to the freeway.

"We didn't. They built that freeway next to our house. It was my parent's house before, you know."

"Why didn't they ever move?"

"They couldn't get a decent price for the house. Still can't. No one, unfortunately, is clamoring to live next to a freeway."

"So what happened to your parents?" Aria asked. "Where are they now?"

"My dad died right after Max was born. You met him when you were a tiny little thing. We went into town, had lunch. You wanted to hold his hand the whole time. It was adorable! And my mom was there, too, always picking you up and kissing you on the forehead. She bought you this little pink dress and matching ruffled socks, and she said she'd carry you all day so you could go shoeless and show them off. Aw, Mom. She lives in Arizona now. Maybe she'll come visit, near the end of the summer, when it's warm."

"She can use my bed," Aria said.

"Well of course, hon. She's not sleeping on that futon. Or the couch." Mother laughed and playfully grabbed Aria's ear. She accidentally grabbed her hair, too, and Aria tried not to wince. "They were never big on coming back to visit. I think after they left they wanted to move on, you know? Forget this place. I think they hated it. Their dream of a little house in this huge valley, all green and big-skied, all quiet and alone, completely ruined by the freeway. But, I don't know. I always thought it was beautiful here. The freeway shouldn't take away from all the good things."

Aria knew what she meant by the good things. Sometimes she secretly enjoyed the purple-tinge of the clouds, the restlessness of the overgrown grass, the ferns along the stream as they first opened up, thinly, fragilely, almost alien in their strange, unfurling shape. Last year, when she was taking her online GED classes, and she was the only one home on most days, Aria would sometimes sit next to the stream. Each season its sound changed—heavy, yelling, and steady beneath the rains; very secretive in the dry season, much like the delicate muddle of hummingbirds. Aria liked to pretend she was a messenger sent here from Deeyae. An explorer. She imagined herself telling Aster about the blue sky, or how easy it was to run. She arranged the words in her mind so she would be ready to tell him all about the Water Planet: "Did you know they have trees, like giant water plants, and they're thick—their bases are like rocks—and they give off these puffy little seeds that float in the air, and you can smell them everywhere—they smell like the Waters, and also like Earth-soil." She imagined telling him this on the shore, sitting with their bare legs touching, his body hair itchy but warm. She would ramble like that, but he would nod and look at the sand as though the images were playing out in front of him. Yes, she would be the one to tell him everything. To unveil the secrets of the Earth. She knew it was unlikely—impossible—that she would be allowed back, but still she dreamed of it. That was why she sat by the stream and tried to match the birds to their songs.

Her laptop beeped. It was a new Facebook message from Max; another link, this one to a YouTube channel called *Aliens_Among_Us*.

Aria closed her computer. She wandered out into the living room and sat next to Max on the couch. He was watching the five o'clock news.

"Where's Mother?" Aria asked.

"The garden." He handed her the remote. Aria rested it at her side without changing the channel.

"Derek?"

"I don't know. Out back somewhere."

The screen door squeaked. Mother walked in wearing a button-up tank-top and oversized khaki shorts. Her cheeks looked yellow, and the wrinkles around her eyes shone like spools of thread. The outside air wafted in. It smelled like cut grass and carrot greens.

"Look what I found," Mother said, holding up a bundle of dark purple, dirt-heavy beets. "First crop of the season. They've been growing all winter. I hope they aren't too tough." She dangled them over the kitchen trash, scrubbing them with a vegetable brush. "Beets for dinner? I could whip up a quick soup."

"That sounds good, Mother," Aria said, even though she hadn't really liked the beets they'd harvested the year before. They'd tasted like earth. Coarse, and minerally.

Max said nothing.

"Veggie soup sound good?" Mother asked as she laid out the knife and cutting board.

"Sure," Aria said. She wished Mother would leave so she could talk to Max. She wanted to ask him why he was helping her when he didn't even believe her. She wanted to ask when he would believe her. What would it take?

But she didn't get a chance to ask him that day, and the rest of the weekend passed quickly. Before Max left on Sunday afternoon, Aria pulled him into her room. "You're leaving already?" she asked. He had his backpack on, and it was obvious he was ready to go.

"Yep."

"Why've you been so quiet? You're not mad at me, are you?" Aria asked. She sat on the bed with her legs crossed while Max stood in the doorframe. The thick light of the windows caught in his pale eyelashes.

"No."

"Well, good. I wanted to ask you—what kind of scholarships should I apply for?"

"Nothing that has to do with academics. Even if you have good grades, they usually don't go for the community college kids." Max took off his backpack. He set it on the floor and let it rest against his ankle.

"So what did you get, then? You went to community college too."

Max crossed his arms. "I got a scholarship and a grant, mostly for being economically underprivileged. The rest are loans."

"Hmm. So I could get a scholarship for being poor?"

"We're not actually poor. We're lower middle class. And I wrote a damn good application essay, that's what got me that scholarship. So who knows if you would get one too. Although, think about it; the poor kidnapped girl, tormented, raised by drug-addicts, and finally returned to her birth family?" He nodded. "You could really make something out of that."

"Yeah, I'm sure I could," Aria said tightly. She shifted to her desk; opened the dusty lid of her laptop. "Well. Have a good time at school, flower-boy. Try and make friends."

"Alright," he said. He came from behind the chair to give her a hug around the shoulders. His breath was clothed in spearmint gum. "I'll see you soon, Alien."

Again, she wanted to ask him if he would ever believe her. Now was the perfect time. Ask him, ask him! But, for some reason, she couldn't, just couldn't, and she listened to his car engine shudder, a low clicking that made Mother worry that it would break down and he'd have to pull over three lanes to get to the side of the freeway. "I wish he'd have done his research," Mother said after Max brought the used car home for the first time. "There must be better options out there." But Max had raised all the money himself through his job at the campus bookstore, and Derek was obviously proud. "There we are," he'd said, rubbing his hand across the chipped paint of the hood. "She's not a beauty, but she'll do, won't she?"

Aria listened until Max's car melded with the noises of the freeway. She spent the rest of the afternoon writing the next blog post; she wouldn't post it until later in the week, but she thought she should at least get started. It was titled *Life On Earth*. She didn't know if she was a good writer. In her manipulated memories, Meredith had taught her the basics of reading and writing. Picture books "borrowed" from the library and never returned. Plushy notebooks from the dollar store that she wrote in with crayons. Word puzzles on the back of kid's menus at Applebee's and Outback Steakhouse. Her GED classes had helped refine her writing skills a little. Vocabulary building. Advanced grammar skills. Spelling. By the end of the course, Aria felt caught up. The closest thing they had to writing on Deeyae were the murals, and each time Aria wrote something, she felt like she was carving into a magnificent white stone. Sometimes it took her hours to write a single paragraph for an essay. Usually her goal was to make it sound like she was talking. Her online GED teacher recommended that she say the words out loud as she typed them. Aria moved her lips but rarely let the words tumble out into sound; she didn't want Mother to overhear.

The next day was class—biology in the morning and speech in the afternoon. Mother dropped Aria off on her way to the animal shelter.

Aria hated walking toward the glass-walled building. She hated the aloneness of it. All the buildings and the occasional cars and the sun on her shoulders. Aria quickened her steps and stared at the grass along the sidewalk. It was easy to walk fast here on the Water Planet. At times she felt like her knees would kick up and she would lift off the ground. She felt light; like she was swimming.

A guy wearing a tank-top walked past her. The pale sides of his ribs flashed as he swung his arms. Then came a very young-looking guy with short curly hair. He laughed with an older woman who carried a potted cactus in her arms. Then came a slim girl in knee-high boots. And an overweight woman with a shaved head and long turquoise earrings, whose breathing sputtered like the engine on Max's car. Aria watched them all without turning her head. She breathed in warm, flowery perfume, concentrating on the way it mixed with the cut grass and the must of someone's backpack. Each smell fastened together to become something new.

A man with a clip-board stood near the doorway, next to the trashcan. He stepped forward. "Sign the petition to stop the logging of old-growth forests?" He pulled a pen from the front pocket of his jeans and held it out to Aria. His face shrunk into a smile.

"Oh," Aria said, her voice unusually nasally this early in the morning. She cleared her throat. "Okay." She had never been to an old-growth forest, but she thought of the trees along the ravine. It sounded wonderful to visit a hill ripe with ancient trees. *They* were this reddish-brown color, she would tell Aster someday. *And all along the ground there were light-green plants in the shadows, and pine cones that had fallen. When I stepped on them, they crunched, but they didn't break all the way. They were a bit like rocks.* Maybe she should collect them. She could bring them back for him! Lay a whole pile of twigs and cones and seeds at his feet. But obviously they wouldn't let her bring them back. She had to keep telling herself—they wouldn't let her come back at all. *You're stuck here you're stuck here you're stuck here.* As time went on she was able to delude herself that maybe, since she was special enough to keep her memories, she would be special enough to return to Deeyae. The Contact liked her, right? Half the time she thought of it that way—maybe it'll happen, maybe—but half the time she felt sure they were all dead. Aster would be sent to Earth someday, but Pittick and Leera, everyone else—she had to be sent back, or else they were dead already. She knew they were out there, up there, alongside one of those stars that glimmered grayly against the lights of the freeway, but if she couldn't see them, or walk with Leera and Pittick from the meal, or stand next to the portation machine as Imari analyzed her next move, or if she couldn't hear Sonlo call her Fish, or swim alone in the Waters, then her old life was just as unreachable as if she had died, or as if they had died, or as if, all at once, the galaxy had expunged itself and these were the last painful moments, and that was why she felt like she was constantly rubbed with gravel, all over her skin until the scratches opened and blood surged forth painting her red, red, red, and each movement was slow even though she finally had energy, and everything was colliding and swelling together until blackness. This was the constant pain she felt. This was why sometimes she just covered her eyes and did nothing, said nothing, tried to stop breathing. No one else seemed to understand that this pain didn't recede. It did nothing but dull for the briefest moments—birds landing on the stream, or Mother stroking her hair. Then everyone would look at her with this lightness in their eyes like, *oh, she's doing better*, but she wasn't, and she never would be, and they seemed unable to understand how much she had lost, or the constant, constant heaviness that had taken the place of Deeyae's oppressive atmosphere, and how, really, she was faking it, and there was no way to remove this panic from her abdomen. Sometimes, as she thought back at everything that had happened, she felt horrified. Absolutely horrified. As though someone had removed her organs while she was sleeping.

The man nodded at the clipboard. He skimmed it with his finger as he read what she had written. "Thanks—Aria?"

Aria nodded and escaped into the building. The air-conditioning clung to her arms. Why had she worn a sweater with quarter-length sleeves? She was always cold. Shouldn't she have known better?

The classroom was arranged with two-person tables. She chose the one closest to the door. Most of the desks were still empty. Two other students were looking at their phones. Aria knew she should probably feel at least a little old, a little behind—twenty-five and a sophomore in college? Community college?—but she didn't. And not even because there were occasionally thirty and forty and fifty year-olds in her classes. Honestly, she felt neither old nor young. She felt only as though she had lost something. And the only time she felt even somewhat better was when she was working on her website. She wished she were there now; the blinds half open, dim light in the room; she imagined leaning forward in her chair, her legs crossed, still wearing her pajamas; the thud of the keys as she finished her blog post.

Soon the empty chairs were filled. As usual, Georgia, an eighteen-year-old who wore a long braid draped over her spine, sat next to Aria. She delicately lowered herself into the plastic chair. "Hey," she said quietly to Aria.

"Hey," Aria repeated. She knew she should ask *how are you?* But she didn't feel like it. They'd gone through those pleasantries the first few weeks of class, and now Aria was bored by it. She flipped through the old text messages on her phone to look like she was busy. They were all from Mother or Max. One from Father.

Georgia pulled a small, glittery notebook from her bag and arranged it on the desk along with a pink pen. Then she rested one hand on each thigh and turned her head toward the teacher. Aria secretly glanced at Georgia's hands. They were the color of wet sand. Maybe caramel.

"Morning, everyone," the teacher—Mrs. Lowry—said. "Let's get started, please." She closed the door to the classroom. Briefly, her eyes skimmed over the rows of desks, the blank walls, the floor-length windows in the back, the newly green tree branches. Mrs. Lowry pulled up the waistband of her slacks, then crossed her arms over her purple, cotton blouse. Aria thought her teacher was tall enough and lanky enough to be a model, but her face wasn't pretty. Her hairline was so far back it almost looked receding, and her cheeks were far too soft, almost shapeless.

"Alright. Today: evolution. Who here has heard of Charles Darwin?" Mrs. Lowry waited for hands. Aria raised hers, thanks to the GED classes. "Good. You all should have. He's what we would call the father of evolution. His theory about the origin of species completely transformed the world; he's responsible for completely revolutionizing the way we perceive ourselves in relation to the other life on this planet. Every animal and plant and even the bacterium on this planet became, under Darwin's theory, our long-lost relatives.

"Now, Darwin wasn't all that popular during his time. Those who believed in creationism thought his theory was incorrect, to say the least, and, of course, some religious folk still believe that today. 'God created man. Man did not come from apes.' Now, I'm not saying that God exists, or doesn't exist, or that some divine force did or did not create the world. All I'm saying when I teach evolution is that this is what Darwin's theory suggested. You can choose to believe it or not. That's a personal choice. But, either way, you need to learn about it for this class.

"And, personally, I think the two viewpoints can easily co-exist. Perhaps God created the world, and got life going, and then, once life was going, the forces of evolution took hold. I probably shouldn't say things like that but," she raised her shoulders, "what are you going to do."

Mrs. Lowry pulled up a slideshow. She talked about Darwin's travels, natural selection, Galapagos finches. Aria kept repeating in her head; *long-lost relatives, long-lost relatives.* The Deeyans, too, were her relatives. Truly, they shared the same lineage. They had evolved from the same ancient species of human. She'd always known this, and yet, hearing someone else pretty much say it—someone human—made it real.

For the first time, Aria felt bad for the Deeyans. They'd been stolen from a planet where all the creatures and plants and bacteria were their relatives, and they'd been transported to some other planet around some other star, an unknown place where they held no kinship with the red-breasted spers or the water creatures. The first Deeyans must have been terrified of that dusty landscape. They'd had the Gods to guide them, of course, but some of them probably still wanted to go back. Some of the first Deeyans probably yearned for Earth, the color green, the shocking blue sky.

Mrs. Lowry tugged at her wedding ring as she spoke; she twisted it over the knobby bones of her finger. "The part of it that people tend to misunderstand is this: an organism cannot evolve during its lifetime. It's not like Pokémon. You were all at least born in the '90's, right? Everyone remember Pokémon? That show with those weird creatures that fought each other and lived inside those balls?" Some of the guys in the back of the room snorted.

Mrs. Lowry ignored them. "And, I can't say I'm clear on the details, but I remember that the Pokémon could evolve from one stage to another; from child to adult; from adorable to beastly. One minute they looked like a raccoon, the next they looked like a giant bear-like monster. That's what I'm referencing. Evolution on command. That's not how it works, folks. It takes random mutations from generation to generation. It takes that mutation being well suited for environmental conditions. It takes luck. And, once it's occurred, there's no going back."

Aria had never seen Pokémon, but she understood what Mrs. Lowry was talking about. That was why the Deeyans had red skin. That was why she did not. Just thinking about it, her skin became—not itchy, but uncomfortable. She had so many questions. Should she ask them? She tapped her foot against the table leg. *Ding ding ding* went her Vans sneaker against the metal. *Ding ding ding*. Georgia glanced at her foot. *Ding ding ding*. Aria rubbed her hand over her thigh. She had to ask. She had to.

"Yes," Mrs. Lowry said. She paused as though she'd forgotten her name. Then, with a short nod and a slight exhale: "Aria."

"I just had a question." She had never spoken out in class before. Sometimes she asked questions face-to-face with the teacher, but never in front of everyone like this. "I had a question about whether, if someone was somehow able to change the genes in their body, they could evolve during their lifetime, or whether it would still have to be passed on."

"Ah," Mrs. Lowry said. "You know, that's really quite an interesting question. Honestly, I can't say I'm a hundred percent positive on the answer to that, but my best guess would be that if you changed your genetic code, you would see instant results, but they might be catastrophic. For instance, cancer is the typical outcome of genetic mutations. But I'm not a geneticist, so I can't say for sure." She squinted at Aria. Her eyes were a muddy green. "I would ask Mr. Cornell, the molecular biology teacher; he knows a bit more about genetics."

Aria knew she would never talk to Mr. Cornell. She was already embarrassed for asking anything at all.

"Yes, Sarah." Mrs. Lowry pointed to a girl two tables behind Aria.

"I don't know if you've seen it, but I was just thinking about that *Ancient Aliens* show, and how they say that aliens came here and tampered with peoples' genetic codes, like it was some big experiment or something. Like, I think there was a big jump in human evolution and that was why they think that?" Sarah tugged at the edges of her knit cap.

Ancient Aliens? Through all her research, Aria had never heard of it. Evidently she needed to watch more TV. She hid her phone under the desk and Googled *Ancient Aliens* so she would remember to watch it later.

Mrs. Lowry opened her mouth, closed it, then spoke. "I can't say I've seen that particular show, but I have heard about it. There was an old movie that came out in the '70's called *Chariots of the Gods*—"

"Oh, I've heard of that," Sarah said.

Mrs. Lowry nodded. "I believe their hypothesis was essentially the same. And, you know, it's hard to say. Human evolution is tricky. It's complicated. There could be many different reasons for a sudden surge forward through the evolutionary ladder, so to speak."

"So—aliens—it's not impossible?" A heavy-set older man asked from the other side of the room.

"No, certainly not impossible. Maybe they helped our ancestors build the pyramids, and Stonehenge. Maybe they enslaved humanity for a time, or abducted a few people. Who knows? There are more than enough questions and few enough answers that no one can rule it out with any certainty." Backpack zippers began to unzip, books slid off desks, a few students scooted back their chairs. "Okay, I'm starting to hear that rustle-rustle. Let's leave class five minutes early, shall we?" Mrs. Lowry soundlessly clapped her hands together. "See you Wednesday. Go watch some TV."

And Aria did. After school she looked up episodes of *Ancient Aliens* online. The ancient humans had it right, calling the aliens Gods—they were Gods, only, they didn't come from Sirius or Orion or the Pleiades, but from the twin stars Aamsh and Jord. Aria spent three hours after class watching the show on her laptop. The megalithic structures. Why did humans build them? And how, with their lack of technology? The vanishing civilizations. Why had they abandoned whole cities? Where did they go? The artifacts and paintings and stories; spacesuits, strange creatures, fire from the heavens. It all made sense. It was the Gods.

A knock at her door. Aria quickly closed her laptop. Mother stood on the other side, folded t-shirts in her arms. "Here you go, hon." She looked into Aria's room for a moment, and then she marched to the nightstand and clicked on the white lamp they'd bought to replace the broken one. "What've you been up to?"

"Homework," Aria said as she slid the t-shirts into the top drawer on her dresser. They smelled sweet, like lavender.

"Alright. Well you can always do it out in the main room, if you want. You don't have to be holed up in the dark in here."

Aria nodded but said nothing.

"Dinner will be ready soon," Mother said, and then she left.

That was how most days went. Class. *Ancient Aliens.* Website research. Blog posts. Aria spent almost all her time in her room, at her desk, on her laptop. It was exactly what she needed. Whenever she was in class she looked forward to this sense of dissolving; this sense of becoming something that was her but not her; she wanted to be numb but also enthralled, to be so absorbed that the scant walls of her room and the grassy hills out the window ceased to close in on her. When she was entranced like this she felt like she was in some dark corner of space, far enough away from stars and planets that they became only soft, gray strings of Christmas lights. After several hours on the computer she could barely focus her eyes. Her knees felt tight from crossing her legs. She hated re-awakening like that. It was like coming out of the Waters. Or, worse: it was the slow, dripping walk home.

Father often called on Sunday nights. He'd stopped making excuses for why he hadn't moved to Oregon yet. In fact, he'd stopped mentioning it at all. Instead he talked about the repairs he needed to make on his car, or how he'd gotten sunburnt on the back of his neck. Or he'd ask what Aria was learning in school. Once, they spent the whole phone call talking about the ocean.

"You ever been there, Aria? They ever take you?"

"No. I don't think so." She didn't ask which "they" he meant.

"The ocean here is warm. It's always summer here. An Oregon summer, not a Florida summer. Florida has two seasons. Hotter and less hot."

"Oh?" Aria liked listening to his voice. It reminded her of an audiobook. "There's an ocean here, right? On the edge of Oregon?"

Father laughed. The phone crackled. "They didn't teach you geography in that GED thing?"

"Well, yeah." Aria rubbed her hand over her lips. "I mean, what's the ocean here like?"

"Windy. Rainy. Rough. It's not the kind of place to go swimming. But the Oregon coast is, yeah—it's kind of—kind of unique."

"But it's warmer in the Florida ocean?" Aria asked.

"A hell of a lot warmer. I'll take you someday. You come visit me this winter. You have a break in December, right? Or are you done with school this year?"

"No—" She wasn't sure she was ready to visit Father. She imagined Florida like a white blanket, harsh, chopped through by buildings. Every time he asked her to visit, school was her excuse. But now she was graduating. "Well, I'll be done after fall term. I just have one class to make up."

"Oh? Which class is that, now?"

"It's a math class. I don't know. I just got lazy the first time I took it."

"Well that's alright. So you're done in the winter?"

"Yeah." There was no way out of it. What would it be like, to be alone with Father for so long?

"Perfect way to celebrate—tell your mother if you want to come visit, and I'll book the ticket."

"I better wait to make sure what the schedule is. When class gets out." Aria knew the Gods could see her from any angle of the Earth, but part of her worried that if she went to Florida, something would change. She would become even more distant from Deeyae. Even more lost.

Father coughed. "Alright. Let me know the dates and we'll get you all set. I love you, girly."

"Love you, too, Father."

Another spiky, crackled laugh. "Alright." Then the click.

The moment right after a phone call always startled her. She pressed the red button on her cell phone and faced the muffled, grainy silence of her room. Max's room. It would never really be hers. The dust on the windowsill was Max's. The spiky lint beneath the bed was Max's. The tapioca colored blanket on the top shelf of the closet was his, too. Each time Max came home he spent less time sitting on the edge of Aria's bed, helping her find alien videos on YouTube. Instead he stretched himself long on the couch. The murmur of TV, a lukewarm bottle of Sprite, a fun-sized bag of Fritos, his crunching louder than the voices of whatever History Channel show he was watching. Max's hair grew so long it touched his shoulders. Even though it was straight and well-combed, it reminded Aria of lamb fur. Maybe because of the color. Maybe because it was thick. There had always been something remotely sheep-like about Max; a certain sleepiness in his eyes. That didn't mean he was docile, though. He was not docile.

Aria was watching *Ancient Aliens* one Friday when Max appeared in her doorway.

"Hey," Aria said. She paused the video. "Another Friday night at home?"

"Finals are next week. I need a break." He crossed his arms and leaned against the wall. His hair fell across his cheeks. Neither of them spoke. Aria knew she should say something—anything at all—or she should at least grunt, or hum, or mutter something about getting back to her show, but she couldn't force herself to emerge from the numbness. Max swung away from the wall and stumbled off. From her room, Aria heard Mother. The fridge opening and closing. Glasses on the off-white countertop. Mother's pitch falling and rising. Aria forced herself to turn off her computer, and she shuffled into the brightly-lit kitchen.

"There she is," Mother said. "I made the Trader Joe's lemonade. The frozen stuff." She grabbed another glass from the cabinet. "Want any?"

"Sure," Aria mumbled.

"We were thinking of pizza tonight. Thin crust. Sound good?" Mother asked. She looked intently at Aria, who nodded. Max loudly gulped his lemonade with his head tipped back.

Mother pushed the glass toward Aria; full to the top, milky yellow and pulpy. It tasted sweet but slightly, just barely, like spinach, or soil, or cardboard.

Mother's scant eyebrows came together. "Hey, Max, wasn't there something you wanted to ask your sister?"

Max stared. Aria could tell what he was thinking—*half* sister. "Mom thinks I should take you to the coast sometime."

"Your father e-mailed me to ask if you could stay in Florida with him. To celebrate your graduation. He said you talked about it on the phone. He mentioned you'd never seen the ocean." Mother sipped her own lemonade. Her lipstick left maroon lines on the rim of the cup. "So why wait until December? The Oregon coast is beautiful. You and Max would have a great time."

"That sounds great," Aria said in her fake-sounding-but-actu-ally-sincere voice. Why hadn't Father listened to her? She'd said she would ask Mother later in the year. Aria wasn't ready for a new place. She was barely used to Oregon. Now she had to pretend to be excited; the plane ticket would be expensive. She had to pre-tend she was grateful. The only good thing, the only good thing, was that Florida would be warm.

"Well, Max?"

"Yeah, sure. I'm in."

"Great, that'll be good for you two. Spend some time together." When Mother said this, Aria thought of how, once, in the middle of the night, she'd had to go to the bathroom, and, as she walked past Mother and Derek's room, she'd heard Mother crying. Mostly she heard Derek's voice. "No," he repeated in a soothingly low register. "No, no." Then sharp gasps that belonged to Mother. Aria could imagine Mother's wrinkled eyes nestled into the crook between Derek's armpit and shoulder. The tear marks on his gray cotton shirt. His voice dropped even lower. Aria only heard fragments ("—wasn't you—") and the vague rustle of fabric. She stood in the half-darkness of the hallway for as long as she could bear. At first she held her breath, but then she realized that if they heard her, she could just keep walking to the bathroom like she'd been doing all along. So Aria listened a moment longer, until their voices and their distant movements died away, and she felt alone in front of their door. It made her think of Leera after the sick-ness. She wondered if, within the stone walls of the house, Leera cried for Agapanthus. What if she fostered another exchanger? What if, in a thousand years, Leera forgot about her?

Sometimes Aria wished she could forget. Perhaps it would be easier to start again.

This is what she thought about on the drive to the coast. Max kept his music loud enough that they couldn't talk over it without yelling. "I made a CD," Max said when they first sat in the car, and that was the last thing he said until they saw the ocean. The music was a mix of acoustic guitars and bass-heavy, screeching electronic music. Max stared ahead at the road as he drove. He nodded his head occasionally—subtly, so subtly that Aria couldn't tell whether it was the music or the jolting movement of the car that was making his head sway. Aria watched the trees grow taller. She made sure to vary her gaze between the side window and the windshield so Max wouldn't think she was curled away into her own world; so he would know that her eyes were there, she was there, and he could talk to her, if he felt like it.

Old-growth forest, Aria thought as the elevation grew, as the car edged along hills and cliffs painted a green so dark she thought of the night sky. They passed thin, mottled trees shading streams from the sun; a bare, red-dirt hill, with one spindly, leggy tree left alien at its peak; ferns and moss dripping together, colliding; and, just beyond a line of trees, a field of broken branches, shorn stumps, all saturated with sunlight, all dry and empty, dust tossed lightly, hanging, floating. This was what the Save the Forests petition guy was talking about. This was what he was trying to stop. It was ugly, certainly. Trees didn't make sounds, or move, or do much of anything, it seemed, and yet Aria intrinsically liked them. Of all that she had seen on Earth so far, all that she had looked over in her fake memories, trees were the most mystifying.

"It's foggy," Max said, "but usually you can see the ocean over there. Just down there, past that hill."

"I kind of see it." Something gray and blue bled through the clouds.

"The sun will probably come out later." Max cleared his throat. "Should we stop and get some coffee?"

"What? I want to see the water!"

"Look who's all enthusiastic all of a sudden." The turn signal clicked. "Don't worry, the ocean isn't going anywhere."

They stopped at a café with soft music playing. It smelled like cinnamon, and there were black-and-white photos taped and stapled and tacked into the wall. Bridges. Foggy streetlamps. A lighthouse. An old-fashioned woman with an umbrella.

"You want coffee?" Max asked, his eyes on the croissants in the glass display case.

"Sure," Aria said. She didn't love coffee, but she didn't hate it.

"Alright. You pay, though."

"For both of us?"

"Well, if you're not chipping in for gas."

Aria blew through her lips. "Fine," she mumbled, although, really, she was happy about it, because it felt like the distance in Max's eyes had lifted slightly.

It lifted even further by the time they had walked a few blocks to the stairs leading down to the beach. Dark sand stretched out below. The fog had lifted just enough to reveal broken, white-tipped waves. The higher clouds passed, came and went, unleashing occasional sunlight which made the sand glisten where it was wet from the tide.

"Wow," Aria said. "It smells—kind of like fish."

"Seaweed," Max said. He led her down the sand-caked concrete stairs. "Take your shoes off." He kicked off his flip-flops and left them scattered.

"You're going to leave them there?"

"It's not like anyone's going to steal them," Max said. "Look, that old lady down there, with the purple rain jacket—she looks like a criminal for sure."

Aria slipped off her sandals, too, and she left them beside Max's. This sand was finer than Yeela's. It felt like dirt but also like sugar; she felt like she wasn't supposed to be walking in it.

"Look, strawberries," Max pointed to tiny round leaves growing straight from the sand. He bent next to it and pinched a leaf. "Strong vein, short terminal tooth. Agh, yes, duh, *Fragraria chiloensis*, and, look, it's in flower! You see? Small, white." Then Max popped up again. Aria followed him closer to the water. The sand became solid, like a slab of stone. Suddenly the wind shoved her hair in her face; she looped it around her shoulder and held a ponytail with one hand. Why hadn't she brought an elastic? This was wild, heavy, powerful wind. It made the loose sand dance. It had, long before, molded the shore trees until they were bent and craggled; all branches pointed inland, away from the water.

"Come feel it," Max yelled over the wind. He was crouched at the edge. Cloudy water slithered toward and away from his feet, venturing closer each surge. Max patted the shallow trickle. "It's freezing!"

Aria walked slowly toward him. Down the beach, a giant sea-rock protruded from the ocean. It was rounded, mossy; capped with a shifting white carpet of birds. "What's that down there?" she asked when she was closer to Max.

"That's Haystack Rock." He pointed to the water. "Come on, feel it. It's fucking freezing."

Another gust of wind pounded over them. It pushed droplets of seawater against their faces. Aria scrunched her nose; she turned away and crossed her arms. Two jackets and she was still freezing. "I'm so cold," she said, biting her lip, letting the cold air enter and exit through her mouth. Then—icy water on her feet. "Max!" she screamed.

"There you go!" Max laughed, sputtering, cough-like. Aria thought his laugh sounded like something he had been trained to stifle; something he had long tried to hide, and was just now learning to let free again. Max kicked at the receding water. "Goddamn that's cold."

This ocean was dark, dark, dark, like the Waters. But it was so different. This ocean was a vast blanket of richness, of swishing and chopping waves, of movement and damp-earth smells and never-ending wind. This ocean came at her all at once. It didn't invite her toward it.

"You can't swim in it?" Aria asked, although she already knew the answer.

"Not really. Too cold. Maybe in, like, late August, but even then—not really."

There was no essence behind it, there was no—it wasn't the Waters. It wasn't the Waters, it never would be, it would never replace the calm, red shore where she had found weightlessness, and been calm and cocooned and warm, always warm. Aster would not find her here. He would not sit on the shore and critique the position of her arms as she swam. She worried she would forget his face. Pittick, Leera, everyone else, she knew she wouldn't forget, but Aster, for some reason—she worried about. Once she tried to draw a picture of him but it was so bad she ripped it up and threw it away.

Aria's smile fell. She backed away from the ocean's arms. Her feet tingled. She stood in the dry sand, arms crossed.

Max turned around. "What, had enough already?" he shouted.

She stepped closer. "It's too cold here. Really, what's the point of this? Who wants to stand around in the freezing wind while their feet turn numb?"

"Um, me," Max said, still smiling.

"Really?" Aria glared at him. "You think this is fun?"

"You're the one who wanted to come here." Max emerged from the now ankle-deep water. His legs were speckled with wet sand.

"Yeah. I wanted to see it once. I was just curious. And now I'm not. So I'm good to leave whenever you are."

"Okay, we'll leave now, right now." Max stomped past her. He funneled through the deep sand, his hands in the pockets of his shorts.

They nestled their shoes back on. The sand on Aria's feet rubbed against the band of her flip-flops.

"Is there somewhere we can rinse our feet?" Aria asked. Max said nothing. "Now you're mad at me?" she asked.

"I drove you all this way and you don't even want to stay for more than two seconds."

"You don't have to get all mad like a little kid. You only drove me because Mother made you."

"So what. I still gave up my whole day for you."

"Well—thank you. Is that what you want? Thank you for bringing me to this boring, empty, freezing place."

"You know what, Aria? You know what your problem is? You're afraid to like anything that's not from your precious *world*. Or, no—you love everything and hate everything at the same time. The stream, the forest, the hills, the ocean; any of us. You're afraid to get attached to this planet, and anything and anyone on it; you're afraid to enjoy yourself or connect with anything because you think you might go back someday. Well guess what, Aria—you're not going back. You're never fucking going back to that place. You're here. This is your planet. This is your life. This is your family. You are never going back."

"You don't know that," Aria whispered.

"You're right, I don't. And, you know what—forget it. I should actually probably be thanking you, because, Mom and Dad, they used to worry about me the way they worry about you."

"They still worry about you. All the time," Aria said.

"Mom thinks you call her Mother because you called Meredith Mom. Meredith was Mom so she can't be Mom."

"But—"

"You could at least fucking pretend. For Mom's sake. Tell them you feel better. Tell them you're not an alien. It doesn't matter if you believe it—it matters if they do. Because, I know you don't care, but Mom's been through hell. That whole time you were gone—wherever the fuck you were—she, she—did you know that, when I was little, she wouldn't even get out of bed some weekends? She'd stay in her room until six at night, sometimes, and

Dad would take me walking outside or into town so I wouldn't hear her crying."

Aria opened her mouth.

"And now you're here and you're messed up so she still can't forgive herself. She can't forgive herself and no one can move on until you get your shit together."

Aria bit her lip and stared back at the ocean. "I don't—" but she stopped there. There was nothing she could say. Nothing at all, in the wind on the beach. Nothing at all throughout the car ride home. Nothing at all when Mother asked how their beach day was. Nothing at all when she was alone in her room; not even in her head as she closed the blinds to shut out the late afternoon sun and the premature, transparent moon. Nothing. That was the best she could do. Nothing, nothing, nothing.

A knock on the door. Derek, breathing heavily, his thumbs looped through the belt loops on his jeans. "You know where Max went?" he asked. He stepped forward into Aria's room. She couldn't remember the last time he was in there. His presence felt bulky, with his heavy stomach, and his wide, stubbled cheeks that seemed, to her, made of iron.

"No," Aria forced herself to say. "I haven't seen him since we got home."

"It's not like him to just leave like that."

"He probably went back to school early."

"Without telling anyone?"

"What, are you worried he ran away? He's an adult. He can do what he wants."

"No, that's not—he would at least have said good-bye. Or left a note, for God's sakes. He wouldn't have just taken off, even if he was in one of his moods." Derek glanced at the corner of the bed. He leaned toward it, and for a moment Aria thought he would sit next to her. Instead he stepped sloppily, absently backward. His hands finally migrated from the belt loops to his pockets. "Did something happen? Was he upset over something?"

"How should I know? He's not exactly emotionally open." Aria had the odd feeling that she was watching herself from a distance; critiquing herself, looking upon her slumped posture and her frizzy hair in disgust. And—what was she *saying*? Emotionally open? What did that even mean?

Derek uttered a phlegmy breath; something between a sigh and a cough. "I'm not saying whether the hell anything did happen. But if something did, seeing as he disappeared right after you two went on your trip together, it might be nice to send him a text and just ask where he is, since he's not answering your mother or me."

"It was his decision. You can't blame me for him leaving."

"I'm not blaming you. I'm asking for your help, Aria." For a long moment, he stared at the blinds. Aria did too. She focused on the tiny, sour lines where the slats were dusty. "I know it's been hard for you," he said. "But we're here. We're here for you, and for Max." He opened his mouth like he would say something more, but he didn't. Then, from the doorframe, he said: "Just let me know if he answers."

Aria rubbed the hem of her sweatshirt. She dug her fingernail into the long stitches; the lines in the fabric. Her phone was on her nightstand. She rolled onto her back and raised the screen above her face. Her father had texted her, asking how her day at the coast went. Did he really keep track of those things? How did he even know about it? Mother?

Aria replied that it was cold and windy. But, thinking back, she thought of the giant rock—Habstack Rock? Holrock Rock? Haystack. Haystack Rock; breathless and unmoving against the constant motion of the clouds and sea. She thought of the smell, sweet but bitter. The tacky consistency of the sand on her feet. The little strawberry growing straight from that sand, spreading, coursing, weaving itself into the beach, reaching its arms through each grain, pushing the chopped up seashells aside, devouring them, groping toward the damp sunlight.

She wrote Max that she was sorry. Just *sorry*. She didn't ask where he was, or why he'd left. *Sorry*.

For a half-hour she closed her eyes, hands folded across her stomach. The rise and fall of water filled her mind. She wished she could dive in. Float on her back, just like this. Aamsh and Jord churning across the redness. Imn, steady as always. The wind—the wind. Lifting spray from the Waters, just like the wind here.

Eventually she fell asleep. It was unusually early, but she was tired from being in the car for so long. The next morning her phone was still on her chest. She checked it, but there were no new texts. In her sweatshirt and jeans, she scuttled into the kitchen. The wood floors felt cold through her socks. A humming permeated everything; the fan was on in the bathroom.

"Morning," Mother said.

Aria looked up. Mother stood at the counter holding a packet of toaster waffles. At the table, gazing into his glass of orange-pineapple juice blend, was Max.

"Where did you go last night?" Aria asked, nearly shouting in her unbending, gruff morning voice.

"Town," Max said.

Today she could think more clearly, and she knew it had been her fault that he'd left like that; it had been their argument on the beach. And Aria didn't care why, or where exactly, or what he'd been doing. She was just glad he'd come home. Mother most likely felt the same way, judging by the lightness of her movements, the way she whipped her bangs from her forehead as she poured herself coffee.

"He was meeting up with a friend from his ecology class," Mother added. "And his phone was low on batteries, so he had it turned off most of the night. Silly boy. You just had to say one word; bye. I'm leaving. If you knew what was going through our minds!"

"Jeez, Mom. I was only gone for a few hours."

"Yeah, Mom," Aria said. It felt weird to call her that, even if she was only mimicking Max's tone. "He's a grown man."

"Oh, Aria—check your Facebook," Max said. He nodded to her, his eyes on Mother.

"Where do you keep finding all this stuff?" Aria asked. She sat beside him.

"Finding what?" Mother asked. With a clang, the waffles popped up from the toaster. They smelled burnt.

"Nothing," Aria said. "Just Facebook stuff."

Mother chuckled; her chin collapsed down into her throat, and, for a moment, she reminded Aria of a plump, jolly frog. "Beyond me," she said.

"Seriously, this is big," Max whispered. "Go check it right now. Like, this instant. Watch the video."

Aria rushed to her room just as Derek emerged from the steamed-up bathroom in his ankle-length navy blue bathrobe. Thank you, he mouthed to her, glancing back at Max. The wood-paneled hallway smelled like a mix of watermelon hand soap and burnt toaster waffle. Aria nodded hectically and shut her door. She waited for her laptop to turn on. Ten, nine, eight, she counted. Facebook. Log in. She checked her messages. There were a list of links from Max; blogs, YouTube videos, podcasts, all based on aliens in some way. WATCH THIS! The most recent message said. She clicked on the link. A man—young in the face, but gray haired—looked straight into the camera. "I'm going to tell you a story," he said. Aria turned the volume down a little. "I'm going to tell you how I got here." He had big lips and the words seemed to get caught in them. A deep breath scratched at the microphone. "I don't care if you believe me or not, because it's true. And if I'm the only one who remembers, then at least I've saved this record of it. You know. Saved it on the interwebs." He smiled. His front teeth were very long. "My, my. Let's see. Deeyae. That was the name of my planet. They used to call me Rhamnus."

Rhamnus was from Lorpan, two islands over from Shre, where he grew up alongside two foster-brothers. When he was older he apprenticed as a boat-builder. "I know it's weird to think that they have boats there too, but our planets have so much in common. It's not even funny."

He was returned to Earth at around age seventeen. "On Deeyae I was much older, because the years are shorter. But when I came here I suddenly knew that I was seventeen in Earth years. I knew other things too. It was like someone shoved all this new information in my brain. But that doesn't mean they deleted the old information."

The door swung open. Aria slapped her laptop closed, but it was only Max. "Did you watch it?" he whispered. "Oh my god, it's just like you. Everything, down to the names."

"I can't believe it." Aria felt like everything was muffled. She lifted the laptop screen again and waited for it to reload. "Where did you find this?"

The bed squeaked as Max sat on the edge of it. "It was just random, when I got home last night. I was looking through YouTube and I clicked on this one—it was way, way down the list of search results—and I watched the beginning, and when he said Deeyae, I freaked the hell out." Max leaned forward. He rested his elbows on his thighs. "I wanted to wake you up but it was late, anyway. Almost morning."

"There's no way this is a coincidence. Or, not a coincidence. I don't know." Aria clutched her hand over her forehead.

"You mean, there's no way this isn't proof."

"You believe me now. You have to believe me now."

Max nodded. "There's no way. There's no other way. You've never met this guy. How could you have the exact same story? I mean, exactly. Red sky. The name of the sun. The Contact guy."

"His is different, though. Each island has one."

"Whatever! You know what I mean. This is—this is big. This is big as fucking hell. Holy crap!" Max rubbed his hands together, his shoulders scrunched up. He bounced up and down. "Aliens, actual, real, aliens. There's no way. There's no way."

"This means I'm not crazy," Aria said quietly. "This means I'm not—" She stepped over to Max and hugged him around the neck. "*Thank you*," she said. She felt like she could cry, but also that she wouldn't be able to.

She had to meet this guy. Rhamnus. She had to talk to him in person. Were they the only two in the world who remembered? Were they somehow the only two ex-exchangers? She had to learn everything he knew. Finally. Someone who had been to the Festival of the Underworld; someone who had dove through the Waters; someone who had lived beneath Aamsh and Jord.

"Max," she said, pulling back. "Max. You have to come with me."

"God. Holy fucking shit."

"You have to!"

"Contact the guy first." Max pointed to the screen, which was paused on Rhamnus, his plump cheeks puffed up, halfway through a word. "Find out how far he is. He could be in Australia, for all we know. E-mail him. Ask if we can visit." Max rubbed his hands together again. "I have to admit, sometimes, when I thought about all the things you told me about your planet, especially, like, late at night, all alone, I would get really creeped out. And that was just not knowing if it was real. Now that I'm pretty sure—"

"*Pretty sure?*"

"I don't know—as sure as I can get without seeing a real alien. Because, you never know; maybe you and this guy were both part of some governmental experiment or something, and you have the same jacked up memories of something that never really happened."

Aria stopped typing so she could glare at him.

"That's just as likely as your story," he went on.

"I thought you said you believed me now?"

"I don't know. I'm open. This shit is crazy. Just got to think things through, you know? But, fuck. Either way, this is insane."

Aria received a reply to her e-mail by the next morning.

Good morning, Aria.

I'm very happy you wrote me. It's good to hear from another exchanger. That is the intent of my videos, on some level.

As for meeting up, I think it would be best if you came to visit me. I will be having a busy time the next few months and I won't be up for traveling. Feel free to stop by my house any time, as I work from home. If you would be more comfortable meeting in a restaurant, that would be O.K. too. Let me know what works for you and what days you would be interested in. Fridays work best but any day will work. We can talk on the telephone or over Skype but I do prefer meeting in person. Let me know.

Best,
Phillip Jorgensen (A.K.A. Rhamnus)

Aria wrote him back:

Dear Rhamnus,

Thanks for your quick reply! Where do you live? If it's not a far drive, I would love to come meet with you sometime.

Thanks again!
Aria (AKA Agapanthus)

He replied with his address. Aria wanted to yell for Max, but it was Sunday, and he'd headed back to school already. Instead she texted him: Washington! And he replied that they were going, that he would drive her.

Can I tell Mother yet? Aria asked.

No. Max replied, and then the phone buzzed.

"Hello?"

"Do not tell Mom."

Aria shut her bedroom door. "Why? She won't think I'm crazy anymore."

"She doesn't need to know. She'll worry. We'll just tell her we're going on a road trip to Seattle."

"Another road trip," Aria said breathily.

"Another road trip," Max echoed.

They left that weekend. The sky opened like a flower; fiercely blue, cloudless, beautiful. Trees glittered alongside the great interstate freeway; hazy black, like the burnt carcass of a snake. The occasional flick of gravel clinked against the side of the car. Max poured open the air conditioning, while Aria bundled into two sweatshirts. She was nervous, but not because of Rhamnus; she knew she would be nervous about that later, but, for now, meeting him seemed incomprehensible, unimaginable, a dark, blurry blotch on the horizon. For now, she was nervous about the ride with Max. She wanted so badly to redeem herself after the coast trip.

"I'll admit it. It is kind of pretty out here," Aria said with a giddiness spurred by expectation, and not by the scenery.

"It's one of those ignorance is bliss things," Max said. He gripped the steering wheel with one hand so he could rub his nose. "I look at those fields, and all I think of are the invasive weeds in there, the cheatgrass, the dandelions, the wild lettuces, the morning glory, the chickweed. Even the planted stuff, like the grass-seed; it's not that great, if you think about how it's completely annihilated the white oak savannah. That's what this all used to be."

"Mmm," Aria mumbled, nodding even though she didn't know what a white oak savannah was, exactly. Or, at least, she couldn't envision one. "The fields are better than freeways all over, though."

Max laughed. The sound lurched forth from deep in his throat, like phlegm. "Anything is better than freeways all over. Freeways are ugly as hell. Even freeway manufacturers would admit to that."

Silence crept over them. It chased them throughout the car trip as their conversation surged and receded.

"For some reason I didn't realize how long I'd have to be driving," Max said, just outside of Portland. "We still have, like, three hours to go. So that'll be five hours total. Fuck."

They stopped for coffee after they crossed the Columbia River into Washington. The enormous, windy bridge scared Aria a little—with its open sides and the great, gaping river far below—but she didn't say anything. Max glared at the road ahead. Sometimes Aria thought she felt his eyes on the side of her face, but whenever she looked, his head was turned.

In the empty moments between conversations, she tried to think of Aster. What would he be doing, right now? Was there even such a thing as right now—shared time between vast distances in space? Was he swimming in the Waters? She tried to think of the delicate lines around his mouth that remained behind after he smiled, how they gradually smoothed away and evaporated into his pale skin. She tried to imagine how their lives would have been if she'd stayed just a little longer. But there was some strange pressure in her chest when she tried to feel these things; something that felt forced, or forgotten. Sometimes she found herself imagining Aster with red skin. Brilliant, saturated maroon like the light of Imn filtered between clouds.

"Head north," a stiff, woman's voice emanated from Max's phone, which he'd propped up in the cup holder.

"Head north? Shut up, lady. Been heading north for three hours," Max spat.

"Do we even need this on anymore?"

"I just need it to know which exit to get off. And if I turn it off now I'll forget about it, and then we'll end up in Canada."

"Alright," Aria said. She leaned back into the seat. Earlier in their trip she would've said more. She would have teased him, said he liked hearing the lady's voice. Instead she resumed her window gazing. Her thoughts turned to Dr. Wendell. She'd almost told him about all of this. Almost.

"Anything else you want to talk about?" he'd asked on her last visit.

She stared at his glasses on top of his head. The magnified strands of hair sticking out. "Well, there is something," she said, and she clenched her hands together in her lap, and she told him about her fascination with *Ancient Aliens*, and her blog, all her research, which, until then, only Max had known about. She wasn't sure why she decided to do this; why now, why right when all her work had paid off, just days before she was about to visit Rhamnus? And she came so close to telling him about that, too— part of her wanted to prove to him that Deeyae was not a cushio- ny false reality her brain had invented. But then Aria remembered the quick shake of Max's head when she'd wanted to tell Mother. So she told Dr. Wendell only half the truth; the pre-Rhamnus truth.

"So we can tell that you're still relying heavily on this—" Dr. Wendell pressed his hand over his lips, and burped or coughed or swallowed or something. "Excuse me. This manifestation. I think it's safe to say that you prefer the false reality to the real one." He nodded slowly, as though he wanted Aria to nod along with him. She breathed in heavily, because she knew this would make it seem like she was thinking about what he was saying. The room smelled like eucalyptus and a faint, foody savoriness.

"My advice to you," Dr. Wendell continued—he smiled as he spoke—"my great, general, key-to-happiness, is to be present, to

forgive those around you, and, more importantly, to forgive yourself. Every moment. Forgive yourself."

"For what? I had no say in it. I had no say in any of it."

"Exactly. Forgive yourself for that. Forgive yourself for being
human."

"I wish I wasn't," Aria said, and each word tightened, withdrew
into the empty pocket at the back of her throat.

"But you are. No matter what, you are."

She clenched her teeth together. Her underarms began to
sweat. Although she wanted to look away, she forced herself to
stare at Dr. Wendell. His eyes were red, cloudy. He wasn't supposed to get tired. He was supposed to always be there, behind
that desk, in his big chair. He wasn't supposed to sit awake at
night and look at the streetlight out the window, or put the TV
on mute while he tried to sleep. Maybe he wore his stupid glasses
on his head as a distraction. Maybe he didn't want to be human,
either.

Max coughed. "I think you need to prepare yourself a little.
I mean, there's always the possibility that this guy told you what
you wanted to hear. Maybe he saw your website first, and then he
made a video saying all the same stuff."

"But his video was dated before mine."

"He could've faked it. You never know."

"You're too skeptical."

"I'm just being realistic. This isn't something that happens every day. Or, like, ever."

More silence. Gas station bag of tortilla chips-scented silence.
Stuffy hours-old-air-scented silence. Aria closed her eyes to pretend she was asleep. She opened them again when the phone voice
told them which exit to take. It was late, late afternoon. Aria was
hungry for dinner already. They drove down a street of widely
spaced one-story buildings; a thrift store, a laundromat, a movie
theater, a car dealership, a pawn shop, two Mexican restaurants,
one of which had an inflatable parrot tied to the roof.

"Turn left on Thoroughgood Avenue," the woman said. "Then, turn right on Maple Drive."

The tick of the turn signal. After a moment: "Your destination will be on the left."

Max parked along the street, parallel to the dry grass lawn. There was a big, square mailbox outside her door. Metal, locked up with a key.

Aria unbuckled her seatbelt very slowly. "We're here," she said. "We are actually here."

Max tilted his head toward the car door as if to say, let's get out. He pressed his palms into his back and stared at the sky. "He knows we're coming, right?"

"Max," Aria huffed. She shook her head.

"Well he said we could come pretty much any time. So I wanted to make sure he knew this was the time we chose."

"I e-mailed him last week. He knows." She adjusted her jeans and pulled her sweatshirt lower over her hips. "He's probably in there waiting for us. I guess I'll knock on the door?"

It was a surprisingly hollow knock for such a large and darkly colored door. A terracotta pot with a dead, shriveled vine was situated next to the welcome mat—a woven rainbow of ragged cloths tinged with chunks of forgotten dirt.

"Hi there," a woman wearing glasses answered the door.

"Oh, is this—does Rhamnus live here?"

"He absolutely does. He just ran to the store for a second there—come on in, come on in. He wanted to get some refreshments for you all. I would've gone but Lydia was crying, and it was easier this way." The woman stepped back as Aria and Max joined her in the hallway. "Although, in hindsight, maybe it wasn't actually easier. Anyway. He told me your names, but I can't quite remember."

"Oh. I'm Aria." She shook the lady's hand.

"I'm Max. I don't know if he even knew I was coming."

"Okay, okay, that's fine. And you guys are—" she pointed one finger at each of them

"Brother and sister," Max said.

"Okay—okay. I'm Shelly. And that little bugger in there is Lydia." She pointed to a half closed door; yellow walls inside. "She's taking a nap now. But don't worry, she's a heavy sleeper."

Aria noticed that Shelly had clear, plastic guards over her teeth—retainers? They made her smile shine in an off, man-nequin-like way. Or maybe they made her teeth look dull and stained. Some combination of both. This is how the rest of the house felt, too. It smelled like powder and old banana peels, but the beige carpets were perfectly clean, still pale with vacuum lines, and the leather couches in the living room felt smoother than any Aria had ever felt.

"Aren't they just buttery?" Shelly said, rubbing the back of one. "We bought them not too long ago, so I'm still waiting for them to get that worn-in feel. The pillows too. You know, they just need to feel lived in. Sometimes I feel like I'm in a furniture show-room. But anyway. You guys are more than welcome to sit down, if you feel like it. I think I just heard the laundry buzz—I better go check on it. I put some delicates in there that will wrinkle if they're left too long. But please—let me know if you need any-thing. I'm right down the hall." Shelly turned and lumbered lithely across the carpet, her thin hair tied back with a mustard-brown, patterned scrunchie.

"I can't believe he's married," Max whispered. "I thought he'd be some sketchy dude living in a basement or something."

"Yeah, it's all pretty normal. I thought—I don't know. I didn't imagine it like this." Aria wiped her palms on her thighs. The couch shook as she tapped her foot up and down. She looked around—a plastic CD tower against the wall, dust gathered on its top; a jean jacket slung across the arm of the other couch; the window, the neighbor's trashcan, the leaf blower coughing farther down the street.

Max turned to her, still whispering. His breath smelled like mustard. "Aria, if you want to talk to him just the two of you, I can sit out in the car."

"No, it's fine."

"I'm not going to know what's going on anyway. All your alien talk. I'll just be in the way."

"It's not all alien talk, Max." She wanted him there. That's all there was to it; she wanted him there. "Just stay and listen. Maybe you'll learn something. Plus I need someone here to be proof, you know? So everyone will know I'm not just making this up."

Max's pale eyebrows scrunched together. "Everyone? Who's everyone?"

The door crashed open. Keys jingled. Paper bags crinkled. Rhamnus and Shelly's voices murmured. "They're *something something* and I told *something something something something* and *something* couch."

Aria held her breath. She glanced at Max.

Rhamnus turned the corner, fresh in a white t-shirt. He looked much stronger than in his YouTube video—his arms were thick and grooved, but also cumbersome, like logs. His gray hair looked fluffy and straight. He smiled at them.

"Agapanthus." He stopped, hands at his sides. "Agapanthus. You never told me your second name."

Aria wasn't sure if she should stand up too. She uncrossed her legs but remained seated. "They call me Aria here."

"No, I meant—Deeyae—"

"Oh. I was Agapanthus Caracynth." She said each word very distinctly, as though they no longer went together.

Rhamnus smiled again. His teeth—yellow compared to Shelly's retainered smile—pushed out from his fleshy lips. "Agapanthus Caracynth." In heavy-breathing silence, he rested a cold hand on her forehead.

"Rhamnus—"

"Porovae."

"Rhamnus Porovae." Agapanthus returned the gesture.

"Always good to revisit the old ways," Rhamnus said. He sat on the other couch and looked at Max. "Oh, and you—did I double book, so to speak? You're not Galium?"

Max's eyes flickered between Aria and Rhamnus.

"You're not an exchanger too?" Rhamnus went on. He flapped his hands in front of his chest as he spoke.

"No, he's not. He's my Earth brother," Aria said quickly, angrily. He was not an exchanger. He was not like her because she was not like him. Not just any human could be an exchanger. There were Deeyans and then there were exchangers and then there were plain-old-humans.

"Just wanted to make sure. I'm meeting with another former-exchanger next week and I wanted to make sure I didn't mess up the dates and you didn't both show up at the same time."

"So there's others?"

"Of course there's others. Thousands. Millions."

"But do they all—why doesn't everyone—"

"Know about it? The great magnificent Deeyae? Why are the earthlings not worshipping us? Why is this world not ripe with Deeyan knowledge? It's because of the transfer process. They wipe memories." He tapped the side of his forehead, just above his ear. "Only sometimes it doesn't work. We're all a bunch of flukes. As you know very well." He paused. When Aria said nothing, he continued. "Unless you were awakened?"

"What?"

"Guess not."

"Wait—awakened?"

"Hypnotized, essentially. It's the only other way to get the memories back. The suppressed Deeyan memories. And to flush out those false ones—memorganda, I like to call it."

"Oh?"

"It's funny. I sat in on a session once that my exchanger buddy was doing. He actually saw and recognized this guy that he'd known on Deeyae, but the guy didn't recognize him, of course, so he acted all normal with the guy, got him to come over, we were having a barbecue, and then my friend just said—" Rhamnus's chin lowered and his register deepened as he switched to Deeyan— "*now you will remember.* That was it. That was all it took. The guy said it was like everything was clear to him again."

"Was your friend the first person to try that?" Max asked. "It seems so random. How did he know what to do?" He glared heavily at Rhamnus as if to say *I don't believe you.*

"Oh, no, it's been in practice for some time. Who knows who came up with it? It's old knowledge, passed on and on."

Aria nodded. She brushed her hair away from her cheeks. This was too much at once. She'd had so many questions; she'd thought of them each night as she tried to fall asleep, but now she couldn't think of anything. "So do you meet a lot of exchangers? That find you? From the videos?"

"Sure, sure."

Shelly walked in with a cup in each hand and a third pressed into the crook of her arm. She handed one to each of them; ice water with lemon. There was no coffee table, so Aria balanced the transpiring cup on her lap. She mouthed *thank you* to Shelly, but her head was already turned, and then she was gone.

"I know you might think there's some underground ex-exchanger community, but there's really not. People like to find out that there's others like them, but they don't really like to go past that. There's only one group I can think of, really, and they're pretty hardcore. But they're—" he shook his head. Sipped his water. "You probably just wanted to reminisce?"

"No, no. Keep going."

Rhamnus rested his ankle against his thigh. His foot seemed incredibly large, in its long, bulky tennis shoe. "There's a group that goes around and awakens—you know, the hypnosis thing—awakens exchangers. And they want to get enough people to make a big stink about it. Get the word out. Safety in numbers. They want some recognition, see. They don't just want to know, they want others to know. They want the government to know. The media. But they haven't done anything big. Yet. Probably because, like I said, most exchangers aren't interested in collaboration."

"Why?" Aria asked. "I mean, what reasons do they give?"

"I don't understand it either way. If word gets out, great. If not, who cares. I don't see what good it'll do."

"Don't you think They would be more likely to notice if people made a big deal out of it?"

"They? You mean the Gods?"

"Or the Contacts."

"All of the powers-that-be over there, They see everything already. They know that some of us remember Deeyae. If They were going to retaliate, keep things quiet, They would have done so by now. You can bet that, if They wanted it, people would start disappearing, and not for a return trip to Deeyae. The Gods are powerful. They can take your life away when you're on the Water Planet just as easily as They can on Deeyae. No use messing with them."

Aria stared at her hands. Her fingernails. The slight chip of dirt under her thumb. What could she even say to that? What could she say? "You miss it, though?"

"What, Deeyae?"

"Yeah. Home."

"Why do you think I have that YouTube channel?" He smiled at the floor. "It's not all bad here, Agapanthus," he said stiffly. Then he leaned forward. "Let me tell you. I couldn't actually remember, at first. When I first got here. It took me a few days. I remembered vague things, but no details. And it was like, like the whole world had opened up, like the sky was finally the right color, like, even though it was summer, there was finally some distant chill to the wind. I hadn't known I'd missed those things until I was surrounded by them. And I just walked around in this weird daze, a little ways out of town, by where my childhood house used to be. I walked in circles, thinking Earth was so much like Deeyae and yet it had that something that Deeyae had been missing. That tether, that pull. I don't know, really. All I know is that, when the stars came out on the first of those nights, no clouds at all, new moon, and I looked up at all of them, I remembered Deeyae. Just like that." Rhamnus smiled delicately, eyes still on the carpet, the corners of his mouth pressing up into his cheeks. He exhaled. "*Now you will remember.*"

"Are they really the same stars you used to see?" Max asked. "How far away is Deeyah?"

"Deeyae," Aria corrected him.

"You can see it from here," Rhamnus said. "Well, you can see Imn."

"Imn?" Max repeated.

"Our home sun," Aria said. "I told you that."

"Follow the constellation Scorpius to its tail, and there ye will find it."

"Aamsh and Jord, too?" Aria asked.

"Imn, Aamsh and Jord, the glow of Deeyae, they all roll into one, from this distance. All it looks like is one, single, faint star." Rhamnus rested his water glass on the floor and then leaned back. The couch creaked. He crossed his ruddy-skinned arms over his chest. Aria suddenly noticed how freckled they were.

"How could you possibly know which star is your star?" Max asked. "There's no way you could possibly know that."

"That friend I was talking about earlier? He got pretty intense about everything. Did some mathematical equation or something."

"What, is he a fucking genius?"

"Well he managed to slim down the possibilities to the Alpha Centauri system or the Gliese star system. I don't remember how he narrowed it down from there. Something about sun strength and distance from Earth, the size of the planet, light intensity, intervals, I don't know. And he tied it in with all this ancient knowledge, all this stuff passed down by other exchangers. But you can see it—Gliese 667 according to scientists. You can see it with the naked eye. Look for it next time you're away from light pollution."

"Doesn't that remind you of the Festival of the Stars?" Aria said.

"Oh, sure it does. Festival of Stars every night out here."

Max snorted. "You're pretty close to the city, here. Suburbs, right? Try farther out, like east of the Cascades. Then you'll see stars. I've been camping out there a few times. There are so many stars it makes me dizzy."

Suddenly Rhamnus leaned back over the couch, his head turned. He shouted down the hallway: "Shelly!" Then he waved an arm toward his torso, nodding, eyes wide. Shelly sat down next to him.

"Shelly grew up in New Mexico. She saw stars all the time."

"Milky Way like you've never seen it," she said, her eyes on the ceiling. And on a very clear night, on a new moon, way out there in the desert, I don't think there's anywhere that can beat that. I really don't."

"You should tell them about the time—"

"Oh, on the horse trip?" Shelly crossed her legs. "Okay, okay. Well, I was out on a solo camping trip, me and Ferddie—my horse—and I think I was only, what, fourteen? We walked along all day, just out in the middle of nowhere, just walking to walk. It started to get all hushed and blue and all, just after sunset, and then, I *swear*, as soon as I hopped down off of Ferddie to make camp, and I looked up at one of the mesas over there, I *swear* I saw the northern lights."

"Wow," Aria said.

Max sat up straighter. "Are you sure? I don't think it's possible to see them that far south."

"Trust me, I've played this over and over again in my head. A million times. The sunset was over already. What else could it have been? And it was just like the pictures, moving red ribbons, just out of nowhere, a little like waves breaking. It gave me goosebumps, watching it. And then, just like that, it was gone. They were ghosts. Ghosts in the sky."

"Isn't that beautiful," Rhamnus said. "I love that story."

Suddenly Aria wanted to leave. She wanted to run out of there with this leg strength she still wasn't used to—something else she could talk about with Rhamnus but didn't want to—and she wanted to drive home and somehow shrivel into blackness, shrivel up, shrivel up, until she no longer existed.

"Well," Aria said, and she looked at Max.

"Are you ready?" Max asked her.

"It's a long drive back," Aria said, looking at Rhamnus.

"Oh, are you sure? You can stay for dinner if you like," Rhamnus said.

"No. We should head back," Aria nodded. "But thank you." She knew she should probably give him a hug or at least shake his hand, but instead she stood, readjusted her pants, smiled at Shelly and Rhamnus, said, "Thank you so much," in a high, emphatic voice, and waited at the car door for Max to unlock it. The sun was just now setting—purple at the highest, frayed-out clouds. Aria hadn't realized how stuffy their house was until the cool air replaced it.

"We were only in there like five minutes." Max unlocked the car. "Are you sure you want to drive back in the dark?"

"You're the one driving," Aria said.

"That's what I mean. But whatever. We can go back now, if you really want."

"What else would you want to do? Stay in a hotel? Stay with *Rhamnus?*"

"Aria. Chill the fuck out. We'll go back now." He started the car, and it growled and churned. Max turned on the radio, but it was static, since the stations were different in Washington. He turned it off again.

They drove through the muffled silence of early night. The sidewalk was partially lit up by solar-powered garden lights at the edges of someone's lawn. A man was holding a hose above his head to reach a hanging basket of flowers. Even through the closed windows, Aria could smell the wet pavement.

"So how do you think it went?" Max asked.

"I don't know," Aria said quickly. She rested her head against the muggy window.

Max said nothing back, which inexplicably annoyed Aria. Everything annoyed her. She glared at the mounting darkness, the dark purples and blues that slowly burned to gray, and the falsely orange signs of gas stations and two-story motels with decorative wire balconies you couldn't even walk on. She hated it all, absolutely everything. And there was the sun, just beyond her shoulder, a red mound burying itself into the grass. The color of Imn.

There was so much to process. The hypnosis thing and the thousands of other ex-exchangers, the watching Gods, the ominousness of it all. Rhamnus and his wife and baby.

Aria knew, then, that she was never going back. Leera, Pittick, Imari, Sonlo, probably Aster, too—she would never see them again. She felt like a seed that had been plucked from some tropical plant and then buried in the desert, expected to grow, far from water, far from the humid air of her birth. People had come and watered her and talked to her and tried to coax her from the ground, but she still refused to sprout. Maybe she couldn't. Or maybe she needed to adapt. Maybe she had already died, and was stunted, and would never again leave the soil.

"Stop the car, Max," Aria said suddenly. "Please, stop the car."

"We're on the freeway, I can't just stop the car."

"It's empty. No one else is behind us. Just pull over."

"Why? Do you have to take a shit?"

"Max, pull the fucking car over, I want to get out!"

Max turned on his emergency blinkers and parked on the side. "What, there's a bunch of fields here. What? *What?*"

Aria wrapped her arms around her chest. She stared at the sky. "Stars," she said. "I wanted to see the stars."

Max stood next to her. The grass ticked against their calves, and their feet sunk into the wet, soddy dirt of the field. Behind the wind, Aria heard crickets or frogs. The field spread before them, dark, breathing, alive. And the stars.

"Where's Scorpius?" Aria whispered.

"Scorpio? I don't know. You're the alien."

"Use your phone. You have that star map thing."

Exhaling, Max held up his phone. "Looks like we can't really see it from here."

"Give me that. You're doing it wrong." Aria grabbed his phone. She compared the star map to the real thing—the few bright, painful dots, and the faint shudderings of light between them, nothing but impressions, transitions, smudges. "There's so many more on here than in the sky."

"It's called light pollution. Even out here, we're close enough to Portland."

Aria shoved the phone back into Max's hands. Her eyes felt hot.

"Don't get upset. I drove you all the way out here. And back. I spent a whole day driving for you. Be grateful."

Aria wiped the tears from her cheeks but pretended she was scratching an itch. She kept her mouth straight. Maybe he wouldn't be able to tell she was crying. "Well I'm sorry I can't just force myself to be happy.

"And, you know," she went on, not giving him the chance to respond, "I remember reading once, somewhere, that if there's a sun storm you can see the northern lights anywhere on Earth."

Max nodded. He stuffed his phone back into his pocket. Another car drove past them down the freeway. It stunk like old rubber.

They were silent for a long, stretched-out moment, before Max spoke again. "If it makes you feel any better, I saw this old TV show once. *Cosmos.* Not the new one, the old one. With Carl Sagan. We watched it in my high school science class. I always remembered this one thing he said. That the stars made up all of the elements that make up everything else. You, me. Trees. Sand. Starstuff, something like that. We are all starstuff. So if you think of it that way, if you think of it like everything's connected, everything comes from the same place."

"If you think of it that way, doesn't everywhere become less special? Everywhere is anywhere?"

"No. That just means everywhere is beautiful. Everywhere is sacred."

Aria looked again at the stars. She sat on the grass, leaned back, and counted the lights, the worlds, the universes. "Let's stay here for awhile," Aria said. "Just to look."

"I don't think you're going to see—"

"No. I just want to look."

8

AGE: TWENTY-SIX EARTH-YEARS

Aria watched the sky darken behind the windows of the airport. The cloud-swaddled winter sunset blew itself out, nothing but a whisper, nothing but a flame doused before anyone but Aria noticed it. The night was replaced by the glare of lights against glass.

She didn't like the idea of flying at night. It felt somehow unnatural, although there had never really been anything natural about airplanes in the first place. The way she thought of it, though, was that most birds didn't fly at night. Owls, nightjars, sure—but not the long-distance travelers. Not geese, not terns, not turkey vultures. When she'd told Max this before she left, Max had said, "Well that's not true. There's hummingbirds. And warblers. They migrate at night."

"How do you even know that? You study plants."

"Birds need plants. Plants need birds. It's a partnership. I've got to know about all of it."

But most birds didn't fly at night. There must be a reason for that.

The very pale woman behind the desk brought her lips to a square microphone. "We'd like to welcome our standard coach passengers on board Alaska Airlines Flight 2544 with service to Denver." Her voice was nasally and airy. People started lining up—an old woman whose floral perfume cluttered the waiting area; a man wearing light-blue jeans and tennis shoes, carrying a sleeping toddler on his back; a woman with very dark skin and a long nose, her hair and half her forehead hidden under a plain black cloth. Aria watched all of them. She was in no hurry. This was her first time flying. From Denver she would take a plane to Miami, where Father would be waiting for her "just outside the security area," as his text said. *Can't wait to see you.*

Aria slumped on her backpack. She held out her wrinkled ticket for the lady to scan. "Thank you," Aria said, but the lady was already looking back to the next passenger.

Cold air leaked through the walls leading up to the plane. It smelled like plastic, with a slight tinge of gasoline. Aria hurried to her seat. 21B. A guy about her age—maybe a little younger—stared out the window. She sat next to him. "Hi," she said.

"Got stuck with the middle seat, huh?" the guy answered. Aria decided he might actually be older than her, despite his round cheeks, and the light-pink babyishness of his mouth. She could smell the fake, orange scent of the gel his hair was combed with. It was arranged so it peaked at the front.

"I didn't even realize," she said. "I've never been on a plane before."

"*Never?*" The guy sat his phone on his lap.

"First time." Aria smiled and held up her chin.

The guy smiled back. He looked at his phone for a second. Then he stood up, pulling down his button-up shirt to cover the exposed sliver of his lower back. "Here," he said with a tilt of his head. "You should sit here. Get the experience. Window seat's always the best."

"Oh no, that's okay—"

"No, no, no. Come on. If it's your first flight, you've *got* to have the window seat." He stepped sloppily over Aria's knees and hunched in the aisle, one hand on the back of the seat. "Seriously, now, don't make me look silly for getting up like this."

Aria laughed. It came out small but not suppressed, from the throat. She slid over. "There won't be much to see at night," Aria said. She hugged her backpack to her stomach. "But thank you."

"Nope. That's where you're wrong," the guy said. "The trick with flying at night is you have to look up. Trust me. It's a decent enough view during the day, but at night? All those stars."

"Well, thank you. So much." Aria shifted to look out the window. All those stars. All those lights. All those other beings, those other skies, those other oceans, those rock-laden expanses. All that distance between. All that empty, dead space where nothing lived. If only she had never loved Deeyae. Maybe, then, it would be easier to live here. If only she had never loved Leera and Pittick. She hadn't yet learned to love them from afar. That certain love of not knowing; that love of hopefulness; that love of entrenched distance, saturated into her being, inescapable, but not crushing. And with Aster—with Aster there was always some small hope that they would meet on Earth.

"And, here." He handed her a square of gum, unwrapped, like a naked white tooth in his palm. "So your ears don't pop."

"Thank you so much," Aria said.

The plane built speed. It rumbled, pulled up. Aria concentrated on chewing her gum.

"Look, you can still kind of see the Columbia," the guy said. He pointed to the window, over her shoulder.

Aria squinted out. Her hands were tight on the armrests. "I think I see it? That line, over there? Oh, I think I see a ship on it."

"Yeah, that one," the guy said, pointing again. "It's kind of hard to see in the dark."

"It's too bad we won't be able to see the mountains, either," Aria said. "I saw Mt. Hood on the drive to the airport, but I'm sure it looks even better from the air."

"Mmhmm. Hood, Helens, Adams, maybe even Rainier. You can see them all. I think Mt. Jefferson, too?"

"There's nothing like that in Eugene."

"Is that where you live?"

Aria told him about their home in the fields, the sheep surrounding them. She told him how she had just graduated community college because she'd gotten a late start, and how she didn't know what was next. She told him about Max, the soon-to-be-botanist, and about Mother, and Derek, and how she was going to be staying with Father in Florida for three weeks. Everything seemed simple as she explained it to him. Simple and comfortable, and even secure. This would not be taken away from her. And as soon as she got a job she would be caught up for her age. She would be normal in some small way. And eventually she would probably stop seeing Dr. Wendell, and maybe live on her own in a little apartment in the city, and meet up with Max for hikes on the weekends. Maybe she would get a scholarship and finish out her Bachelor's degree at a four-year school—Ecology? Environmental science? Geology? Maybe she would travel; somewhere she could see the stars without light pollution.

Eventually the conversation drifted away. The guy fell asleep with his headphones on. His lips were slightly parted and his nose whistled with each breath. Aria continued to stare out the window. The stars unfurled themselves, like flowers waking to the sun. There weren't very many, but the ones that shone were unusually bright.

It was still dark when they arrived in Denver. "It was nice meeting you," the guy said as he pressed his way into the aisle.

"You too." Aria's voice was rough and groggy, although she hadn't even fallen asleep. She cleared her throat.

"I hope you had a good first flight. You didn't seem too scared or anything."

"No. It was fine."

"Well, awesome." He pulled a black rolling suitcase from the overhead bin. His elbow almost hit the middle-aged woman behind him in the face, but he didn't notice. "Did you have anything up here?" he asked Aria.

"No, just my backpack."

"Traveling light. I like it."

"Not really." She laughed. "I just checked in my bag."

The line started moving.

"Have a good rest of your trip," Aria said as he shuffled forward, ahead of her.

"You too," he said over his shoulder. Both of his hands trailed behind him on the rolling suitcase.

She wondered if she should have asked his name, but it didn't matter anymore. Aria joined the back of the plane-exiting horde. Her next flight didn't board for another hour. She wandered the desolate airport, which smelled like a whirling blend of coffee, French fries, and hand sanitizer. Very seldom in the past few years had she been on her own like this. In her room, next to the stream, on the way to class—that was it, and they didn't seem to count, because they were tentative moments in which she was waiting to be interrupted, waiting to be intruded upon. Here, among emptiness and strangers, she was safely alone. It reminded her of the Waters. The swept-over feeling of swimming across the channel.

She found her gate and sat in one of the stiff, black chairs. Someone had left a McDonald's soda cup beneath it. Aria crossed her legs and hugged her backpack again. It was paisley, made of a thick cotton, with leather straps hanging from the top. She'd bought it with Mother at the Saturday Market, from an old man wearing a vest made of the same fabric, his whole booth decorated with purses and tote bags and wallets. After they walked around all the booths, she and Mother had sat at a wooden bench beneath an oak tree, where they ate pizza from one of the vendors. Goat cheese, artichoke, and wild mushroom with a fennel-arugula pesto. A trio of gray-haired women played mandolin music on the stage. And through all of it was this breeze, this wonderful, summer breeze carrying campfire scents and the staleness of sunlight.

Aria knew, then, that she would never tell Mother about Rhamnus. She would never tell Mother that she knew for sure, without a doubt, that her memories of Deeyae were true, that she had never been kidnapped by druggies. Because either way Mother would feel guilty for letting Aria wander away. And, either way, it wasn't Mother's fault, not really. Max was right. Telling Mother wouldn't help anything, and, even if she met Rhamnus, Mother still wouldn't let herself believe that her daughter had grown up on another world. Neither would Father. And what good would it do for them to know?

Two voices cut through the footsteps and whirring airport noises. Aria shifted around in her seat. A blonde woman wearing diamond hoop earrings. A man, back turned, with a bulky heft to his arms. His stature reminded Aria of a Deeyan. Like a mini version of Sonlo, except with tan-white skin and hair the color of coffee beans. He turned his head to the side. His nose was thick. Long eyelashes dolloped up and down as he blinked. His eyes were yellow, gold, brown, red, bound together in a beautiful shade of honey.

"Aster," Aria said so quietly the words didn't carry beyond her lips. She covered her mouth with her hands, leaned forward in her seat. Her backpack fell.

It was him. Aria stood up. With her mouth open she stepped toward him. Her hand was suddenly on his shoulder. Aster. It was him. Really him.

"Hi?" Aster said, eyes wide. His voice was no deeper than before. He glanced at the blonde woman. Together they forced a smile. They waited.

He didn't remember her. He didn't remember Deeyae.

Yet she had found him here. She had found him. This was it. He'd been sent back and somehow they had been pushed together. Of all the people and places in the world, they had found each other.

His hair was longer than it used to be, but his face was just the same. He seemed flatter in this lighting. Under Imn he had been warmer, heftier, graceful. Here he seemed sporadic. Like lightning. Always shifting, feet readjusting, knees locking and unlocking, fingers tapping against his thigh. There was a distance in his eyes. Something irretrievable.

Now you will remember. If she said those words purposefully, sliced them into his ear, her hot breath melting against his skin, then he would remember. Just like that he would be Aster again. Aster, who she had gathered stones with. Aster, who she had floated naked next to in the Waters. Aster, who had kissed her cheek at the top of the cliffs. Who would he be, here? Who was this woman in the flowy turquoise top with French-manicured nails, who he edged closer to as the silence drew on?

Aster was free. He didn't have to think back to the cruelties of his foster-father. There was no ache of displacement. No sadness, no homesickness, no loss of control. *Now you will remember.* Whoever he had become, he wasn't Aster. No, to Aria, Aster would always mean Deeyae. She could not be with him without being stuck there forever. He could not exist apart from the Waters, the red sand, the warm wind. Maybe he wouldn't want to remember. Maybe she didn't want him to either.

"Sorry," she said. "I thought you were someone else."

She walked past them, toward the drinking fountains in front of the restrooms. By the time she returned to her seat, Aster and the blonde woman were gone. *Did you know I swam the rite of passage?* she wanted to ask. She wished she could reach back to the old Aster just for a moment, just one minute, and ask him if he was proud of her. If he knew all their work paid off. But did it matter? She had done it. She had those memories, and she knew that she had proved herself.

The next plane ride passed quickly. She fell asleep this time, and she woke with the thud of the landing. A wonderful heat sunk into the plane. She met with her father at the edge of the security area, just as he'd said. He looked healthier, plumper, more tangible than she remembered. "There you are," he said into her neck as they hugged. "There's my girl." He handed her a little polka-dot bag stuffed with blue tissue paper. "Open it," he said, pausing as the bag crinkled. "Just something small."

Inside was a tiny notebook decorated with metallic stripes. "Thank you, Father," she said. She held it up.

"Just something small," he repeated. Then he led her to the parking lot, never moving his arm from around her shoulders. He smelled sharp and sweet today, like rum and laundry detergent.

His apartment was clean. Modern, leather chairs, stainless steel kitchen, empty white walls. There was only one window, which looked out at a streetlight and the leaves of a palm tree—palm trees were everywhere. She couldn't stop staring up at them as she and Father walked to the beach the next day.

"I like the sound they make," she said. "When the wind blows through them." She could hear the ocean already, too, over car noises, and humming buildings.

"Thank God for the wind. It's humid today. You came at a good time, with this heat wave. Can you believe this is December?"

Why had she been worried about coming here? She loved it. The air smelled constantly like rain, but it was unrelentingly warm. The sky was furrowed by clouds. The light continued to shift, casting shadows upon the sidewalk, upon the sand. She tossed off her sandals. Father did too.

The ocean was a blue she had never seen before, transparent and calm, its shallows crowded with a colorful wash of bathing suits. Farther out, along the horizon, the blue deepened, smoothed out, glistened. The ocean seemed one large, sprawling entity, alive, powerful, but ancient enough to know kindness; ancient like the mountains, ancient like the sky, and the stars, like the Waters and the cliffs beyond.

Aria let the warm water splash up to her legs. Then she brought her arms over her head, she pushed off, and she sprang into the soft ocean. And, finally, she held her breath, and she swam.

ABOUT THE AUTHOR

Francesca G. Varela was raised in Oregon's Willamette Valley. In 2015 she graduated from the University of Oregon with degrees in Environmental Studies and Creative Writing, and she then went on to receive her master's degree in Environmental Humanities from the University of Utah.

Francesca's dream of becoming an author began in third grade, and her writing career had an early start; she wrote her award-winning first novel, *Call of the Sun Child,* when she was only 18 years old, and she wrote her second novel, *Listen,* when she was only 20.

When not writing or reading, Francesca enjoys playing piano, figure skating, hiking, identifying wild birds, plants, and constellations, and travelling to warm, sunny places whenever she can.

visit her at www.francescavarela.com

CPSIA information can be obtained
at www.ICGtesting.com
Printed in the USA
LVOW10s0607260518
578593LV00004B/5/P

AUG 23 2018

man lives.' The park features a serene lake with fishing, swimming and canoe and pedal boat rental; a 7½-mile mountain bike trail; and a few hiking trails totaling 12 miles. Smith Creek is a fine trout stream. Special programs are offered throughout the year, including live music and storytellers on Saturday evenings during the summer and fall. There are also bluegrass and mountain living festivals.

Accommodations include 84 campsites that cost $16 to $18; a nearby trading post sells the basics. A comfortable 100-room lodge/conference center rents rooms for $69 to $134, and 30 one- to three-bedroom barrel-shaped cabins for $95 to $160, plus 12% tax. For reservations, call ☎ 800-573-9659.

The lodge dining room serves breakfast, lunch and dinner at moderate prices. A gift shop sells crafts and regional travel books. There's no standard visitors center here; go to the lodge for information.

A $2 ParkPass is required to enter the park.

ANNA RUBY FALLS & SCENIC AREA

These falls, near Unicoi State Park off GA Hwy 356, occur where two creeks originating atop Tray Mountain plunge 50 and 153 feet over a precipice, joining at the bottom and then flowing into Unicoi State Park. A paved 0.4-mile path leads to an observation deck at the foot of the unusual double falls.

The waterfall is surrounding an 1600-acre Anna Ruby Falls Scenic Area. A 4½-mile trail leads through mountain laurel and rhododendron, crosses several mountain streams and eventually ends at the Unicoi campground.

Rabun County

This county of 15,000 people is a rugged area, with small Appalachian communities, wild white water rafting on the Chattooga River, hiking along the river and a ski resort. It's a dry county: no hard drinks are sold and beer and wine are sold only with

meals. Incorporated towns can overturn this rule and pass their own laws, as did the city of Sky Valley. The population is surprisingly diverse, with many Mexican and East Asian immigrants, but few African Americans.

Information is available at the Tallulah Ranger District Forest Service office (see Clayton, below), or at the Web site www .gamountains.com/rabun. Also contact the Forest Service for mountain biking and trout fishing options. The Rabun County Chamber of Commerce (☎ 706-782-4812), in Clayton, distributes information at their Welcome Center on Hwy 441N.

CHATTOOGA RIVER

Way up high on Whiteside Mountain near Cashiers, North Carolina, cold clear water bubbles up from natural springs and begins its energetic journey to the sea. Melted snow and minor streams join it along the way, forming a powerful tool that carves through stern yet impressionable granite. The Eastern Continental Divide lies along the spine of the Blue Ridge Mountains; here, rivers meet their fate – some will empty into the Atlantic Ocean, others into the Gulf of Mexico. The Chattooga gets an Atlantic Ocean pass and follows the Georgia-Carolina border for another 40 miles to Lake Tugaloo. Starting at an elevation of 3360 feet, the river drops approximately 50 feet per mile to the lake's modest elevation of 891 feet. At times, the river rests in slow-moving pools shaded by hemlock forests, but it soon begins to twist and turn through scattered boulders and narrow gorges, picking up enough speed to plunge effortlessly over steep rock faces.

The Chattooga River is the largest free-flowing mountain river in the southeast and has some of the best white water in the country. Many cliffs, gorges and waterfalls add to the beautiful scenery on the river, and a high rate of rainfall adds to the thrills. The Chattooga's designation as a National Wild and Scenic River prevents motorized vehicles from coming within ¼ mile of its banks, so development is minimal, adding to the pleasantness of the experience.

Things to See & Do

The river is divided into five sections, Section 0 through Section IV. Section 0 is the upper part of the Chattooga River, a rugged stretch closed to boats. Section I is the West Fork, a beautiful area of low falls and deep green pools surrounded by cliffs and forested slopes; the calm Class I water – interrupted by two Class II rapids – is suitable for **tubing, swimming or easy canoeing**.

Sections II through IV contain the white water rafters are looking for. Section II is fairly tame with a Class III rapid. The treacherous rapids of section III might look familiar to movie buffs. *Deliverance* was filmed here and did more damage to the region's reputation than a nuclear reactor spill. Forget the movie's more poignant scenes to concentrate on the 14-mile trip through Class III and IV **rapids** with names like Screaming Left Turn or the Narrows. Near the end awaits Bull Sluice, a Class V rapid. Section III is the one most commonly run by commercial outfitters.

Bull Sluice (near Hwy 76) is a popular put-in for Section IV rafters. The 7-mile stretch of Section IV is for the more experienced rafters and traverses serious Class IV and V rapids such as Sock-Em Dog and Jawbone. Woodall Shoals, a Class VI rapid, has claimed many lives.

The safest way to enjoy the white water is to sign up with a commercial outfitter, all of which are carefully regulated by the federal government. A guide usually accompanies each raft. Trips are offered March through October. Trips of six to seven hours on Section III typically cost $65/75 weekdays/weekends, $20 less at the beginning and end of the season. Section IV trips cost around $80/100 weekdays/weekends, less in the low season. For more information, contact Nantahala Outdoor Center (☎ 800-232-7238, Web site: www.noc.com); Southeastern Expeditions (☎ 800-868-7238, 404-329-0433, Web site: www.southeasternraft.com); or Wild Water Ltd (☎ 800-451-9972, Web site: www.wildwaterrafting.com).

Some adventurers, of course, have gone on the river without using a commercial company, but then, some have died. Only experienced boaters should attempt the river, and even then, only after consulting detailed guidebooks. The Forest Service has strict registration requirements; check with the Clayton office for details (see below). If you want to guide your own boat, you can still join a commercial trip – at least you'll have a margin of safety in the company of their experienced guides.

Numerous **trails** in the area offer plenty to do for hikers, bicyclists and horse riders. The Bartram Trail travels 37 miles from the Chattooga River to the border with North Carolina, with many scenic vistas and waterfalls. Another good option is the 11-mile Chattooga River Trail, beginning where US Hwy 76 meets the river. Most of the trail is within the Wild and Scenic River area. Backcountry campsites are available on both trails. Several short trails lead to waterfalls. For more information, contact the Forest Service's Tallulah Ranger Station (☎ 706-782-3320) in Clayton.

Places to Stay

The Tallulah Ranger District Forest Service office (☎ 706-782-3320), in Clayton, operates seven *campgrounds* in the area – Rabun Beach, Tallulah River, Tate Branch, Sandy Bottom, Wildcat Creek, Sarah's Creek and West Fork. Facilities range from more primitive vault toilets to flush toilets and hot showers. Rabun Beach Campground, off Hwy 441 north of Tallulah Falls, is the largest, with 80 campsites, a bathhouse with hot showers, a beach, boat launch and fishing pier. Sites are $10 to $18. There's nowhere to grab a bite to eat in the Chattooga River area, so you'd better stock up in one of the nearby towns like Clayton.

CLAYTON

pop 2000

This small mountain town makes a decent base for exploring the surrounding mountains, lakes and waterfalls. The historic main street area is only a couple of blocks long, consisting of many old brick buildings alternating between practical (pharmacies, furniture stores) and tourist-oriented (antiques, tea rooms, craft shops) businesses. As with many of Georgia's small towns, the peace is partially ruined by too much auto traffic.

Hwy 76 runs through the town, where it's called Savannah St; the top of the hill is Main St.

The Tallulah Ranger Station of the US Forest Service (☎ 706-782-3320), 809 Hwy 441S, is south of town on Hwy 441, a half mile past the US Hwy 76E intersection. The office sells plenty of maps and hiking and biking books. They can also give you information on trout fishing in the Tallulah River.

In downtown Clayton on N Main St, Virtually Southern Books (☎ 706-212-0014) is one of the best small bookstores in northeast Georgia. It has an excellent selection of regional travel, fiction and nonfiction books, plus bestsellers and lots of mysteries. You can also order books by phone, or over the Web at www.virtuallysouthern.com. It's open 10 am to 5 pm Wednesday through Sunday.

Places to Stay

The hotel tax rate in Clayton is 12% and is not included in the prices quoted here.

Royal Inn (☎ 706-782-4269), on US Hwy 441 a half mile south of Hwy 76E, is a basic, one-story, older-style brick motel in an ugly location on the main highway. But it's one of the cheapest in town, starting at $40 doubles.

A Small Motel (☎ 800-786-0624, 706-782-6488), on US Hwy 76E a half mile from US Hwy 441, is away from the main hotel strip in town, and is popular with rafting groups. All rooms have working fireplaces, are nonsmoking, and a bit dated. The rates start at $49/59 weekdays/weekends.

Days Inn (☎ 800-329-7466, 706-782-4258), at the intersection of US Hwys 441 and 76W, is a modern hotel with standard, decent rooms – it's hardly exciting, and it's located on the ugly hotel strip of 441, but is within two blocks of historic downtown Clayton. Rates start at $49/59 singles/doubles.

Old Clayton Inn (☎ 800-454-3498, 706-782-7722, fax 706-782-2511), on Main St in downtown Clayton, is a cozy historic inn from the mid-1800s, with a spacious and comfortable lobby. The 30 rooms are pleasant but not spectacular. Standard doubles start at $68/78 weekdays/weekends June through September. There's a restaurant on the premises.

The *Beechwood Inn Bed & Breakfast (☎ 706-782-5485),* on Beechwood Dr off US Hwy 76E, is a lovely 1922 house with pine wood floors, wood shingles and a peaceful wraparound porch. Some of the six guest rooms have fireplaces, balconies and good views of Black Rock Mountain. Rates are $85 to $125, higher on holidays and weekends. The inn is open May through October.

Places to Eat

The *Blue Willow Tea Room (☎ 706-782-0790),* in downtown Clayton on Savannah St, features a formal afternoon tea by reservation only, practically a meal in itself (six courses for $13). Tea, scones and desserts are offered throughout the day.

Grapes & Beans (☎ 706-212-0020, 42 E Savannah St) serves basic gourmet coffee (there's no full-service coffee bar, though) and wines (by the bottle or glass). They also serve sandwiches for lunch, including baked eggplant or portobello mushroom ($6).

Clayton Café (☎ 706-782-5438), on N Main St downtown, is crowded every morning with downtown workers eating the simple, inexpensive breakfasts in a nonsmoking atmosphere. Breakfasts cost under $5; Southern lunches are served for about $6.

Mama G's (☎ 706-782-5965), on Duvall St behind the Winn Dixie on Hwy 441 south of town, is a popular Italian restaurant serving pastas ($7 to $8), pizza ($8 for a small) and various subs for less than $5. Specials such as baked ziti and stuffed shells are pricier ($13). Beer is also served here. There's a Mexican grocery store next door.

Nature's Table (☎ 706-782-9557, 91 E Savannah St) serves fresh bread and healthy food, including sandwiches ($3), soups ($2), salads and a fruit plate. There's outdoor as well as indoor seating.

La Pachanga Mexican Restaurant and Cantina (☎ 706-782-7247), at the Days Inn, serves decent Tex-Mex at reasonable prices.

GEORGIA

BLACK ROCK MOUNTAIN STATE PARK

This 1803-acre park (☎ 706-746-2141), 3 miles north of Clayton off US Hwy 441, is named for its sheer cliffs of dark granite. It sits astride the Eastern Continental Divide and, at 3640 feet, is the highest state park in Georgia. Several overlooks have marvelous views of the surrounding Blue Ridge Mountains. There are bountiful spring wildflowers, blooming mountain laurel and rhododendron in early summer and amazing fall colors. A 17-acre lake is stocked with trout.

Ten miles of hiking trails wind through the park. A 0.2-mile trail leads down to the small Ada-Hi Falls. A 7.2-mile backcountry trail follows a mountain stream and slippery granite cliffs. The 2.2-mile **Tennessee Rock Trail** passes through several types of plant habitat. The trail climbs steeply to the Eastern Continental Divide, where the best scenery is found at the Tennessee Rock Overlook – from here, you can see peaks of the Blue Ridge Mountains across a farming valley. Several large boulders make great spots for sunning. Be sure to pick up an informative interpretive trail guide from the visitors center ($1). The guide is a useful introduction to the forest ecology of the Southern Appalachians, with some human history and geology thrown in.

The 64 wooded campsites cost $10 for walk-in tent sites, $15 for regular tent sites and $17 for RVs, vans and pop-ups. Ten cottages rent for $70 to $105.

A $2 ParkPass is required to enter the park.

MOUNTAIN CITY

pop 830

This tiny mountain town is home to the **Foxfire Museum** (☎ 706-746-5828), on US Hwy 441. This small museum, housed in a log building, contains exhibits on Appalachian life: toys, farming implements, household items and tools related to cabin building, blacksmithing, woodworking, wagon building, logging, shoemaking, animal trapping and hunting. A self-

Foxfire

Foxfire – named after a phosphorescent plant – began in 1966 when a newly arrived high school English teacher, Eliot Wigginton, unable to get through to his Appalachian students, suggested they create a literary magazine. The students interviewed older members of their community and recorded detailed accounts of the elders' traditional ways, such as how to make sorghum syrup, build log cabins, shuck corn, make a dulcimer or plow with a horse and mule. These efforts led to the student-published magazine *Foxfire*, which eventually led to the series of books on 'affairs of plain living' that has sold over 8.5 million copies.

This initial experience evolved into a method of teaching known as the 'Foxfire Approach to Teaching and Learning.' The core values of this approach are to involve students in deciding how to meet the required curriculum, encourage active engagement in the learning process, make connections with the surrounding communities and seek an audience beyond the classroom. Although the initial effort was rooted in Appalachian culture, the approach can apply in any culture to any subject. The Foxfire approach is now used in classrooms in 37 states.

Often, Appalachian culture has been portrayed as backward and buffoonish in cartoons like Snuffy Smith and Li'l Abner, or as malevolent and inbred, as in James Dickey's book *Deliverance*. Foxfire was one of the first major organizations to celebrate and present Appalachian culture in a positive light. Recording the old ways in the *Foxfire* magazine has helped give them permanence and respect, and has helped commemorate the lives of the storytellers.

guiding booklet explains each exhibit. Admission is free, but donations are requested.

The museum also documents the 'Foxfire Approach to Teaching and Learning,' which grew out of the *Foxfire* magazine and book series (see the boxed text). A small gift museum sells the *Foxfire* books and other regional products.

On 110 acres of nearby Black Rock Mountain, the **Foxfire Center** is a collection of over 20 buildings dating back to the early 1800s, and provides a glimpse of early mountaineering life. Buildings include a chapel, blacksmith shop, mule barn, wagon shed, one-room cabin, gristmill and smokehouse. The structures are partly original, and partly replicas of traditional log buildings. The buildings are generally locked except during special group tours, but visitors can wander around the outside and walk on trails. The suggested donation is $6 per car. Get a self-guiding brochure at the Foxfire Museum; the museum and center are open 9 am to 4:30 pm Monday through Saturday.
Web site: www.foxfire.org

DILLARD
pop 200
The **Hambridge Center** (☎ 706-746-5718), in Dillard, is Georgia's only residential center for the creative arts. About eight artists are in residence at any one time, and 2000 have stayed here since 1974. A gallery sells pottery, folk crafts, paintings, jewelry and regional books. Public lectures are given on topics such as architecture, art and nature about once a month. The public can also use the center's nature trails and view the Barkers Creek Mill, a water-powered gristmill. It's open the first Saturday of the month, but you can always see the building and the tranquil creek that it is on. The Hambridge Center is off US Hwy 441 about 3.6 miles down Betty Creek Rd.

When Georgians think of Dillard, they usually think of the *Dillard House* (☎ 706-746-5348), a country celebration of gluttony. A veritable institution since 1915, the restaurant serves unlimited plates of fried chicken, cured ham, pork chops, fried okra and other vegetables and lots of relishes and desserts. They have served more than five million guests in the past 85 years. Unfortunately, the sheer quantity of food impairs the quality of preparation; it's not worth going

much out of your way. Prices are set at $10/16/17 for breakfast/lunch/dinner. Children pay less, and weekends cost a bit more. The restaurant is on US Hwy 441.

The Dillard House also offers complete resort facilities, including motel rooms, suites, cottages, swimming pools, tennis courts, fishing ponds, a petting zoo and horseback riding. For more information, contact ☎ 800-541-0671, 706-746-5348 or fax 706-746-3344.
Web site: www.dillardhouse.com

An alternative to the Dillard House is the *Cupboard* (☎ 706-746-5700), on US Hwy 441 in Dillard, featuring Southern cooking, barbecue and sandwiches at moderately expensive prices (less than $10 for lunch; $11 to $16 dinner dishes), plus lots of desserts. Breakfasts are $6 to $10. If you haven't tried pecan-crusted fried catfish, beef livers or chicken livers, here's your chance. This is a nonsmoking restaurant with indoor and outdoor seating.

The *York House* (☎ 800-231-9675, 706-746-2068, fax 706-746-0210, 416 York House Rd), between Dillard and Mountain City, 1/4 mile off Hwy 441, is a charming historic inn that has been in business since 1896. In a quiet location surrounded by trees, the inn is set on 5 acres with walking trails. The 13 large, comfortable rooms are supplemented by a wonderful porch and balconies, great for relaxing and general sitting. Guests can use the kitchen. Rates vary with the season and the type of room, but range from $69 to $149 in the high season, while the cheapest rooms are $79/99 weekdays/weekends. Rates include a full breakfast.
Web site: www.gamountains.com/yorkhouse

SKY VALLEY
In the extreme northeast corner of the state, 15 miles north of Clayton, the Sky Valley Resort (☎ 800-437-2416, 706-746-5303) offers golfing and seasonal skiing. It's the only ski resort in Georgia and the southernmost one in the eastern US. The season traditionally starts the day after Christmas through mid-February, but the temperature and humidity have to be just right before the resort makes enough white stuff to ski

on. Sometimes it's operated weekends only, so *call first!*

When there *is* snow, the resort gets very crowded and is popular with families. Five runs are available, from beginning to experienced; lessons at all levels are offered. They even have a ski-wee program, where you can leave your kids for lessons and lunch. Typical fees are $15/20/28 for night/day/day & night skiing, with rental rates around $20.

Unlike other parts of this dry county, the resort can serve liquor; in fact, the city of Sky Valley was incorporated just for this purpose.

TALLULAH GORGE STATE PARK

This 3000-acre state park (☎ 706-754-7970) is home to a spectacular gorge nearly 1000 feet deep and 2 miles long. It protects six endangered plant species, including the persistent trillium, which grows nowhere but here. More than 500,000 people a year visit the park.

In the mid 19th century, Tallulah Gorge became a resort area for coastal residents escaping yellow fever. The introduction of the railroad in 1882 increased access and ushered in the 'Grand Era' of hotels on the rim of the gorge. The damming of the river in the early 1900s to create electricity for Atlanta reduced the flow by 90% or more and killed off most tourism.

The place to start is the **Jane Hurt Yarn Interpretive Center,** a large, modern education facility that has exhibits with helpful but brief descriptions of the area's natural and human history – from Cherokees to European hunters to settlers to vacationers. You can get maps, lists of activities and permits for climbing down into the gorge.

Although the river is tame compared to what it once was, the gorge still offers gorgeous scenery. Short, easy **hiking trails** lead along the rim to overlooks of the five waterfalls. A couple of 1/4-mile, strenuous trails lead into the gorge; the roundtrip down, along the rocks at the gorge bottom and up is about 2½ miles. To protect the native endangered species, these trails are limited to

100 people a day. To hike down, you need to obtain a permit from the interpretive center; on summer weekends, you'll need to arrive between 8 am and 10 am for a chance at one of the limited permits. At the gorge bottom, Bridal Veil Falls offers a sliding rock and swimming hole.

The 3-mile Shortline Trail is an easy but scenic paved path for hiking and biking that follows an old railroad bed. Five-mile Stoneplace Trail is suitable for hiking, mountain biking and backcountry camping. Tallulah Gorge is also a popular rock-climbing spot, but only 20 permits per day are issued; go to the Jane Hurt Yarn Interpretive Center for permits. Several sections of the Tallulah River are canoeable, but you'll need your own gear. Call the state park for more information.

The average water flow in the gorge is about 35 to 60 cubic feet per second (cfs). On certain days in April, May, September and October, the park provides 'aesthetic releases' from the dam of about 300 cfs. On the first two weekends in April and the first three weekends in November, the dam releases water for white water boating – 500 cfs on Saturday, 700 cfs on Sunday (these flow rates approximate the flow before the river was dammed). The park issues 120 kayaking permits each day.

Other activities here include swimming in the 63-acre lake, fishing and playing tennis. The Terrora Campground (☎ 706-754-7979) offers 50 tent/RV sites set amidst lots of trees, with a moderate degree of privacy. The parking fee for the park is $4.

The **Georgia Heritage Center for the Arts** (☎ 706-754-5989), on US Hwy 441 at the northwest corner of the Tallulah Gorge Bridge, is a pleasant art gallery featuring modern paintings, woven baskets, pottery and wood carvings by Georgia artists. Resident artists frequently give demonstrations and occasionally workshops.

Glen-Ella Springs Inn (☎ *888-455-8896, 706-754-7295, fax 706-754-1560, 1789 Bear Gap Rd),* 2.3 miles down a gravel road off US Hwy 441 2 miles south of the Tallulah River Bridge, is an elegant but isolated country retreat. Glen-Ella was used as an inn until

1915, when the Tallulah Falls traffic dropped off; it was restored and reopened in 1987. Frequently included on lists of best inns in the country, its 16 rooms are individually decorated in a country style. The inn is on 17 acres of carefully manicured lawn and garden, and is equipped for business conferences, groups and weddings. A pleasant deck overlooks the outside pool. There are no TVs in the rooms. Standard room rates are $125/145 weekdays/weekends; suites are also available. Classic American cuisine dinners are served to the general public by reservation.

Web site: www.glenella.com

Central Georgia

Between the northern Georgia mountains and the southern coastal plains lies the Piedmont region. Its southern boundary is the 'fall line' – a sudden drop in elevation at the edge of a plateau. On rivers, this decrease in elevation impeded navigation farther upriver, but also allowed waterpower to be harnessed – Columbus, Macon and Augusta were all established where the fall line intersects rivers. Today, most of these waterways are dammed, creating lakes popular for boating and fishing. Modern waterpower continues to operate textile mills and other manufacturing industries. US military installations also play a major role in the economy of the region.

In the 18th and 19th centuries, the region was populated on the promise of bountiful cotton and the slavery needed to harvest it cheaply. Large antebellum homes were built by wealthy planters. The Civil War ended slavery, and an infestation of boll weevils nearly ended cotton farming a half-century later.

During the last stage of the Civil War, Union general William T Sherman burned factories, homes and sometimes entire towns in his infamous march to the sea. Yet he bypassed some villages and spared others. Many antebellum homes remain and can be visited.

Atlanta lies within the Piedmont region, but native Georgians might say the true heart of the South lies beyond the gleaming office towers and sprawling interstate highways, in dozens of small towns and farming communities that populate the Piedmont's gently rolling hills.

COLUMBUS
pop 186,000

Georgia's third-largest city, 100 miles southwest of Atlanta, was established at the highest navigable point on the Chattahoochee River. In the early 1800s, water powered Columbus' industries; the city was a major producer of Confederate armaments and uniforms during the Civil War.

The news of Robert E Lee's surrender at Appomattox traveled slowly; a week later, Union general James H Wilson launched a night attack against Columbus and burned all property that had supported the Confederate war effort. This is considered the last significant land battle of the Civil War.

Modern Columbus is still mostly industrial. The city has spread out considerably, but most sites of interest to visitors are still near the river. Downtown has historic homes and old industrial brick buildings along cobblestone streets. Ongoing efforts

---

Highlights

- Visit Callaway Gardens, a popular resort with 14,000 acres of attractions, from butterflies to azaleas.
- Revel in the youthful atmosphere and cutting-edge music of Athens, a lively college town

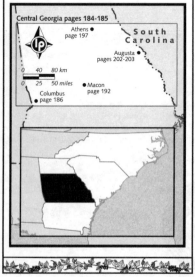

Central Georgia pages 184-185

Athens ●
page 197

South Carolina

Augusta ●
pages 202-203

0   40   80 km
0   25   50 miles

● Macon
page 192

Columbus
● page 186

at downtown revitalization have resulted in housing renovations, new restaurants and nightspots and a new performing arts center.

Famous people from Columbus have included Gertrude Pridgett 'Ma' Rainey, an African-American gospel and blues singer in the 1920s, and Carson McCullers (1917–67), one of the South's finest novelists (see Literature in the Facts about Georgia chapter).

Columbus is also home to Fort Benning, the largest infantry training center in the world. At Fort Benning, the controversial School of the Americas trained 60,000 Latin American soldiers, some of whom became dictators or participated in death squads back home. The group SOA Watch leads annual mass demonstrations that attract thousands of protestors from throughout the country. For more information, see its Web site (www.soaw.org). The school was officially closed in 2000 and replaced with the Western Hemisphere Institute for Security Cooperation; the protests continue.

Information

The Columbus Convention & Visitors Bureau (☎ 800-999-1613, 706-322-1613), 1000 Bay Ave, downtown at 10th St, has plenty of brochures, maps, hotel coupons and a 10-minute video on what to see and do. It's open 9 am to 5 pm weekdays, 11 am to 5 pm Saturday and 1 pm to 5 pm Sunday. Web site: www.columbusga.com/ccvb

Books-a-Million, on Wynnton Rd just west of I-185, has somewhat fewer than a million books, but stocks a good selection of regional books and authors (there's not much written on Columbus itself, however). There's also a coffee shop here.

Internet access is provided at public library branches: The major branch is the WC Bradley Memorial Library (☎ 706-649-0780) at 1120 Bradley Dr; hours are 9 am to 9 pm Monday to Thursday, 9 am to 6 pm Friday and Saturday and 1:30 pm to 6:30 pm Sunday.

Things to See & Do

The downtown residential **historic district** covers 24 square blocks, and is bounded roughly by Victory Dr to 9th St, and from Veteran's Parkway to the Chattahoochee River. The houses date from the 1840s to 1900. Historic Columbus Foundation (☎ 706-322-0756), 700 Broadway, offers tours of several of these houses, including the **Pemberton House**, 11 W 7th St, where the inventor of Coca-Cola lived from 1855 to 1860. The tours are available at 11 am and 3 pm weekdays, and at 2 pm on weekends for $5. Web site: www.historiccolumbus.com

The downtown **Riverwalk** is a pretty, peaceful stroll on a 12-mile paved path along the edges of the Chattahoochee River, stretching to the Infantry Museum at Ft Benning. The path is suitable for walking, jogging, skating or bicycling. Bicycles are available for rent in the summer at the pavilion behind the Iron Works Convention & Trade Center for $6/20 per hour/half day. Hours are 10 am to 7 pm Tuesday to Sunday.

The downtown commercial area starts north of 8th St, where there are several old brick industrial buildings converted to mixed use. The **Iron Works Convention & Trade Center** (☎ 706-327-4522), at Front Ave between 8th and 9th Sts, for example, was a munitions factory during the Civil War; it is now used to hold conventions.

The **Port Columbus Civil War Naval Center** (☎ 706-327-9798), in South Commons at 1002 Victory Dr, contains two old ironclad warships built at the Columbus Naval Iron Works. One was burned and sunk before ever seeing active duty when Wilson attacked Columbus. The ship was salvaged from the bottom of the Chattahoochee River more than a century later. The center is open 9 am to 5 pm; admission is $4.50/3 adults/students. Web site: www.portcolumbus.org

The **Coca-Cola Space Science Center** (☎ 706-649-1470), 701 Front Ave, features planetarium shows, which alternate between astronomy presentations and music/laser productions; there are also a few displays on the US space program. The center is open 10 am to 4 pm Tuesday to Friday, 1:30 pm to 5 pm Saturday and 1:30 pm to 4 pm Sunday. The museum is free; shows cost $4. Call or check its Web site (www.ccssc.org) for a show schedule.

The **Columbus Museum** (☎ 706-649-0713), 1251 Wynnton Rd, not far from downtown, is a combination regional history and American art museum. A film and the exhibits give a good account of local history, including the 19th-century slave-based economic system, and its Civil War era importance as a manufacturing center. Permanent and rotating art exhibits include paintings, sculpture and decorative arts. It's open 10 am to 5 pm Tuesday to Saturday and 1 pm to 5 pm Sunday; admission is free.

The on-site cafe is open for lunch only from Tuesday to Friday.
Web site: www.columbusmuseum.com

Fort Benning Military Reservation

At Fort Benning, the **National Infantry Museum** (☎ 706-545-2958) is an excellent museum containing 25,000 objects, starting with 16th European infantry artifacts and covering the history of wars in the US (as told from a US military point of view, of course). Being surrounded by so many weapons can get creepy. A dress code for

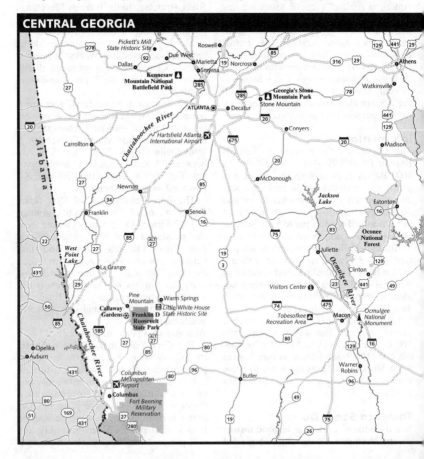

CENTRAL GEORGIA

civilians, posted on the door, prohibits 'tank tops, muscle shirts, sleeveless shirts, underwear worn as outer garments, cut-off military uniforms, shorts without outside pockets, shower caps, shower shoes and hair curlers.' Just so you know. Most visitors are crew-cut recruits in military fatigues. It's open 10 am to 4:30 pm weekdays and 12:30 pm to 4:30 pm weekends; admission is free. To get to the museum, take I-185 south into Fort Benning and follow the signs.

For other public events at Fort Benning, such as the weekly parachute drop, call ☎ 706-545-2238.

Special Events
On the last full weekend in April, Columbus hosts **Riverfest** (☎ 706-324-7417). More than 125,000 people visit the riverfront over three days for folk art, five stages of entertainment and a barbecue contest. Admission is typically $8/2 adults/children.

Places to Stay
The hotel tax in Columbus is 14%.

There are plenty of cheap motels along the very sleazy expanse of Victory Dr south of town. Your best bets are the chain motels

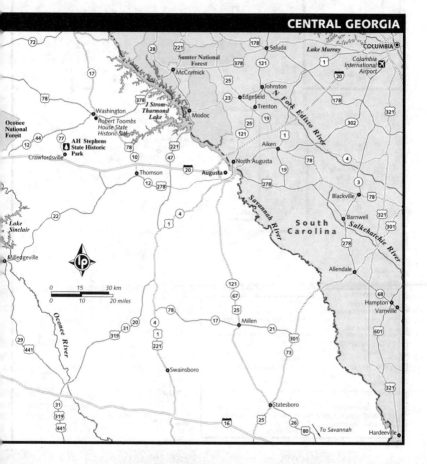

CENTRAL GEORGIA

GEORGIA

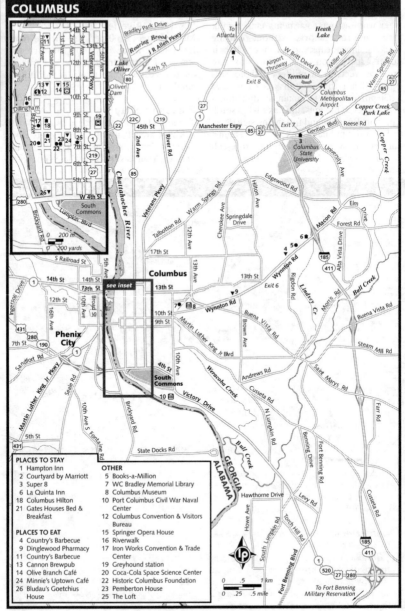

COLUMBUS

PLACES TO STAY
1 Hampton Inn
2 Courtyard by Marriott
3 Super 8
4 La Quinta Inn
18 Columbus Hilton
21 Gates Houses Bed & Breakfast

PLACES TO EAT
4 Country's Barbecue
9 Dinglewood Pharmacy
11 Country's Barbecue
13 Cannon Brewpub
14 Olive Branch Café
16 Minnie's Uptown Café
26 Bludau's Goetchius House

OTHER
5 Books-a-Million
7 WC Bradley Memorial Library
8 Columbus Museum
10 Port Columbus Civil War Naval Center
12 Columbus Convention & Visitors Bureau
15 Springer Opera House
16 Riverwalk
17 Iron Works Convention & Trade Center
19 Greyhound station
20 Coca-Cola Space Science Center
22 Historic Columbus Foundation
23 Pemberton House
25 The Loft

To Fort Benning Military Reservation

clustered around exits 6 and 7 of I-185, a couple of miles east of downtown.

Super 8 *(☎ 800-800-8000, 706-322-6580, 2935 Warm Springs Rd)* provides unexciting budget rooms with small windows and guest washers/dryers starting at $38.

La Quinta Inn *(☎ 706-568-1740, fax 706-569-7434, 3201 Macon Rd),* at I-185 exit 6, is a decent value if you can get the low rate of $49 a night, including continental breakfast. The price can zoom up to $79; at that price, it isn't such a good value. It has 122 standard rooms, plus a laundry room.

Hampton Inn *(☎ 800-426-7866, 706-576-5303, fax 706-596-8076, 5585 Whitesville Rd),* near the airport, has 118 clean, updated, standard business singles/doubles, a complimentary airport shuttle, outdoor pool and continental breakfast for $75/81. It's off the Airport Thruway (I-185 exit 8).

Courtyard by Marriott *(☎ 800-321-2211, 706-323-2323, fax 706-327-6030, 3501 Courtyard Way),* near Peachtree Mall off Manchester Expressway (I-185 exit 7), has standard business rooms. Amenities include a heated outdoor pool, guest washer/dryer, heated spa, small exercise room, evening cookies and 24-hour coffee and tea. Rates start at $82/69 weekdays/weekends; a breakfast buffet is available for $8.

Columbus Hilton *(☎ 800-524-4020, 706-324-1800, fax 706-327-8042, 800 Front Ave),* next to the Iron Works Convention & Trade Center, is the only decent hotel downtown. Located in the old Empire Woodruff Grist Mill built in 1861, it was one of the few buildings spared when Union troops burned Columbus. By 1887, it was the largest meal and flour mill in the South. Today, it's a business-oriented hotel with 177 comfortable rooms, a heated outdoor pool, in-room Internet service ($10/day extra), a shuttle to and from the airport and a restaurant. Doubles start at $79/110 weekend/weekdays.

Gates House Bed & Breakfast *(☎ 800-891-3187, 706-324-6464, fax 706-324-2070, 737 Broadway),* between 7th and 8th Sts, is in the heart of the historic district. Built in 1880, this Colonial Revival house has a beautiful interior furnished with Victorian antiques. Public areas include a screened porch, garden area, parlor and library. Rates for the three double rooms range from $95 to $135, including a full breakfast. Web site: www.gateshouse.com

Places to Eat

Minnie's Uptown Café *(☎ 706-322-2766),* downtown on the southeastern corner of 8th St and 1st Ave, serves inexpensive Southern food. Although the daily selection is somewhat small, it's very popular. A plate of three vegetables costs $4; meat and three vegetables is $6. Minnie's is open for lunch only, from 10:45 am to 2:45 pm.

Columbus takes its barbecue seriously; meat is smoked over blackjack oak, creating a unique flavor. There's none better than ***Country's Barbecue***, with three locations: the original (☎ 706-563-7604) off Macon Rd at 3137 Mercury Dr; downtown on Broadway between 13th and 14th Sts (☎ 706-596-8910); and in Main Street Village at the intersection of Hamilton Rd and Weems Rd (☎ 706-660-1415). The best option at Country's is the barbecue rib platter for $8, including two sides (try the Brunswick stew). A barbecue pork sandwich costs $3. Other options include fried chicken, wings, good pies, beer, wine and an unending supply of sweet tea.

Dinglewood Pharmacy *(☎ 706-322-0616, 1939 Wynnton Rd)* is often full at lunchtime. People stand in line for a scrambled dog – a Columbus tradition consisting of a hot dog buried in chili, mustard, pickles and onion, topped with oyster crackers and eaten with a spoon. Lieutenant Charles Stevens has been serving this succulent dish for more than 50 years from the same spot. The pharmacy also serves up malts, extra thick shakes and ice cream floats. Although a restaurant at the Hollywood Connection is named Lieutenant's, its dogs don't live up to the same standard.

Cannon Brewpub *(☎ 706-653-2337, 1041 Broadway),* between 10th and 11th Sts, is in a nicely adapted old brick industrial building. The brewpub sells pizzas and a wide variety of pub food at moderate prices in a cozy atmosphere, with beer made on site. Look for the cannon out front.

Olive Branch Café (☎ 706-322-7410, 1032 Broadway), between 10th and 11th Sts, is one of the more successful new restaurants downtown. Lunch options include a good selection of salads and sandwiches ($4 to $8), pasta ($8 to $11) and other dishes. It's open for lunch Monday to Saturday, and dinner only on Saturday night.

Bludau's Goetchius House (☎ 706-324-4863, 405 Broadway) is the city's finest restaurant. Diners eat in several rooms of a restored 1839 antebellum house. It's open for dinner only, closed Sunday. Main courses are $15 to $30.

Entertainment

Look for the free *Playgrounds magazine* for a description of events around town.

The Loft (☎ 706-596-8141, 1032 Broadway) is the best option downtown for a pleasant night out. The schedule typically consists of an open mike on Wednesday, comedy on Thursday and jazz or singer-songwriters on the weekend.
Web site: www.theloftlive.com

The *Springer Opera House* (☎ 706-327-3688, 103 10th St), downtown, is a national historic landmark designated as Georgia's State Theatre. The 1871 brick building is decorated with green and gold gilt and was completely renovated in 1997. Its 700-seat theater is a popular venue for ballet and traveling shows, with a smaller 175-person studio for theater-in-the-round.
Web site: www.springeroperahouse.org

Spectator Sports

The 90-acre South Commons sports complex by the river is home to minor league baseball, hockey and fastpitch softball. The Columbus RedStixx (☎ 706-571-8866) are the Class A affiliate of the Cleveland Indians; they play at Historic Golden Park, the 1996 Olympic venue for women's fastpitch softball. The Columbus Cottonmouths hockey team plays at the 10,000-seat Columbus Civic Center. And the Georgia Pride, a women's professional fastpitch softball team, plays at the 2500-seat softball stadium.

Getting There & Away

From the small Columbus airport, Delta services Atlanta, Northwest goes to Memphis, Tennessee, and US Airways Express flies to Charlotte, NC. The main entrance is on W Britt David Rd; access is via the Airport Thruway. Car rental agencies at the airport include National, Hertz, Budget and Avis.

The small Greyhound station (☎ 706-322-7391, 818 Veteran's Parkway), near the intersection with 9th St, provides connections to Atlanta ($17, two hours, 89 miles, five per day), Montgomery ($23, two hours, 92 miles, two per day), and Memphis ($70, 11-15 hours, 399 miles, four per day), as well as other points. Enter from the rear.

PINE MOUNTAIN
pop 1100

The tiny town of Pine Mountain serves as the gateway for **Callaway Gardens**, one of Georgia's most popular and beautiful attractions. In the early 20th century, Cason Callaway, a textile mill owner, and his wife Virginia Hand Callaway developed this land, worn out from decades of cotton farming, into a landscape of lakes, trees, native wildflowers and flowering plants. The best and most popular time of year to visit is from late March to May, when blooming azaleas cover the land.

The gardens now encompass more than 14,000 acres. The **Day Butterfly Center** houses more than 1000 butterflies of different species; they are most active on sunny

afternoons. The **Virginia Hand Callaway Discovery Center** has a helpful information booth as well as rotating nature art exhibits, bird paintings by Athos Menaboni and amazing Georgia wildflower sculptures made from sheet copper, wire and oil paint by artist Trailer McQuilkin. The live bird show at 10:30 am and 12:30 pm is worth catching.

The **John A Sibley Horticultural Center** is a combination outdoor garden and green-house, with a mix of native and exotic orna-mental plants. **Mr Cason's Vegetable Garden**, the filming location of the PBS show *Victory Garden,* consists of 7.5 acres of fruits, vegetables and wildflowers.

Robin Lake Beach, the world's largest inland, man-made beach, is open Memorial Day to Labor Day. You can swim, paddle-boat or play miniature golf here. You can also bicycle the park, play 63 holes of golf, kill skeet at the Gun Club, knock balls around the tennis and racquetball center, rent a fishing boat or take a guided fly-fishing excursion. You can rent just about everything you'll need for these activities.

Popular events are held throughout the year, including the Hot Air Balloon Festival before Labor Day, the Fantasy in Lights in December and the Master's Water Ski Tour-nament on Memorial Day weekend.

A shuttle provides service between the Discovery Center, Butterfly Center and Horticultural Center.

The gardens are open 9 am to 5 pm daily. Rates are $10/5 adults/children weekdays, $12/6 weekends. The price for a two-day ticket is $13/6.50 weekdays, $18/9 week-ends. This will get you into most of the at-tractions, including the beach in summer, but recreational activities (bicycle rental, golf and so on) cost extra.

Callaway Gardens operates five restau-rants inside the gardens and three outside (see Places to Eat).

At the nearby **Wild Animal Safari** (☎ 800-367-2751, 706-663-8744), on US 27 west of Pine Mountain, the animals roam relatively freely. Visitors can drive their own cars through or, for those not interested in buffalo scratches, take a tour bus.

Places to Stay

White Columns Motel (☎ 706-663-2312, fax 706-663-2500), on US Hwy 27 south of downtown Pine Mountain, has clean, modern motel rooms with quaint decora-tions, a microwave and a fridge in each room. Rates are $55/65 on weekdays/week-ends in the high season.
Web site: whitecolumns-ga.com

Callaway Gardens Inn (800-225-5292, 706-663-2281, email: reservations@callaway gardens.com), on US Hwy 27 near the main entrance to the Gardens, is a large complex with almost 400 clean and comfortable – but standard – hotel rooms. There's plenty of greenery and a quiet 'bird study' area on the grounds. Rates are $119 for a standard room, $160 for a junior suite. Two restau-rants and a lounge are located here.

In nearby Hamilton, 5 miles south of Callaway Gardens, *Magnolia Hall Bed & Breakfast* (☎ 706-628-4566) is in an elegant 1890s Victorian house, decorated with an-tiques. Rates for the five cozy double rooms range from $95 to $115.
Web site: www.bbonline.com/ga/magnoliahall

Places to Eat

Callaway Gardens operates several restau-rants inside and outside the park. The five inside range from simple sandwich shops to more formal restaurants overlooking the golf fairways. The brochures you pick up at the gardens' entrance will list the options.

Of the restaurants outside the gardens, *Country Kitchen* (☎ 706-663-2281), near the top of Pine Mountain at the US Hwy 27 and GA 190 junction, serves the simplest and least expensive food. It has the typical Southern platters (meat and two vegeta-bles) for $8, and sandwiches for $6 to $7. Tables near the window have excellent views of the surrounding countryside.

Locals eat at *McGuire's Family Restau-rant* (☎ 706-663-2640) in downtown Pine Mountain. This restaurant has a little of everything, from barbecue, soups and salads, hamburgers and hotdogs, catfish, chicken livers, quail and Brunswick stew, to a dull-looking buffet. Prices range from $5 for sandwiches to $7 to $15 for main dishes.

The *Plantation Room* (☎ 706-663-2281), at the Callaway Gardens Inn, serves a Southern buffet, plus steak, ribs, chicken and fish ($17 to $20). The *Georgia Room* (☎ 706-663-2281) at the inn is a fine dining restaurant serving a fixed menu; $48 per person is typical.

FRANKLIN D ROOSEVELT STATE PARK

This 10,000-acre park (☎ 706-663-4858), sitting atop Pine Mountain, offers 40 miles of hiking trails. One of the better hikes is the 6.7-mile Wolfden Loop, which offers nice views and a walk through mountain woodlands.

To get oriented, stop at the park office, in a stone building built by FDR's Civilian Conservation Corps in the 1930s, on 190 near the western side of the park, 5 miles east of Pine Mountain. It's open 8 am to 5 pm daily.

Many of the 140 camping sites are located on a pretty lake. Rates are $15. There are 11 backcountry sites as well. The park's 21 cottages are $55 to $85. Call ☎ 800-864-7275 or ☎ 770-389-7275 for reservations.

WARM SPRINGS
pop 500

This small town, set among pines and rolling hills between Columbus and Atlanta, became the refuge of US President Franklin Delano Roosevelt after he was paralyzed by polio in 1921 at the age of 39. Although the waters had no special powers, therapy, rest and exercise in the warm waters enabled FDR to learn to stand with assistance and to walk a few steps. From 1924 to 1945, FDR visited often and helped develop the Georgia Warm Springs Foundation for the treatment of polio.

The area became a center for the treatment of polio and, after polio was eradicated in 1955, efforts were redirected toward rehabilitation from strokes, head injuries, spinal cord injuries, neuromuscular disorders, arthritis, sensory disabilities and behavior disabilities. The nearby Roosevelt Institute continues to provide services for 3000 people per year. Visitors can stop by the **Historic Pools & Museum**, where polio sufferers exercised in the 88°F pools.

The **Little White House State Historic Site** (☎ 706-655-5870), ¼ mile south of Warm Springs on GA Hwy 85 alt/US Hwy 27 alt, preserves FDR's home. The site tour starts at a museum, which shows a 12-minute film (politically incorrect in its references to disabilities) on FDR's stay in the area. Displays include gifts given to the president, including more than 100 walking canes.

The house itself is surprising in its modesty and simplicity. It is preserved much as FDR left it in 1945, and models and pictures of ships show his fondness for nautical decorations. You can also see the guest house, servants' quarters and garage, where FDR's 1938 Ford Roadster is displayed.

While at the Little White House on April 12, 1945, FDR had a cerebral hemorrhage while sitting for a portrait. When he died, the woman at his side was not his wife Eleanor but Lucy Mercer. FDR and Mercer had an affair in 1917 and continued to meet secretly during his visits to Warm Springs. The historic site does not cover this bit of gossip.

The gift shop contains videos and books on FDR, Eleanor Roosevelt and disabilities. Hours are 9 am to 4:45 pm; $5/2 adults/children.

The town of Warm Springs itself has a couple of pleasant blocks of gift and collectible shops. The Welcome Center (☎ 706-655-3322) on Broad St has local information.

Places to Stay

Camping and cottages are available at the nearby FD Roosevelt State Park; see that section for details.

Meriwether Country Inn (☎ 706-655-9099), on Spring St at the eastern end of the historic district, was built in 1998. Its 40 modern, comfortable hotel rooms cost $52 per night, plus 11% tax.
Web site: www.meriwethercountryinn.com

Hotel Warm Springs Bed & Breakfast Inn (☎ 800-366-7616, 706-655-2114), at the intersection of Hwys 27 alt, 41 and 85 alt, is a historic inn built in 1907. Rooms with 12-foot ceilings are decorated with Queen Anne antiques, chandeliers and clawfoot bathtubs. There are no phones in the rooms. Singles/doubles start at $60/70, including a silver service breakfast; the honeymoon suite is $145.

Places to Eat

Bulloch House Restaurant (☎ 706-655-9068), off Spring St on the eastern end of town, serves a Southern buffet of fried chicken, fried green tomatoes, stewed tomatoes and the rest for $6; it could use a few more veggies. It seems half the town eats lunch here.

Ivy on Broad Street (☎ 706-655-2319, 70 Broad St) offers a slightly more elegant experience and specializes in buffets, high tea, desserts and coffees.

MACON
pop 97,000

The city of Macon is located on the fall line near Georgia's geographic midpoint. The nearby Ocmulgee River was used as transportation by Native Americans. Fort Benjamin Hawkins was established here in 1806 after the Creeks ceded most of their land; Macon itself was established in 1823. Cotton and railroad prosperity led to the construction of many fine homes. The area had a strong Unionist and peace movement before and during the Civil War. An arm of Sherman's forces passed outside Macon on their march to the sea, so many of Macon's antebellum houses remain today. In fact, this overlooked city has 5500 individual structures listed on the National Register of Historic Places, more than any other city in Georgia.

Macon has several interesting museums and many historic houses that are worth exploring, but downtown is largely deserted on the weekends. Ongoing attempts at downtown revitalization have produced several tourist attractions.

Local colleges include Mercer University (established in 1833) and Wesleyan College (established in 1836), the first college in the US to grant degrees to women.

Orientation

Downtown Macon is located on the western banks of the Ocmulgee River. I-75 approaches downtown Macon from the northwest, then veers off to the southwest. I-475 bypasses Macon on the west. Riverside Drive parallels I-75 and the river and has many hotels and restaurants. Another batch of hotels is clustered on Eisenhower Parkway near I-475.

Information

The downtown visitors center (☎ 800-768-3401, 912-743-3401) is operated by the Macon-Bibb County Convention & Visitors Bureau in the 1916 railroad Terminal Station at the corner of 5th and Cherry Sts, just off Martin Luther King Jr Blvd. It's open Monday to Saturday, and the helpful staff dispenses maps and brochures, including a self-guided walking tour map, a list of African-American heritage sites and hotel coupons.

Web site: www.maconga.org

The I-75 welcome center just northwest of the city also provides information on local and other Georgia sites.

The *Macon Telegraph* is the town's major newspaper, and it has a Web site at www.macontelegraph.com.

Books-a-Million, on Eisenhower Parkway, has a good section of local and regional travel and other books. It's open 9 am to 11 pm daily.

The main branch of the public library (☎ 912-744-0800), at 1180 Washington Ave, offers free Internet access.

Things to See & Do

Macon has a number of museums and other sites within walking or driving distance downtown. The visitors bureau in the Terminal Station sells combination packages to some of the principal sites, slightly cheaper than if you purchased them individually.

The **Georgia Music Hall of Fame** (☎ 888-427-6257, 912-750-8555), 200 Martin Luther King Jr Blvd, showcases the multitude of musical talent that has bloomed in Georgia, from native sons and daughters to groups that got their start here (see boxed text).

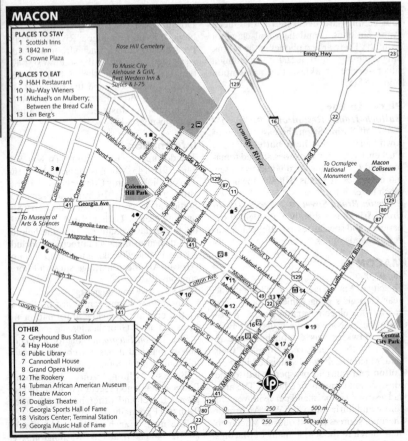

MACON

PLACES TO STAY
1 Scottish Inns
3 1842 Inn
5 Crowne Plaza

PLACES TO EAT
9 H&H Restaurant
10 Nu-Way Wieners
11 Michael's on Mulberry;
   Between the Bread Café
13 Len Berg's

OTHER
2 Greyhound Bus Station
4 Hay House
6 Public Library
7 Cannonball House
8 Grand Opera House
12 The Rookery
14 Tubman African American Museum
15 Theatre Macon
16 Douglass Theatre
17 Georgia Sports Hall of Fame
18 Visitors Center; Terminal Station
19 Georgia Music Hall of Fame

Rose Hill Cemetery
To Music City Alehouse & Grill, Best Western Inn & Suites & I-75
Coleman Hill Park
To Museum of Arts & Sciences
To Ocmulgee National Monument
Macon Coliseum
Central City Park
Ocmulgee River

The museum is a collection of nostalgia-inducing artifacts, listening stations, hands-on exhibits and even a video theater where the audience chooses the video by yelling and clapping. The Music Factory is an interactive exhibit where kids – and adults yearning to be kids – can bang on drums or make music. Hours are 9 am to 5 pm Monday to Saturday and 1 pm to 5 pm Sunday. Admission is $8/3.50 adults/children.

Web site: www.gamusichall.com

The **Tubman African American Museum** (☎ 912-743-8544), 340 Walnut St, pays homage to Harriet Tubman, the escaped slave known as 'the Black Moses' who led hundreds of slaves north to freedom before the Civil War. The museum features a wall mural depicting the journey of African Americans 'from Africa to America,' African artifacts and modern African-American art. Strangely, there isn't actually much information on Harriet Tubman. Hours are 9 am to 5 pm Monday to Saturday and 2 pm to 5 pm Sunday; $3/2 adults/children.

Web site: www.tubmanmuseum.com

The **Hay House** (☎ 912-742-8155), 934 Georgia Ave, is an amazing, elegant Italian

Renaissance Revival mansion built in the 1850s. It is furnished with fine art and antiques; reconstruction of the interior is ongoing. According to legend, a hidden room in a staircase stored the Confederate gold. Tours are offered every half hour from 10 am to 4:30 pm Monday to Saturday and 1 pm to 4:30 pm Sunday, and cost $7/2 adults/children.

Union general George Stoneman fired at the Hay House during the Battle of Dunlap Hill, but hit the **Cannonball House** instead. You can still see the offending projectile resting at the base of the stairs. The house is an outstanding example of Greek Revival architecture of the old South. A Confederate museum behind the house has many relics from the conflict. Hours are 10 am to 4 pm Monday to Saturday; entrance $4/1 adults/children.

The **Ocmulgee National Monument** (☎ 912-752-8257), a 702-acre park managed by the National Park Service, is a memorial to native cultures that inhabited this land starting 12,000 years ago and ending when the Creeks surrendered their land in Georgia in 1826. (The Creeks were later forced out of Alabama in 1836 along their own 'Trail of Tears' similar to the relocation the Cherokee had to endure.) An archeological museum contains exhibits describing the area's cultures, a short film and ancient artifacts. Details on the Creek removal are not prominently displayed; ask the museum staff for a handout or visit the Web site (www.nps.gov/ocmu). You can also visit the Great Temple Mound and a reconstructed earthlodge; hiking trails lead along the river. The park is open 9 am to 5 pm daily.

Black heritage sites include the **Douglass Theatre** (☎ 912-742-2000) at 355 Martin Luther King Jr Blvd. Built in 1921 and recently renovated, it was the premier movie theater and vaudeville hall for and owned by African Americans. In addition to occasional musicals and plays, tours are available by appointment.

Earnest sports fans can get their fill at the **Georgia Sports Hall of Fame** (☎ 912-752-1585), 301 Cherry St, featuring live action footage and sports memorabilia from the

Georgia Music

An astonishing amount of musical talent has originated in Georgia. In addition to musicians born here, clubs and recording studios in Athens and Macon have brought many acts to national attention. The Athens music scene introduced REM, the B-52s and Widespread Panic to the record shelves. Otis Redding, 'Little Richard' Penniman, James Brown and the Allman Brothers got their start in Macon. Other Georgia musicians have included composer Johnny Mercer, Lena Horne, Ray Charles, Dr Thomas Dorsey (father of gospel music), blues great Gertrude 'Ma' Rainey, Trisha Yearwood, the Indigo Girls, Gladys Knight and opera diva Jessye Norman.

state's athletes. Hours are 9 am to 5 pm Monday to Saturday and 1 pm to 5 pm Sunday. Entrance is $6/3.50 adults/children. Web site: www.gshf.org.

The **Museum of Arts & Sciences** (☎ 912-477-3232), 4182 Forsyth Rd, has a planetarium and changing art, science and humanities exhibits. Hours are 9 am to 5 pm Monday to Thursday and Saturday, 9 am to 9 pm Friday and 1 pm to 5 pm Sunday. Admission is $5/2 adults/children; it's free on Monday and from 5 pm to 9 pm Friday.

Special Events
Held the third week of March, the **Cherry Blossom Festival** (☎ 912-751-7429) celebrates the blossoming of 250,000 flowering Japanese Yoshino cherry trees. It's one of the state's most popular festivals. Events include concerts, a balloon launching, arts and crafts, food fairs, fireworks and a tour of homes.
Web site: www.cherryblossom.com

Places to Stay
The closest camping is at Tobesofkee Recreation Area (☎ 912-474-8770), just outside Macon city limits to the west on Hwy 74. Camping fees are $12 for up to four people.

Most of Macon's hotels are along commercial strips on Eisenhower Parkway near I-475 and on Riverside Drive along the I-75. A budget choice is **Knight's Inn** (☎ *800-843-5644, 912-471-1230, 4952 Romeiser Dr),* west of I-475 near Eisenhower Parkway, set back on a quiet street.

On Riverside Drive, **Best Western Inn & Suites** (☎ *912-781-5300, 4681 Chambers Rd)* is a mid-priced ($66) hotel with an indoor pool and continental breakfast about 4 miles from downtown. (The Best Western on Riverside is a bit worn.)

Scottish Inns (☎ *912-746-3561, 1044 Riverside Dr)* is the only decent budget lodging downtown. Doubles start at $37.

Crowne Plaza (☎ *912-746-1461, 108 First St),* downtown, has an outdoor pool, a health club, a restaurant and indoor parking. Rooms are modern and nice but not spectacular; the best feature is the views of historic Macon and downtown. Standard doubles start at $106.

The **1842 Inn** (☎ *800-336-1842, 912-741-1842, 353 College St)* is one of the preeminent historic inns in the state. Set in an 1842 Greek Revival antebellum house and an adjoining Victorian house, the inn has 21 rooms decorated with English antiques, oriental carpets and fine paintings. Extras include complimentary hors d'oeuvres and cash bar in the evening. Singles/doubles cost $190/290, including a continental breakfast, but, oddly for such a place, a hot breakfast costs $6 extra.

Web site: www.the1842inn.com

Places to Eat

Most restaurants downtown are closed on Sunday; finding a place to eat on the day of rest can be challenging.

Len Berg's (☎ *912-742-9255),* set back from the Broadway down an alley between Walnut and Mulberry Sts, has been a Macon tradition since 1908. A conglomeration of tiny rooms, this restaurants serves Southern fried catfish and turnip greens. A plate of meat and two vegetables costs $6 to $7; a vegetable plate is available for $4.20. It's open 11 am to 2:30 pm Monday to Saturday.

Budget travelers, kids and wiener lovers will appreciate **Nu-Way Wieners** (☎ *912-743-1368, 430 Cotton Ave),* an unassuming hot dog stand that makes old-fashioned Coney dogs. A tasty cheese dog with chili costs about $1.50. You can also get burgers here.

H&H Restaurant (807 Forsyth St) was frequented by the Allman Brothers and Otis Redding, and is acclaimed for its great chicken dishes and soul food. This spacious, basic place is open 7 am to 5 pm Tuesday to Friday.

Michael's on Mulberry (☎ *912-743-3999, 588 Mulberry St)* is an expensive but popular diner serving dinner Monday to Saturday. Entrées costing $13 to $18 include grilled salmon pasta, pork chops, duck breast and crab cakes. During the day, their restaurant **Between the Bread Café** serves salads and sandwiches (about $6).

Entertainment

The *Macon Telegraph* publishes an entertainment section every Friday.

The Macon music scene is ongoing at places such as **Music City Alehouse & Grill** (☎ *912-741-1144),* on Riverside Dr just south of Pierce Ave. This is a locally owned restaurant with music posters decorating the walls and live music on Friday and Saturday nights. Burgers, sandwiches, pastas, pizzas, steaks, ribs and seafood are also served daily.

The **Rookery** (☎ *912-746-8658, 543 Cherry St),* in downtown Macon, is a bar that has live music on the weekends ($3 cover) and occasionally on weekdays.

The **Grand Opera House** (☎ *912-301-5470),* downtown, is Mercer University's performing arts center and has a Broadway series, a music series and a family series each year. **Theatre Macon** (☎ *912-746-9485, 438 Cherry St),* downtown, presents seven plays fall through spring.

Spectator Sports

For sports fans, the Macon Braves is the Class A Farm team of the Atlanta Braves. The minor league hockey team, the Macon Whoopee, may have the best name in sports. They play at the Macon Coliseum (☎ 912-751-9232).

Getting There & Away

The Greyhound bus station (☎ 912-743-2868) is at 65 Spring St. There are connections to Atlanta ($14, two hours, 89 miles, 11 per day), Savannah ($37, 3½ hours, 185 miles, two per day), Jacksonville ($51, from 5½ hours, 272 miles, eight per day) and Tallahassee, Florida ($37, from five hours, 200 miles, three per day).

Getting Around

Many of the downtown sites are within walking distance from each other, depending on your energy level. The Macon Transit Authority operates the **Mitsi Trolley** (906-746-1318), which makes a continuous loop every 25 minutes connecting all the downtown sites mentioned previously, and including the Crowne Plaza and 1842 Inn. A one-day pass costs $2; you can get off at any site you wish, then catch the trolley again when you're done. Mitsi operates from 10 am to 6:20 pm Monday to Saturday.

The Macon Transit Authority (☎ 912-746-1318) operates bus services until 7:45 pm Monday to Saturday.

JULIETTE

Thirty miles north of Macon, Juliette is the home of the **Whistle Stop Café**, made famous by Fannie Flagg's novel *Fried Green Tomatoes at the Whistle Stop Café* and the 1991 movie *Fried Green Tomatoes*, which was filmed here. The novel, however, was set in the fictional town of Whistle Stop, Alabama – not Georgia, and the cafe that so many tourists now troop through was an antique shop until the people from Hollywood showed up. Lunch at the cafe (where the food is good, but not great) is $7, and includes one single fried green tomato (as a garnish). A full order will cost you an extra $3.

ANTEBELLUM TRAIL

The Antebellum Trail was a concept developed by the Athens Chamber of Commerce to market the towns between Macon and Athens – Clinton, Milledgeville, Eatonton,

Madison and Watkinsville. The towns have many fine examples of antebellum architecture and give the visitor a good taste of Southern life in a small town.

Web site: www.antebellumtrail.org

Milledgeville

pop 19,000

This little town was the state capital from 1803 to 1868, and it retains some stately buildings from the period, some of which are open for tours. This is a pleasant town to stroll around, with well-preserved Federal, Greek Revival, Victorian and Classic revival houses. Sherman occupied the town for two days in November 1864 on his march to the sea, burning most government buildings but sparing most residences. The welcome center (☎ 800-653-1804, tourism@alltel.net), at the corner of Hancock and Wilkinson across from Georgia College and State University, is open 9 am to 5 pm weekdays and 10 am to 4 pm Saturday.

Downtown has little of interest, but *Brewer's* serves decent burgers, sandwiches and gourmet coffee. A strip of hotel chains is on Hwy 441 north of town.

Eatonton

pop 6800

Another city spared by Sherman, Eatonton is Alice Walker's hometown. Walker's most famous book, *The Color Purple,* was made into a 1985 movie. The tourist information center is at the Eatonton-Putnam County Chamber of Commerce (☎ 706-485-7701), 105 Sumter St, across from the courthouse. A driving map of Alice Walker sites is available.

The **Uncle Remus Museum** is a memorial to Joel Chandler Harris. Born in Eatonton in 1848, Harris grew up listening to folk tales told by plantation slaves. He later published many of these stories as told by 'Uncle Remus.' The antics of Brer Rabbit and the Tar Baby were later featured in Disney's 1946 movie *Song of the South*; controversies over racial stereotyping keep this film from being available.

The current museum consists of two small rooms of objects and some models of characters from the Uncle Remus stories. The museum is housed in former slave cabins, which contain mid-19th-century items. Books and tapes are available.

The museum is open from 10 am to 5 pm Monday to Saturday and noon to 5 pm Sunday, with an hour off for lunch. From September to May, it's closed Tuesday.

Madison
pop 3600
Off I-20, 65 miles east of Atlanta and 30 miles south of Athens, Madison was one of the few towns that Sherman spared on his path of destruction. Part of this picturesque town is a National Historic Site; you can walk a 1.4-mile route through the historic district with a map from the **Welcome Center** (☎ 800-709-7406), on Madison's main square. It's open 8:30 am to 5 pm weekdays, 10 am to 5 pm Saturday and 1 pm to 5 pm Sunday.

ATHENS
pop 100,000
This university town, located south of the Blue Ridge Mountains and 61 miles from Atlanta, is characterized by a vibrant nightlife and world-renowned music scene. Local pop music stars catapulted to national fame have included the B-52's, REM and Widespread Panic.

The University of Georgia (UGA) was chartered in 1785 and opened to students in 1801. The city of Athens was founded in 1806 around the university and named after the Greek center of culture and learning. Today, the University of Georgia has almost 30,000 students and is the largest employer in northeast Georgia. Its mascot is Uga, the bulldog, and you'll see images of him throughout Georgia.

Spared serious damage during the Civil War, Athens has many antebellum homes and 14 historic districts from the 19th and 20th centuries featuring a smorgasbord of architectural styles.

Orientation
Athens is encircled by a highway known as the Loop, but most of the action is concen-

trated downtown. Broad St is a major thoroughfare and separates the downtown area from the North Campus of the University of Georgia. Farther South, Baldwin St is the division between South and North campuses.

Information
The Athens Welcome Center (☎ 706-353-1820), housed in the historic Church-Waddel-Brumby house near downtown Athens at the corner of Thomas and Dougherty Sts, provides basic information to get you started. Hours are 10 am to 6 pm Monday to Saturday and noon to 6 pm Sunday.
Web site: www.visitathensga.com

The University of Georgia Visitors Center (☎ 706-542-0842), on College Station and River Rds, offers campus information, maps and tours. It is not signed well from the road – look for the 'Four Towers' signs. The UGA Web site (www.uga.edu) has information on the school. For continuing education programs, call ☎ 706-542-2056.

Free Internet access is offered at the Athens-Clarke County Library (☎ 706-613-3650) at 2025 Baxter St.

The *Athens Daily News* is the main in-town newspaper. The *Flagpole* has a complete list of events on its Web site (www.flagpole.com) and in a weekly magazine published on Wednesday; it's available free throughout town.

Blue Moon Books (☎ 706-353-8877, 282 E Clayton St) offers a hodgepodge of new and used books, with some regional fiction and travel. If you can't find what you need downtown, Books-a-Million, in the first shopping center on I-78 business/Hwy 10 after the Loop, has a good selection of local authors, regional travel guides and books on Southern life.

A gay and lesbian hot line (☎ 706-546-4611) is operated by several groups.

Things to See & Do
The Welcome Center (☎ 706-208-8687) offers two tours. The **Classic City Tour** departs at 2 pm daily and is an overview of some of the historic houses and sites of

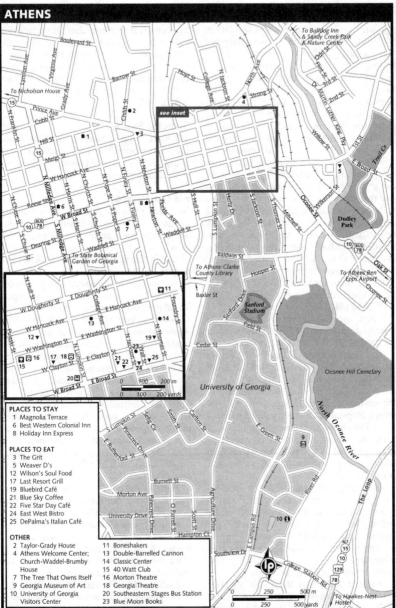

ATHENS

Boulevard St

To Bulldog Inn
& Sandy Creek Park
& Nature Center

To Nicholson House

see inset

To State Botanical
Garden of Georgia

To Athens-Clarke
County Library

Sanford
Stadium

Dudley
Park

To Athens Ben
Epps Airport

University of Georgia

Oconee Hill Cemetary

North Oconee River

The Loop

To Hawkes-Nest
Hostel

PLACES TO STAY
1 Magnolia Terrace
6 Best Western Colonial Inn
8 Holiday Inn Express

PLACES TO EAT
3 The Grit
5 Weaver D's
12 Wilson's Soul Food
17 Last Resort Grill
19 Bluebird Café
21 Blue Sky Coffee
22 Five Star Day Café
24 East West Bistro
25 DePalma's Italian Café

OTHER
2 Taylor-Grady House
4 Athens Welcome Center;
   Church-Waddel-Brumby
   House
7 The Tree That Owns Itself
9 Georgia Museum of Art
10 University of Georgia
   Visitors Center

11 Boneshakers
13 Double-Barrelled Cannon
14 Classic Center
15 40 Watt Club
16 Morton Theatre
18 Georgia Theatre
20 Southeastern Stages Bus Station
23 Blue Moon Books

Athens, including the Church-Waddel-Brumby House Museum (Federal style, 1820s), the Taylor-Grady House (Greek Revival, ca 1845), the Double-Barreled Cannon and the Tree that Owns Itself (the former owner of this tree willed the land around it to the tree itself). The charge for this 90-minute tour is $10. Many of these houses and others can be visited individually.

The **Tour of Historic Interiors**, departing from the Welcome Center at 4 pm on Tuesday and Saturday, includes many of the same historic houses. Call for reservations. The **Double-Barreled Cannon**, in front of City Hall, is remarkable for its morbid design and spectacular failure. Intended to fire two cannonballs connected by a chain to 'mow down the enemy somewhat as a scythe cuts wheat,' it was test fired only once. The two barrels could not be synchronized, so the ball-connecting chain broke, and each ball followed an erratic path. Note that it is pointed due north.

College Ave, between Clayton and Broad Sts, is where the college crowd hangs out; it's a good place for people watching.

Tours of the University of Georgia campus depart from the UGA visitors center (☎ 706-542-0842). Call for the schedule.

The **State Botanical Garden of Georgia** (☎ 706-542-1244), just over a mile south of the Athens loop road on S Milledge Ave, is a tranquil place away from the hubbub of the university. This 313-acre preserve contains a tropical conservatory and 5 miles of trails. The grounds are open 8 am to sunset daily; the visitor center and conservatory are open 9 am to 4:30 pm Monday through Saturday and 11:30 am to 4:30 pm Sunday. A cafe here serves lunch.

The **Georgia Museum of Art** (☎ 706-542-4662), 90 Carlton St, has an impressive array of art exhibits, as well as occasional concerts and film screenings. It's open 10 am to 5 pm Tuesday through Saturday (until 9 pm on Wednesday) and 1 pm to 5 pm Sunday; free admission.

Web site: www.uga.edu/gamuseum

About 1 mile past the Loop on Hwy 441/15N, the **Sandy Creek Nature Center** (☎ 706-613-3615) houses the Environment, Natural Science and Appropriate Technology (ENSAT) center, an educational building constructed using alternative building materials. It offers 6 miles of nature trails through pine forests and marshlands, and a boardwalk. Trails are open sunrise to sunset daily; the office and center are open 8:30 am to 5:30 pm Tuesday to Saturday. Admission is free.

Special Events
The **Kudzu Film Festival** (☎ 706-227-6090), a four-day competitive film festival, is held every October. The **AthFest** is a summer music and arts festival.

Places to Stay
Note that rates are generally higher during football weekends and can be sold out weeks or months in advance. The hotel tax is 14%.

Sandy Creek Park (☎ 706-613-3631) has a walk-in campground with 23 tent-only sites, plus eight tent lean-tos. Campsites cost $5, plus $1 per person park entry. It's open Tuesday through Saturday only.

Hawkes-Nest Hostel (☎ 706-769-0563, eagltavern@aol.com) is located on 7 acres of land near Watkinsville, about 11 miles south of downtown Athens. Operated as an extension of the owner's family house, the hostel has only two rooms, one inside the main house and one in a detached, rustic cottage. These are rented out as private rooms. Guests can use the kitchen and bathrooms inside the main house. Friendly owners Bonnie and Robert Murphy are helpful in planning activities around the area. Singles/doubles cost $10/18; reservations are required.

Bulldog Inn (☎ 706-543-3611, 1225 Commerce Rd) is a budget choice, located just north of the city. Doubles run about $40.

Best Western Colonial Inn (☎ 706-546-7311, 170 N Milledge Ave) has decent, modern hotel rooms on the edge of a pretty, older residential district. Rates start at $49 and include continental breakfast.

Holiday Inn Express (☎ 706-546-8122, 513 W Broad St), 0.2 miles from downtown, has an outdoor pool and exercise center.

Rates start at $69 and include a continental breakfast.

Web site: www.holiday-inn.com

Magnolia Terrace (☎ 706-548-3860, 277 Hill St) is a historic home with eight rooms, and is located in a quiet residential area with good walking opportunities. Rates are $95 to $135 including continental breakfast on weekdays, full breakfast on weekends.

Web site: www.bbonline.com/ga/magnolia terrace/

Nicholson House (☎ 706-353-2200, 6295 Jefferson Rd) is 5 miles from downtown on US 129/Jefferson Rd. Set on large, peaceful grounds, it consists of an original structure built in the 1820s, around which a Colonial Revival house was constructed in 1947. The house is furnished with antique replicas; check out the amazing original wind-up record player. Doubles are $103, including a full vegetarian breakfast.

Web site: www.bbonline.com/ga/nicholson

Places to Eat

Blue Sky Coffee (☎ 706-354-0880, 128 College Ave) has your basic coffee and cappuccino, and is a good place to relax. It also offers bagels, muffins, scones and a small selection of sandwiches.

Five Star Day Café (☎ 706-543-8552, 229 E Broad St) is an unpretentious little cafe with very reasonable prices, serving hot buttered soul chicken with Jamaican seasoning, pot roast, pesto pasta, Carolina barbecue and chicken and dumplings. Dishes cost $4 to $6.

The Grit (199 Prince Ave) is a vegetarian restaurant and popular place for lunch and dinner. Options include Middle Eastern *hummus* and *falafel*, Indian curried vegetables, Italian pasta dishes and Mexican *quesadillas*. Meals are typically $5 to $6.

Bluebird Café (☎ 706-549-3663), on the corner of Clayton and Thomas Sts, is another great international vegetarian restaurant with reasonable prices. It serves breakfast and lunch fare including Spanish omelets, Indian food and avocado and tuna sandwiches. Main dishes are $5 to $6.

East West Bistro (☎ 706-546-9378, 351 E Broad St) is a spacious restaurant that blends Mediterranean and Pacific Rim influences. Dishes include a black bean burger ($6), sandwiches and mustard sesame crusted chicken ($10).

DePalma's Italian Café (☎ 706-354-6966, 401 E Broad St) is a small, popular Italian restaurant that draws a large college crowd. It has inside and outside seating. Pasta, fish and beef dishes cost $7 to $15. They also have pizza and calzones.

Last Resort Grill (☎ 706-549-0810, 184 W Clayton St) has an energetic yet cozy, subdued atmosphere with eclectic Southern cuisine, such as chicken breast stuffed with cheeses and served over grits (the real kind) and covered with a walnut-honey sauce. Several vegetarian options are offered. Main dishes cost $8 to $14.

Wilson's Soul Food (☎ 706-353-7289, 353 N Hull St) is a small cafe serving downhome Southern food for breakfast and lunch. *Weaver D's (1016 E Broad St)* is almost as good. It was made famous by REM, who adopted its motto 'Automatic for the People' as the title for one of their albums. This restaurant serves lunch and dinner.

Entertainment

Athens has an active music scene, with everything represented, including punk, country, rock, blues, hip-hop, pop, Southern rock, alternative, folk, reggae, outlaw-country and rockabilly, to name a few. For the best description of musical acts and locations, check out the weekly *Flagpole* listings.

For the bar scene, your best bet is simply to cruise around Broad and Clayton Sts and check out whatever looks appealing. Many of the restaurants also have bars.

The *Georgia Theatre (☎ 706-549-9918, 215 N Lumpkin St)* is one of the premiere live music halls in the Southeast, with a capacity over 750. Well-known national acts play here frequently, as do popular local and regional bands.

The *40 Watt Club (☎ 706-549-7871, 285 W Washington St)*, on the corner of Pulaski St, is the legendary club where bands such as REM played. Live cutting-edge acts are booked throughout the week, from contemporary R&B to experimental underground bands.

Morton Theatre (☎ 706-613-3771, 95 W Washington St) was once the only black-owned and operated vaudeville company in the country. It has concerts, operas, ballet and the annual Flagpole Athens Music Awards Show.

Web site: www.mortontheatre.itgo.com

Boneshakers (☎ 706-543-1555 events line), on Hancock Ave just east of Thomas St – 'where the men are men and some of the women are too' – is known for its drag shows twice weekly. At other times it's a dance club.

The *Classic Center (☎ 800-918-6393, 706-357-4444, 300 N Thomas St)* hosts traveling Broadway productions, symphony concerts and national touring acts.

Web site: www.classiccenter.com

Spectator Sports

UGA has a full spectrum of college sports, including football, baseball, gymnastics and men's and women's basketball. The 86,520-seat **Sandford Stadium** is typically sold out months in advance when the Georgia Bulldog football team plays (simply the 'Dawgs' to fans). Contact the athletic department (☎ 877-542-1231, 706-542-9036, 706-542-1231) for information and tickets. The 1996 Olympic soccer matches were held in this stadium.

Getting There & Away

Southeastern Stages (☎ 706-549-2255, 220 W Broad St), a Greyhound connection service, has connections to Atlanta ($14, 1¾ hours, 89 miles, 11 daily), Augusta ($48, from five hours, 263 miles, five daily), Columbia, South Carolina ($61, from six hours, 339 miles, five daily), and Savannah ($35, 3½ hours, 185 miles, two daily).

Getting Around

Athens Transit (☎ 706-613-3430) operates 'The Bus' throughout town. You can find schedules at various locations, including the bus kiosk at City Hall. The typical fare is $1. The University of Georgia operates a campus transit system. Bikes can be attached to city buses for no extra charge.

AUGUSTA
pop 195,000

Augusta, Georgia's second-largest city, best known for the Masters Golf Tournament that swamps the town for a week every April, is relatively tranquil the rest of the year. For a city this size, though, it has a nice selection of museums and restaurants, and recent riverfront development and downtown revitalization are giving the town a new vitality.

History

Augusta owes its existence to geography. Here the Piedmont plateau dissolves into the Atlantic coastal plains, forming a rocky edge. The point where the Savannah River tumbles over this edge was used as a river crossing for Native Americans along their trade routes. The rapids here are also a natural barrier to navigation up the river.

Augusta was founded in 1735 by British general James Edward Oglethorpe to provide a first line of defense against the French and Spanish, and to provide access to the lucrative trading routes. Augusta became the state capital briefly during the American Revolution, when it was controlled at various times by the British troops and the patriots.

During the Civil War, Augusta's importance was limited to manufacturing. The Confederate Powder Works was rapidly built along the Augusta Canal and manufactured nearly three million pounds of Confederate gunpowder. The city became one of the world's largest cotton markets at the end of the 19th century and beginning of the 20th century. Augusta was a winter resort for the wealthy at the beginning of the 20th century. Like many Georgian cities, government investment during World War II helped create a new prosperity; several armored divisions trained at Camp Gordon.

Orientation

I-20 passes to the northwest of the city, and I-520 – known locally as the Bobby Jones

Expressway – loops along the southern side. The city is bounded on the north by the Savannah River. Hotels and restaurants are clustered along the Washington Rd exit of I-20 (exit 199). Downtown is about 6 miles from the expressway, but is easy to get to along Washington Rd.

Information

The welcome center (☎ 800-726-0243, 706-724-4067), located in the Historic Cotton Exchange building at 32 8th St, next to Riverwalk, is a good place to get oriented, with many helpful maps, brochures and hotel discount coupons. It's open 9 am to 5 pm Monday to Saturday and 1 pm to 5 pm Sunday.

Web site: www.augustaga.org

The Georgia Welcome Center on westbound I-20 just west of the Savannah River also has information on Augusta and other areas of the state.

Free Internet access is available at branches of the Augusta public library. The main branch (☎ 706-821-2600) is at 902 Greene St.

The *Augusta Chronicle* is the major daily newspaper. Its Web site contains a travel guide to the city (www.augustachronicle .com). *Augusta Focus* is a weekly African-American newspaper. The *Metropolitan Spirit* is a free weekly that contains listings of arts and entertainment; its Web site is at www.metspirit.com. The monthly *Augusta Magazine* issues an annual 'Best of Augusta' guide, where readers vote for the best restaurants and local bands.

Books-a-Million, on Washington Rd near I-20, has local and regional travel and history books and selections by local authors.

Things to See & Do

Guided driving tours (☎ 706-724-4067) are offered from 10:30 am to noon Saturday from the Historic Cotton Exchange Welcome Center. Adult/child tickets cost $10/5.

One of the key features of Augusta's downtown is the **Riverwalk**, a paved path along the banks of the Savannah River, connecting restaurants, shops and museums, and a good place to sit and watch the river. Special events are frequently staged here. The main entrance is at 8th and Reynolds Sts.

At the entrance to Riverwalk, the restored **Historic Cotton Exchange** (☎ 706-724-4067), 32 8th St, built in 1886, houses artifacts from the days of King Cotton, and shows the process of producing cotton in the late 1800s, from planting through manufacturing. Other obscurities include an original blackboard discovered during the renovation, with posted cotton prices. It's open 9 am to 5 pm Monday to Saturday and 1 pm to 5 pm Sunday.

The **Morris Museum of Art** (☎ 706-724-7501), 1 10th St, two blocks west of the Riverwalk entrance, is dedicated to art and artists of the South. The galleries include antebellum portraits, Civil War illustrations, depictions of the African-American presence in Southern painting and contemporary Southern art. It's open 10 am to 5:30 pm Tuesday to Saturday and 12:30 pm to 5:30 pm Sunday. Admission is $3/2 adults/students; free on Sunday.

Web site: www.themorris.org

The National Science Center's **Fort Discovery** (☎ 706-821-0200), 1 Seventh St, on the eastern end of Riverwalk, is a marvelous museum with more than 270 interactive exhibits demonstrating scientific principles. Exhibits include a high-wire bicycle, a lightning bolt generator, robotics and a theater of special effects. This is a good museum for kids or for adults who have forgotten what a gyroscope does. Hours are 10 am to 5 pm Monday to Saturday and noon to 5 pm Sunday; $8/6 adults/children.

Web site: www.nationalsciencecenter.org

The **Augusta Museum of History** (☎ 706-724-5192), 560 Reynolds St, delivers the basics of local history, and has small digestible chunks and exhibits, featuring Indians 10,000 years ago, a 1914 locomotive and 20th-century history. Hours are 10 am to 5 pm Tuesday to Saturday and 1 pm to 5 pm Sunday; $4/2 adult/children.

Web site: www.augustamuseum.org

The **Laney-Walker Historic District** honors educator Lucy Laney. Born into slavery, she later established a school for

African Americans in Augusta. The **Lucy Craft Laney Museum of Black History** (☎ 706-724-3576), 1116 Philip St, is housed in Laney's restored home. Hours are 9 am to 1 pm weekdays and by appointment on weekends; adults/children $2/75¢.

The **Augusta Canal** was constructed in 1845 to take advantage of the rapid fall of the Savannah River near the city on the fall line. The river falls 52 feet over 4 miles as a result. The canal provided transportation, power and water supply for Augusta. It once supplied water to the **Confederate Powder Works**. Today only the chimney remains next to the current Sibley Mill, which manufactures denim. Today, the canal still has practical uses: The city gets half of its drinking water from the canal, and two textile mills use it to generate hydropower; the only transportation is recreational.

Nowadays, city folk escape to the canal on weekends to canoe or to bike, jog or walk on the canal pathway. The best access is at Savannah Rapids, about 10 miles northwest of downtown. Bicycles can be rented from Chain Reaction (☎ 706-855-2024), at 3920 Roberts Rd, for $5/25 per hour/day; or downtown from Andy Jordan's Bicycle Center (☎ 706-724-6777), at 527 13th St. Canoes, kayaks and small boats can be rented from Broadway Tackle & Boat Rental (☎ 706-738-8848), at 1730 Broad. Canoe and kayak rates are $20/30 for 4/24 hours. They will shuttle you to the top of the canal. You can also get fishing gear here. Canoes and kayaks can also be rented from American Wilderness Outfitters Limited (AWOL; ☎ 706-738-8500), 2328 Washington Rd, for similar prices. A shuttle to the canal costs $10; a river shuttle costs $15. AWOL also has a complete line of outdoor and camping equipment and a climbing wall.

During a stroll downtown, check out **Artists Row** on Broad St between 10th and 11th Sts. Art galleries and restaurants in this area are adding to the area's revitalization after years of decline.

Tours are offered in a few historic houses, including **Meadow Garden** (☎ 706-724-4174), 1320 Independence Dr, the last home

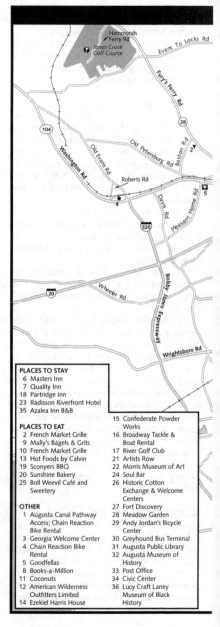

PLACES TO STAY
6   Masters Inn
7   Quality Inn
18 Partridge Inn
23 Radisson Riverfront Hotel
35 Azalea Inn B&B

PLACES TO EAT
2   French Market Grille
9   Mally's Bagels & Grits
10 French Market Grille
13 Hot Foods by Calvin
19 Sconyers BBQ
20 Sunshine Bakery
8   Boll Weevil Café and
    Sweetery

OTHER
1   Augusta Canal Pathway
    Access; Chain Reaction
    Bike Rental
3   Georgia Welcome Center
4   Chain Reaction Bike
    Rental
5   Goodfellas
8   Books-a-Million
11 Coconuts
12 American Wilderness
    Outfitters Limited
14 Ezekiel Harris House

15 Confederate Powder
    Works
16 Broadway Tackle &
    Boat Rental
17 River Golf Club
21 Artists Row
22 Morris Museum of Art
24 Soul Bar
26 Historic Cotton
    Exchange & Welcome
    Centers
27 Fort Discovery
28 Meadow Garden
29 Andy Jordan's Bicycle
    Center
30 Greyhound Bus Terminal
31 Augusta Public Library
32 Augusta Museum of
    History
33 Post Office
34 Civic Center
36 Lucy Craft Laney
    Museum of Black
    History

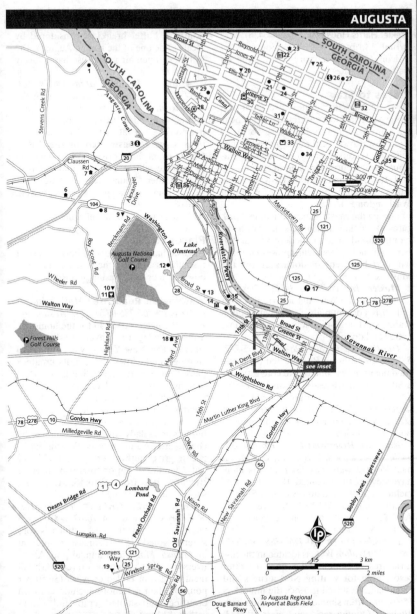

AUGUSTA

of George Walton, the youngest signer of the Declaration of Independence; and the **Ezekiel Harris House** (☎ 706-724-0436), 1822 Broad St, built in 1797. Contact the welcome center for more information on visiting these sites.

Places to Stay

Most of Augusta's hotels are clustered along a particularly unattractive strip near I-20 on Washington Rd, about 6 miles from downtown. Although pitifully ugly, this strip is convenient to the Augusta National Golf Course, many good restaurants and the Augusta Canal. Downtown is easily reached by traveling east on Washington Rd.

During the Masters tournament in April, rates skyrocket and hotels are sold out months in advance. A modern $50 or $60 per night hotel room during normal times will cost hundreds of dollars during the Masters.

Masters Inn (☎ 800-633-3434, 706-863-5566), along the Washington strip just west of I-20, is a decent budget hotel with a pool. Rates start at $45, including breakfast coffee and donuts.

Quality Inn (☎ 800-228-5151, 706-737-5550, 1050 Claussen Rd), located on a side road near the Washington Rd congestion, is a little quieter while still being convenient to restaurants and the golf course. Nice, large singles/doubles with kitchenettes cost $67/78. A continental breakfast and outdoor pool are included.

Radisson Riverfront Hotel (☎ 800-333-3333, 706-722-8900, 2 10th St), downtown next to Riverwalk, has 234 rooms – many have views of the Savannah River. Luxuries include a pool and a fitness center. Singles/doubles start at $112/123 for weekends. Add $13 to these rates on weekdays and another $13 for breakfast.

Partridge Inn (☎ 800-476-6888, 706-737-8888, 2110 Walton Way) is located in the historic area of Summerville, once a winter resort area for visiting Northerners and Canadians. Restored in 1995, the inn offers 155 rooms, from simple rooms to suites with kitchens. Quoted rack rates start at $153,

but with reservations, singles/doubles start at around $89/101. The rates include a Southern buffet breakfast considered by locals to be one of the best in Augusta. The fifth-floor open-air penthouse has a lovely view of Augusta.

Azalea Inn Bed & Breakfast (☎ 706-724-3454, 312-316 Greene St) is located in the Olde Town historic district downtown, providing some nice walking opportunities nearby. The two attractive, Victorian-style houses were constructed in the 1890s. Comfy rooms have private bathrooms, and most have whirlpool baths and gas fireplaces. Other options include kitchenettes, sleeper sofas or a sun porch. Rates are $112 to $168.

Web site: www.theazaleainn.com

Places to Eat

Augusta has a seemingly endless variety of restaurants. Many of the best are clustered downtown or near Washington Rd.

Washington Road Area *Mally's Bagels & Grits* (☎ 706-736-0770, 2742 Washington Rd) – the name says it all for the homesick Yankee trying to convert to Southern cuisine. The New York–style bagels and stone-ground, slow-cooked grits create a place 'where North meets South in perfect hominy.' This cheery place serves breakfast and lunch daily, and dinner Thursday to Sunday. You can get omelets, lox, corned beef hash, pancakes, sandwiches, hot dogs, burgers and salads. And did we mention the cheese grits, Cajun grits, garlic grits, garlic cheese grits, southwestern grits or sausage grits? Or the dozen or so cream cheeses? Breakfast runs from $3 to $8. Most sandwiches with a side are $5 to $6.

French Market Grille (☎ 706-855-5111, 368 Fury's Ferry Rd; ☎ 706-737-4865, 425 Highland Ave), with two locations, is consistently voted the best Augusta restaurant in *Augusta Magazine's* annual poll. Appetizers include Cajun popcorn (crawfish tail meat for $8) or boiled crawfish ($6.50 per pound). Main selections include crawfish etouffeé, soft-shelled crab and Cajun catfish ($14 to $23).

Downtown *Sunshine Bakery (☎ 706-724-2302, 1209 Broad St)* is a small family-owned cafe serving sandwiches, fresh breads, soups and kosher meats for lunch. A sandwich costs $3 to $6. The entire cafe is nonsmoking.

Hot Foods by Calvin (☎ 706-738-5666, 2027 Broad St) is a favorite of downtown office workers and neighborhood residents; this unassuming restaurant has great Southern down-home cooking. If you haven't tried black-eyed peas, candied yams, collard greens or fried okra yet, order a vegetable plate for $4.50 and sample them all. Other specialties include fried or barbecue chicken, catfish and blackened fish. Sandwiches are also available ($1.45 to $5). Typical meals cost $6 to $10; breakfast specials are available for $4.50.

Boll Weevil Café and Sweetery (☎ 706-722-7772, 10 9th St), next to Riverwalk, is best known locally for its fattening and delicious desserts, from white chocolate raspberry cheesecake to the Georgia peach tart, around $4. It also serves salads, crepes, sandwiches and main dishes such as jambalaya ($8 to $13).

Elsewhere *Sconyers Bar-B-Que (☎ 706-790-5411, 2250 Sconyers Way)* is way the heck out of the way off Peach Orchard Rd near the Bobby Jones Expressway, yet it serves barbecue meals to as many as 3000 people a day on the three days a week it's open (Thursday to Saturday). Its selection as one of *People* magazine's 10 best barbecue joints in the US may be an overstatement, but the barbecue – smoked over hickory and oak – *is* good.

Entertainment
The *Soul Bar (☎ 706-724-8880, 984 Broad St)* features live jazz and other music downtown. *Goodfellas (☎ 706-863-5779, 3328 Washington Rd)* has live music, usually Wednesday to Saturday, starting after 9 pm. *Coconuts (☎ 706-738-8133, 469 Highland Ave)* is a popular nightspot for singles looking to shake their groove thing; be prepared for lots of secondhand smoke. The crowd doesn't arrive until late.

Augusta has an opera company, a symphony and a ballet. For a calendar of arts events, contact the Greater Augusta Arts Council (☎ 706-826-4702) or see its Web site (www.AugustaArts.com).

The *Civic Center* often hosts national touring acts, including native son James Brown. Check the listings in the *Metropolitan Spirit.*

Augusta has been a golf mecca since it was introduced during the town's days as a winter resort. The Augusta National Golf Course, where the Masters tournament is played, is private, and your odds of playing there are slim. The area boasts 14 other public or semiprivate 18-hole courses. Popular public courses include Forest Hills Golf Club (☎ 706-733-0001, 1500 Comfort Rd); the new River Golf Course (☎ 706-202-0110), at 307 Riverside Boulevard across the river in North Augusta, South Carolina; and the Jones Creek Golf Course (☎ 706-860-4228), 4101 Hammonds Ferry, in Evans, to the northwest of the city.

Spectator Sports
Golf rules Augusta, but if you think you can actually get tickets to the Masters tournament, we pity you. The Masters gets under way the first full week every April, with practice rounds on Monday through Wednesday and the actual tournament Thursday through Sunday. A waiting list for tickets was established in 1972, closed in 1978 because of the length of the list, and reopened briefly in 2000. Tickets to practice rounds are available on a lottery basis. To apply, send your name, address, daytime telephone number and social security number to: Masters Tournament, Practice Rounds, PO Box 2047, Augusta GA 30903. The deadline is July 15 for the following year's Masters.

The Augusta Lynx hockey team (☎ 706-724-4423) plays October through March in the Civic Center.

Getting There & Away
Delta and USAir offer flights to the Augusta Regional Airport at Bush Field. All Delta's flights pass through their hub in

GEORGIA

Atlanta; a roundtrip flight to and from Atlanta starts at around $260.

The Greyhound terminal (☎ 706-722-6411) is at 1128 Greene St; call ☎ 800-231-2222 for their schedule.

WASHINGTON

pop 4300

This small town, on Hwy 78 between Athens and Augusta, is worth strolling around. Sherman and his forces passed south of here, leaving the antebellum homes undamaged; many still remain. In May 1865, Confederate president Jefferson Davis met with members of his cabinet to sign the last official papers of the Confederacy, thus dissolving the rebel government.

Tourist information is available from the Chamber of Commerce office (☎ 706-678-2013, washcham@nu-z.net) in the City Hall Annex (signed from Hwy 78). They distribute a useful walking/driving map.

The **Robert Toombs House State Historic Site** (☎ 706-678-2226), on Hwy 78 three blocks east of the town square, preserves the story of Robert Toombs, the Confederate Secretary of State and later known as the 'unreconstructed rebel.'

AH Stephens State Historic Park (☎ 706-456-2602), near Crawfordville, has one of the best collections of Civil War artifacts in the state. There are also camping sites ($13/15 tent/RV) and cottages ($55 to $85) available.

Savannah & the Coast

The Georgia coast has a great variety of activities for travelers. The city of Savannah blends history with modernity, with street after street of historic homes, museums, good restaurants and lively nightlife. Farther down the coast, developed islands once used as resorts by the wealthy are now favorites of beachcombers, bicyclists, golfers and history buffs. The coast also has some of the state's most remote scenery – islands where the only access is by ferry or boat, and where you can share miles of beach with only a few other people and wild horses.

All of this variety is set amid a coastal plain of startling beauty – the omnipresent live oak trees; small streams cutting through tidal marshlands, with hundreds of fiddler crabs scurrying for their hiding places and great egrets looking for their next meal; and mile after mile of cordgrass swaying with the wind.

Savannah

pop 130,000
Savannah has been remarkable in its ability to preserve its fascinating history, from its founding as Georgia's first settlement to its revolutionary urban design. Set on the Savannah River amid beautiful scenery, the city is steeped in tradition, yet tourism has helped transform Savannah into a modern city.

HISTORY

Founded in 1733 by James Oglethorpe, Savannah was the first English settlement in the new colony of Georgia. It was strategically located on a high bluff 15 miles upriver from the Atlantic Ocean. The city was laid out in a grid-like pattern of streets, houses and public buildings; in the middle of each ward was an open square. Savannah grew to 24 squares, 21 of which still survive today. This careful urban design is widely studied

Highlights

- Roam Savannah's historic district and relax among well-preserved antebellum homes and lovely parks set amidst beautiful scenery.

- Get lost on Cumberland Island, a national seashore offering peaceful hiking, armadillos, ruins of elegant mansions and wild horses on long stretches of deserted beaches.

- Dive, golf or just explore the history and beaches of the Golden Isles.

and admired for making a livable, beautiful, expandable city.

In 1779, during the Revolutionary War, the British seized the city. American forces attempted to take it back in bloody fighting during the Siege of Savannah, but failed. On Spring Hill (really just a bump in the flat landscape), more than 1000 men died in an hour. The city remained in British hands until the end of the war in 1783.

Savannah became a wealthy shipping center, handling both the export of cotton and the import of slaves. Eli Whitney, a New Yorker, invented the cotton gin here in 1793, expanding the slave trade. In the 19th century, railroads added to the city's wealth, bringing in ever greater volumes of plantation produce for distribution through its ports.

During the Civil War, a successful Union bombardment of nearby Fort Pulaski played a key role in supporting the Union economic blockade. Savannah was the goal of General Sherman's devastating March to the Sea, and the city surrendered to him on December 21, 1864. When Lincoln asked that Savannah be spared, Sherman referred to the city as a Christmas present for the president. Instead of burning the city, Sherman rested his troops there for six weeks before turning north to cut another path of destruction through South Carolina.

The collapse of cotton prices in the late 1800s sent Savannah into a severe economic decline. In the long run, this may have been a good thing – had it prospered, the elegant streets may well have been demolished in the name of development. Still, much was lost to demolition, neglect and decay.

In 1955, the beautiful Davenport House nearly became a parking lot, but was saved by a local campaign that went on to protect and restore significant chunks of the historic downtown. The 2½-sq-mile district now has over 1000 restored Federal and Regency buildings, ranging from churches and private homes to the ornate US Customs House on Bay St.

More recently, John Berendt's hugely successful 1994 murder mystery–travelogue *Midnight in the Garden of Good and Evil*, and the subsequent film directed by Clint Eastwood, made Savannah a huge tourist destination. The book portrays the city as a bizarre remnant of the Old South, where tradition battles with debauchery. Some of the hoopla is finally beginning to die down, and tourism operators are looking for the next big hit.

The city is full of people who come to Savannah, fall in love with the city and stay. The Savannah College of Art and Design (SCAD), downtown, attracts thousands of students from throughout the country. Tourists arrive in Savannah looking for the colorful cast of characters featured in Berendt's book, and they are still out there. Yet, the waiter at a fine restaurant, the young woman serving your coffee, or the clerk at your hotel is more likely to be a SCAD student from Colorado than a native Savannahian.

ORIENTATION

Savannah's Historic District is a rectangle bounded by the Savannah River, Forsyth Park, E Broad St and Martin Luther King Jr Blvd. Almost everything of interest to most visitors lies within or just outside this area. Along the Savannah River, cotton warehouses have been converted into a compact row of restaurants, shops and bars. City Market, on W St Julian St near Franklin Square, is a redeveloped area of shops and restaurants along the western edge of the Historic District.

South of the Historic District, the Victorian District encompasses 50 blocks of two-story wood homes built in the late 19th century. Different areas are in various stages of renovation, and a recently renovated gem can be right around the corner from a sagging eyesore.

Even farther south is the Southside, an uninteresting strip of shopping malls, fast-food joints and hotels. The hotels here, however, are much cheaper than accommodations in the Historic District.

Maps

Many free maps of the city are available at hotels and tourist attractions around town.

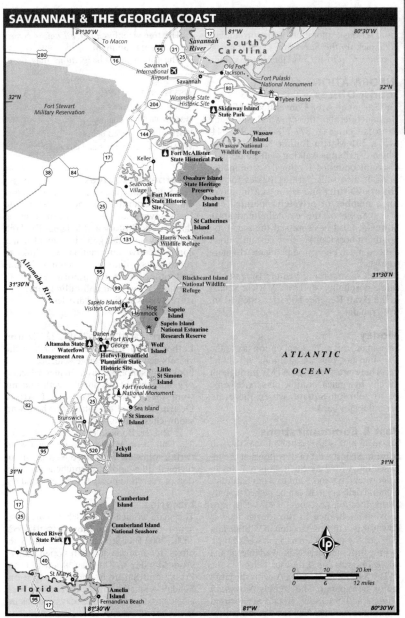

SAVANNAH & THE GEORGIA COAST

To Macon

Savannah River

South Carolina

Savannah International Airport

Savannah

Old Fort Jackson

Fort Pulaski National Monument

Tybee Island

Wormsloe State Historic Site

Skidaway Island State Park

Wassaw Island

Wassaw National Wildlife Refuge

Fort Stewart Military Reservation

Fort McAllister State Historical Park

Keller

Ossabaw Island State Heritage Preserve

Seabrook Village

Fort Morris State Historic Site

Ossabaw Island

St Catherines Island

Harris Neck National Wildlife Refuge

Blackbeard Island National Wildlife Refuge

Altamaha River

Sapelo Island Visitors Center

Hog Hammock

Sapelo Island

Sapelo Island National Estuarine Research Reserve

Darien

Fort King George

Wolf Island

Altamaha State Waterfowl Management Area

Hofwyl-Broadfield Plantation State Historic Site

Little St Simons Island

Fort Frederica National Monument

Brunswick

Sea Island

St Simons Island

ATLANTIC OCEAN

Jekyll Island

Cumberland Island

Cumberland Island National Seashore

Crooked River State Park

Kingsland

St Marys

Florida

Amelia Island

Fernandina Beach

0   10   20 km

0   6   12 miles

GEORGIA

These are good enough if all you plan to do is wander around the Historic District. For more serious exploration of the surrounding area, pick up the *Street Maps of Savannah/Chatham County* for $3 at the visitors center.

INFORMATION
Tourist Offices
The Savannah Area Convention & Visitors Bureau operates the crowded Savannah Visitors Center (☎ 877-728-2662, 912-944-0455), 301 Martin Luther King Jr Blvd, which distributes walking-tour guides and discount coupons for local accommodations. It also sells parking passes for the Historic District and is the starting point for a number of privately operated city tours. *Some* of the overwhelmed staff, however, must have missed the memo on Southern hospitality – they certainly don't expend much energy on being nice to mere tourists.

The Convention & Visitors Bureau also runs a hospitality center on W River St next to the Hyatt Regency hotel. It's open 10 am to 10 pm daily.

Money
Savannah adds a 2% local option tax to the 4% state tax, plus an additional 6% hotel tax. There are plenty of ATMs throughout the city. In a pinch, or for a full-service bank, go to Johnson Square, where there are several major banks.

Post & Communications
The main post office (☎ 912-235-4653) is at 2 N Fahm St, just west of downtown at the intersection with Bay St. It's open 7 am to 6 pm weekdays and 9 am to 3 pm Saturday. General delivery mail can be picked up only at this location (zip code 31402). The most convenient branch in the tourist area is downtown at the intersection of W State and Barnard Sts, open 8 am to 5 pm weekdays.

Free Internet access is available at the public libraries (see Libraries, below).

The *Savannah Morning News* is the city's major newspaper. The weekly *Savannah Tribune* and *Savannah Herald* are focused toward the African-American community.

Web sites: www.savannahnow.com and www.savannahtribune.com

The free weekly *Creative Loafing* covers arts and entertainment.

The following radio stations may be of interest:

WSVH – 91.1 FM, NPR
WIXV – 95 FM, rock
WJCL – 96.5 FM, country
WSIS – 104 FM, R&B oldies
WBMQ – 630 AM, news and talk radio

Internet Resources
The Savannah Area Convention & Visitors Bureau operates a good Web site (www.savcvb.com), with information on things to do, history and lodging. The Web site www.savannahgeorgia.com also has comprehensive information, with links to restaurants, nightspots, accommodations and other items of interest. Savannah Online (www.savannah-online.com) has current news stories and articles.

Bookstores
Ex Libris (☎ 912-525-7550), 228 Martin Luther King Jr Blvd, a block north of the visitors center, has a large selection of art books and supplies, plus a smaller selection of general books. It's popular with students from the Savannah College of Art & Design. There's also a coffee shop here, with sandwiches and desserts.

E Shaver, Bookseller (☎ 912-234-7257), 326 Bull St on Madison Square, is a wonderful, sprawling bookstore with plenty of regional titles and a comprehensive selection of everything else. It's closed Sundays.

Libraries
The main branch of the Chatham-Effingham-Liberty Regional Library (☎ 912-652-3600), 2002 Bull St, between 36th and 37th, offers free Internet access. It's open 9 am to 9 pm Monday to Thursday, 9 am to 6 pm Friday and Saturday and 2 pm to 6 pm Sunday. A smaller branch on Factor's Walk is open noon to 3 pm weekdays and has Internet access.

Laundry

Wash World operates several coin Laundromats in town, with drop-off service. Closest to downtown is the one at 303 Tattnall St (☎ 912-234-3705). The minimum drop-off charge is a steep $10.

Medical Services

The hospitals closest to the Historic District are: Candler Hospital (☎ 912-692-6000), 5353 Reynolds St; and Memorial Medical Center (☎ 912-350-8000), 4700 Waters Ave. Both have 24-hour emergency rooms.

Dangers & Annoyances

The Historic District is safe during the day. However, muggings and drug dealing are common in poorer neighborhoods that surround the Historic District, and Savannah has its share of murders (one concierge admitted hiding the newspaper when the front-page news was too bad). Be aware, too, that criminals know where the well-heeled tourists hang out. At night, use common-sense precautions and stay in well-lit, populated areas. The riverfront is generally OK.

THINGS TO SEE & DO

Savannah is a *great* walking city, and the best thing to do is just walk the squares. The ambiance of Spanish moss hanging from live oaks, entire streets of historic 18th- and 19th-century buildings, and the beautiful squares are Savannah's main attractions. Many of the squares are lovely parks with statues, fountains and greenery and are great for people watching. For an interesting walking tour, stroll along the riverfront, through City Market, along Bull St from City Hall to Forsyth Park, and back along Abercorn St.

The **Savannah History Museum** (☎ 912-238-1779), 303 Martin Luther King Jr Blvd, next to the visitors center, is a good place to start, with a film and exhibits that give a feel for the city's past. The exhibits include the history of the area's rice plantations and railroads, and a replica of Forrest Gump's park bench (which, in the film, was in Chippewa Square). The museum is open

8:30 am to 5 pm weekdays, 9 am to 5 pm weekends. Admission costs $3/2.50 adults/children.

Just a short distance north is the **Ships of the Sea Maritime Museum** (☎ 912-232-1511), 41 Martin Luther King Jr Blvd. The well-done exhibits focus on models of ships, particularly ones associated with the city, and nautical memorabilia. The SS *Savannah* was the first steamship to cross the Atlantic Ocean; much later, the NS *Savannah* was nuclear powered. The collection is housed in one of the South's earliest Greek Revival structures. The museum is open 10 am to 5 pm daily except Monday. Admission is $5/4.

Web site: www.shipsofthesea.org

The **Telfair Art Museum** (☎ 912-232-1177), 121 Barnard St on Telfair Square, is a small but pleasant museum containing several plaster casts of Roman statues, a marvelous rotunda gallery of European paintings, and the bird-girl statue from the cover of *Midnight in the Garden of Good and Evil*. The museum is housed in an 1818 mansion in the neoclassical Regency style. Hours are 10 am to 5 pm Tuesday to Saturday, 1 pm to 5 pm Sunday and noon to 5 pm Monday; admission is $6/2/1 adults/students/children.

Factor's Walk, essentially the upper level of buildings between River and Bay Sts, was the city's 19th-century business center. Now it is a line of shops, mostly selling souvenirs. Nearby are the gold-domed **City Hall** and the **Cotton Exchange** building, guarded by lion statues and once one of the world's busiest exchanges.

Along the waterfront, River Street is home to more touristy shops, restaurants and nightspots of all price ranges. The brick-and-cobblestone waterside promenade is one of the city's highlights. Yachts and boats tie up along the edge.

Several historic houses in Savannah are open for tours. The **Davenport House** (☎ 912-236-8097), on Columbia Square, was the first of Savannah's historic homes to be restored, and its 30-minute tour is still one of the most worthwhile in the city. Its Georgian architecture is some of the finest in the

GEORGIA

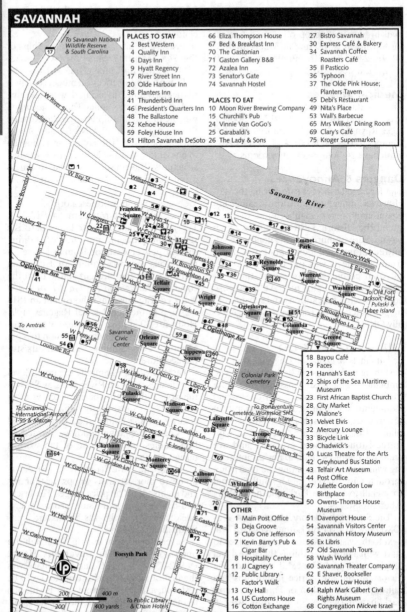

SAVANNAH

PLACES TO STAY
2 Best Western
4 Quality Inn
6 Days Inn
9 Hyatt Regency
17 River Street Inn
20 Olde Harbour Inn
38 Planters Inn
41 Thunderbird Inn
46 President's Quarters Inn
48 The Ballastone
52 Kehoe House
59 Foley House Inn
61 Hilton Savannah DeSoto
66 Eliza Thompson House
67 Bed & Breakfast Inn
70 The Gastonian
71 Gaston Gallery B&B
72 Azalea Inn
73 Senator's Gate
74 Savannah Hostel

PLACES TO EAT
10 Moon River Brewing Company
15 Churchill's Pub
24 Vinnie Van GoGo's
25 Garabaldi's
26 The Lady & Sons
27 Bistro Savannah
30 Express Café & Bakery
34 Savannah Coffee
   Roasters Café
35 Il Pasticcio
36 Typhoon
37 The Olde Pink House;
   Planters Tavern
45 Debi's Restaurant
49 Nita's Place
53 Wall's Barbecue
65 Mrs Wilkes' Dining Room
69 Clary's Café
75 Kroger Supermarket

18 Bayou Café
19 Faces
21 Hannah's East
22 Ships of the Sea Maritime
   Museum
23 First African Baptist Church
28 City Market
29 Malone's
31 Velvet Elvis
32 Mercury Lounge
33 Bicycle Link
39 Chadwick's
40 Lucas Theatre for the Arts
42 Greyhound Bus Station
43 Telfair Art Museum
44 Post Office
47 Juliette Gordon Low
   Birthplace
50 Owens-Thomas House
   Museum
51 Davenport House
54 Savannah Visitors Center
55 Savannah History Museum
56 Ex Libris
57 Old Savannah Tours
58 Wash World
60 Savannah Theater Company
62 E Shaver, Bookseller
63 Andrew Low House
64 Ralph Mark Gilbert Civil
   Rights Museum
68 Congregation Mickve Israel

OTHER
1 Main Post Office
3 Deja Groove
5 Club One Jefferson
7 Kevin Barry's Pub &
   Cigar Bar
8 Hospitality Center
11 JJ Cagney's
12 Public Library -
   Factor's Walk
13 City Hall
14 US Customs House
16 Cotton Exchange

South. It also has a shop with interesting books on architecture, restoration and preservation. The house is open Monday to Saturday and 1 pm to 4 pm Sunday. Admission is $7/3.50.

At the northeastern corner of Bull and Oglethorpe Sts is the **Juliette Gordon Low Birthplace** (☎ 912-233-4501), the 1821 upper-middle-class Victorian home in which the founder of the Girl Scouts of America was raised. Decorations have been restored to match the late 1800s period. Girl Scouts make frequent pilgrimages here. It is open 10 am to 4 pm Monday to Saturday (closed Wednesday) and 12:30 pm to 4:30 pm Sunday; admission costs $5/4.

The **Owens-Thomas House Museum** (☎ 912-233-9743), 124 Abercorn St, features Greek Revival architecture. It's open noon to 5 pm Monday, 10 am to 5 pm Tuesday to Saturday and 2 pm to 5 pm Sunday; admission is $6/2.

The **Andrew Low House** (☎ 912-233-6854), 329 Abercorn St on Lafayette Square, is of classical mid-19th century design and was built in 1848 by cotton merchant Andrew Low (Juliette's father-in-law). It's open 10:30 am to 4 pm Friday to Wednesday and noon to 4 pm Sunday, with guided tours every half hour; admission costs $7/4.50.

Farther south, at Monterey Square, is **Congregation Mickve Israel,** the oldest Reform Judaism synagogue in the USA (the congregation was founded in 1733, though the present building dates from 1878). The original congregation members came mainly from Spain and Portugal. Tours are offered 10 am to noon and 2 pm to 4 pm weekdays; suggested donation is $2.

Colonial Park Cemetery, at Abercorn St and E Oglethorpe Ave, was used as the city's graveyard from 1750 to 1853; several Revolutionary War heroes are buried here. During the Civil War, bored Union soldiers changed dates on some of the headstones as a joke, creating impossibly long lives.

The **Ralph Mark Gilbert Civil Rights Museum** (☎ 912-231-8900), 460 Martin Luther King Jr Blvd, just south of the I-16 overpass, tells the story of African Americans in Savannah, focusing on the Civil Rights struggle. After the first sit-ins in 1960, a 15-month economic boycott, and a 'wade-in' at Tybee Island, the city integrated one year before passage of the 1964 Civil Rights Act. In 1964, Martin Luther King Jr called Savannah 'the most integrated city south of the Mason-Dixon line.' The museum is open 9 am to 5 pm Monday to Saturday; entry costs $4/2.

The **First African Baptist Church** (☎ 912-233-6597), 23 Montgomery St at Franklin Square, the oldest African-American church in North America, was built in 1859 by slaves (after completing their normal days' work). Breathing holes in the floor downstairs are said to have been used by slaves fleeing to freedom. The church is open 10 am to 4 pm Monday to Saturday; church services on Sunday.

Bonaventure Cemetery (☎ 912-651-6843), east of the city on Bonaventure Rd, figures prominently in the book *Midnight in the Garden of Good and Evil.* Here you can walk at the edge of the Wilmington River amid the historic statues, moss-covered oaks, wisteria and azaleas. Songwriter Johnny Mercer and poet Conrad Aiken (look for the bench gravestone) are buried here. The cemetery is open 8 am to 5 pm; no admission charge. To get there, take Wheaton St east from downtown to Bonaventure Rd.

Universities

From its beginnings in 1979, the **Savannah College of Art and Design** (☎ 912-238-2400) has grown to 6,000 students. The college has been instrumental in renovating buildings in the Historic District, and now occupies more than 48 structures. Its artistic students help give vitality to downtown. Many of the tourist industry employees – waiters, hotel clerks etc – are SCAD students. Web site: www.scad.edu

Armstrong Atlantic State University (☎ 912-927-5211) in Southside is part of the state university system and has nearly 6,000 students. Historically black Savannah State University (☎ 912-356-2186) is also part of that system.

PLACES TO STAY

The most attractive accommodations are historic inns and B&Bs in the Historic District, though most of these start above $100 a night and the fancier ones are closer to $200 and above. Be aware that the inns do not typically provide the personal touch of a B&B, where the owners may live in the building.

Many of the historic inns and B&Bs have a very wide range of rates. When making a reservation, you may want to ask why. Cheaper rooms might be a tiny space in the basement with no view (Eliza Thompson House), or they may face an unattractive and noisy parking garage (Planters Inn). You'll pay premium prices for the premium rooms.

Many of the inns are totally nonsmoking; be sure to ask if it's important to you. Some have limits on children aged under 12.

Some hotels' Web sites have pictures of individual rooms so you can choose.

A few chain hotels are located on Bay St, near the riverfront. These are quite expensive for the type of lodging. A few sleazy motels are near the bus station. For standard, decent budget and mid-range chain hotels, you have to travel 5 miles south of Forsyth Park on Abercorn St, an area of Savannah known as Southside. Another concentration of reasonably priced chain hotels is around I-95 exit 94, about 15 miles from downtown.

Whatever type of accommodations you choose, rates tend to be cheaper midweek; making a reservation several weeks in advance is a good idea for any weekend stay. The visitors center and various visitors guides contain discount coupons for the inns as well as the hotels and are probably your best bet for finding a deal.

The Savannah Area Convention & Visitors Bureau Web site (www.savcvb.com) lists many accommodations options, with links provided. Sonja's Bed & Breakfast Reservation Service (☎ 912-232-7787) can also help with reservations.

Budget

For camping, your best bet is to head out to Tybee Island; for a more secluded experience, try Skidaway Island State Park. See the Around Savannah section for details.

The HI-AYH *Savannah Hostel* (☎ 912-236-7744, 304 E Hall St), at Lincoln St near the edge of the Historic District, comes well recommended. It's in a restored mansion and offers dorm beds ($18) and one private room ($36 for one or two people). Guests can use the kitchen, and there's a large Kroger's grocery store across the street. The CAT shuttle stops nearby on Habersham St between Hall and Gwinnett Sts. The office is open 7 am to 10 am and 5 pm to 10 pm daily; guests are expected to leave during the day. The hostel is closed January, February and sometimes December.

The *Thunderbird Inn* (☎ 912-232-2661, 611 Oglethorpe Ave), in a less desirable location near the Greyhound bus station, is a worn but serviceable motel for dedicated budget travelers only. Rates are $40/50 weekdays/weekends including tax.

In the Southside, *Best Western* (☎ 912-355-1000, 45 Eisenhower Dr), outside of town, has 129 rooms from $49. *Baymont Inn & Suites* (☎ 912-927-7660, fax 912-927-6392, 8484 Abercorn St), at Montgomery Cross Rd, has 102 rooms from $59/66 singles/doubles.

La Quinta (☎ 912-925-9505, fax 912-925-3495), at I-95 exit 94, has 120 standard, modern hotel rooms from $59.

Mid-Range

Quality Inn (☎ 912-236-6321, vbqihos@ad.com, 300 W Bay St), between Montgomery and Jefferson Sts, is at the edge of the Historic District and near the riverfront. Its ugly exterior belies its 52 modern rooms. The location is the only justification for its rates of $89/129 low/high season, including continental breakfast. The nearby *Best Western* (☎ 912-233-1011, 412 W Bay St) is similar in quality and price ($70/120).

Days Inn (☎ 912-236-4440, 201 W Bay St), a block from the river, has 253 standard rooms in a large brick building that blends in with the neighborhood's historic character. Rates start at $130, without breakfast. Suites with a full kitchen are available.

There is an outdoor pool and a 24-hour restaurant.

Among Savannah's historic inns, *Bed and Breakfast Inn* (☎ 912-238-0518, fax 912-233-2537, bedbreakfast@travelbase.com, 117 W Gordon St), adjacent to Chatham Square, is in an 1853 Federal row house. Its rooms aren't as posh as others, but then it's less expensive as well. It's decorated in antiques, period reproduction pieces and oriental carpets, and it has a relaxing private garden and deck. Its 16 rooms cost $79 to $150, including breakfast.
Web site: www.travelbase.com/destinations/savannah/bed-breakfast/

The *Azalea Inn* (☎ 800-582-3823, 912-236-2707, 217 E Huntingdon St), a block east of Forsyth Park, is an 1889 Italianate house decorated with period and contemporary pieces. The friendly owners create a casual and unpretentious atmosphere. The inn consists of seven rooms and a two-bedroom carriage house, all with four-poster beds, some with whirlpools. Rates are $129 to $249, including an expanded continental breakfast in the mural-decorated dining room.
Web site: www.azaleainn.com

The *Eliza Thompson House* (☎ 800-348-9378, 912-236-3620, 5 W Jones St), less formal than some other inns, is an 1847 Federal-style home with 25 gracious rooms decorated in antiques, oriental carpets and heart pine floors. The beautiful courtyard is a great place to relax. Rates are $109 to $260, depending on the room and view; the cheapest room is tiny and dim with no view. The rates include a full breakfast, wine and cheese in the evening, and coffee and dessert at night.
Web site: www.elizathompsonhouse.com

Top End

Olde Harbour Inn (☎ 800-553-6533, 912-234-4100, fax 912-233-5979, 508 E Factors Walk), in an 1892 converted warehouse on the riverfront, rents 24 comfortable suites, each with a fully equipped kitchen. The rates are $129 to $229 and include a continental breakfast.

The *Hilton Savannah DeSoto* (☎ 800-445-8667, 912-232-9000, fax 912-231-1633, 15 E Liberty St), near Madison Square, has modern business-class rooms, an outdoor pool and convention facilities. Rates are $129 to $179, plus $7 for parking. Be careful to avoid the silly $50 cancellation fee for leaving before your scheduled departure date.
Web site: www.desotohilton.com

The *Hyatt Regency* (☎ 800-233-1234, 912-238-1234, fax 912-944-3678, 2 W Bay St) has an exit directly onto River St. The hotel offers luxurious, business-class accommodations, but its ugly boxy exterior is a slap in the face to the area's historic feel. It's very popular for business conferences. Rates for its 347 rooms start at $145/205 low/high season, including breakfast.

President's Quarters Inn (☎ 800-233-1776, 912-233-1600, fax 912-238-0849, 225 E President St), near Wright Square, was built in 1855 as a Federal-style townhouse. Its 19 large rooms are furnished with four-poster beds and working fireplaces. The inn is decorated with many presidential pictures. The cozy courtyard is good for relaxing. Rates are $137 to $225 and include breakfast, wine and fruit, and afternoon hors d'oeuvres.
Web site: www.presidentsquarters.com

The *River Street Inn* (☎ 800-253-4229, 912-234-6400, fax 912-234-1478, 115 E River St), in a converted cotton warehouse, is located right on the river in the midst of the River Street restaurants, gift shops and nightspots. The 86 spacious rooms come with wood floors, brick walls and four-poster canopy beds; the rooms on one side have a view of the Savannah River. High-season rates are $149 to $275, including breakfast.
Web site: www.riverstreetinn.com

Planters Inn (☎ 800-554-1187, 912-232-5678, 29 Abercorn St), on Reynolds Square, is an 1890 historic inn with a great lobby and 60 pleasant rooms furnished with historic reproductions. One side of the inn faces an ugly and noisy parking garage; ask for a view of the square. Rates start at $150 and include a continental breakfast.
Web site: www.plantersinnsavannah.com

Senator's Gate (☎ 912-233-6398, 226 E Hall St), with only four rooms and occupied by its friendly, gracious owners, retains the feel of a personal B&B. Opened in 2000 after two years of renovations, this elegant 1885 Italianate house has lots of huge windows, a pleasant parlor, 1880 French wallpaper, 12-foot ceilings and original heart pine floors. The modern bathrooms all have whirlpools and heated towel racks. Rates are $155 to $195, including a full breakfast, and drinks and cheese in the afternoon. There's a two-night minimum.

The *Foley House Inn* (☎ 800-647-3708, 912-232-6622, fax 912-231-1218, 14 W Hull St), on Chippewa Square, is an 1896 five-story Victorian brick house decorated in a fusion of continental and Southern styles. Its 18 spacious rooms are decorated in antiques and oriental rugs, and many have fireplaces, balconies and Jacuzzis, and it's more reserved and private than some others. Rates are $175 to $290, including full breakfast, tea and cookies and evening hors d'oeuvres; the cheaper rooms are in a carriage house and the basement. Web site: www.bbonline.com/ga/savannah/foley/

The *Kehoe House* (☎ 800-820-1020, 912-232-1020, fax 912-231-1587, 123 Habersham St), on Columbia Square, is a formal, quiet historic inn located in a stately four-story Victorian building that was once a funeral home. Its 15 rooms cost $205 to $275, including a full breakfast.

Gaston Gallery Bed & Breakfast (☎ 800-671-0716, 912-238-3294, 211 E Gaston St), is a 19th-century Italianate townhouse on peaceful Gaston St. The spacious public areas, front porch and garden make this a better choice than some of the historic inns, which can be cramped and formal. The 15 rooms are $200 to $210, including a deluxe continental breakfast, wine and cheese; a two-night minimum applies. Web site: www.gastongallery.com

The *Gastonian* (☎ 800-322-6603, 912-232-2869, fax 912-232-0710, gastoniann@ aol.com, 220 E Gaston St), in two adjacent 1868 Italianate Regency mansions, is one of Savannah's premier inns, drawing an upper-class clientele. The romantic setting includes a working fireplace in each room, a lush formal garden, a pleasant deck and huge whirlpool baths. Rates are $225 to $375, including a gourmet breakfast, afternoon tea and wine, and evening cordials. Web site: www.gastonian.com

The *Ballastone* (☎ 800-822-4553, 912-236-1484, fax 912-236-4626, 14 E Oglethorpe Ave), in the heart of the Historic District, is Savannah's grandest and most elegant historic inn. In an 1838 building, the antiques and rich hardwood are complemented by Scalamandre wallpaper, modern baths, a full bar and a beautiful garden. Rates for the 17 rooms are $255 to $465 on weekends in October, March, April and May; $60 less in other months. They include a full breakfast, afternoon tea and evening hors d'oeuvres. Web site: www.ballastone.com

PLACES TO EAT

Savannah has many fine dining experiences, from gourmet Southern food to fresh seafood. Many restaurants are concentrated along the waterfront and in City Market, on W Congress St; you can stroll the strips and pick out what looks good. The riverfront has many seafood restaurants – locals consider these to be overpriced for what they offer. Restaurants are also scattered throughout the Historic District.

City Market Area

The *Express Café & Bakery* (☎ 912-233-4683, 39 Barnard St), a block from the main City Market area, is a simple cafe serving reasonable breakfasts and lunch sandwiches ($4 to $5). It's closed Monday and Tuesday.

Vinnie Van GoGo's (☎ 912-233-6394, 317 W Bryan St), across from Franklin Park, is a popular place for college students. You can get a delicious 14-inch New York–style pizza with two toppings for $12. They also sell pizza by the slice, calzones and domestic and imported beers. This hangout isn't much to look at, but the tables outside are great for people watching. They accept cash only.

Garabaldi's (☎ 912-232-7118, 315 W Congress St) is a Northern Italian restaurant serving pasta, veal, shrimp, fish and chicken dishes ($9 to $16) in an intimate but casual setting. It's open for dinner only.

The Lady & Sons (☎ 912-233-2600, 311 W Congress St) is an excellent Southern-style restaurant, serving delicacies like candied sweet potatoes, butter beans and fried chicken in a pleasant atmosphere. You can go for the outstanding buffet or order off the menu. Lunches are $8 to $10, dinners $16 to $20.

Bistro Savannah (☎ 912-233-6266, 309 W Congress St) is one of the top seafood restaurants in Georgia. The restaurant uses organically grown local and regional produce. Choose from garlic sautéed mussels and asparagus, or barbecued black grouper with peach and pear chutney. Dishes cost $15 to $21; it's open for dinner only.

Il Pasticcio (☎ 912-231-8888, 2 E Broughton St), at Bull St, serves authentic, abundant Italian food in a friendly atmosphere, specializing in handmade pastas. Young professionals meet at the bar after work. Main dishes are $16 to $20.

Historic District

Debi's Restaurant (☎ 912-236-3516, 10 W State St) serves solid, home-cooked meals, sandwiches and burgers (less than $5). It's popular with locals, and has efficient service and super friendly staff.

Savannah Coffee Roasters Café (☎ 912-232-5282, 7 E Congress St), on Johnson Square in the financial center, is a pleasant coffee house, with good people watching, gourmet coffee and sandwiches ($5 to $6).

Wall's Barbecue (515 E York Lane), in an alley between E York St and Oglethorpe St, is a small hole-in-the-wall that serves very good, tender barbecue and enough vegetables to satisfy vegetarians. A sandwich with two veggies costs $6.

Clary's Café (☎ 912-233-0402, 404 Abercorn St), at Jones St, is an inexpensive diner founded in 1903. It figures prominently in *Midnight in the Garden of Good and Evil*. Main dishes such as chicken pot pie cost $9 to $16, but sandwiches ($4 to $7) and soups ($4) are also available. Breakfasts are moderately priced.

Churchill's Pub (☎ 912-232-8501, 9 Drayton St) is popular with a middle-aged crowd, who come for the fish and chips ($11), bangers and mash ($9), sandwiches and burgers ($7); let's hope they've renamed the Mad Cow Burger. Lunch and dinner are served.

The *Moon River Brewing Company* (☎ 912-447-0943, 21 W Bay St), in an 1821 building a block from the riverfront, attracts a young crowd with its homemade brews and local artwork on the walls. The menu ranges from buffalo wing appetizers ($8), corn and crab chowder ($6 a bowl), burgers and sandwiches ($7), and steaks and fish ($18).

For soul food, try *Nita's Place* (☎ 912-238-8233, 140 Abercorn St), just south of Oglethorpe Square. Full meals are a bit pricey, at $10 to $12, for a choice of main dishes such as stewed beef or baked chicken, two vegetables (choose from okra, squash casserole, collards, black-eyed peas and candied yams) and cornbread. The tiny restaurant is cramped, but the delicious food is worth it.

Mrs Wilkes' Dining Room (☎ 912-232-5997, 107 W Jones St) is a longtime favorite for sociable Southern-style breakfasts and lunches. Meals are served family-style to guests packed around long tables. Breakfast is 8 am to 9 am and costs $6. Lunch, served 11 am to 3 pm, includes black-eyed peas, turnips, fried chicken, sweet potatoes, green beans and rice for a fixed price of $12. They accept cash only.

Typhoon (☎ 912-232-0755, 8 E Broughton St) serves unusual Asian cuisine, mostly Malaysian, with some Indonesian and Singaporean; many dishes use a curry based on coconut milk. The atmosphere is sophisticated without being overbearing, and the staff has endless patience in explaining the unusual menu. It's open for dinner daily, and lunch on weekdays. Lunch is about $7; dinner is $11 to $25.

The Olde Pink House (☎ 912-232-4286, 23 Abercorn St), in a 1771 house, is a dignified restaurant serving contemporary Low-country seafood and Southern cuisine. Dishes cost $16 to $25 and are offered in both the elegant dining room and the more casual tavern and piano bar downstairs.

Around the City

Elizabeth on 37th (☎ 912-236-5547, 105 E
37th St), at Drayton St, is one of Savannah's
top restaurants, housed in a beautiful,
elegant 1900 mansion. The cuisine is
modern Southern and changes with the
season. Main dishes cost about $30. It's
open for dinner only. The wine list is impressive, and the desserts are among the
best in the city.

ENTERTAINMENT

Thursday's *Savannah Morning News* lists
weekend activities, as does the weekly *Creative Loafing.*

Jazz

Savannah has several good places for jazz.
Names to look for include Gail Thurmond
and Ben Tucker. *Hannah's East* (☎ 912-233-
2225, 20 E Broad St), behind the Pirates'
House at Bay St, is a legendary jazz bar with
a cozy atmosphere and simple bar foods.
Planters Tavern (☎ 912-232-4286, 23 Abercorn St) features jazz piano in an intimate,
crowded tavern atmosphere. You can order
food from the Olde Pink House upstairs
(see Places to Eat). Be prepared to wait for
a seat. *Chadwick's* (☎ 912-234-3111, 123 E
Broughton St), is a relatively new jazz spot,
with music Thursday to Saturday.

Bars & Live Music

For bars, you can just walk along the riverfront or around City Market and check out
all the places. *Kevin Barry's Pub & Cigar
Bar* (☎ 912-233-9626, 117 W River St), just
west of the Hyatt Regency, has live Irish
music Wednesday to Sunday and food such
as shepherd's pie ($8).

JJ Cagney's (☎ 912-233-2444, 17 W Bay
St) is an excellent place to spot both up-and-
coming local bands and singer-songwriter
types. *Bayou Café* (☎ 912-233-6411, 14 N
Abercorn St), between Bay and River Sts,
across from the Hampton Inn, is a grittier
place, popular with partying students. It also
has music every night, mostly rock and
country-rock.

Malone's (☎ 912-234-3059, 27 Barnard
St), at the east end of City Market, is a

popular bar with customers from a wide
range of ages. It has inside/outside seating,
and sometimes live music. The *Mercury
Lounge* (☎ 912-447-6952, 125 W Congress
St) attracts a college crowd at its bar; sometimes there's live jazz. *Velvet Elvis* (☎ 912-
236-0665, 127 W Congress St), in City
Market, has live music on weekends, geared
toward the college crowd.

Dance

Deja Groove, on Williamson St behind
Quality Inn, is the hottest new singles dance
club near the river.

Gay & Lesbian Venues *Club One Jefferson* (☎ 912-232-0200, 1 Jefferson St) is Savannah's premier gay club, featuring female
impersonators, pool tables and a large
dance floor. Although its clientele is mostly
gay, straight partygoers also come here to
dance. Lady Chablis – the drag queen featured in *Midnight in the Garden of Good
and Evil* – still puts on a show here about
once a month.
Web site: www.clubone-online.com

Faces (☎ 912-233-3520, 17 Lincoln St) is a
laid-back neighborhood bar with a pool
table in the back.

Performing Arts

The *Lucas Theatre for the Arts* (☎ 912-232-
1696, 32 Abercorn St) is a recently renovated theatre, with plays, concerts, musicals
and classic film.

The professional *Savannah Symphony
Orchestra* (☎ 912-236-9536) has a number
of free events at Forsyth Park and River
Street and also plays at the Savannah Civic
Center's Johnny Mercer Theater (☎ 912-
651-6556), on Orleans Square.

The *Savannah Theater Company* (☎ 912-
233-7764, 222 Bull St), on Chippewa Square,
is a community theatre that presents five
comedies, musicals and dramas a year in its
1940s art-deco movie theater.

GETTING THERE & AWAY
Air

The Savannah International Airport (☎ 912-
964-0514) is just about 18 miles west of

downtown off I-16. American Eagle, Delta, United, US Airways, and Continental Express have direct flights to and from Atlanta, Charlotte, Miami, New York, Newark, Washington, DC, Cincinnati, Chicago, Dallas and Houston. Here are some sample fares: Atlanta (from $130), Charlotte (from $230), Miami (from $200), New York (from $200), Newark (from $200), Washington, DC (from $170), Cincinnati (from $210), Chicago (from $200), Dallas (from $290) and Houston (from $210).

Bus

The Greyhound station (☎ 912-232-2135) is just west of downtown at 610 W Oglethorpe Ave. Connections include:

destination	cost	length (hrs)	frequency
Atlanta	$46	5½	5 daily
Augusta	$30	2½	4 daily
Brunswick	$14	1½	6 daily
Charleston, SC	$24	3	2 daily
Columbia, SC	$33	4	4 daily
Jacksonville, FL	$22	2½	12 daily
Macon	$40	4	4 daily

Train

The Amtrak station (☎ 800-872-7245, 912-234-2611) is 4 miles from City Hall and is served only by taxis ($7). Three 'Silver Service' trains per day go south to Jacksonville, Florida, (one-way fares from $40 to $49; 2½ hours), continuing on to Miami ($66 to $129; 12 hours). Northbound, there are two trains per day to Charleston ($18 to $23; 2 hours).

The station can be difficult to find. From downtown, go west on Louisville Rd, turn left on Telfair Rd, then look for signs on the right.

GETTING AROUND

You don't need a car to enjoy Savannah. If you have one, it's best to park it and walk or take tours around town. The visitors center sells a parking pass that covers all city-run parking garages and all metered spaces

where parking is allowed for one hour or more. The pass costs $5, is good for 48 hours, and saves money and running back to feed the meter.

To/From the Airport

Coastal Transportation (☎ 912-964-5999) provides a shuttle downtown for $20. Taxi service costs about $18 to downtown, plus $5 for each additional passenger. The flat rate to Tybee Island is $40.

Bus

Chatham Area Transit (CAT; ☎ 912-233-5767) operates local buses, including a shuttle that makes its way around the Historic District and stops within a couple of blocks of nearly every major site. This is a cheap way to see the city without paying for the tourist trolleys. It circulates about every 20 minutes (every 40 minutes on Sunday). For the location of stops, call or check the Web site (www.catchacat.org). You can also look for it at the following stops: Visitors Center, Forsyth Park at Bull St, on Congress St in front of Franklin Square, or on Bay St in front of the Hyatt Regency.

CAT also has a comprehensive system of buses outside the Historic District. The fare is 75¢ exact change. The Web site has complete route information.

Taxi

The taxi rate is $1, plus $0.25 each ⅕ mile, and $1 for each additional passenger. You'll need to call for a cab; try Yellow Cab (☎ 912-236-1133).

Bicycle

Bicycling is an excellent way to get around the Historic District, but be careful around the squares – cars may not always yield the right of way.

The Old Savannah Tours tourist depot (☎ 912-234-8141), 250 Martin Luther King Jr Blvd, across from the visitors center, rents bicycles for $15 a day, including a lock and helmets. Bicycle Link (☎ 912-233-9401, 22 W Broughton St) is a full-service bike shop that rents bicycles for $20 a day or $80 a week.

Organized Tours

The visitors center is the best place to book tours, whether by foot, trolley, minibus or horse-drawn carriage. Most of the city's tour operators begin and end their excursions from the center's parking lot. The top three operators are Old Savannah Tours (☎ 912-234-8128), Gray Line (☎ 912-234-8687) and Old Town Trolley Tours (☎ 912-233-0083). Old Savannah Tours is the only locally owned company. All the tours are similar, in that they take you around the historic area and down to the riverfront in an open trolley, while the driver explains local history and sites.

Each company has departures every 20 minutes or so between 9 am and 5 pm daily (a good indication of Savannah's popularity as a tourist destination). The basic 90-minute tour is $17, or you can get on and off the trolley all day for $21, which also includes entrance fees to one historic house.

There are also many specialized tours – ghost tours, horse carriage tours, black heritage tours, walking tours, *Midnight in the Garden of Good and Evil* tours, even excursions beyond the Historic District – that are typically more expensive and less frequent. Reservations are often required. See the bulletin board at the visitors center for current options.

Dolphin tours offered by Dolphin Magic (☎ 800-721-1240, 912-352-8697) leave from River Street near the Hyatt Regency. Rates are $20/10 adults/children.

Around Savannah

Several destinations around Savannah offer alternatives to the city scene. The surrounding historic sites, state parks, beaches, national wildlife refuges and forts give you an opportunity to learn some history, hike among tabby ruins, explore the marshes and view wildlife.

WORMSLOE STATE HISTORIC SITE

Ten miles southeast of Savannah's Historic District, this historic site (☎ 912-353-3023) at 7601 Skidaway Rd on the Isle of Hope preserves the tabby ruins (tabby is a building material made of oyster shells, lime and sand mixed with water) of a colonial estate built by Noble Jones, one of Georgia's first settlers, and provides a reminder of the difficult wilderness that met the colonists upon their arrival. An interpretive center presents a film on the founding of Georgia and the Wormsloe site, reminding visitors that the colony was *not* settled by convicts from debtor's prison.

Entry to the site is lined with more than 400 live oaks planted by Jones. A short (less than 1 mile) trail leads through the forest to tabby ruins, a family gravesite and an overlook of the marsh and Jones Narrows. Colonial living skills and crafts are demonstrated during special programs throughout the year.

The historic site is open 9 am to 5 pm Tuesday through Saturday, 2 pm to 5:30 pm Sunday, closed Monday; admission is $2.50. From downtown, take Liberty St east to Wheaton St (veers to right), then take Skidaway Rd. Wormsloe is just past Norwood/Ferguson Aves on the right.

Web site: www.gastateparks.org

SKIDAWAY ISLAND

Separated from the Isle of Hope by Skidaway River, this barrier island is home to a couple of attractions, as well as 'The Landings,' a gated residential community. The 588-acre **Skidaway Island State Park** (☎ 912-598-2300) has two nature trails (1 and 3 miles) that wind through salt marshes, live oaks, cabbage-palmettos and longleaf pines; wildlife here includes fiddler crabs, shorebirds and rare migrating birds. The trails lead to an observation tower overlooking the salt flats and marsh. You can pick up interpretive brochures at the park office. There's also a swimming pool here. Entrance to the park requires a $2 parking fee.

The park's 88 camping sites are in a flat, somewhat exposed area. Flush toilets, showers and laundry facilities are provided. The rate is $18 per site.

To reach Skidaway Island, follow the directions to Wormsloe State Historic Site given previously, but turn south on Ferguson Ave, then left onto Diamond Causeway. After you cross the Skidaway River, the state park is on the left.

Also on the island, the pleasant University of Georgia **Marine Education Center and Aquarium** (☎ 912-598-2496) has a dozen or so small tanks containing aquatic species such as stingrays, turtles, nurse sharks, spiny lobsters, octopuses and cowfish. Also on display are handmade Native American baskets and regional historical photos. Hiking loops of 1/2 or 1 mile wind through the maritime forest and beside the salt marsh. The scenic location overlooks the Skidaway River.

The Marine Education Center is open 9 am to 4 pm weekdays and noon to 5 pm Saturday; admission is $2/1 adults/children. From the Diamond Causeway, turn left at the stop sign after the light onto McWhorter Rd, then another left on Modena Island Rd. The center is at the end of the road, 4.2 miles from the Diamond Causeway.

SAVANNAH NATIONAL WILDLIFE REFUGE

This 27,771-acre wildlife refuge, in South Carolina and Georgia, is part of a string of habitats along the coast administered by the Savannah Coastal Refuges office of the US Fish & Wildlife Service. The refuge consists of freshwater marshes, tidal rivers and creeks and bottomland hardwoods. Once part of a late-1700s rice plantation, the system of dikes is still maintained to provide habitat for migratory waterfowl. The plentiful wildlife here includes alligators, Southern bald eagles, great egrets and blue herons. Migratory birds on the Atlantic flyway also stop

here, including mallards and other ducks, warblers and sandpipers. Birding is best from October through April, but is good year-round.

Hikers and bicyclists can wander more than 25 miles along the dike system. The Cistern Trail leads to Recess Island.

The 4-mile, one-way gravel Laurel Hill Wildlife Drive, off SC 170, offers access into the park along the earthen dikes. Portable toilets and an information board are at the entrance. Look for the alligator pond with the jumping fish 0.9 mile down the drive.

From Savannah, take US Hwy 17 alt across the Eugene Talmadge Bridge into South Carolina; after 5 miles, turn left on SC 17 and follow it for 2 miles. The entrance to Laurel Hill Wildlife Drive will be on the left.

The refuge gates are open sunrise to sunset; no admission charged. For more information, call the Savannah Coastal Refuges office (☎ 912-652-4415) or stop by their office in Savannah (Parkway Business Center, Suite 10, 1000 Business Center Drive), off Chatham Parkway. The US Fish & Wildlife Service Web site (http://savannah .fws.gov) also has information.

OLD FORT JACKSON

Georgia's oldest standing brick fortification, Old Fort Jackson (☎ 912-232-3945, 1 Fort Jackson Rd) was built as an earthen fort during the Revolutionary War. Overlooking the Savannah River, it served as headquarters for the Confederate river defenses during the Civil War.

The fort is still intact, with barracks, a blacksmith shop, cannon and muskets on display. It's open 9 am to 5 pm daily; admission is $3.50/2.50 adults/children.

From downtown Savannah, go east on Bay St 2.2 miles (it merges with President St) to Woodcock Ave, turn left and follow the signs for 1.2 miles.
Web site: www.chsgeorgia.org

FORT PULASKI NATIONAL MONUMENT

This fort on Cockspur Island was completed in 1847 to guard the mouth of the Savannah River. Military engineers thought that such a huge masonry fort, with 7½-foot-thick walls, was impenetrable. The fort was seized by Georgia state troops before the state even seceded from the Union.

On April 10, 1862, the Union opened fire on Fort Pulaski from Tybee Island, 1 mile away, using experimental rifled cannons, which fired bullet-shaped projectiles with great accuracy at long range. The projectiles bore through Pulaski's brick walls, exposing the fort's powder magazine to direct attack. The Confederates surrendered 30 hours after the bombardment began.

Prior to the Civil War, the heaviest ordnance from smoothbore cannons and mortars was effective on heavy masonry walls only within 700 yards. The rapid fall of Fort Pulaski marked the end of conventional masonry fortifications throughout the world. More immediately, its fall tightened the Union blockade, preventing Savannah from exporting cotton and importing military supplies.

After the Confederate surrender, Union commander Major General David Hunter announced that all slaves in Fort Pulaski and the island on which it resides were 'confiscated and declared free.' Several of these freed slaves served in the 1st South Carolina Volunteers, one of the earliest African-American units in the US Army.

Visitors can view the well-preserved fort, complete with moat and drawbridge. From the parapets, you can see the Savannah River, Atlantic Ocean and salt marshes. The visitors center (☎ 912-786-5787) includes a museum, film and bookstore. Trails lead through the dikes surrounding the fort, and there are occasional dramatic Civil War reenactments.

The monument is open 9 am to 5 pm daily; $2 adult admission. The monument is about 10 miles east of Savannah off US Hwy 80; from downtown, head east on Bay St. Web site: www.nps.gov/fopu

TYBEE ISLAND

About 18 miles east of Savannah, at the end of US Hwy 80, Tybee Island is a small beach community sitting on a lot of history. In an important strategic location near the mouth

of the Savannah River, the island was visited by Spanish and French explorers, pirates and British settlers. A hospital for contagious diseases was based here to quarantine slaves and other ship passengers. During the Civil War, Union forces on Tybee fired on Fort Pulaski in April 1862. After the war, the island became a resort area for local Savannahians, and has remained so for 130 years.

The Tybee Island Visitors Center (☎ 912-786-5444, 802 1st St/US Hwy 80), on the right as you come into town, is open 10 am to 6 pm daily.
Web site: www.tybeeisland.com

The island's main attraction is the 3 miles of wide, sandy beach, good for swimming and castle building. The most popular public access is on the southern side of the island near the Tybee Pier and Pavilion, where daily parking costs $7. The pier makes for a relaxing strolling or fishing spot. Another public access point is at the northern end of the island, near the lighthouse; daily parking costs $5. Beach shops and restaurants are concentrated near the village at the southern end of the island (around 14th to 16th Sts).

On the northern end of the island is the 154-foot-tall **Tybee Island Lighthouse** (☎ 912-786-5801), the oldest in Georgia and still in use. The 178 steps to the top reward you with great views of the island and ocean. The nearby **Tybee Island Museum** is in the basement of Fort Screvens, which was in use from 1897 to 1947. The simple museum houses exhibits and photographs covering the island's history. From April through Labor Day, the lighthouse and museum are open 9 am to 6 pm daily except Tuesday (until 4 pm the rest of the year). Admission is $4/3 adults/children.

Note that there are also six-hour parking meters at the Tybee Island Museum and throughout town.

Activities

You can rent bicycles from several locations. Alakai Outfitters (☎ 912-786-4000, 1213 US Hwy 80), 1.5 miles past the Tybee Island bridge on the left, rents multispeed bicycles ($25/day), one-speed beach cruisers ($20/day) and sit-on kayaks ($25/48 singles/doubles). They also offer surfing lessons and lead bike tours to nearby destinations.

Bicycles can also be rented from the Sundance Bicycle Shop (☎ 912-786-9469), on 16th St.

Sea Kayak Georgia (☎ 888-529-2542, 912-786-8732, seakayakga@aol.com) offers kayak trips to nearby Little Tybee Island and Lazaretto Creek ($45, 3 hours) on weekends March through May and daily June through September. The company also offers a limited number of full-day trips ($85), kayak instruction and longer camping trips to Sapelo Island, Ossabaw Island and the Okefenokee National Wildlife Refuge (see the South Georgia chapter for information). The store is 1.8 miles past the bridge on the right.
Web site: www.seakayakgeorgia.com

Places to Stay

The *River's End Campground & RV Park* (☎ 800-786-1016, 912-786-5518, 915 Polk St) is on the northern side of the island just three blocks from the ocean. Tent sites on the northern part of the campground are the prettiest but are close to the noisy pool pump. Sites on the southern side are in a large grassy area near the road and RVs. Rates are $26 for tents and from $30 to $32 for RVs.

Several chain hotels are on the main drag, including the *Best Western Dunes Inn* (☎ 912-786-4591, fax 912-786-4593, 1409 Butler Ave), with rooms from $89 in the high season (September through March), and from $59 in the low season. The *Ocean Plaza Beach Resort* (☎ 800-215-6370, 912-786-7777, fax 912-786-4531), on the oceanfront off Butler Ave at 15th St, has 205 large but unimaginative rooms, some overlooking the ocean. High-season rates start at $105. The restaurant here also has a good view of the beach and ocean.

Places to Eat

The *Breakfast Club,* at the corner of Butler Ave and 15th St, serves a good breakfast, including standard and specialty omelets ($5 to $10), homemade chorizo and waffles. It's an island institution, but the coffee could be better.

The *Crab Shack at Chimney Creek* (☎ 912-786-9857, 40-A Estill Hammock Rd) is a fun restaurant, where huge platters piled with shellfish are served on an outside deck lit up with hundreds of Christmas lights. Customers shovel the shells into a garbage can via a hole in the table's center. The specialty is the sampler platter ($22/35 for one/two people). The Low Country Boil – a moderately spicy mix of boiled shrimp, sausage, potatoes and corn – is also very good ($12). For a very popular place, it seems they could afford to clean the disgusting bathrooms. Turn right 0.7 mile past the bridge onto the island at the Chimney Creek sign.

Tucked away behind the Tybee Lighthouse Museum, the *North Beach Grill* (☎ 912-786-9003, 41A Meddin Dr) is worth the search. Access is through the beach parking lot. Soak up the island atmosphere on the cozy patio or inside. Jamaican dishes and seafood are the dinner specialties – jerk chicken, *ropa vieja,* red beans and rice, grilled okra, sweet potatoes, fruit salsa; main dishes are $12 to $16. The lunch menu ($4 to $9) is simpler – sandwiches, portobello burgers, red beans and rice.

The Georgia Coast

The Georgia seacoast is dotted with 13 large and small barrier islands. Many of these – notably Wassaw, Blackbeard, Sapelo and Cumberland Islands – are nature preserves with abundant wildlife. At the southern end of the coast, several islands have been playgrounds for the wealthy throughout much of their history. The islands have deluxe 'cottages,' beaches and that beloved sport of the rich, golf. These islands – St Simons, Jekyll, Sea, and Little St Simons – are referred to as the Golden Isles.

Historically, this coast was strategically important in the colonization of Georgia and America, in the Revolutionary War and in the slave trade.

SAPELO ISLAND

This island, about 55 miles south of Savannah, is a fascinating combination of history and nature. The fourth-largest barrier island along the Georgia coast, it's home to the Sapelo Island National Estuarine Research Reserve, which focuses on scientific research and education. In the midst of an estuary, the reserve consists of 2,100 acres of coastal upland and 4,000 acres of tidal salt marsh.

The mix of ecosystems includes maritime forest, salt marsh, beaches and dunes. Visitors might sight wild turkey, deer, armadillos and feral cows. The maritime forest is dominated by live oaks and accompanying Spanish moss.

Planter Thomas Spalding purchased land here in 1802 and converted it into a productive antebellum plantation with the help of 400 slaves. When the Civil War ended slavery, ex-slaves established five communities around the island. RJ Reynolds, the tobacco magnate, owned the island from 1934 until 1964. Reynolds forced these five communities into one – Hog Hammock, which still exists today. Its 70 permanent residents are descendents of the Saltwater Geechee peoples (often grouped with the Gullah culture along the South Carolina coast). Due to generations of isolation in the small island communities, the Geechee were able to preserve many customs handed down from their tribal ancestors in West Africa.

Today, the island is owned by the state of Georgia, except for the community of Hog Hammock. The **Sapelo Island Visitors Center,** near the dock in the mainland town of Meridian, has exhibits and books on the island's history. It's closed on Monday.

The only ways to visit Sapelo Island itself are by taking a regularly scheduled state tour, arranging overnight accommodations at a private home in Hog Hammock, or through a group tour. The ranger-led state

Scenic Drive – Georgia Coast

US Hwy 17 winds down the coast of Georgia, paralleling I-95 and passing over coastal plains with pine and hardwood forests and marshes. Diversions and detours lead to historic sites and nature refuges, many of which overlook beautiful salt marshes – you can take as many detours as you'd like or just enjoy the course of the road.

Just south of Savannah, 10 miles east of I-95 on GA Spur 144 (off Route 63/204), **Fort McAllister State Historical Park** (☎ 912-727-2339) has well-preserved Confederate earthwork fortifications on the banks of the Ogeechee River, as well as live oaks, beautiful salt marshes, a Civil War museum, hiking trails and camping. Farther south, on Route 38, **Seabrook Village** (☎ 912-884-7008), open mainly for school groups, is a living-history museum portraying African-American culture from 1865 to 1930. At **Fort Morris State Historic Site** (☎ 912-884-5999), you can view earthworks last used against the British in the War of 1812.

Heading south on Hwy 17, you'll come to a turnoff for the **Harris Neck National Wildlife Refuge**, a peaceful retreat among the salt marshes, with 15 miles of trails and paved roads. Stop in the tiny town of Darien to watch the shrimp trawlers along the waterfront. The nearby **Fort King George State Historic Site** (☎ 912-437-4770) has reconstructed fortifications and a museum explaining what was once the southern outpost of the British Empire in North America. South of Darien, the **Hofwyl-Broadfield Plantation State Historic Site** (☎ 912-264-7333) contains the remnants of one of the rice plantations that once dominated coastal Georgia; you can walk among the rice paddies and dikes, part of a labor-intensive operation once worked by 350 slaves. There's also a nice museum explaining the rice economy.

From here, continue on down to Brunswick, St Simons Island and Jekyll Island.

Note that state historic sites are closed on Mondays.

tours involve a 30-minute ferry ride across Hudson Creek Sound, leaving from the mainland visitors center, and a bus ride around the island, and stopping at sites such as the Reynolds Mansion (called the 'Big House' by locals), ruins of a tabby sugar mill and a lighthouse (some tours only). Half-day tours are offered only at 8:30 am Wednesday and 9 am Saturday. In the summer (June through Labor Day), an additional tour is given at 8:30 am Friday. An extended tour is offered the last Tuesday of the month from March to October. Reservations are required; call ☎ 912-437-3224. The tour cost is $10/6 adults/children. You can get contacts for overnight lodging from the same number.

Groups can arrange overnight lodging at the Reynolds Mansion; call ☎ 912-485-2299 for more information. Southeast Adventure Outfitters, based on St Simons Island, offers overnight kayaking tours here; see the St Simons section later.

Insect repellant is a wonderful thing – bring it.

The state bus tours only scratch the surface of the local culture. For more information about the island's history and fading Geechee culture, see the book *God, Dr Buzzard, and the Bolito Man* by Sapelo Island resident Cornelia Walker Bailey.

BRUNSWICK

Mainly used as a jumping-off point for the nearby islands, Brunswick does have a pleasant downtown historic district with nice live oaks (including the 900-year-old **Lovers Oak** at the corner of Prince and Albany Sts).

The Brunswick-Golden Isles Visitors Bureau (☎ 912-265-0620), at the southeast corner of US Hwy 17 and the St Simons Causeway, has information on all the Golden Isles, accommodations and dining; or see its Web site (www.bgivb.com). There's good eating at the local pit-barbecue places.

The Bookshop (☎ 912-262-6708, 1519 Newcastle St) is an excellent bookstore, with many local titles. You can order by mail. Its Web site has links to local attractions

(www.gacoast.com/hightide/bookshopinc .html).

For free spirits who appreciate communal living, the *Hostel in the Forest* (☎ 912-264-9738) is a brilliant place to stay. The hostel is set on 105 acres in the middle of the forest, and has been here for more than 25 years. Private accommodations are provided in nine rustic tree houses with double beds, electricity, fans and lights, but no air con. The owners have created a natural retreat: Amenities include a duck pond, bushes full of blueberries in June/July, boardwalks through the forest, outside showers, a sweat lodge every full moon, free-ranging chickens, a pool table, laundry and – everyone's favorite – composting sawdust toilets. You'll need insect repellent and flashlights. Rates are $15 per person, including dinner and linens. The hostel is 9 miles west of town and 2 miles west of I-95, on US Hwy 82.

There are many chain hotels around the I-95 exits, especially exit 36 (US Hwy 341), that can be cheaper than accommodations on the islands. Be forewarned that they often fill up from the hordes heading down to Florida.

Greyhound (☎ 912-265-2800) connects Brunswick with Savannah ($15, 1½ hours, 79 miles, 6 per day) and Jacksonville, Florida ($16, 1½ hours, 76 miles, 4 per day).

ST SIMONS ISLAND

With about 14,000 residents, **St Simons Island** is the largest and most developed of the Golden Isles. It's 75 miles south of Savannah and is famous for its golf courses, resorts and landscape of majestic live oaks.

Native Americans on the island traded with the French, who were conquered by the Spanish. In 1736, General James Oglethorpe established Fort Frederica, Georgia's first military outpost, and in 1742 defeated invading Spanish forces in the Battle of Bloody Marsh. The plantation era began in the late 1700s – sea island cotton, indigo and rice were grown on large plantations using slave labor. The loss of that labor after the Civil War made growing cotton unprofitable, but the pleasant climate and proximity to the sea ushered in the age of tourism in the

GEORGIA

1870s. With the island's rich history and plentiful recreation options, summers can be very crowded; the low season is more relaxed, and prices are lower as well.

Information

The visitors center, tucked away in the library complex east of the fishing pier, has useful maps of the island and bike routes, as well as information on lodging. More information is available from the Brunswick and the Golden Isles of Georgia Visitors Bureau (☎ 912-265-0620, fax 912-265-0629).
Web site: www.bgivb.com

GJ Ford Bookshop (☎ 912-634-6168), on the southwest corner of Sea Island and Frederica Rds, is a fine, full bookstore with lots of local titles.
Web site: www.gjfordbookshop.com

Things to See & Do

'The Village,' on the southern end of the island, is a bustling center of good restaurants and shops. The nearby **fishing pier** is popular with locals for fishing, crabbing and relaxing; outgoing folks will find the fishers talkative and friendly.

St Simons Island Lighthouse & Museum of Coastal History (☎ 912-638-4666), near the Village on the southern side of the island, contains exhibits on the lighthouse, a lighthouse keeper's life and island history. The first lighthouse on this spot was burned in 1862 by retreating Confederate soldiers; the current structure was built in 1867, and it remains a navigational aid to boats entering St Simons and Doboy Sounds. The view from the top is well worth the 129 steps. It's open 10 am to 5 pm Monday to Saturday and 1:30 pm to 5 pm Sunday; admission is $3/1 adults/children.

The **St Simons Trolley** (☎ 912-638-8954) offers 90-minute historical tours, which include the lighthouse, Bloody Marsh site, Fort Frederica and Christ Church. Tours leave from the pier in the Village at 1 pm daily, with an additional tour at 11 am in the summer; tours cost $13/7.

The **Battle of Bloody Marsh** occurred on the eastern side of the island. In 1742, the British (including English and Scottish immigrants and Southeastern Indians) ambushed and defeated invading Spanish soldiers (aided by Indians and emancipated slaves). It is said that the water turned red from the blood of the dead. The Spanish permanently evacuated the island a week later and relinquished plans to colonize the eastern coast of North America. There are no facilities here, just an interpretive sign and an overlook of the now-peaceful marsh. The gate, off Demere Rd, is open 8 am to 4 pm; admission is free.

Toward the northwestern side of the island, 7 miles from the Village, the **Fort Frederica National Monument** (☎ 912-638-3639) protects the tabby ruins of a fort and town established in 1736 by General James Oglethorpe, where residents once numbered 11,000. Included are a 25-minute film and interpretive signs on colonial life. Park hours are 8 am to 5 pm daily. Admission is $4 per car or $2 per adult on bicycle or on foot.

Near Fort Frederica, **Christ Episcopal Church** is a simple but beautiful structure built in 1886. You can visit the inside and wander around the old graves. Donations are requested.

The **beaches** on St Simons are sandy and long, but they tend to disappear at high tide. One of the best is near the Coast Guard station on the eastern side of the island at the end of 1st St. There's parking and restrooms here, but no food. Massengale Park also has beach access.

Bicycle paths lead across the flat landscape to many of the island's sights. Single-speed beach cruisers can be rented from the Ocean Motion Surf Company (☎ 912-638-5225, 1300 Ocean Blvd), at Arnold Rd; rates are $8/12 for a half/full day. This company also offers kayak tours of the marshes and creeks. Benjy's Bike Shop (☎ 912-638-6766, 130 Retreat Plaza), in the Retreat Village Shopping Center on the southwestern corner of Frederica and Demere Rds, is a full bike shop that rents mostly single-speed bikes for $7/11 for a half/full day, but they also have a few multispeed mountain bikes. They are closed Wednesday and Sunday.

Because of the area's low wave energy and high water temperatures, it's a good place to learn **sea kayaking.** Southeast Adventure Outfitters (☎ 912-638-6732, 313 Mallory St)) offers kayak tours, rents kayaks and sells outdoor supplies. The best introduction is their three-hour sea kayak trip for $40. The company also offers guided tours to the Okefenokee Swamp and local rivers, and camping trips to Sapelo and Cumberland Islands. The store has complete outdoor supplies, maps and nautical charts; they sell and rent tents, backpacks and other outdoor gear. Rental costs are $25 per day per cockpit for a kayak, and $25 per day for a canoe. If you strike out in your own kayak, keep in mind that the tides are eight feet, and the coastal rivers change direction twice a day.

Web site: www.gacoast.com/navigator/sea.html

The Golden Isles Marina has dive shops, boat rentals, waterway tours, Jet Ski and sailboat rentals and parasailing. Dolphin tours are offered by the St Simons Transit Company (☎ 912-638-5678); admission $17/8 adults/children. Barry's Beach Service (☎ 912-638-8053), near the King & Prince Beach Hotel, rents sailboats, bikes and kayaks and also gives sailboat lessons and rides.

For information on charter fishing, call the Golden Isles Charter Fishing Association (☎ 912-638-7673).

St Simons has several good golf courses. Contact the visitors center for a complete list.

The Island Players (☎ 912-638-3031) presents plays in the summer near the visitors center.

Little St Simons Island

This island is accessible only by private boat. There's just one very charming old resort here, *Little St Simons Island Retreat* (☎ 888-733-5774, 912-638-7472, fax 912-634-1811), starting at $350 plus tax. The 10,000-acre island is a secluded getaway, with good opportunities for nature excursions.

Web site: www.LittleStSimonsIsland.com

Sea Island

On the northeastern side of St Simons, connected by a causeway, Sea Island is largely the preserve of the luxurious *Cloister Resort* (☎ 800-732-4752, 912-638-3611). Rates start at $350, including all meals.

Web site: www.seaisland.com

Places to Stay

Hotel tax in St Simons is 11%. Prices vary drastically between high season (May to September) and low season. Rooms with a view will cost more than rooms without. Several chain hotels are located on Frederica Rd.

Queen's Court (☎ 912-638-8459, 437 Kings Way), near Mallory St in the Village, is a conveniently located, family-owned budget hotel within easy walking distance of restaurants. The 23 singles/doubles are a good value for this location, at $50/56. The hotel is set on grounds with beautiful live oaks draped with Spanish moss, and there's an outdoor pool. Suites and kitchenettes are available.

Epworth by the Sea (☎ 912-638-8688, fax 912-634-0642), just off Sea Island Rd north of the causeway, is a Methodist conference and retreat center, but is open to anyone. Rates start at $45 for simple, older rooms to $85 for a modern apartment with a separate kitchen. It's popular with religious groups. Its strength is its serene setting on the banks of the Frederica River, overlooking the Marshes of Glynn. There's an onsite cafeteria.

Web site: www.epworthbythesea.org

St Simons Inn by the Lighthouse (☎ 912-638-1101, 609 Beachview Dr), across from the lighthouse, doesn't have any views but is a clean, modern hotel in a great location near the Village restaurants. All rooms have a fridge and microwave. Rates at this locally owned hotel are $99 during the high season (May to September) and $70 during the off season.

Sea Gate Inn (☎ 800-562-8812, 912-638-8661, fax 912-638-4932, 1014 Ocean Blvd), has pleasant rooms and an outdoor pool in a quiet location far from the Village. High-season rates are $93 for a modern double room. Rooms with higher rates include wonderful ocean views. The inn also has a separate Ocean House, where all rooms have ocean views, starting at $140.

Web site: www.seagateinn.com

The ***King & Prince Beach and Golf Resort*** (☎ *800-342-0212, 912-638-3631, 201 Arnold Rd*) is an oceanfront resort featuring Spanish Colonial architecture. Some of the 187 comfortable rooms have ocean views. Amenities include indoor and outdoor pools, tennis courts, a fitness center, dining room and lounge. Rates are $145 to $179 weekdays and $160 to $189 weekends, depending on the view. The resort also rents two- and three-bedroom villas starting at $309. Its golf course is on the northern end of the island; prices start at $70 per round (more expensive than Jekyll Island golf courses).

Web site: www.kingandprince.com

Places to Eat

Dressner's Village Café (☎ *912-634-1217, 223 Mallory St*), in the Village, is a cheerful little place with a nonsmoking dining room that serves tasty omelets, pancakes and French toast for breakfast at reasonable prices (under $5). It's open 7:30 am to 2:30 pm weekdays and 8 am to 2:30 pm Saturday. Sandwiches ($4 to $6) are available for lunch.

The ***Fourth of May*** (☎ *912-638-5444*), on the corner of Ocean Blvd and Mallory St, is popular with locals and tourists. Specialties include vegetables, sandwiches, soups, salads, seafood and scrumptious desserts. Veggie plates are $1.15 a vegetable, sandwiches are $5 to $7 and daily specials run about $7. Indoor and outdoor seating is available. It's open 11 am to 9 pm daily.

Brogen's, near the fishing pier, is a laid-back bar & grill, with indoor/outdoor seating. It's frequently recommended as having the best burgers ($5) on the island. There are also lots of munchies, salads and sandwiches at moderate prices.

Locals can barely speak the name of ***CJ's Pizza*** (☎ *912-634-1022*), on Mallery Rd in the Village, without openly salivating. Moderately priced pizzas are the specialty, but subs and pastas are also served.

The ***Crab Trap*** (☎ *912-638-3552, 1209 Ocean Blvd*), just south of Arnold St, is decorated like a shack. The atmosphere is lively, but there's no nonsmoking section.

Seafood specialties – mostly shellfish and a fish of the day – cost $11 to $16. It's open for dinner every day but Sunday.

Blue Water Restaurant (☎ *912-638-7007, 115 Mallory St*), near the pier in the Village, is a popular seafood restaurant with an extensive beer and wine list. It's open for dinner daily except Sunday; main dishes cost $13 to $18.

Getting There & Away

A 5-mile causeway leads from Brunswick on the mainland to St Simons Island. From I-95, exits 29 through 42 will eventually take you to the causeway.

JEKYLL ISLAND
pop 1200

An exclusive refuge for millionaires in the late 19th and early 20th centuries, Jekyll Island is a 4000-year-old barrier island 7 miles long and 2 miles wide, with 10 miles of beaches. French, Spanish, British and pirates have all visited the island, and it was once the site of sea island cotton plantations. Slaves were imported to work on the cotton plantations; the schooner *Wanderer* unloaded 490 slaves from Africa on the northern end of the island in 1858, 50 years after the importation of slaves was outlawed in the US.

In the late 19th century, millionaires including JP Morgan, William Rockefeller, Joseph Pulitzer and William Vanderbilt established an exclusive club on the island; many of their winter 'cottages' are still intact. The club began declining in popularity when the income tax was introduced during the Depression. It closed during World War II, when labor and supplies were low, and the US government feared that such a high concentration of wealth and power in one place invited attacks by enemy subs off the coast.

The island is now owned by the state of Georgia, although there are many private residences on land leased from the state. The island resort is completely self-supporting through tourist fees.

The island has plenty of wildlife, including deer, wild turkeys, hawks, egrets, herons and shorebirds. Good bird-watching sites are indicated by the **Colonial Coast Birding Trail** signs; a list of these is available at the welcome center.

Information

The **Jekyll Island Welcome Center** (☎ 877-453-5955, 912-635-3636), on the causeway to the island, has maps and good brochures on activities and lodging. It's open 9 am to 5 pm daily.

Web site: www.jekyllisland.com

Things to See & Do

The 240-acre **historic area** is a good place to just wander about among the oaks and fancy cottages, although you cannot go inside the houses except on a tour. The **Jekyll Island Museum Center** (☎ 912-635-2762), on Stable Road, is the hub of activity for the historic district and sells walking tour maps. Exhibits explain the history of the island and its conversion to a state-owned resort. The museum is open 9 am to 5 pm; admission is free.

Tram tours leave from the museum center and pass through the historic millionaires' district. Several houses have been renovated with period furniture and decorations; the tours take visitors inside three of the houses, in various stages of renovation, to marvel at the opulence. In the **Dubignon Cottage,** the walls look like leather, wide floorboards are painted to look narrow, and pine boards are painted to look like maple. The 90-minute tours depart every hour from 10 am to 3 pm, and cost $10/6 adults/children.

Alternative ways of touring the district include horse-drawn **carriage rides** (☎ 912-635-9500). The **Landscape Walk** is a guided walking tour of the Historic District, focusing on the gardens and plant life. Tours depart at 9 am on Tuesdays and Thursdays only; admission is $5/3.

You can get access to the 10 miles of **beach** at several locations, including the Central Dunes Picnic Area, which has bathrooms. Note that parts of the beach are completely covered at high tide.

Jekyll Island has 20 miles of dedicated, paved **bicycle paths** around the entire

island, including the Historic District, along the beach and within some of the natural areas. The welcome center distributes maps. Bikes can be rented at the miniature golf course (☎ 912-635-2074) for $4/10 for one hour/half day. Bikes can also be rented at the campground, various hotels and the Jekyll Harbor Marina. It's open 9 am to 5 pm daily. Single-speed beach cruisers, tandems and child seats are available.

The Tidelands Nature Center (☎ 912-635-3636) offers **nature walks** at 9 am Monday, Wednesday and Friday. These walks are to a different destination each day and include the marsh and beach areas. The cost is $5/3 adults/children.

The **Clam Creek Picnic Area & Fishing Pier**, on the northern end of the island, is worth a visit to gaze across St Simons Sound at the St Simons Lighthouse. Eat a picnic while viewing the wading birds in the marsh and stroll along lovely **Driftwood Beach.**

Loggerhead sea turtles nest on the island from May through August. **Turtle walks** are offered by the Sea Turtle Project (☎ 912-635-2284).

The island is Georgia's largest public golf resort, with three 18-hole courses and one nine-hole course. The *Oleander* is ranked among the state's best courses. Daily green fees are $35, half price under 16. Special rates are offered in the winter and special packages are available from many hotels.

Tennis is another big draw. The Jekyll Island Tennis Center (☎ 912-635-3154, jitc@gate.net) was selected as one of the 25 best municipal tennis facilities in the country. Of the 13 courts, seven are lighted. Eight USTA-sanctioned tournaments are held here every year. Court fees are $14 per hour.

The Jekyll Harbor Marina (☎ 912-635-3137), south of the Jekyll Island Bridge, has floating docks, dry storage, boat rentals, bicycle rentals and parasail rides. **Dolphin tours** are offered from the Jekyll Wharf (☎ 912-635-3152) for $17/8. Fishing charters are also available.

Summer Waves (☎ 912-635-2074, Fun@Summerwaveswaterpark.com), near the marsh on Riverview Dr, has more than a million gallons of water in 11 acres of rides. It's open Memorial Day to Labor Day, and on some weekends in May and September. Hours are 10 am to 6 pm Sunday to Friday and 10 am to 8 pm Saturday.

The **Amphitheater** presents plays in the summer.

Places to Stay

Jekyll Island Campground (☎ *912-635-3021, 1197 Riverview Dr*), on the northern end of the island, has 158 sites. RVs are packed closely together on the main part of the campground; some tent sites are well away from the RVs. The campground is near the Clam Creek Picnic Area and Driftwood Beach. Amenities include a camp store, bicycle rental and a coin laundry. Rates are $12 for tents, $17 for sites with electricity, and $20 for full hook-ups.
Web site: www.jekyllisland.com

Seafarer Inn & Suites (☎ *800-281-4446, 912-635-2202, fax 912-635-2927, 700 N Beachview Dr*) is a decent budget motel with 71 rooms, an outdoor pool, guest laundry and a small continental breakfast. It's a short walk to the beach. Rates are $69 plus an 11% tax (as there is for all accommodations on Jekyll Island) for a standard room to $99 for a two-bedroom apartment with a kitchen (cookware not included). Many guests rent by the week here, for $273 for a standard room to $360 for a two-bedroom apartment.

The *Jekyll Inn* (☎ *800-736-1046, 912-635-2531, fax 912-635-2332, 975 N Beachview Dr*), on the beach on the northern end of the island, is a nice modern hotel on a 15-acre property with an outdoor pool, 188 rooms and 75 one- and two-bedroom villas. Standard rooms are $99 to $139; the higher-priced rooms have a lovely ocean view.

Jekyll Island Club Hotel (☎ *800-535-9547, 912-635-2600*), once the exclusive domain of the island's vacationing millionaires, is now a tad more accessible to the rest of us. In the midst of the historic area on the opposite side of the island from the beach, this elegant, turreted hotel has rooms for $139 to $289 during high season (March

through August) and $109 to $259 in low season (December to February).
Web site: www.jekyllclub.com

The Beachview Club (☎ *800-299-2228, 912-635-2256, fax 912-635-3770, 721 N Beachview Dr*), located on the beach, has 38 spacious, recently remodeled rooms, all with an efficiency kitchen. Standard rooms are $134 to $179 in the high season (Memorial to Labor Day), and significantly less at other times; the higher priced rooms have ocean views and a balcony. Suites with luxury amenities are also available. There's even a heated pool and hot tub outside.
Web site: www.beachviewclub.com

Jekyll Realty (☎ *888-333-5055, 912-635-3301, fax 912-635-3303*), with an office in the Jekyll Shopping Center, rents houses on a weekly basis. The houses are individually owned and decorated. Rates range from $450 a week for a simple two-bedroom house accommodating four people to $2,600 for a beachfront house with five bedrooms, accommodating 12.
Web site: www.jekyll-island.com

Places to Eat

The Jekyll Island Club Hotel has two restaurants: *Café Solterra* serves simple breakfasts, pastries, soups, salads, pizza, pita wraps, sandwiches (about $6) and desserts, with plenty of outdoor seating. It's open 8 am to 10 pm. *The Grand Dining Room* is more upscale, serving omelets ($9) for breakfast, seafood, salads, soups and sandwiches ($9) for lunch; and seafood and steak for dinner (dishes range from $19 to $27). The recommended dress code for dinner is a coat and tie for men.

Latitude 31° (☎ *912-635-3800*), at the Jekyll Wharf in the historic district, is the place local islanders recommend most often for fresh seafood. Specialties include the catch of the day, such as grouper, and also shellfish, steak, pasta and chicken. Prices range from $13 to $23.

Getting There & Away

The turnoff for Jekyll Island is 4 miles south of Brunswick on Hwy 17, then another 6 miles on Hwy 520 to the island. As you cross the causeway, you'll need to pay a $3 daily parking fee; multi-day permits are also available.

CUMBERLAND ISLAND

The **Cumberland Island National Seashore** (☎ 912-882-4335, fax 912-673-7747) occupies most of the southernmost barrier island in Georgia. Almost half of the total 36,415 acres are marshland, mud flats and tidal creeks. The island is 17.5 miles long and 3 miles wide. Some private owners still live here; a one-lane dirt road runs almost the entire length of the island.

Web site: www.nps.gov/cuis/

On the ocean side are 16 miles of wide sandy beach that you might have all to yourself. There are shorebirds such as sandpipers, gulls and ospreys, as well as nesting loggerhead turtles. Heading inland, delicate sand dunes protect interdune meadows and shrub thickets. The interior of the island is characterized by a maritime forest consisting of live oaks draped in Spanish moss, other hardwood trees and dense palmetto stands. These shelter a variety of birds, including painted buntings and pileated woodpeckers. On the western side are saltwater marshes containing tall grasses, fiddler crabs and wading birds such as egrets and herons.

Animals include deer, raccoons, feral pigs and armadillos (a recent arrival). Freshwater ponds harbor alligators, and feral horses roam the island and are a common sight around the mansion ruins, in the interdune meadows and occasionally on the beach. There are plenty of sand gnats, too, and they bite.

Indians, Spanish soldiers, missionaries, and British forts have given the island a rich human history. Nathanael Green, a Revolutionary War hero, and his wife built a home here, called Dungeness, in the late 18th century. In 1884, Thomas and Lucy Carnegie built a mansion on the ruins of the original

Dungeness. Their mansion was eventually set afire by vandals, buts its ruins are still visible today. Plum Orchard is an 1898 Georgian Revival-style mansion built for their son George Carnegie.

This is the perfect place to spend a day walking – meandering around the crumbling walls of mansions, along the beach and marshes and through maritime forests and interdune meadows. Visitation to the island is limited to 300 people per day, ensuring a peaceful experience. Most of the day-use areas are on the southern end of the island. The **Ice House Museum, Dungeness Ruins** and **Cemetery** are all worth visiting. The live oaks around **Sea Camp Beach** are worth seeing even if you aren't camping. If time permits, walk north to the end of Old House Road, where there's a dock overlooking **Old House Creek.** Here, thousands of fiddler crabs scurry through the mud and grasses at low tide while wading birds hunt for dinner.

The only public access to the island is via the ferry **Cumberland Queen,** which leaves the St Marys dock. Reservations are strongly recommended (☎ 912-882-4335 from 10 am to 4 pm weekdays). The 45-minute ride is part of the whole experience. The ferry leaves the St Marys dock at 9 am and 11:45 am and returns from the island at 9:45 am and 4:45 pm. During the spring and summer (March 1 through Sept 30), there is an additional departure from the island at 2:45 pm Wednesday through Saturday. During fall and winter (October 1 through February 28), the ferry does not operate on Tuesday or on Wednesday.

Rates are $12/7 adults/children. An additional $4 user fee is charged to go on the island. Bicycles are not allowed on the ferry.

Be aware that there are *no* food or other supplies available on Cumberland Island. Pack your lunch. You'll need sunscreen and insect repellant, too. Ticks here may carry Lyme disease, so check yourself often and know what to do when you find a tick (see Health in the Facts for the Visitor chapter). Restrooms and water are available at four locations on the southern side of the island.

Camping is available at **Sea Camp Beach,** a wonderful, developed campground set among beautiful live oaks. Each of the campsites is surrounded by palmetto stands and comes with a raccoon box (to store your food, not your raccoons). Facilities include flush toilets, cold showers and drinking water. It's a short walk to the beach or the ferry from here, and there are a few carts you can borrow to help move your equipment.

Four backcountry campgrounds are located in the middle of the island, far from civilization. Sulfur water is available from wells for drinking, but should be treated. Campfires are not permitted in the backcountry, so bring a campstove.

Reservations are required for both developed and backcountry camping and the fees are $4 per person per day; call ☎ 912-882-4335 between 10 am and 4 pm weekdays.

The only private accommodations on the island are at the luxurious *Greyfield Inn* (☎ 904-261-6408). Doubles start at $350 per night.
Web site: www.greyfieldinn.com

For other accommodations, see the following St Marys section.

St Marys
pop 14,000

For most travelers, this sleepy little town is just a place to catch the ferry to Cumberland Island. However, it does have a pleasant but small downtown historic area, with a couple of blocks of shops, restaurants, several B&Bs, outfitters and **Orange Hall,** a fine 1829 example of Greek Revival architecture.

Up the Creek Xpeditions (☎ 912-882-0911, 111 Osborne St) is an outfitter offering kayak rental and instruction, and guided tours to Cumberland Island, St Marys River and Crooked River. They also rent bicycles. The store is open 10 am to 5 pm Monday to Thursday and 10 am to 6 pm Friday and Saturday; rentals and tours are available seven days a week by advance reservation.

The *Riverview Hotel (☎ 888-882-1807, 912-882-3242, 105 Osborne St)* is conveniently located right across from the Cumberland Island dock. Although somewhat rundown and in need of maintenance, this historic 1916 hotel has lots of character and a great second-story balcony overlooking downtown St Marys. Rooms do not have phones. Rates for singles/doubles cost $45/55, including continental breakfast. Ask for a room overlooking the dock.

Cumberland Island Inn & Suites (☎ 800-768-6250, 912-882-6250) is a modest but more modern hotel at the intersection of GA Route 40 and GA Spur 40, 4 miles from downtown St Marys. Rates start at $40/50 singles/doubles for standard rooms and include a continental breakfast; suites are available.
Web site: www.cumberlandislandinn.com

You'll find a string of chain hotels 10 miles west of the St Marys dock at the GA Route 40 exit on I-95 (exit 2).

Camping is available at nearby *Crooked River State Park (☎ 912-882-5256, reservations 800-864-7275 or 770-389-7275),* located 10 miles from downtown St Marys on GA Spur 40. This 500-acre park is bordered by large areas of salt marsh. It provides boat access to Crooked River, on which saltwater fishing is popular. Many of the 60 camping sites are in an open area under pine trees, but there are also nice private sites set back among the palmettos. Rates are $14/16 tents/RVs. Cottages cost $75/85/90 for 1/2/3 bedrooms, $10 more on weekends. There's also a swimming pool. It's possible to park a car here and kayak to Cumberland Island. Entrance to the park requires a $2 ParkPass.

South Georgia

Georgia's agricultural heritage lives on in South Georgia. Though this area was once at the bottom of the sea, its predominantly sandy soil is overlain in some spots by richer soils good for growing cotton. Other common crops include peaches, pecans and peanuts. The world-famous Vidalia sweet onion is grown only in the South Georgia town of the same name. Pine trees throughout the region support a vibrant timber industry, and there are many textile mills and pulp and paper plants.

The region has many subtle enjoyments for travelers, and some parts of South Georgia make convenient trips from Columbus, Macon or Savannah. The Okefenokee Swamp is one of the best outdoor regions in the Southeast, where you can canoe with the alligators and search for other unusual wildlife. Living history museums at Agrirama and Westville remind us of a simpler but harder time. Heartbreaking Civil War history is on display at the former Andersonville prison camp.

Highlights

- Canoe in the huge Okefenokee Swamp with alligators and rare birds.

- Visit Plains – the hometown of a former US president – for a glimpse of Georgia's rural, agricultural heritage.

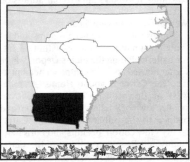

Former US president Jimmy Carter grew up in the tiny town of Plains, where he still lives.

For the true South Georgia experience, be sure to visit in summer, when the high heat and humidity make you want to sit still, but the gnats swarming up your nose make you want to run for cover.

Unfortunately, if you don't drive, South Georgia is not easily experienced. The nearest Amtrak stop is in Savannah, along the Georgia coast. In South Georgia, Greyhound has stops in Albany, Americus, Folkston, Homerville, Thomasville, Tifton, Valdosta, Vidalia and Waycross. Unless you particularly enjoy exploring bus stations and the surrounding neighborhoods, however, you'll need a car for visiting the sites in this chapter. Bicycling is another possibility.

ANDERSONVILLE NATIONAL HISTORIC SITE

The site of the Civil War's most infamous prison lies 10 miles northeast of Americus on Hwy 49. The Andersonville prison camp was in operation for only 14 months in 1864-65, but in that time 12,919 of its 45,000 Union prisoners died from disease, poor sanitation, overcrowding and exposure. Its commander, Captain Henry Wirz, became the only Confederate tried and hanged for war crimes, an act that remains controversial (see the boxed text, later).

Now that it's a national historic site, Andersonville has been expanded to include the **National Prisoner of War Museum** (☎ 912-924-0343), honoring American prisoners of war (POWs) throughout the country's history. The stirring film *Echoes of Captivity* presents interviews with POWs from this century's conflicts and the museum displays moving and sometimes disturbing information on the history of POWs. A small bookstore sells books on Andersonville, the Civil War and other US wars.

Visitors can also tour the field where the Civil War prison stood. All that remains now are a few stockade posts, a reconstructed northeast stockade corner, a few earthworks, some monuments, and the small Stockade Branch stream – once the source of fatal diseases – running through the middle of the field.

Within the park, the **Andersonville National Cemetery** contains the tightly-spaced graves of the Union soldiers who died at the camp. As a national cemetery, it continues to provide a permanent resting place for deceased veterans.

Food is not available within the park. The nearby village of Andersonville has a small sandwich and snack shop next to the prominent Henry Wirz monument.

Admission is free, and the park is open 8:30 am to 5 pm daily.

AMERICUS
pop 17,000

This town is a convenient base for exploring the surrounding rural communities, including Plains. Downtown Americus is set in a historic district with several shops. The headquarters of **Habitat for Humanity International** (☎ 800-422-4828), a nonprofit, ecumenical Christian housing ministry dedicated to building simple, affordable houses, is located on US Hwy 280. The organization operates a museum at 419 W Church St (one street behind the headquarters); tours are offered at 8 am, 10 am, 1 pm and 3 pm weekdays.

Web site: www.habitat.org

Two chain hotels are near the intersection of US Hwys 19 and 280, just west of town. The *Ramada Inn* (☎ 800-932-4430, 912-924-4431, fax 912-924-9602) has modern rooms, an outside pool and a hot breakfast in a dirty dining room. Rates are $57/62 singles/doubles. Other chain hotels are on US Hwy 280 east of town, including a *Jameson Inn* (☎ 800-526-3766, 912-924-2726). Rates are $60 singles/doubles, with a continental breakfast. The hotel has a pool and fitness center.

By far the most impressive hotel in the area is the *Windsor Hotel* (☎ 888-297-9567,

229-924-1555) in downtown Americus on US Hwy 280. This grand Victorian hotel, with its carved oak three-tier atrium and lobby, was built in 1892 and has 53 rooms. Rates start at $90 (plus 13% tax) for a standard room with no view and $159 for a one-bedroom executive suite with a view of downtown Americus.

Web site: www.windsor-americus.com

Nearby, *Dingus Magee's* (☎ 229-924-6333), at the corner of Forsyth and Lee Sts, is a respectable bar and grill with sandwiches and burgers for $5 to $7.

PLAINS
pop 650

This tiny town is best known as the birthplace and current residence of Jimmy Carter, the 39th US president (see the boxed text about him later in this chapter). Downtown consists of little more than peanut warehouses and a few antique stores; it retains the atmosphere of a small, agricultural town.

Many Carter-related buildings are now part of the **Jimmy Carter National Historic Site** (☎ 912-824-4104). The main tourist attraction is the **Plains High School Museum and Visitors Center** (☎ 912-824-4104), on N Bond St. Carter and future wife Rosalynn attended school here. Exhibits and a film on his life, campaign and presidency are presented. In addition, the museum doesn't shrink from an honest portrayal of the difficulties faced by African Americans living in the traditional rural South, when most people did not question the inherent inequalities. It's open 9 am to 5 pm; admission is free.

Web site: www.nps.gov/jica

The visitors center also has maps and information on other buildings within the historic site, including the **Plains Depot,** where Carter housed his 1976 campaign headquarters. The **Carter Boyhood Home,** 2½ miles west of downtown Plains in the even smaller town of Archery, was renovated and opened to the public in 2000; the Carter family grew cotton, peanuts and corn here. Jimmy and Rosalynn still live in the **Carter Home** west of downtown on US Hwy 280,

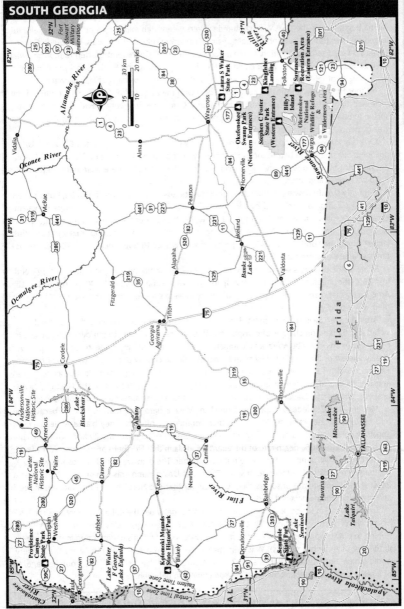

SOUTH GEORGIA

Civil War Prisons

At the beginning of the Civil War, captured soldiers were often exchanged on the battlefield; released captives took an oath not to fight again. This system collapsed in 1863 when Union General Ulysses S Grant refused additional exchanges because freed Confederates often found their way back to fighting units. The North could better afford the losses; the South, short on manpower, could not. Another factor may have been the South's refusal to exchange black prisoners.

Neither North nor South was prepared to deal with the huge influx of prisoners resulting from increased fighting and the cessation of exchanges. Camps became very crowded; both sides resorted to building simple stockades, holding prisoners in an open field without proper shelter. Food was inadequate and diseases rampant.

Officially known as Camp Sumter, Andersonville was a stockade fort covering 26½ acres. Union prisoners began arriving before the camp was fully built or properly stocked with supplies. Prisoners were not provided with any shelter, clothing or eating utensils (there were none to provide). Food was scarce and often rotten.

A muddy stream flowing through the camp was the sole source of drinking water, but it rapidly became a swamp contaminated by the nearby latrines. Dysentery and diarrhea were prevalent. Later, one prisoner wrote, 'We had to strain the water through our teeth to keep the maggots out.' Designed for only 10,000 prisoners, the camp at its peak confined 33,000, making it the fifth largest city in the South. Of the 45,000 prisoners who passed through, nearly 13,000 died, sometimes at a rate of more than 100 men a day.

Some of the prisoners strong enough to survive these conditions went on to meet a tragic end. In 1865, the steamship *Sultana* blew up on the Mississippi, killing 2,000 passengers – still America's worst maritime disaster. Many of the dead were survivors from Andersonville, finally on their way home.

After the war, Swiss-born Captain Henry Wirz, the camp's irascible commander, was tried, convicted and hanged on charges of conspiring with Confederate leaders to murder Union prisoners. Many historians describe Wirz as incompetent rather than malicious; the tragic suffering was largely a result of the inability of Wirz and other officials to cope with the massive influx of prisoners and a lack of supplies throughout the South. Although many prisoners did describe him as abusive, he was also a convenient scapegoat to appease the fury aroused in the North by heartbreaking photos of prisoners nearly starved to death and by the assassination of Abraham Lincoln.

Modern-day Confederate apologists proclaim Wirz a hero and martyr, in part because he refused to implicate Jefferson Davis and other Confederate officials. They blame Andersonville's appalling conditions on Grant's refusal to exchange prisoners, compare the 29% death rate of the prisoners with the 10% death rate of the guards, and claim that Northern prisons were just as bad.

Northern POW camps, in fact, were not much better. The death rate in Union camps was 12% compared to 15% in Confederate prisons. The worst Union camp was Elmira, New York, where 24% of the Confederate prisoners died. Considering that the North had ample supplies of food and medicine, the neglect is disturbing.

Tony Horwitz, in his book *Confederates in the Attic*, describes the debate over Wirz as monster or martyr as 'history as Middle East rug barter': Each side exaggerates the points in its favor, hoping to pull its opponent closer to the middle. Visitors will find this debate often in the South (as in the rest of American politics): Was Wirz malicious or incompetent? Was the war *about* slavery, or did it have nothing to do with slavery? Is the Confederate flag a symbol of a proud heritage, or of a racist heritage? Perhaps the truth lies somewhere in between.

but it is closed to the public. Don't miss the 13-foot-high **smiling peanut** on Hwy 45N, half a mile north of downtown.

The annual **Peanut Festival,** held on the last Saturday of September, is a celebration of the region's favorite legume. Events include a parade, arts and crafts, a peanut recipe contest, book signings by the Carters and a softball game featuring 'Jimmy Carter & His Secret Service Agents.' The city of Plains (☎ 912-824-5445) can provide more information.

Web site: www.plainsgeorgia.com

The Georgia state **visitors center,** on US Hwy 27/280 half a mile east of Plains, has additional local, regional and state travel information. It's open 8:30 am to 5:30 pm.

WESTVILLE

A mile southeast of Lumpkin, **Westville** (☎ 888-733-1850, 912-838-6310) is an authentically-recreated 1850s-era village containing over 30 buildings that were in existence by 1850 and recently relocated to their present site. These buildings are often populated by modern-day craftspeople in historic garb practicing traditional crafts such as blacksmithing, weaving on a loom, woodworking, candle making, quilting and pottery. Be sure to try the greasy but scrumptious biscuits made fresh over the hearth. A horse-drawn wagon makes the rounds through the dirt-packed streets. It's open 10 am to 5 pm Tuesday through Satur-

day, 1 pm to 5 pm Sunday, closed Monday; $8/4 adults/children.

Web site: www.westville.org

The best times to visit are during the fall and spring weekends, holidays and for special events, including the **Fair of 1850,** held every fall mid-October to mid-November, which features special demonstrations of harvest-time activities such as grinding cane and making syrup.

A good place to get a sandwich or stop for a snack between Westville and Providence Canyon State Park is **Dr Hatchett's Drug Store Museum & Soda Fountain,** on the courthouse square in nearby Lumpkin. They'll pack a sandwich and chips to go for about $5, and their old-fashioned ice cream sodas are worth the stop. While waiting for your order, you can look over the drug store memorabilia. They're open 11 am to 7 pm Wednesday through Saturday, noon to 7 pm Sunday.

PROVIDENCE CANYON STATE PARK

This 1109-acre park (☎ 229-838-6202), located 7 miles west of Lumpkin on Georgia Hwy 39C, is an impressive and beautiful environmental disaster. The park is host to 16 canyons, the deepest being 150 feet, that came to be because of poor farming practices in the 19th century. Rows plowed straight into the hillsides gradually became ditches, then gullies. Once the flow of water cut through the hard clay layer, the underlying sand layers eroded rapidly. The Civilian Conservation Corps tried to stem the erosion in the 1930s by planting kudzu and pine trees.

Sometimes known as Georgia's Little Grand Canyon for its multihued soils, the park offers two **hiking trails.** The 3-mile White Blaze Trail follows the canyon rims, then dips down through the canyons. The best views are from the rim. The 7-mile Red Blaze Trail provides access to six **backcountry camping** areas. Camping is $3 per person, and you must register at the visitors center. The rare plumleaf azalea blooms brightly from July to September at the bottom of the canyon.

GEORGIA

From Peanuts to President

Jimmy Carter served as US president for one term, from 1977 to 1981, and has since made his name as an activist for international peace. James Earl (Jimmy) Carter was born in 1924 in the rural town of Plains. His boyhood home in nearby Archery lacked plumbing and electricity. Carter attributes his values of hard work, integrity and family to his rural Georgia upbringing.

Carter attended the US Naval Academy at Annapolis, studied nuclear physics and served as a senior officer on the *Sea Wolf*, the second US nuclear-powered submarine. When his father died in 1952, Carter returned to Plains to run the family peanut business and became involved in local politics. Hampered at first by his stance in favor of Civil Rights legislation, Carter served two terms as a state senator and then became Georgia's governor in 1970. His accomplishments in office included increasing government employment of African Americans and women, opening day care and drug abuse rehabilitation centers and streamlining state agencies.

When his term as governor ended, Carter ran for president in 1976. Little known outside Georgia, he was often referred to as 'Jimmy Who?' His 'Peanut Brigade' campaigned throughout the nation, and his wide grin became a trademark. With his down-to-earth style, Carter charmed a disillusioned country fed up with Vietnam and Richard Nixon's Watergate scandal.

As president, Carter brokered the Camp David peace accords between Israel and Egypt; signed the Panama Canal treaty, which scheduled the return of the canal's control to Panama; signed the Strategic Arms Limitation Treaty (SALT II) with the USSR; developed a comprehensive energy

Hikers on these trails must check in at the visitors center (open 8 am to 5 pm daily) before heading out, where there's also an interpretive **museum** explaining the area's natural and unnatural history. Wildlife includes bobcats, coyotes, the endangered gopher tortoise and armadillos. Wildflowers are common in spring and fall. The park is open 7 am to 6 pm September 15 through April 14, and until 9 pm the rest of the year. Entrance to the park requires a $2 per vehicle ParkPass.

Web site: www.gastateparks.org

KOLOMOKI MOUNDS STATE HISTORIC PARK

This 1293-acre park (☎ 229-724-2150), located six miles north of Blakely (look for the peanut monument!) off US Hwy 27, is both an important archaeological site and a recreational area. Seven earthen mounds within the park were built during the 12th and 13th centuries by the Swift Creek and Weeden Island Indians. The largest, at 56 feet high and 325 feet by 200 feet at the base, was built to be the base for a temple. Kolomoki, with its villages, burial mounds,

temple mound and ceremonial plaza, was the largest ceremonial center in southern Georgia, with a population of perhaps 2000 people.

A small, interpretive **museum** built adjacent to a partially excavated mound has a small display of effigy pottery, a 12-minute slide show and other exhibits. It's open 9 am to 5 pm Tuesday to Saturday, 2 pm to 5:30 pm Sunday, closed Monday; admission costs $2/1 adults/children.

Five miles of **walking trails** wind among the Indian mounds. From the top of the temple mound, you can look over most of the archeological area.

The park also provides recreational activities such as fishing and boating on Lakes Kolomoki and Yohola, picnicking, miniature golf and a swimming pool. Fishing boats, pedal boats and canoes can be rented. The 43 **campsites** cost $13/15 without/with hook-ups. Campsites on the edge of the lake are pretty but have little privacy; the 'rustic' sites are more private. Campsites can be reserved by calling the Georgia central reservations line (☎ 800-864-7275, 770-389-7275).

From Peanuts to President

program; recognized human rights as a key consideration in developing foreign policy; appointed unprecedented numbers of African Americans and women to major government positions; and pardoned Vietnam War draft evaders. His presidency was marred, though, by high inflation and unemployment, the capture of 52 American hostages by Iranian militants, and problems getting his energy program through Congress. Some criticized him for being politically naive and *too* sincere and conscientious. He was handily defeated by Ronald Reagan in 1980.

Since 1981, Carter has continued to pursue issues of peace and human rights around the world. *Time* magazine claimed that he has been 'the best ex-president the US has had since Herbert Hoover.' He has helped monitor elections in Haiti, Panama and Nicaragua, conferred with Middle Eastern leaders, attempted to mediate the Eritrean-Ethiopian civil war, and forged an agreement with Haiti to end military control of the government.

Carter's Presidential Library and Carter Center in Atlanta sponsor programs promoting conflict resolution, human rights, education, agriculture and health care. Carter has also written 14 books, the latest – *An Hour Before Daylight* – a recollection of his childhood and racial separation on a South Georgia farm in the depths of the Depression. Despite his fame, he and wife Rosalynn continue to live in Plains, population 650, where he teaches adult Sunday school at the Plains Baptist Church. They spend a week every summer helping build houses for the poor with Habitat for Humanity.

The park is open 7 am to 10 pm. Entrance to the park requires a $2 ParkPass.
Web site: www.gastateparks.org

LAKE SEMINOLE

At the end of the road in Southwest Georgia, you'll find Lake Seminole, where the Chattahoochee River and the Flint River meet the Jim Woodruff Lock and Dam. This 37,500-acre shallow reservoir offers cool, clear water with a variety of sport fish, including large-mouth bass, catfish, bream, crappie and speckled perch. Duck hunting is also popular. The lake is set among pines, oaks, gums and cypress.

To go boating, locals just put in at one of the many landings on the Chattahoochee or Flint Rivers. Out-of-towners may want to stop at the **Trails End Marina** (☎ 229-861-2060), where state Hwy 253 ends at the Chattahoochee River, for a waterproof map, bait and tackle, a Georgia fishing license and information. Fishing boats can be rented here. There are also rental cabins ($65, sleeps eight), RV hookups ($15) and a primitive campground ($8.50).

Another good place to get started is **Seminole State Park** (☎ 229-861-3137), located near the intersection of Georgia state Hwys 39 and 253. This 604-acre park includes river access, a swimming beach, miniature golf and rental of canoes, paddle boats and bicycles. You might see the threatened gopher tortoise along a 2.2-mile nature trail. The 50 campsites dispersed among the pine trees rent for $13/15 without/with hook-ups. Fourteen two-bedroom, fully equipped cottages are available to rent for $70/80 weekdays/weekends. There's a two-night minimum stay for campsites (three nights on holiday weekends) and a two- to five-night minimum stay for the cottages. For campsite or cabin reservations, call ☎ 800-864-7275 or ☎ 770-389-7275. A $2 ParkPass per vehicle is required.
Web site: www.gastateparks.org

THOMASVILLE
pop 18,000
After the economic devastation of the Civil War and its aftermath, Thomasville became one of the first Southern towns to not

merely welcome but court wealthy Northerners. According to some, 'a Yankee was worth two bales of cotton and twice as easy to pick.' Touted as a region with a healthy climate for pulmonary ailments, 15 grand hotels and 25 boarding houses were built between 1870 and 1906. The cheapest room at one of these palaces was $4 – about four days' average wages back then.

As more and more Northerners came down to pursue hunting, fishing and an active social life, many built 'cottages' as permanent winter retreats.

Throughout the South, antebellum plantations were being sold piecemeal to pay property taxes. In Thomasville, wealthy vacationers bought plantations for a pittance (land was $3 an acre, less than a night's stay at a hotel) and built grand mansions with the plentiful cheap labor. The plantations were used as hunting estates, not farms.

The hotel era ended abruptly in 1906, when the extension of the railroad southward and the eradication of malaria opened Florida as the major winter destination. Even after the tourists left, there was still enough money to keep the plantations going. Today, 71 of the plantations still exist, but only one is open to the public; a few others are operated as B&Bs. Although none of the grand hotels remain, downtown Thomasville offers a pleasant atmosphere of Victorian homes and a historic central business district.

Information

The Destination Thomasville Tourism Authority (☎ 800-704-2350, 229-227-7099) downtown (or 'uptown,' as they say locally) at the corner of Broad and Jefferson Sts, is an excellent place to start. The friendly staff distributes a useful visitors guide and sells a walking/driving guide for $3. They're open 9 am to 5 pm weekdays, until 4 pm Saturdays.

Web site: www.thomasvillega.com

The Bookshelf (☎ 229-228-7767, 108 E Jackson St) has a very good selection of regional books, as well as bestsellers, cards, gifts and a few $1 used books. They even have an audio book trade-in program.

Things to See & Do

The **Lapham-Patterson House State Historic Site** (☎ 229-225-4004), 626 N Dawson St, at Webster St, is one of the few places in the country to be designated a National Historic Landmark on the basis of its unique architecture alone. The house was built in 1885 as a winter cottage for shoe merchant CW Lapham. A survivor of the great Chicago fire, Lapham made sure there were plenty of exits: in all, there are 26 exterior doors and 53 windows in the 19-room cottage. The house is also notable for its fish-scale shingles, oriental-style porch decorations, long-leaf pine inlaid floors and cantilevered spiral staircase that wraps around a double-flued chimney. The 45-minute tours start on the hour. It's open 9 am to 5 pm Tuesday to Saturday, 2 pm to 5 pm Sunday, closed Monday; admission is $4/2 adults/children.

The **Thomas County Museum of History** (☎ 229-226-7664), 725 N Dawson St, offers a comprehensive survey of Thomasville's odd history. The informative two-hour tours offer in-depth perspectives of slavery and plantation life. Included are displays on the grand hotels and cottage retreats. A simple frontier cabin behind the museum and an 1877 middle-class urban house provide a needed reminder that most people did not live the genteel plantation life. The museum can be visited only by taking the tour. It's open 10 am to noon and 2 to 5 pm Monday to Saturday; the last tour is at 3:30 pm; $5/$1.

Going out of your way to see a tree may seem silly, but **The Big Oak,** at the corner of N Crawford and E Monroe Sts, is worth the effort. This whopper of a tree sprouted about 1685, measures 24 feet around the trunk and has a limb spread of 162 feet.

The only plantation open to the public is **Pebble Hill Plantation** (☎ 229-226-2344). Providing a glimpse into an elegant and exclusive past, the impressive 1936 mansion has more than 40 rooms decorated with antique furniture, crystal, porcelain and artwork. The 3000-acre grounds feature a cow barn, stables with a collection of carriages, a historic cemetery and vintage cars.

The plantation is about 6 miles south of the Tourism Authority on US Hwy 319. It's open 10 am to 5 pm Tuesday to Saturday and 1 pm to 5 pm Sunday; closed Monday and the month of September. Admission costs $3/1.50 for the grounds only, and $7/3.50 for the house tour. Children under 6 years old are not admitted to the main house.

Web site: www.pebblehill.com

Special Events

The town's major annual event is the **Thomasville Rose Show and Festival,** held each April. Activities include rose displays, parades, historical home and museum tours, arts and crafts shows, garden tours and, of course, lots of food. **Victorian Christmas** is also a popular event.

Places to Stay & Eat

Chain motels are located on Hwy 19 between Hwy 319 and Remington Ave a couple of miles east of downtown. Rooms at the *Jameson Inn* (☎ 800-526-3766, 912-227-9500, 1670 Remington Ave) start at $53, including a continental breakfast and use of the pool and fitness center.

The best way to appreciate the genteel spirit of Thomasville is by staying at one of the town's bed & breakfasts. The *1884 Paxton House* (☎ 912-226-5197, 445 Remington Ave), at Hansell St, is one of the coziest, in an elegant Victorian house with nine rooms from $110 to $250, plus 10% tax. Furnished with antique and period reproductions, the house also has an indoor heated pool and many fruit trees. A full breakfast is included in the room rates.

Web site: www.1884paxtonhouseinn.com

Dawson Street Inn (☎ 912-226-7515, 324 N Dawson St), at Monroe Ave in the midst of historic Victorian homes, is in a 19th-century house on the National Register of Historic Places. The four suite-size, bright rooms with 13-foot ceilings cost $125 to $190. Amenities include a full breakfast, a nice sitting porch and a mix of antique and modern furniture.

Izzo Pharmacy (☎ 229-226-4411, 122 N Broad St) is a wonderful old-time soda fountain that serves malts and root beer floats, as well as basic sandwiches and burgers.

The Market Diner (☎ 229-225-1777, 502 Smith Ave) has an unusually good buffet with fresh veggies from the farmer's market next door. A meal of all-you-can-eat fresh butter beans, creamy corn, turnips, peas, candied yams and fried chicken costs only $6. From 10:30 am to 1 pm, the buffet is only $4, including a soft drink, possibly the best value in the state.

Mom & Dad's Italian Restaurant (☎ 229-226-6265, 1800 Smith Ave) has a steady stream of regulars for good reason: They serve tasty pastas and veal, beef and chicken dishes in a cozy atmosphere. Dishes cost $9 to $16; closed Sunday and Monday.

Getting There & Away

Thomasville is at the intersections of US Hwys 19 and 84. Greyhound buses (☎ 229-226-4422) stop at 901 Smith Ave.

GEORGIA AGRIRAMA

Near the city of Tifton, Georgia Agrirama (☎ 229-386-3344) is the state's official living history museum. Recalling the 1890's, the museum consists of farmsteads, a rural town and 19th-century manufacturing buildings. Over 35 structures have been relocated to the 95-acre site and restored. Costumed interpreters demonstrate typical activities of the period, including grinding sugar cane using horse power (visitors can try the sweet and odd-tasting cane juice), milking cows and making grits (available for purchase) using a water-powered mill. There's also the upper-class Tiff house, a cotton gin, an operating sawmill, a printing press, a seed store and a non-working outhouse (don't embarrass yourself by trying to use it!). Kids will enjoy the 1.3-mile ride around the site on a steam locomotive. The place is popular with school groups and parents who sign up their kids for a day of chores. This enjoyable museum is an excellent way to learn about South Georgia's rural heritage. The drug store serves snacks and sandwiches.

Agrirama is open 9 am to 5 pm Monday to Saturday; admission is $8/4. To reach

Agrirama, take I-75 exit 63B, turn west and follow the signs from the interstate for 1.2 miles.

Web site: www.agrirama.com

OKEFENOKEE NATIONAL WILDLIFE REFUGE & WILDERNESS AREA

The Okefenokee Swamp is a national gem. The swamp is actually a huge bog trapped within a depression that was once – along with the rest of South Georgia – part of the ocean floor. The swamp area encompasses about 650 square miles, and is home to 234 species of reptiles, including an estimated 9000 to 15,000 alligators; 234 species of birds, such as egrets, ibises, herons, the Florida Sandhill Crane and the endangered red cockaded woodpecker; 49 types of mammals, from the common raccoon to the less common black bear; and 60 species of amphibians.

The term 'Okefenokee' is a variant of a Seminole word meaning 'land of the trembling earth.' Peat deposits that build up on the swamp floor are so mushy that you can cause nearby trees to tremble by stomping on the peat. The swamp water – about two feet deep – is the color of tea as a result of tannic acid released by decaying plants; the swamp has the acidity of a soda. The Suwannee River and St Marys River drain the swamp. A variety of swamp habitat, including islands, lakes, moss-laced cypress forests, scrub-shrub areas and wet prairies support ample wildlife.

The area was inhabited as early as 2500 BC. Israel Barber was the first white settler here, establishing his homestead in 1807. Other settlers followed, farming and logging in the swamp. In the late 19th century, the Suwannee Canal Company attempted to drain the swamp to allow more extensive logging and agriculture; fortunately, they went bankrupt in the process. A railroad was built into the western part of the swamp, and cypress trees were logged for almost 30 years. Since becoming a wildlife refuge in 1937, the swamp has been mostly protected from such manmade momentous changes.

The Okefenokee Swamp has three main entrances, each managed by a different entity. Each entrance has its own activities and charms.

Be warned that biting yellow flies can be excruciating in May or June. Mosquitoes can be a problem after dark.

Greyhound buses serve the towns around the Okefenokee Swamp, including Fargo, Homerville, Waycross and Folkston. To see the swamp, however, you will need a car, a bicycle, a tour or a lift to the water.

Web site: http://okefenokee.fws.gov

Western Entrance

The entrance to the western side of the swamp is at **Stephen C Foster State Park** (☎ 912-637-5274), an 18-mile drive from the tiny town of Fargo along state Hwy 177. The park is named after the composer of 'Way Down Upon the Suwannee River.'

By far the best activity here is to get out on the water. Twenty-five miles of day-use waterways are accessible from here. Alligator sightings are almost certain if you keep alert. Visitors can also canoe to 3140-acre Billy's Island and explore rusting fragments of the area's logging history. Canoes and motorized boats can be rented here; rates are $6/11/15 for 1/4/8 hours for canoes, and $26/36/56 for 4/8/12 hours in a motor boat. There's also a 90-minute guided boat tour, which leaves daily at 10 am, 1 pm and 3 pm; rates are $8/6 for people over/under age 12. You rent boats and catch the tour from near the entrance, at the parks office.

A small **interpretive center** has an introduction to the area's ecology and history. A 1½-mile nature walk leads over a boardwalk into the swamp. There's no food here, so bring your own.

The park's 66 pleasant **campsites** are individually enclosed by palms, shrubs, pine and hardwood trees. Rates are $16/18 tents/RVs from March 1 through May 31, and $13/15 the rest of the year. Cabin rentals are $71/81 weekdays/weekends from March 1 through May 31, and $61/71 at other times; there's a $15 surcharge for one-night-only stays. Campsites and cabins can be reserved through a central phone line (☎ 800-864-7275, 770-389-7275 in Metro Atlanta).

Entrance to the state park costs $5 per vehicle for a seven-day pass (this is also good at the eastern entrance). It's open 7 am to 7 pm in winter, longer in summer; the park office closes at 5 pm in winter, 6 pm in summer.

Web site: www.gastateparks.org

Northern Entrance

Northern access to the swamp is at the **Okefenokee Swamp Park** (☎ 912-283-0583), a private concession and wildlife park eight miles south of Waycross. The park's main attraction is a zoo of live swamp creatures, including alligators (many unfenced), black bears, otters, turtles and deer. Exhibits include a natural history center, a snake display, an educational live reptile show (snakes and gators) and a corny animatronics show for the kids. A railroad runs through the park and provides the only access to Pioneer Island, a collection of buildings and artifacts from the pioneer days. A short boardwalk provides direct access to the swamp.

Once again, a visit to the swamp is hardly complete without a ride on the water. Guided boat tours are a good way to learn about the history, culture and wildlife of the swamp. Canoe rentals are also available.

The park is open 9 am to 5 pm; admission is $10/9 and includes all exhibits and the railroad tour. The guided boat tours are an additional $4/8/20 for 30 minutes/one hour/two hours. Canoe rental costs an additional $6 per person.

A concession in the park provides food, but it may be closed in the off-season.

Web site: www.okeswamp.com

Eastern Entrance

At the eastern entrance, the **Suwannee Canal Recreation Area** (☎ 912-496-7836), 11 miles southwest of Folkston, is the most convenient for visitors who are also exploring the Georgia coast. It has some of the most comprehensive facilities and is the main US Fish & Wildlife Service entrance. The lakes and gator holes dotting the prairies offer promising sportfishing. Gator sightings are a near certainty.

The entrance contains a **visitors center** with exhibits of basic information on swamp culture and wildlife. The 9-mile **Swamp Island Drive** is suitable for exploration by car or bike, and leads to Chesser Island, where the reconstructed homestead of the Chesser family demonstrates how pioneer families lived in the 19th and early 20th centuries. From the island, a boardwalk leads 3/4 mile to an observation tower overlooking a classic swamp prairie and lake.

Much of the canoeing is along the wide Suwannee Canal and is shared with motorboats. For a quieter experience, take the side trails to Mizell Prairie and Cooter Lake if the water level permits. There are a couple of chemical pit toilets on the route.

The private concession Okefenokee Adventures (☎ 912-496-7156) rents canoes and boats, and also sells sandwiches and snacks. Access is available here by water to the swamp lakes and marsh-like prairies. One- or two-hour guided boat tours are offered; for a sense of true swamp mystery, try the night tours.

Entrance to the park costs $5 per vehicle for a 7-day pass (also good at the western entrance). Canoes or single-speed bicycles rent for $14/23 per canoe for four hours/all day. A motor boat costs $26/44 for four hours/all day for up to four people. One-hour guided boat tours are $11/7 over/ under age 12; two-hour tours are $19/11; and night tours are $25/17. Guided canoe tours are also available by prior arrangement for $50/90 half/full day. All these amenities are available from the concessionaire – Okefenokee Adventures. You can bring your own canoe or kayak, but you must register with the concessionaire.

There are no accommodations or camping here; see the Around the Swamp section at the end of this chapter for some nearby possibilities.

Wilderness Canoeing

The ultimate Okefenokee experience is a multi-day trip on the 120 miles of waterways through the swamp. On these trips, canoeists (no motors are allowed) paddle through the swamp all day and camp on platforms over the water at night. Trips can range from two to five days, although they are limited to two nights' length in March and April.

Trips are allowed via permit only by calling Okefenokee National Refuge canoe reservation line (☎ 912-496-3331) between 7 and 10 am weekdays. Permits can be reserved up to two months before your trip, and you must register, send in a nonrefundable fee of $10 per person per night and receive your permit before you can get out

Around the Swamp

You'll find accommodations, places to eat and some interesting things to do in the towns around the Okefenokee.

In Waycross, the **Okefenokee Heritage Center Museum** (☎ 912-285-4260) displays a train depot, a 1912 steam locomotive, local art and exhibits on swamp pioneers. **Obediah's Okefenok** (☎ 912-287-0090) honors Obediah Barber, one of the first white settlers on the swamp's northern border. Exhibits include Barber's homestead and cabin, animal displays, boardwalks over the swamp and nature trails.

on the water. There are only seven platforms in the swamp, so only seven groups per night can register; available space can fill up quickly. Be sure to get the US Fish & Wildlife Service's *Okefenokee National Wildlife Refuge Wilderness Canoe Guide* (☎ 912-496-7836) if you are considering a trip. Canoeists are expected to comply with a number of requirements: no pets or other potential alligator food; no fires in most locations; portable toilets are required (available for rent at the eastern entrance); and you must carry enough drinking water for the entire trip.

Web site: http://okefenokee.fws.gov

For trips that do not begin and end at the same entrance, Okefenokee Adventures at the eastern entrance can provide shuttles (see Eastern Entrance section earlier in this chapter).

Camping is available at the 626-acre **Laura S Walker State Park** (☎ 912-287-4900, reservations 800-864-7275 or 770-389-7275), nine miles southeast of Waycross on GA Route 177. Recreational activities include water skiing, boating, fishing and a swimming pool. The 44 tent and RV sites are set among pine trees at the edge of a 120-acre lake, providing a pretty setting but little privacy. The park also has laundry facilities, a nature trail and a golf course.

Plenty of motels and chain hotels are located on the eastern side of Waycross near the intersection of US Highways 82 and 23. The Waycross Tourism and Conference Bureau (☎ 912-283-3742, fax 912-283-0121) can provide more information on area accommodations and attractions.

Web site: www.gacoast.com/navigator/way cross.html

Nearer the eastern entrance, *private campgrounds* are available near Kingfisher Landing (☎ 912-496-2186), on US Hwy 1, 13 miles north of Folkston; at Okefenokee Pastimes (☎ 912-496-4472, Web site: www.okefenokee.com), on state Hwy 121/23 at the Suwannee Canal Recreation Area turnoff; and at **Traders Hill Park** (☎ 912-496-2536), a county park seven miles south of Folkston on state Hwy 23. *Hotels* can be found in Folkston or at the I-95 Kingsland exit, 22 miles east of Folkston, on state Hwy 40 (see the Savannah and the Coast chapter).

Southeast Adventure Outfitters, on St Simons Island, offers guided tours to the swamp; see the Savannah and the Coast chapter.

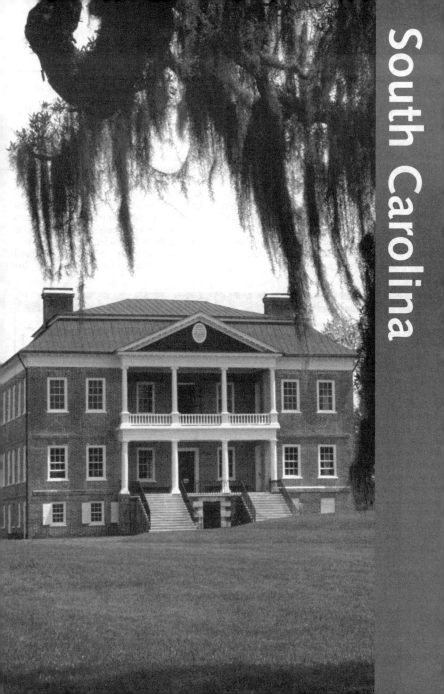

South Carolina

Shaped roughly like a small equilateral triangle, South Carolina seems to be maternally cradled by North Carolina and Georgia. But don't be fooled by this little package – South Carolina has been raising hell since its inception as one of the first English colonies. Always at the forefront of America's early wars, the state clamored for secession from the British Empire and then again from the Union. The reasons for its uprising haven't always been noble – greed propelled many of the early confrontations, sending the state headlong into an unwinnable civil war that has left battle scars on its collective psyche.

An adage says South Carolinians are easily led but rarely driven. Their stubborn resistance to outside influence kept the state from industrializing at the turn of the 19th century and keeps the Confederate battle flag flying in front of the State House today. This unwillingness to bend is coupled with an uncanny ability to take insults and turn them into compliments. South Carolinians often refer to themselves as 'Sandlappers,' which was originally a derogatory term used by the aristocracy to describe poor dirt

Facts at a Glance

Nickname – Palmetto State

Population – 4.012 million

Area – 31,000 sq miles (40th largest)

Admitted to Union – 1788 (8th state to ratify the Constitution), seceded in 1860 and readmitted in 1868, reconstruction ended 1877

Capital – Columbia (112,000)

Birthplace of – Andrew Jackson, Dizzy Gillespie, Mary McLeod Bethune, James Brown, Jesse Jackson, Vanna White and more astronauts than any other state

Famous for – gracious manners, fire-breathing politicians and the world's sweetest peaches

First home for – US golf course (Charleston, 1773), public museum (Charleston, 1773), freestanding campus library (Columbia, 1840)

Highlights – walking the cobblestoned streets of Charleston; eating seafood in rundown waterfront shacks; cruising through two-lane country roads; waterfall hunting in the Blue Ridge Mountains

Most likely overheard -Yes sir, No sir, Yes ma'am, No ma'am (said to anybody old enough to remember rotary phones)

Perfect picnic snack – Carolina-style barbecue sandwiches with coleslaw and Charleston benne (sesame) wafers

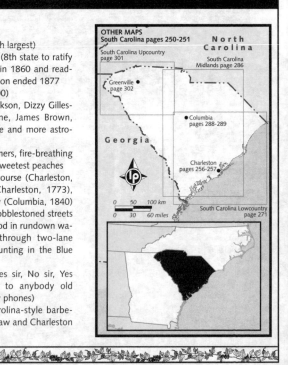

OTHER MAPS
South Carolina pages 250-251

South Carolina Upcountry page 301

North Carolina

South Carolina Midlands page 286

Greenville ● page 302

● Columbia pages 288-289

Georgia

Charleston pages 256-257

0   50   100 km
0   30   60 miles

South Carolina Lowcountry page 271

farmers. Now it proudly denotes patriotism for the state's salt marshes, clean white beaches, sun-baked red clay and granite mountains.

It's not hard to get off the beaten path in South Carolina – in fact, the entire state is off the beaten path. There is not a single major city, and the large population centers are just overgrown towns. The state is most famous for the colonial port of Charleston, with its grand mansions and gracious manners. A string of islands just off the coast shelters the mainland from storms and fosters a truly unique culture called Gullah, created by former slaves who were able to retain many of their African traditions. There are diverse beaches, from tacky and crowded Myrtle Beach and golf-course-crazy Hilton Head to the wild and undeveloped state parks of Huntington Beach and Hunting Island. The interior of the state is dotted with small towns and miles of country roads that wind past farmlands, white clapboard churches, and crumbling sharecropper shacks – an odd mixture of beauty and ugliness. Smack dab in the middle of the state is the capital of Columbia, which was burned by Sherman and resurrected by the cotton mills. The industry hub of Greenville is a new melting pot of European and Asian nationals. Just beyond Greenville are the foothills of the Blue Ridge Mountains, forever wild thanks to a cluster of state parks.

Facts about South Carolina

HISTORY

More than 28 separate tribes of Native Americans have lived in what's now South Carolina. The most influential were the Cherokee, who maintained a permanent settlement in Keowee, in the northwestern part of the state near Clemson. This capital flourished for about 200 years after the first interaction with European traders, and a trading post for Indian-trapped furs and English-made goods was established 96 miles south of Keowee along the Cherokee Path. The Cherokee were eventually forcibly removed during the tragic Trail of Tears. For more information, see the Facts about Georgia & the Carolinas chapter.

The English founded the Carolina colony in 1670; its borders were 36 degrees latitude to 31 degrees latitude and everything west of the Atlantic Ocean. The first settlers came from the overcrowded island of Barbados and built a settlement called Charles Towne, later known as Charleston. They transplanted Barbadian feudal society into the thick coastal mud. A colony of a colony (Barbados was a colony of England), South Carolina's judicial system, slave code and original form of government were based on those of Barbados.

The first cash king was rice. Africans from the rice-growing regions of Sierre Leone, Senegal, Gambia and Angola were enslaved and brought over to the colony to turn impenetrable swamps into cultivated rice fields. Historians estimate that up to 40,000 acres of swamps along the Carolina coast were drained. The wealth this crop created rivaled that of Europe and was, at the time, unparalleled in other parts of the North American continent.

By the 1730s, there existed two South Carolinas: the Lowcountry, a much older, refined community of aristocrats and their attendant slaves; and the Backcountry, a frontier settled by Scotch-Irish and Swiss-German farmers. This split played a major role in choosing sides when revolutionary sentiments began to emerge. Rarely were the battles simply Americans versus British; instead, the Loyalist troops included South Carolinian Tories from the Backcountry who'd received their farmland through royal grants. In South Carolina the Revolutionary War was a civil war, and neighbors and kin often met on the battlefield.

After gaining a foothold in Savannah, Loyalists moved north along the coast and with little resistance took control of Beaufort and Charleston in 1780, and South Carolina was now an occupied zone. The Continental Army had abandoned the state for battles farther north, but guerilla-style militias organized throughout the area. Nipping at the heels of the British were partisan heroes such as Francis 'Swamp Fox' Marion in the Lowcountry, Thomas 'Gamecock' Sumter in the Midlands and Andrew Pickens in the mountains.

One early head-on collision in South Carolina was the Battle of Camden, in which the Continental Army was badly defeated by the Loyalists. The victory at Camden encouraged the British to move north toward Charlotte, North Carolina. Later in 1780, the entire left offensive wing of the British forces was wiped out in less than a day by sharpshooters and frontier militia at King's Mountain, on the border of North and South Carolina, near present-day Rock Hill.

With the route to Charlotte cut off, General Cornwallis sent Colonel Banastre 'Bloody' Tarleton west into the Piedmont. His troops met forces from the Continental Army at Cowpens on January 17, 1781. The Loyalists were a well-oiled machine of mounted infantry headed by Bloody Tarleton, a cruel and ruthless fighter. Lines of foot soldiers backed up by riflemen and flanked by cavalry approached each other in the open space of a cow pasture. The fighting lasted just one hour before Tarleton's men were surrounded and defeated by the rag-tag Patriots.

The British forces were now weakened and met with other defeats farther north; they began to abandon forts in Ninety Six and Camden, and after 2½ years of occupation, they also abandoned Charleston. Surprisingly, more battles and skirmishes were fought in South Carolina than in any other state.

Prosperity followed until the 'late, great unpleasantness' (Charlestonians' euphemism for the Civil War). The first battle of the Civil War occurred in April 1860 at Fort Sumter, a federal base strategically located in Charleston Harbor. The fort fell to the Confederates 30 hours later.

In November 1861, the Union Army crawled up the coast using Hilton Head as a base to overtake Beaufort and Sea Island plantations, freeing the slaves three years

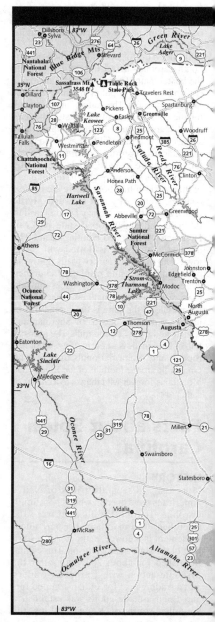

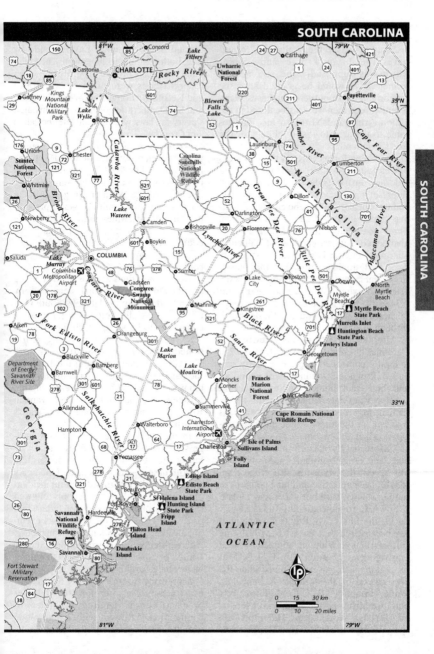

SOUTH CAROLINA

before war's end. The Union seized planters' property on account of back taxes and sold parcels to the plantation's former slaves. The slogan '40 acres and a mule,' which was supposedly the recompense former slaves would be granted after the war, originated from these purchases. Many recently freed men were also enlisted in the Union Army, and Northern missionaries came to the area to found schools for the freed communities.

The Union forces were on the doorsteps of Charleston, a valuable port for the Confederacy. Just outside the harbor, Union ships set up an ever-tightening blockade and later began shelling the city. On Christmas night, 1861, 134 shells rained down. Three years later, the Confederate Army abandoned Charleston. General William T Sherman, torch in hand, was expected any day. Charlestonians shipped all their goods to Columbia for safekeeping and were sadly surprised when Sherman arrived right behind them in February 1865. His troops burned the capital and a 30-mile swath through the middle of the state.

After the fall of the Confederacy, the two Carolinas became Military District No 2, a federally controlled zone. Prosperity had ended. Prominent families were penniless, and their grand homes were auctioned off to repay war debts. While white South Carolinians mourned, black South Carolinians rejoiced, for the long-awaited day of emancipation had finally come.

Unfortunately, racially motivated violence and struggle ensued. Race riots broke out across the state, the Ku Klux Klan (KKK) became active and nine counties in the Upcountry were put under martial law. If South Carolina escaped bitter struggles during the 1960s Civil Rights movement, it was because the state bled so heavily during Reconstruction. White men joined the Red Shirt movement, centered in Edgefield, to reclaim the state government and undo the laws passed by the 'radical' Republicans. Wade Hampton III, a Confederate war hero, was crowned the Democrat's leader, and through intimidation, Hampton won the election of 1876. The Republicans

refused to leave office, rightly claiming that voter fraud had occurred. The two parties carried on government business side by side, both claiming to have won. The stalemate was finally broken in April 1877, when federal troops were officially withdrawn and Reconstruction ended. Wade Hampton and his Democratic government reinstated slavery-era laws, which would later be called Jim Crow laws.

At the turn of the 20th century, poor tenant farmers left the fields to join the mills, where they lived in villages provided by the companies and lost the sun-scorched hue of farmers. William Gregg built the South's first cotton mill in 1845 in present-day Graniteville. Mills sprang up alongside rivers and creeks in the Midlands and Upcountry, and in 1925, the state was the largest cotton goods producer in the country.

By this time, the state was finally coming out of its 100-year stupor and welcomed any and all industry. In the late '50s, South Carolina successfully courted international companies to build high-tech factories. By 1980, 155 foreign companies were represented in the Greenville-Spartanburg area. The US government came in the 1950s for the patriotic endeavor of building a plutonium and tritium plant for nuclear weapons. Located near the banks of the Savannah River, the plant became one of the state's largest employers.

In the 1960s, concerned that new businesses would be scared off by racial violence, the state managed a moderately smooth desegregation. Clemson University was successfully integrated without incident in 1962 and the other state schools followed suit. But economics could not hide white Carolinians' fears of integration, as exemplified by a fatal incident in Orangeburg, where three students were killed and 30 injured by police when they tried to enter a whites-only bowling alley.

Like many Southern states, South Carolina gets media attention for white supremacy but is ignored in times of cooperation. Attitudes will change along with the changing demographics of the state.

The latter part of the 20th century saw an increase in the population for the first time in 150 years. New people were moving in from other parts of the country, and of the state's 4 million residents, just under one-third were born outside of South Carolina.

GEOGRAPHY

There are three distinct regions in South Carolina: the Lowcountry, Midlands and Upcountry. The Lowcountry is the swath of land that follows the coast and is the most tropical in climate and vegetation. Barely above sea level, the land is covered with swamps, marshes and tidal rivers, as well as 182 miles of oceanfront beaches. Moving inland, the land rises gradually to the Midlands, which separates the coast from the Piedmont. Ages ago, the Midlands area was the beach, and the land is largely infertile and dotted with sand hills, piney forests and large swamps. The Upcountry rises still higher, preparing to meet the Blue Ridge Mountains in the state's far western corner. The highest elevation is Sassafrass Mt (3548 ft).

About 830 sq miles of the state are covered by water, including the Congaree, Savannah, Saluda, Edisto, Pee Dee and Broad Rivers and three man-made lakes.

NATIONAL PARKS & PROTECTED AREAS

There are no national parks, but there are three national forests and dozens of state parks. In the Lowcountry, the westernmost part of the South and North Carolina border is lined with state parks, including the popular Table Rock and Caesars Head. On the Georgia border, the Chattooga National Wild and Scenic River is one of the best white-water rivers in the Southeast (see the North Georgia chapter for more details).

GOVERNMENT & POLITICS

South Carolinians typically vote in line with conservative Republicans, although, historically, white Carolinians were Democrats and black Carolinians were Republicans. (Each group chose either to align or distance themselves from the Republicans, the party of Lincoln.) The state's early primary vote for president is credited with helping win the Republican nomination for President George W Bush in 2000.

The state is represented in the US Congress by two senators and six representatives. The popularity and endurance of the state's most famous senator, Strom Thurmond, confounds the rest of the nation. Once an ardent segregationist, he was the first write-in candidate to win a US senate seat (1954) and set a filibuster record to block the 1957 Civil Rights Act. By switching parties in the 1960s in response to the increasingly pro-Civil Rights nature of the Democrats, he ushered many white Southerners into the party of Lincoln. Another turnabout came when he began to embrace more modern attitudes toward race relations. Thurmond is loved by his constituents, who have voted him into office eight times, making him the oldest and longest-serving senator (he'll be 100 years old at the end of his eighth term). He has brought an unprecedented number of military jobs to the state and sends condolence cards to grieving widows.

On a state level, sanctioned gambling has been a frequently debated topic in the legislature, a 170-member body of 46 senators and 124 representatives. Governor Jim Hodges, a Democrat, sauntered into office because of his support for a lottery that would partially benefit education. Until November 2000, South Carolina was one of 11 states without a statewide lottery.

ARTS

An observer once noted that South Carolinians pour all their creative strength into politics instead of the arts. Many of its creative people (such as Dizzy Gillespie and James Brown) left for better opportunities elsewhere. While South Carolina has not contributed nationally to the arts, it does boast the country's largest outdoor sculpture garden (Brookgreen Gardens, south of Myrtle Beach) and the coastal craft of sweetgrass basketry, originally brought to the area by West African slaves. Robert Mills, the nation's first federal architect, was a South Carolinian and designed many of the public buildings in Charleston and Columbia. Charleston is an architectural history lesson, with fine examples of Federal, Georgian and Victorian homes. The old art of kaolin pottery has been revived in Edgefield, and public murals and sculptures decorate the capital of Columbia. There are also many talented painters, potters and writers who are mentioned in more detail later in this chapter.

INFORMATION
Tourist Offices

With 32 million people visiting annually, South Carolina is well versed in providing tourist information. Contact the Department of Parks, Recreation & Tourism (☎ 800-255-2059, 803-734-1700, fax 803-734-0133), which can provide information about parks, attractions and golf courses. Visit its Web site at www.travelsc.com or write to 1205 Pendleton St, Suite 106, Columbia, SC 29201.

Welcome centers are on all major highways and interstates and offer restrooms, tourism information, snacks and brochures. For road conditions, call ☎ 803-896-9621. The state also compiles a B&B guide; call ☎ 888-599-1234. Some state parks rent furnished villas or cabins with air-con and heating. These are very popular, and it can be difficult to get reservations, especially during peak seasons. To make a reservation for the current year, call the park and ask about availability. For next year's rentals, reservations are accepted the first Monday after January 1 through the following Friday. Web site: www.southcarolinaparks.com

Sales Tax & Other State Laws

Sales tax varies by county but ranges from 5% to 7%.

The myriad of so-called blue laws (concerning, among other things, liquor sales) requires a lifetime to understand, but here is an abbreviated version. Beer and wine are sold in grocery stores every day except Sunday. Liquor is sold throughout the state in licensed package stores, which are also closed on Sunday. The exceptions are Beaufort, Edisto, Hilton Head, Greenville, Charleston and Myrtle Beach restaurants and bars, which can sell alcohol on Sunday for on-site consumption only. Bars and restaurants are required to sell alcohol in airplane-style mini-bottles. This means more fluid ounces (about 1.7oz) per drink, but it can also make mixed drinks with two kinds of liquor prohibitively expensive (a white Russian might cost $12).

Special Events

The state fair is held in October in Columbia. In May and June, Charleston hosts Spoleto and Piccolo Spoleto, international and regional arts festivals. Privately owned historic plantations and mansions are opened to the public in the spring and fall (see Charleston and Georgetown). Other smaller festivals celebrate the local harvest; see individual cities for more information.

Charleston & the Lowcountry

Coastal South Carolina, also called the Lowcountry, is part land and part water, with boundaries in constant negotiations. Tides as high as 10 feet donate and steal land on a diurnal basis, and hurricanes and winter storms create sandbars where once was deep water. The residents know the tides as well as they know their family trees. This fecund environment of tropical temperatures and rich loamy soil grew a wealthy and powerful society that once ruled the entire state and helped steer the young nation. Charleston reigned for close to 200 years before the loss of the Civil War reduced it to a quaint colonial town surrounded by small farms and fishing villages.

In the northern corner of the Lowcountry is the tourist mecca of Myrtle Beach, with carnival-like attractions that outshine the Atlantic's gentle surf. Heading south toward Charleston are a string of fishing villages and small seaside communities that collect on Sundays for oyster roasts and to recount the battle scars of past hurricanes. Although most have never traveled far, these residents are sure they live in paradise.

Nothing can beat Charleston for elegance and charm. It is the cosmopolitan center of the state and a romantic getaway for the nation. Restored old homes, horse-drawn carriage rides and a population with impeccable manners are the modern accoutrements of this antique city.

South of Charleston, the land is fractured into a multitude of islands separated by tidal creeks and marshes. Some of these are named, others appear and disappear with the tides. Technically an island, the town of Beaufort is the mainland center for Sea Island dwellers, people who live on Lady's, St Helena, Harbor, Hunting and Fripp Islands. Farther south is Hilton Head Island, the world famous golf capital. Bridges weren't extended to the Sea Islands until the mid-20th century, so culturally and geographically they were cut off from the mainland. Those who traveled did so by boat. A ferryman named Michael transported people from Lady's Island to Beaufort, and it is believed that he is forever immortalized in the spiritual 'Michael, Row Your Boat Ashore.' His passengers were mainly descendants of colonial-era slaves, known as Gullah, who maintained strong African traditions and spoke a hybridization of English and African languages. The author Pat Conroy, an honorary South Carolinian, has captured this region and aspects of the Gullah people in his autobiographical book *The Water is Wide,* a must-read for anyone journeying south of Charleston. His other books, *Prince of Tides* and *The Great Santini,* describe lives tied to the sea and marsh, and Beaufort's genteel poor.

CHARLESTON
pop 89,000

Charleston's historic district is one of the most appealing urban areas in America, with handsome old houses, charming little streets, gorgeous gardens, good restaurants and lively bars. Everyone loves it, though attitudes can be a little snooty.

History

Even well before the Revolutionary War, 'Charles Towne' (named for Charles II) was one of the busiest ports on the Eastern seaboard, the largest 18th-century town south of Philadelphia and the center of a prosperous rice-growing and trading colony. With influences from the West Indies, Africa, France and other European countries, it became a cosmopolitan city that was often compared to New Orleans. It was a wealthy city that held magnificent second homes for planters escaping the plantations during the malarial summers.

Charleston saw some of the first battles of the American Revolution, when British ships attacked Fort Moultrie, at the entrance to the harbor.

The Charleston & Hamburg Railroad began operations in 1833, transporting cotton 136 miles from the inland area to Charleston's ports. At the time it was an engineering wonder, and it secured Charleston's position as a principal East Coast port over rival Savannah.

The first shots of the Civil War were fired at Fort Sumter, in Charleston's harbor, but after the war the city's importance declined, as the labor-intensive rice plantations became uneconomical without slave labor. Natural disasters wrought more damage, with a major earthquake in 1886, several fires and storms, and the devastating Hurricane Hugo in 1989. It's remarkable that so

SOUTH CAROLINA

much of the town's historic fabric has survived, and fortunate too, because tourism is now a major moneymaker, with up to 4 million visitors arriving each year.

Orientation

The Greater Charleston metropolitan area sprawls over a broad stretch of coastal plains and islands, but the historic heart of Charleston is very compact, about 4 sq miles at the southern tip of a peninsula between the Cooper and Ashley Rivers. I-26 goes to North Charleston and the airport. Hwy 17, the main coastal road, cuts across the Charleston peninsula as the Crosstown Expressway, with soaring bridges connecting west to James Island and West Ashley and east to Mount Pleasant.

The Visitor Information Center, at 375 Meeting St, is about six blocks south of the Crosstown Expressway and should be your first stop, if only to park your car for the day ($12). Buses or a tour will take you into town. To walk downtown, take the most pleasant route by going a block west, then turning left (south) down King St, the main shopping thoroughfare. North of the visitors center, the streets are unattractive, and beyond the Crosstown Expressway they can be unwelcoming.

Information

The visitors center (☎ 800-868-8118, 843-853-8000) can help with accommodations, tours and event information, but if the lines are too long, just grab a map and the free *Official Visitors Guide*. The 23-minute *Charleston Forever* audiovisual is worth seeing ($2). Nearby at 81 Mary St, the chamber of commerce (☎ 800-868-8000) is also helpful. The chamber's Web site is www.charlestoncvb.com. The Charleston Preservation Society (☎ 843-722-4630), 147 King St, has history and architecture books, as does the Historic Charleston Foundation (☎ 843-724-8484), 108 Meeting St.

The main post office (☎ 843-577-0690) is at 83 Broad St. Charleston Memorial Hospital (☎ 843-577-0600) is at 326 Calhoun St. Major banks with ATMs and currency exchange in downtown Charleston are Bank

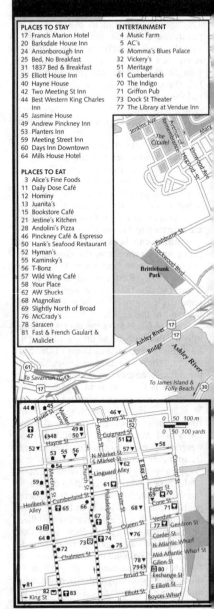

PLACES TO STAY
17 Francis Marion Hotel
20 Barksdale House Inn
24 Ansonborough Inn
25 Bed, No Breakfast
31 1837 Bed & Breakfast
35 Elliott House Inn
40 Hayne House
42 Two Meeting St Inn
44 Best Western King Charles Inn
45 Jasmine House
49 Andrew Pinckney Inn
53 Planters Inn
59 Meeting Street Inn
60 Days Inn Downtown
64 Mills House Hotel

PLACES TO EAT
3 Alice's Fine Foods
11 Daily Dose Café
12 Hominy
13 Juanita's
15 Bookstore Café
21 Jestine's Kitchen
28 Andolini's Pizza
46 Pinckney Café & Espresso
50 Hank's Seafood Restaurant
52 Hyman's
55 Kaminsky's
56 T-Bonz
57 Wild Wing Café
58 Your Place
62 AW Shucks
68 Magnolias
69 Slightly North of Broad
76 McCrady's
78 Saracen
81 Fast & French Gaulart & Maliclet

ENTERTAINMENT
4 Music Farm
5 AC's
6 Momma's Blues Palace
32 Vickery's
51 Meritage
61 Cumberlands
70 The Indigo
71 Griffon Pub
73 Dock St Theater
77 The Library at Vendue Inn

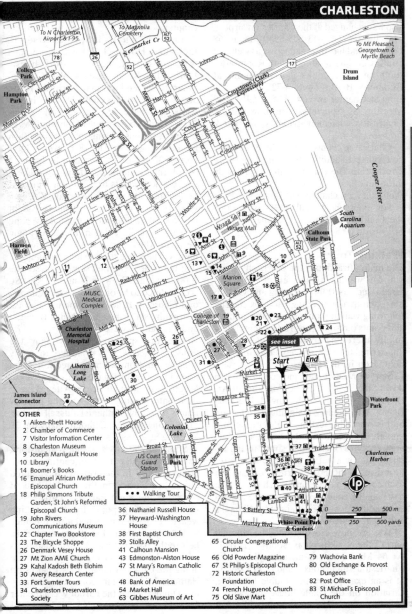

CHARLESTON

SOUTH CAROLINA

OTHER
1 Aiken-Rhett House
2 Chamber of Commerce
3 Visitor Information Center
8 Charleston Museum
9 Joseph Manigault House
10 Library
14 Boomer's Books
16 Emanuel African Methodist Episcopal Church
18 Philip Simmons Tribute Garden; St John's Reformed Episcopal Church
19 John Rivers Communications Museum
22 Chapter Two Bookstore
23 The Bicycle Shoppe
26 Denmark Vesey House
27 Mt Zion AME Church
29 Kahal Kadosh Beth Elohim
30 Avery Research Center
33 Fort Sumter Tours
34 Charleston Preservation Society

••• Walking Tour

36 Nathaniel Russell House
37 Heyward-Washington House
38 First Baptist Church
39 Stolls Alley
41 Calhoun Mansion
43 Edmonston-Alston House
47 St Mary's Roman Catholic Church
48 Bank of America
54 Market Hall
63 Gibbes Museum of Art

65 Circular Congregational Church
66 Old Powder Magazine
67 St Philip's Episcopal Church
72 Historic Charleston Foundation
74 French Huguenot Church
75 Old Slave Mart

79 Wachovia Bank
80 Old Exchange & Provost Dungeon
82 Post Office
83 St Michael's Episcopal Church

of America, 200 Meeting St, and Wachovia Bank, 16 Broad St. Foreign currency can also be exchanged at the Charleston airport. The library (☎ 843-805-6930) is at 68 Calhoun and has Internet access as well as a South Carolina reading room. Room after room of used books can be found at Boomer's Books (☎ 843-722-2666), 420 King St. Chapter Two (☎ 843-824-5910), 249 Meeting St, specializes in new books. Charleston's daily newspaper is *The Post & Courier.*

Charleston claims to have America's first golf course. In addition to the first, there are 22 offspring. The visitors center can provide information.

Web site: www.charlestongolfinc.com

For emergencies, call ☎ 911 or contact the Charleston Police Department, Office of Tourism (☎ 843-720-3892).

Walking Tour

The main attraction is the city itself, where you can wander along elegant thoroughfares – such as Tradd, Meeting and Church Sts – and quaint, winding back streets. The following walking tour should take an hour and points out some historically or architecturally interesting private residences. Items appearing in bold are covered in more detail later in the chapter.

Start at **Market Hall** and continue south down Meeting St to Gibbes Museum of Art (☎ 843-722-2706), 135 Meeting St. This 1905 Beaux Arts building maintains a collection of historic Charleston photographs and miniature portraits of the South Carolina aristocracy ($7). Continue south to the intersection of Meeting and Broad Sts, referred to as the Four Corners of Law. At each corner is a different branch of the law: city hall, the county courthouse, the federal courthouse/post office and **St Michael's Episcopal Church.**

You are now crossing into the colonial part of the city known as 'South of Broad.' At 64 Meeting St is an example of the Charleston 'single house,' and at 59 Meeting St is an example of the 'double house' (a variation on the single house, but with a street frontage that's two rooms wide). For more on this interesting Charleston architecture, see 'The Single House' later in this chapter.

Turn right onto Tradd St. At 106 Tradd St, the Stuart House (1772) has a captain's walk on top of the three-story house. During the Revolutionary War, Colonel Stuart remained loyal to the British Crown, and his property was confiscated by the patriots. It is believed that General Francis Marion jumped from one of the windows to escape a riotous evening of drinking. Turn left onto Legare St. The 1818 Sword Gates House, 32 Legare St, is said to be haunted by a former headmistress trying to prevent her female students from eloping. Turn left on Lamboll St to view the ornate Wedding Cake House, 14 Lamboll St, which was built in 1850. Take a left onto King St. At 21 King St is O'Donnell's Folly, an Italianate home built in 1865 for Patrick O'Donnell's fiancée. The home took so long to complete that the fiancée married someone else. The 1760s-era Miles Brewton House, 27 King St, is considered to be one of the best examples of a Georgian Palladian home in America. A wealthy slave merchant, Miles Brewton and his family were lost at sea in 1775. Notice the spiked ironwork near the house's fence; this was added to many Charleston homes for protection from feared slave revolts in the 1820s. Jog over to Meeting St through Prices Alley. Take a right onto Meeting St to visit the popular house museums **Nathaniel Russell House**, 51 Meeting St, and **Calhoun Mansion**, 16 Meeting St.

Some of the city's grandest mansions, dating from the early 19th century, adorn South Battery. In the evenings the painted ladies are bathed in the golden hue of sunset. White Point Park & Gardens is a pleasant resting point for the walking weary. The garden is named after the huge white oyster bed that flourished here before the battery wall was extended to its present location. From the promenade along the battery you can view **Charleston Harbor,** where dolphins come for a morning meal unaware that the harbor was a theater for some of the country's most important wars. Follow the promenade to 21 E Battery St, **Edmonston-Alston House**, a house museum that has one of the best views in the city.

A little farther north, take a left onto Water St and a quick right onto Church St. Here you'll find the **Heyward-Washington House**, 87 Church St, a house museum that once hosted George Washington. Nearby is the former tenement called Cabbage Row, 89-91 Church St, which served as the model for Catfish Row in *Porgy & Bess*. The character Porgy was based on a crippled man who hung out around the market; he had a mean reputation, and people whispered that he once killed a man.

Church St will eventually return you to Market St, passing several historic churches along the way. (See Historic Churches, below, for more information.)

Historic House Museums

Quite a few fine houses are open to visitors. Discounted combination tickets may tempt you to see more, but one or two will be enough for most people. Most house museums are open Monday to Saturday, 10 am to 5 pm and run guided tours every half hour.

Joseph Manigault House (☎ 843-723-2926), 350 Meeting St, was the showpiece of a French Huguenot family who made their fortune trading rum, sugar and rice. Built on the edge of town in 1803 in a newly expanding subdivision, this Federal house was designed by the owner's brother Gabriel, who is credited for introducing the architectural style to the city. The house was saved from near demolition in the 1920s and now displays period furniture. Admission is $8; see the Charleston Museum section for information on combination tickets.

A good example of the 'urban plantation' is the 1818 **Aiken-Rhett House** (☎ 843-723-1159), 48 Elizabeth St, which includes the main house as well as slave quarters and other outbuildings. The house has been preserved but will never receive a face-lift, resulting in a less pretty but historically interesting tour. This is the only house museum that discusses Charleston's slaves, who made up a little more than half of the city's antebellum population. The house has a self-guided audio tour and is open during the week and 2 to 5 pm on Sunday. Admission is $7 or $12 in combination with the Nathaniel Russell House.

The 1808 Federal **Nathaniel Russell House** (☎ 843-724-8481), 51 Meeting St, is noted for its spectacular, self-supporting spiral staircase. The inside of the house has been restored to show off the ornate and symmetrical woodwork and crown molding. Although not as ostentatious as the Calhoun Mansion, Nathaniel Russell House rivals it for historical accuracy. The garden is an equal attraction. Admission is $7, or $12 in combination with Aiken-Rhett House; also open Sunday 2 to 5 pm.

A financier of blockade runners was the only person in post-Civil War Charleston who could afford a new home. His slap-in-the-face to the blueblood society was the 1876 **Calhoun Mansion** (☎ 843-722-8205), 16 Meeting St. That Ted Turner-style audacity continues with the current owner, a wealthy lawyer, who seems to finance his antique-collecting habit by opening the house to the public. The Victorian glass and woodwork are impressive, and Prince Charles has eaten at the dining room table, but this is *not* a history lesson. Admission is $15; it is open Wednesday to Sunday, 10 am to 4 pm.

Combination Tickets

Combination tickets for various historic attractions are available from the visitor center. The Charleston Heritage Passport ($30/20 adults/children) includes the Nathaniel Russell House, Gibbes Museum of Art, Edmonston-Alston House and the plantation homes of Drayton Hall and Middleton Place.

Holders of the Best of Charleston Pass can pick nine of the city's most popular attractions to visit at about a 20% savings. Call ☎ 843-853-2378 or visit www.bestofcharleston.com for more information.

SOUTH CAROLINA

Wonderfully located in front of the harbor, the 1828 **Edmonston-Alston House** (☎ 843-722-7171), 21 E Battery, has lots of portraits, porcelain and artifacts from a well-to-do family ($8).

The 1772 **Heyward-Washington House** (☎ 843-722-0354), 87 Church St, semiofficially serves as the city's furniture museum, with pieces that include Charleston-made mahogany cabinets. The unrestored house is one of the city's oldest. Admission is $8; see the Charleston Museum section for combination tickets.

Historic Churches

From the city's beginnings, religious tolerance was fashionable in Charleston, and persecuted French Huguenots, Baptists and Jews sought refuge here. The number of churches on Church St alone attests to the city's laissez-faire attitude. Many of these congregations are the oldest of their faiths in the US. Visitors are welcome to attend religious services (call the churches for times).

French Huguenot Church (☎ 843-722-4385), 136 Church St, was founded in 1681, and services were originally timed with the tides for the church members who lived on Cooper River rice plantations.

The Single House

At one stage in its long history, Charleston based its property taxes on the length of street frontage. As a result, many houses were built just a single room wide with a 'piazza' (porch) running down the side of the building instead of across the front. The porch is a traditional feature of Southern architecture, offering a shady, cool and private place to sit. The typical 'single house' is a smallish timber home rather than a grand mansion, and what appears from the street to be a front door actually opens to the end of the piazza. Often there's a narrow garden alongside, with azaleas, wisteria and a shade tree overhanging the street – an essential ingredient of Charleston's unique charm.

Dating from 1680, **St Philip's Episcopal Church** (☎ 834-722-7734), 146 Church St, is the oldest congregation in Charleston. The statesman John C Calhoun and the author of *Porgy & Bess*, DuBose Heyward, are buried in the adjoining cemetery.

A 1752 parish division resulted in the founding of **St Michael's Episcopal Church** (☎ 843-744-1334), 78 Meeting St. George Washington and Robert E Lee sat in pew No 43 when they visited Charleston. In the church's graveyard, James L Petigru, the state's most outspoken Unionist, is buried. A talented and well-respected lawyer, he described South Carolina during the midst of the secession debates as being 'too small for a republic and too large for an insane asylum.' He was never dissuaded from this opinion and was described as the only person in South Carolina who did not secede. When a friend told him that Louisiana had joined the Confederacy, he replied 'Good God, I thought we had bought Louisiana.' His epitaph was read by President Woodrow Wilson at the signing of the Treaty of Paris, ending WWII. The yard is open to visitors daily 9 am to 4 pm.

First Baptist Church (☎ 843-722-3896), 61 Church St, is the oldest Baptist church in the South and was established in 1699; the present structure was designed by Robert Mills, the first federal architect, in 1822.

Emanuel African Methodist Episcopal Church, (☎ 843-722-2561), 110 Calhoun St, is the oldest AME church in the South and the second oldest in the US. During slavery times, free blacks and slaves who had formerly worshiped at white Methodist churches left to join the AME movement. Emanuel's congregation expanded into **Mt Zion AME Church** in 1882. Members of the 54th and 55th Massachusetts regiments worshiped here. Sunday services feature six choirs ranging from classical to early spirituals.

St Mary's Roman Catholic Church (☎ 843-722-7696), 95 Hasell St, is the mother church for Catholics in the Carolinas and Georgia. **Kahal Kadosh Beth Elohim** (☎ 843-723-1090), 90 Hasell St, is the oldest continuously used synagogue in the country. Tours are also available weekdays 10 am to noon.

Market Area

Market Hall Buzzards used to line the rooftops waiting for scraps from the city's meat market at 188 Meeting St at S Market St. A more pleasant site today, Market Hall houses the Confederate Museum on the second floor (when the building isn't undergoing restoration). Continue down either side of Market St, which now has some touristy shops, craft stalls, eateries and bars and is a good place to be at lunch or dinnertime. Keep an eye out for vendors selling benne wafers, a Charleston cookie made of sesame seeds ('benne' is an African word for sesame).

The market is also a good place to watch local women make sweetgrass baskets.

Old Exchange & Provost Dungeon This Palladian structure (☎ 843-727-2165), 122 East Bay St, was built in 1767 as an exchange and customs house for the busy port. As resentment toward England began to boil, Charlestonians met here to protest the controversial Tea Act in 1773 and to elect delegates to the Continental Congress in 1774. The city had more wind in its sails than ammunition in its reserves and was easily occupied by English troops near the start of the Revolutionary War. The prominent patriots were thrown into the building's dungeon, where outlaws and pirates were once detained. Stede Bonnet, the gentleman pirate, was one of the dungeon's famous occupants. For more on this colorful character, see the boxed texts: 'The Gentleman Pirate' in this chapter and 'Pirates of the Atlantic Coast' in the Facts about Georgia & the Carolinas chapter.

A nice break from the historic house routine, the exhibits in the dungeon are especially entertaining for children. Animated figures tell the stories of grizzled pirates and brave patriots. The first floor exhibits covering the Independence movement are in a more traditional museum fashion. It's open daily, and admission is $6/3.50 adults/children.

Old Powder Magazine The oldest building in Charleston, the powder magazine (☎ 843-805-6730), 79 Cumberland St, was built in 1712 just inside the fortified walls that protected the early city from Spanish, pirate and Indian attack. This low-slung building is constructed of tabby, a brick-like material made from crushed oyster shells. Admission is free.

Old Slave Mart Approximately 75% of the African slaves brought to America entered through the port of Charleston. Slaves were sold on the city's streets and docks until 1853, when a building for that purpose was opened at 6 Chalmers St. The Old Slave Mart previously served as a museum but has been 'temporarily' closed for many years. If you take a stroll by the building, notice the blue doors. Painting buildings blue, a Gullah tradition, helps ward off evil spirits, or 'haints.'

South Carolina Aquarium

The aquarium (☎ 843-720-1990), 350 Concord St, presents flora and fauna from the state's major geographic areas, with an emphasis on coastal environments. A three-story, 333,000-gallon tank displays more than 22 different fish species that live in the state's coastal waters. If you get bored of looking at fish, the aquarium has a panoramic view of the Cooper River. Admission costs $14/7 adult/children, and the aquarium is open daily with seasonal hours.

College of Charleston & Around

West of King St and south of Calhoun St, many smaller timber houses are somewhat timeworn, but the streets are a nice contrast with the more posh neighborhoods.

College of Charleston The College of Charleston (☎ 843-953-5507), approximately between St Philip and George St, opened in the 1770s and later became an extension of the city's school system, free to city residents. An interesting mix of Charleston debutantes and artsy out-of-towners now attend this liberal arts college. The college green, referred to as the cistern, is decorated by imposing Greek Revival structures and gnarled live oaks dripping

The Gentleman Pirate

Piracy and an 18th-century midlife crisis immortalized the story of Stede Bonnet, the gentleman pirate. On the little island of Barbados, Bonnet was a member of the landed gentry; he received a classical education, dressed in the finest English fashions and married a respectable woman. Active in civic affairs, Bonnet was a justice of the peace and a major in the island's militia.

In 1716, he made arrangements for what appeared to be an extended business trip. This trip was actually Bonnet's escape route: He had bought himself a sloop (the *Revenge*), outfitted her with armaments of war and hired a crew of 70 men for a new life of piracy.

The Atlantic Ocean bustled with ships carrying valuable cargo to and from Europe, North America and the Caribbean, and piracy had long been a profitable but despised profession that usually attracted destitute sailors. The only pirate in history to buy his own ship, Bonnet knew little about robbing vessels and even less about sailing. That's when he met Blackbeard, who took the novice pirate under his wing for a spree of looting and commandeering. Their most outrageous stunt occurred in Charleston in 1718. With five vessels, Blackbeard blocked the entrance to the port for a week and seized every ship that stumbled into them. One ship carried prominent Charlestonians, including a member of the Colonial council, who were taken hostage. Blackbeard demanded medical supplies, allegedly for syphilis, from the Charleston governor in exchange for the hostages. At the mercy of the pirates, the governor complied.

Bonnet's apprenticeship soon ended when Blackbeard made off with all the booty, and Bonnet followed him, hoping to take back his share. Bonnet was finally captured in the Cape Fear River by Colonel William Rhett, a Charleston planter turned pirate vigilante. The Charleston courts charged Bonnet with taking more than 28 vessels, committing other acts of piracy and murdering 18 law-abiding men. Stede Bonnet was hanged at White Point Gardens on December 10, 1718. Friends from his previous life as a Barbadian aristocrat whispered that it was his nagging wife who drove him to a life of crime.

with Spanish moss. The **Halsey Gallery** (☎ 843-953-5680), in the Simons Center for the Arts on St Phillip St, displays modern works by international and national artists. It's open Monday to Saturday, 11 am to 4 pm. The **John Rivers Communications Museum** (☎ 843-953-5810), 58 George St, covers the history of broadcasting with early animated movies and historical radio speeches; it's open Monday to Friday, noon to 4 pm; donations accepted.

To the west of the college, the **Avery Research Center** (☎ 843-953-7608), 125 Bull St, contains genealogical records, documents and a small museum dedicated to the African Americans of Charleston. The center is housed in the former Avery Normal Institute, a secondary school for African Americans from 1868-1954. It's open Monday to Saturday, noon to 5 pm; donations accepted.

Denmark Vesey House At 56 Bull St, this single house (now a private residence) was the home of Denmark Vesey, alleged leader of a slave uprising. He was a West Indian slave who came to Charleston with his master. In 1800, he bought his freedom with $1500 he won in a public lottery. Supporting himself as a carpenter, Vesey was active in the AME church and began to talk openly about leading other blacks out of bondage. Inspired by the slave uprising in Haiti, Vesey and four close conspirators planned to unite 6000 slaves, rob banks, burn the city, kill the whites and escape via ships to Haiti. The white authorities found out about the conspiracy, and Vesey, along with 34 associates, was sentenced to death in 1822. There is much disagreement over whether a plot really existed or the scheme was concocted by whites to deter possible uprisings and tighten slave laws.

The result was that the Charleston whites were sufficiently frightened, and in response, black churches were closed, manumission was outlawed, curfew laws enforced and free blacks on merchant ships were housed in the city jail during shore leave.

Charleston Museum

The museum (☎ 843-722-2996), 360 Meeting St, opposite the visitors center, offers some good exhibits on the state's history, but see Charleston first. It's in a modern building, but claims to be the country's oldest museum, founded in 1773.

Once conservation work is completed, the Confederate submarine *HL Hunley* will be displayed at the museum. Until then, a model, the history of early submarine technology and coverage of the ship's recent discovery will have to satisfy Civil War buffs. Occasionally, tickets to view the 65,000lb sub are auctioned off; visit the Friends of the Hunley Web site at www.hunley.org for more information.

The museum is open Monday to Saturday, 9 am to 5 pm, and Sunday 1 to 5 pm. Admission is $8; for $12, you can visit the museum and either the Joseph Manigault House or the Heyward-Washington House. For $18, you can visit all three.

The Citadel

North of downtown, along the banks of the Ashley River, the Citadel (☎ 843-953-5000) is South Carolina's state-sponsored military college. Founded in 1842, the young men receiving military training at the Citadel – originally located in downtown Charleston at Francis Marion Square – also acted as guards in case of a slave revolt. Citadel cadets technically fired the first shots of the Civil War in January 1861, when they shot at a Union military ship bringing supplies to Fort Sumter; no retaliation followed, so this event has become an obscure factoid.

The school moved to its present location in 1922. It was forced by the US Supreme Court to accept women in 1996 after a high-profile case in which an applicant, who erased gender references from her high school transcript, was accepted and then immediately barred from full enrolment after the school realized the new cadet was a woman.

Famous graduates include US Senator Ernest Hollings and author Pat Conroy, whose book *The Lords of Discipline* is loosely based on his experience here.

The Citadel Museum (☎ 843-953-6846), on the 3rd floor of the Daniel Library, is open to the public for free, daily 2 to 5 pm except Saturday, 12 to 5 pm. The admissions office in Bond Hall has a walking tour map. Visitors are also welcome to view the dress parade of the cadets at 3:45 pm Friday during the school year.

Charleston Harbor

From the very southern tip of the peninsula, you can view an expanse of water across which cannons were volleyed during two wars, tall ships swollen with cargo crawled into port and pirates laid in wait. When standing at the bend in the promenade near White Point Garden and looking to your left, you will see **Fort Moultrie** on Sullivan's Island. Fort Moultrie was the site of one of the first Revolutionary War victories for the patriots. (See the Sullivan's Island section later in this chapter for more information.)

The pentagon-shaped island in the center of the harbor is **Fort Sumter,** upon which the first shots of the War Between the States were fired. Union troops that had been stationed in Charleston retreated to Fort Sumter when the Ordinances of Secession were signed. Confederate troops lined the harbor and waited for orders to fire upon the strategic fort. The bombardment began April 12, 1861, and the Union contingent surrendered 30 hours later. A Confederate stronghold, Fort Sumter was shelled by Union forces from 1863 to 1865. By the end of the war it was a pile of rubble, and some very forbidding concrete defenses were later added. A few original guns and fortifications and the obviously strategic location give a feel for the momentous history here, and there's a good little museum as well. To get here, take a boat with Fort Sumter Tours (☎ 800-789-3678, 843-722-1691) from Charleston City Marina, on the west side of the peninsula, or from Patriot's Point (see Mt Pleasant, below in the Around Charleston section). A tour from either place takes about 2¼ hours, costs $11 and is first-come, first-served (five trips daily – call for times).

Other Things to See & Do

Wrought-iron gates and decorative works have adorned Charleston's finest homes for centuries. Blacksmithing was a common profession for the city's middle-class freed blacks, and the skill of forming iron into decorative swirls and shapes was passed down from master to apprentice. Philip Simmons is one of the city's only remaining practitioners of this tradition, having started in a blacksmith's shop as a horseshoer in 1920 at the age of 13 and later gaining national recognition for his ornamental ironworks. He has made more than 200 ornamental pieces for homes throughout Charleston, including the **Harp of David Gate** at 67 Alexander St; the **Egret Gate** on Stolls Alley, just off Church St; and a **tribute garden** at 91 Anson St, next door to St John's Reformed Episcopal Church, where he is a member. His work can also be viewed in the American History Museum in Washington, DC, and the state museum in Columbia. Simmons' work is so in demand that he informs the customer when to expect the completed project, and Charlestonians are willing to wait. Now in advanced years, Simmons is training his nephew to carry on the tradition.

A bit of a trek out of town, **Magnolia Cemetery** (☎ 843-722-8638) is as beautiful a city for the dead as Charleston is for the living. Near the marshy shoals of the Cooper River, intricately carved headstones, some dating to 1850, are shaded by old, twisted trees. A lake in the center of the property attracts egrets and herons as well as a few lazy alligators. Confederate soldiers who fell at Gettysburg and the second crew of the *Hunley* are buried here. To reach it, take Meeting St out of town, past the highway ramps to Cunnington St. Turn right on Cunnington and look for signs to the cemetery.

Organized Tours

Bus tours from the visitors center start at $14 for a useful 75-minute introduction to the town. Carriage rides are touristy, but they're very pleasant and start at $15 for a one-hour tour. Each can be arranged at the visitors center. Walking and ghost tours (☎ 843-723-1670) and Civil War tours (☎ 843-722-7033) cost around $14. Black history tours are also available and are the best way to find out about Charleston's freed black community, which numbered more than 3000 in 1860 and were skilled iron, wood and stone workers. Gullah Tours (☎ 843-763-7551) and Sights & Insights (☎ 843-762-0051) both offer educational and entertaining tours.

When touring, keep in mind that you are surrounded by water – from deep dark swamps to windswept shores – and a road can only take you so far. Check out Barrier Island Ecotour (☎ 843-886-5000), which offers crabbing clinics, fishing trips and sunset cruises. Or paddle down the Edisto River, the longest free-flowing blackwater stream in the US; contact the Colleton State Park (☎ 843-538-8206) for trip information. Captain Peter Brown (☎ 843-830-0448) leads fly and light-tackle inshore fishing trips ($300, 1/2 day).

Special Events

Budweiser Lowcountry Blues Bash – The first two weeks in February, Charleston hosts national and local blues acts (☎ 843-762-9125).

Festival of Houses & Gardens – March to April, more than 150 of Charleston's private homes are opened to the public (☎ 843-722-3405).

World Grits Festival – Early April, the small town of St George, near Charleston, hosts a grits-eating contest and crowning of Miss Grits (☎ 843-563-4366).

Spoleto Festival – End of May to June, Charleston's internationally renowned cultural festival celebrates opera, chamber music, theater and dance (☎ 843-722-2764).

Piccolo Spoleto – Coinciding with Spoleto, this offshoot festival hosts street performances, free concert performances by Southeastern musicians and bands, and more popular forms of the arts (☎ 843-724-7305).

MOJA Arts Festival – End of September to October, African-American and Caribbean culture are honored through dance, theater and films (☎ 843-724-7305).

Places to Stay

Staying in the historic downtown is the most attractive option, but it's expensive, especially on weekends and when there are special events in town. The prices quoted below are for the high season, which is typically spring and fall; the hot summer and deep winter months tend to be around $100 less. In general, these rates are for doubles.

Camping Three campgrounds southwest of Charleston offer shuttle service to downtown. On nearby Johns Island, *Oak Plantation Campground* (☎ 843-766-5936, 3540 Savannah Hwy) has tent and RV sites from $14 to $18. A little farther out, *Lake Aire RV Park & Campground* (☎ 843-571-1271), Hwy 17S and Hwy 162, also has full facilities and sites from $11 to $18. Perhaps the nicest is the *James Island County Park* (☎ 800-743-7275, 843-795-9884, 871 Riverland Dr) with a park setting and family amusements; it has tent/RV sites that cost $18/24 and cottages that cost $100.

B&Bs Contact the visitors center or the Historic Charleston B&B association (☎ 843-722-6606) for additional listings of B&Bs. A small, friendly, *pensione*-style place is *Bed, No Breakfast* (☎ 843-723-4450, 16 Halsey St), near Calhoun and Gadsden Sts, with just two rooms and a shared bathroom, from $70 to $95 (cash/check only; call ahead). *1837 Bed & Breakfast* (☎ 843-723-7166, 126 Wentworth St) has two suites from $120 to $145.

Near the College of Charleston, *Barksdale House Inn* (☎ 843-577-4800, 27 George St) has 14 rooms for $135 to $200.

The best B&Bs are well-located historic homes like *Hayne House* (☎ 843-577-2633, fax 577-5906, 30 King St), a block from the Battery, with six rambling rooms, antique furnishings and a Southern breakfast. Rates vary, but expect to pay close to $200. A Queen Anne mansion on the Battery, *Two*

Meeting St Inn (☎ 843-723-7322, 2 Meeting St), is the premier Charleston fantasy. Tiffany stained glass windows, carved oak paneling and an air of exclusiveness can be yours for $165 to $250 (depending on the room).

Inns Larger than a B&B but not as big as a hotel, inns typically have garden piazzas, antique reproductions and Southern or continental breakfasts.

Tucked behind a narrow courtyard, the cozy *Elliott House Inn* (☎ 800-729-1855, 843-723-1855, 78 Queen St) is a Charleston single house with rooms for around $135.

Most inns are geared toward couples, but the bargain *Ansonborough Inn* (☎ 800-522-2073, 843-723-1655, 21 Hasell St) is ideal for families and groups. In a converted warehouse near the aquarium, the inn has large suites, some with lofts, from $110/$160 weekday/weekend.

More posh places like *Planters Inn* (☎ 843-722-2345, fax 843-577-2125), at Meeting and Market Sts, will run from $150 to $250 for a double. The Greek Revival *Jasmine House* (☎ 800-845-7639, 843-577-5900, 64 Hasell St) has broad front verandahs and 10 spacious rooms for $225.

Hotels Downtown chain hotels are generally less expensive than the centrally located inns and B&Bs, but they're also less atmospheric. Even more affordable are the charmless highway motels on the edge of town, a short drive away. East of the Cooper River on US 17, *Masters Inn* (☎ 800-633-3434, 843-884-2814) has spacious rooms from around $55, less with discount coupons. A few miles west on US 17 (Savannah Hwy), near the I-526 junction, a trusty *Motel 6* (☎ 843-556-5144) has singles/doubles for $45/50. There are plenty more motels north of town around I-26 exits 199A and 203.

Days Inn Downtown (☎ 800-329-7466, 843-722-8411, 155 Meeting St) has a good location and standard motel-style rooms from $120/160 weekday/weekend. Prices are similar at *Best Western King Charles Inn* (☎ 800-247-6884, 843-723-7451, 237 Meeting St).

SOUTH CAROLINA

Larger hotels attract conventioneers and business travelers. *Francis Marion Hotel* (☎ 843-722-0600, 387 King St) overlooks the Old Citadel and Marion Square and has standard rooms for around $100. *Mills House Hotel* (☎ 800-874-9600, 843-577-2400), at Meeting and Queen Sts, is a reconstruction of a famous antebellum hotel with rates ranging from $100 to $300, depending on the room.

Places to Eat

The indigenous specialties are referred to as Lowcountry cuisine and include seafood, such as the famous she-crab soup, shrimp and grits, and the popular side dish of red rice. Charlestonians have been compared to the Chinese because they love rice and worship their ancestors. Rice is so integral to their diet that grocery stores maintain a steady stock of 10-lb bags, and home cooks employ a unique Charleston rice steamer.

The restaurant scene is surprisingly cosmopolitan. Young chefs trained in New York come to Charleston to make a name for themselves. Fine dining is easy to find; cheap eats will be harder.

Around Market St The highest concentration of restaurants is on and around Market St. *T-Bonz* (80 N Market St) does steak and seafood dishes for around $11, with a good selection of burgers and sides. Nearby, *Wild Wing Café* (36 N Market St) threatens meltdown with its Chernobyl wings (10 pieces, $5). Put out the fire with a bucket of beer ($9). The well-promoted *Hyman's* (215 Meeting St) and *AW Shucks* (35 S Market St) are passable seafood restaurants, but not worth waiting in line for. Locals go to *Hank's Seafood Restaurant* (☎ 834-723-3474, 10 Hayne St) for she-crab soup or other Lowcountry specialities (main dishes are $15 to $20). A common table near the bar is good for solo travelers.

Just north of Market, *Pinckney Café & Espresso* (☎ 843-577-0961, 18 Pinckney St) is a moderately priced local spot doing fresh variations on Southern cuisine. Smack dab at the end of the Market St in a little blue shack is *Your Place* (☎ 843-722-8360, 6 Market), the best burger joint in town.

Desserts, coffees and other treats can be found at *Kaminsky's* (☎ 843-853-8270, 78 N Market St), right in the heart of the market. Indulge yourself with a little afternoon tea at *Charleston Place* (☎ 843-722-8091, 130 Market St), Monday to Saturday, 2 to 5 pm. Locally grown teas as well as sherries, sandwiches and caviars run $7 to $17.

Around East Bay St Just south of Market, there are fashionable places along E Bay St, like *Magnolias* (☎ 843-577-7771, 185 E Bay St), which offers 'down South dishes with uptown presentation' (from $10 to $20) – try shrimp and grits. Casual dining and 'maverick' Southern cuisine can be found at *Slightly North of Broad* (☎ 843-723-3424, 192 E Bay St) – often shortened to SNOB, a jab at the upper-crust society who live *south* of Broad St. Crab cakes, fish and beef dishes range from $16 to $22.

For an unusual architectural ambience, try *Saracen* (☎ 843-723-6242, 141 E Bay St), a 'Moorish-Gothic' ex-bank building. It has an original menu that has the same influences as the architecture – Morocco and its neighbors – and a comfortable little bar upstairs; main dishes run about $20. It is open Tuesday to Saturday, 5 to 10 pm.

Down a cobblestone alley is *McCrady's* (☎ 843-577-0025, 2 Unity Alley), a big beautiful restaurant of carved wood and leaded glass where restaurant owners and business types hobnob. A four-course prix fixe meal ($35) might be the best way to sample their innovative twists on New American cuisine.

Around King St On the upper-end of King St north of Calhoun St, several good-value places attract more students than tourists. Each location of *Juanita's* (439 King St and 75½ Wentworth St) has a friendly atmosphere and affordable Mexican food. *Alice's Fine Foods* (☎ 843-853-9366, 468-470 King St), a neighborhood gathering place, serves a buffet of Southern and soul food for under $7; catch the jazz brunch on Sunday. *Bookstore Café* (☎ 843-720-8843, 412 King St) has an affordable breakfast of eggs and such ($4) as well as sandwiches ($7 to $9) and their specialty sweet potato biscuits.

Just a block from King St is *Jestine's Kitchen* (☎ 843-722-7224, 251 Meeting St), a memorial to the owner's family cook. Meatloaf, fried chicken and daily specials run $5 to $10.

Across King St, close to the College of Charleston, *Andolini's Pizza* (☎ 834-722-7437, 82 Wentworth St) has slices or pies, day or night. It's open till 11 pm on weeknights and till midnight on Friday and Saturday. The *farmer's market* sets up between Hutson and King Sts on Saturday 8 am to 1 pm, April to October.

At the opposite end of King St is *Fast & French Gaulart & Maliclet*, a tiny bistro with bargain meals. Nightly specials ($12) include a main dish, soup and wine, or try the Thursday night fondues, or veggie lunch sandwiches ($6).

Near the Medical College The area north of Calhoun and west of Rutledge St is the 'transitional' zone of an otherwise languishing neighborhood. Urban pioneers of young professionals and students are moving in, and simple daytime eateries are following in their wake. *Hominy* (☎ 834-937-0930, 207 Rutledge Ave) is a favorite breakfast spot, with heavenly French toast ($5) and an outdoor patio. *Daily Dose Café* (☎ 834-442-8344, 146 Cannon) has turned an old gas station into a vegan and veggie lunch spot for wraps and sandwiches ($5; weekdays 11 am to 4 pm).

Entertainment

The balmy evenings are conducive to late-night dining, drinking and dancing at the various venues around Market and E Bay Sts. *Griffon Pub* (☎ 843-723-1700, 18 Vendue Range) is a popular place with Celtic style and good bar food. *Cumberlands* (☎ 843-577-9469, 26 Cumberland St) has mostly blues acts and late-night food. Later on, try *The Indigo* (☎ 843-577-7383, 5 Faber St), a party place with dance, alternative, reggae and cabaret nights that's also popular with the gay crowd.

A good place to catch the sunset is the rooftop bar at *The Library at Vendue Inn* (23 Vendue Range). A bit of a pickup scene, *Meritage* (☎ 843-723-8181, 235 E Bay St) is a wine bar with interesting tapas dishes ($6 to $8) and a great happy hour for beer drinkers ($1.75 for imports).

Big diner-style booths, ice-cold mugs of beer and greasy burgers attract a mixed crowd of gays and straights to *Vickery's* (☎ 843-577-5300, 15 Beaufain St), near King and Market, a Charleston branch of an Atlanta gay landmark.

There's an endless supply of college frat and dive bars along King St. *AC's* (☎ 843-577-6742, 467 King St) is a beloved dive bar thanks to its happy hour specials ($2.50 pints of Guinness) and everybody-knows-your-name atmosphere. *Momma's Blues Palace* (☎ 843-853-2221, 46 John St) fills the 'quirky Southern' category. Momma, along with Poppa and their band, performs Thursday to Saturday, 10 pm till close.

The weekend section in the *Post & Courier* and the free weekly *Charleston City Paper* provide upcoming music and cultural events. The *College of Charleston* is well-known for its theater and concerts; contact the school's events line (☎ 843-953-8228) for upcoming shows. In the summer, the *Charleston Symphony Orchestra* performs outdoor concerts at Middleton Place; visit its Web site at www.charlestonsymphony.com for the season's schedule. In a former railroad storage depot, the *Music Farm* (☎ 843-722-8904, 32 Ann St) hosts regional bands.

The historic *Dock St Theater* (☎ 843-723-5648), at Church and Queen Sts, presents classical and contemporary works from October to May.

Getting There & Away

The Charleston International Airport (☎ 843-767-7009) is 12 miles outside of town in North Charleston. Five carriers (Continental, Delta, Midway, United Express and US Airways) serve Charleston, and fares to East Coast destinations cost around $250, to the West Coast and London between $400 and $500. Avis, Budget, Hertz and National have offices at the airport.

The Greyhound station (☎ 843-747-5341), 3610 Dorchester Rd, has regular buses to New York City ($120; 18 hours), Atlanta ($100; six hours), Savannah ($44; three hours) and Columbia ($45; 2½ hours).

The Amtrak train station (☎ 843-744-8264) is an inconvenient 8 miles north of downtown at 4565 Gaynor Ave. The *Silver Meteor* and *Silver Palm* travel the coast; fares to New York are $260 (14 hours); to Savannah, $45 (1½ hours). A city bus on Dorchester Rd goes into town from near the bus and train stations – at night, call a North Area Taxi (☎ 843-554-7575).

To reach Charleston from points along the north or south coast, use Hwy 17. From I-95, take I-26 for about an hour. I-26 is also the fastest route from Charleston to Columbia.

Getting Around

To get to the airport, take I-26 west to exit 212-B and follow the signs. Shuttles and taxis go to and from the airport to downtown Charleston and environs; the fare will range from $10 to $20.

Downtown is walkable, but the residents are entirely obsessed by their cars and pay little attention to a pedestrians' right of way. If walking, be especially careful when crossing the street adjacent to a one-way.

DASH, the Downtown Area Shuttle (☎ 843-724-7420), has faux streetcars doing five loop routes from the visitors center ($2 day pass, or 75¢ per trip); pick up a route map from the visitors center.

Students and many old-timers ride bikes, making it fairly safe for tourists to do so as well. The Bicycle Shoppe (☎ 843-722-8168), 280 Meeting St, rents single-speed bikes from $4/15 per hour/day.

AROUND CHARLESTON

Antebellum plantation homes, beautiful public and private beaches, historic forts and retired military technology, as well as dilapidated shacks serving seafood fresh from the trawlers are all an easy drive from downtown Charleston.

Mt Pleasant

Across the narrow Cooper River Bridge is the small community of Mt Pleasant. Here you'll find **Patriot's Point Naval & Maritime Museum** (☎ 843-884-2727), which features the aircraft carrier USS *Yorktown,* WWII's famous 'Fighting Lady.' You can also tour a submarine, a destroyer, a Coast Guard cutter and a recreated 'fire base' from Vietnam. It takes hours to see it all ($11/5 adults/children). To get here from Charleston, take Ashley Ave north to the Hwy 17 Crosstown Expressway, then north to Mt Pleasant. Follow the sign to your right immediately after the bridge.

On the north side of town, 8 miles from Charleston, **Boone Hall Plantation** (☎ 843-884-4371), 1235 Long Point Rd, is a 1935 reconstruction, with costumed guides and touristy tours (daily; $10). Supposedly the house was the inspiration for Tara in *Gone With the Wind.* Nearby, the **Charles Pickney National Historic Site** (☎ 843-881-5516) is the former plantation of Charles Pickney, a famous South Carolinian statesman who helped frame the US Constitution. Exhibits cover archaeological findings on the site and historical descriptions of the slaves and farming techniques they employed on the plantation. The site is 6 miles north of Charleston off Hwy 17 on Long Point Rd.

Shem Creek attracts a lot of visitors for its seafood restaurants. Many locals are critical of the restaurants' prices, quality and owner, who runs a virtual fiefdom on the creek. More 'hidden' is *The Wreck (☎ 843-884-0052),* a no-nonsense seafood restaurant in an old icehouse right on the creek. With the insurance money the owners received after Hurricane Hugo smashed their boat, they opened this restaurant, which serves large portions of shrimp, scallops, clams, oysters, flounder, grouper or shark ($15). Call for opening hours and directions.

Sullivan's Island

Edgar Allen Poe used Sullivan's Island as the backdrop for his tale of buried treasure in 'The Gold Bug.' Perhaps not as wild and eerie as Poe painted it, Sullivan's Island is noncommercial, with elegant early-20th-century beach houses and abandoned military fortifications now covered in moss and weeds. Public beach access is available on certain parts of the island; observe all parking and swimming signs posted or face heavy fines. Even if you don't like books, check out the library, 1921 I'on Ave, which is housed in a old battery fortification.

Poe was actually stationed on the south end of the island at **Fort Moultrie** for 13 months. The first European settlement on the island, Fort Moultrie was built in the 1770s to protect Charleston from a sea invasion. Made of spongy palmetto logs, the fort's walls were able to absorb, without fracture, shells from the British navy in one of the first American victories of the Revolutionary War. A good example of the now defunct coastal defense system, Fort Moultrie was modernized and manned until 1947, when new military technologies made such forts obsolete.

The visitors center (☎ 843-883-3123), 1214 Middle St, is a good place to start a tour of the fort. Admission is $2/1 adults/seniors and kids.

Sullivan's Island is about 10 miles from Charleston. Take Hwy 17 N Bus to Mt Pleasant and turn right on Hwy 703. To get to Fort Moultrie, turn right onto Middle St and follow it for a mile.

Isle of Palms

More accessible to the visitor is the nearby Isle of Palms, with a long, unbroken beach, low-key hamburger and T-shirt stands and a beachside county park (at 14th Ave). At the northeastern end of the island is the **Wild Dunes Resort** (☎ 800-845-8800), a private golfing paradise with courses designed by Tom Fazio. On the main part of the island, there are lots of beach rentals; contact the Charleston visitors center (☎ 800-774-0006, 843-720-5687) for a list of realty agencies.

Frolicking bikinis and flexing hard bodies can be found at **The Windjammer** (☎ 843-886-8596, 1000 Ocean Blvd), a well-promoted bar and restaurant. For breakfast or lunch, **The Sea Biscuit Café** (☎ 843-886-4079, 21 JC Long Blvd) is a quaint local place with quality eats. Proper attire (meaning flip-flops) is required for dinner at **The Boathouse at Breach Inlet** (☎ 843-886-8000). Just across the bridge from Sullivan's Island, right on the Intracoastal Waterway, the Boathouse serves Lowcountry dishes and plenty of seafood in the $15 range.

Isle of Palms is 12 miles from Charleston via Hwy 17 N to Hwy 517 (the Isle of Palms Connector).

Charles Towne Landing State Historic Site

In 1670, a group of English colonists sailed through what would later become Charleston Harbor and into the Ashley River. They landed on the first high ground they encountered and set up a home. This was the original site of the Charles Towne settlement, which would later move south to the peninsula between the Ashley and the Cooper Rivers. Today the site is a cute wooded park with a reproduction sailing vessel, walking trails, a picnic area and a natural habitat zoo of animals once native to the Carolina coast. The site (☎ 843-852-4200) is 3 miles north of Charleston; take Hwy 17 to West Ashley and turn right onto Hwy 171 (Old Towne Rd). Admission is $5/2.50 adults/children.

Folly Island

Only a 15-minute drive from downtown, Folly is an easy day trip for beachgoers. Ira Gershwin came to this narrow island in the 1920s to write the music for the folk opera *Porgy*

& *Bess*. Today the island attracts dropout hippie types and surfers. The area called the WashOut on E Ashley Rd can proudly claim a few ridable waves and even hosts surfing tournaments. At the far east end of the island, the Morris Island Lighthouse is all that remains of a Confederate fort. Follow E Ashley road to find streetside public parking; east of E 8th St the beach no longer has groins (concrete structures built into the ocean perpendicular to the shore to keep sand from eroding). Short-term rentals are available; contact the Charleston visitors center (☎ 800-774-0006, 843-720-5687) for more information. From Charleston, take Hwy 17 S to Hwy 171 W; Folly is the next island after James Island.

Just before the causeway leading to Folly is a sign for ***Bowen's Island Oyster Bar*** (*☎ 843-795-2757*) on the right. This rundown shack sits on an isolated pitch of land overlooking the marsh and serves incomparable seafood for $8 to $16. It's open Tuesday to Saturday, 5 to 10 pm.

Kiawah & Seabrook Islands

The private beach resorts on Kiawah and Seabrook Islands offer golf, tennis, horse riding, pools and fitness centers and a sense of exclusivity. Kiawah is somewhat unique because it maintains a fairly natural, undeveloped setting. For more information, contact the reservation services at Kiawah (☎ 800-845-3911) or Seabrook (☎ 800-845-2475). Both islands are about 20 miles southwest of Charleston. Take Hwy 17 to Hwy 20 through John's Island. Along the way, stop at **Angel Oak,** on John's Island, a live oak believed to be more than 1400 years old. This *Quercus virginiana* is 65 feet high, provides 17,000 sq feet of shade and its largest limb is 11 feet around and 89 feet long.

EDISTO ISLAND

Mainly visited by South Carolinians, Edisto ('**Ed**-is-tow') is as homespun as big Sunday dinners. Families come here for annual beach trips, weddings and reunions. Row upon row of unassuming cottages line the oceanfront and marsh. Relatively little com-

mercial development has occurred, and the island preservation society works to keep it that way. Many of the full-time residents live on parcels of land originally part of plantations that their ancestors once farmed. The Edisto Indians first lived on the island, followed by plantations that were famous for Sea Island cotton and the long thread it produced. The boll weevil and the Civil War permanently ended that phase of the island's history, which has been quiet ever since.

You'll find a remnant of the island's Indian culture at **Edisto Beach State Park** (☎ 843-869-2756/2156). The Spanish Mount is a large shell mound dating to 2000 BC; the cultural purpose of a shell mound is unknown, but similar sites have been found along the Southeast coast. The park rents marshfront *cabins* (sleeping 6) for $180/350 weekend/weekly and oceanfront *campsites* for $22/11 RVs/tents. Short- and long-term rentals are available through ***Edisto Island Vacation Rentals*** (*☎ 800-868-5398*). There are a few places to eat on Hwy 174 as you head toward the ocean, but nothing highly recommendable. Edisto is 50 miles from Charleston via Hwy 17 S to Hwy 174.

Plantations on Highway 61

Up the Ashley River on Hwy 61, **Drayton Hall** (☎ 843-766-0188) is a fine brick mansion built circa 1738, still in original condition. Admission is $10/3 for the house/grounds. **Magnolia Plantation** (☎ 843-571-1266) has a 50-acre garden with azaleas and camellias, and the 60-acre Audubon Swamp Garden, with alligators and cypresses ($16). The well-furnished Reconstruction-era house tour costs $6 extra. A little Disneyfied, Magnolia Gardens is more about presentation than education.

Middleton Place (☎ 843-556-6020) features the country's oldest landscaped gardens, dating from 1741, as well as working horse stables, a slave house and the 1755 guesthouse with interesting items from the illustrious Middleton family. Middleton Place offers more of a museum-like experience than other plantations, with living history demonstrations

($15 to tour the garden and stables, $23 with a house tour).

Francis Beidler Forest

In the heart of Four Holes Swamp, this Audubon sanctuary 40 miles from Charleston off of I-26 is the area's largest remaining stand of cypress-tupelo forest (11,000 acres). There are 1½ miles of boardwalk trails, blackwater streams and more than 300 species of wildlife. The visitors center (☎ 843-462-2150) is open Tuesday to Sunday 9 am to 5 pm. Admission is $5.

Canoe trips are available in season. Visit its Web site at www.pride-net.com/swamp for directions.

BEAUFORT
pop 10,200

The 'Newport of the South,' Beaufort ('**Bew**-fert') is an elegant small town with magnificent antebellum homes, a sleepy downtown and shady lanes where life moves a bit more slowly. Beaufort Bay laps the main streets and sparkles like a million diamonds in the bright sun and glows like

SOUTH CAROLINA LOWCOUNTRY

1 Charles Towne Landing
   State Historic Site
2 Middleton Place
3 Magnolia Plantation
4 Drayton Hall

SOUTH CAROLINA

tiny fireflies in the pale moon. Locals conjecture that the area's high phosphate content is responsible for the water's uncommon reflections. This little gem by the sea is named after Henry Somerset, the second Duke of Beaufort, who left England to come to this chunk of high ground at the mouth of an unnamed river (later named Broad) in 1711, making Beaufort the state's second oldest town after Charleston.

With a naval hospital, Air Force base and Marine recruit center, the military provides the town's main industry, but the movie business and tourism are upcoming rivals. *The Big Chill, Prince of Tides, Forrest Gump* and *White Squall* are but a few of the movies filmed in and around this picturesque town.

The chamber of commerce (☎ 843-524-3163), 1106 Carteret St, distributes maps of the historic downtown and organizes boat, carriage and walking tours. The Gullah Cultural Festival is held in late May.

Hwy 21 turns into Boundary St and then Carteret St as it approaches downtown and the Beaufort River. Most businesses are located on Bay St, which intersects with Carteret just before the bridge to the Sea Islands.

Beaufort Arsenal Museum

The museum (☎ 843-525-7077), 713 Craven St, is housed in the 1798 arsenal built for storing gunpowder and experimenting with explosives. Interesting exhibits cover the city's early Native American inhabitants, the extinct industries of Sea Island cotton, commercial oystering and phosphate mining, as well as the antebellum past. ($2; open every day except Wednesday and Sunday, 10 am to 5 pm)

The Point

A high bluff in the eastern corner of Beaufort became the fashionable residential neighborhood during the height of the cotton boom. Some brochures call this the 'Old Point,' but locals are tender yet firm in pointing out that 'The Point' is the correct term. These old homes all face south to catch the ocean breezes, have wide porches,

raised basements and equally old trees lending a little shade. All of the homes in The Point are private residences, but a leisurely stroll for a bit of guarded voyeurism is a fun pastime.

Start at Bay St east of Carteret St. At 601 Bay St, an 1852 house is a good example of the Beaufort style (raised basements in case of flooding); unlike most families, the original owners were able to reacquire their home after the Civil War. Turn left onto New St. The oldest residence in Beaufort is at 214 New St. Built in 1717, the house has musket slits cut into the foundation for protection against Indian attacks. Turn right on to Craven St. At 411 Craven St, an 1850s solid brick home is known as the Castle because of its imposing Doric columns and stuccoed façade. It was featured on a 1960s promotional US travel poster, and the owners once hosted annual Christmas parties open to the entire town. Turn left onto East St, right on Federal St and then right onto Pickney St. At 501 Pickney St, only the western facade of this 1814 Caribbean-style mansion (called Marshlands) can be glimpsed from the street. The grandest part of the house faces the marsh, which would have been the entrance point for most visitors. Backtrack along Pickney St to King St and take a right. At Short St turn left, then right onto Laurens St. While pretending to look for your lost cat, sneak a peak at 1 Laurens St, better known as Tidalholm, which hosted the reunion of friends in the movie *The Big Chill.* Edgar Fripp built this summer home in 1856, then promptly lost it when Union troops occupied the town. When it was placed on the auction block, a generous Frenchman bought it and unexpectedly signed the deed over to Fripp.

Robert Smalls Memorial

In the yard of the Tabernacle Baptist Church, 907 Craven St, is a bust of Civil War hero Robert Smalls. Smalls never rode beside General Robert E Lee or wore Confederate gray, though he was a slave in Beaufort at the time of the war and worked as a crewman for the Confederate Army on the steamer the *Planter.* Having some prior knowledge of the harbor, Smalls sneaked aboard the Confederate ship and piloted it into the hands of the Union forces. Celebrated by some and vilified by others, Smalls joined the Union forces as part of the 1st South Carolina Volunteers, a regiment of freed slaves. After the war, Smalls invested the money that the Union had paid him for the *Planter* and became quite wealthy. He served in the Reconstruction-era government and in the US Congress for five terms. The wife of Smalls' former owner was elderly and penniless at the end of the war, and Smalls gave her a room in his own house until her death.

National Cemetery

Just outside the historic district, the National Cemetery, at 1601 Boundary St (Hwy 21) at Bladen St, is one of 12 such sites authorized for the burial of Civil War dead by President Abraham Lincoln in 1863. Live oaks and magnolias make this a serene resting place for Confederate and Union soldiers, including members of the African American Massachusetts 55th and 54th Infantry killed in the battle at Folly Beach. Memorial Day services are held in May, when graves are decorated with US flags. The cemetery is open daily during daylight hours.

Places to Stay

Lodging in the historic section of Beaufort is expensive, especially during the tourist season, which is every month except January and February. The small and mediocre *Red Carpet Inn* (☎ 800-251-1962, 843-521-1121, 301 Carteret St), at Port Republic St, is the cheapest place in the historic district, with rates of $50/60 weekdays/weekends.

Even the chain *Best Western* (☎ 800-528-1234, 1015 Bay St), at Newcastle St, is pricey, with rooms from $100 to $120, but it does face the waterfront and is conveniently located.

The homey *Old Point Inn* (☎ 843-524-3177, fax 843-525-6544, 212 New St), at Bay St, is the only B&B in The Point district. This late-Victorian house has rooms of varying sizes for $75 to $135.

The large, dollhouse-like *Beaufort Inn* (☎ 843-521-9000, fax 843-521-9500, bftinn@ hrgray.com, 809 Port Republic St) has spacious rooms that range from $125 to $300 and include a full gourmet breakfast. A formal restaurant is also housed here.

The 1820s *Rhett House Inn* (☎ 843-524-9030, 1009 Craven St), at New Castle St, features a double piazza and grand bedrooms for $175 to $275.

On Hwy 21 outside of town are several chain hotels and motels ranging from new and clean to tired and worn. The nicest of them is the Holiday Inn (☎ 843-524-2144, 20001 Boundary St/Hwy 21), at the junction of Hwy 802. Set away from the highway on a shaded lot, the hotel charges $70 to $90 for a double.

Places to Eat

When locals are asked where to find a good meal, most recommend catching and cooking it yourself. Every Beaufortonian is a well-heeled angler, crabber and clammer. This makes for charming conversation but rarely leads to a dinner invitation. For the tourists, however, there are a handful of fine restaurants serving the fruits of the sea. Most downtown restaurants are closed on Sunday.

The local nook of *Blackstone's Deli* (☎ 843-524-4330, 915 Bay St) serves lunch standards such as sandwiches ($6), salads and shrimp and grits ($8). Java, books and pastries can be picked up at *Firehouse Books & Espresso Bar* (706 Craven St), at Scott St. Housed in the old firehouse, it's open Monday to Saturday, 7:30 am to 7 pm, and Sunday 9 am to 3 pm; lunch is served daily.

Tucked behind the storefronts of Bay St is *Plums* (☎ 843-525-1946, 904½ Bay St), a casual restaurant serving gourmet versions of seafood classics such as blue crab cake with wasabi slaw and Thai pepper sauce ($9) or ginger-crusted grouper ($20). For only $7.50, you can buy a round of beer for the kitchen staff. With a waterfront view, it is open daily for lunch and dinner. A favorite of Hollywood refugee Tom Berenger, *Bistro dejong Peter Patisserie* (☎ 843-524-4994, 205 West St) serves Asian-Lowcountry fusion food. Local seafood gets rolled up with caramelized pecans and spicy sauce for the Bubba Shrimp sushi roll ($9); main dishes include seared tuna with seaweed salad and sushi ($25) and American standards. It's open for lunch Tuesday to Saturday and dinner every day except Sunday; reservations are recommended.

Across the bridge on Lady's Island is **Steamer Oyster & Steak House** (☎ 843-522-0210, 168 Sea Island Parkway). Steamers serves fresh local seafood and Frogmore stew, a famed local dish of shrimp, sausage, corn and seasonings. It's open every day except Sunday for lunch and dinner.

For other local seafood joints, see the St Helena section, below.

Shopping

Souvenir and collectible shops line Bay St between Carteret and Charles Sts. At the east end of Carteret St, Boombears, No 501, is filled with stuffed animals of all shapes and sizes, toy train sets, games and toys. Nearby, Aaron's Beauty & Barber Supplies, 613 Carteret St, has a wide selection of natural and unnaturally colored wigs.

Getting There & Away

The nearest airports are in Savannah, Georgia, 45 miles away, and Charleston, 65 miles away. By car, Beaufort is 25 miles from I-95; take I-95 to Hwy 17/21 to Garden's Corner, then take Hwy 21 to Beaufort.

AROUND BEAUFORT

The string of islands off the coast of Beaufort are crisscrossed by ribbons of sandy roads, shaded by swaying palmetto trees and decorated by produce-laden pickup trucks and veggie stands. Development is creeping in: Strip malls have blossomed along Hwy 21 on Lady's Island, and long lines of cars idle at the Beaufort bridge waiting for sailboats to pass. But the last stoplight is always within sight, and beyond is a bold, blue sky merging with the tongues and fingers of the Atlantic Ocean.

St Helena Island

The largest of Beaufort's Sea Islands, St Helena ('S'int Hellena') is an Anglicization of the original Spanish name Punta de Santa Elenas, so named during a Spanish exploration of the area in 1521. The island's

Gullah Culture

Many parts of the US resemble the European cities from which the founding settlers emigrated. Only in the Sea Islands along the South Carolina and Georgia coast can the same claim be given to Africa. From the region known as the Rice Coast (Sierre Leone, Senegal, Gambia and Angola), African slaves were transported across a vast ocean to a landscape that was shockingly similar – swampy coastlines, tropical vegetation and hot humid summers. The African slaves, who were in the majority on the plantations, had little contact with Europeans and were able to retain many of their homeland traditions. After the fall of the planter aristocracy, the freed slaves remained on the islands in relative isolation until the mid-20th century. Being cut off from the mainland ensured that African traditions were passed on to the descendants of the original slaves.

The result was Gullah, which describes both a language and a culture that persists today on Johns, James, Wadmalaw, Edisto, Hilton Head, St Helena and Daufuski Islands, as well as mainland communities in Georgetown, Charleston and Beaufort.

The Gullah language is a creole of Elizabethan English and African languages (mainly Bantu) and is spoken by about 500,000 people. Some of these Gullah words have snuck into the Southern lexicon, words such as 'cooter' (turtle), 'benne' (sesame), 'bubba' (brother) and 'bad mouth' (to talk badly about someone).

planters were said to have protested the French government's decision to exile Napoleon to St Helena in 1815, only to discover that there is more than one St Helena in the world. At the island's only major crossroads is the small town of Frogmore, named after a long-gone cotton plantation. One or two modest storefronts define the downtown. Farther east, the small dirt roads sport shiny new street signs that read 'Joe Polite Rd' or 'Clarence Mitchell Rd' – when the emergency telephone service (☎ 911) system came, the roads were christened after their longtime residents.

Things to See & Do Right at the crossroads is **Red Piano Too,** an art gallery of local artists. It also sells maps of historic St Helena ($5).

Turn right at Martin Luther King Jr Rd to reach **Penn Center Historic District** (☎ 843-838-2432), the first school for freed slaves in the US. Opened in 1862 by missionaries from Pennsylvania, Penn Center began in a single room on the former Oaks Plantation and quickly expanded to the complex seen today. In the 1900s the school adopted the Tuskegee University curriculum and gave training in agricultural and technical skills. The state assumed responsibility for educating the island's African-American population in 1948, but Penn Center's facilities were used as a school until 1953. In the '60s, Dr Martin Luther King and members of the Southern Christian Leadership came here to plan strategies and train leaders during the Civil Rights Movement.

The 50-acre, 19-building campus provides after-school learning programs to Sea Island children, promotes environmental issues and conducts lectures and courses on the history of the Gullah people. On the campus, the **York W Bailey Museum,** named after a Penn school graduate and the island's first black doctor, covers the school's history and cultural aspects of the Sea Islanders. It's open Monday to Saturday, 11 am to 4 pm; admission is $4. Pick up a self-guided walking tour map of the campus.

Penn Center celebrates Heritage Days in early November with parades, Gullah crafts and gospel performances.

Gullah Culture

Enduring traditions include the making of sweetgrass baskets, which has an identical twin in Sierra Leone handicrafts. Sweetgrass basketry involves three types of materials: the marsh grass called sweetgrass, palmetto fronds and longleaf pine needles. Sweetgrass makes up the bulk of the basket, with strips of the palmetto fronds and pine needles woven into the coiled grass. This tradition is typically passed from mother to daughter, and basket prices are based on the number of hours invested. The Smithsonian Institution in Washington, DC, displays baskets made by the Forman family of Charleston.

Gullah storytellers often relate the exploits of Buh Rabbit, more famously known as Brer Rabbit from the Uncle Remus books. This small yet cunning rabbit is a common character in the trickster tales of West Africa. He outwits bigger and stronger animals and is constantly in danger of retaliation.

The following is an excerpt from *Folk-Lore of the Sea Islands, South Carolina*, by Elsie Clews Parsons.

Oncet Buh Rabbit an' Buh Wolf buy a cow togeder. Den Buh Rabbit kill de cow, an' Buh Wolf didn' know it. Buh Rabbit take de cow tail an' stick un down in de dirt an' run, gone ter call de wolf. An' tell de wolf 'Le' um pull on de cow tail, see ef he could get 'e cow up!' Den, when dey pull, de cow tail come off. Said, 'Cow gone down in de groun'.' After Buh Wolf gone, Buh Rabbit gone to get de meat to kyarry home for his fader.

Places to Eat In lovely downtown Frogmore, *Ultimate Eating – Gullah Style* (☎ 843-838-1314), formerly Gullah House Restaurant, serves honest-to-goodness Gullah food, including bean stew, ribs, sweet potato chips, crabs straight from the marsh and Frogmore stew. It is open 6 am to 9 pm daily and has a mouthwatering lunch buffet ($7).

Just before the bridge to Harbor Island, sitting in a little sandlot, is a simple, blue shack called the *Shrimp Shack*. If you haven't already guessed, its specialty is shrimp – shrimp burgers, that is (something like a crab cake). Something of a regional icon, Shrimp Shack draws people en route to Hunting Island for a leisurely lunch on the screened-in porch, watching the shrimp boats moor at the dock across the way.

Hunting Island State Park

The only public beach in the area, Hunting Island (☎ 843-838-2011) is straight out of a conquistador's diary. The island wasn't settled until the late 1930s, and it still retains its wild appearance. A narrow blacktop road winds through a thick canopy of palm and live oak trees that fracture the sunlight into golden bands – not a house or human in sight. Local planters used the island as hunting grounds for deer and raccoons in the 1800s, hence its name.

This 4-mile-long, 1-mile-wide island also exemplifies the dynamic nature of barrier islands. The islands lying off the coast of South Carolina were formed about 4000 years ago by a buildup of sediment from as far away as the Appalachian Mountains. Tides, hurricanes and storms toss loose sand from one end of an island to another and from one island to another. Because of its front-row seat on the Atlantic Ocean, Hunting Island is more vulnerable to erosion than less seaward islands. It's estimated that the island loses 10 feet of shore a year. The missing beach is evident during high tides when the water rushes into the maritime forest and swallows once high-ground boardwalks. The lighthouse in the center of the island used to be 1¼ miles from the highest tide; now it's less than 400

feet. The receding sea leaves behind carcasses of trees, steals the sand dunes and dumps shells and sharks' teeth for the beachcombers, who can walk for miles and not see a soul.

At the southern end of the island are 14 *cabins* ($200/500 weekend/weekly), many bordering the ocean or the lagoon. At the north end is the *campground* ($22 tent or RV). The park headquarters handles reservations. Public beach access is available at South Beach and North Beach. The park's visitors center features displays on the island's tidal erosion and flora and fauna. A nature center at the fishing pier before the bridge to Fripp Island displays shells, plants and animals commonly seen on the beach as well as exhibits on the loggerhead turtle, which nests on the island. Day use fees are $2 per person.

Parris Island USMC

All new Marine recruits from east of the Mississippi River (and all female recruits nationwide) come here for basic training. The summers are hot, the sand fleas bite and the 13-week regimen is grueling. Visitors are welcome to tour the depot, visit the museum and watch sympathetically during afternoon marching chants. Ask at the gate for directions to the visitors center. The **museum,** in the War Memorial Building, covers the military history of the Marines and Parris Island as well as an archaeological display on the area's early Spanish outpost; it's open daily 10 am to 4:30 pm, and admission is free. From downtown Beaufort, take Hwy 170 to Hwy 280 and follow the signs.

HILTON HEAD
pop 31,000

The state's largest barrier island, Hilton Head is a veritable temple to the game of golf. There are dozens of courses enclosed in private communities called 'plantations,' and the island's great cultural events are the annual golf tournaments. This is one of the few places in the state where the prized word 'heritage' can be used in conjunction with 'golf.' The island's 'golf heritage' dates back to 1961 when Sea Pines Plantation, the first exclusive resort, opened. Ten others have followed, since golf is a year-round business in this subtropical climate.

Before golf was king, William Hilton, an English sea captain, stumbled upon the island in 1663 in search of good land to promote to prospective buyers. Two hundred years later, the island supported 12 plantations raising the famed Sea Island cotton. During the Civil War, the Union Navy sailed into Port Royal Sound, set their sites on Hilton Head and made an amphibious landing of 13,000 troops – a force so large that it would not be duplicated until the invasion of Normandy in 1944. The Union used Hilton Head as headquarters for launching attacks on nearby islands and plantations. Many of the recently freed African Americans remained on the island, bought pieces of their former owners' land and lived a quiet life of farming and fishing; Gullah communities still exist on Hilton Head, tucked behind the neatly landscaped strip malls and gated communities.

The island prides itself on being designed in concert with the natural environment, but summer traffic and miles of stoplights make it hard to see the forest *or* a tree. There are, however, some very beautiful nature preserves, and the beaches are wide and lovely.

Orientation & Information

Hwy 278 turns into William Hilton Parkway when you enter the island. The parkway continues east toward the beach and then heads south toward Sea Pines Circle. The Cross Island Expressway (toll $1) cuts across the island to points on the south end. Sea Pines Plantation is at the southernmost tip and Hilton Head Plantation at the northwestern end.

Right at the entrance to the island is the welcome center (☎ 800-523-3373), 100 William Hilton Parkway, which has maps of the island ($1) showing the private communities, public golf and tennis courts, shopping malls and beach access. The center can also provide golf and lodging guides. Visit its Web site at http://hiltonheadisland.org.

Things to See & Do

Golf is the primary attraction; anything else is a filler between tee times. Rates for 18 holes of golf range from $60 to $180 depending on the course and the season. Call ☎ 888-465-3475 for a golf planner to the island's world-famous, nationally awarded courses.

Public **beach access** is available at the mid-island Folly Field Beach, Driessen Beach and Bradley Beach as well as Coligny Beach, just off Pope Avenue (which has a pavilion and restrooms).

For an introduction to the non-suburban aspects of Hilton Head, stop by the **Coastal Discovery Museum** (☎ 843-689-6767), 100 William Hilton Parkway, with exhibits on coastal history, archaeology and ecology. The museum is on the 2nd floor of the visitors center and asks a $2 donation. Nature and history tours as well as dolphin and kayak trips can be arranged through the museum.
Web site: http://coastaldiscovery.org

Preserved areas on the island give an amazing snapshot of what early explorers and Native Americans might have encountered, a slowly undulating forest floor of former sand dunes now covered in short palmettos, tall palms, ferns, entangled vines and pools of standing water. Covering 50 acres, the **Audubon Newhall Preserve** was set aside during the first invasion of golf courses in the 1960s. A sharp contrast to the nearby traffic circles and manicured lawns, the preserve is on Palmetto Bay Rd, west of Sea Pines Circle. **Pinckney Island National**

Wildlife Refuge protects the small slivers of land that have developed between Hilton Head and the mainland. The main island, Pinckney, is 8 miles long and can be hiked or biked; trails lead through canopied forests and expansive salt marshes. The park entrance is on Hwy 278 just before you reach Hilton Head.

The **Self Family Arts Center** (☎ 843-842-2787), 14 Shelter Cove Lane, hosts plays and musical performances, including the Hallelujah Singers, who perform Gullah songs and storytelling. Interestingly, they appeared in the movie *Forrest Gump*, and the group's founder, Marlena Smalls, played Bubba's mother.

The **Gullah Flea Market,** 103 William Hilton Parkway, operates every day except Sunday and is good place to pick up locally grown produce, eavesdrop on the locals, or browse for books and other junk. The market also hosts the annual Gullah barbecue festival in February.

Places to Stay & Eat

Staying at a resort plantation is the most convenient option, plus it will give you that special feeling of privilege. The resorts offer self-sufficiency with golf courses, tennis courts, shopping and dining. For $5 you can buy a pass into another private resort to see what the Joneses are doing.

Try a real estate agent, such as *Hilton Head Oceanfront Rentals* (☎ 800-845-6132), if these options seem overwhelming. Villas, townhouses and full-service hotels (in some cases) are available at the plantations of Hilton Head (☎ 800-475-2631), Palmetto Dunes (☎ 800-845-6130) and Sea Pines (☎ 800-732-7463). Rates vary widely and are cheaper during the off-season and for non-beachfront property. Independent hotels include *Motel 6 (☎ 800-466-8356, 843-785-2700, 830 William Hilton Parkway),* which charges $60/67 single/double, and *Holiday Inn Oceanfront (☎ 800-423-9897, 1 S Forest Beach Dr),* which charges $130/260.

Every plantation has its own award-winning restaurant, but in general, eating in Hilton Head feels a lot like visiting a mall. *Hilton Head Diner (☎ 843-686-2400),* south of Palmetto Dunes on Hwy 278, is one of the only all-night diners on the island. Popular with the Sunday brunch crowd, the diner also serves liquor and beer all day, every day. Nearby, the national hamburger chain *Fuddruckers,* on Hwy 278 at Shelter Cove Plaza, is a truly American invention. The burgers come in two sizes: big ($1/3$ pound) and bigger ($1/2$ pound). *Old Fort Pub (☎ 843-681-2386, 65 Skull Creek Dr)* serves Lowcountry and American cuisine ($20) in a charming setting overlooking the water and surrounded by live oaks draped in Spanish moss. It's open for dinner and Sunday brunch; reservations for either are encouraged.

Getting There & Around

US Airways offers direct flights from Charlotte to Hilton Head Island Airport (☎ 843-689-5400), on Beach City Rd, for about $250. Savannah International Airport (☎ 912-964-0514) is only 45 miles away and has more frequent and cheaper service (see the Savannah & the Coast section, earlier, for more information).

If driving to Hilton Head, take I-95 to exit 8 (Hwy 278), which will lead directly to Hilton Head. Hwy 170 to Beaufort is a good drive full of scenic water views.

You'll need a car to get to the island, but once you're here, there are bike paths connecting most major attractions and shopping areas. Resorts offer bike rentals.

MYRTLE BEACH
pop 25,500

Myrtle Beach proper is the central area in the 25-mile strip called the Grand Strand, which stretches from North Myrtle Beach to Pawleys Island. Nature lovers would be disappointed by the overdevelopment of the oceanfront, but college students, families and foreigners swarm here for spring break and summer vacation.

If you were to relocate Las Vegas (minus the gambling) to the Carolina coast, you would have a close approximation to Myrtle Beach. The beach is quite lovely, but it's a minor attraction compared to the huge outdoor malls, 100 golf courses, water parks, country music shows, hot dog stands and T-shirt shops.

One of the most popular resorts along the eastern seaboard, Myrtle Beach is successful because it's strangely democratic. Fancy upscale condos reside beside smaller and cheaper family-owned motels, and the beach's carnival attractions are diverse enough to entertain teenagers and grandparents. The few gated communities are easily ignored, and there is an overriding feeling that all are welcome as long as they pay the admission price.

Orientation

Hwy 501 leads into town from the west, and Hwy 17 (Kings Hwy) runs roughly north-south on the eastern side of the Intracoastal Waterway.

The beach is backed by a near-continuous row of 10- to 20-story concrete high-rises, and behind them, along Ocean Blvd, are parking lots, neon signs, tourist shops, bars and restaurants. Kings Hwy runs parallel to Ocean Blvd on the inland side and is the main route to communities north or south of Myrtle Beach.

Just getting into Myrtle Beach will be difficult because of traffic; finding your hotel should be a little easier if you understand the oceanfront's simple grid system. The blocks on Ocean Blvd run by hundreds and are designated north or south depending on its relation to the 2nd Ave pier. If your hotel's address is 2700 N Ocean Blvd, it will be north of the 2nd Ave pier and near the intersection of Ocean Blvd and 27th Ave N.

Information

The main Chamber of Commerce Visitors Center (☎ 843-626-7444) is at 1200 N Oak St, with offices on Hwys 17N and 17S and on Hwy 501 west of town. The library (☎ 843-918-1275) is at 400 14th Ave N, has Internet access and offers temporary library cards to visitors. Modestly discounted tickets or coupons are available through coupon books distributed in area restaurants and hotels, the visitors center and Key Attractions (☎ 800-819-2282).

Myrtle Beach Pavilion & Family Kingdom Amusement Parks

The heart of the resort, historically and geographically, is the Myrtle Beach Pavilion (☎ 843-448-6456), at 9th Ave N and Ocean Blvd, with Coney-Island-style rides and amusements. The pavilion opens daily at 1pm, and all-day ride passes cost $22 for ages seven and older, $13 for ages three to six. Close by, at 3rd Ave S and Ocean Blvd, Family Kingdom (☎ 843-626-3447) might be a better value (an all-ride pass will cost you about $19). Both parks claim to have the biggest, baddest roller coaster, but Family Kingdom can claim Myrtle Beach's only oceanfront water park ($14).

Broadway at the Beach

This is the latest and greatest of Myrtle Beach's quickly outdated outdoor malls. Built around a man-made lake are three thematic villages (Caribbean, New England Fishing and Charleston Boardwalk) with more than 100 specialty shops, 20 restaurants, 6 nightclubs, 2 mini-golf courses, an IMAX and multiplex theater and a water park. It might be more accurately called 'Broadway on the Bypass,' since it is on Hwy 17 between 21st and 29th Ave N and *not* near the beach.

You'll be pleasantly surprised by **Ripley's Aquarium** (☎ 800-734-8888), which isn't as cheesy as expected. Glass-encased tunnels travel through the tanks for an up close view of 10-foot sharks. (It's a little unnerving to stand underneath a shark's belly.) There are also hourly dive and marine education shows and a stingray petting tank. The aquarium claims to be the number one attraction in the state; to avoid those massive shark-loving crowds, come early in the morning or after 7 pm; hours are 9 am to 11 pm. Admission is $15/9 adults/children.

NASCAR Speedpark (☎ 843-918-8725) is the latest, greatest version of a go-cart track. Admission is $22/12.

Barefoot Landing

Built along the Intracoastal Waterway, Barefoot Landing was once the hottest idea to hit the beach. Now displaced by the newer Broadway at the Beach, the Landing is beginning to show its age, although it still sports major attractions such as the Alabama Theatre and House of Blues. Its gimmick is to create the feeling of an old fishing village with weathered wooden buildings and an undeveloped marsh area.

If you visit no other beach in South Carolina, you should take a walk down the marsh boardwalk. Songbirds perched on marsh grass sing in time with the highway noise, turtles sun themselves on nearly submerged logs and the deep black mud emits its salty odors in the summer sun – this is a small example of the true Carolina coast. At the end of the boardwalk is **Alligator Adventure** (☎ 843-361-0789), a commercial zoo of more than 800 alligators, tropical birds and exotic reptiles. Admission is $12/8 adults/children. Barefoot Landing is at 4898 Hwy 17 (Kings Hwy) in North Myrtle Beach.

Children's Museum of South Carolina

Afraid your tot is getting dumbed-down from excessive amounts of cotton candy and miniature golf? Stop by this museum (☎ 843-946-9469), 2501 N Kings Hwy, to jumpstart the old gray matter. For ages 1 to 11, interactive, hands-on displays cover magnets, electricity and even a kiddie ATM. The museum is near the Belk shopping center, across the street from the convention center. Open Tuesday to Saturday, 10 am to 4 pm; admission costs $4.

Places to Stay

Most campgrounds are for RVs, but *Myrtle Beach State Park* (☎ 843-238-5325), 3 miles south of central Myrtle Beach, has cabins (sleeping four to eight) for $200/$400 weekend/weekly, unshaded tent sites ($22) and its own beach. The state park is where you can find the wax myrtle, the shrub after which Myrtle Beach was named.

Myrtle Beach used to be just a summer resort, and the locals had it to themselves the rest of the year. Thanks to the game of golf, the tourist season now extends from mid-October to the end of November and

February to late April as well as the summer months. Accommodations also get tight during Harley week (in May), golf tournaments and national holidays. Hundreds of hotels have prices that vary by the season and the day – a room might cost $25 in January and more than $100 in July. In summer, many will be all booked up, so it might be best to contact the chamber of commerce in advance. The chamber can also help you find monthlong condo and cabin rentals as well as golfotels (lodging-golfing packages). In the low season, you'd do just as well driving on and around Ocean Blvd, looking at the signs for special prices – the big beachfront hotels may be no more expensive than a cheap-looking motel. The prices quoted below are high-season rates only. Most hotels have in-room mini-fridges and air-con, pools and Jacuzzi; rooms advertised as suites are usually 2 bedrooms with a sitting area. In an attempt to deter those rowdy spring breakers, most hotels won't rent to those under 25.

Away from the beach, the *Grand Strand Motel* (☎ 800-433-1461, 843-448-1461, 1804 S Ocean Blvd) has doubles and efficiencies from $50 to $100.

For beachfront accommodations, try the small and friendly *Firebird Motor Inn* (☎ 800-852-7032, 843-448-7032, 2007 S Ocean Blvd), which charges $75 to $120 for oceanfront doubles and efficiencies. The large *Compass Cove* (☎ 800-326-0234, 843-448-8373, 2311 S Ocean Blvd), formerly the Swamp Fox Ocean Resort, has oceanfront suites and efficiencies for $100 to $140.

Close to the Pavilion are the *Chesterfield Inn* (☎ 843-448-3177, 700 N Ocean Blvd), which caters to seniors and families and charges $110 to $130 for motel-style doubles, and the *Beverly Motel* (☎ 843-448-9496, 703 N Ocean Blvd), which is one of the few motels that will rent to people under 25. Rates for the Beverly are around $80 to $100.

Near Family Kingdom, the nice and new *Sandy Beach Resort* (☎ 800-844-6534, 843-448-5522, 201 S Ocean Blvd) has oceanfront doubles and suites for $115 to $140 and side views for $60 to $120.

On the north end of the beach is *Anderson Inn* (☎ 800-437-7376, 843-448-1535, 2600 N Ocean Blvd); rates hang around $100/120 for doubles/efficiencies. The big and modern *Sea Island Inn* (☎ 800-548-0767, 843-449-4102, 6000 N Ocean Blvd) charges $120/135 for a double/efficiency; for an extra $40 to $50 you can add a meal plan to your room rate.

Places to Eat
The 1700 or so restaurants are mostly mid-range and high volume, but competition keeps prices reasonable. For Americana ambience, hit the burger bars on Ocean Blvd near the amusement parks.

Seafood, ironically, is not Myrtle Beach's specialty; it tends to be mass-produced and deep-fried in the Calabash style. According to one local, 'the only good fish is a fried one.' The small fishing village of Murrells Inlet is where locals go for oysters and Lowcountry dishes.

You'll have an endless choice of chain and theme restaurants, including the pyramid shaped *Hard Rock Cafe* (☎ 843-946-0007), *Planet Hollywood* (☎ 843-448-7827) and *NASCAR Cafe* (843-946-7223) at Broadway at the Beach and *Greg Norman's Australian Grille* (☎ 843-316-0000) at Barefoot Landing.

The area north of Myrtle Beach where Kings Hwy and the Hwy 17 bypass rejoin is referred to as Restaurant Row, a name suggesting something different than the endless expanse of strip malls. In these cookie-cutter buildings, however, are some of the area's better restaurants. *Taste Buds Cafe* (☎ 843-497-3643, 9904 N Kings Hwy), a locally owned lunch spot, serves sandwiches, salads and pasta dishes (veggie options, too). *Cagney's Old Place Restaurant* (☎ 843-449-3824), on N Kings Hwy and 71st Ave, is decorated with salvaged antiques and oddities. Open for dinner only, Cagney's specializes in large portions of surf-and-turf ($15 to $20).

Croissants Bakery & Café (☎ 843-448-BAKE, 504A 27th Ave N), at Kings Hwy, serves beautiful pies and desserts, coffee and sandwiches such as chunky chicken salad or prosciutto and marinated artichoke hearts ($6).

Entertainment
The shag, not the bump-and-grind, was born in nearby North Myrtle Beach, see that section for more information. Music variety shows are a Myrtle Beach standard, combining rock, country and bluegrass music with a dose of comedy, Christianity and patriotism. Venues include the *Dixie Stampede* (☎ 800-433-4401), Dolly Parton's dinner and theater show; *Alabama Theatre* (☎ 843-272-1111), a live music and comedy show brought to you by the country-rock band Alabama; and *Carolina Opry* (☎ 843-238-8888), country music with Carolina flavor. *House of Blues* (☎ 843-272-3000), at Barefoot Landing, hosts live music, Monday night football parties and a Sunday gospel brunch.

Bars and clubs catering to the college crowd include *Mother Fletchers* (☎ 843-626-7959, 710 N Ocean Blvd) and *Studebakers* (☎ 843-448-9747, 2000 N Kings Hwy). For laid-back beach ambience, try *Dead Dog Saloon* (☎ 843-445-6700, 404 26th Ave N). An outside deck hosts Saturday cookouts and live music. With pool tables and $1 draft beer specials, *Murphy's Law Sports Bar* (☎ 843-448-6021, 405 S King Hwy), at 6th Ave, fills the dive bar category. *Bummz Beach Café* (☎ 843-916-9111, 2002 N Ocean Blvd) has an ocean view and a swimsuit-clad crowd.

Getting There & Around
Myrtle Beach International Airport (☎ 843-448-1589) is within Myrtle Beach city limits and is serviced by eight airlines. Fares from New York City and Chicago are $160 and from London and the West Coast are $500. The nearest Amtrak station is in Florence, 70 miles west, with connecting bus service; the *Silver* service connects to New York City ($140, 14 hours). Greyhound (☎ 843-448-2471) stops at 511 7th Ave N. Roundtrip bus fares to Myrtle Beach are: from New York City $110 (16 hours), Charlotte $75 (6 hours), Atlanta $85 (11 hours) and Charleston $45 (3 hours). Coastal Rapid

SOUTH CAROLINA

Public Transport (☎ 843-488-0865) has infrequent service up and down the resort area.

Two new highways are nearing completion and should relieve summer congestion along Hwys 17, 501, 9 and 544, the main routes to the beach. Hwy 22 (Conway Bypass) will run from Hwy 17 to Hwy 501 between Conway and Briarcliff Acres on the coast, and Hwy 90 (Carolina Bays Parkway) will connect Hwy 9 with Hwy 501 on the western side of the waterway.

AROUND MYRTLE BEACH
North Myrtle Beach
North Myrtle Beach feels like a beach town – the pace is slow, the buildings are squat and vacationers spend their days doing a lot of nothing. The crowd is much older and has had a longer relationship with the Grand Strand than the average Myrtle Beach visitor. Way back when (in the '40s and '50s), they came as teenagers to the open-air pavilions and dance halls that dotted the oceanfront. With the floors covered with sand and the sweaty bodies packed in thick, they created the dance called 'shag,' which is the courting precursor to the British slang meaning. The shag is a much slower version of swing or jitterbug. Moving in an eight-count step with gentle twists and spins, these teenagers were rebelling against the region's dance-forbidding tradition. The music that inspired the steps was known as race music (rhythm and blues) in the segregated South and outlawed everywhere else except the beach. As times changed, such R&B classics as 'Under the Boardwalk' and 'Give Me Just a Little More Time' came to be known as beach music, a name applied to any shaggable song. The nucleus of the shag culture was Ocean Drive (or 'OD'), the northernmost beaches of the strand, now technically North Myrtle Beach.

Shag's popularity peaked in the early '60s, and its naughty reputation has mellowed into respectability – the shag is now the South Carolina state dance, performed at weddings, debutante parties and country club events. A few originals, known as the Society of Stranders, stay devoted to the shaggin' culture and host two festivals: the Spring Safari and Fall Migration (☎ 888-767-3113). To watch old-timers in action or try your feet at shaggin', head to *Fat Harold's (210 Main St)*, *Ducks and Ducks Too (229 Main St)* and *Spanish Galleon (100 Main St)*, all within a few blocks of each other.

Murrells Inlet
At the south end of the Grand Strand, Murrells Inlet ('Mer-EARLS') is a small, quiet fishing village named after a pirate who would hide amongst the tidal marshes of Waccamaw Neck, a peninsula stretching from Murrells Inlet to Winyah Bay near Georgetown.

If you've never eaten steamed oysters, then visit *Nance's Creekfront Restaurant and Oyster Roast (☎ 843-651-2696, 4583 Hwy 17)*. During the fall and winter months, oysters are at their sweetest; they get plucked from the jet-black marsh mud and steamed over a hot grill. At your table will be a large roll of paper towels and a hole in the middle for discarding the oyster shells. This will be a meal of physical exertion. Armed with an oyster knife, you pry into the gnarled shells and pluck out the tender morsels. Don't let the tight ones go unopened, usually they are the tastiest. A full order of steamed oysters ($15) is enough for two; Nance's is open daily and sits right on the creek with a wonderful sunset view. The town's other restaurants are also good since all serve seafood harvested less than a mile away.

Deep-sea fishing charters and boat rides depart from Murrells Inlet. Contact Captain Dick's (☎ 843-651-3676) for prices and tour information.

Huntington Beach State Park
Broad white-sand beaches, sloping dunes covered by bowing sea oats and a tidal marsh fished by great blue heron, purple gallinule and snowy egret make up one of the state's prettiest public beaches. The park (☎ 843-237-4440), south of Murrells Inlet on Hwy 17, is named after the land's former owners, the Huntingtons. In the 1930s

Archer Huntington, a wealthy philanthropist, and his wife, Anna Hyatt Huntington, a renowned animal sculptor, left the cold winters of New York City for this isolated preserve that was once the Waccamaw Neck's most prosperous rice plantations. Their home, Atalaya, was built in the style of a Moorish fort, with narrow passageways, meandering rooms and a guard tower where bats were kept to eat malaria-carrying mosquitoes. Atalaya can be self-toured during daylight hours, but a guided tour (every hour between 9 and 11 am and 2 and 4 pm) helps explain the details of the house and of the independent and eccentric Huntingtons, who also founded nearby Brookgreen Gardens.

Day use fees are $4/2 adults/children; tent and RV campsites ($11 to $22) are available near the ocean.

Brookgreen Gardens

Just across US 17 is Brookgreen Gardens (☎ 800-849-1931, 843-235-6000), the largest sculpture garden in the country. The gardens were developed as a nature preserve and to exhibit the artwork of Anna Hyatt Huntington, who, along with her husband, owned the majority of the area's former rice plantations. Stone and metal sculptures of classical myths, indigenous animals and fanciful patterns bloom perennially in formal English gardens shaded by majestic live oaks. A waterbird aviary and zoo display the living versions of the statues. This 10,000 acre preserve would take several days to explore and the admission ticket ($8.50/4 for adults/children) is good for seven days.

Pawleys Island

Only 4 miles long and a quarter-mile wide, Pawleys Island is affectionately called 'shabby chic' because of the island's informal, noncommercial elegance. Once a summer resort for wealthy planter families, Pawleys retains its reputation as a getaway for the wealthy, but the huge rustic cottages, some predating the Civil War, lack air conditioning and manicured lawns. Sea breezes enter the sleeping porches, footwear is an

accessory and golf courses are strictly a mainland obsession. Visitors and locals alike might do a little fishing in the morning, read a skinny paperback before an afternoon nap, or follow the sun from one end of the island to another – a worry-free schedule.

For a little excitement, pick up a map of historic homes at the visitors center (☎ 843-237-1921), on Hwy 17, or watch demonstrations of the famous Pawleys Island handmade hammocks at the nearby **Original Hammock Shop** (☎ 843-237-9122), 10880 Ocean Hwy/Hwy 17. Other indigenous crafts can be found at the **Gullah Ooman Shop** (☎ 843-235-0747), on Waverly Rd at Petigru Dr. The shop sells quilts, dolls, sweetgrass baskets and books on the African-American Gullah tradition.

Pawleys Island Chapel is a non-denominational church precariously balanced on the creek bank; the 10 am Sunday service is one of the island's few social functions.

Weekly rentals of beach cottages (sleeping eight to 12) run between $1500 and $3000 during the peak summer season. Contact the following rental companies for a brochure of information on rental properties: *Lachicotte Realty* (☎ 800-422-4777), *James Smith Realty* (☎ 800-476-5651) and *Dieter Company* (☎ 800-950-6232).

The closest commercial hotels are on the mainland. The new *Holiday Inn Express* (☎ 800-830-0135, 843-235-0808, 11445 Ocean Hwy/Hwy17) has modern rooms for $100/$55 high/low season. On the private end of the island, *Sea View Inn* is a rustic guesthouse (no air con) that charges $150/980 for daily/weekly oceanfront rooms, single occupancy; double occupancy is $250/1550, and ocean view rooms are $50 to $100 cheaper. Rates include three meals daily. For a more pampered experience, stay in the *Litchfield Plantation Inn* (☎ 800-869-1410, 843-237-9121, fax 237-1041), a 1750s mansion framed by an alley of live oaks. Six spacious bedrooms and outlying cottages run from a meager $190 to a whopping $400 a night.

Most restaurants are off the island on Ocean Hwy/Hwy 17. *Pawley's Island*

SOUTH CAROLINA

Tavern & Restaurant (☎ 843-237-8465) markets itself as the home for shrimp, beer and blues. This local hangout is on a little dirt road (marked by a tattered pizza sign) off Ocean Hwy. Live bands play weekend nights.

For fine dining, *Frank's Restaurant* (☎ 843-237-3030, 10434 Ocean Hwy) offers an extensive menu of Lowcountry specialties, such as pan-fried cornmeal-and-black-pepper-encrusted grouper with shrimp ($23) and Frank's famous oyster pie ($8).

Pawleys Island is 30 miles south of Myrtle Beach on Hwy 17 and 60 miles north of Charleston.

GEORGETOWN & AROUND

The Spanish tried to settle here in 1526, but soon retreated to St Augustine, Florida. In colonial times, Georgetown became a

Ghost Stories of South Carolina

Almost every corner of the state is filled with tales of the unresting dead. Featuring everything from mourning specters and disappearing hitchhikers to swamp creatures and alien sightings, these tales should be avoided if driving alone down dark, country roads.

The ghost of Alice Flagg has haunted her family home for three generations. A figure clad all in white glides through the hallway to her old room or sits in the garden. Residents have spotted her combing the beach or even standing on the breaking waves. Who was Alice Flagg? She was from a wealthy family who lived in the Hermitage, a well-known plantation home between Murrells Inlet and Pawleys Island. While away at school in Charleston, Alice fell in love with a turpentine salesman who was beneath her family status. She pursued the relationship despite her family's disapproval, sometimes wearing his ring to public functions in Charleston. While at school she caught yellow fever and was sent home to the Hermitage. Her brother saw the ring and was so angry that he took it and threw it into the inlet. She died shortly thereafter but refuses to leave without her ring.

For more than a hundred years, the Gray Man has walked the beach at Pawleys Island, warning residents of impending storms. Dressed in tattered gray clothes, the Gray Man first appeared to a distraught young woman who had just lost her fiancé in a riding accident. The family left the island soon after the appearance to take her to a Charleston physician because of her insistence that the mysterious figure was the ghost of her lover. The infamous storm of 1822 hit shortly after they left and most of the island residents were killed. The Gray Man appeared again in 1893 at the home of a prominent family asking for bread. Not recognizing the man in such a tight-knit community, the family remembered the original story and left the island as a precaution. A disastrous tidal wave followed soon after their departure.

Modern weather prediction might have made the Gray Man redundant, but he changed with the times. People who have spotted or been approached by the Gray Man have suffered little to no damage to their property during storms. Before Hurricane Hazel, the Gray Man knocked on the door of a family that had come to spend the week at their beach house. Heeding the unknown man's warning they left, and the hurricane swept through the island destroying their neighbors' houses but leaving theirs untouched.

center for rice plantations on the estuarine land around the Pee Dee and Sampit Rivers. West African slaves, experienced in rice cultivation, provided the expertise and the labor. The small **Rice Museum** (☎ 843-546-7423), on Front and Screven Sts, has models and maps that explain rice cultivation in the area ($5; closed Sunday). The chamber of commerce (☎ 800-777-7705), 1001 Front St at King St, has brochures on the town's historic homes, including that of Joseph Hayne Rainey, the first African American elected to the US House of Representatives (1871–1879). The old downtown contrasts with the big steel and paper works across the Sampit River. An annual tour of privately owned plantations and historic houses occurs in April (☎ 843-545-8291).

Between Georgetown and Charleston, some old plantation homes give a feel for antebellum life. The privately owned Hopsewee (☎ 843-546-7891), on US 17, 12 miles south of Georgetown, was a rice plantation from about 1740 and the birthplace of Thomas Lynch Jr, a signer of the Declaration of Independence. The house has antique furnishings and atmospheric grounds; both are open Tuesday to Friday, 10 am to 4 pm, and entry costs $6. From the same era, Hampton Plantation State Historic Site (☎ 843-546-9361), off US 17 about 15 miles from Georgetown, is an imposing white building, but unfurnished and unrestored, with overgrown surroundings and big old trees. George Washington visited this home on his Southern tour in 1791; he so admired a live oak that grew in front of the house that he persuaded the plantation owner never to cut it down. Open Thursday to Monday, 1 to 4 pm; admission is $2.

FRANCIS MARION NATIONAL FOREST

Twenty miles from Charleston, a 250,000-acre forest, named in honor of the region's Revolutionary War hero Francis Marion, contains more than 120 miles of recreational trails for hikers, mountain bikers or canoeists. Within the forest, moving west to east, you will find sand ridges and pine forests, then swamps and finally the At-

lantic Ocean. Along the sand ridges that were once ancient beaches grow tall loblolly pines that shoot up for many feet before ever sprouting a branch. Nearer the ocean, blackwater swamps seep into the cypress and palmetto forests. The carnivorous trumpet pitcher plant grows here, and endangered species include the red-cockaded woodpecker, bald eagle and American alligator.

Also managed by the forest service is the neighboring **Cape Romain National Wildlife Refuge,** which encompasses 64,000 acres of wetlands, salt marshes and beaches along the Atlantic Coast. A stop along the Atlantic fly zone, the refuge is essential to migratory bird species as well as recently introduced red wolves and massive loggerhead turtles, which lay their eggs in the beaches' sand dunes. The most popular destination in the refuge is **Bull Island,** a wild island accessible via boat. The boneyard beach is strewn with sun-bleached trees, marking where a forest succumbed to the sea. The island is for day-use only, and visitors should bring drinking water. A private ferry (☎ 843-881-4582) runs Tuesday, Friday and Saturday ($20); call for times and directions to the landing.

The first stop for outdoor enthusiasts or through-travelers should be at the **Sewee Visitor and Environmental Education Center** (☎ 843-928-3368), on Hwy 17N. The center (closed Monday) can provide hiking and camping information and has exhibits on Lowcountry ecosystems.

Midlands

Thousands of centuries ago, everything roughly southeast of I-20 was ancient sea that retreated and advanced, pushing up huge sand hills and creating the mysterious inland Carolina Bays. Today, hills of red clay ripple to the coastal plain in the east and the mountains in the northwest.

This is cotton country, and peach country and soybean country. For a brief time, it was mill country. Along the Savannah River, it's nuclear country, where the government

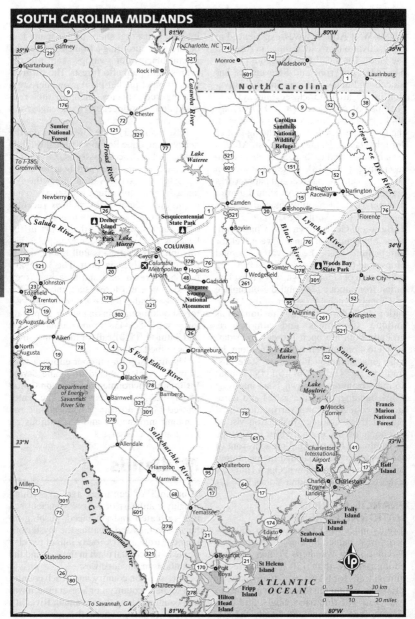

SOUTH CAROLINA MIDLANDS

built a plutonium and tritium plant. Well-educated scientists and engineers filtered into towns that rarely produced high school graduates, and, thanks to the arms race, plant workers were able to afford to send their kids to college and retire by the golf course.

To early Charlestonians, the drier air and rolling hills were a refuge from the 'noxious fumes' of the flooded rice fields, believed to cause malaria. Many came to Aiken, near the banks of the Savannah River; wealthy Northerners followed in the next century and brought a lively equestrian culture. The tall, canopied loblolly pine flourishes in the Midland's sandy soil, and the handsome town of Sumter was built by timber fortunes. Columbia, the capital, is a big small town with a vibrant college community and a Confederate memorial to keep the Lost Cause alive for another century.

A side trip off the interstate to poke around roadside fruit stands, small town festivals and greasy spoons will give you a glimpse of a hardy, unpretentious people who live with poor sandy soils and hot summers, keeping a great sense of humor all the while.

COLUMBIA
pop 112,000

Home to the state legislature and the University of South Carolina, Columbia is a welcome foil to Charleston's classical architecture and celebrated pedigree. All Columbia's pretensions were burned by Sherman's troops, and what remains is unassuming, simple and surprisingly comfortable. Trains still rumble straight through downtown like they have for a century. The town's grandest buildings are the former mills that enveloped the Midlands like kudzu. The avenues are broad and offer spectacular vistas over red-brick buildings, tall scraggly pines and a landscape that melts gently into the sky. Five Points, a funky college district of shops and restaurants, an incomparable state museum and lots of public murals make Columbia worth a few days' exploration.

Columbia was born of compromise and for that reason will never get the respect it

deserves. Just after the Revolutionary War, the state was in danger of splintering into two separate entities: the more populous but poorer Backcountry and the wealthier Lowcountry, which controlled the capital in Charleston. In 1786 a compromise was reached: The state government would relocate to a central place where all citizens would have equal access. The legislature, records, offices and residences moved from the bustling urban center of Charleston to a backwater field near the Congaree River. This new capital would always be painfully inferior to Charleston.

In 1865, General William T Sherman burnt the 'capital of Southern rebellion' to the ground during the encore of his famous March to the Sea. Technically, Sherman didn't order the surrendered city to be burned; his drunken troops undertook the effort on their own. But he was later quoted as saying, 'I never shed any tears over the event.'

Orientation
The heart of the city is the State House, which resides on the aptly named Assembly St (Hwy 48), a north-south route. Main St radiates north from the State House and is a struggling downtown business district. Gervais St (Hwy 1 & 378) is the main east-west artery that crosses the Congaree River. Blossom St, which also runs east-west, leads to the University of South Carolina and to Five Points, a trendy shopping and eating district. Bordering the Congaree River in the western part of Columbia is the Vista, a yuppie district of upscale furniture boutiques and art galleries. The old money district is called Shandon and is south of Devine St.

Information
The helpful visitors center (☎ 803-254-0479) is at 801 Lady St. Information about historic tours is available through the Historic Columbia Foundation (☎ 803-252-1770). The main post office is at 1601 Assembly St. Palmetto Baptist Medical Center (☎ 803-296-5010) is centrally located at 1330 Taylor St. The county library (☎ 803-799-9084),

1431 Assembly St, has Internet access and a well-designed children's reading room. Foreign currency can be exchanged at Wachovia Bank, 1426 Main St. You'll find ATMs at Regions Bank, 1010 Gervais St, and Bank of America, on Harden St in Five Points. The South Carolina library (☎ 803-734-8666), 1500 Senate St, maintains a collection of state documents and nonfiction books and also provides a talking book library (☎ 803-898-5900) for the blind and physically handicapped. The Happy Bookseller (☎ 803-782-2665), 4525 Forest Dr, is

the city's primary independent bookseller. Columbia's daily newspaper is *The State.*

South Carolina State House

The South Carolina State House is a stunning copper-domed, Italian Renaissance structure made of blue granite, the state stone, which was mined and carved in Columbia. Construction on this, the third State House, began in 1851, and in spite of having an incomplete seat for the government, the state leaders still felt prepared to secede from the Union; this decision stalled the

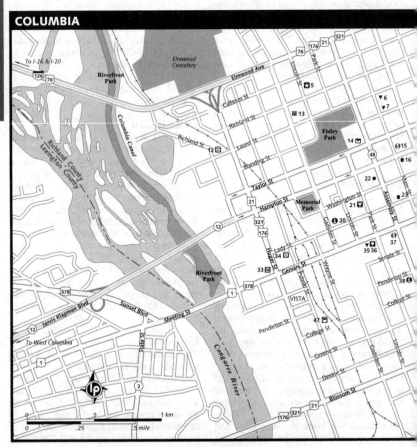

COLUMBIA

building's completion until 1907. Sherman's troops fired on the building and left six scars on the west and southwest facades; these are marked with bronze stars.

It's open to the public Monday to Saturday. The gift shop distributes a detailed brochure and map and conducts tours; call for information (☎ 803-734-2430).

University of South Carolina

From the humble beginning of a class of only 29 students, the University of South Carolina now enrolls 24,000 and is virtually a mini-city within Columbia. Originally founded as South Carolina College in 1801, the school taught the classics, philosophy and chemistry. It was here that the study of political economics was first introduced in the US, and it was here that nullification, the political argument upon which Southern states seceded, became an academic pursuit.

While the early curricula may have been strenuous, the students were by no means refined intellectuals. Drinking, gambling and firing weapons were popular pastimes. The Dish of Trout duel in 1833

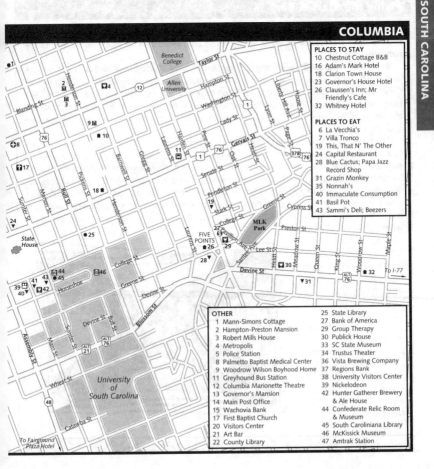

COLUMBIA

PLACES TO STAY
10 Chestnut Cottage B&B
16 Adam's Mark Hotel
18 Clarion Town House
23 Governor's House Hotel
26 Claussen's Inn; Mr Friendly's Cafe
32 Whitney Hotel

PLACES TO EAT
6 La Vecchia's
7 Villa Tronco
19 This, That N' The Other
24 Capital Restaurant
28 Blue Cactus; Papa Jazz Record Shop
31 Grazin Monkey
35 Nonnah's
40 Immaculate Consumption
41 Basil Pot
43 Sammi's Deli; Beezers

OTHER
1 Mann-Simons Cottage
2 Hampton-Preston Mansion
3 Robert Mills House
4 Metropolis
5 Police Station
8 Palmetto Baptist Medical Center
9 Woodrow Wilson Boyhood Home
11 Greyhound Bus Station
12 Columbia Marionette Theatre
13 Governor's Mansion
14 Main Post Office
15 Wachovia Bank
17 First Baptist Church
20 Visitors Center
21 Art Bar
22 County Library
25 State Library
27 Bank of America
29 Group Therapy
30 Publick House
33 SC State Museum
34 Trustus Theater
36 Vista Brewing Company
37 Regions Bank
38 University Visitors Center
39 Nickelodeon
42 Hunter Gatherer Brewery & Ale House
44 Confederate Relic Room & Museum
45 South Caroliniana Library
46 McKissick Museum
47 Amtrak Station

SOUTH CAROLINA

epitomized the students' dubious reputation: Two students grabbed the same platter and refused to yield to the other. The matter was settled in a field – one was shot and killed and the other was dismissed from the school.

Classes were suspended during the Civil War when nearly the entire student body enlisted in the Confederate Army. During the war, it served as a hospital, and for this reason, the campus was spared by Union troops.

The Reconstruction government called for the school to be integrated in the 1870s; in protest, the white faculty and students left. In the last decades of the 19th century, the school would be opened and closed more times than a cut-rate furniture outlet. Stability and growth would not occur until the 20th century, which brought new departments of education, law and engineering as well as female and black students. Now the university boasts a top-ranked international business program and eight

Flying the Stars & Bars

A Confederate monument is a common feature of almost every South Carolina town, and the one in front of the State House would be largely ignored if it weren't for the recent addition of a Confederate battle flag.

But first, let's start at the beginning: The centennial of the War Between the States ironically fell in the midst of the Civil Rights movement. While the South was being forced to dismantle Jim Crow laws, South Carolina passed a resolution to raise a Confederate battle flag over the State House dome in honor of its war dead; it was supposed to be taken down once the centennial celebrations ended. Thirty-some years later, the flag was still flapping in the wind along with the state and national flags.

The state legislature was finally forced to seriously debate the issue when the National Association for the Advancement of Colored People (NAACP) organized a tourism boycott in early 2000. (Small towns that rely heavily on annual family reunions were hit the hardest by the boycott.) In the end, the legislature reached what it called a compromise: the two Confederate flags that decorated the House and Senate chambers would be removed entirely and the flag atop the dome would be moved to the Confederate memorial on the State House grounds. On paper, this seemed like a levelheaded decision, but take a visit to the State House and it will

seem like 'good ol' boy' politics. In its present location, the flag is more noticeable than it was on top of the dome; in fact, on a windy day, it is a major eye-catcher. Not surprisingly, the NAACP was not satisfied with the compromise, so its ban has not been formally lifted, and the South Carolina state chapter had its annual meeting in Charlotte, North Carolina.

branches throughout the state. Famous alumni include talk show host Leeza Gibbons, all members of the band Hootie & the Blowfish and artist Jasper Johns.

The **Horseshoe,** on Sumter between Pendleton and Greene Sts, is a park-like space surrounded by the refined old buildings of the original campus. The brick wall that encompasses the Horseshoe was originally built to fence in the rowdy, all-male student body.

South Caroliniana Library (☎ 803-777-3131) was designed by Robert Mills and was the country's first freestanding collegiate library. At the head of the Horseshoe is the **McKissick Museum** (☎ 803-777-7251), which specializes in Southern folk art and culture exhibits; it's open daily and admission is free. The **Confederate Relic Room & Museum** (☎ 803-898-8095), two blocks southeast at Sumter and Pendleton, is where Carolinians come to check the Confederate credentials of their ancestors (free; open weekdays).

The university's official **visitors center** (☎ 803-777-0169) is on the corner of Pendleton and Assembly Sts; it can provide campus maps, tours (☎ 803-777-2125) and free parking passes.

South Carolina State Museum

The interesting state museum (☎ 803-898-4921), near the riverfront at 301 Gervais St, is housed in a recycled 1894 textile factory building, one of the world's first electrically powered mills. Excellent exhibits on three floors cover science, technology, and the state's cultural and natural history. It's open daily, and admission is $5 for adults, free for children.

Historic Homes & Churches

By torching the city, Sherman's troops made it easy for a modern-day visitor to tour Columbia's historic sites in less than a day. Surviving the burning has also added to the remaining buildings' historic appeal. There are four major historic homes open to the public through guided tours (Tuesday to Sunday); tickets ($4 per house) can be bought at the carriage house of the Robert Mills House (☎ 803-252-1770).

The **Robert Mills House,** 1616 Blanding St, is named after the famous architect Robert Mills, a South Carolina engineer and designer who became the first federal architect (appointed by Andrew Jackson). Along with many of the stately public buildings in Columbia, Mills added the Washington Monument and the US Treasury Building in DC. to his legacy. Next door is the **Hampton-Preston Mansion,** which was built in 1818 by a wealthy slaveholding family. These two homes avoided destruction because they were used to house Sherman's troops.

Mann-Simons Cottage, 1403 Richland St, was owned by a freed black family for more than 100 years. Celia Mann, the matriarch of the family, walked to Columbia from Charleston after being freed by her white father in the 1850s. Celia became one of the city's most respected midwifes, and later generations of her family grew in prominence. Reflecting the family's success, the house grew from one room to two stories in the Columbia-cottage style (high-pitched roof, many windows and a front verandah). The house survived Sherman's fire thanks to neighbors who protected it because it served as their hiding place for valuables.

The only US president to have a PhD, Woodrow Wilson lived in Columbia for four years (1871–75) in what is now the **Woodrow Wilson Boyhood Home,** 1705 Hampton St. The house is decorated in period style, displays the family bed where Woodrow Wilson was born, and has a small museum chronicling the 28th president's life.

Irate Carolinians met at the **First Baptist Church,** 1306 Hampton St, to draw up the Ordinances of Secession, the formal announcement of the Confederacy. First on the Unionists' 'things to torch list,' the church avoided destruction because an African-American Columbian intentionally misdirected Sherman's troops to the old Baptist church nearby.

Special Events

St Patrick's Day – In Columbia's Five Points neighborhood, this is the state's only St Patty's celebration.

Three Rivers Music Festival – In early April, the Vista hosts this music festival of artists great and small; visit www.3riversmusicfestival.org for more information.

Okra Strut – A celebration of okra happens in nearby Irmo in September (☎ 803-781-7850).

South Carolina State Fair – Rides, agricultural exhibits and lots of food can be had in October (☎ 803-799-3387).

Step-Off – In November, USC's Association of African-American Students (☎ 803-777-5780) sponsors this step competition of fraternities and sororities. Stepping is a type of choreographed dance.

Chitlin' Strut – On the weekend following Thanksgiving, the small town of Salley (☎ 803-258-3485) hosts this festival devoted to chitlins (boiled or fried pig intestines); an estimated 124,000 pounds of chitlins have been consumed over the festival's 34-year history.

Places to Stay

You'll need to make reservations far in advance if you plan on visiting Columbia during spring graduation or home football games – call ☎ 803-777-4274 for information on the latter; expect rate increases during these peak periods.

Downtown & University Area A few blocks from the State House, *Governor's House Hotel* (☎ 803-779-7790, fax 803-779-7856, 1301 Main St) has standard rooms for $70. *Adam's Mark Hotel* (☎ 803-771-7000, 1200 Hampton St) caters to business travelers with standard rooms ($80-$150) and suites ($350-450).

The modern, franchise-style *Clarion Town House* (☎ 803-771-8711, fax 803-252-9347, 1615 Gervais St) offers rooms for $80 to $100.

Chestnut Cottage B&B (☎ 803-256-1718, 1718 Hampton St) is the former home of Mary Boykin Chestnut, one of the state's famous diarists. Four spacious rooms range from $175 to $200, and one room is believed to have hosted Confederate President Jefferson Davis in 1864.

Around Five Points Housed in a converted bakery, *Claussen's Inn* (☎ 803-765-0440, fax 803-799-7924, 2003 Green St)

offers large rooms for $125/140 for one/two people.

In a nice tree-lined neighborhood, the big *Whitney Hotel* (☎ 800-637-4008, 803-252-0845, 700 Woodrow St), at Devine St, is close to Five Points and Shandon's upscale restaurants. Standard rooms go for $120 to $160.

Outside of Town There are lots of moderately priced options on the interstates just outside of town. The *Fairground Plaza Motel* (☎ 800-220-2752, 803-252-2000, 621 S Assembly) isn't much to look at, but it does have cheap rooms ($45) close to downtown. *Motel 6* (☎ 803-798-9210), I-26 exit 106, has reliable basics for $37/44.

Dreher Island State Park (☎ 803-364-4152), on Hwy 1 in Prosperity (see the South Carolina Midlands map), sits in the middle of Lake Murray and was used in the 1940s for bombing practice by the Army Air Corps. Campsites ($17) and villas sleeping six to eight ($130/300 nightly/weekend) are available. Closer to Columbia, *Sesquicentennial State Park* (☎ 803-788-2706, 9564 Two Notch Rd) has campsites with electrical hookups ($16).

Places to Eat

Columbia's restaurant scene isn't as adventurous as Charleston's. This is a meat-and-potatoes town, and even the few cutting edge restaurants are sure to include at least one steak item. Thanks to the university, you can eat cheap and late.

Most restaurants are closed on Sunday, but the pubs and bars (listed in the Entertainment section) are open and serve food.

Downtown & University Area Probably more 'gub'ment' business gets done at the *Capital Restaurant* (☎ 803-765-0176, 1210 Main St) than the hallowed chambers of the State House. A favorite with the legislature, the Capital serves breakfast, grilled chops and daily specials. It's open for breakfast and lunch only.

La Vecchias' (☎ 803-376-888, 1736 Main St) bold and beautiful dining area creates the illusion of being at the bottom of the ocean. Grilled salmon ($18) and sesame seared yellowfin tuna ($20) will please any top-of-the-chain feeder. Dinner reservations are recommended; it's also open for lunch.

Serving three meals a day, seven days a week, **Basil Pot** (☎ 803-799-0928, 928 Main) feeds the city's health nuts and vegetarians with homemade breads as well as tofu and fish dishes ($6-8).

Java and sandwiches ($5) are served at the cozy **Immaculate Consumption** (☎ 803-799-9053, 933 Main St).

Sink your sweet tooth into a deep-dish apple pie or chocolate espresso torte ($6) at **Nonnah's** (☎ 803-779-9599, 930 Gervais), in the Vista neighborhood. Nonnah's also has late-night hours, a coffee bar and an attached art gallery.

A side order of family and tradition comes with any main dish at **Villa Tronco** (☎ 803-256-7677, 1213 Blanding). This 60-year-old, family-owned Italian restaurant is in a 19th-century firehouse that still retains its original stable doors and skylights. Menu items, such as lasagna and baked ziti, are based on Mama Tronco's recipes. Lunch items cost $5 to $8; dinner, $13 to $15.

Near the university, there is an endless supply of cheap sub and gyro shops. **Sammi's Deli** (☎ 803-256-7763, 919 Sumter St) and its neighbor **Beezers** (☎ 803-771-7771) do a steady student business.

Around Five Points Blue Cactus (☎ 803-929-0782, 2002 Greene St) provides the following disclaimer: The food is good, but slow. This mom-and-pop joint is a virtual United Nations, offering Korean dumplings and stews ($3 to $6), Puerto Rican red beans ($5), burritos ($3) and good old Philly cheese steaks ($6) as well as lots of veggie and vegan options.

Just around the corner from Claussen's Inn, **Mr Friendly's Cafe** (☎ 803-254-7828, 2001-A Greene St) has reinvented the Southern classics, including pecan crab cakes ($15) and a grilled rib eye with portobello hash ($20). This casual bistro is open for lunch and dinner and has outdoor dining.

Reggae tunes, funky décor and large portions of Caribbean specialities can be found

at **This, That N' The Other** (☎ 803-779-3820, 948 Harden St). Lunch meals run $5 to $6; dinner, $10 to $12.

Grazin Monkey (☎ 803-256-1072, 2406 Devine St) is the Southern interpretation of a tapas bar. A seasonal menu might include fried green tomatoes with goat cheese and red pepper pesto ($9) or pan-seared sea bass ($10). It's open Tuesday to Saturday for dinner only.

An old-style ice cream stand, **Rosewood Dairy Bar** (☎ 803-252-1662, 3003 Rosewood Dr) has helped folks beat the heat since 1942.

Entertainment

The Free Times, available in most restaurants and bars, is the best information source for cultural and music events. The university posts a calendar of events on its Web site at http://events.sc.edu.

Kids will get a kick out of the **Columbia Marionette Theatre** (☎ 803-252-7366, 401 Laurel St).

The few South Carolina-spawned artists, liberals and hippies gravitate to Columbia, and the art scene is better for it. One incubator is **Trustus Theater** (☎ 803-254-9732, 520 Lady St), the only theater in South Carolina to receive funding from the National Endowment for the Arts. Trustus presents modern, cutting-edge and locally written plays. An independent movie house, **Nickelodeon** (☎ 803-254-3433, 937 Main St) often showcases local filmmakers as well as cult and foreign classics.

If you like your music unplugged, the **Unitarian Universalist Coffee House** (☎ 803-799-1746, 2701 Heyward St) sponsors acoustic folk music on the weekends. In West Columbia, **Bill's Music Shop & Pickin' Parlor** (☎ 803-796-6477, 710 Meeting St) hosts weekend bluegrass shows.

The oldest, dirtiest dive bar in Five Points, **Group Therapy** (☎ 803-256-1203, 2107 Greene St) has helped generations of Columbians scratch an itch. Grad students and professors carry on erudite conversations at the **Hunter Gatherer Brewery & Ale House** (☎ 803-748-0540, 900 Main St). Homemade brews and gourmet pizzas make good silence fillers. Live music is held on Tuesday and Thursday nights.

Be as hip as you want to be at the *Art Bar* (☎ *803-929-0198, 1211 Park St)*. Local musicians perform midweek, and weekend nights feature deejays spinning drum & bass, jungle and Latin music.

Publick House (☎ *803-256-2207, 2307 Devine St)* is an Irish-style pub serving chicken wings and sandwiches. A common table near the bar is good for solo travelers, and Sunday night hosts a Celtic jam session.

Signs that the new economy has reached Columbia can be found at the *Vista Brewing Company* (☎ *803-799-2739)*, at Gervais and Park Sts. Sipping homebrews and fancy cocktails, the upscale crowd appears poised and well-groomed in this refurbished industrial space. Appetizers and a bar menu are available.

The unmarked *Rockaway Athletic Club* (☎ *803-256-1075, 2719 Rosewood Dr)* is a little out of the way but has a hometown pub feel. Burgers and oysters keep the drinkers fueled throughout the night, and according to one waitress, 'We wouldn't close on Sunday even if Jesus were coming to town.' Rockaway is in the Shoppes on Rosewood Center, near the Salvation Army.

Columbia does support a very quiet gay culture, many of whom go dancing at the *Metropolis* (☎ *803-799-8727, 1800 Blanding St)*.

Spectator Sports
Whether or not the team wins or loses, the loyal fans of USC's *Carolina Gamecocks* still pack an 80,000 seat stadium. Theirs is a long-suffering relationship: In 1999 USC had a no-win season and held the division's longest losing streak. Lou Holtz, the former coach of Notre Dame, was brought in to break the 'Chicken Curse;' the spell seems to be subsiding, for Carolina recently played in a postseason bowl game and made its intrastate rival, Clemson, break a sweat in the 2000 annual showdown.

Named after the Revolutionary War hero Thomas 'Gamecock' Sumter, the team is often referred to simply as the 'Cocks' – the double entendre is lost on

self-respecting fans. The Gamecocks play at the mammoth Williams-Brice Stadium, and pregame tailgate parties start several hours before kickoff. Tickets for home games are difficult to get; call ☎ 803-777-4274 for information.

In nearby Orangeburg, South Carolina State University (☎ 803-536-7000), a historically black university, fields a football team better known for its marching band.

The first national pastime, baseball, still draws crowds on sticky hot summer evenings. *Capital City Bombers* (☎ 803-254-4487) is a professional minor league team affiliated with the New York Mets.

The *Double Dutch Forces* make dancing through staggered jump ropes look easy. These world champions practice in MLK Park in Five Points, Thursday and Friday, 6 to 8 pm, and Saturday and Sunday, 4 to 6 pm.

Shopping
Refreshingly unique artists call Columbia home. Blue Sky is best known for his outdoor murals, including 'Tunnelvision,' (Taylor and Marion Sts), 'Light at the End of the Tunnel' (Hampton and Bull Sts) and 'Harper's Restaurant Mural 1948' in Five Points. His gallery is at 707 Saluda Ave in Five Points. Ernest Lee, also known as the Funky Chicken Man, sells his chicken-inspired paintings on Harden and Gervais Sts near the bus station. Papa Jazz (☎ 803-256-0095), 2014 Green St in Five Points, is arguably one of the best used record shops in the Southeast.

Getting There & Around
Columbia Metropolitan Airport (☎ 803-822-5000) is on Hwy 302 off of I-26S. It's serviced by eight airlines; fares to destination on the East Coast and Chicago are $250; to the West Coast, $500; and to London, $350.

The Greyhound station (☎ 803-256-6465), 2015 Gervais St, has buses to Charleston ($45; 2½ hours), Atlanta ($85; four hours), and New York City ($115; 14 hours). *Silver Star* trains arrive at the Amtrak station (☎ 803-252-8246), 850 Pulaski

St, and serve New York City ($250; 16 hours) and Savannah ($80, 2½ hours).

To reach Columbia by car, take I-20 W from I-95. From Charleston or Greenville, take I-26. From Charlotte, use I-77 to I-20.

AROUND COLUMBIA

A 100-foot-tall neon sign sporting a plump, happy pig beckons barbecue lovers to *Piggie Park* (☎ *803-796-0220, 1600 Charleston Hwy)*, the first location of what is now an empire. Barbecue baron Maurice Bessinger became famous for his mustard-based sauce in 1953, but has recently become infamous for his outspoken support of the Confederate flag. This simple barbecue hut has been transformed into a personal pulpit to restore state sovereignty: The Confederate flag flies in the parking lot, and pro-flag pamphlets and Civil War videos are sold alongside souvenir T-shirts and hats of dancing pigs (a common motif for quality barbecue). What might have started as Carolina impudence has become rabid conviction – Maurice has fought several legal battles to keep the flag flying, has plastered his Web site with a personal message about saving our constitutional republic and suffered an economic blow when grocery stores pulled his popular barbecue sauce from their shelves after his politics garnered criticism. For the nonjudgmental visitor, there might not be any other place in the US like this, and the barbecue ain't bad.

Pools of algae-covered water, thick tree canopies more than 15 stories overhead and deposits of rich alluvial soil make the **Congaree Swamp National Monument** prime real estate for river otters, wild boar and the pileated woodpecker. This 11,000-acre tract catches the Congaree River when it jumps its banks and is an International Biosphere Reserve, one of the few remaining old-growth floodplains in the US. Six hiking trails (two wheelchair-accessible) lead into the heart of the knobby kneed cypress and tupelo forest. Canoe trails follow the meandering river into silent isolated pockets.

Rangers lead nature hikes and canoe trips; make reservations (☎ 803-776-4396) early for canoe trips, which occur one Sunday a month. The private outfitter Adventure Carolina (☎ 803-796-4505), 1107 State St, Cayce, leads trips down the Congaree and Edisto; visit its Web site at www .adventurecarolina.com for more information. Primitive camping is allowed with a permit. A new visitors center will be opening at 100 National Park Rd, Hopkins, and will provide hiking and canoeing maps. From Columbia, take I-77 S to exit 5 and follow the signs.

SIDE TRIPS ALONG I-20 EAST

One of the major east-west arteries, I-20 connects the capital to I-95 and smaller highways that lead to Myrtle Beach. The eastern route goes through the coastal plain – an ancient ocean floor that yields cotton and tobacco. Early morning fog, standing pools of water and tall reed grasses hint at the land's preparations for meeting the sea. The oldest inland town, **Camden,** claims a longer horse-racing history than the more scenic town of Aiken. Camden's Carolina Cup horse race occurs in the spring, and the Colonial Cup follows in the fall. During the Revolutionary War, Camden served as the British headquarters and was the site of a disastrous battle for the Continental Army. Contact the chamber of commerce (☎ 803-432-2525), 724 S Broad St, for information about touring the town's historic sites. Take Hwy 521 N from I-20 to reach downtown Camden.

The little town of **Boykin** is a quick and scenic drive from I-20. Barely a bend in the road, the town comprises a few simple shacks housing a broom-maker (☎ 903-425-0933), an operating gristmill and an old-fashioned country store. Take Hwy 521 to Hwy 261 and cross the Swift Bridge to reach Boykin.

Cotton fields line Hwy 15 N as you enter **Bishopville,** home to the state's cotton museum (☎ 803-484-4497), 121 W Cedar Lane. Did you know that US currency is made of 75% cotton, or that the boll weevil is the size of a pinhead? Have you ever touched raw cotton? These are just a few of the things you can experience at the museum; open weekdays 10 am to 5 pm, admission is $2/1 adults/children.

NASCAR fans will want to visit the **Darlington International Raceway** (☎ 843-395-8499), on Hwy 151 in Darlington, where the Southern 500 is run. You can visit a commercial museum for $3.

SUMTER
pop 46,000

Wide magnolia-lined streets and spacious Victorian homes built by timber barons define the historic district of Sumter. Founded in 1800, Sumter was named in honor of the region's Revolutionary hero, Thomas 'Gamecock' Sumter. The 200-year-old **Opera House** (☎ 803-436-2616), 21 N Main St, adorned by a 100-foot clock tower, watches over the sleepy downtown of hat shops and 99-cent stores.

Tourist brochures will try to trick you into drooling over historic mansions, but sometimes true grit makes more of an impression. The **Carolina Backcountry Homestead** exhibit at the county museum (☎ 803-775-0908), 122 N Washington St, depicts the way European settlers survived on the frontier. Corncobs instead of toilet paper, soap made of animal fat and not a television in sight will make that dingy apartment you live in seem like a castle. Students from the local high school perform living history demonstrations of blacksmithing, yarn spinning and woodworking. Other museum exhibits include the obligatory displays of silver, antique furniture and other attic collections (a trademark of most regional museums). The museum is open Tuesday to Saturday, 10 am to 5 pm, and Sunday 2 to 5 pm; donations accepted.

The **Swan Lake Iris Gardens** (☎ 803-436-2555), on W Liberty St, hosts the annual Iris Festival in May. Swans from almost every continent live and swim amid the cypress swamp and flower gardens. **Woods Bay State Park** (☎ 803-659-4445), on Hwy 301, exit 146 off I-95, has several Carolina Bays, an egg-shaped depression occurring only in the Southeast. All bays face the same direction (on a northwest-southeast axis), and scientists believe that an ancient meteorite crashed into the coastal plain, creating these depressions.

Shaw Air Force Base is one of Sumter's major employers. The base's four squadrons of F-16 Fighting Falcons have served in Desert Storm and enforced the Iraqi 'no-fly' zone. Want a closer look at these fearsome machines? The public is welcome to view the fighter jets dropping 25-pound dummy bombs on assigned targets Monday to Thursday. Call the range (☎ 803-895-2597) for directions and the daily flight schedule; bring earplugs.

One of the few downtown restaurants is *Caribbean Pepper Pot* (☎ 803-934-8732, 18-20 Liberty St), which offers a lunch buffet of delicacies from the islands ($5) and a kid's menu.

Sumter is only 14 miles from I-95 and makes a nice resting point for Florida-bound snowbirds. *Poinsett State Park* (☎ 803-494-8177), on Hwy 261, 18 miles southwest of Sumter, near Wedgefield, has campsites for $11. *Best Western* (☎ 800-528-1234, 1050 Broad St/Hwy 521) charges $50/55 single/double for clean, simple rooms. *Magnolia House B&B* (☎ 888-666-0296, 803-775-6694, magnoliahouse@sumter.net) is a 1907 Greek Revival home in a quiet residential neighborhood. This pet- and kid-friendly inn charges $75 to $145, depending on the room.

AIKEN
pop 24,000

Miles of undisturbed pine forests and shabby one-stoplight towns can't prepare a visitor for the beauty of Aiken. Graced with antebellum mansions and an air of aristocracy, Aiken was a summer health resort in the early 1800s for wealthy Charlestonians. The town was rediscovered after the Civil War when the South became a sportsperson's paradise. Northern visitors built extravagant homes, which they called cottages, and brought their equestrian hobbies. The town soon became a center for horsemanship and today is the winter training ground for thoroughbreds en route to the Kentucky Derby. A more permanent population of scientists and engineers settled in Aiken when the US government's Department of Energy built the Savannah River Site in the 1950s.

Aiken Chamber of Commerce (☎ 803-641-1111), 121 Richland Ave E, has information and maps for touring the historic homes and the city's parks.

Hitchcock Woods

This 2000-acre preserve in the center of town (☎ 803-642-0528) is allegedly the largest urban forest in the US. Originally, this was the playground for Thomas and Loulie Hitchcock, Aiken's most prominent winter colonists, and their cast of horse-loving friends. Miss Loulie was one of the first women to abandon the sidesaddle and became a master of foxhounds and flew over bridle jumps into her 60s.

The Hitchcocks' land was donated to the city in 1939 and, according to local lore, is protected by a ghost who chases off nefarious speculators. The preserve is diverse, with rambling horse- and footpaths that traverse gentle slopes and eroded clay hills.

Maps are necessary and available from the chamber of commerce or at the main entrance. To get to the main entrance, follow S Boundary Ave west until it terminates in what looks like someone's front yard. An iron gate marks the entrance. A 10-minute walk into the forest will bring you to the site of the annual **Blessing of the Hounds,** 11 am on Thanksgiving Day. Well-groomed horses and their riders collect with the exuberant hounds for some hobnobbing at the start of the foxhunting season. (These days they only use eau de fox instead of the real thing.)

Winter Colony District

If you find a dirt road in the middle of downtown, then you have ventured into the Winter Colony, a neighborhood of wealthy migrants whose livelihood revolves around horses. (The roads are left unpaved for the horses, which have the right of way over cars). During the winter months, the horses, their trainers, vets, psychics, tooth fairies and groomers quietly slip into town and carry on in a self-contained world. The commoner is allowed to peer from the car window at the sleek, muscled thoroughbreds or horse-drawn carriages traveling the red clay streets. The Winter Colony proper is south

of S Boundary Ave and east of Whiskey Rd, which is considered to be the old whiskey-hauling route between Charleston and Augusta; it's also named for the discarded whiskey bottles that once littered the street.

The **Aiken Training Track,** at Two Notch Rd and Grace Ave, has produced such top thoroughbred racehorses as Summer Squall, the 1990 Preakness winner, and Pleasant Colony, the 1981 Kentucky Derby winner. Visitors are welcome to watch the training sessions (usually from dawn to late morning) from the track's sidelines.

Everyone comes out for the **Aiken Triple Crown,** which is held in early March and comprises three events: trials, steeplechase and harness. The most popular, and most important for a young racehorse, is the Aiken Trials, the flat running event. This is the first public viewing of the year's upcoming contenders. For the majority of spectators, the races are an opportunity to let down the tailgate of the new pickup truck and swill down some American beer.

The cultured sport of **polo** is played every Sunday at 3 pm at Whitney Polo Field, at Mead Ave and Two Notch Rd. The polo season is September to November and March to July. Admission is $2 per person.

The neighborhood west of Whiskey Rd is easier to poke around in than the officially designated Winter Colony. From Whiskey Rd, turn left onto Coker Springs Ave, where the spring of the same name provided water for early residents of the area and later served as a stagecoach stop between Abbeville. (Thanks to the modern inhabitants, the spring is permanently blocked off because of contamination.) Horse stables and paddocks abut the narrow road. Old, stately trees provide camouflage, making the neighborhood seem like a newly discovered secret. An underground system of tunnels connects many of these homes to the old railroad depot; homeowners suspect that the tunnels were used to deliver hooch to thirsty citizens during Prohibition.

Hopelands Garden

Antique trees strike dramatic poses in this 14-acre public garden, just off Whiskey Rd on Dupree Place. Formerly a winter estate, the foundation of the main house has been turned into an English formal garden with carp ponds and mold-covered statues. Huge magnolias bend their old limbs to the ground for children to climb. The garden also contains the **Thoroughbred Racing Hall of Fame and Museum** (☎ 803-642-7758), which displays racing silks, memorabilia and photos of champion horses trained in Aiken. The garden is open from 10 am to sunset daily; admission is free.

Places to Stay

Due to the popularity of the Masters golf tournament in nearby Augusta, Georgia, and Aiken's Triple Crown horse races, make reservations far in advance if planning a trip in March.

Aiken State Park (☎ 803-649-2857, 1145 State Park Rd), 16 miles outside of Aiken on Hwy 302, has camping for $11 a night.

Holley Inns (☎ 803-648-4265, 235 Richland Ave W), at the corner of Laurens St, is right in the heart of the historic downtown and still oozes a courtly charm. Rates in the main building, which was built in 1929, are $60/70 during the week/weekend. Rates are $10 cheaper in the adjoining motel.

The true gem is the historic *Willcox Inn* (☎ 803-649-1377, 100 Colleton Ave SW). Built in 1898, the Willcox was the showpiece for such prominent visitors as Winston Churchill, Elizabeth Arden and President Franklin D Roosevelt. Huge magnolia blossoms sweeten the columned front porch, and the inn's aristocratic atmosphere makes one want to 'dress' for dinner. Rates range from $100 for a standard room to $150 for a king-sized suite.

Places to Eat

A good place to eavesdrop on the horsey set is at the *Track Kitchen*, on Mead Ave at Two Notch Rd. Trainers, riders, horseshoers and even mounted city police gather to discuss college basketball, misbehaving yearlings and how those 'Northerners' do things. It's open 5:30am to 2pm.

New Moon Café (☎ 803-648-7088, 116 Laurens St NW) serves fancy coffee drinks,

breakfast and lunch. This might be your best bet for a vegetarian meal.

One of the best barbecue joints in the state is *Carolina Bar-b-que* (☎ 803-652-2919, 109 S Main St), in nearby New Ellenton. A plate costs $5.25 and includes meat, hash and a choice of three sides. Call for directions and opening hours.

If you want to do some fine dining, make reservations at *No 10 Downing St* (☎ 803-642-9062, 241 Laurens St SW). High-dollar main dishes, such as roasted pork loin and sea bass, go nicely with the ambience of this former 1835 residence. No 10 is open for dinner Tuesday to Saturday.

Entertainment

The Alley, which runs between Laurens and Newberry Sts, is the proving ground for new and old drinkers alike. The young kids flock to *Aiken Brewing Company* (☎ 803-502-0707, 140 Laurens St SW), and the business crowd likes to be seen at the *West Side Bowery* (☎ 803-648-2900, 151 Bee Lane).

Getting There & Away

Aiken is about an hour's drive from Columbia via I-20 W. The second Aiken exit (Hwy 19) will take you by former Chicago Bear William 'Refrigerator' Perry's mansion. It sits on a low hill just after the perpetual care cemetery on the right side as you enter town. Look for the brick serpentine wall with football-shaped ironwork.

Augusta, Georgia, just across the Savannah River, is about a 30-minute drive and is accessible via Hwy1 S/78 W, which is called Richland Ave within Aiken's city limits.

Southeastern Stages (☎ 803-648-6894, 347 Barnwell Ave NW) runs frequent buses east and west of Aiken daily. Roundtrip fares to Columbia are $23 and to Augusta, $13.

EDGEFIELD

In the center of peach country, this sleepy town has been a breeding ground for hot-headed politicians, including Ben 'Pitchfork' Tillman and Strom Thurmond. At last count, the town could claim to have produced 10 governors and five lieutenant governors – quite a boast for a population of under 3000.

Long before political tempers flared, patient potters bent over spinning wheels making the famous Edgefield pottery. Along the Savannah River Valley, deposits of clay (locally called 'kaolin') were left behind after the sea receded 30 million years ago. Native Americans were the first to use kaolin, and their knowledge was passed on to Europeans. By the 1820s, the Edgefield pottery village supplied the country with jugs, crocks, jars, tobacco pipes and other stoneware. One famous potter was the slave known simply as Dave. Trained as a typesetter, Dave inscribed lines of poetry on his jars and jugs. One jar bears the instructions: *Fill this jar with pork or beef & Scott will be there to get a piece.* In addition to household crockery, the potters

also made face jugs, which are believed to be a transplanted African tradition. These vessels bear the shape of a face – busts of famous people such as George Washington, monkeys, fearsome monster-like characters. Some face jugs might have been whimsical creations for carrying water, but some suspect that the more gruesome jugs might have played a role in root medicine. Stephen Ferrell, the resident potter at **Old Edgefield Pottery** (☎ 803-637-2060), 230 Simkins St just off the town square, can describe the art and history of alkaline glazed pottery and demonstrate the traditional technique. It's open Tuesday to Saturday, 10 am to 6 pm.

A **village blacksmith shop** also occupies the small downtown. The resident blacksmith

SOUTH CAROLINA

Scenic Drive – From the Coast to Clay Hills via Country Roads

This drive takes you on two-lane country roads from the salt marshes of the coast to the fragrant pine forests of the Midlands. (Places shown in bold type are covered in more detail in this chapter.) From **Beaufort** take Hwy 21 N to Old Sheldon Church Rd; follow signs to Yemassee, which hosts an annual shrimp festival in September. At Yemassee the road turns into Hwy 68 and follows the railroad tracks past abandoned country stores, one-intersection downtowns and clapboard churches within tippling distance of squat, concrete liquor stores. Soon you'll reach Hampton, which hosts an annual mid-summer watermelon festival. Tune your radio to 92.1 FM for a local morning chat show. Hwy 68 will turn into Hwy 278 near Allendale, which hosts an annual spring cooter fest. (A cooter is a turtle.)

As the Spanish moss begins to disappear, you are approaching Barnwell, birthplace of James Brown. The town has yet to erect a memorial to the Godfather of Soul, but he was honored during James Brown Day. JB reportedly was so impressed with the school band that he donated money for uniforms. In Barnwell, take Hwy 3 to get to Blackville and its famous healing springs, just north of town. The former owner deeded the springs to God so private interests couldn't bottle the fine-tasting water. Backtrack to Bus 78/Main St for a late lunch at Miller's, a Mennonite restaurant. Follow Hwy 78 to **Aiken** and tune your radio to 94.7 FM for a mix of Latin, funk and JB tunes. About halfway there, you'll see on the right the Williston Gin, which gins cotton from a tri-county area, October through January.

is hard at work Tuesday to Saturday, 9 am to 5 pm. In the summer of 2001, the **Discovery Center** is slated to open; this state-sponsored history museum will feature exhibits on the county, interpretive living-history displays and visitor information.

The nearby towns of Trenton and Johnston celebrate the peach in June and April, respectively. Contact the chamber of commerce (☎ 803-275-0010) for specific dates.

Many people opt to stay in Edgefield during Masters Week because of the town's proximity to Augusta, Georgia. The *Carnoosie Inn* (☎ *803-637-5107, 407 Columbia Rd*) is in a mid-1800s house and charges $40/45 for one/two people. *Edgefield Inn* (☎ *803-637-2001, fax 637-2020, 702 Augusta Rd/Hwy 25 S*) is a modern hotel with a variety of rooms ranging from $55 to $85. Expect rate increases during the Masters.

There are several lunch spots on the square. The judges and lawyers take courthouse recess at the *Edgefield Billiard Parlor* (☎ *803-637-9941*). Finer dining can be found at *Old Edgefield Grill* (☎ *803-637-3222, 202 Penn St)*, which specializes in New Southern cuisine and features a seasonal dinner menu ($20 an entrée). When making reservations for dinner, ask to be seated in the Strom Thurmond dining room, where pictures of the famous senator decorate the walls. It's open for lunch Tuesday to Saturday and for dinner Wednesday to Saturday. If you'd like to sample some of the sweetest peaches in the world, stop by *Cook's Market* on Hwy 25.

Edgefield is about half an hour from Aiken via Hwy 19. From Augusta, take I-20 to Hwy 25.

Upcountry

In history and attitude, the Upcountry is similar to the Midlands. This was the former backcountry, the domain of the powerful Cherokee Indians and their capital of Keowee, near present-day Clemson. Scotch-Irish and German settlers eventually pushed out the Cherokee and carved the rolling hills into small family farms. By the early 20th century, cotton mills, centered on powerful mountain rivers, created the region's first towns, some of which still bear their creator's names (eg, Spartanburg was named after the Spartan Mill). Thanks to the region's low taxes and low union activity, international high-tech firms now relocate to the 35-mile stretch of I-85 between Greenville and Spartanburg. Former mill workers have been retrained to make BMW roadsters, silicon wafers for semiconductors, plumbing fixtures, tires, polyester fiber and electrical equipment.

Greenville is a concentrated example of the New South, where German sports cars outnumber US pickup trucks on the highway and international cuisine invades everyone's culinary vocabulary. To the west is the bucolic town of Clemson and the state agricultural school bearing the same name and a forbidding reputation in college football.

In the northwestern corner, the rolling hills turn into the voluptuous peaks of the Blue Ridge Mountains, where hiking trails crisscross bubbling streams and mountain ridges and little roads switchback through apple farms and rhododendron groves.

No trip to the region is complete without first reading *Red Hills and Cotton*, a memoir by Ben Roberston, who grew up in the Keowee valley near Twelve-Mile Creek. The book is a meditation on being a South Carolinian, a Southerner, a farmer, a son and a grandson.

GREENVILLE
pop 57,000
At the base of the foothills, Greenville is the nexus of the I-85 boom belt and the economic engine of the state. The injection of new money and foreign blood has created a small town with cosmopolitan accoutrements. Huge performance spaces host national shows, the county art museum is top-notch and the restaurants reflect a culinary diversity rarely found in the state. But a leafy, tree-lined downtown, circuitous streets that crisscross the Reedy River, plenty of country kitchens and a well-ingrained Christian tradition keep Greenville feeling cozy and Southern. Two

SOUTH CAROLINA UPCOUNTRY

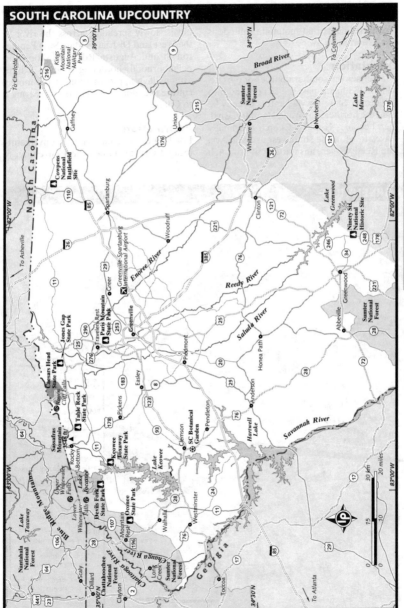

SOUTH CAROLINA

petite skyscrapers share the cityscape with equally demure distant mountains that remind residents that mountain solitude is just a short drive away.

Orientation

I-85 defines the southern border of the city, while I-385 heads past the airport and into downtown. State Hwy 29 enters Greenville from the northeast as Wade Hampton Blvd, then becomes N and S Church and finally leaves town in the southwest as Mills Ave. The Reedy River runs north-south through the center of town. The shopping district is centered along several blocks of Main St but is slowly spreading across the river to the West End District (S Main St to Pendleton St and Augusta Rd). The shops and neighborhoods bordering Augusta Rd are Greenville's approximation of old-money culture (but don't even bother comparing it to Charleston).

Information

Load up on brochures at the conveniently located Greater Greenville Convention &

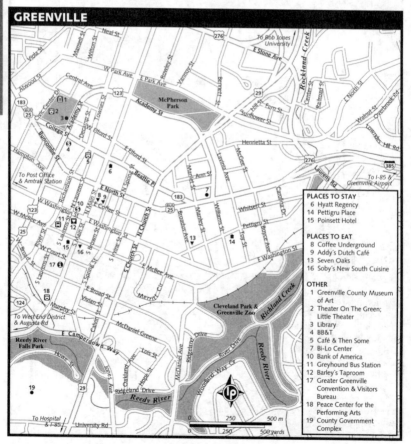

GREENVILLE

PLACES TO STAY
6 Hyatt Regency
14 Pettigru Place
15 Poinsett Hotel

PLACES TO EAT
8 Coffee Underground
9 Addy's Dutch Café
13 Seven Oaks
16 Soby's New South Cuisine

OTHER
1 Greenville County Museum of Art
2 Theater On The Green; Little Theater
3 Library
4 BB&T
5 Café & Then Some
7 Bi-Lo Center
10 Bank of America
11 Greyhound Bus Station
12 Barley's Taproom
17 Greater Greenville Convention & Visitors Bureau
18 Peace Center for the Performing Arts
19 County Government Complex

Visitors Bureau (☎ 800-351-7180, 864-421-0000), 206 S Main St, or visit its Web site at www.greatergreenville.com.

The post office is at 600 W Washington St (☎ 864-282-8401). Greenville County Main Library (☎ 864-242-5000), 300 College St, has Internet access. Greenville Memorial Hospital (☎ 864-455-7000) is at 701 Grove St, southwest of downtown. Downtown banks include BB&T at 301 College St and Bank of America (no ATM at this location) at 7 N Laurens. Many banks are conveniently located along Main St. The town's daily newspaper is the *Greenville News*.

The Open Book (☎ 864-235-9651), 110 S Pleasantburg Dr, is the only independent bookseller in town. Out of Bounds (☎ 864-239-0106), 219-F W Antrim Dr, near Laurens St (Hwy 276), might be a good resource on the complexities of being gay in the Bible Belt.

Greenville County Museum of Art

This is just a darn good museum. The collections are varied, and the price is right (admission is free). The highlight is the collection of 24 Andrew Wyeth watercolors. The Southern-related art collection gives a compelling commentary on the history of the region, from fields of cotton to mechanized looms, and includes work by William H Johnson, a Florence native who taught himself how to draw from comic books. The museum (☎ 864-271-7570), 420 College St, is open Tuesday to Saturday, 10 am to 5 pm.

Bob Jones University

This fundamentalist Christian school was originally established in Florida in 1927 by an itinerant preacher named Bob Jones. The campus moved to Greenville in the '40s and is currently headed by the founder's grandson, Bob Jones III. What is a fundamentalist, you might ask? The official word from the school is that fundamentalists read the Bible literally and consider it an infallible and verbally inspired miracle, the word of God.

BJU's current enrollment is 5000 students from across the country. At one time the majority of BJU graduates went on to become ministers of evangelical churches,

but recently, the school's other colleges – education, fine arts and business, among others – have gained more popularity.

Another fundamental to student life is the extensive set of rules appearing in the closely guarded student handbook. Female students must wear long skirts, and male students, neckties; all dates are chaperoned, and smooching is out; Saturday nights on campus are called 'study breaks' and don't include drinking alcohol, dancing or rock music. In the 1970s the school lost its tax-exempt status because of its whites-only admission policy (apparently the mixing of the races is against God's plan). The school rescinded the rule with the caveat that students from different races could not date and interracial couples would not be admitted as students. That rule was eventually abandoned after a visit from then-presidential candidate George W Bush in 2000. In an effort to discredit the candidate, the media publicized the school's policy toward interracial couples; this in turn unleashed a national uproar, several talk show appearances by Bob Jones III and a few too many news exposés. The students, however, seem happy and content and describe the school as a caring community of like-minded people.

The showpiece of the campus is the **Bob Jones University Museum & Gallery,** a collection of more than 400 religious paintings from the 13th to 19th centuries. Rembrandt, Rubens, Titian and Van Dyck are represented, as well as a healthy cross section of the development of Western art. Bob Jones Jr (the son of the original BJ) began collecting these pieces at the end of WWII when Europe needed cash more than art. When asked why he chose to collect religious art, he responded 'being a fundamentalist was no excuse for unpolished shoes.' In other words, the museum is an educational and cultural tool for the school and the community. Pick up the brochure 'On Looking at Old Master Paintings' for this and other well-tailored responses to the obvious paradoxes of this phenomenal collection. Admission is $5/4/3 adults/seniors/students, free admittance for children. The museum is open Tuesday to Sunday, 2 to 5 pm. The university (☎ 864-242-5100) is at 1500 Wade Hampton Blvd (Hwy 29).

Roper Mountain Science Center

If you've ever wasted a beautiful afternoon watching nature or science TV shows, this place is for you. The center (☎ 864-281-1188), 402 Roper Mountain Rd, exit 37 off I-385, covers almost every aspect of science, from the animal and plant world to stars and space – and it is truly hands-on learning. You can view the surface of the sun through one of the largest telescopes in the country or stargaze in the state's largest planetarium. The living farm raises cotton, hand gins it and turns it into cloth. Depending on the season, the costumed docents will put you to work. There are also animals to be petted, shells to be admired and a rain forest to be explored. Run by the Greenville school district, the center is open to the public the second Saturday of each month; admission is $4/2 adults/students and seniors. The planetarium is open on Friday nights.

Activities

Mountains, lakes and rivers are just beyond the horizon from Greenville and can be attacked on foot, canoe, kayak or raft. Talk to the friendly folks at Sunrift Adventures (☎ 864-834-3019), 1 Center St (Hwy 276) in the burg of Travelers Rest, about 10 miles north of Greenville, about rental equipment, organized hikes and kayak clinics. Web site: www.sunrift.com

There is no shortage of golf courses in the area. For descriptions and contact information for golf courses, obtain a copy of 'Upcountry South Carolina Visitors Guide' from the visitors center.

Places to Stay

Surprisingly, Greenville doesn't have a diverse selection of lodging options in the downtown proper. There are, however, an endless supply of franchise (chain) hotels and motels along the major highways and interstates.

Paris Mountain State Park (☎ 864-244-5565), on State Park Rd, has campsites ($12) and hiking trails. It's 6 miles north of Greenville on Hwy 253.

On Wade Hampton Blvd (Hwy 29), just a stone's throw from downtown, are *Super 8* (☎ 864-232-6416), which charges $35/40 single/double, and the nicer *Travelodge Suites* (☎ 800-578-7878, 864-233-5393, 755 Wade Hampton Blvd), which charges $40/50.

An interesting option is *Phoenix-Greenville Inn* (☎ 800-257-3529, 864-233-4651, 246 N Pleasantburg Dr), a stylishly resurrected motor lodge. Rates range from $85 to $150.

Pettigru Place (☎ 864-242-4529, fax 864-242-1231, 302 Pettigru St) is one of the city's few B&Bs. Housed in a 1920s Federal-style building, this charming B&B has six rooms decorated in different themes; all have private bath and telephones, some have fireplaces. Internet access is also available. Near the downtown attractions, it also caters to business travelers. Rates range from $125 to $185.

The modern *Hyatt Regency* (☎ 864-235-1234, 220 N Main St) charges $150/100 weekday/weekend for a standard double; suites and specialty rooms are also available. There's an outdoor pool.

Once billed as one of the finest hotels in the South, the *Poinsett Hotel* (☎ 864-421-9700, 120 S Main St) was built in 1925 to cater to socialites en route to Miami. The town had never seen anything so grand, and country farmers would stare in disbelief at the marble stairs, crystal chandeliers, vaulted ceilings and ornate ballroom. The coins given as change in the hotel were washed so as to sparkle like jewels. Eventually, the hotel fell into decline and was closed in 1986. A recent two-year, $20 million restoration effort brought the hotel into the Internet age with hopes of reclaiming past glory and most of its original architectural detail intact. Many of the former employees were rehired, but word is that Jesse Jackson, who worked as a bellhop in the '50s, won't be submitting an application. A suite or guest room will vary between $130 to $260. If you can't afford to stay at the hotel, stop by for afternoon tea and the hotel's famous spoonbread (a custard-like version of cornbread).

Places to Eat

A veritable world eating tour can be undertaken in just a few days, but, alas, Sunday is the day of rest, and many downtown restaurants abide by it.

Homemade soups and salads ($5 to $7), hot sandwiches ($6) and loads of desserts feed the masses at *Cottage Cuisine (☎ 864-370-9070, 615 S Main St),* in the historic Falls Cottage, next to Reedy River Falls Park. It's open for lunch weekdays.

McBee's Diner (1005 Buncombe) serves a hearty dose of country cooking ($5 to $7). Fried chicken, macaroni and cheese, sweet potato soufflé, collards and sweet tea will chase away homesickness even if you've never had a country meal before. It's open weekdays 7 am to 3 pm and closed Saturday and Sunday.

Where does the java-drinking counterculturist go in Greenville? Why *Coffee Underground (☎ 864-298-0494, 225 N Main St),* of course. This full-service coffee bar also serves sandwiches and salads (around $5; veggie options available).

Vegetarians will find a much-needed oasis at *Garner's Natural Market & Café (60 E Antrim Dr),* near McAllister Square shopping center on S Pleasantburg Rd.

Soby's New South Cuisine (☎ 864-232-7007, 207 S Main St), across from the Westin Poinsett Hotel, is the place to see and be seen. With a martini in hand and a golf engagement for the weekend, you can enjoy the restaurant's famed fried green tomato appetizer ($7) and New Orleans–style barbecued shrimp entrée ($16 to $18).

Addy's Dutch Café (☎ 864-232-2339, 17 E Coffee St) is a cozy dining space serving Dutch-style meat and potatoes as well as specialty Indonesian and German dishes ($20). There is live jazz on Tuesday nights. It's open daily for dinner.

Surprisingly good sushi and surprisingly affordable prices are the specialities at *Irashiai Sushi Pub & Japanese Restaurant (☎ 864-244-2008, 23 Rushmore Dr).* Call for directions.

Where can you milk the company credit card in Greenville? In a restored mansion, *Seven Oaks (☎ 864-232-1895, 104 Broadus Ave)* specializes in French-Asian fusion such as Asian grilled shrimp ($28) and trout foie gras ($30). Sip a mint julep on the verandah before dinner commences.

Looking for something more exotic? *Yagoto (☎ 864-288-8471, 500 Congaree Rd)* serves Japanese food in a traditional 14th-century-style house (allegedly built without nails). The big draw is the *kaiseki,* a ritualized series of small courses considered Japan's haute cuisine ($30 to $40 per person). The Nippon Cultural Center (☎ 864-288-8471) is also housed here, and visitors can take part in traditional tea ceremonies ($5). The restaurant is open Monday to Saturday, 6 to 9:30 pm, and happy hour is 5 to 8:30 pm; call for directions.

Entertainment

The free weekly *Creative Loafing* is a good information source for music and cultural events.

South Carolinians used to go to New York for theater, but now they go to Greenville. *Peace Center for the Performing Arts (☎ 800-888-7768, 864-467-3000, 300 S Main St)* hosts opera, classical music, national comics and international dance groups. *Little Theater (☎ 864-233-6238, 444 College St)* is inside the Theater on the Green and is the Upcountry's oldest and largest amateur company.

The biggest sports and entertainment venue in South Carolina is the *Bi-Lo Center (☎ 864-467-0008, 650 N Academy St).*

Ever find that some theater groups are just too serious? For a lighthearted approach, catch a show at *Café & Then Some (☎ 864-232-2287, 101 College St).* Previous productions have included the Christmas play 'Away in the Trailer,' which poked fun at the double-wide lifestyle ('Rednecks boasting as they open fire, Cheap rum ripping at my nose…').

With 43 brews on tap, *Barley's Taproom (☎ 864-232-3706, 23 W Washington St)* attracts a diverse crowd, from the good ol' boys who forsake Bud for Newcastle to

Phish-head college students. Order a draft card ($10) and sample 10 beers to find out what grandpa really meant by war wounds. Open daily, it also serves gourmet pizzas ($10 for a medium).

Occasionally Blues (☎ 864-242-6000, 1 Augusta Rd) hosts live blues, zydeco and Cajun music. The night owls go to *The Castle* (☎ 864-235-9949, 8 Le Grande Blvd), off of S Pleasantburg just south of McAllister Square shopping center, for techno and dance music. It's also a rare gay-friendly club in this conservative town.

Getting There & Away

Greenville/Spartanburg International Airport (☎ 864-877-7426) is midway between the two namesake cities, just off I-85 at exit 57. Fares to East Coast destinations and Chicago are $250; West Coast, $400; and London, $550.

Greyhound Bus Lines (☎ 864-235-4741), 100 W McBee Ave, goes to Asheville ($30; 1½ hours), Charlotte ($40; 2 hours), Atlanta and Columbia ($45; 3 hours), among others.

The Amtrak train station (☎ 864-255-4221) is at 120 W Washington St and is served by the *Crescent* en route to Atlanta ($40; 2½ hours) and Charlotte ($40; 2 hours).

Take I-85 to Greenville from points east and west. From Columbia, take I-26 to I-385. From Asheville or other points south, take Hwy 25 for a more leisurely drive.

AROUND GREENVILLE
BMW Zentrum

Every city in South Carolina put on its finery to woo BMW when the German-based company started looking for a US manufacturing base. Greenville-Spartanburg won the coveted $900 million investment and 3000 new jobs. This plant makes Z3 roadsters. A museum and visitors center are open to the public and could be described as BMW's version of a Hollywood fashion show. On display is the Z3 roadster driven by James Bond, the modish bubble car (the first car powered by a motorcycle engine) and classic motorcycles. The virtual factory tour, a three-screen music video, makes working on the assembly line look as glamorous as being a rock star. The museum (free admission) is open Tuesday to Saturday, and factory tours ($5) are through advance reservation (☎ 888-868-7269). To get to the museum, take I-85 S to exit 60 and follow the signs.

Spartanburg

Some day Spartanburg (locally pronounced 'Spah-ten-burg') will get its downtown together and give Greenville a little competition. Until then, there are only a few things worth checking out. That said, Spartanburg is home to the *Beacon Drive-In* (☎ 864-585-9387), the number one reason to come to South Carolina. The drive-in is so loved by the town that its road was renamed John B White Sr Blvd in honor of the recently deceased founder and owner. As soon as you

---

Someone to Watch Your Speed

Travelers Rest is a small town in northern Greenville County with a penchant for traffic safety. According to *Travelers Rest Monitor* (December 6, 2000), the community police made 2776 traffic stops from November 1999 to October 2000. There are, however, only 3065 residents of the town, leading the paper to surmise that nearly every resident has been stopped for a traffic violation. One would hope that this 'zero tolerance' policy would make the streets a model for the nation, but as police were cracking down on missing taillights and red-light runners, burglaries in the area increased. On one unfortunate day in July, the paper reported, three businesses were broken into on the same street while elsewhere the police conducted a speed and safety check. One must assume that the burglars obeyed all traffic rules when making their getaway.

pull into the parking lot, you are met with a carnival-like excitement. Pull around to the right side of the building for the carhop service, which is supervised by a 50-year veteran of the drive-in. Or, for the full food circus, go inside. Incantations of an edible nature fill the air – the sizzle of patties on the grill, the clamor of the kitchen staff, garbled conversations, munching, slurping and dipping. Like a snake-oil hawker, a caller at the front of the line convinces the crowd that they want to order and keep the line moving. Chili cheese-a-plenty, fried chicken, catfish sandwich and variations of such are whispered to the caller, who recites the order in a cribbed language to the cooks. The call is like a song, and the kitchen staff part of a collective machine that deep-fries, flips, wraps and serves all in one continuous motion. Come hungry and leave entertained. The drive-in is at 255 John B White Sr Blvd (formerly Reidville Rd); take Main St away from downtown, cross the railroad tracks and at the crest of the hill take a left.

I-85 NORTH TO CHARLOTTE

During the Revolutionary War, South Carolina quickly fell into the hands of the British and their loyalist army. Kings Mountain (1780) and Cowpens (1781) were two stunning victories for the patriots that marked the end of the loyalists' successes in the South. The patriot victory at Kings Mountain was one of the few that did not involve one member of the Continental Army. A visit to both these battle sites is an easy detour from I-85. The parks provide a good opportunity to stretch your legs, brush up on American history and imagine the tactical elements of Revolutionary warfare. **Cowpens National Battlefield** (☎ 864-461-2828) is 11 miles northwest of I-85 and Gaffney on Hwy 11 W. **Kings Mountain National Military Park** (☎ 864-936-7922) and the nearby state park with camping ($8/15 primitive/RV) and hiking trails are just off I-85 (exit 2) on Hwy 216.

CLEMSON
pop 12,500
This little town revolves around Clemson University like the Moon around the Earth.

The city streets are painted with orange tiger paws in honor of the school's mascot. Evening traffic starts around 3 pm when afternoon classes end; and the evening news starts at 5:30 pm once the professors, administrators and students have returned home. Needless to say, the single, yet worthwhile, attraction is the university.

Clemson University

Rolling hills of green fields and upright red-brick buildings create a spacious and bucolic campus for more than 16,000 Clemson students. Founded in 1889 by Thomas Green Clemson, the school was the first in the state to provide agricultural training. This was a much-needed resource for a state with relatively infertile land that had been badly eroded by poor farming techniques. The educational tradition continues today with a few modern adjustments, and students primarily earn degrees in engineering and agriculture. *Time* magazine was impressed by Clemson's emphasis on writing and communications and gave it a Public College of the Year award in 2000. Clemson also operates agriculture experiment stations throughout the state and has more than 17,000 acres of farms and woodlands on campus for research purposes.

But the school has earned the most bragging rights from its football team, the Clemson Tigers. The second and better half of the state's fierce football rivalry, the Tigers inspire generations of fans to paint their mailboxes orange (the school color), attend football games more religiously than church services and recite mantras such as 'Southern by birth, a Clemson Tiger fan by the grace of God.'

A good place to catch Tiger fever is at the visitors center (☎ 864-656-4789), on Hwy 93 near the intersection with College Ave. Guided walking tours can be arranged by calling the center, or you can pick up a map and have a crack at the campus yourself. Ask the center about the student-made ice cream and blue cheese.

Fort Hill In the heart of the campus is **Fort Hill** (☎ 864-656-2475), the former home of

Thomas Green Clemson. Technically Fort Hill is a plantation home, which suggests a much grander structure. The house started life as a one-room cottage for a traveling clergyman in 1803 and was acquired by the Calhoun family in 1825. The famous statesman John C Calhoun left the home to his son-in-law Thomas Green Clemson, who in turn deeded the house and the surrounding land to the formation of Clemson University. Enlargements and additions of the Upcountry-style columned porticos occurred, but the house retains its rustic, even crude, craftsmanship. The family's original furnishings are on display and give an interesting glimpse into the modest life of the backcountry elite. Fort Hill is open weekdays, 10 am to 5 pm, and admission is $3/2/1 adults/children/seniors.

Clemson Athletics Rising from the earth like an alien landing strip, Clemson Memorial Stadium is one of the largest campus stadiums in the country and can accommodate more than 80,000 screaming, orange-clad fans. Legend states that during construction, coach Frank Howard put a plug of chewing tobacco in each corner of the stadium. The talent of the team or the spit-christened stadium created an unbeatable force, and losing opponents soon nicknamed the stadium Death Valley.

Death Valley is as steeped in ritual as a Catholic Mass. Before rushing onto the field, the Tigers gather at the top of the hill in the east end zone and one by one rub 'Howard's Rock,' believed to impart good luck and athletic prowess on the field. The football gods must be pleased, because Clemson has been to a bowl game 11 of the past 14 years and has held the 'King of the ACC' title 13 times (more than any other team).

Having a healthy bank account might be the real fuel behind the team's success. IPTAY ('ip-TAY') is the athletic fundraising body; it collected $10 million in 1999. The name originated as the acronym for the slogan 'I Pay Ten a Year,' referring to the annual membership dues; inflation has changed the dollar amount to $30, but the name still works. Donations of all sizes come from alumni, Tiger supporters and even posers who need the respect that an IPTAY bumper sticker provides.

Call the ticket office (☎ 800-253-6766) for ticket information.

South Carolina Botanical Garden Not every flower in South Carolina is a magnolia. To become versed in the language of the state's rich flora, take a stroll through the botanical garden (☎ 864-656-3405). The drab winter landscape is set ablaze by the camellias, then azaleas and daffodils soon follow to announce spring, and wildflowers soak up the summer's heat. The dry landscape garden displays plants that are well-suited for drought conditions. The garden is open dawn to dusk and is free of charge. Take Hwy 76 toward Anderson and turn right at Perimeter Rd. The garden will be on your left.

Next door to the garden is the **Bob Campbell Geology Museum** and the **Discovery Center,** one of four history museums sponsored by the state tourism department. The Discovery Center will open in the spring of 2001, and the museum is open Thursday, Friday and Sunday, 1 to 3 pm, and Saturday 10 am to 5 pm; free.

Places to Stay

If visiting Clemson during football season or graduation, make reservations far in advance and expect a rate hike. *Clemson Motel* (☎ *864-654-2744, 835 Greenville Hwy/93 N)* charges $28/35 low/high season for an itty-bitty room. Higher up on the food chain is *Clemson Suites* (☎ *864-654-4605),* on Hwy 123 N and Hwy 93, which charges $35 for two beds. *Sleep Inn* (☎ *864-653-6000, fax 864-653-3790, 1303 Tiger Blvd/Hwy 123)* has quality rooms for $60 to $70. *Hampton Inn* (☎ *864-653-7744, 651 Tiger Blvd/Hwy 123)* charges about the same.

Places to Eat

Big appetites get friendly with the steak and seafood dishes at *Pixie & Bill's* (☎ *864-654-1210, 1058 Tiger Blvd/Hwy 123),* next to the Baskin Robbins. The dinner menu features Greek and American dishes (spanakopita

$7, green peppercorn strip steak $20). Go for a lighter lunch of a salad (with chicken, apple and smoked gouda, $7) or a black and bleu burger (with blue cheese, $6). Lunch is served weekdays 11:30 am to 1:30 pm, and dinner is offered Monday to Saturday, 5:30 to 9:30 pm.

Entertainment
In a converted gas station, *The Esso Club,* just across campus on Old Greenville Hwy, has been the tailgate bar for generations of solid orange fans; it also has live music and once hosted an annual spittooning contest (which has now moved to a larger venue).

Getting There & Away
The *Crescent* train stops in Clemson at the Amtrak station (☎ 864-653-3410), on Hwys 123 and 133, en route to Greenville ($12; 30 minutes). By car, take Hwy 123 from Greenville to Clemson. From I-85, exit at Hwy 76.

PENDLETON & AROUND
Curvy country roads lead to the picturesque town of Pendleton, once a mountain retreat for wealthy Charlestonians and a new opportunity for Scotch-Irish farmers from Northern colonies. The town square is the focal point for Sunday strolling and gossiping. Plenty of lunch spots and antique shops keep hard-earned cash in healthy circulation, and churches outnumber doctors' offices (11 to 4). A little town like this could easily entice folks away from the fast-paced life of a city, or at least soothe their nerves after hours of travel on I-85. On a low hill adjacent to the square is **Hunter's Mercantile & Warehouse,** the remnants of a famous 1800s all-in-one store. From the porch of the two-story clapboard warehouse, you can sneak a view of the gentle blue slopes of the Blue Ridge Mountains. Visit the Pendleton Historic District (☎ 864-646-3782), 125 E Queen St, in Hunter's Mercantile, to find out about touring the town's historic homes and mansions or obtaining a self-guided walking tour map.

The **Farmers Society Hall,** on the village green, is the oldest such hall in continuous use in the country. In the second-floor meeting room, Thomas Green Clemson started talking about the formation of an agricultural school to train young farmers; the school would later bear his name and dominate the state in college football. Grab a cup of tea or light lunch in the first-floor *restaurant* and think about all the things farmers must talk about.

Liberty Hall Inn (☎ 800-643-7944, 612 S Mechanic St) provides a lovely respite for business or interstate travelers. Decorated with farmhouse-style crafts, the rooms are spacious and run $70/130 in the low/high season. The large Lowcountry-style verandah and surrounding gardens lend themselves to wasting time with a trashy romance novel or just waving to passing cars.

Imagine this: a crowded greasy spoon, a beer-soaked hot dog covered with chili, an 8-oz glass bottle of Coke and a bill that comes to a whopping $2. This could be your reality, if you take exit 19A off I-85 to *Skins Hotdogs* (in the Marketplace Shopping Center, behind the Red Lobster on Hwy 28/76). A sign on the wall states 'The language you use in church is good enough for here.'

A 20-minute drive from I-85, **Split Creek Farm** (☎ 864-287-3921) is a working goat dairy that produces award-winning cheeses and fudge. With a little advanced warning, large groups can get a tour of the farm; late spring is a good time to see the kid nursery. Tours cost $2 per person with a $10 minimum; walk-ins are also welcome to visit the on-site store. From I-85, take exit 14 and turn right onto Hwy 187 (Wild Hog Rd). At the Texaco station just before the Clemson Research Park, take a right onto Centerville Rd. The farm is 1/4 mile down on the left.

NINETY SIX NATIONAL HISTORIC SITE
The first foothold that European settlers acquired in Cherokee Country was Ninety Six, a convenient resting point along the Cherokee Path. Soon Ninety Six emerged as a major trading post, and as many as 90

wagons a day came to barter away goods such as blankets and guns for animal hides. By the 1750s, relations between the Cherokees and the white settlers had turned violent, and the trading post became a fort to protect against Indian attacks. Before the Revolutionary War, Ninety Six became one of the first courthouse districts in the backcountry and served the western portion of the state.

How did Ninety Six get a number as a name? According to the unadorned version of the story, the outpost was roughly 96 miles from the Cherokee capital of Keowee. Romantics, however, added the legend of a Cherokee woman riding across 96 creeks and streams to warn her white lover of an Indian attack.

This crossroads community would see more war as the colony prepared for its impending split from England. Loyalists, under Lt Colonel John Cruger's command, built a star-shaped fort at Ninety Six because of its strategic location between Charleston on the coast, Augusta, Georgia, to the west, and Cherokee Country to the north. General Nathaniel Greene of the Continental Army attempted to oust the loyalists from the fort on May 21, 1781. Starting 200 yards away, patriot forces dug a series of parallel ditches so that the army could advance to the fort with a degree of protection from cannon and musket fire. This was a textbook formula for formal European warfare. Once they were within firing range of the fort (close to a month later), an attack was launched, most of it hand-to-hand combat. The siege attempt was unsuccessful, and Greene's army was repulsed two days later. The loyalists later abandoned the fort in July as the British were weakened elsewhere.

The parallel trenches have been restored, and descriptive markers give a clear image of the advancement of Greene's army. The site (☎ 864-543-4068) is on Hwy 248, 2 miles south of the town of Ninety Six.

THE BLUE RIDGE MOUNTAINS

The Blue Ridge Mountains drape across 600 sq miles of the state, through the northern portions of Oconee, Pickens and Greenville Counties. Technically only foothills, the peaks loom over the Piedmont with seemingly awesome proportion – from 1400 to 3500 feet – a compact range for a compact state. The Chattooga, Saluda, Eastatoe and Toxaway, among other rivers, ride this range from the summit to the base, creating waterfalls, shootable rapids and popular hangouts for tasty fish. Oaks, gums, hickories and other deciduous trees clothe the mountains in spectacular fall color. Rhododendrons and mountain laurel as big as trees line the switchback roads and crooked creek beds with spring blossoms.

While South Carolina doesn't have the rugged peaks of its neighboring states, there are plenty of places to get drunk off the scenery, and the state parks that line the North-South Carolina border keep most of the region wild and remote, free from neon and golf courses.

Highway 11: Cherokee Foothills Scenic Drive

More functional than scenic, the Cherokee Foothills Scenic Dr (Hwy 11) connects six state parks, a national forest and a handful of county parks along the South-North Carolina border. The route is also an interesting east-west alternative to I-85. Stretching from Hartwell Lake near the Georgia-South Carolina border to Gaffney and I-85, this 130-mile road shoots along the base of the pine-clad foothills and was once used by English traders visiting Cherokee country. The eastern portion has a higher concentration of mountains, and the entire stretch is haphazardly decorated by gas stations with folksy names and unadorned trailers. If you're looking for crooked-as-a-politician mountain roads, take any of the connecting highways to get lost for a spell.

Most visitors to the area stay in the cabins or campgrounds of the state parks, so hotels and B&Bs are not abundant. ***Rocky Bottom Camp of the Blind*** (☎ 864-878-9090, 123 Hancock Rd, Sunset, nfbsc@logicsouth.com), a retreat center for members of the National Blind Federation, also rents lodge space to individuals and groups for rates ranging from $45 to $150. The camp is tucked back in the woods on Hwy 178 at the base of Sassafras Mt. On Hwy 11, across from Table Rock State Park, is the **Schell Haus** (☎ *864-878-0078, fax 864-878-0066*). Schell Haus has antique-decorated rooms and a full view of Table Rock Mt, and charges $85 to $165. Rates increase slightly in October and November. Between Table Rock and Caesars Head is **A Nice Little Motel** (☎ *864-878-9949*), on Hwy 11. The name fits and so do the prices ($45 to $55). Near Caesars Head State Park, **The Log Cabins on Foxfire Mountain** (☎ *864-836-6712*), on Hwy 276 just north of the state park visitors center, cater to daytime outdoor enthusiasts who are nighttime indoor enthusiasts.

There are so few restaurants along Hwy 11 that you certainly won't get fat, and if traveling on a Wednesday or Sunday, you'll be lucky to find anything open at all. The gas stations usually have lunch counters that serve barbecue and short-order items. **Table Rock State Park Lodge** (☎ 864-878-9065) is the most permanent full-fledged restaurant in the area. The food is ordinary American fare (fried chicken or fish and hamburgers), and some items are served family style. In the park proper, the lodge was built by the Civilian Conservation Corps (CCC) in the 1930s and has its very own resident ghost; don't worry, she's much too busy teasing the wait- and kitchen staff to bother the customers. The lodge is open Tuesday to Saturday, but hours vary according to season. **Mountain House**, on Caesars Head just before the state park visitors center, is open May to November. **Gourmet Peaks & Perks** (☎ 864-836-0021) is a catering company that prepares meals and picnics ($25 per person) for local delivery. The nearby towns of Walhalla and Pickens also have a few options (see below).

Sumter National Forest – Andrew Pickens District

Filling the northwestern corner of the state, the third district of the Sumter National Forest protects a wild and remote country. The free-flowing Chattooga and

SOUTH CAROLINA

Scenic Drive – From I-85 to the Mountains

Just west of Anderson on I-85 is the northern stretch of Hwy 24. The drive passes through beautiful, sloping farmland and offers brief glimpses of the Blue Ridge Mountains in the distance. North of Westminster, Hwy 24 becomes Hwy 76, the apple orchard route. In early spring, the delicate pink and white apple blossoms burst from the previously naked branches, and the earth smells new and fresh. Picking time comes in the fall, and makeshift roadside stands sell apples, cider and apple butter. Westminster hosts the annual Apple Festival during the Labor Day weekend. You are now in the very thin sliver of the state's mountainous region, once called the Lost Corner. Continue following the switchback road to the North Carolina border, and pull over at the small parking lot next to the bridge. Below you is the **Chattooga River**, one of the best white-water rivers in the Southeast.

Cross back into South Carolina and take Hwy 76 to Chattooga Ridge Rd (follow the signs for Oconee State Park). The road dips and crests past small mountain homes and trailers, eventually leading to a ridge that overlooks the North Carolina mountains. Take a right onto Hwy 28. At the first stop sign, you are now in Mountain Rest, which hosts the annual Hillbilly Festival on July 4. Follow Hwy 28 south and you'll pass Hillbilly's Country Store, where local musicians and curious onlookers come for Saturday night bluegrass jams. Farther down the road, Hwy 28 intersects with Hwy 107, and a left turn will lead to **Oconee State Park**, a good base for mountain hikes. As you come down off the mountain, keep your eyes peeled for the sign for **Stumphouse Tunnel & Issaqueena Falls** on your left. After a full day of mountain driving, head into **Walhalla** for some grub.

Chauga Rivers dip and pool through a slowly eroding landscape of house-sized boulders and leafy, flood-weary trees. Old Indian trails that crisscross mountain peaks and plateaus have been transformed into popular hiking paths. The rivulets and streams that feed larger waterways teem with swiftly moving bass and trout. Pick your activity – rafting, canoeing, fishing, hiking, horseback riding – and plunge headlong into the forest. Please be advised that the trails and rivers require proper preparations and precautions; be able to spot and avoid the poisonous copperhead and timber rattlesnake.

Camping is allowed at least 50 feet from the trail and waterways. Contact the district office for information on more developed sites. The office (☎ 864-638-9568) is 6 miles north of Walhalla on Hwy 28 and has maps, trailhead directions and other helpful information. Visit its Web site (www.fs.fed.us/r9/fms) for additional help.

Chattooga River

More stringent protective status is given to specially designated areas throughout the forest. The Chattooga River's designation as a National Wild and Scenic River prevents motorized vehicles from coming within 1/4 mile of its banks. The river trail roughly follows the path of the river and connects with the Chattahoochee National Forest in Georgia and the Nantahala National Forest in North Carolina.

The Chattooga River is the largest free-flowing mountain river in the Southeast and has some of the best white water in the country. The river is divided into five sections designating specific uses and activities. Sections III and IV can be used for rafting and hiking. See the North Georgia chapter for more information.

Foothills National Recreation Trail

This 80-mile trail follows the ridges of the Blue Ridge Escarpment from Oconee State Park to Table Rock State Park and connects to trails leading to Caesars Head and Jones Gap State Parks. A rugged and strenuous route, the trail hits all the region's highlights: Chattooga River, Whitewater Falls, Jocassee Gorge, Sassafras Mt and Table Rock State Park. Interested in undertaking the entire trail? Write to the Foothills Trail Conference (PO Box 3041, Greenville, SC 29602) for guidebook information. Like short hikes with lots of scenery? Starting at one of the six vehicle access points can make a nice day hike.

Oconee State Park

A popular access point for the Foothills Trail or a base camp for trips down the Chattooga, Oconee State Park (☎ 864-638-5353) sits atop a plateau near the small town of Mountain Rest. One of South Carolina's first state parks, Oconee was built by the CCC and still boasts the corps' legendary craftsmanship. Rustic cabins (sleeping 6, $180/360 weekend/weekly) and campsites with electrical hookup ($15) are available; the park also has a small swimming and fishing lake. The park staff are helpful and can provide loads of area-specific brochures. To get to the park from Hwy 11, take Hwy 28 to Hwy 107.

Stumphouse Tunnel & Issaqueena Falls

It must have taken one smooth talker to pitch the idea that a railroad tunnel could be dug through the Blue Ridge Mountains from South Carolina to Tennessee in an attempt to link the Mississippi River with the Atlantic Ocean. Stumphouse Mt proved to be a significant granite barrier, and in 1853 workers started blasting, digging and drilling their way to nowhere. Only 1600 feet of the planned 5900 feet were completed before funds dried up in 1859, and the Civil War put an end to hopes of reviving the project. The tunnel has been sealed, but a visit to the site is good for a laugh and a quick peek at the nearby Issaqueena Falls on Oconee Creek. The falls were named after a Creek Indian woman who was being pursued by an angered party of fellow tribe members. She eluded capture by making it look like she had fallen off the edge of the falls – a 200-foot drop; but in fact, she was hiding on a nearby ledge. The tunnel and falls are 6 miles northwest of Walhalla on Hwy 28.

Walhalla

Stop for a spell in the cute town of Walhalla. Founded in 1850 as a German settlement, Walhalla was named after the mythological Norse heaven, Valhalla. The town celebrates its German heritage with an annual Oktoberfest on the third weekend of October.

Walhalla Motel (☎ 864-638-2585, 901 E Main St) is one of the few places for non-camping lodging. The rooms are small and basic ($30).

According to Norse legend, slain warriors brought to Valhalla for their valiance in battle were nursed back to health with mead and roast beef. You won't find any heavenly roast beef, but you will find fried chicken at *Steak House Cafeteria (316 E Main St)* and Central American food at *Rio Grande (604 Main St)*.

Whitewater Falls & Other Falls

Straddling the North/South Carolina border, Whitewater Falls is one of the highest cascades in the Eastern US. At a combined height of 800 feet, the waterfall is actually two consecutive falls of equal height. The falls viewing area is just across the state border on Hwy 130, a fairly steep drive past huge stands of rhododendrons. The map 'Finding the Falls' provides the location of 25 waterfalls in the upstate; to order send $2 to SC Wildlife/Marine Resources Dept, PO Box 167, Columbia, SC 29202.

Lakes Keowee & Jocassee

Lake Keowee and Lake Jocassee were both created by Duke Power's hydroelectric dams in the 1970s and have now become playgrounds for boaters and anglers. At 18,500 acres, Lake Keowee ('key-o-wee') covered Keowee, the Lower Cherokee's capital city. Longer than its sister lake and more developed, with several private resort communities, Lake Keowee isn't as attractive or accessible for the average visitor. *Keowee-Toxaway State Park (☎ 864-868-2605)* is half a mile from the lake and has 1000 acres of protected forests. Hiking trails lead to the lake, along pine ridges and beside creek beds. Wildflowers, including trillium and wild orchids, bloom in abundance in the spring, and wild turkeys and

foxes are reluctant local celebrities. Near the visitors center, the **Cherokee Interpretive Trail** winds through the woods to kiosks with displays on the Cherokee culture and history. The park rents rustic cabins and tent and RV sites.

Lake Keowee Marina (☎ 864-882-2047) rents pontoons and houseboats. Lake Jocassee ('**Joe**-cass-ee') filled the cliff-rimmed basin called Horsepasture, where livestock had grazed since Cherokee times. The valley had many naturally occurring caverns where animals could easily be hidden if their rightful or unrightful owners came inquiring. Now these lairs are lost under the deep waters of Lake Jocassee, which fittingly means 'Place of the Lost One.' Anglers come to the lake for prized trout fishing, and paddlers tour the lake's finger streams. Easily spotted from the lake is Jumping-off Rock, a high cliff where rejected lovers of romantic days past leaped to their deaths.

On the southern end of the lake is *Devils Fork State Park (☎ 864-944-2639)*. Surprisingly comfortable and modern villas have two or three bedrooms and screened-in porches (some with lake views). Rates start at $100/260/740 night/weekend/week. Less comfortable tent ($10) and RV ($18) sites are also available.

Hoyett's Grocery & Tackle (☎ 864-944-9016), 516 Jocassee Lake Rd, Salem, rents boats, sells bait and hot dogs and organizes

fishing and sightseeing trips. James Couch (☎ 864-944-9292) also leads fishing and boating trips and provides shuttle service to the lake access points of the Foothills Trail.

Jocassee Gorges

Swift-moving rivers carved a series of deep scars into the smooth face of the Blue Ridge Escarpment. In these gorges (collectively known as the Jocassee Gorges), an elevation change of 2000 feet can happen in a couple of miles. Mosses from as far away as Central America grow thick along riverbeds due to the abundant rainfall (more than 75 inches per year). Once harvested for timber, the forest still feels wild with large stands of hemlock, white pine and sturdy oaks. The Foothills Trail goes through the heart of the gorges, roughly between Devils Fork and Table Rock State Park, and can be accessed via Hwy 178, just after the Eastatoe Creek Bridge. The brochure 'Jocassee Gorges: A Partnership in Conservation' describes several interesting hikes and driving tours through the area and is available from the state Department of Natural Resources (☎ 864-654-1671).

Sassafras Mt

The tallest peak in South Carolina is Sassafras Mt (3548 feet). The streams borne from its peak feed the Santee, Savannah and Tennessee Rivers. To get to the trailhead parking lot from Hwy 11, take Hwy 178 to the second right, onto Van Clayton Rd.

Table Rock State Park

The most prominent and well-known peak in the state's mountain jewelry box is Table Rock. According to Cherokee legend, the Great Spirit dined at the mountain's long, flat surface while sitting upon neighboring Stool Mt. The view from the summit is so legendary that possibly more South Carolinians can claim hiking Table Rock than having Confederate ancestry. The CCC converted more than 3000 acres of surrounding mixed pine and hardwood forest into parkland in 1935, creating one of the most popular and accessible parks in the state system. Rustic cabins ($160/330 weekend/

weekly) and campsites ($15 RV space, $3 per person tent space) provide lodging, and an obligatory meal should be had at Table Rock State Park Lodge (see the Cherokee Foothills Scenic Drive section, earlier). The visitors center (☎ 864-878-9077) is across from the park entrance on Hwy 11.

If you prefer views from parking lots, head up to Table Rock reservoir. This spring-fed lake is tucked behind Table Rock and supplies the city of Greenville with drinking water. (People claim it's the best municipal water in the country.) From Hwy 11 E, take a left at Aunt Sue's Country Store on to S Saluda Rd, which will turn into Table Rock Rd. Turn left at Table Rock Rd Extension, just after the Greenville County sign.

Caesars Head & Jones Gap State Parks

Collectively, these two state parks are referred to as the Mountain Bridge Wilderness Area, but only park officials know this term. Everyone else knows Caesars Head Mt, which has been a destination for tourists since the late 1800s. At the pinnacle of the 3266-foot mountain is a rock outcrop said to resemble the profile of Julius Caesar (this is believed to be the origin of the mountain's name). If you can't piece a human profile out of the shapeless cluster of exposed rocks, another story has been conveniently circulated. A prized hunting dog named Caesar plunged to his death here while pursing his prey, and his heartbroken owner named the mountain in the dog's honor. From the profile overlook, the neighboring tree-covered mountains stand like unmoving waves imperceptibly breaking on the shore. A drop of 1400 feet below the cliff face is the Dismal – a valley of wilderness that swallows time and space. The overlook is a prime spot for sunsets.

Atop Caesars Head Mt is a strenuous 2-mile hike that leads to Raven Cliff Falls, which cascades for 420 feet. Hiking trails connect to Jones Gap State Park and the Foothills Trail.

The visitors center (864-836-6115) is on Hwy 276, 5 miles from Hwy 11, and park naturalists lead bird walks and nature hikes.

Jones Gap State Park lies in the shadow of Caesars Head within a rockbound gorge that once served as the wagon trail between Greenville and Brevard, North Carolina. Hugging the shoulder of the boulder-ridden creek, portions of the original trail still remain. Pristine forests of beech, hemlock and poplar shade the park's 3300 acres, creating a milder climate than elsewhere in the area. The Middle Saluda River, one of the state's first designated scenic rivers, draws anglers for its rainbow trout fishing. The visitors center (☎ 864-836-3647) is just off Hwy 11 on Hwy 276.

Trailside primitive camping ($2) is available in both parks but requires advanced registration with park offices.

Other Things to See

Pretty Place Chapel lives up to its name. This open-air pavilion is built on the extreme peninsula of the Cleveland ridge overlooking the South Carolina foothills and the Piedmont. On a clear day, Greenville and Spartanburg are visible just where the land begins to level out. The exposed rock face to your left is called Hospital Rock and is frequently the site of climbing rescues. Offering one of the best views around, the chapel is no secret, and hundreds of couples get married here each year. Pretty Place is north of Caesars Head on Hwy 276. Turn right at the state line and follow signs to the YMCA camp. The chapel's real name is Symmes Chapel, and it's on the camp's grounds.

Half the fun of getting to **Twin Falls** is the drive. Take Hwy 178 north of Hwy 11 and turn left at the crumbling wooden shack called Bob's Bar. This road follows the twisted course of the Eastatoe Creek for a couple of miles before straightening out at the intersection with Cleo Chapman Hwy, named in honor of the postal worker who faithfully delivered the mail along this route for 50 years. Only once did weather prevent her from making her rounds. Take a right onto Cleo Chapman, and a little farther down the road turn right onto White Falls Rd. Follow the wooden signs for the falls, and drive carefully, as the road passes too close to people's backyards for comfort. The falls are a 5-minute walk from the parking area. After your visit to the falls, if you're still in the mood for cruising, continue back the way you came on Cleo Chapman, but follow it to the end. The road snakes through farms and pastures, log cabins succumbing to gravity and sculpted mountains.

Pickens & Around

If you need supplies or a little lunch, come down out of the mountains into the small town of Pickens. While you're here, visit the **Pickens County Museum** (☎ 864-898-5963), 307 Johnson St at Hwy 178, which is housed in a castle fit for a criminal. Once used as the county jail, this early-20th-century building has castle-like turrets, a copper-colored tin roof and hand-rolled bricks. Inside, an old jail cell still remains intact; a list of infamous criminals, many of whom were moonshiners, gives an idea of the building's former life. Other thoughtful exhibits cover the Cherokee Nation and the town's early history. The museum also operates the **Hagood Mill,** a 1700s water-powered gristmill. Once the gathering place for the community, the mill is being developed as a living history museum and hosts festivals and musical events in the summer. Hagood Mill is 5 miles from Hwy 11 on Hwy 178 S.

North Carolina

North Carolina

Stretched like a giant tarpaulin along the borders of Virginia, Tennessee, Georgia and South Carolina, the wondrous state of North Carolina is pulled in many directions. Rustic mountain folk, New South workaholics and beach bums all find solace here. Its remarkable landscape – plains sandwiched between mountains and a long, bulgy shoreline – is that of the US, but in miniature.

Sweeping generalizations are out of place here. Visitors puzzle at how the climate can range from sub-Arctic (in the highlands) to sub-Saharan (on the coast), or that the politics can shift unexpectedly from New Age liberal to Stone Age fossil. One way to describe North Carolina is as a compromise between North and South, the best of both worlds right there on the Mason-Dixon line (hence the term 'half-way backs' – for Northerners who moved to Florida, wrinkled their noses and decided the Tarheels offered a better mix of climate and culture).

The urban areas of the Piedmont can seem a tad provincial until there's a major festival or cultural event, and travelers will do well to plan accordingly. Charlotte is surprisingly cosmopolitan and fast-paced, and likes to think of itself as a southern New York; it certainly has enough banks and restaurants to try. Yet North Carolinians have a huge appreciation for the arts, and this is felt in museums and performance halls across the state. The many universities add spice to life; Chapel Hill, and to a certain extent Durham, both college towns, stand out for music, sports and a dash of the alternative.

In terms of numbers, most travelers are drawn to either the mountains or the coast. The Appalachians, especially along the Blue Ridge Parkway and in the Smokies, are a treasure-trove of natural wonders and wildlife. Whether you're a tenderfoot or a seasoned outdoors type, your views and experiences here will be stored for life. Amid the peaks, the town of Asheville shines like an art-deco jewel and has a sumptuous chateau – George Vanderbilt's amazing Biltmore House.

The barrier islands of the Outer Banks offer some of the wildest, most beautiful beaches along the Atlantic Coast, with extensive nature reserves. These fragile strips of sand are worlds away from the rest of the state, and the many shipwrecks recall the region's stormy, pirate-filled past. On the mainland, New Bern, Bath and Edenton are old colonial towns, but the port of Wilmington to the south comes as a bit of a surprise: Pleasantly familiar and Southern, it's also an eastern hub of America's film industry.

Facts about North Carolina

HISTORY

In precolonial times, Iroquoian groups including Cherokees and Creeks inhabited much of the coastal plains and mountains, coexisting with Algonquians along the coast and islands. The first Europeans to visit the coast were explorers led by Giovanni da Verrazano, a Florentine sailing under a French flag, in 1524. The Spanish followed two years later and tried without success to establish a colony on the Cape Fear River. In 1540, a gold-hunting expedition led by Hernando de Soto crossed through what is now western North Carolina and went on to discover the Mississippi River.

The first European settlement was established by the English. In 1584, Sir Walter Raleigh arrived with a shipload of settlers at Roanoke Island. A second group set sail from England in 1587, this time including women, and the first English child in the New World, Virginia Dare, was born in North Carolina. But by 1590, the community had vanished, and to this day the fate of the 'Lost Colony' remains a mystery (see the Outer Banks section for more details).

Facts at a Glance

Nickname: Tarheel State
Population: 8.049 million (11th largest)
Area: 52,700 sq miles
Admitted to Union: 1789 (12th); seceded 1861; readmitted 1868.
Capital: Raleigh (pop 281,000)
Birthplace of: James Polk, John Coltrane, Thomas Wolfe, Ava Gardner, Andrew Jackson, Andrew Johnson, Michael Jordan
First Home For: ice cream cones; Pepsi-Cola; Roanoke Island, the first English colony in the New World
Famous for: NASCAR racing, civil rights sit-in, Wright Brothers' first flight, pirates
Highlights: a night on Wilmington's lively waterfront; the thunder of surf on the Outer Banks; everything about the Great Smokies; the Biltmore Estate in Asheville, America's largest home
Most Likely Overheard: Jesse Helms quotes, roaring basketball fans, barbecue twisting over the coals

NORTH CAROLINA

Kentucky

Virginia

Tennessee

Great Smoky Mountains
National Park
pages 382-383

Wiston-Salem
page 340

Greensboro
page 346

Durham
page 332

Chapel Hill
page 336

Raleigh
page 329

Asheville
page 372

Charlotte
pages 354-355

North Carolina Mountains pages 364-365

Wilmington
page 405

Outer Banks Shipwrecks
page 393

Central North Carolina
pages 326-327

South
Carolina

North Carolina Coast
pages 386-387

Georgia

ATLANTIC
OCEAN

0   50   100 km
0   30   60 miles

OTHER MAPS
North Carolina pages 320-321

The first enduring English settlements were in the mid-17th century in the Albermarle region. The settlers called their new home 'Carolina' (from the Latin *Carolus,* or Charles, for the English monarch). Initial problems, however, led to the formation of separate colonial charters for North and South Carolina in 1712. In the Tuscarora Wars (1711–13), the colonists defeated and displaced the Indians in a series of battles, making room for more European colonists. Inland settlement was mostly by Scots, Irish and Germans migrating from northern colonies on the Great Wagon Road. An early industry was the extraction of 'naval stores' like tar, pitch and turpentine from coastal forests, followed by cultivation of tobacco and cotton.

The town of Edenton, on the Albermarle Sound, was one of the first places to protest British taxes on tea and was at the forefront of the American independence movement. Pro-British troops suffered an early defeat at Moore's Creek Bridge, near Wilmington, in 1776, which secured North Carolina and much of the South for the revolutionaries. Though well represented in the constitutional conventions, North Carolina lan-

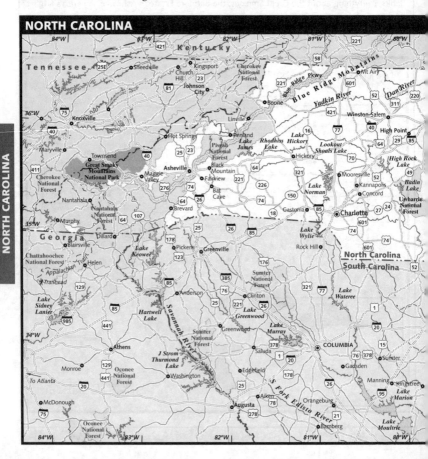

NORTH CAROLINA

guished as an agrarian backwater in the early years of the republic, earning the nickname Rip Van Winkle State (this was later changed; see 'Tarheels' boxed text). Most activity was on small farms that focused on labor-intensive tobacco, rice, cotton and indigo. Slavery was less common in North Carolina than elsewhere in the South, but slaves still made up about a third of the population in 1790.

In 1835, the federal government ordered 15,000 Cherokees to leave their homes in the Appalachians and march toward a new reservation in Oklahoma. Thousands per-

ished on what came to be called the 'Trail of Tears.' Those refugees who managed to escape hid in the mountains and formed the core of today's Eastern Cherokee.

The North Carolinians were divided on slavery, between the plantation society of the coast and the small landholders and workers of the Piedmont, and the state seceded reluctantly in 1861. During the Civil War, the Outer Banks and most ports fell early on, but Wilmington remained in Confederate hands, sustained by blockade-running supply ships. Fierce battles were fought at Fort Fisher, and other notable clashes included Fort Hatteras

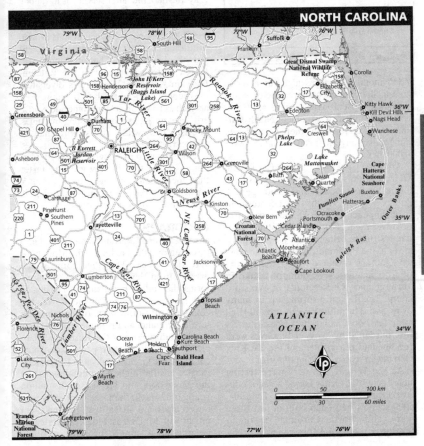

Tarheels

In the 19th century, North Carolina was a big producer of pitch, tar and turpentine, meeting almost two-thirds of the colonies' needs. The sticky pine extracts gummed up the workers' shoes, which at some point usually stuck fast to the ground.

Legend has it that during one of the fiercest battles of the Civil War, North Carolina's troops held their ground while a regiment from Virginia fled. Jefferson Davis, the Confederate president, was rumoured to be buying tar to brush on the heels of fightin' boys throughout the South.

Hearing of the incident, General Robert E Lee remarked: 'God bless the Tarheel boys.' The nickname stuck.

and Plymouth. During his infamous march to the sea, Sherman encountered the only real resistance at Bentonville, where 4,000 soldiers were killed or wounded. North Carolina ended up providing more Confederate soldiers than any other state – and lost over 40,000 men.

After the Civil War, a North Carolinian, Andrew Johnson, served as president during much of the Reconstruction period. Until recently he was the only US president to be impeached. The Democratic party took over the legislature as the state began to industrialize, bringing new jobs and prosperity to the Piedmont. The era of the powerful factory owner dawned, led by the tobacco magnates Washington Duke in Durham and RJ Reynolds in Winston-Salem. Textile mills sprung up in many towns, as did furniture makers around High Point. The boom had its dark sides: Farmers were burdened by heavy debt; slaves were free but had few rights; and the Ku Klux Klan began its covert reign of terror.

As the Wright Brothers were testing their first craft at Kitty Hawk, a major educational reform got underway. By 1904, 1,000 schools had been built in just three years, and North Carolina began to develop a reputation for academic excel-

lence that still prevails at higher institutions today, such as Duke, the University of North Carolina and NC State. Still, segregation persisted in the schools and universities long after it was officially abolished. In 1960, black students in Greensboro staged the first sit-in at a local Woolworth's, launching similar peaceful protests across the country. The resulting integration was largely peaceful but would not be completed until the 1970s.

WWII brought some new industries and large military bases, including Camp LeJeune (Jacksonville) and sprawling Fort Bragg (Fayetteville), the latter serving as a training hub for Operation Desert Storm. Agriculture remains key, although tobacco is becoming less so (mentioning class-action suits around Winston-Salem isn't a good idea). The recent growth of finance in Charlotte and of research and development in the Raleigh-Durham Research Triangle has diversified the economy; bio- and high-tech multinationals such as IBM, Glaxo-Wellcome and Northern Telecom act as job-generating machines. Tourism, meanwhile, draws more than 42 million visitors every year.

Once plagued by emigration, North Carolina's population is now growing faster than the national average, but this state is far from rich: Poverty remains a problem in many rural and mountain areas.

GEOGRAPHY

North Carolina can roughly be divided into three regions: the Piedmont, the Mountains and the Coast. The Piedmont, which extends from New York State to Alabama, forms the rolling heartland and is dotted with lakes, forests and golf courses. It's the country's fifth-most-populous region, has fertile farmland, and is home to the state's largest industries and the Research Triangle. The worn-looking Appalachians, which comprise the Great Smoky and Blue Ridge ranges, are the highest mountains east of the Mississippi and are some 500 million years old. Back then the Appalachians towered around 40,000 feet, putting them on par with Mt Everest today. Dark, steamy swamps lie a stone's throw from lonely beaches off the sandy coastal plain, and the necklace of islands called the Outer Banks is forever shimmering in the breezes.

No other state east of the Mississippi covers a greater breadth (560 miles), and none has more paved roads (78,000 miles).

NATIONAL PARKS & PROTECTED AREAS

The most interesting protected areas are at opposite ends of the state: the Great Smoky Mountains National Park, of course, and the national seashores of Cape Lookout and Cape Hatteras. The Blue Ridge Parkway is managed by the national park service, too. National forests are in abundance, the main ones being pretty Pisgah (with the Blue Ridge Parkway running right through it), Uwharrie in the Piedmont, and Croatan in the boggy Albemarle region. There are 34 state parks, which draw 12 million visitors a year; for something a bit off the beaten track, try Pilot's Mountain or Hanging Rock between Winston-Salem and the Virginia border.

For a useful companion in the wild, pick up *North Carolina Hiking Trails* by Allan Hart, which covers the state from the Smokies to the Outer Banks.

The *North Carolina Atlas,* edited by Douglas Orr and Alfred Stuart, gives a good general overview of history, culture, demographics and so on.

GOVERNMENT & POLITICS

As in most Southern states, North Carolina's political landscape was ruled by conservative Democrats after the Civil War. In 1972, as Republican president Richard Nixon was being grilled for Watergate, voters gulped and elected the Republican Jesse Helms to the Senate, a prickly journalist with a daily radio show from Raleigh. Now in his eighth term, the head of the Senate Foreign Relations Committee is still firing off memorable salvos ('Democracy is a good thing, but now it's gotten into the wrong hands' – a mild example). Liberal North Carolinians tend to smirk rather than steam in reaction.

Democrat Jim Hunt's tenure (1984–2000) made him the longest-serving governor

since colonial times. In the 2000 gubernatorial election, the socially moderate, pro-business Democrat Mike Easley narrowly defeated Richard Vinroot, a Republican former mayor of Charlotte. It was neck-and-neck in the weeks before the ballot – that is, until popular actor Andy Griffith came out for Easley in a campaign ad. Supporters dubbed it the 'Mayberry Miracle' and celebrated with 16 cases of Biltmore Estate wine and 900 dozen Krispy Kreme donuts at the inaugural party. North Carolina's first-ever female lieutenant governor, Democrat Beverly Perdue, took office at the same time.

ARTS

North Carolina has had an active community of artists ever since George Vanderbilt imported hundreds of European artists to work on his Asheville estate. Many visitors come just to see a sampling of the 200 arts-related festivals held annually. The classical music and performing arts scenes are good, but what really sets the state apart are its handmade crafts and contemporary music.

The Penland School of Crafts is the largest crafts school in the country, and the Appalachians are peppered with the cabin studios of fine artisans. A good way to learn about them is in the *Craft Heritage Trails of Western North Carolina,* by Asheville-based arts group HandMade in America (☎ 828-252-0121).

As for music, bluegrass pickers such as Doc Watson or Pat Donohue have an international following. Chapel Hill has produced some good pop and alternative bands in recent years, including Ben Folds Five (which folded in 2000) and the wonderfully named Squirrel Nut Zippers. Jazz greats born here have tended to move elsewhere, just as John Coltrane and Thelonius Monk did.

North Carolina's literary legacy, though not as rich as Georgia's, is still considerable. Thomas Wolfe (1900–38) shared scenes of his Asheville home in *Look Homeward, Angel* and *You Can't Go Home Again,* which are regarded as modern classics. William Sydney Porter (1863–1910), better known as O Henry, produced some of the most masterful short stories ever written.

Among the living, North Carolina Writers' Network numbers 1800 members, the largest statewide organization of writers in the country. Leading lights include Charles Frazier, whose best-selling Civil War epic *Cold Mountain* won the National Book Award for fiction in 1997. Fred Chappell, on the staff of UNC-Greensboro, is known for his folksy fiction and poetry. Jerry Bledsoe writes humorous nonfiction and true crime tales set in North Carolina. Other notable figures to look out for are Paul Green, Charles Chesnutt, James Boyd and Inglis Fletcher.

INFORMATION

The North Carolina Division of Tourism (☎ 800-847-4862, 919-733-4147), 301 N Wilmington St, Raleigh, NC 27601, sends out good maps and information. For highway information, call ☎ 919-549-5100. The state's Web site (www.visitnc.com) covers attractions, accommodations, maps and oodles of facts and figures. The North Carolina department of commerce has a good private Web site (www.nccommerce .com). For North Carolina tourist offices abroad, see the Facts for the Visitor chapter.

Welcome centers are located on all major highways and interstates and offer rest rooms, tourism info, snacks and brochures.

Sales Tax & Other Laws

The state sales tax is 6%, with the exception of Mecklenburg County, where it's 6.5%. Where it applies, the local tax on accommodations is generally 3% to 6%.

Alcohol laws are similar to elsewhere in the Southeast, with one big exception – any establishment that makes more than half its revenue from alcohol must call itself a 'private club,' charge membership fees and enforce a three-day wait before that membership takes effect. For tourists, the usual way around this inconvenience is to hang around outside and kindly ask an approaching member to invite you as a 'guest.' You'll pay the guest fee, which is usually cheaper than membership, and

everyone's happy. Clubs in some towns waive the three-day grace period.

Special Events

January

Edge of the World Snowboard Series – Boone, January 7; board geeks from around the globe descend on an area resort, usually Sugar Mountain or Hawksnest, to strut their stuff.

April

The North Carolina Azalea Festival – Wilmington; on the first or second weekend in April, homes and gardens are thrown open to the public.

June

American Dance Festival – Durham, through July; perhaps the best modern dance event in the country.

Brevard Music Festival – Brevard, through August; the finest in classical music.

July

Appalachian Summer Festival – Boone, throughout the month; Doc Watson, Newport Jazz Festival All-Stars and Willie Nelson are but a few of the past guests.

Grandfather Mountain Highland Games – second weekend in July; Pole-throwing, kilt-clad he-men battle at the base of the mount, for the multitudes.

August

Mountain Dance and Folk Festival – Asheville; held the first weekend, with stage shows of folk and bluegrass music and traditional dance.

September

Bull Durham Blues Festival – Durham; on the second weekend, get bluesy to the likes of Buddy Guy, Wilson Pickett and up-and-coming talent.

October

Outer Banks Stunt Kite Competition – Nags Head; on the first weekend in October, test your ground-to-air skills with the best of them.

November

Christmas at the Biltmore Estate – Asheville; from November, big bows and a truly huge Christmas tree adorn the Biltmore House for concerts and other events.

Central North Carolina

The gently rolling foothills of the northern Piedmont were once powerhouses of tobacco and textiles; these industries still exist, but it's the research and high-tech industries of the Research Triangle that call the shots nowadays. Created in the 1950s to promote business, the Triangle (as it's commonly called) comprises the cities of Raleigh, Durham and Chapel Hill, each with its own university. The region is growing like crazy and, to a certain extent, overshadows the neighboring 'Triad' cities – Winston-Salem, Greensboro and High Point.

To the southeast, the Sandhills region is a venerable mecca for golfers. Several attractions are scattered in the central heartland, including the barbecue capital of Lexington and Seagrove, with its passel of potters. Down on the South Carolina border, Charlotte is a linchpin of the banking world, second only to the Big Apple; its charms are mainly culinary.

RALEIGH
pop 281,000
Named for the man John Lennon called 'a stupid git,' Raleigh has a handsome old state capitol, a trendy-looking pedestrian mall and a decent cultural scene. Urban renewal has given parts of downtown a shot in the arm, and while even Sir Walter wouldn't have described it as lively, the capital city does offer a few good diversions.

Orientation
Raleigh, in the Triangle's eastern corner, is encircled by the I-40/440 loop. Downtown is a smallish grid a few miles square and home to the bulk of worthwhile sights. Downtown is bisected north to south by the pedestrian Fayetteville St Mall, with the State Capitol at the north end.

Information
The convention and visitors bureau (☎ 919-834-5900), 225 Hillsborough St, hands out a list of hotels with discounts. The Capitol Area Visitors Center (☎ 919-733-3456), 301 N Blount St, has a walking-tour map of the government buildings and the old Oakwood district.
Web site: www.raleighcvb.org

Banks with ATMs can be found along Fayetteville Mall.

The most central post office is Century Station (☎ 919-833-7879), at 300 Fayetteville Mall. The county library's Electronic Information Center (☎ 856-6690), at 334 Fayetteville Mall, has 16 Web terminals for free public use (Monday to Friday only).

The *News & Observer* is Raleigh's big regional daily and has a Web site at www.news-observer.com. Free listings handouts include the *Spectator, The Independent* and *This Week Magazine,* all of which can be picked up in bars and restaurants. Gays and lesbians should check out *The Front Page,* which covers the Carolinas.

Local radio stations include WKNC 88.1 FM (alternative, reggae & pop), WCPE 89.7 (classical & jazz) and WQDR 94.7 FM (country).

American Express travel services are handled by Capitol Travel Designers (☎ 833-3254) at 1101 Oberlin Rd. Its 24-hour information line is ☎ 919-871-5668.

The best independent bookshop is Quail Ridge Books (☎ 828-1588), 3522 Wade Ave about 3km west of downtown. It has an extensive arts and travel section and hosts readings and book signings by authors.

White Rabbit (☎ 919-856-1429), at 309 W Martin St, is the top gay and lesbian bookshop.

Raleigh has good medical facilities, including Raleigh Urgent Care (☎ 919-231-3131) east of downtown at 2610 New Bern Ave.

Things to See & Do
Built in the Greek Revivalist mould, the **State Capitol** (☎ 919-733-4994), on Fayetteville Mall, is basically unchanged from its completion in 1840. Visitors can walk round the old legislative chambers, state library and state geologist's office; the current legislature meets in the State Legislative Building just north. Check the statue of George Washington in Roman garb in the main hall.

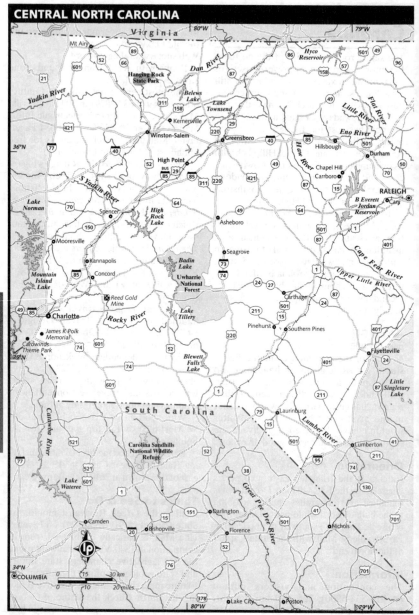

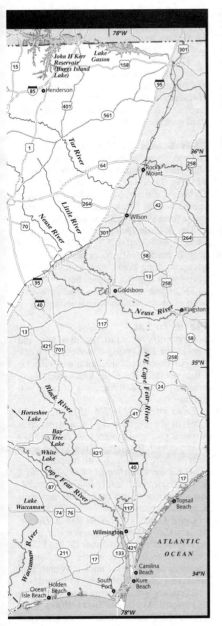

It's open daily; admission is free. Governor Mike Easley works here too, but resides in the swanky Victorian-era **Executive Mansion** (1891) at 301 N Blount St (open by group appointment).

Museums All the following museums are closed on Monday and Sunday morning. The **North Carolina Museum of History** (☎ 919-715-0200), at 5 E Edenton St, has a good chronological exhibit, including a 700 BC dugout canoe, flags, Civil War photos, a Wright Brothers plane model, a Sports Hall of Fame and much more. Hours are 9 am to 5 pm Tuesday to Saturday and noon to 5 pm Sunday (closed Monday); admission is free.

The world's only dinosaur specimen with a heart is kept at the modern, airy **North Carolina Museum of Natural Sciences** (☎ 919-733-7450), at 11 W Jones St. There's also a unique and scary Acrocanthosaurus, five habitat dioramas and lots of well-done taxidermy. In the Discovery Room, live animals are brought out for kids to stroke. It's open 9 am to 5 pm Monday to Saturday and noon to 5 pm Sunday; admission is free.

There are several big hands-on, kid-oriented museums in the state, but **Exploris** (☎ 919-834-4040), at 201 E Hargett St, is the best one. This 'global experience center' is aimed at children, but adults will also enjoy some of the exhibits, which include a 4-ton section of the Berlin Wall, a gizmo-filled Japanese bathroom and a multimedia center where you can design your own Web page. Hours are Monday to Saturday, 9 am to 5 pm, and Sunday, noon to 5 pm. Admission is $7/5 for adults/children.

The **North Carolina Museum of Art** (☎ 919-839-6262) is inconveniently located on the western fringe of town at 2110 Blue Ridge Rd, but it's well worth visiting for its fine collection of antiquities and baroque and Renaissance paintings spread over several levels. In the European section, don't miss the Girl Defending Herself Against Love (1880), by Adolphe-William Bouguereau – so realistic that it's omitted from some tours. There's also a representative selection of the best-known American artists, and traveling exhibits such as Ansel

NORTH CAROLINA

Adams' photography. The one-hour free guided tour is offered regularly throughout the day. It's northwest, off exit 5 of I-440. Hours are 9 am to 5 pm Tuesday to Thursday and Saturday, 9 am to 9 pm Friday and 11 am to 6 pm Sunday.

By 2002, the city plans to convert the former **City Gallery** into a contemporary art museum. It'll be at 409 W Martin St.

The areas around City Market and Moore Square feature several art galleries, including **Artspace** (☎ 919-821-2787), 201 E Davie St, which has more than 40 artists' studios, and the **Art Trace Gallery** (☎ 919-851-8234), 222 S Blount St, which has some very quirky stuff indeed.

Other Attractions Mordecai Historic Park (☎ 919-834-4844), north of town at 1 Mimosa St, features an old plantation house and several other old buildings that give a feel for antebellum life. There's a reconstructed village street, and the birthplace of hapless Andrew Johnson is also preserved here. It's open daily; admission is $4/2 for adults/children

Places to Stay

Camping The nearest camping is at *Umstead State Park* (☎ 919-787-3033), north off US 70, 2 miles west of town; call for directions. The woodland tent sites cost $9.

Hotels & Motels Capital Blvd, north of town, has plenty of motels, with the most basic places charging $40 plus. There are others along I-440, especially at I-40 to the southwest and Hwy 70 to the northwest.

Motel 6 has two locations, both about 8 miles from downtown: in Cary (☎ 919-467-6171, 1401 Buck Jones Rd) and to the northwest of town (☎ 919-782-7071, 3921 Arrow Dr). Singles/doubles cost around $40/46 in high season.

The *Regency Inn* (☎ 828-9081, 300 N Dawson St) is the cheapest downtown option, charging $46 for a king-size bed and $48 for two singles. Rooms are basic but clean.

The *Microtel Inn* (☎ 919-462-0061), at I-40 exit 284B to the west, is quite good for $48/54, and often discounted.

The *Brownstone Hotel* (☎ 919-828-0811, 1707 Hillsborough St), near the university, is an average-looking tower complex but has very nice, plush, renovated standard rooms for $79 to $99.
Web site: www.brownestonehotel.com

Convenient in the center of town, *Holiday Inn* (☎ 919-832-0501, 320 Hillsborough St) caters to the business crowd. Standard rooms cost $89 to $129.

B&Bs & Inns There are two historic accommodations in the heart of Raleigh. The Victorian *Oakwood Inn* (☎ 919-832-9712, 411 N Bloodworth St), in the pretty Oakwood district, has six nicely furnished theme rooms (Polk, Linden etc). Prices range from $95 to $150, including breakfast.

The *William Thomas House* (☎ 800-653-3466, 919-755-9400, 530 N Blount St) is slightly fancier, with room telephones and tranquil sitting areas, such as an old-style parlor with a piano. Rooms here cost $115 to $142; some are dearer on weekends.
Web site: www.williamthomashouse.com

Places to Eat

For a country breakfast, try cured ham and eggs at *Big Ed's* (☎ 919-836-9909, 220 Wolfe St), with checkered tablecloths and a jocular Ed in overalls. The place looks like a farm museum. It's closed Saturday evening and Sunday.

Lily's (☎ 919-833-0226, 1813 Glenwood Ave), at the north end of the street, is a screamingly popular pizza joint catering to a young crowd. Its pizzas (from $7 for a 10-inch pan) are piled high with toppings.

At *Cooper's Barbeque* (☎ 919-832-7614, 109 E Davie St), friendly folk serve barbecue sandwiches for a mere $2 at simple, if somewhat greasy tables.

Caffé Luna (☎ 832-6090, 136 E Hargett St), on Moore Square, is a popular place, serving creative Italian dishes ($11 to $15) in chandeliered rooms of subtle pink, among the owner's artworks. Lunch is available all week, and dinner Wednesday to Saturday.

There are some alluring places up in the Glenwood Ave area. *Sushi Blues Café* (☎ 919-664-8061, 301 Glenwood Ave) is good for evening jazz and mouthfuls of good, if pricey, sushi. ***Rockford*** *(☎ 919-821-9020)*, upstairs and barely visible at No 320½, offers truly huge sandwich platters for about $6 and quaffable foreign brews. Both places are open for lunch and dinner.

518 West *(☎ 919-829-2518, 518 W Jones St)* serves refined Italian meals ($13 to $24) and gets seriously packed and trendy in the evening. Grab a table on the upstairs gallery and watch posers eat pasta.

The ***42nd St Oyster Bar*** *(☎ 919-831-2811)*, at West and Jones Sts, is a very popular downtown eatery with music, dancing, a raw bar and seafood restaurant – lunch is $6 to $9, dinner $11 to $15.

Irregardless *(☎ 919-833-8898, 901 W Morgan)* is a one-time veggie bastion that now also serves steak, seafood and poultry amid a West Coast decor. Mains cost $14 to $23. It's open all day (dinner-only on weekends).

The ***Five Star*** *(☎ 919-833-3311, 511 W Hargett St)* serves up Maoist morsels such as General's Chicken, smothered in spicy sauce with sesame seeds. Meals average $10 to $13. The interior is an artsy former warehouse,

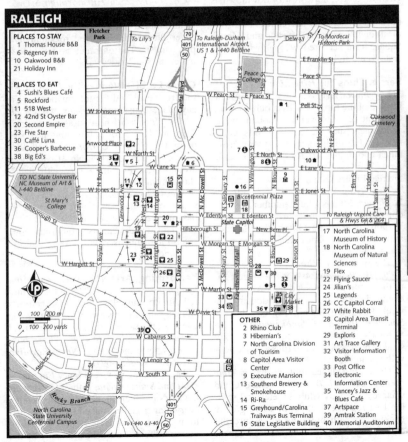

RALEIGH

PLACES TO STAY
1 Thomas House B&B
6 Regency Inn
10 Oakwood B&B
21 Holiday Inn

PLACES TO EAT
4 Sushi's Blues Café
5 Rockford
11 518 West
12 42nd St Oyster Bar
20 Second Empire
23 Five Star
30 Caffè Luna
36 Cooper's Barbecue
38 Big Ed's

OTHER
2 Rhino Club
3 Hibernian's
7 North Carolina Division of Tourism
8 Capitol Area Visitor Center
9 Executive Mansion
13 Southend Brewery & Smokehouse
14 Ri-Ra
15 Greyhound/Carolina Trailways Bus Terminal
16 State Legislative Building
17 North Carolina Museum of History
18 North Carolina Museum of Natural Sciences
19 Flex
22 Flying Saucer
24 Jilian's
25 Legends
26 CC Capitol Corral
27 White Rabbit
28 Capitol Area Transit Terminal
29 Exploris
31 Art Trace Gallery
32 Visitor Information Booth
33 Post Office
34 Electronic Information Center
35 Yancey's Jazz & Blues Café
37 Artspace
39 Amtrak Station
40 Memorial Auditorium

NORTH CAROLINA

and jazz or New Age music is played until around 3 am (dinner only).

Opposite the NCSU campus, the *Rathskeller* (☎ 919-821-5342, 2412 Hillsborough St) is a popular student hang-out serving vegetarian, seafood, poultry and beef dishes. Most mains cost $12 to $15, and burgers and sandwiches run $7 to $8.

For the ultimate splurge, *Second Empire* (☎ 919-829-3663, 330 Hillsborough St) serves fantastic French food at royal prices (dinner only).

Entertainment

Glenwood Ave, northwest of downtown, is developing some good nightlife, while Hillsborough St, near the university, has droves of student bars. City Market and Moore Square have been redeveloped with shops, restaurants and galleries.

Bars & Clubs The *Hibernian* (☎ 833-2258, 311 Glenwood Ave) is arguably the most enjoyable of the three new Irish pubs in town. Celtic music wafts over the wooden booths, and you can suck the cream top off a Guinness on the dining terrace. It's open for lunch and dinner. *Ri-Ra* (☎ 919-833-5535, 126 N West Ave) has great Joycean nooks in the rear library section.

The *Flying Saucer* (☎ 919-821-7401, 328 W Morgan St) has a huge number of beers, domestic and foreign. Slurp on a Belgian Trappist beer or an Oktoberfest Märzen and ponder the plates stuck on the walls and ceiling.

The gimmick at *Rhino Club* (☎ 919-831-0400, 410 Glenwood Ave) is the longest bar in the Southeast – cooled by a row of mechanical handfans. There's dancing on weekends (membership $8). Nearby, the *Southend Brewery & Smokehouse* (☎ 919-832-4604, 505 W Jones St) makes good steaks and brews, but also runs a dance floor with live music behind the vats.

The hottest dance spot in town is *Time* (☎ 831-9222, 901 Tryon St), behind Good Charlie's Comedy Club. Its elevated split-level stages, laser light shows and groovy backlit bar with bubbling tubes lure the crowds on weekends, and there are frequent

lines. Members cost $5 and nonmembers $8, but everyone gets in free till 10:30 pm (closed Wednesday).

Yancey's Jazz & Blues Café (☎ 839-1991, 205 Wolfe Street), in the City Market, has live jazz and blues bands several times a week. There's a good selection of microbrews and imported beers.

In the mood for pool, shuffleboard or volleyball? After 5 pm, go to *Jillian's* (☎ 919-821-7832, 117 S West St) and let off steam for $3.50 to $6 per hour. There are interactive games upstairs.

Across from the NCSU campus, *Five-O* (☎ 821-4419, 2526 Hillsborough St) is a sleepy bar during the week but fills with gyrating students on weekends. Theme nights cover alternative, industrial, rockabilly and punk music. The entrance is half-hidden under the sign 'Hideaways.'

Gay & Lesbian Venues The *Front Page* is the freebie to find for information on the gay and lesbian scene. *Legends* (☎ 831-8888, 330 W Hargett St) hosts drag shows from 8 pm and has a groovy fountain-filled back patio. *CC Capital Corral* (☎ 755-9599) a couple of doors down at No 313, has been around for a quarter century, with nightly shows from 9 pm.

Flex (☎ 832-8855, 2 S West St) is a gay bar with a rough edge – hurricane fencing at the basement entrance sets the tone. Dig the urinal filled with peanuts in the front room. It has theme nights – leather, drag, uniform etc – and is open nightly from 5 pm.

Performing Arts The *North Carolina Symphony* (☎ 919-733-2750), in the Memorial Auditorium, plays about 185 concerts annually and attracts a stable of high-profile talent. At the same venue, you might attend *Oklahoma!* or *The Best Little Whorehouse in Texas* performed by the *North Carolina Theatre* (☎ 919-831-6941).

The sparkling new, very fancy *Entertainment and Sports Arena,* with 21,000 seats, is the city's premier big-ticket venue, hosting everything from Barenaked Ladies concerts to monster truck rallies and wrestling thump-a-thons. Buy tickets directly at the box office, at Ticketmaster outlets or by phone at ☎ 919-834-4000. It's near the junction of I-440 Beltline and Hillsborough St, west of downtown.

Spectator Sports
You can catch the midday practice sessions of the North Carolina Hurricanes hockey team at the Iceplex (☎ 878-9002), 2601 Raleigh Blvd. Call for dates and times; admission is free. The official games are held at the Entertainment and Sports Arena (see Performing Arts in the Entertainment section).

Getting There & Away
Air Raleigh-Durham International Airport (☎ 919-840-2123) is served by 14 airlines, including American, Continental, Delta, and United. Delta Airlines offers good deals to New York ($99 roundtrip including a Saturday and $198 without a Saturday).

Bus & Train The Greyhound/Trailways station (☎ 919-834-8410) is at 314 W Jones St. Sample fares include Durham ($5.50, 40 minutes), Winston-Salem ($20, from 3 hours), Charlotte ($30, from 4¼ hours) and Wilmington ($29, from 6¼ hours).

The Amtrak station (☎ 919-471-3399) is at 302 W Cabarrus St. Sample destinations include Charlotte ($25, 3¾ hours), Washington, DC ($66, from 7½ hours) and Durham ($5, 40 minutes).

Getting Around
The Triangle Transit Authority (☎ 919-549-9999) runs bus No 101 from the airport to Moore Square in downtown Raleigh ($1.50, 40 minutes, half hourly). Taxi fare to downtown from the airport (20 to 30 minutes) will cost around $28.

Capital Area Transit (☎ 919-828-7228) runs a bevy of routes that converge at the Capital Area Transit Terminal on Hargett St. Buses run every half-hour, or hourly after 6 pm. Fares cost 75¢, with free transfers.

There's also a free touristy trolley that loops around Martin and Davie Sts, and again around Glenwood and West Sts.

Taxis in Raleigh cost $2.85 for the first mile and $1.85 for each additional mile. Call

Wake Taxi (☎ 919-231-0367) or National Cab (☎ 919-704-7122).

DURHAM
pop 172,000
In the late 19th century, Durham's stock rose with the fortunes of the newly established American Tobacco Company, one of the first big tobacco companies, owned by Washington Duke and his sons. The Dukes had an instinct for PR as well as business, and in 1924 the founder's son Buck donated a wad of cash to a small college that grew into Duke University.

Durham is a lively student town with an active black community, at the northeast corner of the Triangle. Durham is home to the Durham Bulls, a minor-league baseball team that shot to fame after the 1988 flick *Bull Durham*. The lilting Piedmont Blues were pioneered here by Blind Boy Fuller, and the performing arts scene is pretty vibrant. Downtown can be quiet or raucous, depending on where the students (and sports fans) are.

Orientation & Information
There are two hubs of activity. Brightleaf Square on the east side of downtown is a recycled tobacco warehouse with restaurants and upscale shops, and a half-mile northeast, adjacent to the Duke campus, is the student-filled Ninth St District. It's best to park near either and walk, rather than driving between shops and other attractions.

The helpful visitor information center (☎ 800-446-8604, 919-687-0288) is at 101 E Morgan St. There's also a 24-hour voice recording of events and activities (☎ 919-688-2855).

Web site: www.durham-nc.com

The post office is on the corner of Pisgee and Chapel Hill Sts; the public library, with free Internet terminals for email, is east of the visitor center on Holloway. Among downtown banks, there's a Bank of America ATM at the main entrance of Brightleaf Square.

The Regulator Bookshop (☎ 919-286-2700), 720 9th St, is the hippest bookstore around, with good travel, history and alternative living sections.

Local radio stations include WNCU 90.7 (NPR, classical & jazz) and WDNC 620 AM (news & talk). Free listings mags include the *Spectator* and *The Independent*.

Things to See & Do

Generously endowed by the Duke family's cigarette fortune, **Duke University** (☎ 919-684-2572) has a Georgian-style East Campus and a neo-Gothic West Campus with an impressive 1930s chapel (211 feet), looking very much like a one-up on Canterbury Cathedral. The Flentrop organ inside has over 5000 pipes. Students juggle, play soccer and pretend to read on the front concourse.

The chapel is best reached by a walk through the very pleasant **Sara P Duke Gardens** on the west side of the campus (☎ 919-684-3698). This beautifully sculpted, 55-acre tract was the crowning achievement of Ellen Shipmen, a landscape architect. Highlights include an **Asiatic arboretum, rose garden, garden of native plants,** and a set of carefully framed **terraces** decked out in azaleas, camellias and a waterfall. The arboretum has a network of lacy bridges and

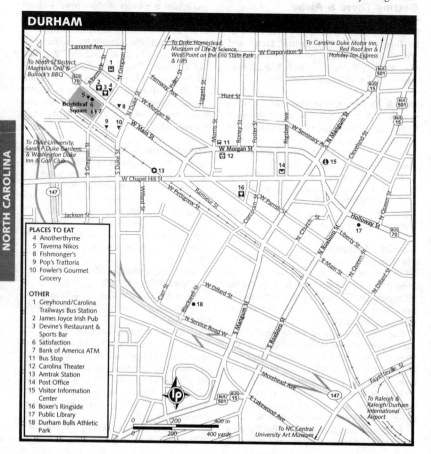

DURHAM

PLACES TO EAT
4 Anotherthyme
5 Taverna Nikos
8 Fishmonger's
9 Pop's Trattoria
10 Fowler's Gourmet Grocery

OTHER
1 Greyhound/Carolina Trailways Bus Station
2 James Joyce Irish Pub
3 Devine's Restaurant & Sports Bar
6 Satisfaction
7 Bank of America ATM
11 Bus Stop
12 Carolina Theater
13 Amtrak Station
14 Post Office
15 Visitor Information Center
16 Boxer's Ringside
17 Public Library
18 Durham Bulls Athletic Park

pathways, as well as a stunning garden pond. The free map guide is essential for finding your way around (available at all entrances). You might also drop by the shiny new Doris Duke horticultural center near the main parking lot. The park closes at dusk; admission is free.

See the humble origins of the Duke family and have an uncritical look at the tobacco industry at **Duke Homestead** (☎ 919-477-5498), 2828 Duke Homestead Rd, on the north side of town. When Washington Duke, a penniless farmer, trudged home from the Civil War, he remembered how popular the area's bright-hued tobacco leaves had been with his soldier buddies. Brightleaf Tobacco became his company's trademark brand, and the Dukes became mega-rich. The video plays up the family's community spirit; the Dukes sponsored the first major hospital in the 19th century, paving the way for the university medical school. There are amusing old ads, cigarette-rolling machines (the invention that made it all possible) and a Liberty Bell made out of tobacco. It's off Duke Street north of I-85. It's open daily; admission is free.

The **Museum of Life & Science** (☎ 919-220-5429) has two floors of hands-on exhibits and an outdoor nature park. Kids will enjoy testing rocket propulsion, watching mini tornados form and the petting zoo. At the back of the grounds is the **Magic Wings Butterfly House**, with lepidoptera fluttering madly as you enter (note the hanging chrysalises). Butterflies native to North Carolina bear intriguing names such as mourning cloak, question mark and red admiral. Many feed on the rotting fruit laid out on feeders. The butterfly house is open daily; admission is $8/5.50 for adults/children.

Just east of downtown lies the NCCU campus. There you'll find the **NC Central University Art Museum** (☎ 919-560-6211), with a good permanent display of 19th- and 20th-century African-American artists.

West Point on the Eno State Park

This pretty state park (☎ 919-471-1623), 6 miles north of downtown, is 371 acres of leafy calm on the scenic Eno River and a magnet for tired urbanites. The grounds have several museum-piece buildings including a mill, blacksmith shop and tobacco barn, but most people come to picnic or hike (there's a 1½-mile trail along the river). The park is open daily; the buildings open only on weekends, when craft workshops, concerts and demonstrations take place. From I-85, take N Duke St/Hwy 501 N exit and drive 3½ miles.

Special Events

Some 15,000 listeners show up for the renowned **Durham Blues Festival** (☎ 919-683-1709), which is held the second weekend in September. The **Festival for the Eno,** at West Point on the Eno, is a bonanza of crafts and concerts on a weekend in late August. The **Duke University Jazz Festival** (☎ 919-660-3300) runs from January to April and September to December, with high-profile talent.

Places to Stay

The cheapest motels line I-85 north of downtown. The *Carolina Duke Motor Inn* (☎ 800-438-1158, 286-0771, 2517 Guess Rd) is the cheapest good motel option in town, with singles/doubles for $40/45. All 182 rooms are spacious and have TV and air con. Web site: www.citysearch.com/rdu/carolina duke

Some 3 miles northwest of town is the *Red Roof Inn* (☎ 919-471-9882, 1915 N Pointe Dr) charging $40/60 for rooms in low/high season.

The *Holiday Inn Express* (☎ 919-313-3244, 2516 Guess Rd) has the usual comforts, a pool and a free breakfast bar. Singles/doubles cost $59/69, jumping to $89 for peak periods (Duke U homecoming).

The swishest option is the *Washington Duke Inn* (☎ 800-443-3853, 919-490-0999, 3001 Cameron Blvd) just off Hwy 15/501 by the Duke campus. Rooms with a park view cost $175 ($200 with a golf-course vista). Prices drop to around $120 in slow periods. Web site: www.washingtondukeinn.com

Places to Eat

There's a good selection of places to eat in the Brightleaf and Ninth St districts and on Main St on both sides of the Duke University East Campus. Head to *Fowler's Gourmet Grocery* (☎ 919-683-2555, *112 S Duke St*) for stylish self-catering from the deli counter, and the inviting back terrace for coffee and the strains of piped-in jazz.

Fishmonger's (☎ 919-682-0128, *806 W Main St*) is a seafood and crab joint. It's nothing special really but pleasant for a midday munch. Oyster, crab and fish sandwiches run $5 to $8 (closed Monday lunch).

Tasty, good-value Greek fare is available at *Taverna Nikos* (☎ 919-682-0043, *905 W Main St*) in the Brightleaf complex. Standard dishes such as spanakopita, dolmas or moussaka start at $5; a rabbit stew in port wine sauce will set you back $14. It's open for lunch and dinner (closed Sundays). Reserve ahead.

Pop's Trattoria (☎ 919-956-7677, *810 W Peabody St*) has good pizzas (starting at $9), pricier pastas ($13) and a well-stocked bar (closed Monday evening).

Opened in the 1930s, *Bullock's Bar-B-Que* (☎ 919-383-6202, *3330 Quebec Dr*) is an institution. Lines start to build from 6 pm most evenings for cheap BBQ sandwiches, seafood and chicken. Almost everything on the menu costs under $10, but there's nothing stronger to drink than ice tea (open for lunch and dinner, closed Monday). It's northwest of the Duke campus, off Hwy 70 and behind the Eckerd's pharmacy.

Moving upmarket, *Anotherthyme* (☎ 919-682-5225, *109 Gregson St*) does multi-culti cuisine, slightly pretentious but good, with little bonuses like smoked mozzarella or porcini mushrooms to tickle the palate. Mains cost about $15 to $23 (dinner only).

In the Ninth St District, grub doesn't get much cheaper than at *Bank's* (☎ 919-286-5073, *750 9th St*), a simple joint serving a few Chinese and Vietnamese dishes for under $4. *George's Garage* (☎ 919-286-4131) at No 737 is a warehouse-sized fish restaurant, selling fresh bouillabaisse ($19) but also big salad-bar portions for $6. Both are open for lunch and dinner.

On the edge of a lovely old residential district stands the *Magnolia Grill* (☎ 919-286-3609, *1002 9th St*). The owners grow their own bio-veggies. The imaginative choices might include roast *poussin* (young chicken) in brandy with cranberry-apple chutney ($20). Reserve ahead, or come right at the 5 pm opening.

The *Fairview* in the Washington Duke Inn (see Places to Stay) is regarded as one of the best restaurants in town, with views of lush golf greens. Mains, such as stuffed saddle of rabbit with pine nuts, spinach and truffles ($23) run $21 to $28. A credit card's a good idea.

Entertainment

Bars & Clubs Get a sense of literary despair at *James Joyce Irish Pub* (☎ 919-688-6189, *912 W Main St*). Photos of the great man, signs in Gaelic and the stained paneling make you want to down a stout right away. It's open all day (and a good part of the night!) until 2 am.

DeVine's Restaurant & Sports Bar (☎ 919-682-0228, *904 W Main St*) is filled with raucous students on game nights, hurling abuse at botched plays on the big screen TV. There's live music on weekends (closed Sunday).

Across the road in Brightleaf Square, there are burgers and pizzas at *Satisfaction* (☎ 919-682-7397, *905 W Main St*), amid the auto memorabilia and music posters. Here, too, most people come to watch sports and chug beers.

The lesbian and alternative crowd hits *Boxer's Ringside* (☎ 919-680-2100, *3033 W Main St*), in an old converted stone building downtown, with sofas, lounges and yet more sports screens. There are other places that welcome gay closer to downtown, in the 300 block of W Main St.

Classical Music The *Durham Symphony Orchestra,* the *African-American Dance Ensemble* and other groups are sponsored by the well-funded Durham Arts Council (☎ 919-560-2787). Theatre events are also staged at local universities and other venues in the Triangle.

Film The beaux-arts *Carolina Theater* (☎ *919-560-3030, 309 W Morgan St)* hosts the North Carolina symphony, repertory cinema and other events.

Spectator Sports

College basketball and football is like religion here, but locals work up the greatest fervor for the Durham Bulls, the single-A affiliate of the Atlanta Braves. The old stadium where actor Tim Robbins pitched to Kevin Costner still stands, but games are now played at the spanking new Durham Bulls Athletic Park (☎ 919-956-2855). The season runs from April to early September, but you'll need to buy tickets months ahead of time.

Getting There & Away

The Triangle Transit Authority (☎ 919-549-9999) runs bus No 101 from Raleigh-Durham airport to downtown Durham ($1.50, 30 minutes, half hourly). The stop is on the corner of Morgan and Main Sts. A taxi to the airport will cost about $23.

Greyhound/Carolina Trailways (☎ 919-687-4800) is a seedy but harmless station at 820 Morgan St. Fares include Raleigh ($5.50, 40 minutes), Richmond ($33, 3 hours) and Asheville ($44, 7 hours).

The Amtrak station (☎ 800-872-7245) is at 400 W Chapel Hill St. Services go to Raleigh ($5, 40 minutes), Greensboro ($7, 1¼ hours) and Charlotte ($19, 3¼ hours).

Getting Around

The 13 local bus lines of the Durham Area Transit Authority (☎ 919-683-3282) run along Main St (inbound) and Chapel Hill St (outbound). Fares are 75¢ (children 35¢).

For a taxi, call Orange Cab (☎ 919-682-6111).

CHAPEL HILL

pop 44,000

An attractive university town, Chapel Hill is conspicuously more affluent than the other corners of the Triangle. The University of North Carolina, founded in 1789, was one of the nation's first state universities and has several fine old buildings. The music scene –

particularly for grunge, jazz and pop – is smokin', as is the basketball; Michael Jordan rose (or rather leaped) to fame here.

Orientation & Information

Downtown lies about 2 miles northwest of the Hwy 15/501 bypass. The main drag is Franklin St, lined with funky clothing shops, bars and eateries on its north side and the UNC campus to the south; the same street enters Carrboro to the west. Murals are sprinkled around town, such as a gigantic yellow No 2 pencil along the wall on Church St.

The Chapel Hill–Orange County Visitors Bureau (☎ 888-968-2060, 919-968-2060) is at 501 W Franklin St, or see its Web site (www.chocvb.org). The visitors center at Morehead Planetarium's west entrance (☎ 919-962-1630) does free 1-hour walking tours of the UNC campus.

The main post office is at Henderson and E Franklin Sts. The Davis Library (☎ 919-966-3260) on the UNC campus has lots of Internet terminals; just walk in and sit down at one. There's a Wachovia Bank at 165 E Franklin St.

Local radio stations include the great student-run WUNC 91.5 (world music to reggae, NPR) and WXYC 89.3 FM (alternative rock & folk). For entertainment listings, pick up the free *Spectator* or *The Independent* weekly papers.

Chapel Hill has good independent bookstores. Run by volunteers, the Internationalist (☎ 919-942-1740), at 405 W Franklin St, has a good selection of progressive and alternative literature and is a great source of tips on the local gay scene. The Bookshop (☎ 919-942-5178), 400 W Franklin St, is a bit more mainstream.

The Skylight Exchange (☎ 919-933-5550) at 405½ W Rosemary St, is an offbeat bookstore-cum-diner that sells and trades used books, CDs, tapes and records. You'll find gems here such as *The Gulf War Reader* or *Inside Tar Heel Basketball 1992*.

Council Travel (☎ 919-942-2334), 137 E Franklin St in the back of the Bank of America complex, has good deals to Europe and Asia. STA Travel (☎ 919-928-8844) is a couple of doors down at No 143.

Things to See & Do

With science exhibits, celestial shows and kiddy extravaganzas in its 68-foot dome, **Morehead Planetarium** (☎ 919-549-6863), on the UNC campus, is the finest planetarium in the state ($4.50/3.50 adults/children; call for schedule). The building itself is grand, and behind the visitors desk downstairs there's a hall with giant portraits of historical greats.

The university's **Ackland Art Museum** (☎ 919-966-5736), on S Columbia St, has an eclectic, oft-overlooked collection – European paintings and sculpture (including Rubens, Degas and Pissarro), Asian and African-American works and local folk art. Hours are 10 to 5 pm Wednesday to Saturday; admission is free.

On the southeast edge of the campus, the **North Carolina Botanical Garden** (☎ 919-962-0522) is the largest, and probably most varied, botanical garden in the state. Wildflowers, carnivorous plants, and aquatic and herb gardens are among the highlights, all neatly sorted by zone (mountains, Piedmont, and coastal plains). It's open mid-March to mid-November, 8 am to 5 pm weekdays, 10 am to 6 pm Saturday and 2 to 6 pm Sunday; admission is free.

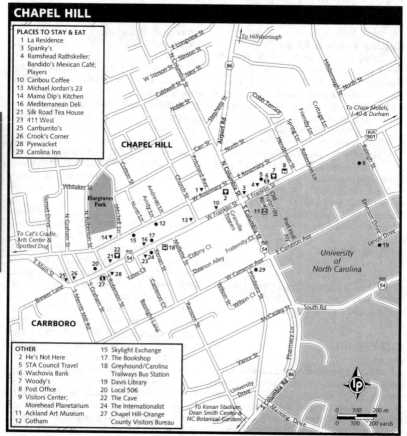

CHAPEL HILL

PLACES TO STAY & EAT
1 La Residence
3 Spanky's
4 Ramshead Rathskeller;
   Bandido's Mexican Café;
   Players
10 Caribou Coffee
13 Michael Jordan's 23
14 Mama Dip's Kitchen
16 Mediterranean Deli
21 Silk Road Tea House
23 411 West
25 Carrburrito's
26 Crook's Corner
28 Pyewacket
29 Carolina Inn

OTHER
2 He's Not Here
5 STA Council Travel
6 Wachovia Bank
7 Woody's
8 Post Office
9 Visitors Center;
   Morehead Planetarium
11 Ackland Art Museum
12 Gotham
15 Skylight Exchange
17 The Bookshop
18 Greyhound/Carolina
   Trailways Bus Station
19 Davis Library
20 Local 506
22 The Cave
24 The Internationalist
27 Chapel Hill-Orange
   County Visitors Bureau

Special Events

The **Weaver St Market** in Carrboro is a fun place to be on Thursdays and Sundays in summer, with food vendors and groups playing jazz to keep the diners lingering. The **Sleaze Fest** in August gathers 60-odd grunge bands over a three-day weekend in a handful of area clubs.

Places to Stay

Cheap accommodations are scarce; consider staying in Durham if you're really stumped. Campers can try the full hook-up sites at the **Southern Country Inn** (☎ 919-732-8101, 122 Daniel Boone St) in pretty Hillsborough, 12 miles northwest of town.

The **Red Roof Inn** (☎ 919-489-9421, 5623 Chapel Hill Blvd), is a comfortable chain motel with singles/doubles starting at $48/53. It's 4 miles north, at Hwy 15/501 before I-40.

The **Days Inn** (☎ 919-929-3090, 1312 N Fordham Blvd) is an attractive new place off the east end of Franklin St near Europa Dr. Doubles start at $75; there are occasional cheaper deals.

The classiest place is the historic **Carolina Inn** (☎ 919-933-2001, 211 Pittsboro St) in the heart of town, with plush rooms from $139 to $169 and an elegant restaurant. Web site: www.carolinainn.com

The slick **Siena Hotel** (☎ 800-223-7379, 919-929-4000, 1505 E Franklin St) has doubles starting at $169 (10–15% in slower periods). For marble-topped desks, faux-Euro balconies and good business facilities, stay here. Web site: www.sienahotel.com

Places to Eat

Most of the eateries and nightspots are along Franklin St, which is upscale at the top of the hill but has less fancy places at the west end. Java fiends will love **Caribou Coffee Company** (☎ 919-933-5404), at No 110, with an eclectic clientele of relaxed, bagel-hungry students. For something more exotic, try the **Silk Road Tea House** (☎ 919-942-1533, 456 W Franklin St), which is strewn with Himalayan pillows and floor cushions. It's open from 5 pm weekdays, 3:30 pm weekends.

For a quick bite, the **Mediterranean Deli** (☎ 919-967-2666, 410 W Franklin St) has falafel, spinach pie and souvlaki for around $5 (open for lunch and dinner).

'Downhome' is the word for **Mama Dip's Kitchen** (☎ 919-942-5837, 405 W Rosemary St), with favorites such as smoked ham with okra and black-eyed peas served at diner booths. Mama Dip, the owner, sells her own cookbook. More Southern cooking is available at the popular **Crook's Corner** (☎ 919-929-7643, 610 W Franklin St), behind the quirky pig facade (lots of main dishes for about $10).

Spanky's (☎ 919-967-2678, 101 E Franklin St) is a popular cafe, with jazz, ceiling-high windows and a great view of Franklin St from upstairs. Lunch specials run about $5 to $9.

Down a flight of stairs at 159 E Franklin St, the **Ramshead Rathskeller** (☎ 919-942-5158) is a very studenty, sprawling, pseudo-German place with sort-of-quaint wooden booths, a fake cave and tons of memorabilia. Next door to the Rathskeller, shredded beef is the thing at **Bandido's Mexican Café** (☎ 919-967-5048).

For good Mexican fare, seek out **Carrburrito's** (☎ 919-933-8226, 711 W Rosemary St), with a small wrought-iron gate and courtyard off Franklin St. A fat burrito and a Dos Equis will set you back $8.

In Carrboro, the **Spotted Dog** (☎ 933-1117, 111 E Main St) has art lining the walls and paws creeping across one side. Mains start at $8 (try a 'Veggie rollover,' a sun-dried tomato tortilla with spinach and red cheddar). It's open 11:30 am to midnight daily.

Fine French meals can be had at **La Residence** (☎ 919-967-2506, 202 W Rosemary St) for $19 to $33 (evenings only). The menu might include highlights such as tuna crusted with Asian spices in orange-ginger butter. Top-end Italian is available at the trendy **411 West** (☎ 919-967-2782, 411 W Franklin St). The ever-popular, bistro-like **Pyewacket** (☎ 919-929-0297, 431 W Franklin St) has a wide range of seafood, steaks and poultry dishes from about $14.

Entertainment

Bars & Clubs Popular grunge outfits such as Bus Stop or Superchunk started out in Chapel Hill, and the tradition lives on.

Cat's Cradle (☎ 919-967-9053, 300 E Main St) hosts big-name local and visiting bands such as the Tom Tom Club, Warren Zevon, Joan Osborne and the Squirrel Nut

His Royal Airness

Widely considered to be the greatest basketball player of all time, Michael Jeffrey Jordan inspires awe even among folks who don't know dunks from Dinks. A native of Wilmington, Jordan enrolled at the University of North Carolina at Chapel Hill in 1981, and as a freshman, the 6-foot, 6-inch guard scored the winning basket in the national championships. He went on to be named College Player of the Year in both his sophomore and junior years, and in 1984 and 1992, he led the US team to Olympic gold medals in Los Angeles and Barcelona, Spain.

After his junior year, Jordan was drafted by the Chicago Bulls in 1984. In his first season he was named Rookie of the Year, and after the next season (which was injury-plagued), Jordan was the top NBA scorer for seven years running, averaging 32 points per game. This talented shooter was only the second player to score 3,000 points in a single season, after Wilt ('the Stilt') Chamberlain. Along the way, the lucky Bulls racked up six NBA championships. Jordan's extraordinary leaps on the court earned him the nickname 'Air Jordan,' and he became the hero of a generation of dribblers (not to mention sportswear makers).

Since retiring in 1998, the living legend makes the odd appearance at his restaurant, *Michael Jordan's 23* (☎ 919-960-9623, 200 W Franklin St), where patrons sit under a huge sky-lit basket. You can learn more about Jordan and other UNC greats at the Blue Heaven Basketball Museum (☎ 919-929-5877), 1840 Airport Rd.

Zippers. Cover is usually around $12, Thursday to Sunday.

Web site: www.catscradle.com

Other venues worth checking are *Skylight Exchange* (see Places to Eat) and *The Cave* (☎ 919-968-9038, 452½ W Franklin St), a great grad student and local hangout with pool tables to complement the rock and roll, bluegrass and country (weekends only). *Go! Rehearsal Studios* (☎ 919-969-1400, 100 Brewer Lane) in Carrboro has practice rooms as well as a stage venue.

He's Not Here (☎ 919-942-7939, 112½ W Franklin St) has a cool courtyard with live jazz in summer, and 33oz cups of beer ($1 specials). It's open daily till late.

The smallish *Local 506* (☎ 919-942-5506, 506 W Franklin St), hosts local and visiting bands, and has sports TV. *Woody's* (☎ 919-968-3809, 175 E Franklin St) is another good place to watch Tar Heel basketball (two dozen screens).

Players is a popular dance club upstairs from the Rathskeller. *Gotham* (☎ 919-967-2852, 306 W Franklin St) is a happenin' gay and lesbian nightclub. Doors open at 9 pm.

Performing Arts The aptly named *Arts Center* (☎ 919-929-2787, 300 E Main St) in Carrboro (next to Cat's Cradle) has a wide and varied program of lectures, art exhibits and concerts. Schedules are available around town. Also check the Carolina Union (☎ 919-962-1449), the student union building near the library, for events.

Spectator Sports

UNC's temple of basketball is the Dean Smith Center (☎ 919-962-7777) on Skipper Bowles Drive. Named for the legendary coach who retired in 1987, this huge arena seats nearly 22,000 Tar Heels fans, and also contains the Carolina Athletic Memorabilia Room, with tons of UNC sporting artifacts. It's open weekdays; admission is free. On South Rd, the Kenan Memorial Stadium (☎ 919-966-2575) hosts more Tar Heels action, this time for football. Tickets for all UNC events can be ordered on ☎ 800-722-4335, 919-962-2296.

Getting There & Away

The Triangle Transit Authority (☎ 919-549-9999) runs bus No 401 to/from Raleigh-Durham airport to/from Chapel Hill ($1.50, 1¼ hours, half hourly). Buses stop on Franklin St in front of the UNC campus. A taxi to the airport (20 minutes) will cost about $28.

Greyhound/Carolina Trailways (☎ 800-231-2222) stops on Franklin St. Sample fares include Raleigh ($9, 1¼ hours via Durham), Winston-Salem ($16, 2¼ hours), Wilmington ($35, 9¾ hours).

The closest Amtrak station is in Durham, 6 miles northeast.

Getting Around

Chapel Hill Transit (☎ 919-968-2769) covers the area with 10 bus routes; services become less frequent after 6:30 pm. The fare is 75¢ (children 35¢), with free transfers. Several buses run up and down busy Franklin St.

'Tarheel Express' buses are laid on for UNC sports events and concerts at the Smith Center. Buses depart from the University Mall at Estes Dr and Hwy 15/501, among other places. A roundtrip costs $4.

For a cab, call Access One Taxi (☎ 919-942-8580) or Airport & Intown Taxi (☎ 919-942-4492).

WINSTON-SALEM
pop 173,500

The grouping of Winston-Salem, Greensboro and High Point is known locally as the Triad, an answer to its bigger and better-known rival to the southeast. The competition leads to headlines such as 'Triangle Tops Triad' or vice versa. Of the three Triad cities, Winston-Salem probably deserves the most of your attention.

In the mid-18th century the Moravians, a group of German-speaking religious dissidents from Bohemia and Moravia, bought 100,000 acres of land in the Piedmont and called it *der Wachau*, after their leader's ancestral home. (This label became 'Wachovia,' now one of the largest US banks.) The Moravians, a group sometimes compared to the Quakers or Mennonites, number about 20,000 here and have left their mark everywhere, from the quaint steepled churches to the Moravian sugar cookies sold in local shops.

Richard Joshua Reynolds built his first tobacco factory in the town of Winston in 1875, just as the railway was laid. By 1913, Winston and nearby Salem had grown to the extent that they were merged. The RJ Reynolds empire named two of its cigarettes after the city – the Winstons and Salems that dangled so carelessly from young, sophisticated fingers in the 1950s.

Winston-Salem makes a nice breather if you're passing through the area. Reynolda House alone is worth the trouble.

Orientation & Information

Downtown sits on a hill, making its skyscrapers seem even higher than they are. The Wachovia Bank tower is a useful landmark and lights up like a beacon at night. The grid system of streets is fairly easy to navigate.

The friendly Winston-Salem Visitors Center (☎ 800-331-7018, 336-777-3796) is located at 601 N Cherry St. Pick up a free map of town.
Web site: www.wscvb.com

Banks with ATMs downtown include the Wachovia Bank at 100 N Main St. The well-equipped Wake Forest University Baptist Medical Center (☎ 336-713-0000), on Medical Center Blvd, is close to downtown.

There's a post office at 200 Town Run Lane. The public library, at 660 W 5th St, has Web terminals for walk-in use. It's open 9 am to 9 pm Monday to Thursday, 9 am to 6 pm Friday and Saturday and 9 to 5 pm Sunday.

The local paper is the *Winston-Salem Journal*; its Web site is at www.journalnow.com. *El Bilingüe*, the regional Spanish-English daily, is readily available. The free *Triad Style* and *ESP* are weekly entertainment mags. Radio stations include WFDD 88.5 FM (NPR, classical, jazz & folk), WTQR 104.1 FM (country) and WKZL, 107.5 FM (rock).

Encore Books (☎ 723-2525), 1138 Burke St, is a pleasant new and used bookshop with comfy chairs for browsing.

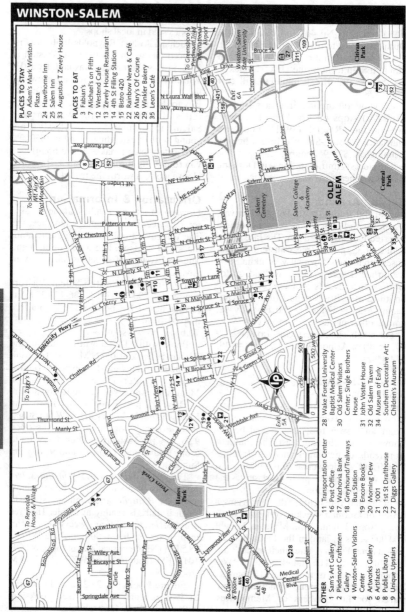

WINSTON-SALEM

PLACES TO STAY
10 Adam's Mark Winston Plaza
24 Hawthorne Inn
25 Salem Inn
33 Augustus T Zevely House

PLACES TO EAT
3 Fabian's
7 Michael's on Fifth
12 Westend Café
13 Zevely House Restaurant
14 4th St Filling Station
15 Bistro 420
22 Rainbow News & Café
26 Mary's Of Course
29 Winkler Bakery
35 Leon's Café

OTHER
1 Sam's Art Gallery
2 Piedmont Craftsmen Gallery
4 Winston-Salem Visitors Center
5 Artworks Gallery
6 Artifacts
8 Public Library
9 Unique Upstairs
11 Transportation Center
16 Post Office
17 Wachovia Bank
18 Greyhound/Trailways Bus Station
19 Encore Books
20 Morning Dew
21 1001
23 1st St Drafthouse
27 Diggs Gallery
28 Wake Forest University Baptist Medical Center
30 Old Salem Visitors Center; Single Brothers House
31 John Voster House
32 Old Salem Tavern
34 Museum of Early Southern Decorative Art; Children's Museum

Things to See & Do

Almost all the sights are strewn outside of downtown. The main draw here is the **arts district** on Trade St between 5th and 7th Sts, which has two dozen galleries and artists' studios. It's not exactly Greenwich Village but it's fun poking round some of the offerings; favorites include the Artworks Gallery (☎ 336-723-5890), at 560 N Trade St, and Artifacts (☎ 336-761-8833), at 528 N Trade St.

Reynolda House Northwest of downtown, the Reynolda House Museum of American Art (☎ 336-725-5325) is the jewel in Winston-Salem's crown. This historic home of tobacco baron RJ Reynolds is a treasure trove of paintings and sculptures, and a favored site for concerts. The house itself – an elegant, 64-room mansion with splendid antique furnishings, paintings and pretty gardens nestled in a sprawling estate – has enough charms for any visitor.

Georgia O'Keeffe, Grant Wood, Frederick Church and Thomas Cole are some of the more famous artists whose works are displayed here. Some lesser-known gems, such as *The Old Hunting Grounds* by Worthington Wittredge, are unexpected delights.

Other highlights include a basement of amusements and a Chesterfield sofa (President Truman napped here in 1951). Music was a favorite pastime in the Reynolds family and there's a self-playing organ that pumps out tunes hourly, not to mention a complicated aeolian organ with 2566 pipes. Reynolds himself passed away in the den, after a prolonged struggle with cancer (of the pancreas, not the lungs).

The fun-filled basement includes a quaint bowling alley (don't those wooden pins look fragile), a squash court, an odd art deco bar with convex and concave mirrors, and a glassed-in wing with a swimming pool.

Hours are 9:30 am to 4:30 pm Tuesday to Satuday and 1:30 pm to 4:30 pm Sunday. Admission is $6/3 for adults/children. Web site: www.reynoldahouse.org

Old Salem The original Moravian settlement of Wachovia has been restored as Old Salem, a 'living history museum.' A few blocks from the skyscrapers, the cobblestones, white picket fences and brick-and-clapboard facades seem fake until you realize that the homes are still occupied. You can stroll through for free or buy a ticket for the seven guided tours of individual homes led by docents in period costume. Keep an open mind and you'll enjoy it.

The visitors center (☎ 336-721-7300) at 600 S Main St hands out maps and sells tickets to all attractions. Hours are 9 am to 5 pm Monday to Saturday and 1 to 5 pm Sunday. If you've got a day or more, the 'all in one' ticket is best; it's good for two days, covers all sights and costs $20/11 for adults/children. All the historic buildings are open 9:30 am to 4:30 pm Monday to Saturday and 1:30 to 4:30 pm Sunday.

Highlights include the **Single Brothers House,** located in front of the visitors center, which was a boarding school for boys learning skills such as blacksmithing, tailoring and tannery. The **John Vogler House,** on the corner of West and Main Sts, was a silversmith's residence (the jewelry in the ground floor is good). The **Winkler Bakery,** at 529 S Main St, still bakes yummy breads and cookies in a wood-fired oven. On the main square, the **Moravian Winston Church** is thought to have the largest Moravian congregation in the world, and visitors are welcome at services.

The **Museum of Early Southern Decorative Art (MESDA)** (☎ 336-721-7300), on the south side of Old Salem at 924 S Main St, leads you through a legacy of Southern furniture, ceramics, silver, textiles and other metalwares on display in 24 period rooms and seven galleries. Admission with a one-hour guided tour costs $10/6 for adults/children.

The **Children's Museum,** at the same address, is a fun place for kids 4 to 9 years. There's a miniature Moravian house, a maze sculpture, self-teaching musical instruments and more. Admission is $4/2.

Should your whistle need wetting, stop by the **Old Salem Tavern,** at 800 S Main St, open for lunch and dinner from Monday to Saturday. George Washington stayed here in 1791, and was delighted.

NORTH CAROLINA

Other Attractions The **Diggs Gallery** (☎ 336-750-2458), at 601 Martin Luther King Dr, on the Winston-Salem State University campus, has a good collection of African-American art and special exhibits. The displays seem to span centuries, from naive African carvings to slick, sophisticated wall prints. Next door, in the university library, the intriguing **Bigger Murals** are indeed huge and loaded with deep thoughts. Hours are 11 am to 5 pm Tuesday to Saturday; admission is free.

The **Southeastern Center for Contemporary Art** (☎ 336-725-1904), at 750 Marguerite Dr, is housed in a comely old stone mansion on the estate of the late underwear king, James G Hanes. Exhibits can be daring and unexpected, such as a huge two-sided video presentation of a man vanishing in flames (the reverse showed him washed away). It's open 10 am to 5 pm Tuesday to Saturday and 2 to 5 pm Sunday; admission is $3/2. To get there, take University Parkway north, turn left on Coliseum Dr and right again on Peters Creek (it's about 2 miles from downtown).

Historic Bethabara Park (☎ 336-924-8191), at 2147 Bethabara Rd, is more of an archeological site, with ruins of the first Moravian settlement in North Carolina. The 175-acre park has reconstructed buildings, including a 1788 church. There's a slide show at the visitors center, and costumed docents roam. Hours are 9:30 am to 4:30 pm weekdays and 1:30 to 4:30 pm weekends; admission is free. Some buildings close in winter. It's about 5 miles north of downtown off University Pkwy.

SciWorks (☎ 336-767-6730), at 400 W Hanes Mill Rd, is a whizbang science museum for kids. Features include do-it-yourself chemical reactions, a marine tank with otters, a planetarium and a 15-acre nature park with petting zoo. It's open 10 am to 5 pm, Monday to Saturday. Admission is $8/6. It's located about 6 miles north of downtown off Hwy 52.

Activities

The 1300-acre Tanglewood Park (☎ 336-778-6300) has recreational options including paddleboats, horseback riding, fishing, hiking and swimming in an Olympic-sized pool. Its biggest draw is its Championship golf course, which hosts a regular PGA tournament. Green fees are $57 for out-of-state visitors; the less challenging Reynolds course costs $16 to $18. Park admission is $2.

Special Events

Winston has several music programs that run from late July to late October, including **Alive After Five** for rock and pop on Thursday nights, **4th St Jazz & Blues** on Friday nights, and **Summer on Trade** for roots music on Saturdays. The **National Black Theatre Festival** is a showcase of local talent every other year in early August.

Places to Stay

Budget chains are clustered along I-40 south of downtown. Watch out for the High Point furniture market in April and October, when prices skyrocket.

Budget The *Motel 6* (☎ 336-661-1588, 3810 Patterson Ave), on Hwy 52 6 miles north of I-40, has weekday/weekend rates starting at $38/40.

The *Microtel Inn* (☎ 336-659-1994, Hanes Mall Blvd), at I-40, has rooms with one or two queen-size beds, data ports, and continental breakfast for $45.

The *Tanglewood Lodge* (☎ 336-778-6370, 4061 Clemmons Rd), in Clemmons about 7 miles southwest of downtown off I-40, is a small, rustic, aging motel complex with rooms for $50, single or double.
Web site: www.tanglewoodpark.org

Mid-Range The newly refurbished *Salem Inn* (☎ 336-725-8561, 127 S Cherry St) has nicely appointed doubles from $61 to $65, with special deals from $48.
Web site: www.saleminn.com

The *Hawthorne Inn* (☎ 800-972-3774, 336-777-3000, 420 High St) is a good business hotel with useful touches such as data ports and hair dryers, and continental breakfast delivered to your room. Rates are a standard $79, with specials from $59.

Top End The *Adam's Mark Winston Plaza* (☎ 336-725-3500, 425 N Cherry St) offers luxury in 600-plus rooms spread over two towers. Amenities include a sauna, exercise room and various lounges. Doubles start at $89/79 for weekdays/weekends, zooming to $200 during special events.
Web site: www.adamsmark.com

The *Augustus T Zevely House* (☎ 800-928-9299, 336-748-9299, 803 S Main St) is a restored 19th-century home with lots of original furnishings, heated brick floors, iron bedsteads and more. Single or double rooms start at $80.

Lady Ann's B&B (☎ 336-724-1074, 612 Summit St) offers nice rooms in a Victorian home with full breakfast for $55 to $95.
Web site: www.bbonline.com/nc/ladyannes

Places to Eat

Winston is the headquarters of *Krispy Kreme Doughnuts,* doughnuts so sinfully delicious that the Smithsonian has one of their doughnut-making machines on display. Outlets around town include one at 5901 University Pkwy.

The cutest breakfast haunt is *Mary's of Course* (☎ 336-725-5764, 301 Brookstown Ave), with the day's specials nearly obscured by all that colorful pop art. Two eggs with Canadian bacon, hash browns and biscuits will set you back $4. It's open 7 am to 3 pm daily (10:30 am to 2 pm Sunday).

Bistro 420 (☎ 336-721-1336, 420 W 4th St) has a relaxed ambience and cheap, good fare, such as burritos, meat pies and veggie dishes, for $5 to $8. There's no liquor license. It's open for lunch 11 am to 2 pm Monday to Friday and for dinner 5:30 pm to 10 pm Wednesday to Saturday.

The *Rainbow News & Café* (☎ 336-723-5010, 712 Brookstown Ave) is a vegan-oriented cafe and bookshop located in a turn-of-the-century home. Mains run $8 to $16, with organically prepared lasagna, humus and salads, and also chicken and ordinary sandwiches. It's not as offbeat as it once was before some pipes broke and seriously flooded the place, but it's still fun. It's open for lunch and dinner (closed Sunday).

The *West End Café* (☎ 336-723-4774, 926 W 4th St) is a family-oriented joint serving reasonably sandwiches, burgers, and steaks. Try a downhome dish such as molasses-glazed pork chops with sweet potatoes and hash browns ($15). Mains run $14 to $19. It's perennially packed at lunch and dinner, daily.

Built by a Moravian cabinetmaker, *Zevely House Restaurant* (☎ 336-725-6666, 901 W 4th St) serves dinner in a cozy, antique-filled room with hearth. Seafood is a good bet (fried trout with pine nuts and capers, $19) but the duck and beef dishes are also tempting. It's open 5:30 pm to 9 pm Tuesday to Saturday, and for Sunday brunch (11 am to 2 pm).

The *4th St Filling Station* (☎ 724-7600, 871 W 4th St) has a semirustic interior with an open fireplace and exposed wooden beams. The fare includes salads ($4 to $8) and pizzas, steaks, seafood and pasta ($7 to 22). It's open 11 am till around midnight daily (closed Sunday).

Leon's Café (☎ 336-725-9593, 924 S Marshall St) has its fish flown in daily. The menu is inventive (French, of course) and the wine list copious. Some starters ($7 to $10) are meals in themselves, and mains cost $16 to $25. Their baked salmon in ginger-orange sauce is heaven. The cafe is open 6 pm to 11 pm. Reserve ahead to avoid disappointment.

Noble's Grill (☎ 336-777-8477, 380 Knollwood St) has an upper-crust menu (rump steak, pecan-crusted trout, woodfire roast pork tenderloin), a copious wine list and a snazzy but simple interior. The mains ($20 to $30) aren't overpriced given the high quality, or reputation. It's open for lunch and dinner daily. To get there, take I-40 west to exit 2 (Knollwood St).

For fab French dining, try *Michael's on Fifth* (☎ 777-0000, 858 W 5th St) or *Fabian's* (☎ 336-723-7700, 1100 Reynolda Rd). Both serve by reservation only and are closed Sunday.

Entertainment

Bars, Cafes & Clubs Burke St has a few good spots; and 1st St around Hawthorne

Rd west of downtown, bustles with student bars. *Morning Dew* (☎ *336-723-5282, 1140 Burke St)*, with its bohemian patrons and 40 types of coffee, would have fit right into old Haight-Ashbury. There's live music and poetry slams (contests with judges) on Thursday nights. Hours are 7 am to at least 10 pm weekdays and 9 am to 8 or 9 pm weekends.

North of downtown, *Ziggy's* (☎ *336-748-1064, 433 Baity St)* is a funky saloon-cum-concert hall in a clapboard house. It pulls in alternative talent but also older bands such as Styx or .38 Special. Admire the autographed photos as you down your shots. The cover varies. Take Cherry St north, and the first right after Deacon Blvd (Ziggy's is behind the Wendy's hamburger joint).

The *1st St Drafthouse* (☎ *336-722-6950, 1500 W 1st St)*, west of downtown at Hawthorn Rd, is a popular college bar with trendy beers (Newcastle, Sierra Nevada Wheat, Hoegaarden) and pub grub (burgers, burritos and chicken, $5 to $8). Hours are 11 am to 2 am.

Unique Upstairs (☎ *324 4th St)* is a cool jazz lounge–bar spread over two levels, with a soothing landscape of stuffed chairs and chessboards. Upstairs has great acoustics and recalls the big-city jazz clubs of yesteryear. Admission is free till 9 pm and $5 to $7 later.

Gay & Lesbian Venues There's not much of a scene in Winston-Salem. *1001* (☎ *336-724-4644, 916 Burke St)* has pool tables, a well-stocked bar and male dancers. It's open 8 pm to 2:30 am Wednesday to Sunday.

Club Odyssey (☎ *336-774-1077, 4019 Country Club Rd)* has DJs spinning techno and house, as well as regular drag shows. Take I-40 and Hwy 421 west to the Jonestown Rd exit, turn right and right again into Country Club Rd.

Performing Arts The *North Carolina School for the Arts* (☎ *336-721-1945, 1533 S Main St)* features a big menu of drama, dance and musical productions. The *Piedmont Opera Theatre* (☎ *336-725-7101, 305 W 4th St)* stages two long-running productions a year.

Shopping

Sam's Art Gallery (☎ 910-777-1954), 701 W Northwest Blvd, is run by an old survivor named Sam McMillian. He didn't start painting till in his late '60s, and now he's a renowned folk artist who daubs his naive, patriotic motifs around the country. His shop doesn't keep set hours, but you might get lucky if you stop by (Sam owns the house next door).

The Piedmont Craftsmen Gallery (☎ 336-725-1516), 1204 Reynolda Rd, is a wonderful outlet for over 130 of the Southeast's craft artists. Stop in even if you don't want to buy. It's open 10 am to 6 pm Tuesday to Saturday.

Getting There & Away

Air The Piedmont Triad International Airport (☎ 336-721-0088) is 22 miles east of downtown off I-40. It's served by 7 airlines, which post special offers on the airport Web site (www.ptia.org). Despite the name, there are virtually no international or West Coast flights; Raleigh or Charlotte might be a better option if you're coming from farther afield. Sample roundtrip fares in high season include Baltimore ($159), Chicago ($179), New York ($148) and Toronto ($263).

Bus The Greyhound/Trailways station (☎ 336-724-1429) is at 250 Greyhound Court. Sample fares include Charlotte ($16.50, 1¾ hours), Raleigh ($20, 3 hours), Asheville ($33, 3¼ hours), Colombia ($41, 4¼ hours) and Atlanta ($59, 6¼ hours).

Getting Around

The Airport Express shuttle (☎ 336-668-3606) stops at many hotels and costs $22 to $28. A taxi from the airport to downtown will cost $32 to $38.

The Winston-Salem Transit Authority (☎ 336-727-2000) runs a good local bus network from its transportation center at 100 W 5th St. The fare is $1 with free transfers.

Old-fashioned trolleys operate in Old Salem during the day; the fare is 25¢.

For a taxi, call Blue Bird Cabs (☎ 336-722-7121) or Dallas Taxi (☎ 336-788-9999).

AROUND WINSTON-SALEM
Körner's Folly

A German-born interior decorator, Jule Körner, set out in 1878 to build an all-in-one bachelor's pad, including artist's studio, office, billiard and ballroom, carriage house and stables in his adopted home of Kernersville. Dubbed **Körner's Folly** (☎ 336-996-7922), at 413 S Main Street, the oddball, mazelike result (21 mostly claustrophobic rooms over 7 levels) is now a historic landmark. There are 15 fireplaces of differing design, classical murals, rococo sculptures, a private theater and scores of nooks and crannies. Some sections are badly run down but undergoing restoration. It's open 10 am to 3 pm Thursday, 10 am to 1 pm Saturday and 1 pm to 5 pm Sunday; admission costs $6/3. From downtown, take the Business I-40 east to the Kernersville–South Main St exit, turn left onto S Main St and drive 1 mile.

State Parks

The 1400-foot summit of the **Pilot Mountain State Park** looms like a monk's shorn head from the verdant surrounds. The Indians called it *Jomeokee* for 'pilot,' but early European settlers preferred 'Ararat,' after the mountain where Noah's Ark came to rest. There are actually two summits: the taller quartzite knob and a shorter one that can be reached from the main park road by a short foot trail. The section of the Yadkin River that flows through the 3703-acre park is quite scenic, and there are nice trails and fishing along its banks. The 49 wilderness campsites, with hand-pumped water and port-a-johns but no showers, cost $12 per night. Campers (no RVs) must arrive by closing time (9 pm in summer). The local park office (☎ 336-325-2355) is off I-52, about 24 miles north of Winston-Salem.

Hanging Rock State Park (☎ 336-593-8480) is just the ticket for secluded hiking along rocky outcrops and waterfalls. There's an easy 1½ mile trail that takes in three sets of falls, and another of similar length that ends with a panoramic view atop Moore's Knob. There's swimming in a marked lake area; many crags are climbable; and fishing is allowed in the Dan River. Six cabins are available for weekly rental in summer. There are 73 sites with rest rooms and bathhouse for tents/RVs ($12), and facilities for picnicking and grilling. It's about 30 miles north of Winston-Salem, between Hwys 66 and 89, close to Danbury.

Mount Airy
pop 8500

This sleepy community is the birthplace of Andy Griffith, star of the TV show of the same name that beamed Opie, Aunt Bea and other homespun characters into millions of living rooms. Mount Airy was the inspiration for the make-believe town of Mayberry, and every year droves of fans shuffle down Main St to visit **Floyd's Barber Shop** (quite real, although the actor who played Floyd, Howard McNear, died in 1969), and line up for a pork-chop sandwich at **Snappy Lunch,** which Andy used to frequent as a boy. Local retailers hawk spinoffs such as *Barney Fife's Guide to Love and Defense,* and plenty of residents seem to live out the Mayberry myth, rocking on their front porches and shooting the breeze. By the way, Andy Griffith's appeal is undiminished; a campaign ad by the aging actor helped swing the 2000 gubernatorial election for Mike Easley.

Mount Airy is 50 miles northwest of Winston-Salem, just south of the Virginia border.

GREENSBORO
pop 208,000

The third-largest city in the state, Greensboro was settled by Scottish-Irish farmers who came to the Piedmont from the northern colonies in the 18th century. The moniker derives from Nathanael Greene, a Revolutionary War hero whose forces met the British at Guilford County Courthouse to the north. Greensboro later made a name for itself by promoting higher education for African Americans and women, and the numerous colleges here helped to sow the seeds for the first civil-rights 'sit-in' in 1960. The burbs sucked the life out of the center in the '70s, but downtown is now revitalizing. Plan one day here.

GREENSBORO

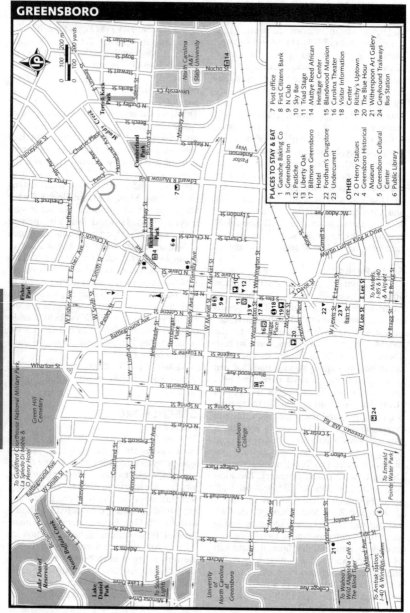

PLACES TO STAY & EAT
1 Ganache Baking Co
3 Greensboro Inn
12 Pastiche
13 Liberty Oak
17 Biltmore Greensboro Hotel
22 Fordham's Drugstore
23 Undercurrent

7 Post office
8 First Citizens Bank
9 N Club
10 Sky Bar
11 Triad Stage
14 Mattye Reed African Heritage Center
15 Blandwood Mansion
16 Carolina Theater
18 Visitor Information Center
19 Ritchy's Uptown
20 The Blue Hour
21 Witherspoon Art Gallery
24 Greyhound Trailways Bus Station

OTHER
2 O Henry Statues
4 Greensboro Historical Museum
5 Greensboro Cultural Center
6 Public Library

Orientation

With the exception of a few points downtown, you'll need wheels to reach most attractions, which are scattered. Old Greensborough, in the southwest corner, brims with pretty turn-of-the-century architecture and listed buildings. The area around Market St between Church and Greene Sts has several restaurants and nightclubs. South of the railway line, S Elm St is a treasure trove of antique shops.

Information

The visitor information center (☎ 800-344-2282, 336-274-2282), 317 S Green St, is open 8:30 am to 5:30 pm weekdays, 10 am to 4 pm Saturday and 1 to 4 pm Sunday. Web site: www.greensboronc.org

The main post office is at 201 Edward R Murrow Blvd. The public library, at 219 N Church St, has Web terminals for walk-in use. Just register at the counter.

There are several banks along Market Street, including a big First Citizen's bank, which has an ATM, at the corner of S Elm St.

The *News & Record* is Greensboro's daily newspaper; its Web site is at www.newsrecord.com. *Triad Style* is a freebie listings mag, which covers Greensboro and has a Web site (www.triadstyle.com). Local radio stations include WNAA 90.1 FM (classical, jazz) and WKSI 98.7 FM (rock).

Things to See & Do

Housed in a pretty Romanesque church, the newly refurbished **Greensboro Historical Museum** (☎ 336-373-2043), at 130 Summit Ave, has displays on the life and works of homeboy William Sidney Porter, the short-story writer better known as O Henry, and also on the life of a fashionable first lady, Dolley Madison. Another big draw is the exhibit on civil rights and the Woolworth sit-in, including a replica of the famous lunch counter. Less compelling are the sections on local history – transportation, furnishings, pottery, textiles and military weaponry. It's open 10 am to 5 pm Tuesday to Saturday and 2 to 5 pm Sunday; admission is free.

Take a gander at the nearby **O Henry statues** at the corner of N Elm and Belle-meade Sts. The three bronzes depict Greensboro's famous literary son, a 7-by-14-foot open book of his short stories and his dog, Lovey. After he died of alcoholism in New York, age 47, Porter was buried in Asheville.

The **Mattye Reed African Heritage Center** (☎ 336-334-3209), 1601 E market St, houses one of the most extensive collections of African art in the country: over 6,000 artifacts including sculptures, masks, figures, musical instruments and textiles from 35-odd countries. There's a library with a large stock of books, photos and slides, and the gallery hosts regular exhibitions. Hours are 10 am to 4:30 pm; admission is free. It's in the Dudley Bldg on the NC A&T University Campus.

The **Witherspoon Art Gallery** (☎ 919-334-5770), at Spring Garden and Tate Sts, has a good collection, including bronze sculptures by Henri Matisse and modern classics by Andy Warhol and Willem de Kooning. Check the rotating exhibits. Hours are 10 am to 5 pm Tuesday to Friday (till 8 pm Wednesday) and 1 to 5 pm weekends; admission is free.

Blandwood Mansion (☎ 910-272-5003), 447 W Washington St, is a Tuscan-style villa dating from the 1790s that was home to a former governor, John Motley Morehead. The furnishings aren't spectacular, but the costumed docents make its history come alive. It's open 11 am to 2 pm Tuesday to Saturday and 2 to 5 pm on Sunday; admission is $5/3 for adults/children.

By 2002 the **International Civil Rights Center & Museum** (☎ 336-274-9199) will open its doors at 134 S Elm St, site of the former Woolworth store and the historic sit-ins (see 'The Greensboro Sit-Ins' boxed text). The three-floor center will chronicle civil rights history and current developments around the world. Hours are likely to be 9 am to 5 pm weekdays (call ahead).

Guilford Courthouse National Military Park

On March 15, 1781, General Nathanael Greene deployed 4400 rebels against General Earl Cornwallis' force of 1900 in a

NORTH CAROLINA

The Greensboro Sit-Ins

On February 1, 1960, four African-American college students nervously sat down at the whites-only counter at the Woolworth's in downtown Greensboro. It wasn't the first organized challenge to 'Jim Crow Laws' in the US – remember Montgomery, Alabama in 1955 – but it played a key role in the Civil Rights movement.

Over the next few days the four students (Franklin McCain, Joseph McNeil, Ezell Blair Jr and David Richmond, all freshmen at North Carolina A&T State University) were joined by other youths, both black and white, at Woolworth's and another lunch counter a half-block away. Within a week, students were staging 'sit-ins' in Winston-Salem, Durham, Charlotte and Raleigh; in two months the movement spread to 54 cities in 9 states. The tactic worked: By the summer of 1960 the downtown lunch counters in Greensboro were serving both African-Americans and whites. Later, the sit-in would be adopted by anti-war protesters and the women's liberation movement.

Decades afterwards, Franklin McCain said that he'd expected to be arrested, beaten to a pulp or worse. 'I really didn't think about whether I was ever coming back,' he told the Greensboro News & Record, 'because life the way it was, wasn't worth living.' The Woolworth branch eventually closed, but the historic 8-foot section of lunch counter is on display at the Smithsonian Institution in Washington, DC.

bloody two-hour battle. Cornwallis' redcoats held their ground but lost a quarter of their number, a turning point that hastened the defeat of the British at Yorktown seven months later. Today the site (at 2322 New Garden Rd, off Battleground Ave, 4 miles north of downtown) is a national military park with a 200-acre wooded tract and a 2½ mile self-guided tour, with push-button audio programs, of 28 monuments. The visitors center has a 20-minute video on the pivotal battle as well as displays of military artifacts. Hours are 8:30 am to 5 pm daily; admission is free. It offers plenty of pleasant hiking trails.

Activities

The fun Emerald Pointe Water Park (☎ 336-852-9721) is the largest waterpark in the Carolinas, with giant wave pools, drop slides, tube rides, cable glides and a good children's area. Hours are 10 am to 8 pm daily (till 9 pm Saturday) May to early September. Admission is $17/25 for adults/children (cheaper after 4 pm); parents wanting a break can buy a 'dry ticket' for $10. It's off I-85 near exit 121.
Web site: www.emeraldpointe.com

Places to Stay

Camping The well-equipped *Greensboro Campground* (☎ 800-274-4143, 336-274-4143, 2300 Montreal Ave), east of downtown Greensboro, has large, shaded tent/RV sites with sanitary and recreation facilities for $12. Cabins are for rent in summer for $30/34 for one/two-bedroom. Take I-85 east to exit 128, drive ¼ mile southeast on Lee St, a mile west on Sharpe Rd and ¼ mile north on Trox St.

Hotels The *Greensboro Inn* (☎ 336-370-0135, 135 Summit Ave) is a crumbling flat-top motel with a convenient, if loud, location opposite the historical museum. Singles/doubles are cheap and clean at $36, but don't expect much more.

The *Motel 6* (☎ 336-854-0993, 831 Greenhaven Dr), at the junction of I-40 and I-85, has rooms starting at $38. The *Days Inn Central* (☎ 336-275-9571, 120 Seneca Rd), along I-40/I-85 at exit 125, has singles/doubles starting at $45/50. There are other budget options around exits 210 and 217B.

The *Biltmore Greensboro Hotel* (☎ 800-332-0303, 336-272-3474, 111 W Washington St) has faded old-world elegance with high ceilings and free continental breakfast. Year-round weekend/weekday rates start at $50/99 for small rooms; larger rooms are $75. Check out the huge portrait of the Napoleonic character in the walnut-paneled lobby; no one knows who he is.

The boutique *O Henry Hotel (☎ 800-965-8259, 336-854-2000, 624 Green Valley Rd)* has 131 large, plush, well-equipped rooms in a stylish new art deco complex. Doubles start at $179, although it runs specials for $99 to $119. It's about a mile northwest of downtown, off Benjamin Pkwy. Web site: www.o.henryhotel.com

Places to Eat

Soda fountains live on in the Southeast, and *Fordham's Drugstore (514 S Elm St)* is a quaint place to ruminate over a milk shake (closed Sunday).

Ganache Baking Co (☎ 336-230-2253, 403 N Elm St) does excellent fresh breads, cakes, pastries and light lunch fare. It's open for breakfast and lunch (closed Sunday).

The airy, relaxed *Pastiche (☎ 336-272-3331, 223 S Elm St)* serves sandwiches, salads, steaks, pastas and seafood under a curvy tin ceiling to strains of soft jazz. Evening meals run $16 to $54 (for a 16oz Chateaubriand). It's open daily for lunch and dinner.

The *Liberty Oak (☎ 336-273-7057, 100 Washington St)* has fresh pastas, fish, duck, salads and a chic polished wood bar. Lunchtime salads and sandwiches cost $6 to $8, and mains average $13 to $16. It's open for lunch and dinner (closed Sunday).

For inventive fusion, go with the flow at *Undercurrent (☎ 336-370-1266, 600 S Elm St)*. The lunch specials are hard to beat (for example, citrus-chili shrimp and scallops with bacon-bean ragout, $12). Mains cost $17 to $27 at dinner. The desserts are delicious, too. It's open Tuesday to Friday for lunch and dinner, and Saturday evening.

Southern Lights (☎ 336-379-9414, 105 N Smyres Place) is a casual bistro with Californian flair, good for sandwiches ($6 to $10), full meals ($10 to $19) or just a drink. The in-house collection of weird fish crafted from metal objects is itself worth a visit. Lunch is served Monday to Friday, and dinner 5:30 to 10 pm nightly. It's about a mile west, off W Friendly Ave.

Spiedo Di Noble (☎ 336-333-9833, 1720 Battleground Ave) is a high-class affair serving refined Italo-French dishes. Expect to pay from $40 per head for dinner with wine. There's live jazz Wednesday to Saturday (closed Sunday). Reservations are a good idea.

Entertainment

Bars & Clubs The Elm St area is a small hub of downtown nightlife. Try *Ritchy's Uptown (☎ 336-275-8113, 106 W McGee St)* a pleasant upstairs bar-restaurant with a zigzagging bar, tin ceilings and an air of inexorable decline. There's live R&B Thursday to Saturday (closed Sunday).

The *Sky Bar (☎ 336-275-1006, 221 S Elm St)* has DJs spinning '80s hits. It's open 10 pm to 3 am Wednesday and Friday to Sunday. The *N Club (☎ 336-333-9300, 117 S Elm St)* pulls in the urban legends with its late-night diet of Top 40. There's one floor for over 18s, another for over 25s. Members/nonmembers pay $5/8. It's open 10 pm to 3 am Wednesday and Saturday.

Several good college bars are out near the UNCG campus, about a mile west of downtown. Take Spring Garden St and turn right on Walker Ave, the first street after the campus. Get into the R&B groove at *Wild Magnolia Café (☎ 336-378-0800, 2200 Walker Ave)*, a wildly popular place with lots of music memorabilia and a good choice of microbrews. It also does po'boys, seafood and hot snacks.

Close by at No 2115, the rough-looking *Blind Tiger (☎ 336-272-9888)* has pool tables and live bands Wednesday to Saturday nights. *Wahoos (☎ 336-333-0094)*, at No 2120, is full of delinquent students at exam time.

Feeling kind of blue? Check out *The Blue Hour (☎ 336-378-2583, 360 Federal Place)*, a cool jazz bar with plush designer furniture, wild art and fine cocktails. It's open evenings only (closed Sunday).

Performing Arts Greensboro has a pretty lively performing arts agenda. The *Greensboro Cultural Center (☎ 336-373-2712, 200 N Davie St)*, in Festival Park, is a hive of activity with four levels of galleries, studios and concert halls.

The *Greensboro Symphony Orchestra (☎ 336-335-5456)* and the *Greensboro*

NORTH CAROLINA

Opera Company (☎ 336-273-9472) both perform at the huge, well-equipped *Greensboro Coliseum Complex* (☎ 336-373-7474, 1921 W Lee St), which hosts a variety of events throughout the year.

The *Carolina Theatre* (☎ 336-333-2600, 310 S Greene St) is a restored vaudeville theater, fun even to look at, with a varied diet of drama, dance, concerts and films. The *Triad Stage*, a fancy theater and music complex, is due to open on Elm St in late 2001 and pump more life into downtown.

Getting There & Away

The Piedmont Triad International Airport (☎ 910-665-5600) is 12 miles east of downtown. See the Winston-Salem section for sample fares.

The Amtrak station (☎ 336-855-3382) is on Oakland Ave. Bus No 1 runs to/from downtown, one long block north on Spring Garden St.

The Greyhound Trailways bus station (☎ 336-272-8950) is at 501 W Lee St. Sample fares include Raleigh ($16.50, 2½ hours), Charlotte ($12, from 2 hours) and Richmond, VA ($38, from 4 hours).

Getting Around

The Airport Express (☎ 336-668-3606) charges $15 from the airport to downtown Greensboro; a taxi will cost about $18.

The Greensboro Transit Authority (☎ 336-332-6440) runs 15 bus lines from downtown to the suburbs. The one-way fare is $1, with free transfers. Pick up schedules and route maps at the visitors center.

For a taxi, call Blue Bird Cabs (☎ 336-722-7121) or Dallas Taxi (☎ 336-788-9999).

AROUND GREENSBORO
North Carolina Zoological Park

The best and biggest zoo in the Carolinas (☎ 336-879-7200) squashes North America and Africa into a lush 500-acre tract for a good day out. There's an alphabet soup of the wild kingdom – alligators, bison, chimpanzees, dragonflies, elephants and so on, all the way up to zebras – as well as sheltered habitats such the Sonora Desert or the bird-filled African aviary. When the mercury dips the African beasts retreat to heated quarters, but there's plenty to see year-round. You can ride a tram around the entire zoo and catch some of the big game out there grazing. Hours are 9 am to 5 pm daily (4 pm in winter). Admission costs $8/5 for adults/children. It's about 5 miles south of Asheboro, off Hwy 220.

Seagrove
pop 253

During Prohibition, people needed a place to store their moonshine, and Seagrove obliged with innocent-looking vessels churned out by over 250 potteries. About 90 remain today, and you can find some exquisite bowls, pitchers and vases by local artisans, some of them sixth- and seventh-generation potters. The blue-veined clay in these hills makes great material. Stop by the modern, skylit **North Carolina Pottery Center** (☎ 336-873-7887), at the junction of Hwys 220 and 705 about 9 miles south of Asheboro, to see exhibits and get a map of the local studios. Most of them are along Hwy 704. Follow the hand-painted signs nailed to fence posts, pointing down dirt roads.

HIGH POINT
pop 79,000

Named for the highest point on the North Carolina railway, this former Quaker town is best known for the two-week, twice-yearly International Home Furnishings Market, the largest event of its kind in the world. In fact, it's a good idea to avoid High Point during the market (April and October), as the town swarms with tens of thousands of retailers, and hotels fill up for a hundred miles around. Cavernous outlets sell furniture at cut-rate prices, which for many folks is the chief reason for visiting.

Orientation & Information

The downtown area is several miles north of Business I-85, off of S Main St/US Hwy 311. The High Point Convention & Visitors Bureau (☎ 800-720-5255, 336-884-5255), 300 S Main St, has free town maps and other brochures.

Web site: www.highpoint.org

Things to See & Do

Right behind the visitors bureau, the **Furniture Discovery Center** (☎ 336-887-3876) at 101 W Green Dr, is a mock-up factory showing how furniture is made. It's tame stuff, with the main rush being a hands-on demo of an air-powered nail gun. Admission is $5/2 for adults/children. At the same address is the **Angela Peterson Doll & Miniature Museum** (☎ 336-885-3655), with over 1700 dolls (including 120-odd figurines of Shirley Temple). Admission is $3/1.50. Both places are closed Sunday morning.

A mile or so to the north stands the **World's Largest Chest of Drawers,** a three-story 1926 building which has been restored as an 18th-century bureau. It's now home to the High Point Jaycees, at 508 N Hamilton St. At N Main St, turn east on Westwood St.

John Coltrane grew up in High Point in the 1930s, and there's a **commemorative marker** to the legendary jazz saxophonist at the corner of Centennial St and Commerce Ave, near his former home.

Places to Stay & Eat

Budget accommodations are in short supply in High Point. The central **Super 8 Motel** (☎ 336-882-4103, 400 S Main St) offers singles or doubles for $40 to $65. The **Atrium Inn** (☎ 336-884-8838, 425 S Main St), adjacent to dozens of furniture showrooms, charges a standard $75 for doubles, with deals for $63.

Web site: www.atrium-inn.com

The **Grateful Bread Baking Co** (☎ 884-4424, 1506 N Main St) is a great little bakery and sandwich shop, open till 6 pm (closed Sunday). The ample, hearty Mexican dishes at the **Azteca Restaurant** (☎ 882-0066, 712 S Main St) more than outweigh the cheesy decor. It's open for lunch and dinner daily.

The **B Flat Café** (☎ 887-0094, 3805 Tinsley Dr) is a great jazz cafe that serves po'boys, gumbo and other Louisiana fare. It's two miles north of downtown off Eastchester Dr: turn right on Sutton Way and your first left is Tinsley Dr. It's open for lunch and dinner.

J. Basul Noble's (☎ 889-3354, 101 S Main St), in the glass pyramid next to the big GE Capital building, is one of the Triad's best restaurants – French-Italian food with Southern accents, smoke-free and stocked with tasteful art. Starters cost $6 to $12 and

---

Pulled Pork as Art

Barbecue has been raised to an art form in the Piedmont region, and there's no better place to savor it than Lexington, a town of 19,000 souls and 18 barbecue joints. The tradition dates from the 1920s, when a couple of shrewd fellas, Sid Weaver and Varner Swicegood, put up cookers near the Lexington courthouse to feed the masses on court days.

Local experts (and they're everywhere) will tell the uninitiated that barbecue 'is a noun, not a verb' and proudly relate what makes theirs unique. Lean pork shoulder is smoked over a hickory fire and then pulled from the bone, hence the term 'pulled pork' familiar in parts of the South. The 'dips' or sauces are vinegar-based, with perhaps a dash of sugar, as opposed to the tomato-based stuff consumed elsewhere. Coarsely chopped or sliced, the meat is made into sandwiches that are typically served with coleslaw, but also hush puppies or fries. When ordering, be sure to ask for some crispy outside bits.

If you're driving through, a good place to pig out is **Lexington Barbecue** (☎ 336-249-9814) on Hwy 70/29 at I-64, which has served the likes of Ronald Reagan and Tom Cruise. For serious addicts, the **Barbecue Center** (☎ 336-248-4633, 900 N Main St) also does mail orders.

You can pick up a map of barbecue restaurants at the helpful Lexington Visitor Information Center (☎ 336-236-4218), 305 N Main St. By the way, the annual Barbecue Festival attracts some 125,000 people on the third weekend in October.

Web site: www.visitlexingtonnc.org

NORTH CAROLINA

mains $20 to $30. There's often live jazz (open for dinner, closed Sunday).

Getting There & Away

The Amtrak station (☎ 336-841-7245) is downtown at High St and S Main St. Sample destinations include Greensboro ($10, 20 minutes) and Raleigh ($45, 2½ hours).

The Greyhound bus (☎ 336-882-2000), 100 Lindsay St, takes about as long but is cheaper ($8 to Greensboro, and $26 to Raleigh).

AROUND HIGH POINT

A must for locomotion buffs is the interesting **North Carolina Transportation Museum** (☎ 704-636-2889), in the cute little town of Spencer, is housed in a former repair shop of the Southern Railway. Stroll round the exhibits of transportation history (going back to Blackbeard and the pirate era), a bulletproof 1935 police car and a seaplane. In summer a restored locomotive puffs passengers around a loop of the property (50 minutes). Hours are 9 am to 5 pm daily (1 to 5 pm Sunday) in summer and 10 am to 4 pm in winter, when it's closed Monday. Spencer is about 22 miles southwest of High Point (exit 79 off I-85).

CHARLOTTE

pop 507,000

Founded at the junction of two old Indian trails, Charlotte was described as a 'hornet's nest of rebellion' against British rule in the 1770s. Miners burrowed under the town in the early 1800s, and banks were founded to handle the gold. Today, Charlotte is the second-largest US banking center after New York, complete with futuristic highrises and elevated walkways, but its downtown isn't quite as engaging as the Big Apple. Charlotte is primarily a business town, and its appeal consists of a few good museums, excellent restaurants and a scattered but lively music scene.

Orientation

The heart of the city is called Uptown, a 1½ by 2 mile, skyscraper-filled grid ringed by I-77 and I-277 (known jointly as the 'inner beltline'). Neighborhoods and main streets radiate from this core. To the south is Dilworth, a spruced-up residential area, and to the southwest lies South End, a hub of trendy eateries, shops and nightlife. Closer to the South Carolina border is Myers Park, an old-money suburb, and South Park, a mall-filled commercial district. North of Uptown, the North Davidson or 'NoDa' district is the center of the arts community, with galleries, alternative bars and cafes. Off the main roads, Charlotte is tricky to navigate and some streets may change names five or six times. Seriously consider buying a booklet-type city map, even if you're visiting just a few days.

Information

The friendly Info! Charlotte visitors center (☎ 800-231-4636, 704-331-2700) is located at 330 S Tryon St. Pick up a copy of the *Charlotte Visitors Guide,* which contains some useful fold-out maps. The office is open 8:30 am to 5 pm weekdays, 10 am to 4 pm Saturday and 1 pm to 4 pm Sunday. Web site: www.charlottecvb.org

Money There are banks and ATMs sprinkled along Tryon St and its cross-streets, including the Bank of America at 100 N Tryon St. The Wachovia Bank has a branch at 400 S Tryon St, opposite the visitors center. Sales tax in Charlotte is 6.5%; accommodation tax is 3%.

Post & Communications The post office upstairs in Founders Hall, 100 N Tryon St, is open 9 am to 5 pm Monday to Friday. General delivery is best at the main post office at 201 N McDowell, Charlotte, NC 28204. It's open Saturday, too.

The main public library, at 301 N College St, has a couple of dozen Web terminals with free printing. Hours are 9 am to 9 pm (till 6 pm Friday and Saturday, 1 pm to 6 pm Sunday).

The *Charlotte Observer* is the Carolinas' largest newspaper with good daily entertainment listings and a Web site (www .charlotte.com). Local radio stations include:

Huntington Beach State Park, SC

Sweetgrass baskets are a traditional Gullah craft.

Drayton Hall, SC, built in 1738

RICK GERHARTER

Murrell's Inlet – a lobster landed on my truck!

CHINA WILLIAMS

Abandoned sharecropper shack, Edgefield, SC

OLIVER STREWE

A farmer with a truckload of June Gold peaches, Santee, SC

OLIVER STREWE

Getting there & away the old-fashioned way, Blue Ridge Mtns

OLIVER STREWE

A crop of Hard Winter Red wheat

WBAV 101.9 FM (classic rock, R&B), WEND 106.5 FM (alternative rock), WFAE 90.7 FM (NPR) and WSOC 103 FM (country, NASCAR racing).

Travel Agencies American Express Travel (☎ 704-362-3373) has a full-service outlet several miles southeast of Uptown, at 4735 Sharon Rd. AAA Carolinas (☎ 800-888-3262, 704-569-3500), 6600 Executive Circle, offers travel planning for all and free maps and assistance for members; its Web site is at www.aaacarolinas.com. The Sunday edition of the *Charlotte Observer* is a good source of travel ads and information.

Bookstores The Little Professor Book Center (☎ 525-9239), 4139 Park Rd in the Park Road Shopping Center, is the city's best-stocked independent bookseller. There's a Barnes & Noble (☎ 535-9810) at 5837 E Independence Blvd.

White Rabbit (☎ 704-377-4067), 834 Central Ave, is the leading gay and lesbian bookstore and a great source of information on the local scene.

Laundry A good coin-operated laundry near Uptown is Coin Mach, at 521 E Morehead St in Dilworth, about half a mile south of I-277.

Medical Services The Carolinas Medical Center (☎ 704-355-2000), 1001 Blythe Blvd, about a mile south of Uptown, has a 24-hour emergency ward.

Things to See & Do

Most sights are clustered in the northeast part of Uptown and can easily be seen on foot. At the intersection of Tryon and Trade Sts, the main arteries of Uptown, **Independence Square** marks the point where the Indian trails crossed centuries ago. Scotch-Irish settlers later set up a trading post, and the Revolutionary War raged in this area. Today, the corners are graced by four Raymond Kaskey sculptures that represent industry (a textile worker), commerce (a gold prospector spilling money onto the head of a banker),

transportation (a railroad worker) and the future (a mother holding an infant aloft). Does the banker look familiar? The face was modeled on Federal Reserve chairman Alan Greenspan.

With its 60 floors, the **Bank of America Corporate Center** is the tallest skyscraper in the Southeast. The grand lobby contains a colorful **Ben Long fresco** with three huge sections (measuring 18 by 23 feet each) depicting the construction of the center, an unruly crowd and Long's own son. The artistic concept is Buddhist, although you may find it vaguely socialist, with all those workers in the picture. Long has painted frescoes in rural churches throughout the Blue Ridge Mountains, and there are four in Charlotte alone – the visitors center has a pamphlet. Attached to the BOA to the west is **Founders Hall,** a six-story glass atrium with two floors of restaurants, shops and businesses catering to the Uptown crowd.

In the mid-1800s the **Fourth Ward** was home to merchants, ministers, physicians and several churches. By WWII the district had lost its shine and was becoming downright sleazy until high-minded citizens began a restoration project in the 1970s. Today it's a showcase of Victorian style, and there are several historic sites worth a look. The visitors center has a free map guide.

Museums & Art Centers

The **Mint Museum of Craft & Design** (☎ 704-337-2000) presents pure imagination in the form of glass, metal, wood and other handcrafted materials, as well as highlights of the design world. A sample of 2002 exhibitions includes 'Czech Glass Masters' and 'American Modern Design, 1920–50.' A permanent collection gives a historical overview of studio crafts. It's well worth the $6/3 admission for adults/students. Hours are 10 am to 5 pm Tuesday to Saturday and noon to 5 pm Sunday (closed Monday). The craft museum's sister museum, the **Mint Museum of Art** (same phone number), at 2730 Randolph Rd southeast of Uptown off Independence Blvd, has a good, varied collection of art in the Americas; admission is $6/4. Web site: www.mintmuseum.org

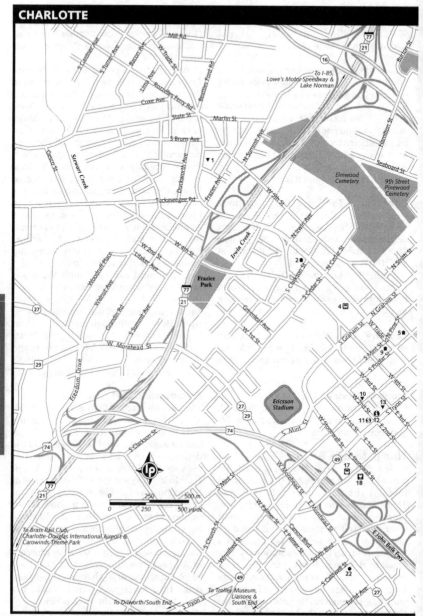

CHARLOTTE

CHARLOTTE

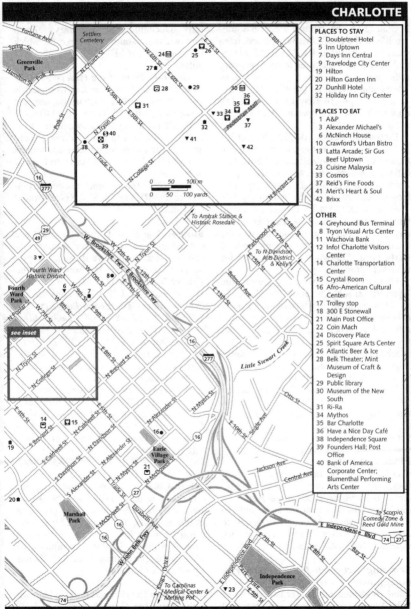

PLACES TO STAY
2 Doubletree Hotel
5 Inn Uptown
7 Days Inn Central
9 Travelodge City Center
19 Hilton
20 Hilton Garden Inn
27 Dunhill Hotel
32 Holiday Inn City Center

PLACES TO EAT
1 A&P
3 Alexander Michael's
6 McNinch House
10 Crawford's Urban Bistro
13 Latta Arcade; Sir Gus
    Beef Uptown
23 Cuisine Malaysia
33 Cosmos
37 Reid's Fine Foods
41 Mert's Heart & Soul
42 Brixx

OTHER
4 Greyhound Bus Terminal
8 Tryon Visual Arts Center
11 Wachovia Bank
12 Info! Charlotte Visitors
    Center
14 Charlotte Transportation
    Center
15 Crystal Room
16 Afro-American Cultural
    Center
17 Trolley stop
18 300 E Stonewall
21 Main Post Office
22 Coin Mach
24 Discovery Place
25 Spirit Square Arts Center
26 Atlantic Beer & Ice
28 Belk Theater; Mint
    Museum of Craft &
    Design
29 Public library
30 Museum of the New
    South
31 Ri-Ra
34 Mythos
35 Bar Charlotte
36 Have a Nice Day Café
38 Independence Square
39 Founders Hall; Post
    Office
40 Bank of America
    Corporate Center;
    Blumenthal Performing
    Arts Center

NORTH CAROLINA

Get to know King Cotton at the **Museum of the New South** (☎ 704-333-1887), at 324 N College St. The exhibits focus on Southern life in the post–Civil War period, from sharecropping through to NASCAR racing, and headsets let you listen to contemporary radio programs. Visitors are encouraged to leave comments about the place. Hours are 11 am to 5 pm Tuesday to Saturday. The museum was set to reopen in 2001 following a face-lift.

Discovery Place (☎ 704-372-6261), at 301 N Tryon St, has a better-than-average collection of hands-on science exhibits. You can see how astronauts work in space, peer inside a huge eyeball and sample liquid nitrogen ice cream in the chemistry lab. There's an OMNIMAX theater ($2 extra) and planetarium with shows throughout the day. Some exhibits are a bit dated – the Health section still features pictures of Betty Ford. Admission costs $6.50/$5 for adults/children.

Formerly a Presbyterian church, the **Tryon Visual Arts Center** (☎ 704-332-5535), at 721 N Tryon St, now hosts contemporary arts shows including works by a resident artist colony. Ask if you can see the second-floor exhibition space, normally open for special events, just to peek at the architecture. Hours are 11 am to 5 pm Tuesday to Saturday. Admission is free.

The **Afro-American Cultural Center** (☎ 704-374-1565), at 401 Myers St, hosts temporary art exhibits, performances and films. It's open 10 am to 6 pm Tuesday to Saturday and 1 to 5 pm on Sunday.

Places to Stay

Charlotte is a business town, so hotels charge more during the week than on weekends. Look out for special deals, even from the luxury hotels – you might be able to sleep in silk sheets at budget prices. Note that rates skyrocket during special events, especially NASCAR races.

Camping *McDowell Nature Preserve & Campground* (☎ 704-588-5224, 15222 York Road) is located off the verdant shores of Lake Wylie. You can rent tents, cots and other gear on site. Tent/RV sites cost $9/18 per night. It's open year-round (weekends only December to February). From Uptown, drive south on S Tryon St, which becomes York Rd/Hwy 49 – it's about 12 miles.

The *Duke Power State Park* (☎ 704-528-6350, 159 Inland Sea Lane), in Troutman, is about 45 miles north of Charlotte, just past Mooresville off I-77. The pretty 1400-acre park offers hiking trails, swimming, boat rentals and access to Lake Norman. There are separate campsites for tents and trailers (both $12). It's open mid-March to the end of November.

Carowinds Theme Park has wooded, full-service tent/RV sites for $23/28 (see Around Charlotte).

Budget The closest budget motels are outside the center, clustered around I-77 and I-85, and many have discount coupon deals. Coming from the south, try the *Cricket Inn* (☎ 704-527-8500, 219 Archdale Dr) off exit 7 of I-77, with rooms for $50 ($40 in winter). The *Econo Lodge* (☎ 800-228-5160, 704-523-0633, 575 Clanton Rd) is also out here, and charges $55.

The *Travelodge* (☎ 704-398-3144, 3200 I-85 Service Rd), near exit 33, is among the best values of the many places out here, at $41 for rooms year-round.

The area around Sugar Creek Road, 1 mile north of I-77 off exit 41 of I-85, has a few good-value options. The *Best Western Luxbury Inn* (☎ 704-596-9229, 4904 N I-85 Service Rd) charges from $45 per double with children, including a continental breakfast. The *Red Roof Inn* (☎ 704-596-8222, 5116 N I-85 Service Rd) starts as low as $39.

East Charlotte offers a number of cut-rate places in the 2000 and 3000 blocks, including the 130-room *Masters Inn* (☎ 800-633-3434, 704-377-6581, 2701 E Independence Blvd/Hwy 74) about 2½ miles from downtown. Singles or doubles cost $40, including continental breakfast. There's a pool and a restaurant.

Mid-Range The cheapest hotel in Uptown is the *Days Inn Central* (☎ 800-329-7466,

704-333-4733, 601 N Tryon St), charging a standard $59, with deals for $49.

The **Travelodge City Center** (☎ *800-578-7878, 704-377-1930, 319 W Trade St)* is in a refurbished low-rise in Uptown. The walled-in parking lot gives it a military compound feel, but comforts are good for the price and location. Rooms cost a flat $66.

The **Ramada Inn** (☎ *800-488-9110, 704-527-3000)*, south of town on I-77 near exit 7, charges $50 (as low as $39 with coupons).

Near the university, the **Microtel Inn** (☎ *800-276-0613, 704-549-9900, 132 E Mc-Cullough Dr)*, off exit 45 of I-85, has standard comforts in a pleasant modern complex. Singles/doubles cost $53/59, including free continental breakfast.
Web site: www.microtelinn.com

Some eight blocks west of Uptown, the 187-room **Doubletree Hotel** (☎ *704-347-0070, 895 W Trade St)* has a richly decorated marble-and-wood lobby, very comfy rooms and, if grandma's been baking, chocolate chip cookies at reception. Standard rates are a great deal at $69.
Web site: www.doubletree.com

Top End There's always room for another swanky hotel in Charlotte, judging by the construction of the 30-story, 700-room Westin Hotel across from the convention center.

The **Holiday Inn City Center** (☎ *704-335-5400, 230 N College St)* is in the thick of the Uptown entertainment district. Rooms cost $170 Monday to Thursday, but drop to $89 or $99 on weekends.

Now dwarfed by skyscrapers, the 10-story **Dunhill Hotel** (☎ *800-252-4666, 704-332-4141, 237 N Tryon St)* towered over the scene when it was opened in 1929. Restored to its original elegance in the 1980s, it's noted for its period furnishings and original art. Doubles start at $139/209 for weekends/weekdays.
Web site: www.dunhillhotel.com

The 22-story **Hilton** (☎ *704-277-1500, 222 E 3rd St)* has all the posh amenities you'd expect and is linked to several banks and corporations via an overstreet walkway. Standard doubles cost $189.
Web site: www.charlotte.hilton.com.

The **Hilton Garden Inn** (☎ *704-347-5972, 508 E 2nd St)* offers similar luxury to the Hilton but is cheaper – rack rates start at $109, with special deals as low as $59.
Web site: www.charlotteuptown.gardeninn.com

B&Bs & Inns Most B&Bs in Charlotte are snazzy affairs costing upwards of $85. An exception is **Roswell Inn Bed & Breakfast** (☎ *704-332-4915, 2320 Roswell Ave)*, in a pretty yellow colonial-style house 2 miles south of Uptown. Its three rooms, with hardwood floors, fireplaces, oriental rugs and plenty of nice touches, cost $75 per night. The owner is friendly.

The Inn Uptown (☎ *800-959-1990, 704-342-2800, 129 N Poplar St)* is good for an intimate Uptown splurge. The six rooms in this 1890 villa have gas-log fireplaces, and the top suite has a black-tiled Jacuzzi. Doubles start at $129 year-round.
Web site: www.innuptown.com

Places to Eat

Charlotte's choice of eats has big-city girth. From barbecue to burritos, pancakes to penne, and steaks to sushi, there's something here for every taste and budget, but the focus here is on the standout Southern restaurants. Reservations aren't a bad idea at the upscale places.

Uptown For self-catering in style, visit **Reid's Fine Foods** (☎ *704-377-1312, 225 E 6th St)*, in the 7th St Station. Apart from designer groceries – vintage olive oils, fine wines, deli wares, sun-dried-this-and-that – you can pick up a good salad, sandwich or hot meal. Touch the glass sculpture that surrounds the store, and you'll get a goofy sound. Hours are 7 am to 8 pm Monday to Saturday.

For standard groceries, the **A&P** (☎ *704-376-6563, 1600 W Trade St)* is the closest supermarket to Uptown.

Mert's Heart & Soul (☎ *704-342-4222, 214 N College St)* does definitive Lowcountry and soul food – pork chops, thickly breaded Southern fried chicken, cornbread, and fried green tomatoes ($6 to $10 for most mains). Big wooden painted creatures, eclectic prints and photos set an artsy mood. It's open for lunch Sunday to Friday, and also dinner Thursday to Sunday.

Sir Gus Beef Uptown (☎ 704-347-5741, *324 S Tryon*) in the Latta Arcade, is a bistro-type place that serves up generous portions of Southern home cooking (mostly under $10) to the business crowd. The roast beef is thick enough to knock someone unconscious. It's open for lunch weekdays only.

Crawford's Urban Bistro (☎ 704-375-5990, *322 S Church St*) serves tasty Cajun and Creole fare such as jerk chicken, lemon-pepper catfish, collard greens and candied yams for $8 to $14. There's great live blues and jazz four nights a week (see Entertainment), and at dinner it's packed to the gills. It's open for lunch and dinner Monday to Saturday, and noon to 4 pm Sunday.

In the Uptown clubbers' district, *Brixx* (☎ 704-347-2749, *225 E 6th St*) serves up great wood-fired pizzas and pastas (mostly $10 to $17) in a classy bistro ambience (all black-and-white tiles and soft orange lighting). It has several branches around town, and is open daily for lunch and dinner (till at least 2 am). Also out here is *Cosmos* (☎ 704-348-9876), near College and 6th Sts, a trendy cafe with tapas, pizza and sushi, where stretch limos often disengorge merry-makers for the night. It's open till 2 am daily (closed Sunday).

Warm wood paneling and candlelight make *Alexander Michael's* (☎ 704-332-6798, *401 W 9th St*), a tavern-restaurant in a former general store in the 4th Ward district, a favorite for atmosphere. Southern-style dishes include blackened chicken and crawfish burritos, with mains averaging $11 to $14. It's open for lunch Monday to Saturday, and for dinner nightly (closed Sunday, April 1 to Labor Day).

Bistro 100 (☎ 704-344-0515, *100 N Tryon St*), in Founder's Hall, is decorated in French country style, with a lovely frescoed ceiling. Mains (such as ragout of braised rabbit with seared scallops and hazelnut whipped potatoes) cost $15 to $25. Lunch and dinner are served daily (closed Sunday).

Peel off the C notes at the Victorian-era *McNinch House* (☎ 704-332-6159, *511 N Church St*). Six-course continental meals are served with antique china, crystal and starched linen; reckon on several hours and $100 to $150 per person, including wine and dessert. It serves dinner only, by reservation only, Tuesday to Saturday.

Dilworth/South End Once bleak and dangerous neighborhoods, Dilworth and the adjacent South End now hum with activity long after much of Uptown has closed for the night.

The *Southend Brewery & Smokehouse* (☎ 704-358-4677, *2100 South Blvd*) is a trendy converted warehouse with huge brewing vats. Smoked ribs, wood-fired pizzas and grilled seafood are the specialties; wash it all down with one of 8 house beers (also see the Entertainment section). Main dishes cost $7 to $16. It's open for lunch and dinner.

Cuisine Malaysia (☎ 704-372-0766, *1411 Elizabeth Ave*), on the corner of E Independence Blvd, is a light, airy place serving tasty Malaysian and Japanese dishes for lunch ($6 to $7) and dinner ($7 to $18). It's open 11 or 11:30 am till midnight (10 pm on Sunday).

There's a big choice of places around the intersection of South and West Blvds. Among them, *La Paz Cantina* (☎ 704-372-4168, *1916 South Blvd*) serves up tasty Tex-Mex – quesadillas, tostadas, burritos and tacos – all at reasonable prices. The awesome margaritas are reputedly the best in town; Monday nights they're half-price. It's open for lunch and dinner daily.

Melting Pot (☎ 704-334-4400, *901 S Kings Dr*), in the Kings Court Plaza, serves up high-class fondues (lobster tails or teriyaki sirloin) for $14 to $26. There's even chocolate fondue for dessert, if you really want to overdo it. It's open 5 pm to 11 pm daily (till midnight on weekends).

The *Pewter Rose* (☎ 704-332-8149, *1820 South Blvd*) has a wacky decor and a great menu. Enjoy New Orleans and fusion dishes such as goat cheese arugula, blackened tea duck and whiskey gumbo, under illuminated paper stars and light strands strewn across colorful vases. Mains cost $14 to $25. It's open 5 pm to midnight daily.

North Davidson *Kelly's* (☎ 704-372-0103, 3100 N Davidson St) is a cute alternative cafe with several galleries. It takes part in gallery crawls on the first and third Friday of each month. Its salads, Tex-Mex and veggie dishes are awesome, and there's a great Sunday brunch. Mains cost just $5 to $8. Lunch and dinner is served Tuesday to Saturday, and lunch on Sunday (no credit cards).

Entertainment

Creative Loafing is the free arts and entertainment weekly you'll find lying around in bars and restaurants around town.
Web site: www.cln.com

Uptown nightlife is focused on College St between 6th and 7th Sts, but bars and clubs are scattered through other areas, especially South End.

Bars & Clubs – Uptown *Ri-Ra* (☎ 704-333-5554, 208 N Tryon St) is an Irish pub with authentic Irish furniture – perhaps too authentic. All is forgiven, for the selection of beer, whiskey and cigars is excellent. Tap your toes to folk music on weekends. Hours are 11:30 am to 2 am Monday to Friday and noon to 2 am weekends.

Atlantic Beer & Ice (☎ 704-339-0566, 330 N Tryon St) is a popular restaurant-bar with a lively agenda of roots, jazz and rock groups. Downstairs are pool tables and bands, upstairs there's a cigar and scotch bar. The bar is open till midnight (2 am on weekends). There's usually no cover.

Crawford's Urban Bistro (see Places to Eat) has live blues and jazz on Tuesday, and Thursday to Saturday nights.

At *Bar Charlotte* (☎ 704-342-2557, 300 N College St), see college girls clamber onto the bar to dance while the bartender swoops back and forth on a rope swing. Cover is $4 to $6. It's open 8 pm to 2 am Thursday to Saturday. Minimum entry age is 18 (21 on Thursday).

Put on your smiley face for the *Have a Nice Day Café* (☎ 704-373-2233, 314 N College St), an overdose of '70s culture with posters of Farrah Fawcett, John Travolta, Erik Estrada and the Bee Gees. One bar is an ice-filled VW Beetle. Hours are 8 pm to 2 am Wednesday to Saturday. Cover is $6.

Mythos (☎ 704-375-8765, 300 N College St) is the sizzling club of the second, with DJs spinning house, techno and European dance music for fashion victims. Membership costs $15. Security is tight; prepare to have your bags searched. Hours are 10 pm to 3 pm Tuesday to Thursday and Sunday, and 10 am to 4 pm Friday and Saturday. Cover varies.

Bars & Clubs – Dilworth/South End Stevie Ray Vaughan and Eric Clapton played at the *Double Door Inn* (☎ 704-376-1446, 218 E Independence Blvd), which serves up live blues, zydeco and rock in a 1920s clapboard house. Expect serious decibels; the goons at the door sell earplugs. It's open 8 pm to 2 am nightly. Cover is usually $5.

The *Southend Brewery & Smokehouse* (see Places to Eat) is a haven for Panthers fans and players, and post-game tailgate parties are a feature. There's live music Wednesday to Saturday. It's open till 10 pm Sunday to Tuesday, to 11 pm the rest of the week and till the wee hours on game nights.

Tutto Mundo (☎ 704-332-8149, 1820 South Blvd) is a cool drinks lounge playing retro jazz next to the Pewter Rose (see Places to Eat). Relax in the soft leather chairs and ponder the gigantic tree murals. Hours are 5 pm to 2 am daily.

Bars & Clubs – Other Districts *Jack Straw's* (☎ 704-347-8960, 1936 E 7th St), a restaurant-bar about 1 mile east of Uptown, draws college students and yuppies with its triple-whammy of rock, reggae and rhythm & blues. There's canned jazz on Thursday, and live music on Friday and Saturday, always with cheap beer. Hours are 5 pm to 1 am (2 am weekends).

Up in the NoDa district, *Fat City* (☎ 704-343-0240, 3127 N Davidson) is an alternative music club hosting groups with in-your-face names such as Snagglepuss,

NORTH CAROLINA

Nuke, and Hotplateband. It's open till 2 am daily. Cover is $5 to $10.

Gay & Lesbian Venues *Liaisons (☎ 704-376-1617, 316 Rensselaer Ave)* gets rave reviews for its great sound system, fab costume contests, and balcony view of Uptown skyscrapers. On Mondays there's free pool and no cover. Hours are 9 pm to 3 am daily. Cover varies. It's off South Blvd, about ³/₄ mile southeast of I-277 ring.

300 E Stonewall (☎ 704-347-4200, 300 E Stonewall St) is a hopping club with multiple bars and dance floors, spiral staircases and a glass cage with rainbow-colored birds. Members ($10 to join) get in free before 10:30 pm, while guests pay $8 to $12. Hours are roughly 9 pm to 3:30 am Friday and Saturday, but the hard-core stick around till sunup.

Scorpio (☎ 704-373-9124, 2301 Freedom Dr/Hwy 27), about 1½ miles west of Uptown, draws a mixed crowd of 20-somethings who strut their stuff to light and video shows. Enjoy $1.50 beers at the patio bar. Hours are 9 pm till at least 2 am Tuesday to Sunday. Membership costs $10 and cover is $5.

The *Brass Rail (☎ 704-399-8413, 3707 Wilkinson Blvd/Hwy 74)*, the only jeans-and-leather bar in town, has good theme nights (uniforms, costumes etc). Hours are 5 pm to 2:30 am nightly (Sunday from 3 pm). There's no cover. Take Wilkinson Blvd west from Uptown about 2 miles.

The Crystal Room (☎ 704-334-3762, 431 E Trade St) is a lesbian sports bar and dance club with regular DJs, pool and foosball tables. It's open 9 pm to 2:30 am Friday and Saturday. Admission is $5/8 for members/nonmembers.

Comedy Split your sides at the *Comedy Zone (☎ 704-568-4242, 5317 E Independence Blvd)*, which draws regional and national talent such as Jerry Seinfeld or James Gregory. Shows are at 8 pm Wednesday, Thursday and Sunday; 8 pm (nonsmoking) and 10:15 pm Friday; and 7 pm, 9 pm and 11 pm Saturday. It's 4 miles east of Uptown.

Concert & Theater Venues For classical concerts and drama, check out the *Spirit Square Arts Center (☎ 704-372-7469)*, on N Tryon St between 6th and 7th Sts. The complex includes three galleries and two theaters.

Nearby, the *Belk Theatre (☎ 704-372-1000, 130 N Tryon St)* hosts a variety of dramatic and musical performances.

The *Blumenthal Performing Arts Center (☎ 704-372-1000, 100 E 5th St)*, located in the bowels of the Bank of America building, stages performances by big-ticket artists and elaborate productions such as *Godspell*. It also hosts the town's own cutting-edge troupe, the Charlotte Repertory Theater.

The *Neighborhood Theater (☎ 704-358-9298, 511 E 36th St)* is an intimate venue tucked away in the funky NoDa district. The eclectic program spans everything from Celtic instrumentals to Cajun roots rock. There's a bar and a pool table for use at intermission. Cover is $8 to about $30.

The *Charlotte Coliseum (☎ 704-375-7300, 100 Paul Buck Blvd)* hosts rock and pop concerts. The *Tremont Music Hall (☎ 704-343-9494, 400 W Tremont Ave)* at S Tryon St, about 1½ miles south of Uptown, is the town's largest live music club, hosting anything and everything from top national acts to local alternative gigs. Concerts begin at 9 pm or 10 pm.

Spectator Sports

The men's Charlotte Hornets (☎ 704-424-9622) and the women's Charlotte Sting (☎ 704-357-0252) play professional basketball at the Charlotte Coliseum (☎ 704-357-0489), off the Billy Graham Pkwy. Prices range from $9 for a rafter seat to $85 courtside. The best Hornets seats sell out early in the season.

The Carolina Panthers football team plays at Ericsson Stadium (☎ 704-358-7800) on S Mint St.

Insanely popular NASCAR races are held in Concord north of town (see Lowe's Motor Speedway in the Around Charlotte section).

Shopping

Charlotte's malls are flashy and numerous. The South Park area (south of Dilworth) alone has four malls, including the upscale South Park Mall with over 100 stores on Sharon Rd, off Providence Rd. For more off-beat tastes, try 7th Street between Pecan and Hawthorne Sts (southeast of Uptown), with galleries and shops selling retro lamps, didgeridoos, South American carvings, furry backpacks and more. Paper Skyscraper (☎ 704-333-7130), 330 E Blvd in Dilworth, is known for its irreverent cards and funky gifts.

Getting There & Away

Air The modern, trilevel Charlotte Douglas International Airport (☎ 704-359-4000) is one of the top-rated airports in the country. High-season fares to the East Coast, Chicago and the West Coast cost around $270 to $300, and to London between $400 and $500. A total of 11 airlines serve Charlotte, including American, British Airways, Delta, Northwest, United and US Airways. Web site: www.charlotteairport.com

Bus The Greyhound station (☎ 800-231-2222, 704-372-0456), not far west of Uptown at 601 W Trade St, has regular connections to Raleigh ($30, 4¼ hours), Atlanta ($42, 4 hours), Charleston ($43, 4¾ hours) and Washington, DC ($66, 7½ hours).

Train The Amtrak station (☎ 800-872-7245, 704-376-4416) is north of Uptown at 1914 N Tryon St. City bus No 11 links the station with Uptown.

There are snail-like services to Atlanta ($51, 4½ hours) and Raleigh ($25, 3¾ hours). Express trains go to destinations including New York, ($134, 2 hours) and New Orleans ($170, 4½ hours).

Getting Around

To/From the Airport For just $1, the City Bus (Route 5) makes the 30-minute run to the Charlotte Transportation Center (CTC) in Uptown. It departs hourly from the east end of the upper level of the main terminal, usually at 52 minutes past the hour, till almost 2 am. The Carolina Transportation Airport Express (☎ 704-359-9600) also runs a shuttle to major hotels and various neighborhoods; a one-way ticket to Uptown costs

$8. The taxi fare to the Uptown area is roughly $14.

Bus & Trolley The Charlotte Area Transit System (CATS; ☎ 704-336-3366) operates 30-odd lines from its sparkling Charlotte Transportation Center at 310 E Trade St. Single fare is $1, with free local transfers; a 7-day pass costs $10. Express buses link the suburbs to downtown ($1.40), with stops at many park-and-ride lots. There's also a free Uptown shuttle bus, the Center City Circuit, that runs weekdays till 6:30 pm.

An old streetcar clangs its way along a 3-mile stretch of track between Southend and the lower edge of Uptown every half-hour ($1 each way) 10 am to 9 pm Friday and Saturday and till 6 pm Sunday. It's based at the Trolley Museum (☎ 704-375-0850), in the old Atherton Mill at 2104 South Blvd.

AROUND CHARLOTTE
Latta Plantation

This restored clapboard mansion was owned in the early 1800s by James Latta, a local merchant and cotton farmer. Today it's a 'living history museum' (☎ 704-875-2312), with 13 outbuildings, a working farm and craft demonstrations. Admission is $4/3 for adults/children, including an optional guided tour. Just as interesting is the **Carolina Raptor Center**, in the adjacent park, a refuge for hundreds of injured birds, including owls, eagles and falcons. Take I-77 north to exit 16B, then Sunset Rd west; at the third stoplight turn right into Beatties Ford Rd, and drive about 5 miles to Sample Rd – it's signposted. Admission here costs $5/3.

Both places are open 10 am to 5 pm weekdays (closed Monday), and afternoons on weekends.

Carowinds Theme Park

This amusement park (☎ 704-588-2600) has a fine assortment of rides themed on Carolinian history and Paramount movies. Stomach-spinning roller-coasters include Top Gun, License to Thrill and Vortex, and a fancy water ride simulates tidal waves and tropical falls. Yet the place retains a downhome feel, with regular stage shows and musical reviews.

NORTH CAROLINA

Admission is a hefty $39/27 for adults/children. It's closed in winter and runs weekends only in spring and fall. Take I-77 to near the South Carolina border, about 10 miles south of Uptown. Carowinds Connections buses go from the CTC to the park for $1.40.

Reed Gold Mine

John Reed used a 17-pound chunk of yellow rock as a doorstop for three years before a shrewd jeweler snapped it up for $3.50. This was in fact the first documented gold find in the US and triggered a gold rush nearly half a century before California's. The family ran their own mining operation, and today the Reed Gold Mine is a state historic site offering free guided tours of the underground tunnels, mining equipment exhibits and films about the discovery. You can pan for treasure yourself, too ($2 per pan). Hours are 9 am to 5 pm daily from April to October (closed Sunday). The rest of the year it's open 10 am to 4 pm Tuesday to Saturday. Take Hwy 27 east from Charlotte (19 miles).

Lowe's Motor Speedway

NASCAR racing, in the words of one critic, carries 'as many stereotypes as chicken bones tossed against the grandstand fence.' Yet there's no denying the insane popularity of the sport, which now draws more millions (of spectators and sponsors' cash) than football, baseball or basketball. Catch the ear-splitting action at Lowe's Motor Speedway (☎ 704-455-3200), which hosts three Winston Cup and two Busch series races at its 200,000-seat stadium. Tickets cost anything from $12 to $113. It's about 12 miles northeast of Charlotte in Concord, off I-77.

James K Polk Memorial

This memorial (☎ 704-889-7145) to 'Young Hickory,' as the 11th president was tagged in his youth, features guided tours of a reconstructed cabin, outbuildings and grounds. The visitors center runs a short film on Polk's life and presidency. It's on Hwy 521 in Pineville, about 10 miles south of Charlotte. Hours are 9 am to 5 pm Monday to Saturday and 1 pm to 5 pm Sunday from April to October. The rest of the year it closes at 4 pm and all day Monday.

PINEHURST & SOUTHERN PINES
pop 9250 & 11,300

The Sandhills region in the southern Piedmont got its name from the flat-topped, sandy ridges formed by the sea millions of years ago. Scottish Highlanders settled here in the mid-1700s and carved up the vast forests for timber, lopping choice pines for use as masts of Royal Navy ships. As a result, most of the virgin longleaf pines disappeared from the Sandhills by the late 19th century.

About the same time a Boston philanthropist, James W Tufts, built a New England–style health resort and invited Frederick Law Olmsted, the famed architect of New York's Central Park, to design the village of Pinehurst. Gentle hills make for good golf, and in 1900, Tufts got the idea of hiring Scotsman Donald Ross to lay out the greens. Pinehurst was soon calling itself the St Andrews of the US (sorry, Augusta), and today a staggering 720 holes lie at the end of 165 miles of fairways studded with 2900 bunkers. The annual PGA Women's Open is now held here. Equestrianism is also big business, and horse farms abound.

Less genteel than Pinehurst, Southern Pines is an old-fashioned town close by with a pretty main street. All told, the region is attractive, but unless you swing clubs or ride horses, you'll want to make this a short stopover.

Orientation & Information

Pinehurst is loosely separated from Southern Pines, some 5 miles east, by Hwy 1. The

Artful Barns

About 15 miles north of Southern Pines lies tiny Cameron, which once prospered from the unlikely pairing of turpentine distilling and dewberry farming. The sticky stills and berry patches have dried up, and today Cameron's sights are trained firmly on the antiques shops of its pretty main drag, Carthage St.

The painted barns down the road have a more original charm. David Ellis, a local artist, recruited 15 painters from New York, Canada, Japan and Korea to give 15 Cameron barns a face-lift. Ellis was inspired by the graffiti he'd admired in Europe as a teenager. The result is like pieces of the Berlin Wall transplanted to rural North America. The visitors' center in Pinehurst has a basic map of the locations, and from Cameron you'll need only about a half-hour to see them all.

From Southern Pines, take busy Hwy 1 north to Hwy 24/27 and turn left (west). Follow the highway a few miles until it veers right into Red Hill Rd. At the dogleg junction of Stanton Hill Rd (on your right) and Nickens Rd (about 50 feet farther, on the left), the first colorful structures appear. The corner of Stanton Hill Rd features a spoof cigarette ad, 'Welcome to Flavor Country,' with the brand 'Espo' clearly visible; across the road are some freaky faces on the haybarn that Ellis first daubed when he was 14. At this point, continue west on Red Hill Rd to see some flying pigs and psychedelic cows, or bear left (south) on Nickens Rd and right again onto Hwy 24/27. Past Cranes Creek Rd, you'll spot more wacky images on the right – look for the vinyl record nailed over the door of the first barn.

visitors bureau (☎ 800-346-5362, 910-692-1600) is at 1480 Hwy 15/501, about a half-mile northwest of Hwy 1, and has a forest of pamphlets, including area maps and golf guides. Green fees on the cheaper of the region's 30-odd courses start around $25. Web site: www.homeofgolf.com

Things to See & Do

Opened in 1901, the **Pinehurst Resort & Country Club** (☎ 910-295-6811) is a sparkling white palace topped with playful domes and a shiny copper roof – worth a look, even if 'mashie niblick' sounds like a potato dish to you. The famously tricky courses 2 and 7 are closed to nonmembers, but for a hefty green fee ($90 to $160), you can play six other classic courses. There are also four lawn courts for regulation croquet. The adjacent **Pinehurst Village** is a minefield of touristy shops, craft galleries and eateries housed in old New England–style buildings.

The **Sandhill Horticultural Gardens** (☎ 910-695-3882), at 2200 Airport Rd by Sandhills Community College in Pinehurst, has 32 acres of wonderfully varied and sculpted landscape. There's a wetland trail on a wooden boardwalk, an acre-sized English garden and tracts of conifers, roses, hollies and even fruits and vegetables. It's free for a stroll, dawn till dusk.

Also good for walks is the **Weymouth Woods Sandhills Nature Preserve** (☎ 910-692-2167), with sandy paths and boardwalks crisscrossing 676 acres of lush parkland. The good, and short, Bog Trail loops from the visitor center through a carpet of ferns, pitcher plants and shrubs. The preserve is a mile southeast of Pinehurst – look for signs along Hwys 1 and 211. It's open daily; admission is free.
Web site: www.ils.unc.edu/parkproject/wewo.html

Places to Stay & Eat

Hwy 1 around the junction of Hwys 501/15 teems with chain eateries and hotels. In Pinehurst Village, *Dugan's Pub (☎ 910-295-3400, 20 Market Square)* serves up big tasty sandwiches and pints of the good stuff. Try the steaming Irish Wake, made of hot corned beef and sauerkraut, for $8. Hours are 10 am to 11 pm daily (closed Sunday).

NORTH CAROLINA

Theo's Taverna (☎ 910-295-0780, 140 *Chinquapin Rd*) in Pinehurst Village is a good, somewhat pricey, Greek place with good dishes such as moussaka, rabbit or sea bass. Specials cost $15 to $20. It's closed Sunday.

In Southern Pines, try *Sweet Basil Cafe*, on NW Broad St, for lunch, with good quiches or sandwiches for around $5.

Budget hotels are a bit thin on the ground. The *Motel 6* (☎ 910-944-5633, 1408 *N Sandhills Blvd*) about a quarter-mile south of the junction to Hwy 1, charges $40/44 weekdays/weekends for one to two people. The *Inn at Bryant House* (☎ 800-453-4019, 910-944-3300, 214 N Poplar St) in Aberdeen, 5 miles south, is a comfy 1913 house charging $50 to $85 for a room with breakfast.

Getting There & Away
Greyhound (☎ 910-692-4191) stops at the BP station at 912 W Pennsylvania Ave. Services include Raleigh ($16, 1¾ hours) and Charlotte ($24, 2½ hours). Most buses into South Carolina go via Charlotte.

Amtrak (☎ 800-872-7245) has an unstaffed station at 235 NW Broad St, smack in the middle of Southern Pines. Destinations include Raleigh ($27, 2 hours), Camden, SC ($29, 2 hours) and Richmond, Virginia ($51, 5 hours).

AROUND PINEHURST
82nd Airborne War Memorial Museum
This modern museum (☎ 910-432-3443) in the army town of Fayetteville covers the missions of the 82nd Airborne from WWI through Desert Storm and beyond. A scene from the Battle of Normandy is cleverly done, and there are aircraft, artillery and other equipment on display. Check out the CG-4A Waco glider, which disgorged an Army Jeep. Various videos are shown throughout the day. Fort Bragg military base is nearby, so you'll see lots of crew cuts among visitors. The museum's at the corner of Ardennes and Gela Sts, signposted from Hwy 210 and I-95. It's closed Monday; admission is free.

North Carolina Mountains

With their cool summers, gentle breezes and spectacular scenery, the western mountains of North Carolina work like a shot in the arm on weary urbanites. The southern section of the Blue Ridge Mountains, which forms part of the Appalachians, has massive peaks of over 5,000 feet. Early European settlers took the name from the 'blue' haze hanging over it (caused by rising damp from the forest below).

For the plantation colonials, the mountains formed a frontier to Indian country to the west. During the late 18th century, settlers from Ireland, Germany and England moved into the area and formed isolated farming communities that had almost no link with the African slave labor that was so typical of the Southeast. Meanwhile the Cherokee Indians occupied much of the region into the early 1800s, hunting in the mountains they considered sacred. As the settlers pushed toward their Manifest Destiny, President Jackson had 16,000 Cherokees removed in 1838, and a quarter of them died on the Trail of Tears.

During the 1930s, the Blue Ridge Parkway was authorized as a Depression-era public works project and gradually extended to link the Great Smoky Mountains with central Virginia. The new route revealed a world of mountain culture for outside visitors, and sleepy backwoods towns such as Boone or Valle Crucis suddenly found their visitors included more skiers than lumberjacks. Still, the old-time folk music, crafts and other traditions live on, and turning off the main roads can land you in the back of beyond.

Natural sights and options for outdoor activities abound: The Appalachian Trail

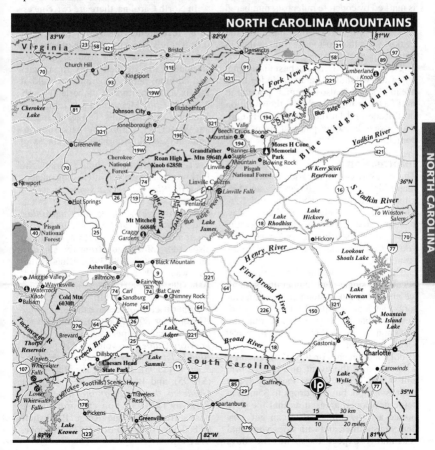

NORTH CAROLINA MOUNTAINS

roughly follows the state's western border; there's great white water around Nantahala; and the Great Smoky Mountains National Park draws thousands of hikers (and RVs) every year. Of the four ski areas south of Boone, Sugar Mountain has the longest runs and a snowboard park.

BLUE RIDGE PARKWAY

The Blue Ridge Parkway traverses the ridge of the southern Appalachians for 469 miles, from Shenandoah National Park in Virginia to Great Smoky Mountains National Park in North Carolina. The two-lane, paved road is marked by concrete mileposts, numbered north to south. With nearly 20 million visitors per year to various parts of the Parkway, it's the most visited site in the US national park system.

The Parkway is at its best in spring, when the wildflowers and rhododendrons are in bloom. It's also extremely popular in mid-October for fall colors – the variation in altitude and latitude means that there will always be some place at its peak of comeliness.

Information

The Parkway can be accessed from several major highways in North Carolina and Virginia, including I-40, I-81, I-77 and I-26. There's no fee to enter or use the Parkway. Its many breathtaking overlooks, especially in the section south of Boone, will entice you to get off the main road and explore the scenery.

The road is sometimes closed in winter because of single-digit temperatures, wind, ice and snow, but in summer, the temperatures can soar into the 90s (F). This is understandable when you realize that the elevation of the Parkway varies from 650 feet to 6000 feet.

For emergencies, or for information on what to do in the event of a breakdown, call ☎ 800-727-5928. The Parkway speed limit is 45mph, but this drops to 35mph in some developed areas; note that the state police are vigilant. Traffic can get *very* heavy in summer, and with stops, you could reasonably expect to spend two days

driving the full length. There are three gas stations on the Parkway, but prices are exorbitant so fill your tank elsewhere. An 11-mile section between Miles 270 and 281 near Boone will be closed until summer 2002 for bridge repair.

Bicycling on the Parkway isn't a good idea, due to the narrowness of the road and frequent poor visibility. If you're undeterred, take commonsense precautions (layered clothing, proper lights or reflectors and a helmet). Some sections climb as much as 1100 feet in 3½ miles, so be realistic about your fitness before setting out.

In North Carolina, there are two concessionaires operating **lodges and cabins,** and three **restaurants,** open May to October only. There's also a huge range of activities available – walks vary from simple 'leg stretchers' to extended hikes. In summer and autumn, ranger programs are held at the six **visitor centers** – Cumberland Knob, Moses H Cone Memorial Park, Linn Cove Viaduct, Linville Falls, Craggy Gardens, and Waterrock Knob. The park superintendent (see following) has an overview of what's on.

Free publications help make the Parkway journey more interesting, including *The Blue Ridge Parkway Directory,* complete with strip maps and bloom calendar, and the NPS's *Official Map and Guide.* The publications can be picked up at concessionaires along the Parkway. You can also order information from the superintendent (☎ 828-298-0398), Blue Ridge Parkway, 199 Hemphill Knob Rd, Asheville, NC 28803.
Web site: www.nps.gov/blri

Other useful sources are the *Blue Ridge Almanac* (☎ 800-877-6026), published six times a year ($3 per issue), *Blue Ridge Parkway Guide* (two volumes, $16 per set), *Blue Ridge Parkway: The Story Behind the Scenery* ($8.95), *Bicycling the Blue Ridge* ($10.95), and *Walking the Blue Ridge: A Guide to the Trails of the Blue Ridge Parkway* ($12.95). You can order these books from the Blue Ridge Bookshelf (☎ 800-548-1672), PO Box 21535, Roanoke, VA 24018.

Cumberland Knob

Located on the oldest segment of the Parkway (1936), Cumberland Knob has a useful National Park Service visitors center at Mile 217.5 on the Virginia border. It's a good introduction to the park and distributes a range of brochures and literature, and there's camera film available. It's a short walk from the knob itself.

There are some good roadside observation points to the south. At Mile 232.5, pull into the **Stone Mountain Overlook** to examine the 500-foot granite patch opposite, which looks like a bump on the head. It's a heavenly spot for a picnic, too. Three miles on, the **Devil's Garden** is the gap formed by two crags, with rattlesnakes and copperheads its sole residents.

Moses H Cone Memorial Park

This former estate of Moses H Cone, Mile 292, is a pretty 21-room Victorian manor that's now an Appalachian crafts center, visitors center and museum. Cone was the 'Blue Denim King,' who owned a pants factory in Greensboro. The house is a hive of activity in summer, when hot hikers and equestrians come in off the nearby trails to sit on the porch and admire the panorama.

Grandfather Mountain

This privately run park (☎ 800-468-7325) is owned by Hugh Morton, a spunky conservationist who for years fought the construction of the final segment of the Blue Ridge Parkway around Grandfather Mountain (see 'The Linn Cove Viaduct' boxed text). There are miles of picturesque walking trails around the old man (5964 feet) and a dizzying **Mile High Swinging Bridge**, which spans a 100-foot chasm to Linville Peak. There are also a small animal refuge, a nature museum and a restaurant with stunning views from the rear balcony. The Scottish Highland Games held here in mid-July attract thousands of visitors, including many people of Scottish descent, for caber-tossing, highland wrestling and clan tugs-of-war. Admission to the park, at Mile 305.1 off the Parkway on Hwy 221, is $10/6 for adults/children.

The Linn Cove Viaduct

The Blue Ridge Parkway is a marvel of engineering, and the jewel in its leafy crown is undoubtedly the Linn Cove Viaduct. After 30-odd years of work, by 1967 the Parkway was completed but for a 7½-mile stretch near Grandfather Mountain. The question of how to tackle this 'missing link' created a lengthy and heated controversy between private conservationists (led by Hugh Morton, owner of Grandfather Mountain) and the National Park Service. They finally agreed on a complicated, snaking design that required a minimum of drilling into the craggy Linn Cove beneath, and the only trees cut were directly under the structure. Unveiled in 1983, the viaduct took four years and $10 million to build, as each of its 153 concrete sections had to be cast individually.

Linville Falls

This lovely recreation area at Mile 316.4 features a visitors center and hiking trails to the overlooks of the falls. The explosive rush of water from the falls is one of the most popular sights along the Parkway. The falls are divided into upper and lower sections, which can be reached via three paths (1 to 2 miles roundtrip). It's a lovely spot to picnic and camp year-round, too (see Places to Stay, later in this chapter).

Near the falls, the mineral deposits in **Linville Caverns** (☎ 800-419-0540) resemble the interior of a cathedral. It's always cold here (52° F), so wrap up. It's open year-round, but weekends only from December to February; admission is $5/3 for adults/children.

Penland School of Crafts

Southwest of Linville Falls, about 9 miles north of the Blue Ridge Parkway off the Hwy 226 by Spruce Pine, the Penland School of Crafts (☎ 828-765-2359) is the oldest and largest crafts school in the US. It was started in 1929 by Lucy Morgan, who recruited a first-class weaver, and soon

NORTH CAROLINA

courses including pottery, woodworking, weaving, and glassblowing were added. All told there are some 42 buildings over 400-plus acres, hundreds of students and staff with international reputations. Two-month courses are offered in spring and fall, but for a brief taste, there are guided tours on summer afternoons. From Spruce Pine, take Hwys 19E or 226 – it's signposted, with a visitors center at the end of it (closed Monday).

Mt Mitchell State Park

The highest peak east of the Mississippi (6684 feet), Mt Mitchell has a climate more like Canada than North Carolina, and snow isn't unheard of in July. The state park (☎ 828-675-4611) has an observation tower with a fantastic view right on the summit, a restaurant, small nature museum, a good picnic site and oodles of hiking trails. It's named after geographer Elisa Mitchell, who fell to his death while measuring the mountain in 1857 (and was subsequently buried here). It's 5 miles off Mile 355.5 on Hwy 128 – you can drive almost to the summit. There's a nine-site campground and pack-in primitive camping is permitted.

Craggy Gardens

A great place to marvel at the wildflowers is the Craggy Garden Trail, Mile 364.5. Look out for Indian pipe (white to pink), bee balm (red), spiderwort (blue), Turk's cap lily (orange), jewel weed (yellow or orange), fire pink (red) or dodder (orange vine, white flower) and dozens of other varieties. There's a visitors center, breathtaking vistas and good hikes of half a mile to 4 miles in length.

Folk Art Center

Open year-round, this airy gallery (☎ 828-298-7903), Mile 382, is one of the oldest and best centers of Appalachian crafts. Check the listings for its changing exhibits and special events (Clay Day, Wood Day, the biannual Chair Show and more). Craft demonstrations take place April to December. The gift shop has pottery, wood, glass, jewelry and other wares fashioned by hundreds of artists.

Web site: www.southernhighlandguild.org

Pisgah National Forest

South of Asheville, the Parkway winds into the Pisgah National Forest. Railway magnate George Vanderbilt's purchase of 125,000 acres included Mt Pisgah (5749 feet) at Mile 408.6. There's a good 1½ mile trail leading up to the peak from the parking lot of the Pisgah Inn (see Places to Stay, later). It's named after a smaller mountain near the Dead Sea in Jordan.

Several minor sights beckon in the forest to the south of Mt Pisgah. At Mile 412, the **Cold Mountain Overlook** affords a view of the 6030-foot peak popularized in Charles Frazier's Civil War–era novel. Near the same spot you'll see a turnoff east on Hwy 276 for the **Cradle of Forestry in America** (☎ 828-877-3130), the country's first forestry school (founded in 1898 by Vanderbilt). It's good for kids, with live demonstrations of, say, basket weaving and a short film. The guided tours through the surrounding woods are more interesting for grown-ups. Admission is $4/2.

This region is renowned for its waterfalls (of which there are more than 300 in North Carolina). About a mile southeast of the forestry school on Hwy 276, **Looking Glass Falls** is a 30-foot-wide watery curtain that cascades 60 feet into a ridiculously clear pool, accessible by a short set of steps. Two miles later, **Sliding Rock** is an enduring attraction, with lifeguards to watch over the masses zipping down the 60-foot natural waterslide. (Even Lassie slid down once, in her TV series). An old pair of jeans is the best outfit for sliders, as the surface is tough on swimsuits. Parking costs a couple of bucks in summer.

Southwest of the forest and straddling the South Carolina border, the magnificent cascades of **Whitewater Falls** are definitely worth a detour. The two-tiered falls tumble 411 feet down a craggy mass, higher than Niagara Falls (but quite a bit narrower). From Brevard, take Hwy 64 southwest for about 23 miles to Hwy 281 and turn south.

Places to Stay

Camping The Parkway has nine campgrounds along its length; five of them are in North Carolina. These are *Crabtree Meadows* and *Doughton Park* (both Mile 241.1); *Julian Price Memorial Park* (Mile 300); *Linville Falls* (Mile 316); and *Mt Pisgah* (Mile 409). They are open from May to October, except Linville Falls, which is open year-round. To make reservations, call the state park system (☎ 800-933-7275).

Campground fees are $12 for families or groups with two adults, plus $2 for each extra person over 18. There are no hookups or showers. There are also 7 picnic grounds in developed areas and tables at some of the overlooks.

Grandfather Mountain (☎ 828-733-4337) at Mile 305.1, has privately run sites for $5 per night, plus a $10 entrance fee to the park.

Hostels Just over the Virginia border, the *Blue Ridge Country HI-AYH* (☎ 540-236-4962) is on the Parkway at Mile 214.5 (a mile north of Route 89). Reached by a paved driveway on the eastern (right-hand) side, this is a quaint 20-bed place with dormer windows and panoramic views. Beds for members/nonmembers cost $13/16. The hostel is closed in January and February. It has a music room, a meeting room, a 'clogging' barn and nearby hiking, canoeing, rafting, horseback riding, skiing and mountain biking opportunities. There's a bike-repair shop in Woodlawn, 12 miles away.

Cabins & Motels Lodgings directly on the Parkway are open early May to October only.

In Virginia, the *Doe Run Lodge* (☎ 540-398-2212), at Mile 189 near Fancy Gap, is a mountaintop resort with the most basic of the rooms starting at $87/109 for two during low/high season; the log cabin starts at $169. There are tennis courts, a pool, a dining room and a lounge bar.

Bluffs Lodge (☎ 336-372-4499), at Mile 241.1, has quarters at the old Brinegar Cabin in an isolated mountain setting.

In Blowing Rock, the basic, backwoodsy *Elk Motel* (☎ 828-264-6191, 321 Blowing Rock Rd) starts as low as $25 per night. The *Green Park Inn* (☎ 828-295-3141, Hwy 321S), at the top of the pass, is a fine alternative to the usual motels. Rooms start at $99/69 in summer/winter. Guests at the white Victorian manor inn included FDR and JD Rockefeller.

The *Big Lynn Lodge* (☎ 800-654-5232), at Mile 331 in Little Switzerland, is an old-style mountain resort with motel-style rooms starting at $86. That's not a bad deal as it includes breakfast and dinner. Web site: www.biglynnlodge.com

Pisgah Inn (☎ 828-235-8228), at Mile 408.6, is the highest lodge on the Parkway, with spectacular views at 5000 feet. Standard singles or doubles cost $73, complete with rocking chairs on the balcony. It's a sprawling place, with guest entertainment that includes square dancing. Web site: www.pisgahinn.com

The *Balsam Mountain Inn* (☎ 800-224-9498, 828-456-9498), on Hwy 74/23 around Mile 443, is a wonderful place up a mountaintop drive, with a lobby with a fireplace, clapboards, sprawling porches and a very good restaurant. It's luxurious but manages to keep downhome charm and holds regular shows of Appalachian art. Singles/doubles with breakfast start at $85. Web site: www.balsaminn.com

BOONE & BLOWING ROCK

Six miles west of the Blue Ridge Parkway, Boone (pop 14,000) offers good access to the surrounding area, and the Appalachian State University (ASU) is a bonus. The visitors bureau (☎ 888-251-9867, 828-262-3516), 208 Howard St, has information about canoeing outfitters, ski areas, parks and so on. Web site: www.visitBooneNC.com

The **Appalachian Cultural Museum** (☎ 704-262-3117), on University Hall Dr off Blowing Rock Rd, is a serious attempt to present mountain life and history beyond the hillbilly stereotypes. It has some first-class exhibits and thoughtful interpretive material. It's closed Monday; admission is $2.

The *Horn in the West* (☎ 828-264-2120) is a musical drama that lets you 'relive the frontier days with Daniel Boone' at an amphitheater off Blowing Rock Rd. It's open June through August; admission costs $12.

Hwy 321 from Blowing Rock to Boone is studded with tourist traps – the cutesy **Tweetsie Railroad** (☎ 828-264-9061) is the best of them. It's open in summer only; tickets cost $16/13.

Blowing Rock (pop 5600) makes a big deal out of the same-named attraction (admission costs $4/2) – a constant wind returns light objects dropped from the rock – but the views are just as good elsewhere on the Parkway.

More worthwhile is a visit to the **Mast General Store** (☎ 828-963-6511) on Hwy 194 in Valle Crucis (about 30 minutes' drive west of Boone). It's a quaint, old-fashioned place with a potbelly stove, just this side of contrived but stacked to the gills with everything from thick woolen socks to gout cures. Here you can pick up mountain toys such as the 'gee-haw whimmy diddle,' a stick with a propeller that turns when you rub the notches on the stick.

Skiing

The area between the Blue Ridge Parkway and the Tennessee border has four major ski resorts with downhill slopes. This ain't exactly Aspen, but it's certainly cheaper and the snow machines keep the pistes open for business in winter, even for night skiing.

Appalachian Ski Mountain – on Hwy 221/331 between Boone and Blowing Rock, this is the most family-oriented range with 9 gentle downhills and an ice-skating rink (☎ 828-295-7828).

Hawksnest – on Hwy 105 in Seven Devils, the toughest pistes in the area are found here, including the pulse-quickening Top Gun with an average 38-degree grade; it's open late weekends, and good for snowboarding (☎ 800-822-4295).

Ski Beech – on Hwy 184 near Sugar Mountain, this full-blown resort has restaurants, boutiques, a sports shop and mock Alpine village, as well as 14 slopes and a snowboard park (☎ 800-438-2093).

Sugar Mountain – on Hwy 184, two miles southeast of Banner Elk, skim over 19 trails and enjoy steepest vertical drop in the state (1200 ft) and the longest run (1½ miles); all skill levels (☎ 800-784-2768).

Weekday/weekend lift tickets range from $13/15 per day on Hawksnest to $28/45 on Ski Beech. Ski rentals cost $11 to $17 per day, snowboards $20 to $25. Beech Mountain also runs a lodging hotline (☎ 800-258-6198).

Other Activities

High Mountain Expeditions (☎ 800-262-9036, 828-295-4200), on Main St, offers white-water rafting, biking, caving, hiking and kayaking in the Pisgah and Cherokee National Forests and surroundings. Some trips (such as rafting on the Watauga) are good for families with small children. Tours range from $35 to $75.
Web site: www.highmountainexpeditions .com.

The area is good for horseback riding, too. Blowing Rock Stables (☎ 828-295-7847) charges $30 an hour for riding and $40/50 for 1½ hours/2 hours. You can camp here for $8 a night.

Special Events

Boone has a lively agenda. **Appalachian Summer** (☎ 800-841-2787) is a well-regarded festival of music, theater, dance and the visual arts that takes place in July. Past headliners have included Arlo Guthrie, Pinchas Zukerman and Kenny Rogers. Boone also serves as a base for events such as the **Edge of the World Snowboard Series** (☎ 800-789-3343), on January 7.

Places to Stay & Eat

For camping, the Boone *KOA* (☎ 828-264-7250) is 4 miles north, off Hwy 194, with nice mountain views. The cheapest accommodations are found at the basic *Boone Trail Motel* (☎ 828-264-8839, 820 E King St), where a small room starts at $25/30. See the Boone Lodging Web site (www.boonelodging.com) for more information on the following.

Better places are on Blowing Rock Rd/Hwy 321. Rates at the *Scottish Inns* (☎ 800-524-5214, 828-264-2483), at No 782, start at $34. *Red Carpet Inn* (☎ 800-443-7179, 828-264-2457), No 862, has rooms from $38.

The very nice, ASU-run *Broyhill Inn & Conference Center* (☎ 800-951-6048, 828-

262-2204) has a sparkling location at the top of a wooded hill above Boone. Rooms here start around $60, jumping to $120 in high season.

Web site: www.highcountryhost.com/nc/broyhill

In Boone, *Macado's* (☎ 828-264-1375, 539 W Kings St) has great beer specials, big burgers and burritos for $5 to $7 and a fun selection of movie mementos. Check out the Mark Twain look-alike in the bumper car. The *Angelia Restaurant* (☎ 828-265-0809, 506 W King St) is a New Age veggie joint with a juice bar. We hadn't reckoned on toasted seaweed sheets up here ($5 to $8).

The *Harvest Café* (☎ 828-264-6075, 415 Blowing Rock Rd) opposite the ASU, is an inexpensive, studenty place with vegetarian dishes. Other congenial eateries include the *Mellow Mushroom* (☎ 262-9733, 957 Rivers St) at King St, with hand-tossed pizzas, and the *Caribbean Café* (☎ 265-2233, 489 W King St), which is also a popular watering hole for ASU students.

ASHEVILLE
pop 68,000

Over a century ago, millionaire George Vanderbilt raved that Asheville was the 'most beautiful land in the world.' Whatever your means, it's hard not to be impressed with this surprisingly liberal town, which retains a certain 1920s charm in a fabulous setting. Everywhere you turn there are gorgeous, wooded Blue Ridge Mountains and sparkling blue skies. And by the way, the nightlife is among the liveliest in the state. Don't be surprised if you extend your stay, just as Vanderbilt did.

History

In the late 1700s, Asheville was but a crossing of two Indian trails when homesteaders from northern Ireland dubbed the valley 'Eden Land.' A real estate broker developed the area, and tiny Asheville was founded in 1797, after North Carolina governor Samuel Ashe. At first, the town became not a resort, but a stopover for cattle farmers driving their herds to market. Growth was slow in those early, mud-caked years.

Asheville remained a backwater until the railroad came to town in 1880. Virtually overnight Asheville was transformed as trains chugged in thousands of tourists from the East Coast and beyond. One carriage disengorged 26-year-old George Vanderbilt, heir to a vast railway fortune, and the rugged beauty of the region opened both his heart and wallet. Vanderbilt purchased 125,000 acres of land, from Asheville to the present-day Pisgah National Forest, and in 1890, he asked Richard Morris Hunt to draw up plans for Biltmore House. Hundreds of artisans and builders from Europe would spend six years fashioning the interior and exterior of this grand chateau, now the largest private residence in the world.

Ritzy inns were needed to meet the rising tide of well-to-do visitors. In 1913 Edwin Grove, a millionaire inventor of health tonic, constructed the grand Grove Park Inn in the Blue Ridge Mountains nearby, and celebrity guests such as F Scott and Zelda Fitzgerald, Henry Ford and Thomas Edison were drawn like moths to the light. Meanwhile, downtown became a mecca for up-and-coming architects such as Douglas Ellington, who popularized the art deco style he'd admired in Paris.

When the stock market crashed in 1929, Asheville crashed with it, and the town was left with the greatest per-capita debt of any US city. This was a blessing in disguise, for empty coffers meant that many crumbling historic buildings were spared from 'urban renewal.' Several generations would pass before the last debts were paid off in 1976.

In recent years Asheville has regained much of its Jazz Age allure. Dozens of architectural gems have been restored, and the crisp mountain air now draws a varied crowd of bohemians, outdoors enthusiasts and retirees. Fortunately, mutual tolerance is in ample supply, and a good time is had by all.

Orientation

The town sits in a valley at the confluence of the Swannanoa and French Broad Rivers. I-40/I-240 forms a loop around downtown, which is relatively compact and

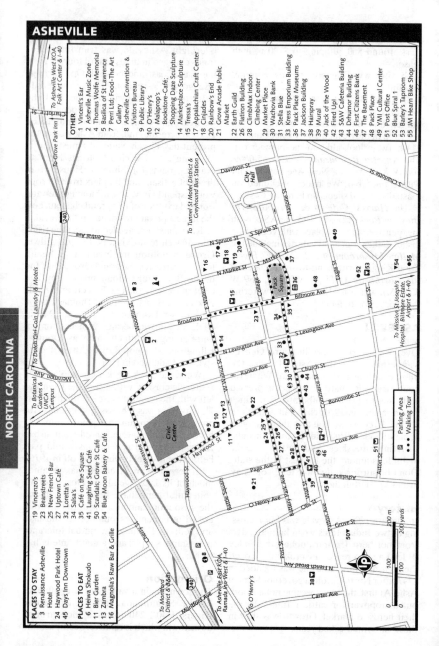

ASHEVILLE

PLACES TO STAY
3 Renaissance Asheville Hotel
24 Haywood Park Hotel
45 Days Inn Downtown

PLACES TO EAT
6 Heiwa Shokudo
11 Bier Garden
13 Zambra
16 Magnolia's Raw Bar & Grille
19 Vincenzo's
23 Beanstreets
25 New French Bar
27 Uptown Café
32 Loretta's
34 Salsa's
35 Café on the Square
41 Laughing Seed Café
50 Scandals; Grove St Café
54 Blue Moon Bakery & Café

OTHER
1 Vincent's Ear
2 Asheville Music Zone
4 Thomas Wolfe Memorial
5 Basilica of St Lawrence
7 Perri Ltd; Food-The Art Gallery
8 Asheville Convention & Visitors Bureau
9 Public Library
10 O'Henry's
12 Malaprop's Bookstore-Café; Shopping Daze Sculpture
14 Marketplace Sculpture
15 Tressa's
17 Appalachian Craft Center
18 Cinjades
20 Rainbow's End
21 Grove Arcade Public Market
22 Earth Guild
26 Flatiron Building
28 ClimbMax Indoor Climbing Center
29 Market Place
30 Wachovia Bank
31 Stella Blue
33 Kress Emporium Building
36 Pack Place Museums
37 Jackson Building
38 Hairspray
39 Mural
40 Jack of the Wood
42 Fired Up!
43 S&W Cafeteria Building
44 Drhumor Building
46 First Citizens Bank
47 The Basement
48 Pack Place
49 YMI Cultural Center
51 Post Office
52 Blue Spiral 1
53 Barley's Taproom
55 JM Hearn Bike Shop

easy to negotiate on foot. The sprawling Biltmore Estate lies on its southern boundary.

The city is renovating the Grove Arcade Public Market between O'Henry and Page Aves. Due for completion in 2002, this Gothic-style complex will house oodles of shops, eateries, and market stands. The interior is a riot of frescoes, gargoyles and other original details.

Information

The Asheville Convention and Visitors Bureau (☎ 828-258-6101) is at 151 Haywood St on the north side of downtown. Pick up a copy of the *Guide to the Visual Arts and Fine Crafts of Asheville,* with a map of local galleries.

There's a First Citizens Bank at the corner of Coxe and Patton Aves. The Wachovia Bank at 1 Haywood St is one of the few banks in western North Carolina that readily exchanges foreign currency.

The main post office is at 33 Coxe Ave. The public library at 67 Haywood St has Web terminals for free public use with a proper ID. It's open 10 am to 9 pm Monday to Friday, till 6 pm on Saturday and 2 to 6 pm Sunday (September to May only).

The *Asheville Citizen-Times* is the biggest daily in western North Carolina. It's Web site is at www.citizen-times.com. The *Mountain Xpress* freebie listings mag is available in local bars and restaurants.

Local radio stations include WCQS 88.1 FM (NPR, folk), WQNQ 104 FM (classic rock) and 99.9 FM KISS (country).

The epitome of alternative bookstores, Malaprop's Bookstore & Café (☎ 828-254-6734) has an excellent stock including regional maps, cookbooks and gay & lesbian literature. For many patrons days pass like minutes in the cafe, over a good book and cups of espresso. It's open till 9 pm (11 pm on Friday and Saturday) and till 6 pm on Sunday.

Rainbow's End (☎ 285-0005), 10 N Spruce St, is a great source of gay-oriented books, videos and information on the local scene.

Wash your undies at the Dutch Girl Coin Laundry, 954 Merrimon Ave.

The Mission St Joseph's Hospital (☎ 828-213-1111), 509 Biltmore Ave, has a 24-hour emergency ward and walk-in care services from noon to 10 pm.

Walking Tour

Asheville has the largest number of art deco buildings of any town in the Southeast, and they're a delight to view on foot. The following 1½ mile tour of architectural highlights (marked on the Ashville map) takes about 45 minutes at a leisurely pace. Some of the items described here can be found in the *Asheville Urban Trail* leaflet available from the visitors bureau.

Start at the **Basilica of St Lawrence** (1909), on Flint St, a landmark church with two Spanish Renaissance towers sheathed in colorful tiles. It claims to have the largest free-standing dome in North America (52 by 82 feet), crafted without a single nail; look up and feel your head spin. The ornate carved altar is topped with an 1800lb block of Tennessee marble. Most of the stained-glass windows were made in Germany. At the rear of the chapel lies the crypt of the Italian architect Rafael Guastavino, who had previously worked on the Biltmore House.

Moving south into the Haywood St shopping district, in front of Malaprop's Bookstore, you'll see one of Asheville's collection of intriguing sculptures, the bronze **Shopping Daze**, which consists of three fashionable ladies and their pooch. Take the first right into Battery Park Ave, and you'll be confronted with the **Flatiron Building** (1926), which looks like a shrunken version of the building on New York's Times Square. Just past Page Ave and on the left, seek out a staircase next to the parking garage and descend to Wall St. Almost opposite you'll spot a huge **mural** with a variety of wacky figures, and several bronze cats next to the low wall (catwalks once linked sections of Wall St). There are several inviting restaurants and galleries along here (see Galleries & Folk Art, later in this chapter).

Turn east on Wall St and take the next staircase (near the entrance to Essential

Arts) down to Patton Ave and the heart of the historic business district. At the bottom of Haywood St you'll pass the former **S&W Cafeteria** (1929), a marvelous art deco structure by Douglas Ellington, with gleaming Romanesque arches. There's a stunning mosaic replica of one arch embedded in the sidewalk in front of the Wachovia Bank across the street.

A few steps farther east you'll pass the elaborate Romanesque facade of the **Drhumor Building** (pronounced **droo**-mor, 1895), with a striking frieze including angels, maidens and dragons. Cross Church St to admire the rich ceramic tiles and neoclassical motifs of the **Kress Emporium** (1928; ☎ 828-281-2252) on your left. It's now a showcase of regional artists and craftspeople.

Continue on Patton Ave to **Pack Square,** once the crossing of Indian trade routes but now a busy traffic circle with an obelisk monument to Zebulon Vance, an early governor of North Carolina, at its center. The more remarkable features here include the **Jackson Building** (1924), a slender skyscraper with gargoyles and upper floors that resemble a Tuscan palace. Thomas Wolfe's hard-drinking father ran a monument shop here. Gaze eastward, and you won't fail to see the octagonal, pink-tiled roof of the giant **City Building,** an Ellington creation that caused a storm of controversy when it was unveiled in 1928.

From Pack Place, turn north up Broadway, a pleasant avenue filled with restaurants, New Age shops, galleries and antique stores – you could easily lose yourself here for an afternoon. Go left on Walnut St and note the double doors on many buildings; in the 19th century this was a market street, with produce stands and livery stables. At the corner of N Lexington Ave you'll spy the **Marketplace** sculpture, a bronze bonnet and basket of apples resting on a bench. From here it's a short stroll back to Haywood St.

Pack Place Museums

The Pack Place Education Arts and Science Center (☎ 828-257-4500), at 2 S Pack Square encompasses four museums. The **Asheville Art Museum** has several small galleries, changing exhibitions and a permanent collection of 20th century works – paintings, bronzes, lithographs and textiles. Next door, the **Health Adventure** takes kids on a journey through the human body with galleries called Bodyworks and Miracle of Life (don't miss the size 23EEE shoes of basketball star Shaquille O'Neal). In the Creative Playspace kids can don costumes and role-play. The **Colburn Gem & Mineral Museum** features a galaxy of precious gems and stones from throughout North Carolina.

Around the corner, the **YMI Cultural Center** (☎ 828-252-4614), on the corner of Eagle and S Market Sts, features airy galleries with African-American masks, sculptures and other art, as well as high-profile travelling exhibits. This refurbished Tudor building was built by George Vanderbilt as a community center for the black craftsmen who worked on the Biltmore Estate.

Museum hours are 10 am to 5 pm Tuesday to Saturday and 1 to 5 pm Sunday. The YMI center also opens Monday. Admission is $4/3 for adults/children per museum, but there are package tickets for two to four museums.

Thomas Wolfe Memorial

In Wolfe's first novel, *Look Homeward Angel,* he remembered this rambling clapboard structure as an 'old dilapidated house with 18 or 20 drafty, high-ceilinged rooms.' But Wolfe, who lived here from 1900 to 1920, would never call a room his own – his cheapskate mother kept moving him around to accommodate her boardinghouse guests. Wolfe's father, an alcoholic stonemason, wanted nothing to do with the place and lived down the road. The 1929 novel was largely autobiographical, and its references incensed so many residents that the public library banned it for seven years.

Sadly, in 1998 an arsonist's attack reduced most of the furnishings to cinders, and restoration of this historic site is ongoing. Some of Wolfe's original artifacts, including his writing desk and Remington typewriter, are on display in the adjacent visitors center (☎ 828-253-8304), at 52 N

Market St, which also shows a video on the novelist's life.

Biltmore Estate

If the United States had a royal family, its members would undoubtedly reside at Biltmore House. The 1895 French chateau is almost indescribable in its scale and sumptuous furnishings; the only other place that comes anywhere close is Hearst Castle (165 rooms), in California.

The 'cottage,' as its filthy rich owner, George Vanderbilt, called the 250-room mansion, took over a million man-hours to build; every one of those chambers would be needed to accommodate the 70,000 objects that Vanderbilt and architect Hunt purchased in Europe and the Orient. There's art by Renoir, Dürer, Whistler and Sargent, furniture by Sheraton and Chippendale, a chess board frowned over by Napoleon, 16th-century Flemish Gobelins – the list staggers the mind. Despite the grandeur, the overall impression tends to be low-key, for the Vanderbilts valued discretion just as their European forebears did. ('Bildt' was the region in Holland where the Vanderbilts originated, while 'more' is Old English for 'rolling hills.')

Biltmore was considered a marvel of modern engineering, with some of Edison's first lightbulbs, elevators, refrigerators, a fire alarm system and a telephone. The 43 bathrooms had flush toilets (but curiously few sinks – Mrs Vanderbilt and the servants had to make do with pitcher and jug). Above all, the rooms are *big*; the banquet hall, for instance, measures 72 by 42 feet and has a 70-foot ceiling; the entire floor space of Biltmore totals more than 4 acres. Henry James, the realist author, complained during a 1905 visit that his bedroom was at least a half-mile from the library. Be sure to save time for the cavernous basement, which housed the bowling alley, swimming pool, kitchen and servants' quarters.

Numerous attractions await outside the main house, including a **winery** (with tastings and sales, in the former dairy), several restaurants and shops (in the ex-stables), and sprawling **gardens** of sophistication.

The 70-acre gardens were laid out by Frederick Law Olmsted, the architect of Central Park. The greenery includes a 16th-century Italian garden with reflecting pools, and the English Walled Garden, where 50,000 tulip bulbs are planted every year.

The self-guided tour of the house covers all four floors, and docents are available to answer questions. Allow at least 1½ hours for the house and an afternoon, if not a full day, for the entire estate. Admission costs a hefty $32/24 for adults/children. Tickets can be extended for a second day for $7. Don't bother with the guided 'Behind the Scenes' tour ($12/6) if you've only got one day. Near the entrance to the estate, the 'Historic' Biltmore Village is an uninspiring collection of tourist-targeted shops, galleries and eateries.

The front gates to the estate (☎ 800-543-2961, 828-274-6230) open at 8:30 am (9 am in winter), with last entry at 5 pm daily; the house closes at 6 pm. The winery (about a mile from the house) is open till 7 pm. Try to visit during the week to avoid the crowds, and note that it's especially popular before Christmas, when the mansion is decked out in Yuletide regalia.

Web site: www.biltmore.com

Botanical Gardens

Located on a 10-acre site north of downtown, the Botanical Gardens (☎ 828-252-5190) is a year-round show of blossoms, buds, fruits or leaves, depending on the season. The displays of Appalachian plants and flowers are a botanist's dream, but anyone will enjoy a stroll on shady, leaf-covered paths beneath giant sycamores and along babbling brooks. There's a Garden for the Blind with labels in Braille. Located at 151 Weaver Blvd, off Broadway next to the UNCA campus, the gardens are open dawn to dusk, and admission is free.

Galleries & Folk Art

Perri Ltd (☎ *828-281-1197*), 65½ N Lexington Ave, is a quirky 'floral decor studio' that's more like a gallery. Its stylish owner has made bows for actor Andie McDowell (who has a house in the Biltmore Forest), and keeps a live rooster in the store. Next door is **Food – The Art Gallery** (☎ 828-281-1190), 63 N Lexington Ave, a converted warehouse space with wacky items such as large antique birdcages.

Blue Spiral 1 (☎ 828-251-0202), 38 Biltmore Ave, is a huge three-level hall displaying fine arts and crafts of the Southeast (mostly expensive, but quality stuff), including the estate of landscape painter Will Henry Stevens.

Earth Guild (☎ 828-255-7818), 33 Haywood St, offers courses from knitting to papermaking and sells weaving machines, arts and crafts supplies and folkwear patterns.

Activities

Scale the heights at **ClimbMax Indoor Climbing Center** (☎ 828-252-9996), 43 Wall St, for $12 for 2 hours ($16 per hour if you need instruction). It's open 3:30 pm to 10 pm Tuesday and Thursday, noon to 10 pm Wednesday and Friday, 10 am to 10 pm Saturday and 1 pm to 6 pm Sunday.

Fired Up! (☎ 828-253-8181), 26 Wall St, is a 'creative lounge' that allows you to paint and glaze your own porcelain. Most pieces cost $8 to $15, plus a studio fee of $6 per hour including all colors and materials. It's open 11 am to 7 pm Tuesday to Saturday (to 11 pm Friday) and 1 pm to 6 pm Sunday.

Organized Tours

The parks and recreation department (☎ 828-259-5498) runs historic tours of the Asheville Urban Trail (see Walking Tour, earlier) on the second Friday (4 pm) and third Sunday (3 pm) of the month, for $5. Tours start at Pack Place, at the southeast corner of Biltmore and Patton Aves.

Sure-footed, gentle llamas make great companions in the mountains. Road's End Llamas (☎ 828-680-9429), 5051 E Fork Rd in Marshall, runs half-day hikes for $25 per person ($31 with picnic lunch). Call ahead to reserve.

Special Events

Festival of Flowers – throughout April, the Biltmore Estate is awash in spring blossoms (☎ 800-543-2961).

Black Mountain Music Festival – the last weekend in May, arts, crafts and dance feature at this wingding northeast of Asheville (☎ 800-669-2301).

Brevard Music Festival – from mid-June to early August, this is one of the Southeast's best classical music festivals (☎ 828-884-2011), held 30 miles south of Asheville.

Mountain Dance and Folk Festival – the first weekend in August, there are stage shows of folk and bluegrass music, as well as traditional dance (☎ 828-258-6107).

Shindig on the Green – on most Saturday evenings, July through Labor Day weekend, this festival features outdoor clogging and music (☎ 828-258-6107).

Christmas at Biltmore Estate – from early November to early January, concerts and other performances are held amid stunning decoration (☎ 800-543-2961).

Places to Stay

Note that prices really jump in October, at the height of the leaf-peeping season.

Camping *Bear Creek Campground* (☎ 704-253-0798, 81 S Bear Creek Rd), right next to the Biltmore Estate, has full facilities (clubhouse, laundry, pool etc), RV sites ($20) and nice tent sites ($18). Westbound on I-40, take exit 47 and proceed from the signal to the campground; eastbound, take exit 47 and turn right at the signal and left again into S Bear Creek Rd. It's open year-round.

The *Asheville East KOA* (☎ 800-562-5907, 828-686-3121, 102 Hwy 70 E, Swannanoa) is 10 miles east of town. Take I-40 exit 59, drive north one block to the signal, turn right on Hwy 70 and go 2 miles. Web site: www.koakampground.com/where/nc/33116.htm

Budget For a touch of Davy Crockett, try *Log Cabin Motor Court* (☎ 704-6450-6546, 330 Weaverville Hwy), north of town, where rustic singles/doubles start at $32/35.

Chain motels cluster north of downtown on Merrimon Ave, and east on Tunnel Rd. Here you'll find inexpensive places such as *Skyway Motel* (☎ 704-253-2631, 131 Tunnel Rd), *Townhouse Motel* (☎ 704-253-8753, 141 Tunnel Rd) and the *Mountaineer* (☎ 704-

254-5331, 155 Tunnel Rd), all in the \$35 to \$45 ranges. Farther out, the *Motel 6 (☎ 800-466-8356, 828-299-3040, 1415 Tunnel Rd)* offers its standard charms with singles/doubles starting at \$33/38.

Days Inn Downtown (☎ 704-254-9661, 120 Patton Ave), is the cheapest downtown option with clean, if unexceptional, rooms starting at \$60/80 for weekdays/weekends in high season. Off-season prices begin around \$43.

Mid-Range *Ramada Plaza Hotel West (☎ 800-272-6232, 828-665-2161, 435 Smoky Park Hwy)* has a 6-story atrium lobby with fireplace, an indoor-outdoor pool and standard amenities. It's reasonable value with singles or doubles for \$78/99 in low/high season. Take I-40 to exit 44 – it's 15 minutes southwest of downtown.

The comfortable, 160-room *Quality Inn Biltmore (☎ 800-228-5151, 828-274-1800, 115 Hendersonville Rd)* has a pretty setting and good comforts. Doubles cost \$135 (as low as \$70 off-season). Take I-40 to exit 50.

The *Renaissance Asheville Hotel (☎ 828-252-8211, 1 Thomas Wolfe Plaza)*, in a 12-story high-rise downtown with excellent mountain views, offers singles or doubles with Marriott-style luxury for \$115/99 in high/low season – a pretty good deal. Web site: www.renaissancehotels.com

Top End The *Haywood Park Hotel (☎ 800-228-2522, 828-252-2522, 1 Battery Park Ave, hotel@haywoodpark.com)* is in a modernized Georgian structure with lots of polished brass, oak and marble fittings. Standard singles/doubles cost \$140/165, graduating up to \$325 for a double grand suite.

You can stay in F Scott Fitzgerald's room at the *Grove Park Inn (☎ 800-438-5800, 828-252-2711, 290 Macon Ave)*. As fancy as all get-out, the hotel is practically a mountain colony, with 510 rooms, including 12 suites and 42 conference chambers. Simple singles or doubles start at \$195/135 in high/low season. One-bedroom suites start at \$375. Web site: www.groveparkinn.com

The sparkling new *Inn on Biltmore Estate (☎ 800-858-4130, 828-274-9600, Biltmore Estate)*, has 72 double rooms and 132 'king' rooms. It's the next best thing to staying at 'George's Place.' Rates for standard rooms go from \$179 to \$289. Web site: www.biltmore.com

B&Bs & Inns The *Asheville Bed & Breakfast Association (☎ 828-252-0200, 877-262-6867)* handles bookings for 21 B&Bs in the Asheville area, from Victorian mansions to mountain retreats. Web site: www.bbonline.com/nc/abba

Inn on Montford (☎ 800-254-9569, 828-254-9569, 296 Montford Ave) is in a Victorian building designed by the architect of the Biltmore House. It has four antique-filled guestrooms; three bathrooms have whirlpool baths, and one even has a claw-foot tub. Midweek rates start at \$115 and soar to between \$230 and \$400 on weekends – and this is one of the cheaper places.

Places to Eat
Cafes Broadway, Lexington and nearby streets are chock-a-block with hip hangouts. *Beanstreets (☎ 828-255-8180, 3 Broadway Ave)* is the most eclectic of Asheville's coffeehouses, with curious lighting (a foot gripping a lamp), funky art and a mix of patio and living room furniture. It serves up java, hot snacks and occasional poetry readings. The *Double Decker Coffee Co (☎ 828-255-0441, 41 Biltmore Ave)* is another great place, just south of downtown – located inside a double-decker bus.

In summer, the sidewalk at *Café on the Square (☎ 828-251-5565, 1 Biltmore Ave)* is as fashionable as a catwalk. The meat, seafood and pasta dishes aren't bad either.

Restaurants & Eateries Long like a shoelace and about as wide, *Loretta's (27 Patton Ave)* does cheap and tasty salads, soups and sandwiches (lunch only). The *Blue Moon Bakery & Café (60 Biltmore Ave)* has good salads, European-style breads and sidewalk characters ready for a chat.

The *Bier Garden (☎ 704-285-0003, 46 Haywood St)* is perfect for a late evening bite or drink. Their sandwiches, salads, burgers and Tex-Mex dishes ($6 to $9) all have a special twist, such as honey-lime sauce or caramelized onions. There's a copious beer menu and occasional live music. Hours are 11 am to at least midnight (closed Sunday).

The vegetarian **Laughing Seed Café** (☎ 828-252-3445, 40 Wall St) is an institution known across North Carolina. Apart from cheap tofu, tempeh and bean dishes, they have wine and organic Green Man beer. Big eaters go for the Blue Ridge plate. Come early for lunch or dinner, or reserve a table.

Late's the best time to hit **Zambra** (☎ 704-232-1060, 85a W Walnut St), a laid-back Spanish eatery with tapas for $4 to $7 and mains for $12 to $15. Hours are 5 pm to whenever, depending on the crowd (closed Sunday).

Salsa's (☎ 828-252-6042, 6 Patton Ave,) serves well-priced Mexican fare ($8 to $13) with a Caribbean feel (fajitas with coconut sauce) under fake palms and seaweed decor. Hot sauce got the place started – the story's a good one. Lunch and dinner are served daily (closed Sunday).

There's more than sushi to **Heiwa** (☎ 828-254-7761, 87 N Lexington Ave) but those $3.50 morsels *are* tempting. The seafood dishes such as salmon teriyaki ($12) win hearts and stomachs. Dinner is served Tuesday to Saturday.

The **Uptown Café** (☎ 828-253-2158, 22 Battery Park Ave) has a multiple personality that spans Mexican, Asian, Italian and pub food. Lunch specials, served Monday to Saturday, cost $6 to $8 and evening meals (Friday to Sunday) run $10 to $16. Sunday brunch is also good.

The **New French Bar** (☎ 828-252-3685, 1 Battery Park Ave) is a Paris-style cafe serving hot croissants at breakfast, and cheap soups, baguettes and salads for lunch ($3 to $8).

Vincenzo's (☎ 828-254-4698, 10 N Market St) is an elegant, comfortable Italian place with a voluminous menu of pastas, fish and meats. Starters average $12, and mains cost $16 to $24. Lunch is served Monday to Friday, and dinner is always served. Jazz pianists tickle the ivories in the bistro.

For a truly memorable meal, try **Gabrielle's** (☎ 828-252-7313, 87 Richmond Hill Dr), at the fancy Richmond Hill Inn. A five-course dinner that might include stuffed quail, garlic-crusted rack of lamb and burgundy pear compote costs about $65. It's just off River Rd/Hwys 19/23, about three miles north of downtown (open nightly). Another good choice for *haute cuisine* is **Horizon's** at the Grove Park Inn (see Places to Stay).

Entertainment

Bars Sample 42 brews, and ignore the consequences, at the busy **Barley's Taproom** (☎ 828-255-0504, 42 Biltmore Ave). There's good pizza ($9 to $13) and live music. It's open till at least midnight.

Hidden at the rear of a tiny courtyard, the proudly grungy **Vincent's Ear** (☎ 828-259-9119, 68B N Lexington Ave) is a favorite haunt of the alternative crowd. Its quirky agenda features poetry readings, live jazz and hard rock. Hours are noon (3 pm on Sunday) till at least midnight daily (1 am Friday and Saturday).

Jack of the Wood (☎ 828-252-5445, 95 Patton Ave) is a paneled English-Irish brewpub with live music throughout the week. There are munchies on the menu, but the Laughing Seed Café up the rear stairs, offers more choices (see the Places to Eat section).

Magnolia's Raw Bar & Grille (☎ 828-251-5211, 26 Walnut St) is best for a late-night drink on the covered, open-sided patio (open till 2 am). There's live music on weekends.

You won't experience many jazz sushi bars, so be sure to visit **Tunatini's** (☎ 828-285-9110, 161 Biltmore Ave). It hosts small groups nightly (blues, jazz or folk). Try the Saktails (sake cocktails) or sushi for $2.50 to $7.

Music Clubs Asheville's music scene manages to span hillbilly to Motown. Be sure to check the listings in the freebie *Mountain Xpress*.

The decor of **Tressa's** (☎ 828-245-7072, 28 Broadway St) is pleasantly old-fashioned, with a grand piano on a tiny stage. It hosts blues and jazz bands, as well as swing dancing and other events nightly. Membership costs $25, but they're lenient with newcomers. It's open 4 pm to 2 am daily, with live music from 9 pm.

The *Asheville Music Zone* (☎ *828-255-8811)*, at the corner of N Lexington Ave and Hiawassee St, has eclectic concerts at 8 pm or 9 pm, with soul, funk, jazz mandolin, grunge and folk. Cover is roughly $6 to $15. Check the listings.

Stella Blue (☎ *828-236-2424, 31 Patton Ave)* is another popular venue offering rock, blues and jazz from Thursday to Saturday.

The Basement (☎ *828-285-0808)*, under Almost Blue records at the corner of Coxe and Patton Aves, is only a tiny room, but a cool spot to catch local bands and some national acts.

Cinjades (☎ *828-254-0835, 22 N Market St)* is a hot dance club for 20-somethings (behind Magnolia's Raw Bar, at the back of the parking lot).

Gay & Lesbian Venues For a smallish town in the mountains, Asheville is sophisticated and quite gay-friendly. Recently moved, *O'Henry's* (☎ *828-254-1891, 232 Haywood St)* is the city's oldest gay bar. It offers a diverse program, from goofy hat parties to theme nights. Relax at the oak bar and admire the paintings.

Scandals (☎ *828-252-2838, 11 Grove St)*, in the Grove St Café, has a big techno-fed dance floor with laser shows and attracts a mixed crowd. It's open 6 pm to 2 am Wednesday to Sunday.

Hairspray (☎ *828-258-2027, 38 N French Broad Ave)* has pool tables and two dance floors. There's techno/house on Thursday nights. The crowd is college age, older on the weekends. It's open 8 pm to 2:30 am daily (Fridays from 4 pm, with happy hour).

Performing Arts The *Asheville Civic Center* (☎ *828-298-7928)*, on Haywood St, hosts a variety of musicals, concerts and periodic shows of traditional and contemporary crafts.

The *Diana Wortham Theatre* (☎ *828-257-4530, 2 S Pack Square)*, in the Pack Place complex, is an intimate 500-seat venue hosting 150-odd varied performances a year.

For a bit of intrigue, *The Players Theatre* (☎ *828-683-9928, Lipinsky Auditorium)*, on the UNCA campus, puts on classics like British comedies and Agatha Christie murder mysteries.

Getting There & Away
The closest Amtrak station is in Spartanburg or Greenville, South Carolina, 59 miles to the southeast.

Asheville Regional Airport (☎ 828-684-2226) is 9 miles south of town. It's served by three airlines – American Eagle (United), Atlantic Southwest (Delta) and US Airways. There are direct links only to Atlanta, Charlotte, Cincinnati, Pittsburgh and Raleigh.

The Greyhound bus terminal (☎ 800-231-2222, 828-253-2222) is at 2 Tunnel Rd. Sample fares include Winston-Salem ($31, 3¼ hours), Knoxville ($23, from 2 hours), Columbia ($30, 1½ hours), and Atlanta ($32, 5½ hours with a long layover).

Getting Around
The Sky Shuttle Service (☎ 800-582-7868, 828-253-0006) charges $15 per head for trips to/from Asheville Airport.

The Asheville Transit Authority (☎ 828-253-5691) operates 10 lines in the greater Asheville area (75¢). Downtown is a 'free fare zone,' meaning you'll only have to pay if you ride a bus beyond it (maps are posted). The transit point is on Coxe Ave next to the post office.

JM Hearn (☎ 828-253-4800), 34 Broadway, rents out mountain bikes for $35 to $45 per day.

Call Yellow Cab (☎ 828-253-3311) or Jolly Taxi (☎ 828-253-1411) for a taxi.

AROUND ASHEVILLE
Chimney Rock
The photogenic 'chimney,' complete with US flag, is a widely publicized rock spire about a 20-minute drive southeast of Asheville. A long dark tunnel leads to the elevator, which whisks visitors 258 feet up

the chimney in 42 seconds, as your elevator operator will relate. Up top, flee the gift shop to get a staggering view of Hickory Nut Gorge, the surrounding mountains and pretty Lake Lure. The real attraction, though, is the exciting hike around the cliffs to the 404ft Hickory Nut Falls – allow at least two hours here. Scenes of *The Last of the Mohicans* with Daniel Day Lewis were shot around here.

Entrance to the private Chimney Rock Park (☎ 828-625-9611) is $11/5 for adults/children in summer, or $7/4 in winter, when some trails are closed.

Places to Stay & Eat The main street in Chimney Rock Village, Hwy 64/74A, is a strip of touristy shops, eateries and hotels on the admittedly nice Rocky Broad River. If stuck here, a decent budget choice is the *Geneva Riverside Lodging & Grill (☎ 828-625-4121)*, on Hwy 64/74A, which has an outdoor bar and grill open during the warm months. Standard rooms range from $49 to $69, efficiency flats $65 to $129.
Web site: www.genevarivermotel.com

For something better, 5 miles to the southeast there's the small, classy *Lodge on Lake Lure (☎ 800-733-2785, 828-625-2789)*,

on Charlotte Dr at the end of the road and right on the water. Its 12 swanky rooms start at $139/night, including breakfast.
Web site: www.lodgeonlakelure.com

Not much to look at outside, *Lakeside Pizza (828-625-1457)*, on Hwy 64/74A about a quarter mile east of Lake Lure beach, serves good New York–style pizzas. The *Point of View Restaurant (☎ 828-625-4380)*, on Hwy 64/74A, has great lake views, and seafood and steaks (about $12 to $20). Both serve lunch and dinner.

Carl Sandburg Home

In Flat Rock, about an hour's drive south of Asheville, the pretty white farmhouse of Carl Sandburg (☎ 828-693-4178), on Little River Rd off Hwy 25, is a national park site open for viewing. The poet, Lincoln biographer and social critic moved to North Carolina from the Midwest in 1945 in search of the solitude to write. It seemed to work, for Sandburg (who was originally Swedish) published over one-third of his life's work during his 22 years here. The estate, named Connemara for the mountain range in Ireland, is as much a natural attraction as a cultural one, with lakes, hiking trails, woods and pastures. Although Sandburg died here

Scenic Drive – Along the Drovers' Road

This route takes you through Hickory Nut Gap, one of two passes in the Blue Ridge Mountains that early settlers took to reach the Asheville plateau in the 18th century, and on into orchard country. Early farmers drove their flocks to market through the gap. This curvy, at times steep, drive is about 14 miles long and takes half an hour.

From Asheville, follow Hwy 74 southeast to Fairview; just after, the tall peak on your left, **Little Pisgah Mountain** (4412 feet) gives you a taste of the climb through the gap. Along the way, well-scrubbed clapboard homes peek out from mature hardwood forests speckled with wildflowers such as trillium and mountain laurel. As you descend from the gap you enter Hickory Nut Gorge, and soon you're in the tiny village of Gerton, with crafts shops such as the Manual Woodworker selling an eclectic mix of wares. The craggy sides of the gorge are covered with trees and rhododendrons; one tree with lavender blooms, the Paulownia, was introduced here by George Vanderbilt.

A few miles later you'll reach the junction of Hwy 9 and Bat Cave. As big as a bump on a log, this town is about as easy to miss, as the signs are often stolen. Drop by the venerable Old Cider Mill here for a swig of the local best. The region teems with roadside stands selling fresh produce, apples or pumpkins. Continue on Hwy 64/74 to Chimney Rock and Lake Lure, or turn north on pretty Hwy 9 to return to Asheville (via Black Mountain).

in 1967, the interior seems stuck in a time warp, with magazines from the 1940s lying around. The site is open daily. Admission costs $3; children are free.

CHEROKEE
pop 12,500

Some of the Cherokee people escaped removal on the Trail of Tears by hiding here in the Great Smoky Mountains. Most of their vast territories have vanished, but their descendants – some 11,600 members of the Eastern Band of the Cherokee – now occupy a 56,000-acre reservation, at the edge of the national park.

The small town of Cherokee caters to the lowest common denominator of the tourist trade, with ersatz Indian souvenir shops, tacky attractions, and fast food joints. The visitors center (☎ 800-438-1601, 828-497-9195) on Main St has local maps and can help find accommodations. The biggest moneymaker is Harrah's Cherokee Casino (☎ 800-427-0427-7247), with parking lots the size of football fields on Hwy 19.

More worthwhile is the **Museum of the Cherokee Indian** (☎ 704-497-3481), Drama Rd/Hwy 441N, which has a special interpretive exhibit on the Trail of Tears. There are good special effects: In one display, a holograph of a medicine man explains his herbal remedies over a campfire. The realistic, well-lit displays wend their way through the stations of Cherokee history with traditional music playing in the background. Note the examples of written Cherokee language, which is again being taught in local schools. It's open daily; admission is $6/4 for adults/children.

Across the road, **Qualla Arts & Crafts** (☎ 828-497-3103) sells authentic Indian handicrafts, most of them quite expensive.

The **Oconaluftee Indian Village** (☎ 704-497-2111) is a replica of an 18th-century Cherokee village where Cherokees demonstrate traditional crafts It's open mid-May through October 25; admission costs $12/5. The outdoor show here, *Unto These Hills,* dramatizes the history of the Cherokee from the first European contact up to the Trail of Tears. Seats cost $14 to $16 (children

$6) and can be reserved on ☎ 828-497-2111 (mid-June through late August).

Places to Stay & Eat

The nicest campgrounds are in the national park, but one decent local option is the 40-site, riverside **Cherokee Campground** (☎ 828-497-9838) on Hwy 19N at Hwy 441. It's well-equipped and charges $20 for two people. The **Indian Creek Campground** (☎ 828-497-4361, 1367 Bunches Creek Rd), off Big Cove Rd about 8 miles north, also costs $20 per rough site.

The town has 40-odd motels, with some under $40 in low season. In summer, prices rise above $60 as thousands of Great Smoky Mountains visitors stream through. The adequate **Riverside Motel & Campground** (☎ 828-497-9311), on Hwy 441S, charges $35/65 for rooms in low/high season. *Craig's Motel* (☎ 828-497-3821), on Hwy 19N one mile north on a pleasant creek, is close to the attractions and charges $49/75 for cabins. Near the entrance to the park, **Comfort Suites** (☎ 800-228-5150, 828-497-3500, 35 Hwy 441N) offers its comforts for $69/99.

Cherokee's culinary scene is, shall we say, underdeveloped. Try the **Tee Pee Restaurant** (☎ 828-497-5141), on Hwy 441N next to *Unto These Hills,* for traditional Indian fare and a good country-style buffet (specials $5 to $12, open all day). For a memorable meal you'll need to go farther afield; try the **Balsam Mountain Inn** (see the Blue Ridge Parkway section earlier in this chapter).

GREAT SMOKY MOUNTAINS NATIONAL PARK
National Park Area

Western North Carolina's most famous attraction is its mountains, centered on Great Smoky Mountains National Park, the most visited park in the country. The 520,000-acre park, which spreads into Tennessee, was established in 1934 and now draws some 10 million visitors a year. The park rises from an elevation of 840 feet to over 6600 feet. This, and its position at the point where northern and southern foliage and climate patterns meet, give the park a particularly large variety of flora and fauna. There are more than 1500 species of flowering plants inside the park and 125 tree species. Over the course of a year, about 200 kinds of birds can be seen. There are also some 60 species of mammal, including the bears for which the park is famous.

Summer is the peak season, and you can expect the park to be extremely crowded at any time from mid-May to the end of September. There's a visitors center at Oconaluftee (☎ 423-436-1200) on the main Hwy 441, which crosses the park for 35 scenic miles as Newfound Gap Rd between Cherokee and Gatlinburg, Tennessee. On the northern side of the park, the Sugarlands Visitors Center (☎ 865-436-1291) is on the main access road from Gatlinburg. A useful NPS pamphlet to pick up is *Day Hikes* ($1), with brief descriptions and a park-wide map of 32 hikes. Entrance to the park is free.

The park's best-known sights are **Clingman's Dome,** definitely 'on top of old Smoky' at 6643 feet. It's the highest point in the park: You can see seven states on a clear day, and the dramatic twin summits of **Chimney Tops** are breathtaking. These and the popular

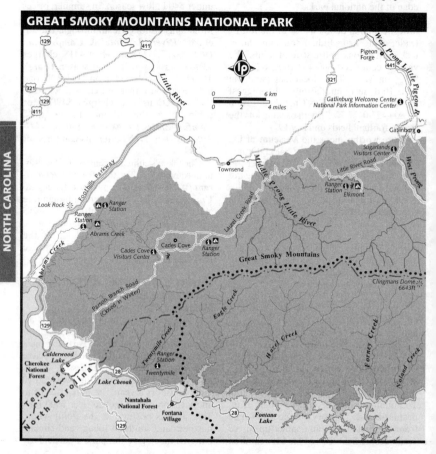

GREAT SMOKY MOUNTAINS NATIONAL PARK

hiking trails around Mt LeConte are all fairly close to Gatlinburg, Tennessee. In the mood for a *real* hike? The Mountains to Sea Trail begins at Clingman's Dome and ends 908 miles later, in the Outer Banks.

The less-visited **Cades Cove** area features an 11-mile, one-way driving loop that's very popular with cyclists. It's an easy route through a one-time farming community, and set back off the road are picture-postcard barns, churches, log cabins, mills and a smokehouse. You can rent bicycles for $3.25 per hour from the Cades Cove store near the campground. Horses can also be rented

here (and other points in the park) for $15 per hour. Cades Cove is in the western end of the park, reachable via the small town of Townsend.

Another good place to escape the crowds of Newfound Gap Rd is **Greenbrier Cove,** which offers waterfalls, hiking trails and bouldery mountain streams. It's six miles east of Gatlinburg, off Hwy 321. Two miles from Cherokee, the **Mountain Farm Museum** has lots of original log buildings and gritty agricultural demonstrations. The Mingus Mill sells stone-ground grain a half-mile north of the museum.

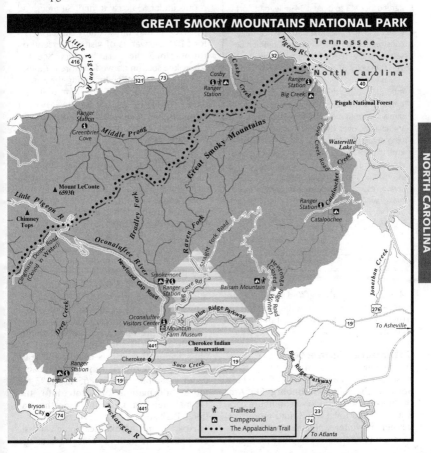

GREAT SMOKY MOUNTAINS NATIONAL PARK

NORTH CAROLINA

The Road to Nowhere

Work has resumed on a spooky, long-abandoned road along the north shore of Fontana Lake, the southern boundary of the Great Smoky Mountains National Park. Currently, the 6¹/₂-mile 'Road to Nowhere' leaves Bryson City, enters the park through a tunnel – and ends.

The construction of the Fontana Dam as a power source drove thousands of people off their land during the 1940s, and isolated more than 20 cemeteries where generations laid their kinfolk to rest. Federal agencies agreed in 1943 to build a 34-mile road north of the lake, but opposition by environmentalists and the National Park Service halted construction in the late 1960s. Communities settled in the 1830s have melted away into 200,000 acres of roadless wilderness.

Families of people who had to leave their mountain homes during the war are prodding public officials to finish the road. The 700-family North Shore Cemetery Association led the charge, over the heads of park officials who argue that the work would hurt wildlife and expose acidic rock that could poison streams and require extensive grading.

Visiting the graveyards requires a park service escort. Once a month, park officials make available boats to cross the lake and vehicles to drive descendants to cemeteries on the north shore. The trip can take up to 12 hours.

Backcountry hiking and camping are your best bet for avoiding the worst of the crowds (see Places to Stay, later in this section).

Gatlinburg (Tennessee)

On the Tennessee side, the best known and most crowded gateway town is Gatlinburg. Because the **Ober Gatlinburg Ski Area** (☎ 865-436-5423, fun@obergatlinburg.com) is just outside town, you'll find more services here in winter, when many of the shops, restaurants and motels at other park gateways may be closed. The ski area itself is small (three lifts, eight trails), and its season is short. In summer, you can take a chairlift up the mountain and ride a simulated bobsled.

There's a visitor center (☎ 800-267-7088, 865-436-2392) on Hwy 441 at the third stoplight in town; it's open 8 am to 6 pm daily (till 8 pm Friday and Saturday, 10 pm in summer).

Places to Stay

Accommodation costs in any of the gateway towns vary greatly from season to season. Spring is the cheapest time, with motel rooms under $35 easy to find. Summer and the brief fall-foliage season are the most expensive. At that time, rooms can easily go for $100, as swarms of visitors descend into towns along the park borders. See the Cherokee section above for more options.

You can streamline by calling the Smoky Mountain Visitor's Center (☎ 800-432-4678), on Hwy 441 S in the town of Franklin, NC, which runs an accommodation hotline 7 days a week.
Web site: www.smokymtnhost.com

Camping There are over 1000 campsites inside the national park, but it can be hard to find one in summer. Sites at the 10 developed campgrounds may be reserved – bookings are taken five months in advance by telephone (☎ 800-365-2267, 301-722-1257) or via the central Web site (http://reservations.nps.gov). Otherwise, it's first come, first served. Camping fees are $17 to $20 per night, except for the five horse camps, which charge $30 to $35 per site. There are no showers or hook-ups. Of the park's 10 campgrounds only Cades Cove, Elkmont and Smokemont are open year-round.

The rest are open from spring (usually March or April) through October. Cataloochee, in the east, is usually the least crowded. A permit is required for backcountry camping; call ☎ 865-436-1297 for more information or drop into the Oconaluftee visitors center (see the National Park Area section, earlier).

Apart from Cherokee, camping is possible outside the park at places such as the

Great Smoky Mountains National Park

Hikers on the Appalachian Trail

Souvenir shop, Cherokee, NC

Great Smoky Mountains National Park

Horseback ride near Blue Ridge

Re-created Cherokee community at Oconaluftee Indian Village, NC

Cape Hatteras is one of North Carolina's least lonely seashores.

Relaxing in the afternoon at the Southend Brewery & Smokehouse, Charlotte, NC

You can camp and fish on Lake Cheoah, Nantahala National Forest, NC.

KOA (☎ 865-453-7903, 2849 Middle Creek Rd) in Pigeon Forge, 6 miles north of Gatlinburg, open April through November.

Other Accommodations The cheapest place with a roof near the park is probably the HI-AYH *Smoky Mountain Ranch Camp (☎ 423-429-8563, 3244 Manis Rd)* in Tennessee. It's about 10 miles southwest of Pigeon Forge and charges $12/15 for members/nonmembers.

The only sheltered accommodation in the park is *LeConte Lodge (☎ 423-429-5704, 250 Apple Valley Rd)*, very much away from it all on the 6593-foot summit of Mt LeConte, the third-tallest Appalachian peak. Its rustic cabins are equipped with two double bunk beds, and there are flush outhouses but no showers. It charges $75 per night, including breakfast and dinner. Reserve at least six months in advance or hope for a last-minute cancellation.

Cottage rental is available at places such as *Freeman's Motel & Cottages (☎ 828-488-2737, Hwy 28N)* in Almond by Bryson City, 15 miles southwest of Cherokee. Prices here start at $35.

NANTAHALA
About 25 miles southwest of Cherokee, the Appalachian Trail crosses the fast-flowing Nantahala River, creating a natural focus for outdoor activities. The Nantahala Outdoor Center (☎ 800-232-7238, 828-488-2175), on Hwy 19/74 near Bryson City, provides equipment as well as services for hiking, mountain biking, canoeing and white-water rafting. In particular it offers a great range of white-water rafting trips on nearby rivers including the French Broad (closest to Asheville), Chattooga, Nantahala, Nolichucky, Ocoee and Pigeon. The Pigeon River offers the closest real thrills, with Class III and IV sections. Allow three to seven hours for a trip, and prepare to get wet. Summer rates with guide start around $28/52 per person for a half/full day, depending on the river and duration. Lunch is included in some full-day outings. For excursions on the Chattooga – and you'd better be in shape – see the North Georgia chapter.

Accommodations include several cabins (starting at $140), simple motel-style units ($55 to $65) and dormitory beds ($14). Call the Nantahala Outdoor Center for reservations. There's also a good little riverside restaurant, a laundry and an outfitter's store. The clientele is a congenial mix of Appalachian Trail hikers, outdoor enthusiasts and passing travelers. It's 45 miles west of Asheville.

Web site: www.noc.com

North Carolina Coast

Mountains are a distant memory by the time you roll into the coastal plain, a two-day drive from the eastern Appalachians. Barrier islands run the whole length of North Carolina's coast, with miles of pristine sandy beaches facing the Atlantic. Looking inland across Pamlico Sound, you're confronted with a series of estuaries, sounds, enclosed tidal lagoons and maritime forests – as disorderly as frayed burlap. The landscape made perfect hiding for Blackbeard, the wild-haired pirate who lurked around the Outer Banks until the English surprised him in 1718.

The area is also rich in firsts – the first English colony was established here, the first town in the state, and the first manned, powered flight. While the Wright brothers sought sand, solitude and steady winds to get them off the ground in the Outer Banks, most seafarers hoped to avoid the islands altogether. Their common failure is noted in the 2000-plus shipwrecks which have accumulated in shoal-filled waters. Some of the hulks can be viewed from the beach but shift nearly as often as the storm-pounded coastline.

To the south, the seashores of Cape Hatteras and Cape Lookout are showcases of wildlife, with over 400 species of birds. These protected seashores stand in contrast to the swarms of motels, holiday homes and tacky eateries that have invaded other parts of the coast. The drowsy, sometimes

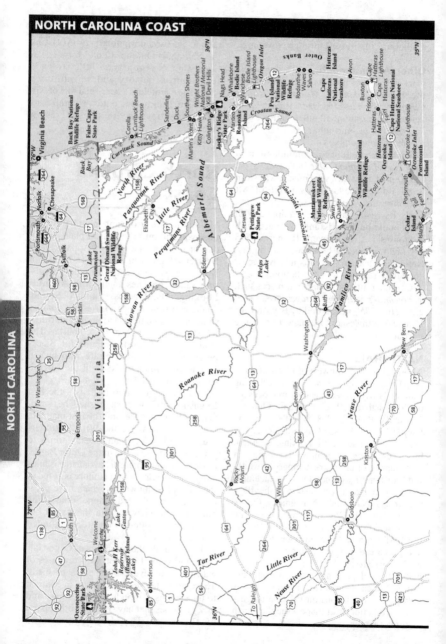

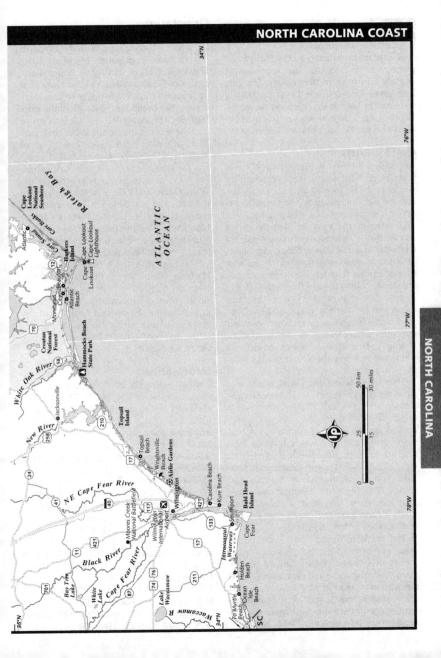

NORTH CAROLINA COAST

NORTH CAROLINA

swampy Albemarle, where the first settlements in the state took hold, today seems forgotten by comparison.

Southern hospitality meets Hollywood pizzazz in Wilmington, the second-most popular film town in the country. The glitz hasn't gone to their heads, though, and movie stars and locals rub shoulders on the street. Nearby Cape Fear is an answer to South Carolina's Myrtle Beach, without the neon glare.

OUTER BANKS

In geological terms, the fragile necklace of islands called the Outer Banks is relatively young, probably formed after the end of the last ice age – previously the Atlantic extended to present-day Pinehurst. Given their fierce battle with the elements, it's a marvel that the islands even exist. Winds relentlessly lash the dunes, lifting mountains of sand and depositing them on the eastern shores; in this manner, the barrier islands are slowly rolling toward the mainland. Big storms can change the lay of the land overnight, carving a bay here and swallowing a beach bungalow there. Sometimes but not often nature spares the worst; in 1998, Hurricane Hugo flooded the inland as far as Charlotte but left the Outer Banks relatively unscathed.

Twenty years ago, the Outer Banks was still a near-virgin territory with scant hotels, condos or restaurants. Only in 1984 was a major public road opened – Hwy 12, which runs along the island chain east of Albermarle and Pamlico Sounds, forms a 100-mile arc. From north to south, Bodie Island, Roanoke Island, Hatteras Island and Ocracoke Island are linked by bridges and ferries. The islands are low sand dunes, less than one mile wide in most places, with long sandy beaches on the ocean and lagoons and marshes on the inland side.

The northern islands are heavily developed, with holiday homes, beach resorts and hordes of summer visitors. Out of season, many businesses close and the region's 27,000 residents are spread very, very thinly. Much of the central islands is protected as national seashore, with over 400 bird species, a few small towns and a wild, windswept beauty.

Orientation

Most of the tourist attractions and facilities are along a 16-mile strip of Bodie Island, in the virtually contiguous towns of Kitty Hawk, Kill Devil Hills and Nags Head. Highway 12, also called Virginia Dare Trail or 'the coast road,' is a two-lane road running close to the beach for the length of the strip. Highway 158, also called the Croatan Hwy or 'the Bypass,' is a four-lane road running parallel but farther inland. Locations are given in terms of Mileposts, starting from Milepost 1 at the north end of the tourist strip, where Hwy 158 crosses to the mainland on the Wright Memorial Bridge. At the south end of the strip, just past Milepost 16, Hwy 64/264 connects to the mainland via Roanoke Island, which has two communities – upscale, tourist-oriented Manteo and the functional fishing town of Wanchese.

The next stop, south over the bridge, is Hatteras Island, where the Cape Hatteras National Seashore begins in earnest. The small towns of Rodanthe, Waves, Salvo, Avon, Buxton, Frisco and finally Hatteras are spread out along the coast. Farther south, and accessible by ferry only, lies tiny Ocracoke Island.

Information

The best sources of information are the visitors centers in Kitty Hawk (☎ 252-441-8144), at Milepost 1½, and Manteo (☎ 800-446-6262, 252-473-2138), at 704 Hwy 64/264, which are open all year. The Manteo office has got to be the only drive-through tourist information point in the country – it's a former bank and the safe is open for viewing. Pick up the free Getaway card, which entitles you to discounts at a number of hotels, restaurants and shops. Other visitors centers in Nags Head are open April to October. Web site: www.outerbanks.org

The public library at 700 Hwy 64/264 has Internet terminals for free use with ID (open 9 am to 6 pm Monday to Saturday, closed Sunday). There are post offices on the Hwy 158 bypass at Milepost 4 in Kitty Hawk, and at Milepost 8½ in Kill Devil Hills.

Banks with ATMs include Centura Bank at Milepost 3 on the Hwy 158 bypass, and the East Carolina Bank at Milepost 10½ in Nags Head.

The *Carolina Coast* is a local free weekly with scads of entertainment listings.

Wright Brothers National Memorial

The dunes of Kill Devil Hills are unspectacular, but the site has some of the excitement of this historic achievement. The memorial

is near Milepost 8, where there's a heavy-looking, art-deco-style, granite monument atop a sand dune. It's inscribed:

In commemoration of the conquest of the air by the brothers Wilbur and Orville Wright. Conceived by genius, achieved by dauntless resolution and unconquerable faith.

Exhibits at the visitors center (☎ 252-441-7430) trace the painstaking development

---

The Wright Stuff

No technical innovation, with the possible exception of the automobile, had a more profound impact on the 20th century than powered human flight. Not surprisingly, there have been plenty of attempts to share in the Wright Brothers' legend, a story of quiet determination if ever there was one.

By the early 1890s, Orville and Wilbur Wright had settled into a respectable existence as the owners of a bicycle shop in Dayton, Ohio. Tinkers by nature, in a second workshop they built kites and pored over complex glider designs. Fascinated with aviation, they followed the wobbly experiments of German birdman Otto Lilienthal (who was killed in a glider crash in 1896) and of Samuel Langley, a secretary of the Smithsonian Institution, whose successful launch of an eagle-sized, powered model earned him a grant from Congress.

In 1899, the self-taught engineers built a biplane kite which they fitted with wings that could be mechanically tilted – providing a lever against the tricky forces of pitch, yaw and roll that had made aircraft inherently unstable. (Wilbur got the idea from observing birds and idly twisting a cardboard box.) Over the next four years and with meager funding, they tested gliders in over 1000 flights on the Outer Banks, near Kitty Hawk. With its isolated dunes and strong winds, Kill Devil Hills was an ideal site, and the locals didn't treat them like crackpots. They shared their beach camp living quarters with their glider, sleeping in burlap slings hung from the rafters.

In the early morning of December 17, 1903, their first powered plane, a frail, cumbersome 12hp contraption dubbed *Kitty Hawk*, lifted off with Orville lying flat at the controls. The aircraft nosed up at a gentle 7mph, covering 120 feet in 12 seconds as Wilbur jogged along behind. 'Damned if they ain't flew!' cried one of the few witnesses. There wasn't a single reporter around at that historic moment, as a much-heralded aircraft built by Langley had plunged into the Potomac River nine days earlier, making aviation seem like folly. After the fourth test of the day managed 852 feet, a wind gust caught the landed *Kitty Hawk* and destroyed it. The Wrights continued their work back in Ohio, where flights of a half-hour or more soon became routine.

Acknowledgment of their feat was elusive at first. In 1905, Orville and Wilbur offered their flyer to a skeptical US Army, which refused to even meet with them; three years later the Wrights were performing for ecstatic crowds in the US and Europe, and the military finally coughed up a contract. The Smithsonian didn't acknowledge the record until 1942, arguing that Langley's aircraft would have flown if the launch mechanism had worked properly.

Tempers are flaring again in the run-up to the 100th anniversary of the event in 2003. Ohio, where the brothers built their prototypes, stamps 'Birthplace of Aviation' on its license plates, while North Carolina cars proclaim 'First in Flight' on their license plates and Raleigh won the exclusive right to use the motto 'First Flight' on US limited-issue quarter coins. Take that, Columbus.

work in Dayton, Ohio, and the experiments conducted at summer camps here over several years. Replicas of their 1902 glider and 1903 powered *Flyer* are displayed, with informative hourly talks. The distances of the first powered flights on December 17, 1903, are marked (also see The Wright Stuff boxed text). The center opens daily ($2 per person or $4 per car).

You can take a spin yourself with Kitty Hawk Aero Tours (☎ 252-441-4460), whose light craft depart from the airstrip next to the monument. A half-hour tour with pilot's comments costs $29 per person for two people, less for larger groups. Hops in Red Baron–type biplanes cost $58 per person, for two people. Reservations and tickets are available at the booking booth.

Fort Raleigh National Historic Site

This site on Roanoke Island saw the first English colonies in North America meet with total failure. The fate of the 'lost colony' remains a mystery, but the visitor center (☎ 252-473-5772) has exhibits, artifacts and a free film on Native Americans.

The Lost Colony

The first European settlers, sponsored by Walter Raleigh, arrived in 1585, but most of them returned to England after only a year. The next group, a shipload of 117 men, women and children, landed in the summer of 1587. Supplies ran low a few months later, and John White, the new colony's governor, set sail to fetch provisions, but got held up at home as war had broken out with Spain. When White returned three years later the colony had vanished, leaving nothing but the word 'Croatan' carved into a tree. This could refer to a place or the name of a Native American group – no one knows. The settlers may have starved or died in attacks by natives, but some historians suggest the colonists intermarried with the Lumbee Indians.

and English settlers that will fuel your imagination. Look for the prints based on 1585 illustrations by John White, which are now some of the best-known depictions of pre-European North America. A small mound nearby is meant to recreate the earthworks of the original fort.

The **Lost Colony Outdoor Drama** is an immensely popular and long-running show that dramatizes the debacle. It plays from mid-June to August, at 8:30 pm in the Waterside Theater (☎ 252-473-3414 for reservations; $16/8). If you spot a face in the audience, it could be Andy Griffith (aka *Matlock*) – the actor owns a house in Manteo and attends the drama each year.

Also nearby, the **Elizabethan Gardens** (☎ 252-473-3234) make a pretty association with the England of 400 years ago; admission costs $5/1 for adults/children. There's always something in bloom – hydrangeas, azaleas, the Lost Colony climbing rose, you name it. Other features include a sunken garden and an Elizabethan rose garden. Note the statue of Virginia Dare, the first child born of English parents in the New World, in 1587 – her grandfather was the colony's first governor, John White (see 'The Lost Colony' boxed text).

Yet another piece of recreated history is **Elizabeth II,** a 69-foot sailing ship built in the style of an old English vessel. It gives a good feel for sea travel in the 16th century, as do costumed docents, exhibits and a film in the visitors center (☎ 252-473-1144). It's open daily April to October, closed Monday in other months; admission costs $4/2.

Jockey's Ridge State Park

The star of this park (☎ 252-441-7132) is a pile of sand – the largest dune in the eastern US. The Wright Brothers came here to test their gliders, and today visitors crawl over its powdery slopes. It's about 100 feet high, depending on the wind and the dune's mood that day, and the best way to get your mind off the searing, reflected heat is to play Lawrence of Arabia music in your head. Kite lovers, hang gliders and sandboarders flock here to practice. The boardwalks behind offer paths through a nice array of myrtle, bayberry and live oak trees. It's off the Hwy 158 bypass, at Milepost 12 in Nags Head. It's open daily; admission is free.

Cape Hatteras National Seashore

Saving much of the Outer Banks area from overdevelopment, this national seashore (☎ 252-473-2111) extends some 70 miles, encompassing the southern end of Bodie Island and nearly all of Hatteras and Ocracoke Islands. Visitors centers at the north and south ends of the seashore open only in the summer season, but the Hatteras Island Visitor Center, near Cape Hatteras itself, opens year-round.

Hatteras Island Natural attractions include local and migratory waterbirds, marshes, woodlands, dunes and miles of empty beaches. One of the best places for wildlife watching is **Pea Island National Wildlife Refuge** (☎ 252-473-1131), at the northern end of Hatteras Island, where there's an informative visitors center, nature trails and a boardwalk leading to observation platforms. Some 265 bird species rest and nest here, including the majestic tundra swan. There's also a red-roofed kiosk out front, one of the stops on the Charles Kurault trail that wends its way along the Atlantic coast (the late journalist was from North Carolina).

Lighthouses are spaced all along the Outer Banks, including the horizontally striped **Bodie Island Lighthouse**, where the keepers' quarters are open March to September. At Buxton, the spirally striped **Cape Hatteras Lighthouse** is open for climbing (268 steps) from April to October, and its visitors center (☎ 252-995-4474) is open all year, with interesting displays on the area's checkered maritime heritage. Erosion advanced so far that, in 1999, the lighthouse was moved half a mile inland on a flatbed truck (great postcard material).

Built in 1874, the **Chicamacomico Lifesaving Station** in Rodanthe is one of seven lifesaving stations along the Outer Banks. Its heroic staff had the spine-tingling job of retrieving survivors from shipwrecks, and more than a few rescuers went to Davy Jones' locker trying. There's a beach lifesaving drill at 2 pm every Thursday afternoon.

Other things to look for include the old village of Avon and the privately owned **Native American Museum** (☎ 252-995-4440) in Frisco, with an extensive, ill-sorted but engaging collection. It's closed Monday; admission is by $2 donation.

Ocracoke Island South across Hatteras Inlet, Ocracoke Island exudes isolation. Over the 12-mile stretch leading to the village of Ocracoke there's not a single building, and the only inhabitants you'll see are the **ponies** kept in pens five miles south of the ferry landing. They're descendants of the wild horses that swam ashore from sinking Spanish vessels and can be viewed from a boardwalk. The beach is

wonderful for beachcombing, especially in the shoulder seasons, as the surf pounds and the salt sea breeze tickles the dune grasses.

The village of Ocracoke revels in its pirate past – Edward Teach, also known as

Blackbeard, used to hide out in the area. Pick up the map directory from the National Park Service Visitors Center (☎ 252-928-4531), opposite the ferry to Cedar Island. With its gnarled live oaks and old frame houses, the area around the harbor is

Graveyard of the Atlantic

Ships traveling along the Atlantic Coast tend to sail close to the Outer Banks. That's risky business, for the waters here are shallow and filled with shoals that are constantly shifting. The seas run very rough around Cape Hatteras, where the icy Labrador Current clashes with the warmer Gulf Stream as it flows north from Florida. All told, over 600 ships – some say as many as 2000 – have found a watery grave along the Outer Banks, typically in a gale and hurricane, or at treacherous Diamond Shoals. On the adjacent map we've highlighted some notable disasters and some shipwrecks that are still visible. A few are documented in David Stick's authoritative book, *Graveyard of the Atlantic: Shipwrecks of the North Carolina Coast.* Note that shipwrecks often appear and disappear during storms.

One of the earliest wrecks on record was the *Tiger*, an English flagship that stranded in Ocracoke Inlet while trying to reach Sir Walter Raleigh's colonists in 1585. More recently, modern researchers have sighted what they think is *Queen Anne's Revenge*, the flagship of pirate Blackbeard, who was beheaded by the English in 1718. Blackbeard's head itself has been rumored to be swimming these waters for years.

Bound for Brazil, the *Metropolis* was a rickety freight steamer that sank in 1878 with 85 passengers on board. Bodies and wreckage, which was pillaged, washed up on Currituck Beach, and the local lifesaving service was ill-prepared to deal with either the survivors or the ensuing scandal. A year earlier, the man-of-war steamer *Huron* had struck ground near Kill Devil Hills, claiming 103 passengers. These accidents hastened plans to open lifesaving stations along the North Carolina coast, and by 1879 a dozen had been built. A violent hurricane is credited with taking the steamboat *Home* to the ocean floor with 90-odd men, women and children, but the real disaster may have been the fact that there were only two life preservers on board. Congress soon passed a law requiring ships to carry one preserver per passenger.

Perhaps the most celebrated loss was that of the Federal gunboat *Monitor*. Likened to 'a cheesebox on a raft,' the Civil War ironclad sank while being towed on New Year's Eve, 1862, about 17 miles off Cape Hatteras.

Among the currently visible wrecks is the *Laura Barnes*, a five-masted schooner out of Maine that shipwrecked in a storm in 1921. The stranded hulk was stripped, but some rotting timbers can still be seen at Coquina Beach on Bodie Island. Not far away, on the north side of the Oregon Inlet, lie the remains of the *Lois Joyce*, a fishing trawler that went down in 1981. The stove pipe spout of the *Oriental*, a federal transport vessel that sank in 1862, sticks out of the breakers near Pea Island National Wildlife Refuge. Further south, a few sodden parts remain near boat ramp No 27 of the *GA Kohler*, a massive 4-masted schooner that washed up on the beach in 1933. Its hull was melted for armaments during WWII.

However, not all sinkings were accidental: The outdated battleships *Virginia* and *New Jersey* were blown to smithereens in aerial target practice in 1923. And aside from Blackbeard's roaming head, other stories of ghost ships abound; the *Carroll A Deering*, a handsome five-masted schooner, was sighted under full sail in 1921 without a hand on board.

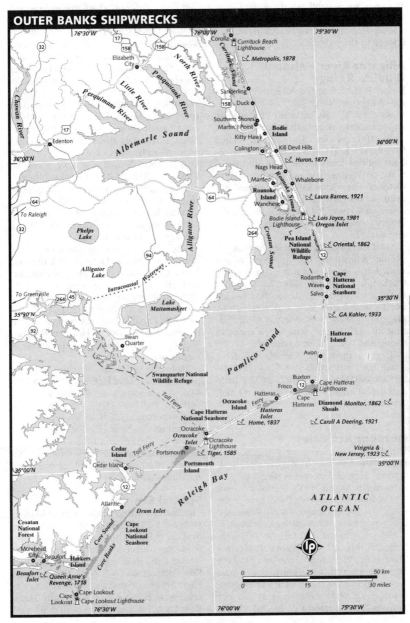

OUTER BANKS SHIPWRECKS

Corolla
Currituck Beach Lighthouse
Metropolis, 1878

76°30'W
76°00'W
75°30'W

32
17
158
158

Elizabeth City

North River

Currituck Sound

Sanderling

158
Duck

Southern Shores
Martin's Point
Bodie Island
Kitty Hawk
Colington
Kill Devil Hills

36°00'N

Huron, 1877

Nags Head
Manteo
Whalebone
Roanoke Island
Wanchese
Laura Barnes, 1921

Edenton

17

Perquimans River
Little River
Pasquotank River

Albemarle Sound

64

64

Roanoke Sound

Bodie Island Lighthouse
Lois Joyce, 1981
Oregon Inlet

To Raleigh

32

Phelps Lake

264

Pea Island National Wildlife Refuge

Oriental, 1862

12

Alligator River

Alligator Lake

94

Croatan Sound

Rodanthe
Cape Hatteras National Seashore
Waves
Salvo

35°30'N

To Greenville

264
45

Intracoastal Waterway

Lake Mattamuskeet

GA Kohler, 1933

35°30'N

92

Hatteras Island

Swan Quarter

Pamlico Sound

Avon

Swanquarter National Wildlife Refuge

Buxton
Cape Hatteras Lighthouse

Toll Ferry

Hatteras
Frisco
12

Ocracoke Island
Hatteras Ferry
Cape Hatteras
Diamond Monitor, 1862
Shoals

Cape Hatteras National Seashore
Hatteras Inlet
Home, 1837

Caroll A Deering, 1921

Ocracoke
Ocracoke Inlet
Ocracoke Lighthouse
Tiger, 1585

Cedar Island
Toll Ferry
Portsmouth

Virginia & New Jersey, 1923

35°00'N

Cedar Island

Portsmouth Island

35°00'N

Raleigh Bay

Atlantic
Drum Inlet

ATLANTIC OCEAN

Croatan National Forest

Core Sound

Cape Lookout National Seashore

Morehead City
Beaufort
Harkers Island

Core Banks

Beaufort Inlet
Queen Anne's Revenge, 1718

Cape Lookout
Cape Lookout
Cape Lookout Lighthouse

0   25   50 km
0   15   30 miles

76°30'W
76°00'W
75°30'W

NORTH CAROLINA

charming for a stroll. At the west end of Point Rd stands the **Ocracoke Lighthouse,** a squat-looking, 75-foot beacon from 1823 (closed to the public).

Alligator River National Wildlife Refuge

Before it feeds into the Albemarle Sound, the Alligator River and its tributaries snake through 150,000 acres of wetlands, and the creeks and canals here make for a wonderful paddle. The refuge office (☎ 252-473-1131) in Manteo runs three-hour **guided tours** of the area starting at 9 am on Wednesday and Friday, May to October. The cost is $30/15 for adults/children, kayak included. Or drop by the office, on Hwy 264/64 near the public library, to pick up a trail map and strike out on your own.

Staff also organize so-called **howlings** – evening educational outings about the red wolf. Participants are driven in pick-up trucks into the bush to learn, among other things, how to bay at the critters (which usually howl back). Summer howlings take place at 8 pm every Wednesday from mid-June to mid-August, with a few dates in spring and fall. Call for a schedule.

To get to the refuge from Manteo, drive a half-hour east on Hwy 64/264 (Hwy 64 farther east), and turn left at the little parking lot on Milltail Rd, near East Lake. The howlings depart from the start of the Creef Cut Wildlife Trail.

Outdoor Activities

Popular outdoor activities include kayaking on the sounds, fishing, sailing, windsurfing, hang gliding and cycling – all well catered for in the northern resort areas. The visitors bureau has a list of bike paths of up to 6 miles in length – some dedicated cycle-only trails, others along highways.

Ocean Atlantic Rentals (☎ 800-635-9559, 252-441-7823), Milepost 10 Virginia Dare Trail, offers good deals on rentals of any and everything – baby, beach and water sports equipment, VCRs, linens, you name it. Cruising bikes cost $10/35 per day/week, two-person kayaks cost $30/90,

and surfboards are $15/45. You can reserve on its Web site (www.oar-nc.com).

Kitty Hawk Kites Outdoors (☎ 800-334-4777, 252-441-4124), at Jockey's Ridge State Park, offers beginners' hang gliding lessons from $65, training to USHGA Hang One standard from $399. It also rents kayaks ($60 per day), sailboats ($80), bikes ($15) and in-line skates ($10) and has a variety of tours and courses. Other outfits such as Kitty Hawk Sports (☎ 252-441-6800) rent boats, surfboards, bikes and other equipment at similar rates.

Adventure Bound Kayak & Camping Center (☎ 252-255-1130) caters to beginning kayakers, campers and ecotourists. Kayak tours are also available from Coastal Kayak Touring (☎ 252-441-393), with 2-hour beginners' tours from $35 and full day tours from $66.

Surfing on the numerous beach breaks is best from August to October, with the East Coast championships in early September, and the hurricane season starting in October bringing the really big waves. Whalebone Surf Shop (☎ 252-261-8737), 4900A N Croatan Hwy, has equipment and information. Canadian Hole, in Pamlico Sound just south of Avon, is a serious windsurfing site.

Dolphin- and whale-watching are also popular. Nags Head Dolphin Watch (☎ 252-449-8999) takes visitors on 2-hour tours in a 40ft covered boat ($20/15 for adults/children in summer, $15/10 in low season). It's located on the Nags Head/Manteo Causeway in the Caribbean Corners store.

Pleasure flights are available at the Wright Brothers National Memorial (see that entry earlier).

Special Events

The **Roanoke Island Festival Park** in Manteo (☎ 252-475-1506) is the site of several outdoor dramas, childrens' plays and art festivals, from July through October. On the first weekend in October, the **Outer Banks Stunt Kite Competition** (☎ 252-441-4124) in Nags Head brings out some awesome-looking aircraft. A week later there's the **Kitty Hawk Kites Fly-In** for hang gliders of all skill levels.

Places to Stay

Sales tax is 6%, plus accommodation tax of 4% – so add 10% to your bill. The area has hundreds of motels, plus efficiencies and B&Bs, but many close in winter and most are booked up in summer – the chamber of commerce (☎ 252-441-8144) offers referrals. Rodanthe, Buxton and Ocracoke are less busy areas, with some smaller inns and B&Bs. Bodie Island, especially the upmarket towns of Corolla, Sanderling and Duck, have plenty of fancy options, but places down south tend to be quieter and slightly cheaper.

Weekly rentals can work out cheaper for groups of four people or more. Two reputable outfits are Sun Realty (☎ 252-261-3892) and Atlantic Realty (252-261-2154), both in Kitty Hawk. The rock-bottom for a simple cottage or cabin is around $600 in high season (and probably no air con). The visitors centers have more details on rental agencies. These companies' Web sites are www.sunrealtync.com and www.atlanticrealty-nc.com.

Camping National Park Service and private campgrounds are spread all along the Outer Banks. The NPS campgrounds (summer only) have no hot showers and little shade – the *Ocracoke campground* (☎ 800-365-2267) can be reserved, but the others are on a first-come, first-served basis. Many private campgrounds open only in summer, and some are mainly for RVs.

On Hatteras Island, the *Frisco Woods Campground* (☎ 252-995-5208, friscowd@pinn.net), on Hwy 12 in Frisco, has sites for tents and RVs from $14 to $22. There's a laundry, pool and convenience store. One- and two-room camping cabins with air con are also available.

Adventure Bound (☎ 252-255-1130, Milepost 4½), is the only campground in a forest (not a bad idea for shade, in summer). Tent sites ($12 for two people) are pretty basic but equipped with hot showers, and you can rent tents. It's open all year.

Colington Park (☎ 252-441-6128, Milepost 8½) in Kill Devil Hills has a boat ramp, store, laundry and electric hookups. It charges $14 for two people ($18 with RV)

and opens year-round, with 30 tent sites and 20 RV sites. Close by, *Joe & Kay's Campground* (☎ 252-441-5468, Milepost 8½) charges similar rates.

The sprawling, 400-site *Camp Hatteras* (☎ 252-987-2777), in Waves, has oodles of facilities – even an indoor/outdoor pool. It's open year-round, and charges $16 for two people.
Web site: www.camphatteras.com

On Ocracoke Island, one good option is *Beachcomber* (☎ 252-928-4031), on Hwy 12, which has water, BBQ grills, hookups and a camp store. Fees are $18/20 for two people in a tent/RV.

Other Accommodations The 40-bed HI *Outer Banks Hostel* (☎ 252-261-2294, 1004 W Kitty Hawk Rd) near Milepost 4½ is in a pleasant location near the Wright Brothers Monument. Coming from the north, take Hwy 158 east, cross the Wright Memorial Bridge, turn right at the traffic light onto The Woods Rd, go 2 miles to the end, and then turn right onto Kitty Hawk Rd. It has a communal kitchen, air con, camping area and 24-hour access. The friendly management arranges kayak trips, bicycle rentals and summer campfires. Dorm beds cost $15/18 for members/nonmembers, and private rooms start at $28/35.
Web site: www.hiayh.org/hostels/northcar/kittyh.htm

Budget Host Inn (☎ 252-441-2503, Milepost 9), on the Hwy 158 bypass in Kill Devil Hills, has rooms starting at $30 in low season.

Chart House (☎ 252-441-7418, email charthousemotel@hotmail.com, Milepost 7), nearby, is a smaller place charging $32/50 in low season and $89/99 in high season.

The *Dolphin Motel* (☎ 252-441-7488, Milepost 16) in Nags Head may vaguely remind you of Norman Bates, but you can't argue with rooms on the ocean for $34 in low season ($70 in high season).
Web site: www.dolphinmotel.net

The oceanfront *Days Inn Mariner* (☎ 252-441-2021, Milepost 7) on the Beach Rd in Kill Devil Hills, is open most of the year and has a variety of rooms from $35/45 in low season to $115/140 in high season.

In Ocracoke, the *Island Inn* (☎ 877-456-3466), on Hwy 12 at Point Rd, is a grand old turn-of-the-century clapboard inn with – get this – Ocracoke's *only* heated pool. Most doubles cost $75 in summer with full breakfast, $48 in winter.
Web site: www.ocracokeislandinn.com

The *Silver Sands Motel* (☎ 252-441-7354, *Milepost 14*) in Nags Head has clean, standard rooms with a queen bed for $59/79 on weekdays/weekends. All rooms have air-con, fridges, cable TV and microwave ovens. There's a swimming pool, too.

Ocean House (☎ 252-441-2900, *Milepost 9½*) has a collection of designer rooms with color TVs and fridges. Summer rates are $65 to $86 for a double – one of the better deals at this level.

The *Quality Inn John Yancey* (☎ 252-441-7141, *Milepost 10*) is a nice place with direct beach access and pool. Rates dip as low as $39 for rooms in winter; standard summer rates are $109.
Web site: www.johnyancey-nagshead.com

The *Cape Hatteras B&B* (☎ 252-995-6004), Old Lighthouse Rd in Buxton, is a multilevel beach house with 6 rooms in traditional and oceanside styles. All rooms have cable TV, air con and private bathrooms. Singles or doubles cost $109 in season, and $69 to $79 the rest of the year.

In Hatteras Village, the *Seaside Inn* (☎ 252-986-2700), on Hwy 12, was the island's first hotel. There are 10 rooms (5 with sitting areas), oil paintings, antique furniture and tongue-and-groove walls. Some bathrooms have Jacuzzis. Singles or doubles cost $85 to $125 in season.

Places to Eat

The main tourist strip in Bodie Island has the most choice and the most nightlife, but only in the season. Most of the following are open year-round on the Beach Rd. A lot of the restaurants have live music one or more nights a week.

Black Pelican (☎ 252-261-3171, *Milepost 4*), does good seafood dishes such as steamed oysters, blackened tuna steak, and mussels (mains $12 to $18) and excellent wood-fired pizzas ($10 to $12). The restaurant, in an old lifesaving station and telegraph office, opens lunch and dinner.

Awful Arthur's Oyster Bar (☎ 252-441-5955, *Milepost 6*) is another sure-fire bet for seafood and a hopping atmosphere. The baked wahoo is terrific ($14). Bulging fish po'boys start at $5, and mains run $10 to $15. Lunch and dinner are served.

Jolly Roger (☎ 252-441-6530, *Milepost 6¾*) is a small family place, good for breakfast, lunch or an inexpensive dinner. It serves Italian meals and prime rib ($10 on Friday). It closes only at Christmas.

As well as being a friendly bar, *Goombays* (☎ 252-441-6001, *Milepost 7½*), serves seafood ($6 at lunch, $10 to $15 at dinner), good sandwiches and surprises such as coconut chicken in pineapple cream sauce ($11). There's live music on Wednesday nights.

Bob's Grill (☎ 252-441-0707, *Milepost 9*) on the Hwy 158 bypass is *the* place to go for a thick, juicy, cheap steak (from $14). Service is friendly, considering the sign out front (*Eat And Get the Hell Out*). It's open all day long.

At the top end, the *Flying Fish Café* (☎ 252-441-6894, *Milepost 10*) on the Hwy 158 bypass does nouveau American–Mediterranean 'in a casual cafe setting' – you'll easily drop $50 just on the wine, but it *is* good. Lunch and dinner are served daily, and reservations are a good idea.

Entertainment

Kelly's Restaurant & Tavern (☎ 441-4116, *Milepost 10½*), on the Hwy 158 bypass is a comfy place with lots of memorabilia and rustic wood. It has a raw bar (the snow crab legs are good) and standard fare such as filet mignon, pasta or chicken. It's open 5 pm to 2 am daily. Live music (usually Motown or Top 40) starts from 10 pm.

A popular surfers' bar, *Hurricane Alley* (☎ 252-926-4021, *Milepost 9½*), has a good selection of pasta, grills, the obligatory seafood and live music in summer.

The *Port O'Call Restaurant & Gaslight Saloon* (☎ 252-441-7484, *Milepost 8½*) in

Kill Devil Hills is so over the top that it's a must for a drink. Eclectic music (Irish *and* reggae) starts around 9 pm.

The bright, artsy **Rundown Café** (☎ 252-255-0026, Milepost 1), at the north end of Kitty Hawk, does Caribbean dishes such as jerk chicken as well as salads and sandwiches (mains $8 to $14), and has regular live entertainment. 'Rundown' refers to a Jamaican soup, not the state of the place. It's closed off-season.

Getting There & Around

No public transport exists to or on the Outer Banks. Free car ferries between the Hatteras and Ocracoke Islands run at least hourly from 5 am to 10 pm, and more frequently in the summer. Bookings for the 40-minute trip aren't necessary, but expect waits in summer.

Ferries between Ocracoke (☎ 800-345-1665) and Cedar Island (☎ 800-856-0343) run every two hours or so and should be reserved, especially in summer ($10 per car, 2¼ hours). Ferries also link Ocracoke and Swan Quarter, on the mainland ($10 per car, 2½ hours, twice daily); for Swan Quarter reservations, call ☎ 800-773-1094.

The speed limit on the Outer Banks is 55mph, but drops to 45mph through the national seashore. Bear distance in mind: the town of Hatteras is 66 miles from Kill Devil Hills, or more than an hour's drive; coming from the Beaufort, the trip to Kill Devil Hills, including ferry crossings, will take about 6 hours.

For a taxi, call Beach Cab (☎ 800-441-2503) in Nags Head.

CRYSTAL COAST

The southern Outer Banks, comprising several coastal towns, sounds, islands, inlets and barrier islands, are collectively called the Crystal Coast, at least for tourist office promotional purposes.

Cape Lookout National Seashore

This 55-mile-long barrier island system – a low ribbon of dunes, scattered grasses and shifting sands – is a great place to get away from it all. Waves are constantly reshaping the geography, and a single big storm can change the face of the three islands overnight. The outlying shoals are treacherous, and early maps called the area *promontorium tremendum* – 'horrible headland'. The beachcombing is among the best of the Atlantic Coast, and surf fishing is also popular for flounder, sea bass, drum and sea trout.

There are virtually no facilities for visitors, and the only way to get there is by boat. You can kayak your way over. Outfitters include AB Kayaks (☎ 252-728-6330) at 320 Front St in Beaufort, which has two-person kayaks for $45/65 per half/full day, and tours to the islands.

The visitors center (☎ 252-728-2250) on Harkers Island near Beaufort is accessible by bridge from the mainland.

There are seasonal nesting sites for turtles and shore birds. Box turtles and terrapins are fairly common, and you'll see the toad or tree frog on the Core Banks, the two long eastern islands of the national seashore. Sandpipers and plovers abound, but you might also see egrets, terns, and herons.

Core Banks The picturesque abandoned village of **Portsmouth** sits on the northernmost tip of the national seashore. Founded in 1753, this was one of the first settlements in the region, a fishing village that swelled to 1000 residents by the mid-19th century. Fortunes declined as competition grew from the town of Ocracoke across the inlet, and the last few souls departed in 1971. Today Portsmouth is a national historic site; more details can be had at the visitors center in the restored Dixon/Salter House.

At the southern end of the seashore, Cape Lookout protrudes like a fishhook, with the distinctive diamond pattern of the **Cape Lookout Lighthouse** visible from the ferry landing. The beacon's 201 steps aren't open for climbing, but there's a small museum next door with island history and seashells.

Camping is permitted, but there are no developed campgrounds and you'll have to bring in all your supplies, including food, water, and long tent pegs. Insect repellent is a must, for the mosquitoes, chiggers, sand gnats and occasional ticks. Be sure to dispose of human waste in cat holes, and take all trash out with you (especially plastic bags, which can kill sea turtles). Swimming isn't recommended due to the strong currents and riptides. A single concessionaire, Morris Marina Kabin Kamps (☎ 252-225-4261), in Atlantic, has a few 6-person cabins to rent on the islands, starting at $100 per night.

Ferry boat day trips run from Harkers Island. Local Yokel Ferry (☎ 252-728-2759), 516 Island Rd, and Sand Dollar Ferry (☎ 252-728-6181), 1390 Island Rd, usually charge $10/6 one way for adults/children; campers with gear may be charged extra. They run regularly, usually on demand, in high season; call ahead in low season. Farther north, ferries also run from the coastal towns of Atlantic (☎ 252-225-4261), Davis (☎ 252-729-2791) and Beaufort (☎ 252-728-6888).

Four-wheel drive vehicles are allowed on the islands, but you'll need a permit from the visitors center on Harkers Island if you stay overnight. Return ferry fares cost about $75 to $130; the cheapest is from Davis.

Shackleford Banks & Around Several smaller islands close to Beaufort are fun for shorter excursions (no vehicles allowed). **Wild ponies** graze the dune grass and gallop the beaches; they're descendants of Spanish survivors from shipwrecks of the early 17th century, and are looked after by the parks service (but they're definitely not for petting).

Nine miles long and wooded at its core, the island of **Shackleford Banks** offers good beachcombing, hiking, swimming and surf fishing, and is home to over 100 horses. At the western tip there's a good picnic spot at Mullet Pond, named for the fish that were caught, salted and shipped from here in the 19th century. You can spot the Cape Lookout Lighthouse in the distance. The ocean side of the groves is dotted with stunning 'ghost forests' – skeletons of trees killed by salt and sand from the shifting coastline. It's a 15-minute ferry ride from Beaufort Harbor on boats run by, among others, the Outer Banks Ferry Service (☎ 252-728-4129), on Front St, across from the Maritime Museum; and Island Ferry Adventures (☎ 252-728-7555), on the dock between Queen and Pollock Sts. Both charge $14/6 for adults/children roundtrip.

Ferries also go to tiny **Carrot Island** ($8/4, 5 minutes), which has a half-mile nature trail on a wildlife reserve and some horses, but few beaches. **Bird Shoals** ($10/5, 10 minutes), at the back side of Carrot Island, has two miles of lonely, wind-swept sands and a few dozen ponies. **Sand Dollar Island** ($12/6, 15 minutes) is known for its bird sanctuary and (surprise) sand dollars, especially at low tide, but visitors are encouraged to limit their take.

Beaufort
pop 3800
One of the oldest towns in the state, Beaufort (bow-fort) was originally called Fish Town and still trades off its maritime heritage. The harbor road is lined with pleasure boats and seafood restaurants on one side, and cute cottages and clapboard houses on the other.

The welcome center (☎ 252-728-5225) is run by friendly costumed docents in the Beaufort Historic Site, at 138 Turner St. It conducts tours of a dozen restored 18th-century buildings, and offers 1½-hour history tours by double-decker bus ($6/4 for adults/children).

The real highlight here is the **North Carolina Maritime Museum** (☎ 252-728-7317) at 315 Front St. There are diverse displays on lifesaving, outboard motors, local fishing, and more – all are very well done. One exhibit features the search for Blackbeard's flagship, the *Queen Anne's Revenge,* which is believed to lie just off Beaufort Inlet (see the 'Graveyard of the Atlantic' boxed text, earlier). Also, check out the screen display of weird fish recipes – how else will you know how to prepare electric eel? It's free and open daily (closed Sunday morning).

The welcome center has a list of B&Bs that start around $85 in season. The *Innlet Inn* (☎ 800-554-5466, 252-728-3600, 601 Front St) has big, comfy rooms with a seating area, fireplace and harbor views starting at $110/65 in summer/winter. Cheaper places are available in nearby Morehead City and Atlantic Beach.

Front St has an assortment of bars and eateries and can be lively on a warm evening. The neatest place is *Amos Mosquito's Swampside Café* (☎ 252-247-6222, 509 Evans St), with moss hanging from the rafters. Sandwiches (crab, blackened fish or shrimp creole) cost $6.50 to $10, and evening meals run $10 to $23. It's closed Sunday night.

Look around Front St for boats and excursions to the islands (see the Cape Lookout National Seashore section, earlier).

Morehead City
pop 7500
An unappealing industrial-commercial stretch of Hwy 70 goes through Morehead City, but it's worth a short detour to the town's waterfront. The town fills with shiny pates during the annual Bald is Beautiful convention held in September.

The Crystal Coast Visitors Bureau (☎ 252-726-8148), 3407 Arendell St (Hwy 70), has tons of area leaflets and is open daily.

So many ships have been sunk along this coast that it's called the 'Graveyard of the Atlantic' (see the boxed text, earlier). Some wrecks are superb for serious divers, especially around June to September when the water is warm and clear. Olympus Dive Center (☎ 252-726-9432), 713 Shepard St, runs dive charters from $55/100 for half/full day trips – drop in to see its collection of artifacts.

Less costly motels include *Econo Lodge* (☎ 252-247-2940, 3410 Bridges St), near Hwy 70, with rooms starting at $35/40 on weekdays/weekends in low season, rising to $69/89 in summer. Web site: www.moreheadhotels.com

Closer to the water, the *Charter Motel* (☎ 252-726-3256, 404 Evans St) is a little cheaper. The basic *Morehead Motor Inn* (☎ 252-726-5141, 3300 Arendell St) charges $32 per room in low season, and about $39/69 on weekdays/weekends in summer.

The *Sanitary Fish Market* (☎ 252-247-3111, 501 Evans St) on the waterfront has been serving seafood to appreciative locals since 1938. It's a raucous place with basic decor, and mains such as poached mullet start at $10. The *Calypso Café* (☎ 252-240-3380, 506 Arendell St) is an excellent choice for Caribbean fare.

Fort Macon
A bridge from Morehead City crosses to Atlantic City, a heavily developed seaside resort on Bogue Island that gets awfully crowded in the warmer months. At the east end of the island, **Fort Macon** (☎ 252-726-3775) will interest Civil War buffs with its old fortifications and exhibits on army life. Built in 1834 to ward off Spanish raids, the five-sided brick fortress was captured by Union forces in 1862 and used as a coaling station for ships, then as a federal prison. The structure was pressed back into service during the Spanish-American War, and again in WWII.

NORTH CAROLINA

Fort Macon is now North Carolina's most popular state park, drawing 1.5 million visitors a year. Push-button audio exhibits can be activated in the WWII barracks, gunpowder magazine and living quarters, and the complex also houses a good little bookstore. Outside, you can explore the quarter-mile nature trail, public swimming beach and rock jetties. It's open daily till sunset; admission is free.

Hammocks Beach State Park

This little gem of a state park (☎ 910-326-4881) features unspoiled sand dunes, beaches and undeveloped *campsites* ($8). The beach, on 892-acre Bear Island, is regularly voted one of the nicest on the Atlantic Coast, but thankfully the masses gravitate toward sands farther east. Accessible only by ferry from Swansboro ($2, 25 minutes), this barrier isle also offers swimming, picnicking, hiking, fishing and park-run nature programs. Canoeists or kayakers can follow the 2¾ mile ferry route to the island or a marked canoe trail, which leads through tidal creeks (maps available at the park office). Watch for the sea turtles that nest here. Access in winter is sporadic, via a private ferry service.

Close by, the smaller, park-owned Huggins Island is completely different – covered by thick maritime forests, with an abandoned Confederate battery. It's reachable only by private boat.

GREAT DISMAL SWAMP NATIONAL WILDLIFE REFUGE

Anything but dismal, this huge tract of fascinating muck (☎ 757-986-3705) on the Virginia border is a national wildlife refuge rich in flora and fauna. Exploration – allowed only by day – is rewarding.

Evidence of human occupation of the swamp area dates from some 13,000 years ago, but by 1650, there were few Native Americans in the area. The earliest settlers showed little interest in the swamp until 1665, when William Drummond discovered the lake that still bears his name. In 1728, William Byrd II led a surveying party into the swamp to draw the dividing line between Virginia and North Carolina. George Washington examined it in 1763 and then organized the Dismal Swamp Land Co, with a view to future draining and logging. It was subsequently logged right through to 1976, and the draining has left the swamp at half of its original size.

The swamp contains five major forest types (pine, Atlantic white cedar, maple–black gum, tupelo bald cypress, and sweet gum–oak-poplar) and three non-forested types of plant communities (remnant marsh, sphagnum bog and evergreen shrub). The dwarf trillium, found in the northwest section of the swamp, blooms briefly every March for a two-week period.

More than 200 species of bird are found in the swamp, and of these species 93 are nesting. Bird watching is best from April to June (spring migration), when the greatest diversity of species occurs. Local mammals include otters, bats, raccoons, minks, gray and red foxes and gray squirrels. The white-tailed deer are common, but black bears and bobcats are rarely observed.

There are three species of poisonous snake (cottonmouth, canebrake, and copperhead) and 18 nonpoisonous species, yellow-bellied and spotted turtles and an additional 56 species of turtle, lizard, salamander, frog and toad.

Hiking and biking are options on the many timber roads here; Washington Ditch Rd is the best for bikes. Also near Washington Ditch Rd, the Boardwalk Trail passes through a mile of representative swamp. Boating and fishing are possible on the water-filled crater of Lake Drummond (a Virginia license is required). Access is via the Feeder Ditch, which connects the lake with the Dismal Swamp Canal. White-tailed deer are legally hunted in the fall.

The 107,000-acre refuge is open from 30 minutes before sunrise until 30 minutes after sunset daily; overnight use is not permitted. To get to the swamp, stop off at the Dismal Swamp Canal Visitor/Welcome Center (☎ 252-771-8333), just south of the Virginia border on Hwy 17, some 21 miles north of Elizabeth City. For boaters, the refuge is 5 miles north of the South Mills Locks.

Web site: www.icw.net/DSCwelcome

THE ALBERMARLE

The wild, swampy region around Albermarle Sound was the unlikely site of the state's first European settlement, in Bath. Beginning in the 18th century, it became a focus for canals that provided protected transport routes north to the Chesapeake and south to Wilmington. Despite its closeness to the silky sands of the Outer Banks, the area remains underdeveloped; the mosquitoes drive (or carry) some people away.

Edenton

pop 5300

Founded in 1712, this small town at the west end of Albermarle Sound was the center of economic, social and political life in early colonial times. In the 1774 'Edenton tea party,' 50 local society ladies swore off tea in protest at British taxes. The town provided signatories to the Declaration of Independence and the Constitution, as well as two state governors and one of the first Supreme Court judges. Within 50 years, development bypassed Edenton, leaving pretty streets of 18th-century buildings.

See the visitors center (☎ 252-482-2637), 108 N Broad St, for a guided walking tour ($6) or a self-guided tour map. It's closed Monday in winter.

Web site: www.edenton.com

Hope Plantation (☎ 252-794-3140) was built in 1803 by David Stone, an exceedingly popular governor who served seven terms in the late 18th century. The interior is lovely, especially the library. Admission is $6.50/3 for adults/children (closed Sunday morning and January). It's on Hwy 308, five miles east of Hwy 13.

Another good historic site is the **Newbold-White House** (☎ 252-426-7567) a two-story Quaker farmhouse from 1730 with period furnishings and a great lindenwood fireplace. Admission is $2/0.50 for adults/children (closed Sunday morning and Monday, and from Thanksgiving to February). It's on tiny Hwy 1336, off Hwy 17.

There are several cheap motels along Broad St. The **Coach House Motel** (☎ 252-482-2107, 823 N Broad St/Hwy 17N), has clean, basic rooms from $36. For something unusual, seek out **The Trestle Inn** (☎ 800-645-8466, 252-482-2282, 632 Soundside Rd), which overlooks a wildlife refuge on a private lake. Singles/doubles cost $65/85. Take Hwy 32 south 2 miles, right on Soundside Rd and continue 3 miles to the inn. The visitors center also has information about seven B&Bs, especially along Queen St and Broad St, with rates from $65 to $175.

Near the waterfront, **Watermann's Grill** (☎ 252-482-7233, 427 S Broad St) is screamingly popular, with frequent lines in the side deli. Try the grilled dolphin in orange ($13) and other innovative dishes (closed Sunday).

No-nonsense Mexican fare is available at **Mamasitas** (☎ 252-482-6892, 1316 N Broad St) in the Edenton Valley Shopping Center (mains average $8 to $15).

Elizabeth City

pop 18,300

On Pasquotank River, Elizabeth City became a shipping and transportation center after the Dismal Swamp Canal was completed in 1803. The west side of the river was deep enough to found an inspection port, and hemp, flax, lumber and other products were unloaded at Mariners Wharf.

The Museum of the Albermarle (☎ 252-335-1453), 2 miles southwest of town on Hwy 17, gives a good account of the canal's and the area's history. It's closed on Monday; admission is free. The museum is moving to a larger site downtown in 2002, at the corner of Southern Ave and E Ehringhaus St.

The downtown area is pleasantly old-fashioned, especially along the waterfront. The chamber of commerce (☎ 252-335-4365), 502 E Ehringhaus St, has a walking-tour map, B&B lists and other tourist information.

Web site: www.elizcity.com

Motels are on the N Road St/Hwy 17N bypass road. At the north end, **Travelers Inn** (☎ 252-338-5451), at No 1211, has clean singles/doubles starting at $40/45. The **Vicki Villa Motel** (☎ 252-335-2994), at No 1161, nearby charges similar rates.

For a quick bite, **The Daily Grind** (☎ 252-375-7600, 507 E Main St) is a busy little cafe with cheap sandwiches and salads. **Mulligan's Waterfront Grille** (☎ 252-331-2431, 400 S Water St), at Mariners Wharf, has good lunch specials starting at just $5, and evening meals from $5 to $15. East of downtown, just over the bridge on Hwy 158/Camden Causeway, is the **Marina Restaurant** (☎ 252-335-7307) with popcorn shrimp and breaded flounder from $5 at lunch (closed Saturday midday).

Creswell
pop 1764

On the low-lying peninsula south of Albermarle Sound, the tiny town of Creswell is a throwback to another era, and haunting in its dilapidation. Most travelers pass through on Hwy 64 en route to the Outer Banks, but seven miles south it's worth a detour to **Somerset Place** (☎ 252-797-4171), a state historic site notable for its detailed depiction of the slave community on a Southern plantation. You can tour the onetime owner's house, a reconstructed slave's cabin, smokehouse, kitchen and other structures till 4 pm, but the grounds are open any time. Admission is free. The light over adjacent Lake Pettigrew is terrific at dusk.

Overlooking the lake, **Pettigrew State Park** (☎ 252-797-4475) is a wildlife sanctuary with some Indian artifacts, fishing and a pretty campsite ($12).

Bath
pop 200

On the north bank of Pamlico River, 16 miles east of Washington, lies the historic village of Bath. A mere pinprick on the map, this was North Carolina's first town, established in 1705. Three years later it became the first port of entry into the state. Blackbeard kept a home here, as did Edna Ferber, who lived at the **Palmer Marsh House** on Main St (open daily, admission $1). Ferber wrote her best-selling 1926 novel *Showboat* after talking to the boat's crew and cast near Bath, but changed the location in the book to Mississippi. Not surprisingly, there's no mention of Ferber in Bath's tourist brochures.

The Historic Bath Visitors Center (☎ 252-923-3971), on Carteret St east of the sole traffic light on Main St, hands out a decent walking-tour map of town. Near the harbor, the spick-and-span **Olde School House** (☎ 252-923-0339, 101 N Main St) does killer subs ($8, enough for two people) and has just opened an upscale restaurant (closed Monday). The **Old Towne Country Kitchen** (☎ 252-923-1840), on the other end of Main St, offers downhome fare.

MATTAMUSKEET NATIONAL WILDLIFE REFUGE

Lake Mattamuskeet is a yawn in the landscape off Pamlico Sound, with an interesting history. In 1909 the landowners of Hyde County set out to drain about 100,000 acres of wetlands, including the entire lake, inspired by examples of Dutch land reclamation. Soya and wheat were cultivated on the soggy lake bed, but the operation never turned a profit, and the lake was allowed to refill. In 1932, the property was sold to the US government, which turned it into a bird refuge.

Today Lake Mattamuskeet is the winter birding capital of the Carolinas. Starting around mid-September, thousands of waterfowl pour into the area, including Canada and snow geese and 22 species of duck. It's famous for the huge flocks of migrating tundra swans that arrive in early December – up to 100,000 at a time, an incredible and thunderous experience. You can observe them on the causeway that spans the lake, or seek out more removed hides near **Mattamuskeet Lodge,** the handsome former pumping station off the main road. It's signposted from Hwys 94 and 264. Information is available from the Mattamuskeet National Wildlife Refuge office (☎ 252-926-4021). They'll tell you about the **Swan Days Wildlife Festival** held the first weekend in December.

NEW BERN
pop 21,000

Some 40 miles northwest of Morehead City, New Bern was settled in the early 18th century by German and Swiss colonists. Named for the city of Bern, the present-day capital of Switzerland, the city was a middling river port when the first colonial capital of Carolina was established here in 1770. The royal governor, William Tryon, had a fine palace built here in 1774.

Downtown, New Bern is an archetypal Southern town, relaxed and slow-moving, with broad, tree-lined avenues and an old harbor that bathes the old town on two fronts. Tryon Palace is really the sole attraction, mostly for day-trippers from the coast. Few people realize that this was also the birthplace of Pepsi-Cola (although there's curiously little razzmatazz about it). The visitors center (☎ 800-437-5767, 252-637-9400) at 314 S Front St is open daily. Web site: www.visitnewbern.com

Tryon Palace

The first permanent seat of colonial government in North Carolina, **Tryon Palace** (☎ 252-767-1560), at 610 Pollock St, was an early symbol of King Charles' power in the New World. William Tryon filled the palace with fancy furnishing upon its completion in 1774, but moved to New York the same year. Anti-British feelings were running high as his successor, Josiah Martin, ended up fleeing the colony in 1775, on the eve of the Revolutionary War. The mansion burned down in 1798, four years after the capital was moved to Raleigh, but detailed plans of the palace and its furnishings survived, and the state had it rebuilt at great cost in the late 1950s.

The courtyard and garden are of 18th-century European design, although the brick-lined walkways from the 1950s renovation are pure New World, with a somewhat sanitized feel. The real joy of the Georgian-style mansion lies in the 40-minute guided tours, which include some amusing anecdotes by costumed docents. Take the story of the guests' party games: A pea in the cake determined who would host the following year's bash.

There are two other restored homes just outside the palace gates, the **Dixon-Sevenson House** (1833), which served as a hospital for Union troops during the Civil War, and the **John Wright Stanley House** built by a wealthy Revolutionary War patriot.

Admission is $15/6 for all buildings and gardens, or $8/3 for the gardens, kitchens and stables only. The site is well-marked.

Pepsi Birthplace

Two blocks from the water, the **Birthplace of Pepsi** (☎ 252-636-5898), at 256 Middle St, serves pop from a soda fountain on the spot where the forerunner, 'Brad's Drink,' was unveiled in 1898. The inventor, Caleb Bradham, went bust in 1921, and the Pepsi company moved to New York in 1935. There are the usual trinkets, and a plaque outside – not much fizz overall.

Places to Stay & Eat

The basic **Curtis Motel** (☎ *252-638-3011, 113 Broad St)* has rooms for $38. The **Harvey Mansion** (☎ *252-638-3205, 211 S Front St)* has spacious singles or doubles equipped with antiques and bathrooms with Jacuzzis for $85. It has a good restaurant (mains $15 to $25) and cellar pub, both open evenings only, as well as regular exhibitions of art. Web site: www.harveymansion.com

The **Chelsea Restaurant** (☎ *252-637-5469, 335 Middle St)* is a fun place, with an old-style drugstore feel and plenty of burgers and sandwiches for $6 to $8 (closed Sunday). The Pepsi mural inside is worth a look – ask the owner to point out the exhibitionist in the picture. Another good choice for salads and sandwiches is the **Gallery Garden Café** *(309 Middle St)*, lined with historic photos of New Bern (closed Sunday evening and Monday).

CROATAN NATIONAL FOREST

Between New Bern and the Crystal Coast, the Croatan National Forest encompasses almost 160,000 acres of coastal forest, estuaries, bogs and pocosins (raised swamps). The forest has several carnivorous plants, including the Venus flytrap (which is protected by law), sundew and pitcher plant. Critters include deer, black bears, ospreys, alligators and even wild turkeys. Hiking

NORTH CAROLINA

trails perforate the soggy landscape, and the park headquarters (☎ 252-638-5628) on Hwy 70, about 9 miles southeast of New Bern, hands out trail descriptions. Picnicking, fishing and rough camping (free) is possible at Fishers Landing on the Neuse River; turn off Hwy 70 opposite Riverdale Fuel Market. Another mile south there's a developed campsite at Flanners Beach ($10), and still more sites can be found elsewhere in the forest.

WILMINGTON
pop 76,000

Wilmington is a busy little port town with factories, a university, film studios and a neat old downtown and waterfront area. Its pretty historic district is one of the country's largest, and the oak-lined streets are fun to peruse. It's one of the best places to stop along the coast, and the surrounding area has a wealth of historic interest.

Giovanni da Verrazano explored the Cape Fear area in 1524, but it was 200 years before the first European settlement was established here on the Cape Fear River. The area prospered as a provider of naval stores (turpentine, pitch and tar) for the Royal Navy, and Wilmington grew as a seaport and as a trading center for goods brought downriver on flatboats.

The town was an early leader in the American independence movement, and one of the first decisive battles of the Revolution was fought nearby at Moore's Creek. In the Civil War it was an important Confederate port, supplied by blockade runners that sped in under the protection of the guns around the mouth of Cape Fear River. Federal forces did not take the city until 1865, after a massive naval bombardment of Fort Fisher.

Information

The Cape Fear Visitors Center (☎ 910-341-4030), in the 1892 Courthouse building at 3rd and Princess Sts, has a walking-tour map, information about historic houses and other attractions. In summer an information booth opens on the waterfront near Market St. Web site: www.cape-fear.nc.us

Banks downtown include a Bank of America at 155 N Front St and First Citizens Bank at 315 Market St.

The post office (☎ 910-313-3251) is at 152 N Front St (for General Delivery: Zip 28402). You can access the Web for free at the public library (☎ 910-341-4390), 201 Chestnut St. Hours are 9 am to 9 pm weekdays (till 6 pm Friday), 9 am to 5 pm Saturday and 1 to 5 pm Sunday.

The *Wilmington Star* is the local daily and has a good entertainment supplement on Friday and a Web site (www.wilmingtonstar .com). Free listings mags include *Encore* and *The Beat,* a monthly for music events, with a Web site at www.thebeatmag.com.

Local radio stations include WHQR 91.3 FM (classical, jazz, NPR), WRQR 104.5 FM (contemporary rock), WLOZ 89.1 FM (UNC radio, world music to rap) and WLGX 106.7 FM (jazz).

The Coastal Dry Cleaners & Coin Laundry, Kerr Ave, at Market St, has plenty of coin-operated machines and is open daily.

For medical treatment, the New Hanover Regional Medical Center (☎ 910-343-7000) is about 1½ miles southeast of downtown at 2131 S 17th St. The larger Cape Fear Hospital (☎ 910-452-8100) is at 5301 Wrightsville Ave, about 4 miles from both Wilmington and Wrightsville Beach.

Dangers & Annoyances

Wilmington is a pretty safe place, but avoid walking the higher-numbered streets after dark – between 13th and 20th Sts, which are well away from downtown.

Things to See & Do

Museums In an attractive old corner of downtown, St Johns Museum of Art (☎ 910-763-0281), 114 Orange St, focuses on North Carolina artists and is known for its exceptionally good collection of prints by Mary Cassatt, the impressionist. The rear section, reached via an underground passage, is a pleasant hall with exhibits by local artists. Also, have a look at the giant head sculptures in the back yard. Admission is $3/1 for adults/children (closed Monday). The museum will move to a larger location

NORTH CAROLINA

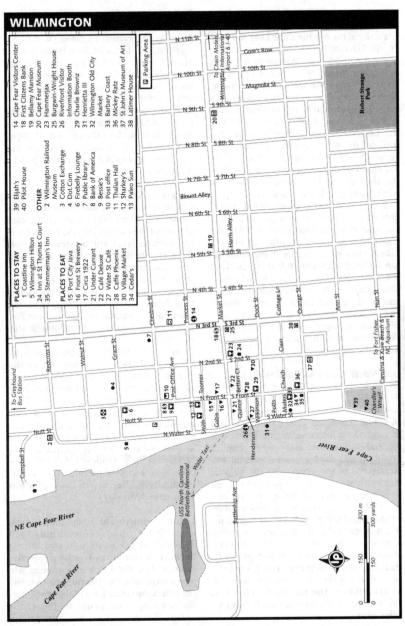

WILMINGTON

PLACES TO STAY
1 Coastline Inn
5 Wilmington Hilton
24 Inn at St Thomas Court
35 Stemmerman's Inn

PLACES TO EAT
15 Port City Java
16 Front St Brewery
17 Circa 1922
21 Under Currant
22 Café Deluxe
27 Water St Café
28 Caffe Phoenix
30 Village Market
34 Cedar's

39 Elijah's
40 Pilot House

OTHER
2 Wilmington Railroad Museum
3 Cotton Exchange
4 Dot.Com
6 Firebelly Lounge
7 Public library
8 Bank of America
9 Bessie's
10 Post office
11 Thalian Hall
12 Sharkey's
13 Paleo Sun

14 Cape Fear Visitors Center
18 First Citizens Bank
19 Bellamy Mansion
20 Cape Fear Museum
23 Hammerjax
25 Burgwin-Wright House
26 Riverfront Visitor Information Booth
29 Charlie Brownz
31 Henrietta III
32 Wilmington Old City Market
33 Barbary Coast
36 Mickey Ratz
37 St John's Museum of Art
38 Latimer House

Ⓟ Parking Area

outside downtown from late 2001 – phone for directions.

For local history, the **Cape Fear Museum** (☎ 910-341-4350), at 814 Market St, includes a terrific model of Wilmington in the blockade-running 1860s. There's a showcase on local legend **Michael Jordan,** including photos, his graduation hat and college basketball uniform (for UNC at Chapel Hill), as well as a kids' interactive eco-display of the Lower Cape Fear Region called the Jordan Discovery Gallery (sponsored by guess who). Look for travelling exhibits, and the maritime display (a row of sea skiffs in the shed outside). Admission is $4/1 for adults/children (closed Monday).

Wilmington was a major rail transport hub during the Confederacy, but the line was shut down in 1960 when the Atlantic Coast railroad moved its office to Florida. Like the locomotive out front, the **Wilmington Railroad Museum** (☎ 910-763-2634) at Water and Red Cross Sts is a bit of a relic. The paraphernalia includes lanterns, signs and good black-and-white disaster photos, and the scale-model railway upstairs is a hit with kids. It's open daily in season, closed Wednesday in winter; admission costs $3/2 for adults/children.

USS *North Carolina* Battleship Moored on the north side of the Cape Fear River, this 44,000-ton monster (☎ 910-251-5797) was the epitome of sea power when she was launched. A self-guided tour takes you through the pilothouse, engine room, sick bay and coding room, and you can clamber around inside the big 16-inch gun turrets. Renovated in the 1960s with the help of children's milk money, it's just old enough to be enjoyed as a technological relic, and the 1940s background music and exhibits on shipboard life provide lots of human interest. Note the lifelike dummies – opening a pack of Chesterfields in the Officers' Statesroom. It's open 8 am to 8 pm daily, mid-May to mid-September (till 5 pm the rest of the year) and charges $8/4 for adults/children. You can take a river taxi ($2 roundtrip, 25 minutes each way) or drive over.

Bellamy Mansion *Gone With the Wind* comes to mind when you lay eyes on this stunning antebellum mansion (☎ 910-251-3700), at 503 Market St. John Bellamy was a planter, and he stuck to a plantation recipe of Corinthian columns, wide porches and droves of servants. Most of the furnishings were gutted by a fire in 1972, and tours stress the restoration and architecture of the rooms, which are used for exhibitions. Movie directors love the location. It's open 10 am to 5 pm Wednesday to Saturday, and 1 to 5 pm Sunday. Admission costs $6/3 for adults/children.

Burgwin-Wright House John Burgwin, a wealthy colonial treasurer, built this town house in 1770 on the massive stone foundations of the old city jail (the damp, claustrophobic cells can still be viewed outside, down the steps). General Cornwallis kept prisoners here during the Revolutionary War and made the house his personal headquarters in 1781, just weeks before his final defeat at Yorktown. Burgwin himself lived out at a plantation on the Cape Fear River and did quite well for himself after the war.

Today this attractive home (☎ 910-762-0570), at 224 Market St, is open for viewing after a restoration by the Colonial Dames of America (who have an interest in many of Wilmington's historic buildings). There are many interesting features here, such as a ridiculously heavy tea set, a nice parterre garden for strolling and a reconstructed kitchen (check out the intricate wood carving on the pie cabinet). Admission, including an excellent narrated tour, is $6/3 for adults/children (open daily 10 am to 4 pm, closed Monday).

Latimer House The sumptuous furnishings of this greystone 1852 residence (☎ 910-762-0492), at 126 S 3rd St, bridge the gap between Victorian and Italianate styles. Zebulon Latimer was a businessman who wed a local belle, and the sumptuous interiors reflect the gentle pace of the times, from the drawing-room piano to the chaise lounge. Today it houses the Lower Cape

Fear Historical Society, offering daily tours ($5/2 for adults/children).

Thalian Hall A grand Italianate edifice completed in 1858, Thalian Hall (☎ 910-343-3660, box office 343-3664), at 310 Chestnut St, is a combined city hall and performing arts center. The public sections house two theaters and a ballroom, and most evenings it's a hive of activity. You can take self-guided tours ($1) from noon to 6 pm daily (2 pm to 6 pm weekends), and it's worth the modest entrance fee just to view the old-fashioned theater. Look up at the balcony: It's said that two seats are always folded down by resident ghosts.

Screen Gems Studio Tours These two-hour studio tours (☎ 910-343-3433) afford some fascinating insights into the goings-on behind the scenes at 'Hollywood East.' There's a film, tour of the studio sound stages (with a long look at *Dawson's Creek*), and parts of projects currently in production. The guide is full of anecdotes, including an explanation of the freak accident that killed actor Brandon Lee on set. Tours meet at noon at 2 pm on Saturday and Sunday, at the studio gate at 1223 N 23rd St, near the airport ($10).

Wrightsville Beach

The sun, sand and chance to strut make for nonstop buzz in Wrightsville Beach, 6 miles east of Wilmington. It's just 1 mile long, but for many it's the height of Cape Fear cool: a wide, impeccably clean beach with shallow surf, decent seafront hotels and eateries with lots of space in between, and a nightlife with a relaxed, flip-flop feel. The north end is mainly residential, with spiffy villas and stilted homes (Michael Jordan bought his mother a nice place here). The hotels here can hurt your wallet, so consider staying in Wilmington and commuting.

Organized Tours

In the summer, Wilmington Adventure Walking Tours (☎ 910-763-1785) will show you the town in a detailed 2-hour tour at 10 am and 2 pm daily. Historic 1½ hour

Walk and Talk Tours (☎ 910-762-0492) leave from Latimer House, 126 S 3rd St, at 10 am on Wednesday and Saturday. Both tours cost $10.

For chills, try Ghost Walk and Unusual Tours of Old Wilmington (☎ 910-602-6055), whose 90-minute tour is quite popular ($12, children under 7 free). Meet at Water and Market Sts, on the waterfront for both.

Wilmington Trolley Co (☎ 910-763-4483) runs 45-minute narrated trolley-bus tours geared toward TV and movie locations such as *Dawson's Creek, Blue Velvet* and *Sleeping with the Enemy*. Tours go hourly except at noon, from 10 am to 5 pm Tuesday to Sunday. Tickets are $10/4 for adults/children. Departure is at Dock and S Water Sts.

Narrated horse-drawn carriage tours (☎ 910-251-8889) depart from the bottom of Market St, just off the waterfront. The 45 minute tours depart hourly from 10 am to 10 pm in season daily (till 4 pm on Monday) and cost $9/4 for adults/children.

Cape Fear Riverboats (☎ 800-676-0162, 910-343-1611) operate 1½ hour narrated cruises on the *Henrietta III*, a New Orleans-style steamboat. Departures are at noon and 2:30 pm Tuesday to Sunday, April to October, from the waterfront on S Water St at Dock St. Tickets cost $10/5 for adults/children. There's also a 1½ hour lunch cruise at noon and a variety of other trips.

Kayak Carolina (☎ 910-458-9111, 910-262-1141) offers kayak rentals, a two-hour guided tour of the coastal marshlands ($35), day trips ($60) and a variety of other outings. Web site: www.kayakcarolina.com.

Special Events

North Carolina Azalea Festival – every April, the beds come alive at Orton Plantation, Airlie Gardens and other area gardens.

Battleship Blast – on July 4, a huge choreographed display of fireworks over the old warship, with riverfront celebrations.

Cape Fear Blues Festival – in late July, enjoy four days of gettin' down in the city and along the Cape Fear River banks.

Holiday Flotilla – in late November, a lighted parade of sailboats, motorboats and yachts strut their stuff for judges in Wrightsville Beach.

NORTH CAROLINA

Places to Stay

Camping The closest camping is at the 83-site *Carolina Beach State Park* (☎ 910-458-8206), on Hwy 421 18 miles south of town, with tent spots for $12. Facilities include showers and rest rooms but no RV hookups. Hiking and nature trails are nearby, and you can fish for flounder in the Cape Fear River. Availability is on a first-come, first-served basis.

Budget & Mid-Range The least expensive accommodations are along Hwy 17/Market St, east of downtown; Wrightsville Beach tends to be pricey. If the town's getting booked up, you can usually find something on the Carolina/Kure Beach motel strip for $30 to $40.

Travel Inn (☎ 910-763-8217, 4401 Market St), has rooms for around $35/38 in low season and $55 on busy weekends.

The trusty *Motel 6* (☎ 800-466-8356, 910-762-0120, 2828 Market St) has singles/doubles starting at $45/51 in high season and $35/41 in low season.

Some hotels run winter specials with doubles for $35 to $40, such as the motel-style *Greentree Inn* (☎ 800-225-7666, 910-799-6001, 5025 Market St) about 4 miles from downtown. It has a pool, free breakfast bar, and several restaurants next door. The *Sunset Lodge Travelodge* (☎ 800-884-4118, 910-762-4426, 4118 Market St) is another sure bet.

A nicer place, not a typical chain hotel, is the *Best Western Carolinian* (☎ 800-528-1234, 910-763-4653, 2916 Market St), with rooms from $52 to $75, depending on season.

The *Coastline Inn* (☎ 800-617-7732, 910-763-2800, 503 Nutt St) has spacious, comfy rooms, most with kitchenette, in a quiet spot behind the railway museum. Many have harbor views, and there's a private pier behind. Rooms start at around $79, and from $99 in high season.
Web site: www.coastline-inn.com

Just before the bridge at Wrightsville Beach, the *Waterway Lodge* (☎ 800-677-3771, 910-256-3771, 7246 Wrightsville Ave/Hwy 76) offers a good range of amenities for $60 in low season and $70/90 on weekdays/weekends in high season.

Top End The top dog is the *Wilmington Hilton* (☎ 910-763-5900, 301 N Water St), in an enormous complex with several bars and restaurant, and lots of comforts. Rooms start around $129, with deals from $89 in low season.
Web site: www.wilmingtonhilton.com

Out at Wrightsville Beach, the 150-room, high-rise *Blockade Runner* (☎ 910-256-2251, 275 Waynick Blvd) runs specials from $109, and all rooms have ocean views and balconies.
Web site: www.blockade-runner.com

The *Shell Island Resort Hotel* (☎ 910-256-8696, 2700 N Lumina Ave) offers top-end luxury in a big complex on Wrightsville Beach. Rooms start at $129/99 in high/low season. Note the sandbags next to the parking lot; man-made jetties are wreaking havoc with the currents here.
Web site: www.shellisland.com

B&Bs & Inns The visitors bureau has a list of historic B&Bs in the area, mostly in the $85 to $160 range.

Smack downtown, *Stemmerman's Inn* (☎ 888-588-7776, 910-763-7776, 132 S Front St) has nice efficiency apartments with gobs of amenities for $99 to $149 – but look out for off-season prices down to $69.
Web site: www.stemmermans.com

The swanky *Inn at St Thomas Court* (☎ 800-525-0909, 910-343-1800, 101 S 2nd St) charges from $129.
Web site: www.innatstthomascourt.com

Down in Kure Beach, the *Ocean Princess B&B* (☎ 910-458-6712, 824 Fort Fisher Blvd S/Hwy 421) is a sheltered, richly furnished place with a pool and private Jacuzzis; doubles rent from $119, or $99 in off-season. Web site: www.lookingup.com/ocean princessb&b

Places to Eat

Downtown has a dazzling array of restaurants, often full to bursting on warm summer nights. Front St offers lots of quick bites – subs, pizzas and diner-style burger joints.

The closest thing to a supermarket downtown is the *Village Market* (☎ *910-762-6229, 26 S 2nd St*) at Dock St. More a convenience store, it's open till 1 am or 2 am daily. There's a big Food Lion several miles out at 8207 Market St.

Get your caffeine fix at *Port City Java* (☎ *910-762-5282, 7 N Front St*). It's a good spot to plan your day or read the paper while sipping a juice or espresso (open till 10 pm, midnight on weekends).

Cedars (☎ *910-763-5552, 128 S Front St*) is an oft-overlooked delight, with good Lebanese dishes for $8 to $10. There's belly dancing on some evenings in summer, and lunch and dinner daily.

The *Water St Café* (☎ *910-343-0042, 5 S Water St*) is a waterfront institution, with good sandwiches, soups and salads ($6 to $8) at lunch and more substantial fare later (closed Monday and Tuesday evening). Bits of *Dawson's Creek* were filmed here – this was Dawson's mother's restaurant. There's sidewalk dining, and Dixieland, blues and flamenco music are played in the evenings.

For a splurge, try *Under Currant* (☎ *910-815-0810, 10 Market St*) for progressive Franco-American fare with a Southern twist (mains about $14 to $25). There's a great upstairs bar, and the wine list is copious. It's closed on Sunday. In a similar vein, *Café Deluxe* (☎ *910-251-0333, 114 Market St*) does *nouveau* cuisine à la West Coast (dinner only, closed Sunday evening).

Circa 1922 (☎ *910-762-1922, 8 N Front St*) is a laid-back, low-lit, deep-paneled eatery focussing on tapas; most dishes run $8 to $9, but you'll need to order two. It's open for lunch and dinner.

Two sprawling seafood restaurants with deck-top seating and harbor views pull the crowds at Chandler's Wharf. *Elijah's* (☎ *910-343-1448*), S Water St, is fixed on Lowcountry sandwiches and seafood (crab cakes, catfish, shrimp) and has a good oyster bar (around $6 to $8 for lunch mains, $12 to $20 evenings). Next door, *Pilot House* (☎ *9210-343-0200, 2 Ann St*) occupies a his-

toric house and is more expensive and formal, although you can show up in shorts.

Caffe Phoenix (☎ *910-343-1395, 9 S Front St*) exudes Californian sophistication, with regular art exhibits and the occasional film star (Michelle Pfeiffer loved the place). The sidewalk's a fine place summer evenings, but atmosphere tends to takes priority over the cuisine ($10 to $20). It's open for lunch and dinner (closed Sunday midday).

Mainstream pub food and steaks are available at *Front St Brewery* (☎ *910-251-1935, 9 N Front St*). Wash it all down with brews such as Weissbier, Irish stout or the house raspberry wheat (an acquired taste).

Out at Wrightsville Beach, *The Oceanic* (☎ *910-256-5551, 703 S Lumina Ave*) serves fancy seafood ($14 to $23) over three levels, with a tremendous variety of seating, good beach views and live music.

Entertainment

Downtown sizzles with options, with a few scattered lights in the 'burbs. Don't show up too late, cause most places close at 2 am. As throughout the state, some clubs are members-only, but you can usually latch on to someone to get you in.

Bars & Clubs The flickering neon sign and battered metal door of *Barbary Coast* (☎ *910-762-8996, 116 S Front St*) give you some an idea of what lies beyond – funky decor (check out the Styrofoam skeleton, a movie set relic), funky patrons (Dennis Hopper) and grungy bathrooms.

Bessie's (☎ *910-762-0003, 133 N Front St*) is a humming basement club with two bars, Civil War doo-dads, pool tables and a great live program. There are usually regional and national R&B groups on weekends, comedy on Wednesday and Thursday nights, and theater at other times. Check the listings for clues.

The *Firebelly Lounge* (☎ *910-763-0141, 265 N Front St*) hosts local alternative talent and R&B, as well as comedy. It's open till 3 am, 7 days a week.

An Aztec god watches over the trendy clientele of *Paleo Sun* (☎ *910-762-7700, 35 N Front St*), a jazz cafe with performances

NORTH CAROLINA

several nights a week. Cover is a couple of bucks, payable to the gruff bouncer.

Hipsters pound the pavements between Market and Orange Sts. You might catch a bleach-blond R&B, pop or jazz band on the small front stage of *Charlie Brownz* (☎ 910-254-9499, 21 S Front St). Or munch a pizza in the worn booths while watching sports TV (open nightly).

The charms of *Hammerjax* (☎ 910-343-9090, 2nd St) at Market St, include shocking South Sea hut decor, cocktails, and a cavernous dance floor. College night is Thursday ($5/7 for members/nonmembers), Friday is ladies' night, and Saturday is for dance contests. Another favorite student hangout is *Sharkey's* (☎ 910-251-8265, 21 N Front St) with DJs from Wednesday to Sunday nights (from 9 pm).

About 3½ miles east of downtown, clearly visible to the right off Market St, *Alleigh's* (☎ 793-0999, 4925 New Centre Drive) is an entertainment complex with restaurant, tiki cafe and a great games room with all sorts of interactive gadgets (including 'virtual baseball' and an electronic drum kit). There's frequent live music – look out for one of the state's few flamenco guitarists, Bill Strickland.

Also outside downtown, *Rusty Nail* (☎ 251-1888, 1310 S 5th St) is the local blues and jazz hub (mostly blues). Down-and-dirty bands play here from 9 pm. There are live concerts on Friday; other nights see jam sessions, blues 'cutting' contests, big-screen sports, karaoke, and open mikes. 'Membership' (cover) is $5.

When everywhere else in Wilmington dies, the action shifts to *Dot.Com* (☎ 910-342-0266, 121 Grace St). A blaze of neon and psychedelic art, the club only serves juice and cokes after 2 am (although the barkeeps, infuriatingly, can keep imbibing). It thumps till 6 am on weekends, for candy kids, aging yuppies and whoever else needs a nocturnal kick.

At Wrightsville Beach, *Clarence Fosters* (☎ 910-256-0224, 22 N Lumina Ave) is a popular bar and restaurant early on, especially with 20-somethings, even before the tables are cleared away for dancing.

Gay & Lesbian Venues The only gay club for miles is *Mickey Ratz* (☎ 9210-251-1289, 115 S Front St), which is renowned for its drag shows and nonstop dance floor. You can cool your heels on the back patio, too. Gays, lesbians and straights crowd the high-energy dance floor. It's open from 10 pm to 2 am Thursday to Saturday. It's members-only ($25).

Theater & Classical Music *Thalian Hall* (see Things to See & Do, earlier) hosts several hundred performances a year, with anything from Patti Page's pop to Irish tenors to gentle chamber strings.

Shopping

For trendy shops and a couple of restaurants and shops in a recycled building, check the Cotton Exchange (☎ 910-343-9896), at 321 N Front St. The Wilmington Old City Market complex down at Chandler's Wharf, at the south end of Water St, has some interesting places, too. The blocks of Front St between Market and Orange Sts are sprinkled with antique shops and commercial galleries.

Getting There & Away

Greyhound's station (☎ 910-762-6073) is north of downtown at 201 Hartnett St (off Front St). It has daily buses to Raleigh ($27, 4½ hours) and Charleston ($38, 5 hours).

Wilmington International Airport (☎ 910-341-4125) is located about 3 miles northeast of downtown on 23rd St. Carriers include ASA (a Delta partner), US Airways and Midway/Corporate Airlines. See the Web site (www.airport-wilmington.com) for details. Some hotels have free shuttle services.

Getting Around

The Wilmington Transit Authority (☎ 910-343-0106) runs six bus lines, most of which stop at 2nd St between Princess and Market Sts. Fares are 75¢, plus 10¢ for transfers. Bus No 4 runs east-west the entire length of Market St.

Port City Pedi Cab (☎ 910-362-0222) runs a free, charming rickshaw service around downtown, sometimes pedaled by aspiring actors (ask for prices farther afield).

Local taxi companies include Port City Taxi (☎ 910-762-5230) and Yellow Cab (☎ 910-762-3322). A taxi to Wrightsville Beach costs about $14, and to Carolina Beach, around $20. Flag fall is $1.35 plus $1.60 per mile.

Parking meters have invaded downtown, but the parking deck at the east end of Chestnut St is free after 5 pm.

AROUND WILMINGTON
Pleasure Island
The coast between Wilmington and Cape Fear is known collectively as the Cape Fear Coast and consists of a string of barrier islands down to the cape itself. For a good day's detour, go south of Wilmington to Pleasure Island, with possible stops at **Carolina Beach** and **Kure Beach.**

Carolina Beach's specialty is pure, prepackaged nostalgia. There's an amusement park, boardwalk, merry-go-round and oodles of souvenir shops. Kure Beach is a bit quieter and has a 711-foot **fishing pier** (free, or $5 to enter with gear). On most days anglers line the rails to cast and chat, and the crabbing is great, too. Just to the

north is Carolina Beach State Park (see Places to Stay in Wilmington), with nature trails that are home to the ferocious looking Venus flytrap, an indigenous plant.

South of Kure Beach, the earthworks and exhibits of the **Fort Fisher State Historic Site**

(☎ 910-458-5538) explain its vital Civil War role. The two land-and-sea battles here were just about the fiercest in the whole war, with 40,000 projectiles fired on both sides. It's open daily (free). The **Fort Fisher State Recreation Area** (☎ 910-458-5798) is an oasis of calm after the hubbub of Carolina and Kure Beach. The park office conducts nature hikes throughout the year. Several evenings a month in summer the gates are closed, to allow the loggerhead sea turtle to nest undisturbed.

The nearby **North Carolina Aquarium** (☎ 252-247-4003), on Hwy 421, will have elaborate biotopes with sharks, alligators, 6-foot-long catfish, schools of glowing jellyfish and much more when it reopens in April 2002 (admission $6/3). Until then, special educational programs are offered; see its Web site (www.ncaquariums.com) for details. It's located about 20 miles south of Wilmington.

From here, catch a ferry across the mouth of Cape Fear River ($3 per car) to the old fishing village of Southport, which like lots of places around here, sees lots of movie production activity. From Southport, there's a ferry to car-free **Bald Head Island,** which lies just south of Pleasure Island. Bald Head Island is mainly an upmarket resort and retirement community, and most residents get around on golf carts. Cape Fear, the bane of seamen for its tricky currents, lies at the tip.

Orton Plantation
Return north on the Hwy 133 and stop at Orton Plantation & Gardens (☎ 910-371-6851), with its exceptionally colorful gardens. The striking Southern mansion (1725) lies well removed from the road, at the end of a dirt drive that winds under oaks strewn with Spanish moss. Built by English Colonel Roger Moore in 1725, the 20-acre estate was a leading rice producer until the 19th century and has had several functions since. The house (closed to the public) was originally built of brick; the antebellum Doric columns and a second story were added in 1840. The rice flats around the house were flooded in the winter to give migrating waterfowl a home. In 1983, movie

NORTH CAROLINA

producer Dino de Laurentis arrived in Wilmington to film *Firestarter,* and a full-scale replica of Orton House was built and subsequently burned down.

Laid out in 1910, the gardens are a terrific and varied sight, with explosions of azaleas, rhododendrons, camellias and other flowers – a must during the spring Azalea Festival. The network of paths embraces the bird sanctuary and a cypress-filled lagoon in which a few alligators lurk. Other features include a colonial cemetery, the Moores' family tombs, and a chapel. Hours are 8 am to 6 pm daily (5 pm in winter); admission costs $8/3 for adults/children.

Topsail Island

Despite enticing place names like Surf City and Topsail Beach, this island about 25 miles north of Wilmington is mostly a middling mass-market holiday destination, without the natural attractions of the Outer Banks or the tacky appeal of South Carolina's Myrtle Beach. The beaches *are* good, though, and in the shoulder seasons it's fine for catching some rays or fishing from its numerous piers.

Airlie Gardens

These pretty gardens (☎ 910-793-7531) encompass 67 acres of 'post-Victorian' landscaping and 12 acres of lakes. There's an intoxicating 1⅛ mile self-guided path flanked by azaleas, camellias, Airlie live oaks and other delights. It's a major area attraction during the annual Azalea Festival in April. Admission costs $8/2 for adults/children (closed Monday and Sunday morning). It's 2 miles west of Wrightsville Beach, off Hwy 76.

Moore's Creek National Battlefield

This historic site (☎ 910-283-5591) marks the first decisive rebel victory of the Revolutionary War, in February 1776. The battle pitted 1000 rebels against 1600 redcoats, and the British (a Scottish regiment) were so thoroughly trounced that they scrubbed plans to invade at Brunswick to the south. Shortly thereafter the colony became the first to vote for separation from the crown. There's a small museum with a film, and self-guided trails. Located 20 miles northwest off Hwy 421, the site is open daily; admission is free.

Glossary

AAA – American Automobile Association
antebellum – the period prior to the Civil War (Latin for 'before the war')

beach music – a relaxed, nostalgic form of pop music derived from R&B and soul; ostensibly from the Carolina coast
benne – an African word for sesame
blackwater – swamps or rivers that contain high concentrations of tannic acid from fallen hemlock and red spruce needles
bluegrass – a form of Appalachian folk music that evolved in the bluegrass country of Kentucky and Tennessee
blue laws – based on an English statute from the reign of Charles II, laws limiting business activity on Sundays in parts of the South, especially South Carolina and Louisiana
booster – a person who promotes the interests and growth of his or her town or city, usually with a personal business angle

carpetbagger – a derogatory name given to itinerant financial or political opportunists, particularly Northerners in the reconstructed South, who carried their possessions in heavy cloth satchels
cataract – a waterfall
CCC – Civilian Conservation Corps, a Depression-era federal program established in 1933 to employ unskilled young men, mainly on projects aimed at the conservation of US wildlands
CDW – collision/damage waiver; optional insurance against damaging a rental car
chicken-fried – a breaded and deep-fried piece of meat, usually steak or pork chops, served with gravy
chitlins – pork large intestine, eaten as a kind of offal meat
clog dancing – a folk dance derived from *square dancing* and a variety of Scotch, Irish and English steps, probably originating in western North Carolina

Confederacy – the 11 Southern states that seceded from the United States in 1860 and 1861
Continental Army – the cooperative army put together by the different colonies in the Revolutionary War
contra dancing – a form of American folk dancing, usually accompanied by Celtic tunes, popular in mountain and rural regions of the US
cracklins – fried strips of pork skin and fat, considered a snack food
CSA – Confederate States of America

dirty rice – white rice cooked with small quantities of chicken giblets or ground pork, along with green onions, peppers, celery, herbs and spices
DUI – driving under the influence of alcohol and/or drugs

efficiency – a small, furnished apartment with a kitchen, often for short-term rental

feed-and-seed – a store selling livestock feed and crop seed
French Huguenots – in this book, French ethnic Protestant refugees who settled in the South from the late 17th century, particularly in South Carolina

grits – coarsely ground hominy prepared as a mush and served with breakfast throughout the South, often with butter or gravy
Gullah – a culture that reflects strong African traditions, as well as a language by the same name that is a hybridization of English and African languages; still spoken on some South Carolina coastal islands

half-way backs – Northerners who moved to Florida and moved 'half-way back' up the coast, especially to North Carolina
HI/AYH – Hostelling International/American Youth Hostels, a term given to hostels affiliated with Hostelling International, a

member group of IYHF (International Youth Hostel Federation)

hookup – a facility at an *RV* campsite that connects a vehicle to electricity, water, sewer and sometimes even cable TV

hush puppy – a bread substitute served with many Southern meals; made from deep-fried balls of cornmeal and onion

Jim Crow – an old pejorative term for a black person

Jim Crow laws – in the post–Civil War South, laws intended to limit the civil or voting rights of blacks

joggling board – a long bench on rockers used in the days of porch courting

KOA – Kampgrounds of America, a private chain of campgrounds with extensive facilities popular with RVers

Ku Klux Klan – an organization, founded in 1866, that espouses white supremacy

kudzu – a weedy, invasive vine brought from Japan to the US in the late 19th century

live oak – an evergreen oak indigenous to Mexico and the US

Mason-Dixon line – the boundary between Pennsylvania and Maryland, partly surveyed by Charles Mason and Jeremiah Dixon in the 18th century; popularly regarded as the dividing line between North and South

mayhaw – a cranberry-size fruit that grows in wet areas of southwest Georgia and parts of Florida and Alabama; often used for making jelly

meat-and-three – a set-price meal that includes a meat dish plus three side orders

Moon Pie – chocolate-covered, marshmallow-filled cookie treat popular in the South

NAACP – National Association for the Advancement of Colored People

NHS – National Historic Site

NPR – National Public Radio; a listener-supported broadcast organization that produces and distributes news and cultural programs via a network of loosely affiliated radio stations throughout the US

NPS – National Park Service

nullification – the theory formulated by South Carolina statesman John C Calhoun that states of the US are sovereign entities and thus have the right to void national laws; was used to justify secession

Piedmont Blues – a type of Ragtime-influenced blues popular in 1930s North Carolina

R&B – abbreviation for rhythm & blues, a musical style developed by African Americans that combines blues and jazz

raw bar – a restaurant counter that serves raw shellfish

Reconstruction – the postwar period (1865–77) during which the states of the *Confederacy* were controlled by the federal government before being readmitted into the *Union*

redneck – derogatory term for a working-class right-winger

root medicine – a mixture of herbalism and conjuring used to promote health, love, success and other wishes

RV – recreational vehicle; also known as 'motor home'

Sandlappers – term once used to describe poor South Carolina dirt farmers; now used with pride by SC residents

scalawags – Southern whites with Northern sympathies who profited under *Reconstruction* after the Civil War

shag – a form of touch dancing derived from the jitterbug, popularly danced to *beach music* in the Carolinas

sharecropper – a Southern tenant farmer in the post–Civil War era who paid a share of his crop as rent

shotgun shack – a small timber house with rooms arranged so that you could (theoretically) fire a gun from front to back; once a common dwelling for poor whites and blacks in the South

soul music – the musical heir to R&B of the 1950s, characterized by unrestrained vocals and stage acrobatics

Spanish moss – an epiphyte plant found on *live oaks* in the South

speed trap – an area known for the likelihood of getting a speeding ticket there; usually, a sudden decrease in the speed limit where police lurk

square dancing – a Southern folk dance similar to but older than clogging, with groups of couples arranged in simple geometric formations, usually accompanied by fiddle or banjo

strip mall – a collection of businesses and stores that are situated around a parking lot, in a square or 'strip'

swamp – a permanently waterlogged area that often supports trees

tabby – a bricklike material made from crushed oyster shells

Tarheels – North Carolina natives

Trail of Tears – the route taken by native American tribes who were forcibly removed to western reservations by the US federal government

TTY, TDD – telecommunication devices for the hearing impaired

Union – the United States of America during the Civil War

USFS – United States Forest Service

USGS – United States Geological Survey; provides detailed topographical maps to wilderness areas

USWFS – United States Wildlife and Fisheries Service

WPA – Works Progress (later Works Projects) Administration; a Depression-era program established to increase employment by funding public works such as road building and the beautification of public structures

ZIP code – a five or nine-digit postal code introduced under the Zone Improvement Program to expedite sorting and delivery of US mail

Lonely Planet Guides by Region

onely Planet is known worldwide for publishing practical, reliable and no-nonsense travel information in our guides and on our Web site. The Lonely Planet list covers just about every accessible part of the world. Currently there are 16 series: Travel guides, Shoestring guides, Condensed guides, Phrasebooks, Read This First, Healthy Travel, Walking guides, Cycling guides, Watching Wildlife guides, Pisces Diving & Snorkeling guides, City Maps, Road Atlases, Out to Eat, World Food, Journeys travel literature and Pictorials.

AFRICA Africa on a shoestring • Botswana • Cairo • Cairo City Map • Cape Town • Cape Town City Map • East Africa • Egypt • Egyptian Arabic phrasebook • Ethiopia, Eritrea & Djibouti • Ethiopian Amharic phrasebook • The Gambia & Senegal • Healthy Travel Africa • Kenya • Malawi • Morocco • Moroccan Arabic phrasebook • Mozambique • Namibia • Read This First: Africa • South Africa, Lesotho & Swaziland • Southern Africa • Southern Africa Road Atlas • Swahili phrasebook • Tanzania, Zanzibar & Pemba • Trekking in East Africa • Tunisia • Watching Wildlife East Africa • Watching Wildlife Southern Africa • West Africa • World Food Morocco • Zambia • Zimbabwe, Botswana & Namibia
Travel Literature: Mali Blues: Traveling to an African Beat • The Rainbird: A Central African Journey • Songs to an African Sunset: A Zimbabwean Story

AUSTRALIA & THE PACIFIC Aboriginal Australia & the Torres Strait Islands • Auckland • Australia • Australian phrasebook • Australia Road Atlas • Cycling Australia • Cycling New Zealand • Fiji • Fijian phrasebook • Healthy Travel Australia, NZ and the Pacific • Islands of Australia's Great Barrier Reef • Melbourne • Melbourne City Map • Micronesia • New Caledonia • New South Wales • New Zealand • Northern Territory • Outback Australia • Out to Eat – Melbourne • Out to Eat – Sydney • Papua New Guinea • Pidgin phrasebook • Queensland • Rarotonga & the Cook Islands • Samoa • Solomon Islands • South Australia • South Pacific • South Pacific phrasebook • Sydney • Sydney City Map • Sydney Condensed • Tahiti & French Polynesia • Tasmania • Tonga • Tramping in New Zealand • Vanuatu • Victoria • Walking in Australia • Watching Wildlife Australia • Western Australia
Travel Literature: Islands in the Clouds: Travel in the Highlands of New Guinea • Kiwi Tracks: A New Zealand Journey • Sean & David's Long Drive

CENTRAL AMERICA & THE CARIBBEAN Bahamas, Turks & Caicos • Baja California • Belize, Guatemala & Yucatán • Bermuda • Central America on a shoestring • Costa Rica • Costa Rica Spanish phrasebook • Cuba • Cycling Cuba • Dominican Republic & Haiti • Eastern Caribbean • Guatemala • Havana • Healthy Travel Central & South America • Jamaica • Mexico • Mexico City • Panama • Puerto Rico • Read This First: Central & South America • Virgin Islands • World Food Caribbean • World Food Mexico • Yucatán
Travel Literature: Green Dreams: Travels in Central America

EUROPE Amsterdam • Amsterdam City Map • Amsterdam Condensed • Andalucía • Athens • Austria • Baltic States phrasebook • Barcelona • Barcelona City Map • Belgium & Luxembourg • Berlin • Berlin City Map • Britain • British phrasebook • Brussels, Bruges & Antwerp • Brussels City Map • Budapest • Budapest City Map • Canary Islands • Catalunya & the Costa Brava • Central Europe • Central Europe phrasebook • Copenhagen • Corfu & the Ionians • Corsica • Crete • Crete Condensed • Croatia • Cycling Britain • Cycling France • Cyprus • Czech & Slovak Republics • Czech phrasebook • Denmark • Dublin • Dublin City Map • Dublin Condensed • Eastern Europe • Eastern Europe phrasebook • Edinburgh • Edinburgh City Map • England • Estonia, Latvia & Lithuania • Europe on a shoestring • Europe phrasebook • Finland • Florence • Florence City Map • France • Frankfurt City Map • Frankfurt Condensed • French phrasebook • Georgia, Armenia & Azerbaijan • Germany • German phrasebook • Greece • Greek Islands • Greek phrasebook • Hungary • Iceland, Greenland & the Faroe Islands • Ireland • Italian phrasebook • Italy • Kraków • Lisbon • The Loire • London • London City Map • London Condensed • Madrid • Madrid City Map • Malta • Mediterranean Europe • Milan, Turin & Genoa • Moscow • Munich • Netherlands • Normandy • Norway • Out to Eat – London • Out to Eat – Paris • Paris • Paris City Map • Paris Condensed • Poland • Polish phrasebook • Portugal • Portuguese phrasebook • Prague • Prague City Map • Provence & the Côte d'Azur • Read This First: Europe • Rhodes & the Dodecanese • Romania & Moldova • Rome • Rome City Map • Rome Condensed • Russia, Ukraine & Belarus • Russian phrasebook • Scandinavian & Baltic Europe • Scandinavian phrasebook • Scotland • Sicily • Slovenia • South-West France • Spain • Spanish phrasebook • Stockholm • St Petersburg • St Petersburg City Map • Sweden • Switzerland • Tuscany • Ukrainian phrasebook • Venice • Vienna • Wales • Walking in Britain • Walking in France • Walking in Ireland • Walking in Italy • Walking in Scotland • Walking in Spain • Walking in Switzerland • Western Europe • World Food France • World Food Greece • World Food Ireland • World Food Italy • World Food Spain **Travel Literature:** After Yugoslavia • Love and War in the Apennines • The Olive Grove: Travels in Greece • On the Shores of the Mediterranean • Round Ireland in Low Gear • A Small Place in Italy

Mail Order

Lonely Planet products are distributed worldwide. They are also available by mail order from Lonely Planet, so if you have difficulty finding a title please write to us. North and South American residents should write to 150 Linden St, Oakland, CA 94607, USA; European and African residents should write to 10a Spring Place, London NW5 3BH, UK; and residents of other countries to Locked Bag 1, Footscray, Victoria 3011, Australia.

INDIAN SUBCONTINENT & THE INDIAN OCEAN Bangladesh • Bengali phrasebook • Bhutan • Delhi • Goa • Healthy Travel Asia & India • Hindi & Urdu phrasebook • India • India & Bangladesh City Map • Indian Himalaya • Karakoram Highway • Kathmandu City Map • Kerala • Madagascar • Maldives • Mauritius, Réunion & Seychelles • Mumbai (Bombay) • Nepal • Nepali phrasebook • North India • Pakistan • Rajasthan • Read This First: Asia & India • South India • Sri Lanka • Sri Lanka phrasebook • Tibet • Tibetan phrasebook • Trekking in the Indian Himalaya • Trekking in the Karakoram & Hindukush • Trekking in the Nepal Himalaya • World Food India **Travel Literature:** The Age of Kali: Indian Travels and Encounters • Hello Goodnight: A Life of Goa • In Rajasthan • Maverick in Madagascar • A Season in Heaven: True Tales from the Road to Kathmandu • Shopping for Buddhas • A Short Walk in the Hindu Kush • Slowly Down the Ganges

MIDDLE EAST & CENTRAL ASIA Bahrain, Kuwait & Qatar • Central Asia • Central Asia phrasebook • Dubai • Farsi (Persian) phrasebook • Hebrew phrasebook • Iran • Israel & the Palestinian Territories • Istanbul • Istanbul City Map • Istanbul to Cairo • Istanbul to Kathmandu • Jerusalem • Jerusalem City Map • Jordan • Lebanon • Middle East • Oman & the United Arab Emirates • Syria • Turkey • Turkish phrasebook • World Food Turkey • Yemen **Travel Literature:** Black on Black: Iran Revisited • Breaking Ranks: Turbulent Travels in the Promised Land • The Gates of Damascus • Kingdom of the Film Stars: Journey into Jordan

NORTH AMERICA Alaska • Boston • Boston City Map • Boston Condensed • British Columbia • California & Nevada • California Condensed • Canada • Chicago • Chicago City Map • Chicago Condensed • Florida • Georgia & the Carolinas • Great Lakes • Hawaii • Hiking in Alaska • Hiking in the USA • Honolulu & Oahu City Map • Las Vegas • Los Angeles • Los Angeles City Map • Louisiana & the Deep South • Miami • Miami City Map • Montréal • New England • New Orleans • New Orleans City Map • New York City • New York City Map • New York City Condensed • New York, New Jersey & Pennsylvania • Oahu • Out to Eat – San Francisco • Pacific Northwest • Rocky Mountains • San Diego & Tijuana • San Francisco • San Francisco City Map • Seattle • Seattle City Map • Southwest • Texas • Toronto • USA • USA phrasebook • Vancouver • Vancouver City Map • Virginia & the Capital Region • Washington, DC • Washington, DC City Map • World Food New Orleans **Travel Literature:** Caught Inside: A Surfer's Year on the California Coast • Drive Thru America

NORTH-EAST ASIA Beijing • Beijing City Map • Cantonese phrasebook • China • Hiking in Japan • Hong Kong & Macau • Hong Kong City Map • Hong Kong Condensed • Japan • Japanese phrasebook • Korea • Korean phrasebook • Kyoto • Mandarin phrasebook • Mongolia • Mongolian phrasebook • Seoul • Shanghai • South-West China • Taiwan • Tokyo • World Food Hong Kong • World Food Japan **Travel Literature:** In Xanadu: A Quest • Lost Japan

SOUTH AMERICA Argentina, Uruguay & Paraguay • Bolivia • Brazil • Brazilian phrasebook • Buenos Aires • Buenos Aires City Map • Chile & Easter Island • Colombia • Ecuador & the Galápagos Islands • Healthy Travel Central & South America • Latin American Spanish phrasebook • Peru • Quechua phrasebook • Read This First: Central & South America • Rio de Janeiro • Rio de Janeiro City Map • Santiago de Chile • South America on a shoestring • Trekking in the Patagonian Andes • Venezuela **Travel Literature:** Full Circle: A South American Journey

SOUTH-EAST ASIA Bali & Lombok • Bangkok • Bangkok City Map • Burmese phrasebook • Cambodia • Cycling Vietnam, Laos & Cambodia • East Timor phrasebook • Hanoi • Healthy Travel Asia & India • Hill Tribes phrasebook • Ho Chi Minh City (Saigon) • Indonesia • Indonesian phrasebook • Indonesia's Eastern Islands • Java • Lao phrasebook • Laos • Malay phrasebook • Malaysia, Singapore & Brunei • Myanmar (Burma) • Philippines • Pilipino (Tagalog) phrasebook • Read This First: Asia & India • Singapore • Singapore City Map • South-East Asia on a shoestring • South-East Asia phrasebook • Thailand • Thailand's Islands & Beaches • Thailand, Vietnam, Laos & Cambodia Road Atlas • Thai phrasebook • Vietnam • Vietnamese phrasebook • World Food Indonesia • World Food Thailand • World Food Vietnam

ALSO AVAILABLE: Antarctica • The Arctic • The Blue Man: Tales of Travel, Love and Coffee • Brief Encounters: Stories of Love, Sex & Travel • Buddhist Stupas in Asia: The Shape of Perfection • Chasing Rickshaws • The Last Grain Race • Lonely Planet…On the Edge: Adventurous Escapades from Around the World • Lonely Planet Unpacked • Lonely Planet Unpacked Again • Not the Only Planet: Science Fiction Travel Stories • Ports of Call: A Journey by Sea • Sacred India • Travel Photography: A Guide to Taking Better Pictures • Travel with Children • Tuvalu: Portrait of an Island Nation

Index

Abbreviations

Text

Bold indicates maps.

Bold indicates maps.

Boxed Text

MAP LEGEND

ROUTES

City   **Regional**

.... Freeway
.... Toll Freeway
.... Primary Road
.... Secondary Road
.... Tertiary Road
.... Dirt Road

.... Pedestrian Mall
.... Steps
.... Tunnel
.... Trail
.... Walking Tour
.... Path

TRANSPORTATION

.... Train
.... Metro
.... Bus Route
.... Ferry

HYDROGRAPHY

.... River; Creek
.... Canal
.... Lake
.... Spring; Rapids
.... Waterfalls
.... Dry; Salt Lake

ROUTE SHIELDS

80 Interstate Freeway
F7 US Forest Service Road
95 State Highway
1 California State Highway

101 US Highway
2 Mexico Highway
G4 County Road
375 Nevada State Highway

BOUNDARIES

.... International
.... State
.... County
.... Disputed

AREAS

.... Beach
.... Building
.... Campus
.... Cemetery
.... Forest
.... Garden; Zoo
.... Golf Course
.... Park
.... Plaza
.... Reservation
.... Sports Field
.... Swamp; Mangrove

POPULATION SYMBOLS

NATIONAL CAPITAL ... National Capital
State Capital ... State Capital
Large City .... Large City
Medium City .... Medium City
Small City .... Small City
Town; Village .... Town; Village

MAP SYMBOLS

.... Place to Stay
.... Place to Eat
.... Point of Interest

.... Airfield
.... Airport
.... Archeological Site; Ruin
.... Bank
.... Baseball Diamond
.... Battlefield
.... Bike Trail
.... Border Crossing
.... Buddhist Temple
.... Bus Station; Terminal
.... Cable Car; Chairlift
.... Campground
.... Castle
.... Cathedral
.... Cave

.... Church
.... Cinema
.... Dive Site
.... Embassy; Consulate
.... Footbridge
.... Gas Station
.... Hospital
.... Information
.... Internet Café
.... Lighthouse
.... Lookout
.... Mine
.... Mission
.... Monument
.... Mountain

.... Museum
.... Observatory
.... Park
.... Parking Area
.... Pass
.... Picnic Area
.... Police Station
.... Pool
.... Post Office
.... Pub; Bar
.... RV Park
.... Shelter
.... Shipwreck
.... Shopping Mall
.... Skiing - Cross Country

.... Skiing - Downhill
.... Stately Home
.... Surfing
.... Synagogue
.... Tao Temple
.... Taxi
.... Telephone
.... Theater
.... Toilet - Public
.... Tomb
.... Trailhead
.... Tram Stop
.... Transportation
.... Volcano
.... Winery

Note: Not all symbols displayed above appear in this book.

LONELY PLANET OFFICES

Australia
Locked Bag 1, Footscray, Victoria 3011
☎ 03 8379 8000 fax 03 8379 8111
email talk2us@lonelyplanet.com.au

USA
150 Linden Street, Oakland, California 94607
☎ 510 893 8555, TOLL FREE 800 275 8555
fax 510 893 8572
email info@lonelyplanet.com

UK
10a Spring Place, London NW5 3BH
☎ 020 7428 4800 fax 020 7428 4828
email go@lonelyplanet.co.uk

France
1 rue du Dahomey, 75011 Paris
☎ 01 55 25 33 00 fax 01 55 25 33 01
email bip@lonelyplanet.fr
www.lonelyplanet.fr

World Wide Web: www.lonelyplanet.com *or* AOL keyword: lp
Lonely Planet Images: lpi@lonelyplanet.com.au